Acclaim for Kessler's docu-novel on John Lennon, Shoulda Been There:

"Massive work…written in a factual approach to accurately recreate situations and conversations" in Lennon's life.
Jerry Bozajian, Beatlelinks.net

"The research is meticulous, down to the tiniest detail…the reader can almost imagine oneself in the room! Indeed, it is this "fly on the wall" approach that is most interesting and endearing…Kessler manages to bring the people and places to vivid life with her charming narrative style."
Susan Ryan, daytrippin.com

"A real tour de force!"
Bill Harry, MerseyBeat, The Ultimate Beatles Encyclopedia

"Truly extraordinary…for 795 pages, the reader is John's shadow. Each reader is John's comrade."
Dave Haber, whatgoeson.com

"Really impressive!"
Mark Lewisohn, The Complete Beatles Chronicles

"It's an unusual literary form. The reader has a peephole on events that shaped Lennon's childhood and the beginnings of the Beatles."
Ken Hoffman, Houston Chronicle

"Jude Kessler has painstakingly researched this epic fact-novel about John's formative years that helps to complete the story of Lennon…one of the most important figures of the Twentieth Century."
Mark Lapidos, Founder of The Fest For Beatle Fans

"A master storyteller!"
Goldmine Magazine

Shoulda been there

a novel on the life of
John Winston Lennon

Jude Southerland Kessler — 17 September 2017

jude southerland kessler

foreword by Bill Harry

To Suzanne and David —
True fans, true rockers, true friends.
Shine on!
Jude

OnTheRock Books

"When You're Smiling" Copyright ©Alfred Music Publishing. All rights administered by Alfred Music Publishing, 16320 Roscoe Blvd., Suite 100 Van Nuys, CA, 91406. All rights reserved. Used by permission.
"Owl George" by John Lennon, reprinted by kind permission of Bill Harry.
"Without You" by Jude Kessler, © 2007, Penin Inc, LLC.
"Sweet Sixteen Lisa" by Rande Kessler. Copyright © 1997, Preferred Risk-Collection One.

Penin Inc Publishing, LLC
Copyright © 2008 Jude Southerland Kessler

All photographs courtesy of the author.
Cover artwork by Shannon, copyright $hannon McDonald. With sincere appreciation to Shannon for the original portrait of John designed for this book. Her talent is exceeded only by her generosity.

All rights reserved. Published in the United States of America

Shoulda Been There / Jude Southerland Kessler
Library of Congress Control Number   2007936909

ISBN 978-0-9799448-0-2
Cover design and prepress work by Tim Coulter

This book may be ordered by mail from the publisher.
Please include $3.75 for postage and handling.

    10 9 8 7 6 5 4 3

OnTheRock books
732 Ontario Street
Shreveport, LA 71106

For my husband Rande, who took me to Liverpool seven times, took notes at all my interviews, drove 700 miles in the city of Liverpool alone, formatted this book, and lived with the Lennon saga his entire life. You **were** there.
ONE.

Acknowledgements

Over the past 20 years, so many people have generously given their time, knowledge, memories, and talents to make this book a reality. It is really a joint effort for us all, and I hope that you are pleased with its outcome. You are (in alphabetical order):

Beryl Adams, for sharing information about NEMS and Brian Epstein... and for always making me feel welcome in Liverpool.
Helen Anderson, for the kind interview at her home in Chester and the first-hand look at "The Daily Howl."
Jean Beck, who helped me locate Nicky Cuff for information on the Sunnyside Skiffle Group.
Dave Bennion, for sharing stories from his days at Quarry Bank with John Lennon and for reading and editing my chapters on Quarry Bank.
Pete Best, for chatting with me on the telephone during our first visit to Liverpool, 1993.
Bryan Biggs, Director of the Bluecoat School, whose information on Fred Lennon and Stu Sutcliffe was invaluable.
Dick Clark, who graciously shared his John Lennon stories with me (including John's interesting handshake) at his club in Overland Park, Missouri.
Nicky Cuff for his wonderful, helpful interview regarding the Empire and Manchester auditions with The Beatles.
B. Davies, Headmaster of Calderstones, 1993, (formerly Quarry Bank) for the tour of Quarry Bank, letting me review the infraction book from John Lennon's days there, showing me photos of William Pobjoy, speaking with me about John's days at Quarry Bank, and introducing me to Dave Bennion.
Rod Davis, for his help in locating information about the Sunnyside Skiffle group and for generously reviewing chapters on The Quarry Men.
Colin Fallows, Head of the Art Department at John Moore's University, whose direction, instruction, introductions, and guidance helped in a thousand ways. Thank you for the introductions to **Rod Murray** and **Bill Harry** as well!

Joe Flannery, for the interview and information about **Pete Best** and The Beatles' venues in Liverpool.

Richard Farrar, founder and chairman of the Kansas City Beatlefest, who introduced me to Louise Harrison, Ruth McCartney, and Charles Rosenay!!!

June Furlong, whose stories of the Liverpool College of Art years, whose help and direction, and correction of my chapters on the Liverpool College of Art days have led to a dear friendship.

Tim Coulter, our friend of twenty-plus years and our webmaster, who took Shannon's amazing artwork and created the new cover against all odds, in the middle of the night. No one could have worked under such adverse conditions and created such a masterpiece. You are not only remarkably gifted, but a good man. Thank you for being so dedicated and talented!

Louise Harrison, for generously giving of her time during Beatlefest, Kansas City, to share her memories of her brother, George, with me.

Bill Harry, who corresponded with me in August of 2007, just as this book was going into print. He was gracious enough to share many additional details of stories I had heard, and some I had not. His offer to write the foreword of this book is deeply and sincerely appreciated.

Jere Hinton, for information about the Liverpool College of Art days.

Ruth Horn and **Joy Voellinger,** my dear friends, who did the final edits on the manuscript.

The late Mr. George Jardine, for the kind interview about John Lennon at Liverpool College of Art.

Ray Johnson, of Cavern City Tours, thank you for arranging for us to see The Casbah with **Roag Best**.

Dimitri Korziouk, for arranging for us to attend the Liverpool premier of "BackBeat," and the premier party at the John Lennon Bar, Mathew Street, where I met Lord Woodbine and Tony Jackson.

Ruth McCartney, for her candid memories of John and Paul from her childhood.

Dr. Peter Muelleman, for "staying on my back" about publishing, for information about publishers, and for always believing in me!

Rod Murray, for his guidance, stories, and corrections of chapters regarding the days at Gambier Terrace.

Diana Nolan, my Philadelphia editor, for revising and correcting this enormous work, at a tiny fraction of what you should have charged. You are a genius.

Jim O'Donnell for encouraging me to self-publish.

Eddie Porter of Cavern City Tours in Liverpool for the many tales. And thank you for introducing me to **Charlie Lennon**!

Margaret Plowman, who checked my Scouse and kept me on the right track, in more ways than one! Ta!!

John Rauch at Rockstore for helping me connect with Retna for the Astrid Kirchherr photo rights. Thank you!

Radio Merseyside for helping me locate information on Nicky Cuff.

Terrie Taylor, who typed a great deal of this manuscript, gratis! That was a gift of love.

Allan Williams, whose many colourful interviews and "evenings on the town" are truly appreciated and valued.

Woody, "Lord Woodbine" whose information about The Beatles' first trip to Hamburg was as interesting as it was helpful. (And yes, I do have a strange brother.)

To the late Bob Wooler and the late Charles Lennon, whose wonderful stories about John and whose warmth touched my heart.

To all the people of Liverpool, who shared stories with me about the Cavern Club, the early Beatles, and the beginning of the Mersey movement. You are the warmest, most wonderful people in the world!

And to my family...

Dr. and Mrs. Tom Paul Southerland, my sweet parents, for encouraging me and teaching me to believe in myself, giving me funds towards my first trip to Liverpool...and who listened to me read the book aloud, chapter by chapter, for two years. Without you, this would have only been a dream.

Cliff, my wonderful son, for constantly "hammering" me to get the book finished. For years, you have made my dream your dream. No one could ask for a better agent...or better son, dude.

Paige, my sweet daughter (in law), for encouraging me and being my friend!

Lisa Southerland Allen, my *swister*, who edited and formatted the book, chose the fonts, dotted my "I's" and crossed my "T's"...and whose servant heart is pure gold.

Rhea Kessler, my sister-in-law, who both read and edited the early manuscript and directed me to describe the characters in more detail.

Ron Kessler, my father-in-law, for teaching me how to write dialogue.

Rose Kessler, my mother-in-law, for graciously babysitting during my many Liverpool trips!!

Thank you to everyone who has been patient and waited for me to finally finish the book. I know you said, "Just push print," but I hope you find it worth the wait.

Ken Bloom, special thanks for his careful and painstaking editing of the first edition of *Shoulda Been There*.

Bob Felten, for reading the first edition with a scrutinizing eye and making sure that my dates and John's ages corresponded.

Foreword

There are currently over 3,000 books about the Beatles – and I can't say I've read all of them, but I have digested a tidy few.

One merges into the other as they cover the same events. As most people weren't privy to these events, they are just depicted in a standard style.

Now here comes a book which attempts to breathe a little more life into the story by presenting the events as if the author were a fly-on-the wall, introducing dialogue and creating a sort of factional approach to the legendary tale

This is a rather dangerous thing to do in many ways. Even people who were present at the events can't remember conversations verbatim so many decades later. There is also the rhythm of the speech, the Liverpool dialogue, the Scouse sense of humour.

It's a difficult act to carry off, but at least it's a worthwhile venture.

Personally, I can vividly remember so many of the incidents I lived through. They come into my mind as clear pictures, I can recall the times and the places and the gist of what was said, but I can't remember detailed conversations.

Sitting in Ye Cracke when John, Stuart, Rod and I decided to call ourselves the Dissenters and make Liverpool famous is an event I remember. I know what we talked about, but can't remember that evening in a word-for-word manner: just the essence of what happened. And that is what counts.

If the essence of what was said is there, then the exact dialogue doesn't necessarily prohibit an expression of conversations, presented in a way to entertain.

Which is where this book comes in and I say, hey Jude, carry on!

Bill Harry, founder of Mersey Beat

Mersey Beat - *Merseyside's Own Entertainment Paper*
The Beatles, The Liverpool Sound, The Swinging Sixties...
It's still happening, man: **http://www.mersey-beat.net**

Imagine, and it's true.™

"History is slippery. Different people remember different events in different ways. The best anyone can do in trying to reconstruct a past time is to piece together a fabric composed of many memories...fabrics from hundreds of lives, vividly and generously recalled for the author and then interwoven into the fabric of the story."

Morgan Llywelyn, 1949

Prologue

Every epic begins in mystery. No one is quite sure how Beowulf was born, or even if he was born. Legend is the hero's birthright. Fable, his swaddling clothes.

And so it is with John Lennon.

Pick up any "Beatles book," and there you'll find it: the well-worn legend – the story of how John's Auntie Mimi ran, amidst one of Hitler's unrelenting bombing raids, from Newcastle Road to the Oxford Street Maternity Hospital to catch a first glimpse of her new nephew. You'll read how Mimi darted in and out of makeshift shelters, weaving her precarious way to her sister's Liverpool hospital room, searching for John, her someday son. It is the story of a woman's incredible journey and devotion against all odds...a touching tale.

But it just isn't true.

Ask Liverpool's Cavern Tours guide, Eddie Porter. If anyone would spin a yarn, Eddie would. He's a master storyteller. But he will tell you that Mimi Smith laughed with him at the fable, chuckled to think that anyone would believe such a fantastic legend.

"Me – running in a bombing raid?" She would cluck her tongue over tea. "Why the police would've had none of it, I'll assure you. It wouldn't have been allowed, that sort of thing."

And I must agree.

You see, I've driven the path from Newcastle Road down the main thoroughfare, Smithdown, straight into the heart of the city. I've passed the great shadow of the Anglican Cathedral and the Art College and found my way to narrow Oxford Street. So I know how far it really is. And I know that even an avid runner would find the route an adequate challenge. It is over three and a half miles. And Mimi Smith was a thirty-four year old housewife in an era when housewives were not athletes!

Furthermore, a quick glimpse into Rodney Whitworth's Merseyside at War will set the record straight. There was no bombing raid on the night of October 9, 1940! (There was a small encounter over rural Garston and Aigburth, but no offensive over

Liverpool proper.) That night Hitler's guns were silent. I'd like to think the moratorium was offered in honour of John; common sense tells me it was coincidence.

The same disheartening attention to detail may be given to other "Beatletales." Was Stu Sutcliffe really attacked in an alley following a Beatles performance? Did Raymond Jones really exist? And who was "the one" actually sent by John to invite Paul to join The Quarry Men? The Beatles themselves, especially the Beatles themselves, have muddied the facts about the events that shaped their lives.

Over the last 20 years, I have accumulated an extensive Lennon/Beatles library of newspaper clippings, books, periodicals, audio recordings, DVD's and CD's in an effort to find THE TRUTH in the mysterious maze surrounding The Beatles. I have made 7 trips to Liverpool to interview John's friends, associates, fans, and contemporaries, in an attempt to separate the truth from fluff. I have established comparative tables, checked facts, and rechecked facts and worked to provide the reader with a novel that is an accurate portrayal of things as they truly were.

But as Peter Berger so aptly observed, "The past is malleable and flexible, changing as our recollection interprets and explains what happens."

And so, I realize that no matter how firmly rooted in fact any writer of historical fiction may desire to be, our subjects will always be swathed in exaggeration, fable, legend, and mystery.

And so…

Let us begin John's story with that oft-repeated trek of Mimi Smith, whose passion for her nephew compelled her to seek the infant she would eventually call her son.

But lest you think the story offered here is conjured up, let me assure you, Mimi *was there!* You see, she caught the late transport into town against her family's better judgement and risked being caught in a bombing raid (How could she have known Hitler would take the night off?) to hold her "beautiful boy."

And so, the story is still magical. It is still goose bumpy in all the right places.

Mimi holding John – that much is really true.

Even if the resonance of bombs only lingers in your mind.

9 October 1940
Oxford Street Maternity Hospital
Liverpool, England

"Calm down now, dearie, y'er hyperventilatin'." The fat, musty nurse patted her hand condescendingly. Julia jerked her arm away.

Unendurable and inescapable! Some professor, undoubtedly referring to something tragic and Shakespearean, had said it once. Julia couldn't remember who. *Unendurable and inescapable!*

Unendurable and inescapable! The blinding, gut-wrenching pain tore at her body, and as her mind wandered through bizarre, jumbled catalogues, Julia remembered some mythological creature springing full-grown from its father's head. Any minute now, *she* would burst open. She couldn't hold on much longer.

She thought if somehow she could just leave this place, the pain would subside. But tubes and bottles, needles and machines tethered her. And there was no one to help her escape. No one.

Julia was alone.

Sweat plastered her auburn hair into sticky, unsightly strands on her forehead and wet pillow. Pain turned her dark lips into thin, white lines of concentration. Agony and loneliness invaded her – and fear – fear of the unknown and fear of the known, too. In undulating waves of fear and agony, Julia was going to have her first baby.

A baby! What a penalty for a night of Christmas cheer! Talk about the punishment not fitting the crime! Julia felt unjustly served. *A baby! Well, where's Freddy's punishment, then? And why's he not sentenced to concentrated labour? Why's he not required to share in this ordeal? And where the bleedin' hell is he anyway?*

"I'll breathe any way I please!" Julia snapped. "I still have a choice in *that*, now, don't I?" Then the pain dug its claws in, and she fell into the silence of suffering.

"Not much longer, then." The nurse was not fazed by the girl's hostility; she'd seen plenty of it – plenty. These flighty young things with their absent husbands – most of 'em were a handful. She checked Julia's dilation again and then jotted notes on the clipboard chart which hung at the foot of the bed.

After a moment, Julia could breathe and speak again. "Not much *longer*?!" she spat. "And I'm supposed to be encouraged by that? *That's* your good news, then? How bleedin' much longer *exactly*? It's been thirty effin' hours as it is!" She took a breath. "Do I need a Cesarean or what?"

"I'll go after the doctor for you, luv." The nurse was a clever evader. She replaced the chart and sidled towards the door. "He's already in hospital, y'know, so you needn't worry. He'll be right along. And trust me, luv, y'er doin' fine, just fine." She smiled a smarmy smile. "In fact, y'er doin' better'n yer sister, that one. She's called at least a dozen times in only a coupla hours. Practically frantic, she is! A regular worrier, now ain't she? Dyed-in-the-wool worrier, that one. Threatenin' us with our very lives…thinks we don't know what we're doin'. She's. . ."

"*Not now!*" Julia screamed, really screamed, as the pain and an overwhelming urge to push pulled her down once again. She gasped for air, gasped and arched her swollen body against the spasm that darkened her vision.

"The doctor!" the nurse mumbled in earnest this time. And she disappeared as Julia howled to no one.

Daylight began to tiptoe into the tiny, austere room with its single iron bed, metal night stand and chair, and sterile washbasin. Everything was steel grey, and the thin October sunrise offered few splashes of colour, minimal cheer. Julia concentrated on a chaotic host of dust specs dancing in a shaft of light, and she panted in and out, in and out to their mesmerizing movement.

She tried to hold on.

"Well, Mrs. Lennon, " the doctor breezed in, smiling, "how are we this morning, then?"

"You," Julia hissed, "are fine. I'm…in agony."

"Is that right?" He looked at her chart and not at her.

"She's completely dilated, sir." The nurse was at his elbow.

"Um-hmmm. Right." He cleared his throat and scribbled, "6:50 A.M. – patient coherent and fully dilated" on the clipboard. Then he looked at Julia over the top of his glasses. "Ready to begin, then, Mrs. Lennon?"

"More than ready," she snapped. "Have been."

He motioned to the nurse, "Let's get her down to the operating theater…just in case."

****

Outside the old brown-bricked edifice that was Oxford Street

Maternity Hospital, war-weary government workers, merchants, and college students had already begun their nervous scuttle homeward. At sunset, all transport systems shut down, and the tense commuters raced to their homes before the evening bombing raids began once again.

Mothers hurried Liverpool's remaining children inside – the few who had not been sent into temporary exile in country homes or safe caves outside the city. Women nervously eyed the skies and pulled their draperies together. They latched heavy shutters across their windows.

Hitler's henchmen would be coming soon. The deafening terror would begin all over again.

Liverpudlians, one after another, extinguished lights, gathered into interior rooms, and hunkered down into frightened silence. But Julia awakened to the sounds of a baby sobbing. He was screaming angrily, wailing loudly in the ominous hush.

"Ah, Mrs. Lennon," a student nurse popped her head in at the doorway. "Y'er awake, then! Yer sister called a while back, and we told her yer wee one's been born already. We told her, and she could barely believe it was a boy, sure enough. If I was a bettin' lady – which of course the church views rather dim – I'd be bettin' she's on her way here right now. . .right this very minute! Why, she was delighted, just thrilled and delighted she was."

"Water," Julia croaked.

"Right, yeah," the girl nodded and filled an old half-pint, holding the glass to Julia's lips.

Quietly, with an experienced smile, the senior staff nurse strolled in and took her post at the foot of Julia's bed. "Cheers, as y'say in Liverpool, Mrs. Lennon," she pronounced.

Her thick accent hinted at Dun Laoghaire or thereabouts. It was definitely Irish; it was definitely rural. It was warm and welcoming, an earthy benediction on the day's proceedings. "Congratulations on the job well done!" she said again.

Julia nodded, feeling that she deserved kudos – kudos and then some. The whole ordeal had been harrowing.

"Well, just look at him, won't you?" The senior nurse peered under Julia's bed and grinned. "Yer son's after bein' a lovely, lusty lad, isn't he?"

"I...I haven't seen him." Julia tried to lift her head. Her arm dangled off the bed in the direction of his cries.

"Sure, you have. You fed him a while back, now didn't you?" the nurse reminded her. "But you were awfully anesthetized, weren't you, now? A little overly groggy, shall we say?"

"I...I don't remember. I..."

"Well, here..." The nurse bit her lip as she carefully lifted the infant from his trundle beneath his mother's bed. "We can remedy that predicament, can't we?" She held the boy a moment and shushed him, then handed him to his mother.

"John," Julia inhaled deeply, smelling his skin, "John Winston."

"Ah, John!" The staff nurse nodded towards her student, "We'd wondered who he'd be."

"I had bets on Corey...or young Sean," the younger girl grinned.

"It's John." Julia touched his tiny lips with her finger. "John Winston Lennon." The baby whimpered into an interested silence and nuzzled in tighter.

"Here, I'll help you with the feedin' then." The staff nurse lifted Julia gingerly, and the student arranged three pillows behind her back. Julia slipped the worn hospital gown down off one shoulder. "'ullo there, John," the nurse patted his head as Julia moved him awkwardly to her breast. Instinct failed the new mother, but the baby knew what to do.

The staff nurse grabbed Julia's chart and sat beside her. "Oh, he's got lungs, that one!" She wagged a finger at the baby.

"Just like his father," Julia offered.

"A singer?" The younger nurse was interested.

"He seems to think so." Julia threw her eyes to the ceiling.

"Ah, one of those. Bathroom baritone, eh?"

"Exactly," Julia smiled a little.

"Well, speakin' of which..." the senior nurse pointed to the line on Julia's chart that read "name of father." Julia squinted to see it and then complied.

"Freddy...Alfred...Alfred Lennon of Liverpool."

"Address?"

"Mine or his?"

"Well, I..."

"He's aboard a transport liner these days. Carryin' lads to the front 'n all," Julia explained.

"God bless him, then."

"Oh, it only sounds noble," Julia made a face. "He's livin' the life, is Fred."

The brief glimpses that Freddy's erratic letters had provided Julia had left her bitter and resentful. While she had spent the last nine months growing round and toddly, Freddy had been busy with ships' concerts and parties for "our brave lads headed for the front."

"I was quite a hit last night, luv!" one letter several months ago had bragged, "They conned me into performin' me famous version of 'Begin the Beguine' for the troops, y'know...I could hardly say 'no' luv, now could I? I mean, the brave lads 'n all, you know how it is! And well, naturally there was cheers all 'round when I was done. Because... well, it truly wasn't half-bad, if I say so meself. (All fact, no brag, Julie girl!) I should've been a professional singer, as we've said from time to time – not some ship's steward, barely makin' the means and scrapin' by."

Julia could just imagine Fred in action – right in the middle of the fray, front and center, the light and life of all those raucous parties at sea. She could see him lifting a toast and grinning his carefree, easy grin. She could hear him laughing and telling tales and putting everyone at ease.

Freddy danced in light while Liverpool was cold, dismal, and frighteningly dangerous. He lived in transit while she was mired in her parents' home with a tongue-clucking assembly of unimaginative moralists. Julia had come to full term with anything but joy in her heart. Day in and out, bombs fell all around her.

The lights in the hospital were going out now, and the nurse collected John, trundling him safely under Julia's bed for protection. It was almost sundown, and Julia stared out the window at the deep purple and orange of the sky. She sighed and sank back into the pillow mound.

"That's right. Close yer eyes, luv," the nurse patted her foot comfortingly, "and try to get some sleep now. Hopefully we'll have a quiet night here in honor of yer wee one there. Hopefully you'll both be able to rest a bit."

And Julia tried. But a growing, pinching pain and a thousand assorted worries kept her in an uneasy drowse. She thought of her mum, full of outdated, conventional values, full of rules from another decade. Julia would have to stand between John and such nonsense from Day One. She'd had to insist that he make his own way.

And Pop...he'd never approved of Freddy, never wanted Julia to fall for the smooth talker with the bowler hat and almond eyes. Now it wouldn't be easy going home to Pop with Freddy's son to rear. Pop had never seen any good in the Lennon clan, and he rarely changed his mind about anything.

And Mimi. Ah, Mary Elizabeth.

Last year when her sister, Mimi, had finally married her long-time companion, George Smith, Julia had hoped that Mimi's attention would be diverted to her own household for a change. Certainly George had waited long enough for Mary Elizabeth Stanley to focus on him; they had dated for over ten years before she'd consented to the marriage. But George's daydreams and Julia's hopes had been dashed when just days after Mimi's wedding on 15 September 1939, George had been shipped overseas for war duty.

So husband or no, Mimi had continued to live at home. She'd continued to dominate the unfolding of Stanley family events. Not even Mum ruled as authoritatively as stern, skinny Mary Elizabeth did. Mimi, Julia mused, was one of the famous dictators of the decade.

The worst of it was, Julia knew she had little real defense against Mimi's criticisms or her parents' misgivings about her marriage. She'd heard nothing from Freddy lately, nothing except the usual monthly paycheck waiting for her at the shipping office. As ship's steward on a liner between Canada and New York to the warfront in Europe, Freddy was rarely ever in port for any length of time, and he was almost never in Liverpool. Julia had faced the war, her pregnancy, and her family without him.

"Judy?" The familiar voice was at her bedside. Only one person called her by that pet name.

"Mimi!" Julia's eyes flew open guiltily. She was afraid that her sister could guess what she'd been thinking.

But oddly enough, in a moment of uncharacteristic emotion, Mimi was smiling, ear to ear, and though she would deny it later, tears even pooled in her eyes. She reached for Julia, and the two sisters clung in an embrace that violated every rule of the Stanley clan. They finally let go, but reluctantly.

Mimi looked at her sister – pale in the last rays of sunlight, paler even than her pillow. Julia was always so robust and energetic, her slanted eyes dancing, her high cheekbones arched in smiles. It was strange to see her so subdued. Julia's sly, flirtatious grin was gone. Her arms seemed to have lost their youthful strength. Mimi reached out and moved a wisp of hair from her sister's forehead. They smiled at one another.

"So…where's our golden boy, then?" Mimi whispered. "Where's he off to so soon after his arrival?"

"Under the bed," Julia pointed weakly. "He must've fallen asleep. The last thing I remember before hearin' your voice was the sound of him whimperin'."

"Under the bed?!" Mimi dropped to the floor as if one of Hitler's stray bullets had found its way to her heart. She reached for the trundle and pulled it to her, gasping as the tiny boy emerged from the shadows.

"Oh…look at him!" she hesitated before picking him up. "Just look at him, Judy. He's perfect…absolutely perfect."

"Perfect like Fred, or perfect like me?" Julia teased, reveling in her sister's elation.

"Just…perfect," Mimi pronounced, thinking how much he looked like a John Winston, thinking how well the name they had selected suited the child. "It's all right…to pick him up, then?"

"Why not?" Julia smiled, "If you're to be my number one nanny, then you'd better get started straight away. I'm quite well-known for being infamously demandin', aren't I?"

"Pfft!" Mimi talked directly to the baby in her arms now. "We won't let that prissy Mum tell us what to do *or* how to do it, will we young John? We'll be the best of friends, won't we just? And for starters…we'll have off with this nasty, rough blanket here. Who'd put such a scratchy thing on such a tiny baby?"

"I can see you're out to ruin him, that's what."

"Nothing of the sort," Mimi shot back, never taking her eyes off of John, "Like as not, *you'll* be the one to ruin him, Judy, and I'll be the one to keep him in line. Good ole Auntie Mimi, the doer of homework, the keeper of rules – the only logical, sensible one in the entire family, as it were!"

Julia shook her head and smiled. Her sister was probably right. Mimi *would* be John's stability. She'd be his straight and narrow. And to tell the truth, that was nice.

It was good to know that although he had a mum who didn't own a watch, who didn't ever pay a bill on time, who didn't keep a calendar – and although he had a dad who could only be relied upon to be unreliable, John would always have rock-solid Mimi at his side. Mimi would be there to change him, feed him, and tie his little shoes. It was an awfully good feeling…safe and warm and…

As Julia slept, Mimi rocked the baby carefully in her arms, humming the haunting "Coventry Carol" and watching John's dark eyes following her every move – following her with an impossible degree of awareness that Mimi knew a newborn could not have. Together they waited for night to fall and for the percussion of bombs to begin, but for the moment Liverpool was quiet. Now and again, muffled booms sounded from the suburbs, but for the most part, Merseyside took a civil tea.

Mimi shifted John in her arms, thought for a second. Then she changed her song to "Silent Night."

"Sleep in heavenly peace," she sang tonelessly to the boy. "Sleep in heavenly peace."

****

It had only been a half hour or so, but it had been enough. Mary Elizabeth Stanley was helplessly under her nephew's spell.

As the news of a Garston air raid and an Aigburth air skirmish spread through the wards, nurses had come and whisked John away to safety, demanding that Mimi and all other visitors evacuate to the basement immediately or seek proper shelter. Mimi had insisted upon leaving.

Now she hurried towards the final transport to the suburbs, navigating the familiar, rubble-strewn streets and thinking of little else besides the baby she'd left behind.

A boy! A boy! Half-stone, seven ounces…not too measly, not overlarge, just the proper size for a little boy…a lovely, beautiful boy! It was a rare gift in the Stanley clan.

Mimi had only sisters, four of them, all born just months apart between 1906 and 1916. And she was the "little mother" of the cluster, the eldest girl – followed in rapid succession by Mater, Nanny, Judy, and Harrie, the baby. Her father, George Stanley, had spent most of his time away from home, first as a seaman and then later as an insurance investigator for the Liverpool Salvage Company. Mimi had always lived in a world of women –

a matriarchal sorority of sorts – until now…until John.

Even her marriage to the shy dairyman, George Smith, had been a bit of a paper marriage so far. When the war ended, they would, of course, have a home of their own. And then perhaps, in the traditional style, there would be children. But for now there was only John Winston, and for Mimi, John was enough.

She walked a bit faster in celebration of the good fortune that had befallen them that day. *A boy's exactly what this family needs to give it new lifeblood and hope in the face of this damned war!* she mused. It would be an experience for them all, watching John grow. It would give heart back to the Stanleys once again. John would change their lives. She just knew he would.

****

"He's beautiful! Incredibly, absolutely beautiful!" Mimi called from the front door. She pulled off her coat and gloves and rubbed her hands together, blowing warm breath on them. "He's alert, intelligent, and really quite aware!" Mimi flopped onto the lumpy, old sofa.

"Oh, hell!" Pop eyed her skeptically from the overstuffed chair where he sat trying to make out the day's headlines by moonlight. "They *all* say that, y'know. He'd naturally *have* to be better than any other, our John."

Mimi's mum smiled as she fiddled with the radio dial, trying to find a station in the crackle of static. She was thrilled to be a grandmother again – thrilled to see her Mary Elizabeth so happy. Mimi rarely, if ever, bubbled above a simmer. This overt joy was remarkable.

Annie was also relieved to have her daughter safely back home. It had been madness to let her go out so late in the afternoon! A Junkers 88 had been shot down only moments ago over nearby Aigburth. Travel after dark was never safe in England these days.

But trying to stop Mimi was like trying to stop the march of time. Her eldest daughter was relentless. No one could curb her.

"He *is* better than all the others, Pop!" The spitfire turned her ire on her father. "Don't laugh about it; it's true! All babies are all wrinkled and red, you know, and more than a little ugly. But our John wasn't wrinkled a bit – he was simply beautiful." She turned to her mother, her eyes twinkling. "Just wait 'til you see him, Mum. A boy…a grandson for you! Can you believe it? It's real and true at last! He's here! He's the one we've all been waiting for!"

Annie Stanley finally picked up Radio Luxembourg, fuzzy but audible nonetheless. "I know, I know," she nodded earnestly, " a boy, our boy. I can't wait to see him, Mary Elizabeth. Can't wait to have a child 'round this house once again . . ."

"Yeah, and I'll be off with him to the picturedrome with him, won't I!" The new grandfather gave way to enthusiasm at last.

"No picturedromes! Nothing of that sort for John Winston!" Mimi cut his vision short. "He's going to be a scholar, not a slacker – John. There'll be no filling his head with useless nonsense when books will do quite nicely, thank you. I'm not allowing that sort of thing."

"Well," Pop Stanley fluffed the evening *Echo* in the dark, "we'll have to see about those grand plans, little Miss Mimi." He peered at his eldest daughter above his newspaper edge. "After all..." he paused for dramatic effect, "he is *Judy's* boy, now, isn't he?"

And three miles away, a weary Julia nursed her infant son, the object of plans, dispute, and turmoil.

You can read the traditional version of this story (Mimi running from Woolton to the Oxford Street Lying In Maternity Hospital in downtown Liverpool) in Ray Coleman's classic biography, Lennon.

John was born at 7:04 A.M., and my guess is that Mimi probably visited Judy (Julia) a bit earlier in the afternoon. But by repeating here the legend that Mimi visited John at dusk, I wanted to highlight the unusually quiet Liverpool night of 9 October 1940...an uncanny symbol of peace in the midst of world war.

All conversations are conjecture.

November 1941
Mendips
Woolton, England

She had every reason to be happy. Autumn filtered long, patterned rays of sunlight onto the living room floor, making her new home surrealistically lovely. It was a delightful place…a seven-room semi-detached house with a walled-in garden, tilled and ready for the planting of winter bulbs. It was more house than she'd ever imagined, growing up first in the meagre shadows of Liverpool 8 and later in the none-too-fancy Wavertree section of Liverpool 13. Compared to those old haunts, Woolton – with its stately Tudor dwellings arranged neatly in a row – was a glorious suburb.

Mimi Smith should have been ecstatic. She was thirty-five years old, slim and attractive. Her husband, though they had been married for three years, was as new as her house; he had been inducted into the army only days after their wedding ceremony in 1939, and having him home for good now was really their first honeymoon.

George was good-looking but, more than that, he was kind. Thwarted from an occupation in his field of choice – art – and tied to a family dairy business that he didn't "give a whit for," George was nonetheless thoughtful, congenial, and outgoing. Everyone in Woolton knew him, and everyone liked him.

George had done well for himself, and he had done well for Mimi. Their new house at 251 Menlove Avenue was extravagant by middle-class tastes. Its leaded, stained glass bay windows tinted the sunlight; its thick oak door with intricately beveled panes was warm, rich, and inviting. Fat, brick chimneys rose arrogantly from the centre of the roof, and graceful trees arched over the low, front wall. Mimi had every reason to be proud.

If she stood at her rear window, she overlooked a small but appealing garden, complete with trellises that ached for roses. If she stood upstairs and looked out the front window, she could view, across the dual carriageway, four large, newly constructed houses with neatly crosshatched, leaded windowpanes. And just to the left, the Allerton Golf Course sprawled lazily, showing off its sloping hills and small man-made lakes.

Today it was all especially lovely.

John was there.

Julia had dropped him off in her usual hurried manner, rushing off for a day of shopping with Ann Stout and Dolly Hipshaw. Mimi knew Julia needed the rest. Since she'd left home and moved out on her own, into a small residence owned by George at 102A Allerton Road, Julia had been under a great deal of stress.

John was a little handful. He generally refused to be fed, insisting upon completing the messy task all by himself. And if anyone ventured to assist him, he flared into a nasty temper.

He had begun to walk extremely early and had quickly learned to explore and investigate, despite efforts to thwart his curiosity. Interference always met with defiant ire; he stomped his small feet and shouted "No!" with real authority, and Mimi had quickly realized that the happy-go-lucky, free-spirited Julia was no match for the determined thirteen-month-old. John was firmly rooted in will, and his exhausted mum, with a shrug of her slim shoulders, had begun to relinquish control of her son. Rather than fight him, Julia simply let John do as he pleased. Mimi, however, would not.

Mimi smiled at the food-smeared child gobbling up his lunch from the high chair George had purchased and painted for him. John smiled back, delighted with his progress. He waved a fork at her.

"Now chew properly, John," she warned him, "chew and chew and chew and chew! Twenty-seven times."

She smiled and began to count. The baby grinned. He was tied to the chair with one of Mimi's best scarves so that he couldn't wriggle free and try to get down. Mimi knew the rascal well; she anticipated his problems before they became crises. But under her shrewd eye, the baby sat relatively still.

After lunch he lay on a large patchwork quilt on the floor looking at Mimi's picture books. John loved the big, old Mother Goose volume with its worn corners and bold, colour illustrations. Over and over he turned the pages, babbling to himself and singing little nonsense tunes while Mimi worked around him, cleaning, dusting, ironing the clothes. She was much too busy to sit and read aloud, but John clung to the book anyway, knowing that George would be home soon. And when Mimi insisted that her nephew nap, the book went along, too.

It was quiet while John slept. Mimi folded the wedding-ring quilt and put it away. She put John's other discarded picture books back onto the shelf as well. But as she clipped into the kitchen to think about supper (*pot roast again?*), she caught a quick glimpse of a Monarch butterfly landing on a trailing vine. It paused, then moved away rapidly, as if it knew exactly where it was going.

Mimi sighed, but she couldn't say why. She felt unhappy, but she didn't know why. It was loneliness, a longing for something, something she was just about to identify, something she wanted…something…but then she busied herself with the peeling of new potatoes.

The feeling disappeared quickly into regimen, and as Mimi worked, the longing vanished.

Photos that I took of Mendips in 1993 are in the appendix. Since then it has been restored and is open for tourism. When I requested a private tour of the premises in March of 1993, I was turned away by the owner, but she lovingly wrote by hand a letter detailing every feature of the home for me. A copy of that letter also appears in the appendix.

November 1943
Woolton

"Mimi's house! Mimi's house!" The child marched resolutely around and around the bed where Julia lay, trying against all hope to catch a "spot of kip." It was a fuzzy, lazy afternoon, ideal for doing nothing.

Why *must he go on so?* Julia yawned and tried to shut him out. She pulled the pillow over her head in an attempt to block out the never-ending noise.

"Mimi's house! Mimi's house!" He put his hands on the bed and rocked it forcefully as he yelled. His wide, brown eyes were determined and intent. His chant was absolutely relentless.

"Not now, John. Later." Julia rolled over, her back to him. She closed her eyes.

He scampered across to her side, standing with his elbows on the bed, staring directly into her face. She opened one eye and looked at him groggily.

"Mimi's house," he repeated again. His lips pursed in unwavering decision. Julia closed her lids and sighed a long, surrendering sigh. Then she sat up on the bedspread, knees up, arms looped over her knees. She looked at her son with frustrated fatigue.

"Mimi's house, Mimi's house," she mocked him, turning her lips down at the corners and making an ugly face. "I'm right weary of that, John Winston. What's wrong with *here*? What's wrong with Mummy's house? Why can't you just run along and find something pleasant to do and let me rest a bit, y'know? I was out half the night...my head's a bell tower at midday, and I don't feel a bit like gettin' up and goin' over to the much-demanded Mimi's house, y'know. I'm not in the mood for her, John...all those damn puritanical lectures of hers! I just don't want to hear it today, that's all. I'm simply not up for it."

She spoke sharply and watched him closely. *Did any portion of it sink in?*

"I want Mimi's house," he stated simply.

Mimi's house! Julia wanted to scream. *What on God's green earth does he find so infernally fascinating at my sister's? There're no toys over* there, no teeter-totters, no games or swings...and other than a currant scone or two, Mimi never gives him anything tempting. What on earth makes Mim's "Mendips" so compelling?

Julia swung her shapely legs down from the bed and planted them firmly in worn, terrycloth slippers. She paused for a moment, studying her reflection in the bureau mirror, pulling her face tighter beside her ears, massaging the puffiness underneath her eyes.

"Mimi's?" John hounded her, standing sentinel on her actions.

"We're going," Julia repeated sluggishly. "We're going to Mimi's." But she didn't move.

Julia flashed a smile at the mirror, turning her head slowly from side to side, looking for wrinkles. She was only thirty, and her appearance was paramount to her. With Freddie still away and largely estranged these days, Julia hadn't a husband at home, and she depended heavily upon being attractive. Her wide mouth and brilliant teeth had to beckon flawlessly. Her crescent-shaped eyes had to dance. Her rich "chocolate 'n cherry" hair had to shine. She couldn't afford to look the way she felt today. She had to sparkle.

"Ready," John pronounced, as if he'd made some grand preparations for the journey. Actually, he had been ready for quite some time. He hadn't budged from the spot or changed a thing. He simply wanted to bring his mother back to the moment.

She got up and rearranged her shirt and skirt, smoothing out the rumples, twisting this way and that. Her toes wriggled into her shoes, and she took a brush vigorously to the long, auburn hair. John watched, fascinated.

"You just want to go visit your Uncle Ge'rge!" Julia begrudgingly smiled at the stubborn interrupter of her stolen afternoon. "I'll wager you think he's got a sweet treat for you...or perhaps another chapter of that naughty book you've been reading..."

"*Just William!*" John smiled enthusiastically. "*Just William* stories!" He rocked up on his tiptoes at the thought of the mischievous tales George had been reading him about the rebellious little boy whose adventurous nature constantly led him astray.

Julia shook her head but smiled at his animation. She had to agree with John. George Smith was a treat for everyone. In fact, she'd never known a sweeter, gentler man.

"We read news, too!" the boy bragged, gathering up his mother's old blue umbrella, just in case. He was ever cautious. "I know sounds now...th, sh, ch, tr, bl, br, thr, dr...Ge'rge says I'm fast."

"Ah, the oft-quoted gospel according to Ge'rge," Julia said, taking her son's hand and half-heartedly moving towards the door. John looked at her and frowned with puzzled eyes. He understood very little of what Mum said, but she smelled lovely, and she was beautiful when she smiled. She was funny, too, even when he wasn't sure what the joke meant or why they were laughing. And now they were off on an outing to Mimi's, just the two of them, alone – no strange men, no chatty friends, no naps to while the afternoon away, just Mum and him, off on an adventure. John smiled and pulled her along.

George was still at the dairy when they arrived, but Mimi ushered them in, clucking her tongue at Julia.

"Aren't looking at all brilliant today, are we, Judy?" Mimi honed in on the dark circles under Julia's eyes. "Late night again?"

"John Dykins," Julia offered a smug smile, "Dinner, dancing, wine and flowers! Quite the dandy, that one."

"And our John?" Her sister interrogated, "What of him, then?"

"Oh, he stayed with friends. No problem, really. They were glad to have him. Isn't that so, John?"

Caught in the act of pulling off his Sunday shoes and knee socks, John compliantly nodded. Though he had spent last evening completely alone in front of the radio, he didn't dream of turning his mother in. She had prompted him on the bus on the way over; he knew just what to say.

Mimi, however, was skeptical. She realized the boy adored – no, worshipped his mother. He would say anything, and like as not, Judy had left the child alone again. Something simply had to be done.

"Where's Ge'rge?" John changed the subject.

"You know good and well where he is." Mimi never answered foolish questions, even for the sake of pleasant conversation. "So why don't you put those socks and shoes right back on and run out in the fresh air until he gets home? You can watch for him and meet him at the walkway."

John did just that. He liked Menlove Avenue – so much to see on the busy dual carriageway and even more to get into. On recent visits, he'd even discovered several local boys about his age who were allowed to come over and play with him. They were just his type – pliable souls whose easy-going nature bent under his firm direction.

That afternoon, the script was the same.

"All right," John instructed them, hands on his hips, "I'm the Indian. You're cowboys."

"But I want to be an Indian, too," one brave boy with a jagged Prince Albert managed to stammer.

"Shut up. You're not." John was firm. "I'm the Indian. You're a cowboy. Right?"

"Yeah, right," the child scuffled his toe across the lush grass of Mimi's walled-in garden.

That battle won, John pressed on, "If you're shot, fall down. No getting up, no getting well."

The neighbourhood gang nodded in unison. Even those who had two years on John's three acquiesced to his dictatorial leadership. The games commenced under Lennon scrutiny and bulldog supervision.

Around teatime, the ceremonious arrival of Uncle George interrupted the play. He swung John up in the air like a sack of feed for one of his prize dairy cows. John giggled joyously, all his Indian deviousness forgotten, his commander's role abandoned. He was immediately a little boy again.

"Stand back now," George put him down, "and let me see how much you've grown, our John." John stretched up to his full height, shoulders back like a miniature soldier. "Goodness gracious me, inches and inches in only one week! Why you'll be tall as the tower of London before you're through, won't you?"

"That big?" John delighted in the fantasy. He had seen the tower in Mimi's *All About London Town*. It was a beautiful colour illustration, two full pages.

"Big enough to rescue a fair princess, I'd say," George added with a smile.

"Big enough to kill cowboys?" John threw a sideways glance at the boys waiting on the sidewalk.

"Well, all mixed metaphors aside, I'd say that's possible. Anything's possible if you're taller than the Tower of London!"

George took John's hand and began leading him into the house. The cluster of cowboys behind him was forgotten as easily as they had been corralled. John's eyes were locked on his uncle's.

In the pristine Mendips foyer, George hung up his jacket and slipped off his work shoes, placing them neatly outside the front door, in the glassed-in vestibule, just as Mimi desired. John put his foot alongside his uncle's socked one, measuring carefully, looking critically for some perceptible change.

"See there," George praised him, "getting bigger and bigger all the time, then." John basked in the unaccustomed recognition.

"'Home the hunter, home from the hill!'" Julia quoted Stevenson as she sauntered towards them, coat and umbrella in her hand. She gave George a wrap-around hug and peck on the cheek.

"Hello, Judy!" George was ever pleasant.

"I don't *want* to go now!" John's voice, full of rage, cut through their small talk. "Ge'rge is home. I want tea! I want to read! I won't go now! I *won't*!" His eyes were locked on Julia's coat and parasol, and he shook with outrage.

"Hush, John," Julia's brow instantly wrinkled. "Mind yer manners. No need to throw hysterics; y'er not off without yer Uncle George. In fact, our Mimi's offered to let you stay the night."

"Oh." The boy now seemed as disconcerted to remain behind as he had been to leave only moments earlier. He wanted it all...George and Mimi and his mother, too. *Why did she have to leave? Why couldn't they just all stay and visit? Why did it always have to be one or the other?*

"I don't want to stay all by myself," he muttered very quietly, "I don't want to."

"Well, well – we'll have a listen to 'Dick Barton, Special Agent', won't we?" George bribed him with one of his favourite radio programmes, "and I might, just might have a brand new sketch pad and colours for some very, very good and talented, young lad."

"You might?" John's mood lightened a bit.

"Besides," Julia knelt down close to her son, rubbing his back comfortingly, "I'll be back bright and early tomorrow morning, first thing, won't I?"

"No," the three-year-old said flatly. "You never are."

"Much ado, John; much ado," Mimi intervened, one hand on an aproned hip. "Come along right now and wash up for tea. You'll see Mum tomorrow, then. And you're much, much too old to be homesick on a mere evening sleepover, are you not?"

No one ever disagreed with Mimi. No one. So despite the empty, sick feeling in the pit of his stomach, John nodded and started to obey.

Halfway down the hall, however, he turned and ran back to Julia, almost knocking her over with the force of his hug, clinging to her like a frightened animal. She hugged him back, but only for a brief moment. Julia was the first to let go.

She stood and smiled and ruffled John's hair. With George's help, she put on her coat and in convincing tones promised the boy, "I'll be waiting to hear the latest adventures of that bad, bad Just William, y'know. Listen to George carefully! Don't miss a bit of the episode!"

"William's not bad," John wrinkled his brow. "just in-cor...incor..." Struggling with the grown-up word George had been teaching him, John glanced at his uncle.

Julia laughed, buttoning the last button. "Incorrigible, John!" She said it for him. "Incorrigible. And that's *you* any day of the week, pet. Just William-John. My own incorrigible boy!"

"Not in this house, he's not," Mimi beckoned John to her. "He's as good as bread and," she checked before she said it, "no dirt behind the ears."

"He's delightful, our John," George agreed. "Just absolutely delightful."

Julia raised her eyebrows in disbelief and then tossed them all a parting smile and a wave.

"Good luck, then," she half-teased, "but I'm willing to wager you'll find it's not all that easy, livin' with Mr. Delightful." And with that, she breezed out the door.

John walked to the window and watched her go. Her step was light and rapid, almost a dance. Her hair bounced on her shoulders as she walked, and John could imagine the clicking sound her high heels made on the sidewalk as she quickly disappeared. He tapped with his fingernail on the window, imitating the sound her shoes made. But over the tapping, he could hear the muffled voices coming from the kitchen.

"Well, he's better off here, and you know it, George."

"Perhaps so, but is he *happier*, Mimi? You know as well as I do how he blindly dotes on Judy."

"Yes, of course. But she's inconsistent George, in and out, flighty as a sparrow. She's no sense of responsibility whatsoever, and she's no inkling how to raise a child. Judy's overly affectionate one minute and then totally unavailable the next, larking about with her girl friends and staying out all night with God knows whom, God knows where. She's far too permissive, but only because she doesn't want to struggle for discipline. And she's unbelievably frustrated with a child as precocious as John is. You've got to be honest about it, George – in every aspect, our Judy's ruining John."

"But," the firm male voice reminded her, "he loves her."

"Yes, well," Mimi closed the subject once and for all, "the things we love are not always the things that are good for us, you know."

The voices hushed. Julia had gone. The sidewalk was empty now, and dusk and a seasonal fog had turned the yard a smoky grey. John blew hot breath upon the cold window and frosted a portion of the pane. Mimi always fussed, but George, nevertheless, had taught him to draw snowflakes in the hazy patch of icing.

Now his small, nimble fingers produced not artwork but lettering, well formed and clear; it was excellent for a three-year-old. Anyone could read it. "J-O-H-N" he had written in tall, lovely letters. And underneath, in penman's best, the child had carved a second word. "M-U-M," was all it said.

All events are documented; all conversation is conjecture.

January 1944
Allerton
Gateacre District

John Dykins was a glamorous man, a swashbuckling, devil-may-care figure with all the polish and romance Julia Stanley could desire. Wearing his brown trilby rakishly over one eye, he sized up the ladies with a mustached smirk and a nod of his tousled head. Julia, working part-time as a waitress to make ends meet, had been captivated by him from the moment he'd first set foot in her café.

At first, he'd been attracted to her chum, Ann Stout. But that romance had been short-lived, and when Dykins actually asked Julia out and pampered her like royalty, she'd become hopelessly infatuated. Though she was still, on paper, wed to the invisible Freddy Lennon, Julia was more than ready to move on, and John Dykins seemed a delicious prospect.

Pop Stanley was shocked.

The Lennon liaison had been disgraceful enough. He'd never approved of the smooth-talking, ne'er-do-well orphan from The Bluecoat School. But Julia had insisted on Freddy; in fact, she'd married the chap right under her father's nose without so much as a "by your leave." Now, with Freddy's name still linked inexorably to hers, she was equally insistent upon "Bobby" Dykins – stating that with or without family approval, she was going to move in with the man.

The Stanleys were not naive. They knew Fred Lennon well enough to know the score; he would never give Julia a divorce. For all of his absences, wanderlust, and ill fortune, Fred still loved his wife. He clung to the shredded thread by which his marriage hung and was content to pop in and out of Julia's life indefinitely, giving her what he could of his erratic personality – a phone call from Southampton or a post card from the South Seas.

In all fairness, Fred had not always been willingly absent. Twice he'd been arrested and had spent time in prison for alleged "ship-jumping" and vandalism while drunk and disorderly. He was certainly no angelic creature, but he was not entirely a wayward husband. Adverse circumstances had kept him away from home, and as things will, one episode had led to another.

No matter. Fred's feelings hadn't changed. He hadn't a thought of surrendering his claim to the flippant Julia Stanley. As far as he was concerned, she would remain Julia Lennon for the rest of her life. Come what may, they were married, and for Fred, that was that. It was inviolable.

Julia wrote to Freddy, pleading for a divorce, painting vivid scenes of her discontent, but Freddy never answered. On one of his rare visits to Liverpool to see his seldom-acknowledged son, Freddy refused Julia a divorce right to her face. The sailor demanded loyalty from his wife. He brooked other alternative.

It was impossible, however, to force Julia Stanley Lennon to do anything. She had no regard for reputation or public opinion. And she cared even less for Freddy's antiquated morality. Standing firm in the face of family disapproval, she moved in with Bobby Dykins with all the glee that a three-year-old feels in stomping her feet and shouting, "You can't *make* me do it!" For Julia, life was not over simply because she'd made one hasty decision.

Julia wanted Bobby Dykins with his ruffled shirts and Latin good looks. She wanted the life of ease that his steady job as a steward at City Centre's elegant Adelphi Hotel provided. She wanted the wine and fruits and only slightly wilted flowers he brought home from work. She wanted romance. She wanted fun. She wanted Bobby. And no one was going to stop her – not her father, not Freddy Lennon, not anyone. Julia had made up her mind.

****

Bobby Dykins was a determined and clever man. He saw right off that Pop Stanley could be courted, that he could win the old man over, given some time.

But his attempts to appease Mimi – the family matriarch since her mother's death – were all but futile. Mimi cared nothing for hotel chocolates or long-stemmed "glads" from some fancy wedding reception, and she doted even less on yesterday's flattery. She kept a keen eye on Dykins and on his relationship with her nephew, and Mimi did *not* like what she saw.

John Winston was far from fond of the man. The child mistrusted the suitor's magnanimity. Few material possessions had ever been showered on John. The boy had never had toys other than a rubber duck for the bath from Uncle George and, later, a stack of sketchbooks and colours. He'd never been given expensive gifts. And as a result, John was wary of those who offered baubles.

Moreover, John resented Julia's preoccupation with the dark stranger, resented the laughter that bubbled from her when Dykins was around. John was a serious boy, thoughtful and introverted in many ways. And he was even more reserved around the gregarious, outgoing Dykins. The man's gaiety somehow offended him.

The truth was, John was jealous. When "Bobby" came around, Julia brightened, revved, even delighted, but alone with her child, Julia was often tired and low-key. Oh, John *tried* to make her happy. He reenacted his most entertaining episodes from "The Goon Show," making his voice old and crackly as he imitated the speech of his favourite character. "I'm the famous Eccles," he would dramatize, acting out the part with real ability. And Julia would smile, pleasantly enough. Sometimes, Julia would even laugh, but never once did she bubble.

No matter what he tried or how hard he tried, John felt he was losing his mother. He could feel it. Dykins was winning her away. And when she announced that she and Bobby had taken a small flat together – for the three of them, of course – John nodded politely through a wave of nausea.

Mimi was not as amenable.

"What are you *possibly* thinking?" She raved at Julia, her eyes blazing. "You've got a *son*, Judy! A son! How can you do this to him? Taking him to live in some…love nest…while all the while you've got another husband, and he's got another father?"

"Some father! Some husband!" Julia snapped back, hands defiantly on her slim hips. "I haven't seen him in eight months of Sundays, have I? And when I do see the lout, it's all rave and rumble with Fred. There's nothing there anymore, Mimi. It's all finished, all done – that relationship."

"So you'll just live in sin, then?"

"If that's what it comes to, yes!" Julia lit an Embassy cigarette, her hands shaking. "Look Mimi, don't be an ass. You know I've asked Fred for a divorce, over and over again, but he's turned me down flat. He's bound and determined to wreck the rest of my life, y'know…to run it his own way, as it were. He won't come 'round and be a proper husband, but he won't let me have another one either! So that's the lay of the land. You tell me, then…what'm I supposed to do?"

"Live by your decisions, Judy; live by your choices. You chose Fred. You chose him against all our warnings and all our pleadings; you were dead set on having the cad as your own. And now *that's* the way it is. You're Mrs. Lennon, and you've his boy to rear. Straighten up and live with it!"

"In a pig's eye!" Julia was firmly entrenched in stubborn resolve. She stared at her sister with open animosity.

"Fine, then," Mimi hissed. "You can destroy your own life, but you'll not destroy John's." She folded her arms. "The night he was born I crossed the city under the very real threat of bombs to catch a glimpse of that boy, and when you let me hold him, I realized it was absolutely worth it. Now I won't shy away from a fight – even a fight with you – for John's sake. Listen to me, Julia…see that you mind that child first and foremost, or very honestly, sister mine, I'll do it for you."

****

The foreboding never left Julia as she and Bobby moved their belongings into the small row house in the Gateacre District. She found herself looking over her shoulder, waiting for Mimi to swoop down like one of the Harpies and snatch John up under her wing.

But Mimi never appeared.

And for several months after that, things actually seemed lovely. John saw little of his rival since Bobby worked late evenings at the hotel, and when they were together, Bobby was wonderful with the child. And John was quiet and polite.

Once, after they had been settled in for a time, Mimi even popped by for a visit, and though she wasn't entirely herself, at least Big Sister didn't make waves. Julia let out a slow sigh of relief.

"Where's John this afternoon?" Mimi cleaned Julia's counters for her, wiping under the canisters Julia never bothered to move when tidying around.

"Over to Dolly Hipshaw's." Julia watched her sister work. "They have him to tea most afternoons now. Dolly has three children of her own, y'know…Pauline who's just a tad older 'n John, then Helen who's three or so, and the baby Carol, two and a half."

"That's nice." Mimi wiped the kitchen sill. "And John gets on well with them, does he?"

"I suppose," Julia lied. "As well as can be expected, y'know. He's a boy, after all, and they're three little girls."

"Dolly rang me up, Judy." Mimi revealed the reason for her visit. She turned from the window, rested the sponge against her apron, and looked her sister straight in the eye. "Dolly rang because she's concerned about our John."

Julia groaned and threw her eyes to the ceiling.

"She's worried about him, Judy. She thinks he's under…an emotional strain."

"Get off!" Julia had heard this all before. Dolly was dramatic – a mewling worrywart. She expected too much of a three-and-a-half-year-old boy.

"She says," Mimi accused, "that John's frightening her girls, attacking them, pinching them, jumping out at them – making them hysterical."

"Hysterical, bushwa!" Julia shook her head. "They're lovin' every minute of it, I'm sure. Very probably, John does startle them, but all in good fun. And what older child hasn't, at some time, taken advantage of a younger one? John's no saint, Mary Elizabeth...I'll give you that. But he's no disturbed delinquent either. And he's *not* havin' problems at home!"

"No one said he was," Mimi returned quietly.

"Implied but not stated!" Julia stood up from her chair and walked indicatively towards the front door. "So I'll thank Dolly Hipshaw to keep her big, fat gob buttoned, and I'll thank you, Mimi Smith, to mind your own business."

Julia opened the door and waited for her sister to take the hint.

Mimi removed the apron, picked up her purse, and walked to Julia's side. "Dolly said you'd refuse to discipline John, Judy. She said you let him run wild and do whatever he pleases. She said he's quite upset about something...that he's showing signs of hostile behavior – more so each day. She said John's dreadfully, dreadfully unhappy, and that *you* refuse to admit it. And if this is true, Judy, you know I'll find it out, and you know I'll not hesitate to act. Because if you're wrong about nothing else, you're wrong about one thing: John *is* my business!"

The crash of the door behind her left no uncertainty as to Julia's reaction, but Mimi was unruffled. She made her way to the Hipshaw home and talked at length with Dolly, just as Julia knew she would. Mimi was a woman on a mission. That was crystal clear.

When George Smith came home that evening, he became a hesitant but consenting co-conspirator. He had to agree with his logical, unemotional wife; John probably would be much better off living with them, if only for a time. The Smiths could provide the child a safe-haven, a place of calm in the whirlwind of Judy's complex life...just until Judy could get her bearings, just until John could mellow a bit. George had to give in to Mimi. They could take John temporarily.

Coleman says Julia and John Dykins moved in together in 1945. Julia Baird, John's younger half-sister puts the date at 1943. I have placed the incident in the winter of 1943-1944 as a compromise. Other documentation tells us that it occurred some time just prior to John's entering Mosspits Infants' School in the autumn of 1945), so I must assume that 1944 is a reasonably good estimate.

All events in this chapter took place just as detailed in my footnoted sources. Only the actual conversation between Mimi and Julia is imagined.

Spring 1944
Allerton

The pounding on the front door was a counterpoint to the pounding in Julia's head. She had just barely managed to get John off to Mosspits Infants' School, and then the warm blankets had lured her back for a morning nap. Bobby had entertained her last night; her pint at the Brook House Pub had never been empty; all songs went to coda. Now she needed a rest.

Whoever's at the door can simply go away.

But they didn't.

"Who's there?" Julia called curtly through the keyhole. Her shilling-thrift dwelling afforded no peephole.

"Mimi." The voice was blunt, strangely aloof.

God, not today, not this early. Julia moaned, holding one hand over her eyes. *Go the hell away*! she wanted to say. Instead, she flung open the door with obvious irritation.

Mimi was not alone. A grey-skinned woman, wearing a uniform not unlike a nurse's attire, nodded at Julia appraisingly. Instantly, the vanity in Julia imagined what the stranger saw…rumpled house clothes, disheveled hair, blurred makeup, bleary eyes.

"Mind if we come in?" Mimi took one step forward.

"No, uh…not at all." Julia stepped back to admit the pair.

The tiny house, really more of an apartment, was a mess. Dirty dishes were stacked by the sink and a plant drooped on the windowsill. The unmade bed made a spectacle of itself, and this time it didn't entice Julia; it embarrassed her. She looked around with the eyes of the stranger, and she saw upheaval…tossed shoes, clothes draped over a chair, a discarded newspaper, a half-read novel. She picked up a few dishes off the breakfast table and nodded for the ladies to have a seat.

"Tea or coffee?" Julia stammered, wondering whom the stranger was.

"No, nothing thanks," the lady smiled warmly.

"Judy, we've come about John." Mimi shattered the warmth. She let her words sink in for a moment.

"Mrs. Lennon," the stranger offered her hand, "I'm Beryl

Tewksbury..."

"...the social worker assigned to this area," Mimi interrupted.

Julia's face went garishly white as Mimi explained. "I contacted her about our John several weeks ago, and after some interviews with the Headmaster at Mosspits, she became concerned and wanted to talk with you directly."

"I see." Julia steeled herself for a fight.

"Mrs. Lennon," the social worker began again, her voice kind and genuine, "I know you're as worried about your son as your sister is. I know you realize he's going through a very difficult transition period right now, a time of..."

"I realize nothing of the kind!" Julia retorted, her cheeks flushed and angry. "John's as happy as a lark! He's always singing! He even sings himself to sleep."

"Nevertheless, you must admit he's been in a great deal of trouble at school," Mrs. Tewksbury asserted, "at school and in the neighbourhood. You're aware of that, of course?"

"He's a boy, Mrs...." Julia was never much for names, especially when she didn't want to remember them. "A *boy,* you understand. He's a bit mischievous, and yeah, full o' the devil at times – but quite normal. What of it?"

"Pfft!" Mimi stepped in. "I've watched him grow, Judy, and this isn't our John! Lashing out at the neighbours' children, doing vicious things at school...pulling shenanigans just to get attention! That's never been John at all. How can you say that's normal?"

The social worker cut Mimi short, trying desperately to bring the conversation back to a calm, even keel. She looked at Julia sympathetically. "I understand how hard it must be to be a single parent, Mrs. Lennon...to be on call twenty-four hours a day without any relief, without anyone to help you. And I do believe that you deserve the right to a fulfilling life of your own – someone to care for romantically, someone to love and share your life with. No one's judging you for that or pointing fingers or condemning you for any of the choices you've made, Mrs. Lennon. I'm just offering to help you where John's concerned."

"But I don't *need* any help!" Julia lashed out, glaring at her sister. "My son is perfectly happy here; John is perfectly fine!"

"Mrs. Lennon," the grey lady laid out the facts, "John is being considered for expulsion from Mosspits Infants' School. His behaviour is uncontrollable. He terrorizes the other children and cannot be cajoled into acceptable actions. Your neighbour, Mrs. Hipshaw, has, in fact, *withdrawn* her little girl from the kindergarten until John has been duly disciplined. It seems John has been hiding under the steps of the Hipshaw home and jumping out at the child each morning. The girl's utterly terrified of your son. All in all, things have reached a rather serious stage."

"He's merely four years old," Julia whined, collapsing into the only vacant chair, a ladderback at the table where her two opponents sat. She laid her head in her hands and spoke to no one in particular, "He's not old enough to be expelled from school. He isn't even in real school yet!"

"I realize this is upsetting. Our children mean so much to us," Mrs. Tewksbury continued. "Perhaps you need some time alone, some time to sort out the matter of how to best manage John. Perhaps you need a holiday from being 'Mummy' for a while – a chance to see things in a new perspective, to rejuvenate, as it were." She paused. "Your sister and her husband have volunteered to keep the boy for a time for you, to give you an opportunity to sort things out…so that perhaps in a few weeks or even a few months, you'll be more readily equipped to deal with the demands of parenthood…"

Julia cut in, *"No one's taking John away from me!"*

"It wouldn't be a permanent arrangement, you understand," the social worker began.

"And it won't be a temporary one, either!" Julia snapped. "Forget the whole bleedin' thing. Chuck it, Mimi! It won't work! He's mine! You can try as you like to manipulate this whole entire family, but you won't get control of my child! John's not goin' with you! He's staying here with me, do y'understand?

"Look, Mrs…whatever your name is," Julia raged on, "Mimi's after my child – she always has been, right from day one. She hasn't one of her own, and chances aren't bleedin' likely that she ever will! So she's out to cash in on what I've got. Big Sister always has to have the best. Big Sister always gets what she wants!"

"Mrs. Lennon, it's not a question of what Mrs. Smith wants or even of what you want, but what's best for John. I stand in the gap for the children. I care very little about the wants and desires of other family members; I care only about the child."

Mrs. Tewksbury handed Julia a tissue and waited as she gathered her control. "Mrs. Lennon, I want to make life a winning proposition for your John, and right now he's not winning. Your sister tells me that John's father hasn't seen the boy for some time…that John has lived alternately with you, your sister, your husband's brother, Charles…with friends and other relatives…"

Julia sobbed, her head on the table now. "John needs me. He loves me. Just ask him. He utterly adores me. We get on famously, John and I."

"Well then," Mrs. Tewksbury patted Julia's arm and sighed, "let's leave things as they are then and see how it goes, why don't we? We'll stay in close contact with you and with his school. We'll give it a try. Perhaps John will adjust after all. Perhaps you're right, and things will even out."

****

But Julia wasn't right, just desperate. She was a whirlwind, and John was a hurricane. She fed his furor, never diminished it. She could no more control her son than a snowstorm could halt the progress of an avalanche. Julia was whimsical, flighty, and unrestrained. And under her tutelage, John grew impetuous and headstrong.

By April 1945, he was officially expelled from kindergarten, and Julia began to sort out his things, preparing for the visit that she knew would come.

"Mrs. Tewksbury." Julia let her in without any emotion in her voice. "How nice to see you. Hullo Mimi. Grand to see you, too. How lovely of you both to pop over for a chat."

"I'm sure you know why we've come." Mimi was ever honest.

"Indeed," Julia nodded towards John's little valise, packed and ready on the floor. And then she began to cry.

Mimi's tone was unwavering, "I'll broach no interference in this, Julia. John needs a firm hand and an unchanging code to live by. He needs stability and something familiar to hold on to. And George and I will give him just that. I'll be there for him…every single day when he comes home from school…for the next fifteen years of my life, if it takes that long. And though it's not the way *you* would rear the child, it's my way."

"Just *love* him," Julia choked.

"I've never done anything else," Mimi said quickly, embarrassed by the emotion. "And…George dotes on the boy…thinks John was created solely for his delight."

"The Smiths will be good to your son," Mrs. Tewksbury picked up the tiny valise at Julia's feet and handed it to Mimi. "They've worked very hard assembling a new room just for him."

"George has installed an extension speaker up in John's room so he can listen to his favourite radio programmes while he paints or reads. He's even purchased a little post office set so John can write you letters and keep you up to date on everything…" Mimi's tone had softened. "And after a bit, when John's settled in and accepted things as they are, well…I don't see why you shouldn't come 'round to check on him now and again."

Julia cried softly, never looking at the women who were holding her son's belongings.

"Mrs. Lennon," the mellow voice of Mrs. Tewksbury pronounced a benediction on the proceedings, "there will be plenty of opportunities to see John. You'll visit your sister often. You'll come 'round for tea at Mendips after John gets home from school. You'll pop 'round on a Saturday for the evening meal. And though it's not what you want from life at this particular moment, it's what we're obligated to offer John. He must be given a chance."

"George'll take him to the dairy, Judy…and I promise to see him to Sunday school and church." Mimi took a step towards the door. "He'll have established chores, and…and if he's still with us when he goes to school, there'll be a set time to do homework and a set time to eat. He'll read something every day, and he'll eat sensibly and dress warmly and have a place to call his own. In every aspect, we'll do all we can to make John comfortable and wanted…to give him a regular, ordinary life."

Julia looked up at last, her face blotched white and red, her eyes puffy and full of tears. "How very awful," she stammered, weeping not for herself now, but for her son. "How absolutely dreadful."

"Don't be ridiculous." Mimi pursed her lips.

Julia stood, gathering anger and resolve. "You have the gall to propose 'a regular, ordinary life' for John Winston Lennon as if it's a good thing, and you tell *me* not to be ridiculous? What could be more ridiculous than offerin' a boy like John a life like that?"

"Stability is nurturing for all children, Mrs. Lennon," Mrs. Tewksbury began.

"Not for all!" Julia hissed. "Not for all and certainly not for John! He's a free spirit, a child who lives in the land of make believe…a child of handcrafted paper characters and made-up songs. He's as far from routine and doldrums as I am, is John!"

"Hence," Mimi held up the valise, "the need for a change."

"Why don't we all just agree to give this arrangement a try, for John's sake, and see if it produces the desired results down the road?" Mrs. Tewksbury reached for the door.

"This isn't an effin' science experiment you're dealing with!" Julia shrieked. "It's my son's life, for God's sake!"

"Well, I can't imagine," Mimi ached to have the last word, "that a bit of routine will do the boy any harm."

"And I can't imagine 'the boy' havin' to endure it," Julia began to cry all over again. "My heart aches at the thought of John havin' to live that way. It's ghastly – absolutely awful! I honestly, truly can't think of anythin' worse."

"Well, I can," Mimi buttoned the top button of her coat as she stepped out on to the small, concrete stoop, "but graciously those days are over. John will have the life he needs, the life every child deserves."

"He'll wither and die," Julia whimpered.

"More than likely," Mrs. Tewksbury offered a weak smile, "he'll find his own way, somewhere in between the two. Children always do. They manage to find a way to make the pieces fit."

But neither Julia nor Mimi, equally convinced that the other was wrong, believed a single word Mrs. Tewksbury said.

Julia Baird, John's half-sister, tells this story in her book, John Lennon, My Brother. *She does not, however, give the name of the social worker. The name (not the character) is completely fictional as are the actual words exchanged by Mimi, Julia, and the social worker.*

June 1946
Woolton

Julia despised compromise. The duplicity inherent in "means serving the end" thinking infuriated her. Julia was an advocate of honest, open warfare.

But in a desperate attempt to "set things right," the headstrong redhead persuaded Bobby to move back into her family home on Newcastle Road where Pop Stanley's presence and influence would help her win custody of John once again. Under the family roof, Julia moved heaven and earth to demonstrate that she was stable and prepared to care for her son, and the strategy worked. Mrs. Tewksbury acquiesced, and John packed his bags one more time – to return home.

But if Julia was relentless, Mimi was even more so. She resolved to extract John from the ongoing drama of Judy's life.

Her assistance came from an unlikely source, an unexpected player in the game – Fred Lennon. Mimi lost no love on the "on-again-off-again" sailor who popped 'round once a year when the tide rolled towards Liverpool. But he was, after all, John's father, and as such, he held fifty percent company stock in the boy.

If only I could acquire that fifty percent, Mimi mused.

"Fred, we've a problem." Her curt tone cut through the usual small talk that might have opened the conversation.

"I didn't figure you'd rung to chat me up, Mary Elizabeth."

"Indeed not. It's quite serious this time. *Quite* serious, let me assure you."

"Well, I'm well acquainted with serious, now aren't I? I mean, it don't get more serious than losin' yer wife 'n spendin' two effin' weeks of shore leave tryin' to convince her to come home again!"

"Obscenities aside, Alfred, I realize you've been under quite a strain."

"*A strain*!" He exploded. "Here all these years I bleedin' stuck by Julie through thick'n thin…through all sorts o' temptations you'll never even know of, in ports o'call you've never even imagined, and I was virtually true blue – was I.

And more 'n that, I've done what she's asked, haven't I? Signin' away all responsibility for her debts'n all...givin' her emancipation, as it were – walkin' away with me head hung low, so she's free as a bird to live with Dykins...just like she wanted, just like she has.

But I'm *not* bleedin' divorcin' her, if that's what you're after, Mary Elizabeth! Not me. I'm hangin' in fer the long haul, as it were, hopin' she'll soften 'er heart...waitin' on the changin' of the tide."

"You're a fool, Alfred!" Mimi warned. "Julia's mind's made up, and her decisions are as irrevocable as a day past and gone. There's no altering her now, as much as you'd like to. You simply have to accept what *is* and go on. Make the best of the situation, as it were. But be that as it may, we have other things to think about right now."

"Other things! What other things! What the fuggin'ell are you goin' on about now Mary Elizabeth? What bleedin', lousy things could be more important that losin' me wife or endin' me effin' marriage?"

"Your son." She let the simple words sink in for a moment, giving Fred time to think.

"Our Johnny? What's up with our John, then?"

"He's run away, Fred."

"Fuggin'ell, Mimi! Why didn't you say so before now! Run away? Have you called the constables? Have they started out after him? When'd he go? What's. . ."

"He's here, Fred; he's here. He ran away to Mendips...to George and me...walked all the way from 9 Newcastle to Mendips, all by himself, through all those busy streets – through all those crowds of strangers."

"But he's only five years old! He couldn't have possibly navigated all that way without help from anyone!" Freddy's voice was husky with anger.

"Well, he did...just yesterday. He'd actually been here for hours before Julia missed him. Your son may be five, Alfred, but he's becoming quite self-reliant now that Julia and Bobby are involved. And why not? They're off in a world of their own."

"Yeah, right."

"And now that Judy's pregnant again..."

"Yeah, I'd heard as much. She wrote to say that Dykins is 'completely thrilled.' It's all a long string o'misery, ain't it?"

"After the baby's born..." Mimi ignored his whining and went on, "well, it doesn't bode..."

"Dammit to bleedin'ell! Everyfuggin'thing's fallin' to fuggin' pieces...and right on the verge of me gettin' the best berth of me *whole entire* career – a chance to sail on the *Queen Mary* as a night steward! I've finally got the chance to make somethin' of me effin' life for once...and now this! What the hell am I supposed to do?"

"I'll let you talk to John, Fred." Mimi handed the phone to the precocious little boy.

"Hullo, John here." It was a small, quiet voice.

"Hello, our Johnny!" Freddy put a smile in his words.

"Hello, Daddy. When're *you* coming home?"

"In a while, Johnny boy – you know how it is. I'm off on a big, big boat this time, the biggest, the very best! It's the *Queen Mary*, y'know, a very fancy ship, a tremendous ship! And Daddy's got the most important job of all, well…next to the captain, that is."

The small voice reached out from Liverpool all the way to Southampton, "When are you coming back for me?"

"Well, Johnny, it'll be a while, son. I'm sailin' in only an hour now. And we're off to New York City. New York, mate! America, y'know! It's a long, long trip! A long trip."

"And then you'll come and get me?"

Fred sighed. He paused and thought of what to say.

"Two weeks, our John. Two weeks, luv. Be a good boy for your Auntie Mimi until then, right? Stay with her and Uncle George, and I'll be there just as soon as I can, luv. Two weeks, I promise."

"Right. All right. See you soon."

"Soon, Johnny boy. Take care now, pet. Be awfully good for Mimi, then. Be extra, awfully good."

****

John kept the official countdown on Uncle George's immense wall calendar. His red crayon marked through the days each night before bedtime. It was better than a barley sweet; it was a ceremony.

Only five more days 'til Daddy returns! Only four! Only three…

But bedtime was bedtime, and whatever the occasion, Mimi held unswervingly to rules. At half-six exactly, John was ushered off to bed, prayers said, tucked in tight.

"You can see your Daddy tomorrow morning," she said in her no-nonsense voice. It was useless arguing.

"He might not even come, you know," she answered her husband's disapproving frown. "Letting the boy wait up *could* have been the cruelest of indulgences, George."

"Perhaps," George pretended to stare at the *Echo*, "but John was awfully disappointed."

"Well that's the way of the world, now, isn't it? We all live with disappointments, and John might as well learn early. Besides, it's not earth-shattering, George, not really. John'll get over it." Mimi popped the dead ends off her potted begonias and poked the soil for moisture.

George got up from his chair and flicked on the porch light for Fred. It was his only reply, but it was a protest nonetheless. Mimi bristled, as silently as he.

Half an hour later, the bell rang. "Fred's here," George said as he strode across the living room to the front door foyer.

And he was. The *Queen Mary* had docked in Southampton a few hours earlier, and Fred had taken the first train to Liverpool, eager to see his son.

"John's in bed," George gestured towards Mimi accusingly, without actually saying a word.

"Well, let's have 'im up then! It's early yet!" Freddy moved towards the stairs, grinning with mischief.

"Certainly not!" Mimi intervened, pinching at her brother-in-law's shirt sleeve. "He's asleep by now, and you'll set him off his schedule. Anyway, you can see him tomorrow morning as easily as tonight."

"Tomorrow morn…"

"Besides," Mimi interrupted, "the three of us need to talk alone tonight, to make some plans for the boy. We need to decide what's to be done for John."

"Well…all right then," Fred relented, moving reluctantly away from the landing, "I suppose you're right in that. We do need to hash it about a bit, as it were – and to come to some agreement 'n all. I mean, it's clear *we've* got our Johnny's best interests at heart – he's the one that matters around here, now, isn't he?"

"Absolutely, Fred," George Smith folded his *Echo* and put it away in the small mahogany magazine rack. "John's a special little lad; he's toppermost of the poppermost in every respect. You know how we feel about him. I suppose that's obvious."

"You're too good, George…both o'you, really. I don't know what I would've done these past few weeks if you hadn't kept him here with you, y'know. As it is I've been half out of me mind, trying to decide what's to become of the boy…what with Julie hell-bent on Dykins…and me always livin' life from port to port. It's a bum fuddled mess – that's what it is."

"We were more that happy to have John here with us." Mimi took control of the conversation. "He's always fit very nicely into our routine. In fact, John's never given us a moment's bobble."

"Now that doesn't sound a bit like our Johnny!" Fred smiled, attempting levity. "He's always bobblin' – John is. Headstrong as his mother, always doin' exactly as he pleases."

Mimi ignored the comment. "But unfortunately, Fred," she went on, "George and I are not independently wealthy, you understand. Since George's brother inherited most of the family money, and, well, in light of other recent disappointments," she glanced at George ruefully, "we're, well, ill-equipped to support the child without some financial assistance, you understand."

"Financial assistance?" Fred wrinkled his brow. He'd never dreamed his sister-in-law would ask him for money for keeping his boy. She'd always seemed inordinately fond of John. This was a surprise.

"Yes." Mimi fished a slip of paper out of her dress pocket. She handed it to Fred.

"What's this, then?" Fred looked at the facts and figures before him with incredulous eyes. He couldn't believe what he was seeing! It was an itemized bill for well over £ 20. Mimi was dunning him for the lodging of her own nephew! Two weeks at £20...for a relative...and a little boy at that! It was unthinkable! It was unheard of! He glared at the Smiths with dangerous eyes.

"He came to us with only the clothes on his back, you know," Mimi hastened to explain, pointing out the items on the list as she talked. "He needed shoes and play clothes – things I hesitated to go over and ask Julia for. You understand, Fred. It would've caused a row; she'd have wanted him back right then and there. I thought it best to simply avoid Judy and Bobby altogether...to get the things myself. But nothing's cheap anymore, you know..."

"Indeed, Mary Elizabeth," he pulled out his wallet to make amends, separating the notes slowly, expecting George to step in and refuse the proffered cash. But nothing was said, and Mimi received the notes with a banker's stoicism. She folded them and put them into her pocket where the hand-written bill had just been.

"Fred, you know you can rely on George and me to look after John." Mimi moved on to the next order of business.

"We're concerned that John isn't completely happy in his mother's house," George added, filling his pipe with meticulous care, "and it's led to bad reports from school – incidents of John bullying and picking on younger children. John's behaviour seems to indicate...well, resentment and unhappiness, Fred. And let's be honest. For the past two years, the boy's been left in the hands of a multitude of sitters and relatives and friends – passed from one hand to the next..."

"What are you suggestin', then?" Freddy could guess, but decided to hear them out anyway. He could make his decision later. He knew his brother, Sydney, or his brother, Charles, would care for John, too. That was still an option. And perhaps he himself could even make arrangements to take Johnny, to get a shore job, to rent a little flat just for the two of them.

"We'd like you to sign custody of John over to us," Mimi spelled it out. "Not adoption, mind you. We know how you feel about that. We'd never ask you to give up your son."

"Fuggin' considerate of ya, Mary Elizabeth! It isn't likely you'd get an answer you'd care to hear, if you struck up the courage to broach that conversation."

She wrinkled her nose a notch at Fred's insolence, but continued her speech, unruffled. "We have everything John could ever want here, Alfred – a room of his own, a yard to play in, and the park just blocks away. We've music, books, and the wherewithal to give him a good, if modest, education…"

"And he's already quite at home here," George Smith interjected, his voice less dispassionate and logical. "I mean, we take walks; I give him his bath. We're good friends, you know. He's a lovely boy, Fred, when he's not so blasted rattled, that is. He's had quite a turn here lately, but we'd like to undo that if we could."

"Well, it's a thought, isn't it?" Freddy leaned forward, his head in his hands. He reeled with fatigue and confusion.

Weary from sitting on trains and taxis, weary from decisions, Fred stood up and stretched. "Just let me sleep on it a bit, all right? I'll run it 'round in me brain and look it over a bit, y'know. And since it's changin' his whole little world, I'll have to ask our John about it as well, won't I? I mean, he'd have a say in it all, naturally. You'd expect that."

"Fine, then," George stood up as well, walking to the kitchen as he spoke, "Whatever you work out, Fred. Whatever John wants to do."

"But," Mimi lowered her voice so that George couldn't overhear, "it can't be a gratis arrangement, Alfred, no matter how much we'd like to make it so. George just isn't prepared to take on another mouth to feed without some sort of monthly stipend. It isn't a matter of greed, you understand; it's simply a matter of necessity. We just can't manage to make ends meet otherwise."

"Right, yeah, I see how it is." Freddy picked up his suitcase and ambled towards the extra bedroom. "I see how it is exactly."

****

"It's morning! It's morning! It's morning, Daddy!" The bed rocked and rolled like it never had at sea. John jumped all around Fred, falling on him at last in a heap of giggles.

"Barely, I believe." Fred opened one eye and peeked at the clock. Quarter past six. *Ungodly! No wonder the boy went to bed with the wrens!* Fred tackled the giggler and wrestled him down among the pillows. John laughed even harder, clinging to his father for dear life.

"Good heavens, now! What's this, then? Y'er much too strong for Daddy these days! Stand back and let's have a look at those muscles, now. Come on, mate, show us what you've got!"

John tightened a bicep fiercely, his almond-shaped eyes intent and serious. Fred gleamed with unashamed admiration, and he poked the tiny muscle respectfully.

"Very dangerous, that!" He feigned fear. "I'll be on me guard from now on, won't I? It's got 'round y'er quite a mixer, y'know! Now the truth is out; now I see exactly why!"

John fell into giggles again, pushing his father back into the pillows and thumping him with tiny fists. Fred wailed and howled as if suffering the worst of a barroom brawl. He rolled and covered his head with a pillow while John jumped and collapsed on his back. The laughter never ceased. It was one continuous sound.

After a while, conversation punctuated the giggles. Freddy spun sea yarns, recreating the delights of New York City, the brass-and-wood elegance of the *Queen Mary*, the smooth sounds of a new American singer named Frankie Sinatra while John sat cross-legged on the bed, imagining diamonds on the ocean and music swirling around the Grand Ballroom. He could hear the places his father had visited; he could smell them, too.

But before long, Fred's stomach called an intermission. "We'd best be up and dressed before yer dear ole auntie comes and turns us both out, Johnny." He swung his feet to the floor, reaching for the robe George had loaned him.

"Tell me more stories, Daddy! Tell me about those tall, skinny buildings and the fast, fast automobiles!"

"Over Twinings and toast, yeah?" Fred pulled the boy to his feet, too. "We'll chat then. We'll chat it all up, every bit of it, y'know."

John stretched in his nightshirt and bare feet, rubbing the sleep from his eyes like his favourite old cat. Freddie smiled. "Scoot off now and put on some of those clothes yer Auntie Mimi bought you, all right?" He swatted the child playfully. "And we'll be dandies for breakfast, you and me! I'll be Pat, and you'll be Mike. . .and we'll stir things up a bit, as it were!"

"Like coffee?" John teased, smiling broadly.

"Yeah, and tea, too," Freddy winked. "Tea, too!"

And as John pattered off to fetch his clothes, Fred rubbed his hands across his eyes, sighed resignedly, and made the final decision about what to do with his only son.

****

"Do I have to call you *Pater*, Daddy?" John walked beside him, holding his hand. "Mimi says I must...because that's what my cousin Stanley calls his father."

Fred looked this way and that, afraid someone would recognize them, afraid Mimi herself would materialize out of nowhere. It was hard to concentrate on John's soft chatter. They had to walk rapidly and keep their heads down; they had to be unobtrusive in the close-knit community of Woolton. It was difficult to do, and Fred was perspiring heavily.

"Must I, Daddy? Must I really?"

"Must you what?" Fred wove around slow pedestrians, pulling John along, double time.

"Call you *Pater*!" The sound of Stanley frustration filled the boy's voice.

"I'd much sooner you didn't, luv," Fred finally answered, reaching the roundabout only minutes before the bus was due to arrive. "And from here on out, there's no more listenin' to Mary Eliz…to your Auntie Mimi, Johnny boy. We're just two free men off on our own…off to see the world, as it were. We'll make up our own rules as we go along. How's that for a change? And you can call me Daddy…or Fred or Freddy or whatever strikes your fancy. But *Pater*? Bah! That's posh stuff. We'll have no truck with that, eh?"

"Right!" John squeezed his father's hand in silent partnership. "No truck with posh stuff. We're just plain."

That fact became painfully evident as the summer-hot, slow motion day wore on. The two "men" endured a bumpy bus ride and an even more cramped economy train trek down to Blackpool.

For lunch they shared one bacon butty and a single bottle of pop, and John napped on his father's shoulder, unable to spread out and sleep comfortably. Both of them ached for a chance to stretch their legs. Hunger pains increased with each hour.

Fred wished for the twenty pounds he'd surrendered to Mimi. Every time he thought it, the incident infuriated him more. *But, oh well…no matter now. Twenty pounds is only twenty pounds…and I've got Johnny with me.*

"Fifteen two!" Fred whispered his pet expression. "Let bygones be bygones, I always say." And he smiled, relieved that he had whisked John away before Mimi even knew they were gone.

By the seaside, in Blackpool, he knew he'd find some way to take the boy under his wing. If it meant abandoning a life at sea, well then, he'd "have a go at it." If it meant settling for some landlubber's job without glamour or excitement, then that would be his lot. Whatever the consequences of having his son with him from now on, Fred knew he could accept it without complaints. He was ready.

As the train rolled into Blackpool, he harmonized to the wheels' screaming halt. Humming his favourite tune and gathering up John's valise, shoes, and socks, Fred roused the sleeping child and tousled his hair lightly.

"C'mon, luv. Off we go!" he grinned. And with the strange scent of the sea in his nostrils, John obeyed, holding his father's hand and singing along now and then to the bright lyrics of Daddy's song, "One Fine Day."

****

Blackpool, England

Billy Hall and Alfred Lennon were kindred spirits. Cheerful dreamers whose thunderclouds always had silver linings, they rumbled from one downpour to the next, seeing only the beauty of the rain. Always on the verge of making a fortune or "hitting the big time," the two rambling sailors found perfect company in each other's visions. They plotted and planned in easy idleness; they schemed together.

It was Billy who had suggested the black market nylon trade. "There's plenty of money to be made in nylons, isn't there!" he had boasted. "Easy money, Fred…enough to spot us a brand new start in New Zealand in the blink of an eye!" Billy guaranteed it.

"Right. But what would I fuggin' want with New Zealand?" Fred swigged his Carling with currant. "New Zealand of all places! Where the fuggin'ell is it, anyway? And what's it to us – Northern boys to the bone?"

"It's only a bleedin' gold mine, Lenny – the fuggin' land of opportunity, as it were! Cheap land. Good wages. Great women. Me parents are even thinkin' of emigratin' over, y'know. We've kicked it 'round a bit, and me dad's put it to me that if I could make enough for their fare over, they'd meet us both in New Zealand, and we'd all start a little business together – a sure thing, a thing destined to set us all in fuggin' silks!"

"*Meet* us there?" Freddy missed no details.

"Yeah, I was figurin' you 'n me could go over free of charge, sailin' as ship stewards on some fancy luxury liner. That's how we'd go, you 'n me...free of charge and full of class!"

"Oh, we would, would we?" Fred chuckled at the idea, finishing off his pint. "But…what were yer plans for our Johnny then, with us sailin' off to kangaroo land, happy as two fat koalas in a bleedin' eucalyptus tree?"

"Actually," Billy smiled at his brilliant forethought, "I'd planned for that, as well."

"Yeah?"

"Yeah," he walked to the bar for another round. "Me parents are rather fond of the lad, y'know. I guess you've gathered that from the way me mom's gone on about him the last few weeks."

"She's spoilin' him rotten, is what," Fred winked, letting Billy get the lagers.

They raised their glasses.

"Cheers, mate."

"Cheers." Billy wiped his mouth on his sleeve before going on. "And me dad, well, he's daft over the lad, too. In fact, he's the very one what suggested bringin' Johnny along with them in a few weeks."

"With *them*?" Freddy felt uneasy. He was constantly worried about letting John out of his sight. Even though his brother, Stanley, was the only person who knew where he and John had relocated, Fred lived in terror of discovery. Living each day cautiously, he avoided constables, combed crowds for acquaintances, and most of all, feared running into Mimi or Julia. The idea of letting John go anywhere with anyone frightened him.

"Look, Len, it's like this," Billy spelled out the plan, "you could grant me parents guardianship of John, just for practicality's sake; you know, legal matters 'n all. Then they'd take the money we're goin' to bring in off the stockin's, and they'd high tail it for New Zealand on the quiet – bringin' Johnny along where your Julia'd never find him. Then, just a short while later, our 'ship would come in,' so to speak, and we'd join them – ready to spend the rest of our lives livin' in the bleedin' lap o' luxury!"

"And what if it went sour – this plan?" Fred had become more practical since John's arrival.

"Then we could always go back to sea," Billy admitted. "Me parents'd have legal custody of John anyway. So they could just step in and see the lad through the separation times, so to speak...be sort of adoptive grandparents, as it were."

"Hell, he's had more 'n enough of those." Fred wrinkled his brow in hesitation. "Relatives aren't exactly a problem in John's young, little life." He thought of his brother as he spoke; Sidney and his wife had, more or less, intimated a similar arrangement. They, too, wanted to take John into their childless household; they, too, wanted to provide for John while his father was away. It was a confusing situation, all in all.

Fred didn't know what to do.

So he ordered another lager.

****

They had just about seen all there was to see in Blackpool – the seaside fair with its coloured lights and calliope sounds, the painted "day trippers" strutting the boardwalk and smiling feverishly at any available men, and the cold ocean waves that pounded night and day with a grey, relentless fury. John had rolled up his pants' legs and waded out far, doing what Mimi would never have allowed. He had eaten fish and chips from discarded newspaper wrappers, slept in late, and refused to go to bed early. Billy had taught him to whistle through his teeth; Daddy had taught him the hands in poker. It was a man's life, this. But it was almost over.

Daddy had announced that they were all leaving soon – in a day or so – leaving for a faraway country named New Zealand. John had a picture book of New Zealand with zebras in it. Mrs. Hall had shown him the platypus duck and the strange "Mars-soup-ials." John wondered what Mars soup tasted like and how these animals got it anyway. He thought about it quite a lot.

And he'd had plenty of time to think, too. For the last two weeks he'd been off at Uncle Sydney's house. It was quiet there, a grownups' kind of place, orderly and calm like Mimi's, but without the books, drawing pads, radio shows, and wonderful Uncle Ge'rge.

Uncle Sydney's home was a polite place, a place of "Would you like?" and "Oh, yes, why of course!" but to tell the honest truth, it wasn't very much fun.

Besides, John had missed his daddy very much. John was ever mindful of money and knew that jobs were all very necessary, but he had been sad anyway to see his daddy go with Mr. Billy down to Southampton to sell ladies' stockings – even if it meant a fantastic ocean voyage on a big, enormous ship.

Thankfully, all of that was over now. Daddy had returned with his pockets crammed full of notes and toffees; Billy Hall had booked his parents' passage on the finest of ocean liners, and John was all packed to accompany the senior Halls on an adventure to the land where summer comes in winter. It would be splendid fun, from beginning to last, and at the journey's end, John would meet his daddy in New Zealand, finished with separations forever – for well and for good.

No more counting on the calendar. No more "Daddy, come home." John would be part of a family.

The doorbell interrupted his daydream. Downstairs there were voices, a man's – probably Daddy's – and a woman's, too. He seemed to know the woman's voice. It sounded familiar.

There were ugly tones, angry voices – the kind of voices landlords used on radio shows when the rent was overdue and out of pocket.

"Give me what's mine!" John pretended by himself with his best landlord's baritone.

"But I can't, I simply can't," he replied in falsetto. "Have mercy on me, dear kind sir. Have mercy!"

"No mercy! Hand it over! Hand it over now, or I'll call the authorities on you!"

The one-man drama was interrupted by a knock on the bedroom door. John immediately fell silent. He was supposed to be napping, and he closed his eyes quickly, trying not to let flickering eyelids give him away. But the knock came again, and almost simultaneously, his daddy opened the door. Fred came to the edge of the bed, and wiggled John's big toe, the way he always did.

"Johnny lad," he began, his face all white and sickly, "you'd best get up now. Get up and chuck the nap, yeah? You've got a visitor downstairs – someone who wants to talk to you, as it were."

"A visitor? For me? Really?" John popped up.

Freddy nodded, but said nothing else. From the look on his father's face, John thought that perhaps the hideous landlord *really might* have come after all...the landlord or someone far worse besides. His father's silence was frightening. John was afraid to go downstairs.

The last person he expected to see was his mother. But there she was, looking tired and unhappy. It was not her usual face. It was not her usual smile. John hadn't seen her since the day he'd run away to Mimi's house, well over two months ago, and he was afraid she was still angry. He was afraid she'd come to punish him, to scold him for his incorrigibility. John stood stock still, feeling his daddy's comforting presence just behind him, reaching for his hand.

"Hullo, Mummy," he offered quietly.

"Hello, John." Her smile was painful.

John retreated to his father's lap, putting his arms around Fred's neck and burying his face in the rough collar. No one said anything.

"Well, then," his mother's voice cracked a bit, "I guess I've seen what I came to see. It looks as if he's decided to stay."

Julia turned quickly and took a step towards the door. Frantically, her husband leapt to his feet, almost dumping John on the floor in the process. Fred grabbed Julia's arm, and John howled, "Mummy, Mummy, don't go!" burying his head in her skirt. Both men clung to her with strong-willed love.

But they were no match for Julia.

"There's absolutely no reason for me to stay." She remained stiff and unyielding. John continued to claw at her, trying to get her to pick him up.

"Look at 'im, Juliet," Fred tried an old endearment. "Our Johnny needs you! We both do! For the last time, for our John's sake, let's have another go at it, why don't we?"

"It's no use, Fred." She pulled John into her arms, "I don't want to."

"Then John'll have to decide for himself." Freddy pried John away from her and set the boy on the floor between the two of them. "Johnny, now listen, mate. Yer mummy here's goin' away, and she won't be comin' back again, y'see. Do you want to go back to Liverpool with her...or stay with me and go on off to New Zealand as we'd all planned?" He knelt beside the child, staring into his eyes prayerfully. "Which is it, luv?"

"I'm stayin' with you, Daddy." John's eyes never left Fred's own...not until the door thundered like cymbals...not until he realized what he had lost.

"Come on, Daddy!" he screamed in utter panic. "Let's go after her! Let's go and bring Mummy back!"

Fred stood and watched his son barrel down the sidewalk. He watched John running hysterically, rending the quiet, ocean air with shrieks of horrific pain. Once John stumbled and fell, but Fred watched the boy struggle to run again – never pausing, never looking back, never diminishing the screeching wails of, "Mummy, Mummy, don't go!"

Fred watched until he saw Julia turn at the sound of the boy's voice. He watched her scoop the sobbing child up into her arms and clutch him like a gold-plated trophy. Then Fred turned and nodded to Mrs. Hall, who had come to his side without speaking. "Johnny'll be returnin' to Liverpool," he said. "He'll leave on the afternoon train."

****

"Here we are!" Julia's bright voice roused the sleeping child from a dream of kangaroos and koalas. John was irritable and grumpy from the tedious journey home, but his mother sounded so delightfully cheery that he managed a squiggled smile.

"Home again, home again, jiggerty jog," she sing-songed, fishing in her purse for the taxi fare, and glancing helplessly at the driver as she fumbled. John rubbed his eyes and stared at the sleep-distorted scene outside the black city cab.

It seemed to be Mendips. It was Mendips! There was Mimi now! John waved wildly to her, and she waved back. Uncle George came out and opened the taxi door. He clapped his hands and reached out as John inched bit by bit off the long, uncomfortable seat.

"Welcome home, young man! Welcome home!" George winked and smiled, giving the boy a warm hug and slipping John a prohibited Cream-line toffee all wrapped in golden foil.

"Hello, John Winston." Mimi seemed unsure quite what to do. "You'd better run out back and say 'Hello' to your Sally as well," she directed. "The little mutt's rather missed you all these weeks. She wasn't at all sure where that frolicsome boy of hers had gotten off to!"

"All right, then. I'll go tell her about it." John started to run towards his dog, but he stopped in midstream, turning back to Julia, "Just don't forget about me when you go, Mummy." His voice quivered a bit. "Don't forget about me, now."

But by the time John had told Sally about the flock of hungry seagulls on the Blackpool beach and the smelly, hurdy-gurdy man at the seaside fair, Julia was already gone. This time, it was for good. John had come home to live at 251 Menlove Avenue.

****

"Nightmares again?" Mimi raised an eyebrow at her husband as he descended the stairs.

"The same one," George sighed, "only in a different location. This time they were all in Blackpool on the beachfront. John had tripped and fallen – 'plunk' – into a frightening hole in the sand. He said some naughty boy must have dug it just to catch some unfortunate someone. As usual, of course, *he* was the unfortunate someone...trying to climb out, dig out, find any means of escape. He called for Julia, but she never answered him. And he tried Fred, too...just as always. But then, hours later, they both appeared with rescue lines, asking him to choose which one would pull him out and take him home. It's horrid, Mimi, absolutely horrid, that dream. I'd do anything to take it away from him. I'd…"

"He'll grow out of it, George." She plodded away at her embroidery, methodically repeating the basket weave stitch. "He'll have to come to grips with the harsh realities of life, you know. All of us do."

"Not all of us." George spoke almost to himself.

He picked up the letter from John's Headmaster and read it one more time. *"Violent behaviour, surly remarks, indignant responses to teachers,"* it said. John was not coming to grips. He was not managing. Things in John's little world were, in fact, falling apart.

"Well? What did you say to him?" Mimi flipped her handwork over and unraveled a pesky knot in the yarn.

"Not much I could say, is there?" George sighed, rubbing his forehead with tired fingertips. "I just tucked him in, and I sang to him."

"Coddled him, then," Mimi snipped.

"Yes, I suppose so." George listened for any noise from the tiny room upstairs.

"Shut off the landing light now and come away from there," Mimi directed. "He's quite fine by now, I'm sure."

"I only wish I thought so, Mary Elizabeth." George stared at the inflammatory letter in his hand. "For all our sakes, I only wish that that were true."

The accounts of Freddie's reunion with his son in 1946 differ drastically. Pauline Lennon (Freddie's second wife) paints it as rescue; Julia Dykins Baird (Julia's daughter) calls it abduction. Other less biased biographies neither condemn nor applaud the action. Davies (p. 8), for example, says that Freddie Lennon had Mimi's permission to take the boy to Blackpool, as does Ray Coleman (p. 20). There is no documented record from any of the principal players in this drama. All conversation is conjecture.

1947
Mendips
Woolton

John's new life at Mendips was anything but unpredictable. Twice a week, the hired man from the dairy would arrive to tend Mrs. Smith's well-planned garden. Every other afternoon Mimi marketed, methodically selecting the freshest meats and produce from a detailed list and a clear-cut budget.

Every evening John was given a single barley sweet after supper, and he read the newspaper with Uncle George, page by page, in order. At bedtime, John would recite his rote memory prayers; then he would ritually call down to his aunt from his room above the enclosed front porch, "Don't waste the light, Mimi!" and she would turn out the soft glow that invaded his room. The Smiths and their little Lennon boy were creatures of regimentation and routine.

Even their leisure was well rehearsed. John retired to his room each day at the appointed time, to draw, read, and listen to "Up the Pole," his favourite radio programme. He found little joy in outdoor sports, but lived embryonically in an imaginary world of books and fantasy.

Above his bed, he fastened cut-out sketches of monsters and skeletons and attached thin strings to their legs which, when pulled, caused the creatures to throw dancing shadows on the wall. He filled his room with the figures he made and spent countless hours absorbed in their intricate creation.

Books, too, beckoned. Mimi was an avid reader, belonging to a book-of-the-month club and completing each novel well before the next one arrived. John found her solitary pursuit easy to emulate; he devoured books as eagerly as other children devoured candy.

He had even started writing his own book – "a rather incredible endeavor," his uncle had proclaimed. Silently, John had quite agreed with G'erge. The boy was proud of his creative efforts.

"What's it about, then – this book?" George squatted down beside the child, giving John his complete attention.

"Well," John drew himself up to his full seven-year-old height and displayed the stapled paper book as if he were giving a classroom presentation, "It's known as *Sport and Speed Illustrated* by J. W. Lennon. It's a serial book, y'know."

"A serial book? Oh, I see." George tried not to look amused.

"That's right," John thumbed through it slowly. "It's full of pictures…and bits of excitin' stories that go right on in the next edition."

"Oh, continued tales!" George nodded.

"Right," the boy explained, "each one ends at the scariest moment, right when somethin' is about to take place. Then I write, 'If you liked this, come again next week. It'll be even better...'"

"Hmmm," his uncle covered his chin with his hand, "Great idea, y'know. It's sort of a radio programme in print, isn't it? Not quite a short story, but not a novel either. Yes, I think you're on to something there, our John. I'd keep it up if I were you."

He did. John wrote something every day, and he sketched as if it were a scheduled event. For an odd change of pace, he played with his dog, Sally, or with Mimi's three Persian cats, talking to them as equals and involving them in all sorts of miraculous adventures.

"Just imagine!" he instructed them, and then the games began.

Make believe was increasingly important to the child, and when he found himself in the presence of others, John merely inducted the local Woolton children into his fantasies. The neighbourhood gang regularly congregated at Mendips, awaiting John's plan of action for the day. It was John who concocted and directed their magical worlds, turning rubbish piles into mountains and transforming abandoned air raid shelters into haunted houses. He was the dream master, and they were the idle dreamers.

Amenable Ivan Vaughn easily succumbed to John's command, and Nigel Whalley, accustomed to guidance from his police sergeant father, also fell cooperatively into line. But John struggled for the respect from Peter Shotton, a ringleted blond renegade from nearby Vale Road.

Pete had commanded the troops himself before the arrival of this new little general, and he resented John's encroachment into his territory. He was jealous of the more articulate boy from the semi-detached dwelling on Menlove Avenue, and though he dared not confront John physically, Pete prepared to challenge him on another front. He needed only to wait, watch, and bide his time.

****

With the clockwork regularity they applied to every other facet of life, the Smiths and their surrogate son attended church every Sunday. In Woolton, church meant one place only: the red sandstone spires of St.

Peter's Parish Church, that large, looming symbol of Christ, rising Gothically above the quiet middle-class neighbourhood on Church Road. The Whalleys, the Vaughns, the Smiths, and the Shottons all worshipped there, and it was there, in the presence of God, that Pete Shotton was given his long-awaited miracle.

"Good mornin'," the round, kindly soul spoke with honeyed-sweetness. "I'm your Sunday School teacher for this year – Mrs. Clark. I'm very excited to be here, you know. So much energy, so much joy!" She clapped her hands together and beamed. "This *will* be fun, won't it?"

She got little response from their sleepy-eyed faces.

"So…" she tried again, "before we begin our lesson for the day, as it were, I'd like to take a moment to get to know you personally, right? If you wouldn't mind standin' then and sayin' your complete Christian name and tellin' us just a little bit about yourself, well – I think it would help us all to become fast friends…right? Well, at least it's a start, isn't it? All right, then, let's start with you."

The girls breezed through the exercise with relative ease; John, slyly nursing a forbidden wad of gum, made faces at them and tried to distract them from their boring dissertations.

Who cares who they are or what they do anyway? John fidgeted. *It's a lot of rot – this.*

But all too soon, the boys were standing up, one after another, telling their own tales, talking of their families. And long before John was ready, it was his turn. John despised this. This was humiliation.

All the others had parents or at least one – he didn't even live at home! He hadn't accomplished anything extraordinary at Dovedale Primary – with the exception of a few canings for insubordination – and he didn't have a team sport to boast about. Even his name presented problems. The room swam as he stood.

"John Winston Lennon," he muttered, "Menlove Avenue, Dovedale Primary. I write and draw things."

"I'm so sorry, luv," Mrs. Clark smiled gently, " but I didn't quite catch your name, and I'm sure some of the other boys and girls didn't either..."

"John…John Winston Lennon," he complied, this time much too loudly.

Someone snickered…a brave someone. John looked around quickly, and silence resumed.

"How lovely…Winston, is it? After our beloved Mr. Churchill, I presume. Thank you John Winston. Thank you so much," Mrs. Clark cooed. And the agony moved on to someone else.

But the damage had been done. Pete Shotton grinned victoriously from across the room and folded his arms in smug self-satisfaction. Now he had an indefensible strategy; he was armed and ready for action.

After services, from the secure circle of his family, Pete called to John across the church grounds. "Hey, Lennon, see ya soon, *Winnie!*"

John's eyes issued threats, unveiled and dangerous, but in the presence of his rigid aunt, John was helpless.

Pete grinned wider and pressed his luck again, "Oh and *Winnie,* don't forget to bring your bike next time. I've decided we'll *not* be playin' that cowboy game again."

What Pete had expected from these challenges, he honestly couldn't say. But it felt good to assert authority once again, to have control again, to lead as he'd once led. John stared at him coolly for a long moment, and then turned his head and ignored the thrown gauntlet. Walking alongside Uncle George, John slowly moved away, leaving Pete with an uncomfortable sense of foreboding.

Pete's intuition was not wrong. John hadn't run from the battle; he'd merely selected the battlefield.

Six days later, as Pete ran carelessly across "The Tip" between Menlove Avenue and Vale Road, his enemy emerged. John had been waiting patiently for him, perhaps for hours, hiding in a thick mulberry bush.

"Listen you," the nasal voice threatened Pete, "if you keep callin' me Winnie, I'm goin' to have to smash you up."

Pete's insides churned. *Who the hell cared about leadership anyway? Wasn't it better to be safe and alive?* But running now would be cowardice.

Pete planted his feet, shoulder width apart, and squared himself at John. "Well, then, Winnie," he spat out nastily, "you'll have to prove it! In fact, I'd really like to see you try."

It was a showdown, but the rivals were miserably mismatched. Pete fought for hierarchy, for a place in his peer group, for recognition.

But John fought for survival; he fought for respect.

John fought this one battle so that the other more important battles would never materialize. He fought so that no one would question him again, so that no one would discover that he couldn't really remember his father...that his mum was living her own life in Liverpool while John lived with Mim and G'erge.

With a force that flashed spots before his eyes, John slammed Pete to the ground. Struggling to catch his breath, he scrambled, pinning Pete's arms helplessly beneath his knees.

And Pete, on the very verge of consciousness, vaguely realized that he was about to be violently beaten.

Then nothing happened. Pete opened one eye, afraid to look, but even more ashamed to hide. John's face was calm and unreadable.

"Right, then," John spoke in carefully chosen words, "you'll not be callin' me that name any more, right?"

Pete was speechless. *The wack had him! Why the bloody hell didn't he strike?*

"Let's hear it." John persisted, pressing even harder.

"Nah...I wouldn't...it was all just a joke, really." Pete couldn't believe this was taking place. He would have creamed Lennon, if he'd been in Lennon's place.

"You're sure of that, Shotton?" the inquisitor went on, never relinquishing the pressure.

Pete felt like a mouse dangling delicately from a claw. He squirmed a bit and summoned his last bit of courage. "You've proved your bleedin' point, y'know. If y'er goin' to blast me, then just go ahead and get it over with."

"Say you won't use that name again...and you won't tell anyone else, either? Promise it. Promise, and I'll let you up."

"Yeah...promised," Pete reluctantly agreed.

"Y'er sure now?" The victor eased his grasp.

"Right, yeah. Cross me effin' heart 'n hope to effin' die!"

And with that, the battle ended. John got up and extended Pete a hand. Pete took it, and they brushed off together.

"Want to ride to the churchyard and hide behind the graves and make eerie sounds at people?" Pete offered a suggestion.

"Yeah, sure, why not?" John agreed.

"We could ask the others if they'd like to come along as well."

"Yeah, all right. Go find Nige and Ivan," John instructed, "and then come 'round to my house, and we'll all go from there."

Little had changed. John was still holding the reins. But somehow, the grip was lighter, less demanding.

John smiled and turned towards Menlove Avenue. Pete headed off on his assignment. But at ten paces or so, Pete turned.

"Hey, Lennon!" Pete called loudly, and John stopped to hear, "See ya in a few, eh Winnie-Winnie?"

John stared at Pete with a critical eye, and Pete began to grin. Without knowing why, John grinned, too. "You're a dead man, Shotton," he snarled, but not a move was made.

"Only if y'catch me first."

Each day after that, Pete and John walked partway to school together, John diverging to Dovedale Primary, Pete to Mosspits. And each afternoon, they sat on the old stone bridges or the low grazing tree branches that arched the busy Woolton streets and dangled their legs daringly at double-decker buses darting underneath. They agreed to swear the vilest swear words known to man. They whispered the raunchiest poems and jokes about girls, and as often as they could engineer it, they "sagged off" school together.

They saw each other through thrashings; they shoplifted toffees and delicacies from unsuspecting grocers. And though they resembled each other in no physical way, people began to get them confused.

John was mistaken for Pete, and Pete was often called John. The duo of Shotton and Lennon became a team. It was, at last, John who turned the friendly confusion into poetry. "Shennon and Lotton" he christened them. After that, either one would answer to either name.

John's Auntie Harrie, who lived farther down Menlove Avenue, began to expect two for tea and biscuits. And John's cousins accepted Pete as part of the family. Bessie and George Shotton, ever leery of John's brand of mischief, gradually grew accustomed to his presence. Even Mimi Smith tolerated the duo.

One afternoon, six or seven months after their fight on The Tip, Pete encountered a stranger at the door of Mendips. Her copper hair shone as brightly as the smile she flashed, and she hugged Pete warmly as he came in the door.

"Peter Shotton of the golden hair! You *have* to be Pete!" she exclaimed, radiant and enthusiastic.

"Yeah…yes mum…is…is John home?" Pete was at a genuine loss for words.

"Oh, absolutely – come in and join us, luv! We're wild with makin' costumes for the school play! John's determined to be an Indian, you know, so he's in the kitchen, mixin' up a batch of real war paint from gravy brownin'…and as a matter of fact, you'd be the absolute perfect 'brave' to test it out on, I believe. Come on. This way, then."

Pete wanted to hesitate. He wanted to say that he had just come by to get John for a bike ride. He wanted to say that he had no intention whatsoever of wearing gravy browning as war paint. But somehow this woman was just like John; there was no saying "no" to her. You simply went along.

"So," John eyed him a little suspiciously as Pete entered the kitchen, "you've met me mum, then?"

No wonder! Surprise showed on Pete's face.

"Sorry," she shrugged and giggled girlishly, stirring brown goo in a mixing bowl, "I must've forgotten to tell you who I was." She wiped her hands on her slacks and extended a hand. "Julia," she winked. No Mrs. Anyone for her.

Pete smiled, mesmerized, and shook her hand in amazement. He couldn't think of anything clever or appropriate to say. He just stared at her thick, dark hair and her laughing eyes; he stared wordlessly and blushed a deep red.

But there was little time to gawk and much havoc to be had. The three Indians mixed up "war paint" in a dozen colours with cups and spoons. And using Mimi's best pastry brush, they painted John first; then Pete was decorated. Julia made herself up as an Indian squaw and wrapped in the kitchen rug for the *piece de resistance*. Whooping and hopping around the kitchen, she let the boys fall in line behind her –John carrying a wooden spoon tomahawk and Pete, armed with a meat mallet. There was enough noise for a whole tribe in the Woolton kitchen, and enough spatter and mess as well.

By nightfall, Julia was gone. With a kiss and a quick, "T'rah luvs!" she was off to catch the bus, leaving the boys to clean up before Mimi discovered it. "But no matter," she'd grinned at them confidently. "Just give it a spot and a tap and a swish and a rinse...and it'll be fine, I'm sure!"

Bowls were overturned in the sink. Bottles of food colouring had spilled on the counters. Dirty butter knives and stained dishtowels were thrown helter-skelter. Mimi's throw rug was stained brown and red, and utensils that had once been weapons were scattered across the floor. Even John and Pete were a shamble...doused in gravy browning.

The sudden quiet inside the house brought Mimi to the kitchen door. She stood in her cable knit cardigan, her gardening apron, and gloves – still slightly damp from a long afternoon of composting roses – and stared.

"Mum had to go home straight away, Mim." John was ever Julia's expiator. "She had to get home before dark'n all. You know how it is."

"And what of *this*, John?" Mimi asked, meaning more than the words implied. "Who will see to this mess now that she's off and gone again?"

Pete shuffled uneasily and looked away. John looked guilty, but said nothing. There was really nothing anyone could say, and both boys were too young to know that the question was primarily rhetorical.

Sighing deeply, Mimi removed her gardening attire and reached for the apron hanging on the iron hook behind the kitchen door. She put it on. Her lips were pinched and tight. Her movements were crisp and purposeful. She clucked and shook her head and looked years older than her sister.

"Goodnight then, Peter," Mimi said pointedly, "unless, of course, you intend to stay and assist in the clean-up process."

Pete didn't volunteer. And neither did John.

At precisely 7:00 p.m. that evening as every evening, supper was served in Mendips. It wasn't fancy, but it was nutritious and warm. It was served at the family table on the traditional evening china with the traditional condiments, including a small bowl of Branston Pickle and a plate of assorted cheeses. All had been prepared in a kitchen that was spotlessly clean, a kitchen in which no trace of mayhem lingered.

After dinner, John tiptoed upstairs to listen to the wireless. He read two chapters of *Alice's Adventures in Wonderland* and laid out his school clothes for the following day. He worried a little about the Indian costume...worried that he'd have nothing to wear after all. But under the circumstances, he didn't think it wise to ask Mim about it. He just worried and gnawed his fingernails.

By half-eight, Mimi had finished the supper dishes, watered her plants, and fed Sally and the cats. Then she returned her apron to the hook behind the door and flipped off the light.

"Done for the night then, Mary Elizabeth?" George studied her face above the newspaper. She'd been unusually quiet at dinner.

"No," she snatched up her sewing basket and long, silver shears, "Not by a long shot, I'm not."

George waited.

"Judy, you understand, was supposed to help John with his costume for the school play tomorrow. He wanted to be an Indian. He wanted to dress in full regalia."

"Wanted?" George raised an eyebrow. "I take it something went wrong, then."

Mimi turned on the lamp next to her chair. "Judy got caught up in the moment..." she huffed.

"And never finished the task?" George suggested.

Mimi waved him off with one hand. "It's all too much to go into now, and things being as they are, I haven't time to chat, George. You see, *I* have a costume to make, as it were!"

"Oh dear," her husband sighed.

"Yes, 'oh dear' as always." Mimi sat down and adjusted her glasses. "Judy can conduct herself as she pleases – here and there, this and that, now and again! But eleventh hour, last minute, night before the show, end of the rope...we're the ones responsible for John, aren't we, George?"

"Right," he said softly. "We can't afford to let the boy down,"

"No," Mimi began to work. "We wouldn't dream of it."

All events are documented. All conversation is conjecture.

September 1948

251 Menlove Avenue
Woolton, England
September 1948

Dear Dottie,

It was lovely to hear from you after all this time! Incredible how the years have slipped away without our noticing. It seems like yesterday we were in nursing school, preparing to conquer the world.
Your life sounds wonderful...three children, the perfect number to keep one happy and occupied. I have given up nursing full time, also...though I suppose one never gives it up entirely...always the neighbourhood doctor of sorts, aren't we? I'm married now to George Smith. You remember him? His father owned the local dairy, and George has taken it on these days. He does well, is a good provider, and on most occasions, remains an equal-tempered man. (You know most Northern men; I count myself fortunate.)
Like you, I have a child...actually, my sister Julia's son, John. You remember Julia, no doubt...cares to the wind. Well, John is the product of Julia's unhappy marriage to Alfred Lennon, a sailor who's had many ports o' call, but no home. Suffice it to say that Julia was never one to sit by the fireside knitting.
In short, she's settled in now with another chap, a glamorous, fly-by-night, swashbuckling sort who's given her a new baby and the kind of life Julia's always desperately desired. And so, John has come to me to rear.
John moved in with George and me several years ago and is as much a part of our family as if he were born to it. And in all honesty, Dot, he's both a blessing and burden...but isn't that the story

with all children?

    Our John's a bright child...reads voraciously. He's only seven, and yet he's read most of the classics. Believe it or not, he adores Balzac and has read the collected works. I struggle with Balzac, and most people have never even glanced at his writings without a professor's prodding. But John devours him like Christmas pudding! So to say that our John is far above average is not boast; it's simply the truth.

    For the most part, he's a quiet child, withdrawn to own his little nook upstairs, always busy with painting, sketching, reading...some sort of creative work. This week he has "chicken pots" (as he calls them), and he's hardly complained a whit. A regimented sort when he chooses to be, our John doesn't attempt to violate doctor's rules. I haven't even seen him scratch a single time. That's John.

    But, like Julia, he's more complex than that. In increasing amounts, he's prone to pranks and misbehaviour. Sometimes I feel he's so intelligent that he concocts these little schemes simply to keep himself amused. Other times, I fear it's something far deeper, far worse. I worry about the scars left by the separation from his mother and father. I worry that he rarely mentions either one of them or expresses loss or complaint. He seems in great part so well adjusted and accepting, and then at other moments, so frighteningly rebellious. Our John's a grand contradiction, Dottie...a miniature but intricate mystery.

    Last week I was on my way home, loaded with packages, hurrying up Penny Lane to get to Mendips before John returned from school. In an alley, I happened to see two common scruffs battling full tilt, and in utter disgust, I started to look away. But at the last minute, something familiar about one of the ruffians caught my eye. I looked again. **It was Lennon!** No rough and tumble boy this...it was my own charge. I was horrified!

    That is the life I lead.

    George is steady as a rock and good for the boy. But John is up and down with the wind...one moment, chattering happily about a scene from The Wind In The Willows; the next, suspended for arrogant behaviour. He is gentle and loving to our three cats and his little dog, but he is fisticuffing his way through school, determined to *take on the world. He writes stories and poems, reads far above his grade level, captains every group...and yet his school report reads, "Certainly on the road to failure...hopeless." I cannot mesh these contradictions, Dot. I only hope your three are more predictable than this.*

To tell you the truth, I worry that my own inability has fostered much of this trouble. It haunts me. I never intended to have children. To be honest, I never really planned to be married at all; you know I hardly fancied being tied to a kitchen or to a sink! But then the war came along, and one thing led to another...I was truly fond of George...and, all things considered, it's been a good partnership.

Then from the moment I first saw him, I loved our John. He was the boy we Stanley girls had long awaited, an incredibly beautiful child.

But he is part-and-parcel Julia and Fred – inexplicable, unpredictable, and nothing like me. I've tried discipline. I've tried decorum and routine. I've tried to make environment rather than heredity count for something. But I wonder, have I been too rigid, too exacting? Have I caused this upheaval? Have I demanded too little? What am I doing wrong?

Do you ask yourself these things? Are your girls as perplexing to you as John is to me? I keep telling myself that it all comes back to an unwavering set of rules to live by, but John seems untouched by the boundaries of such rules. He moves through my little world, but doesn't really exist in it. Oh, there are moments of compromise, Dottie, but they are thinly tolerated, shallow pantomimes of compromise.

Mimi lifted the pen from the notepad. *What in heaven's name am I about? I can't post this! Pouring my heart out like a character from a melodrama to some friend I hardly even remember!*

She tore the letter from the tablet and skimmed it briefly one more time. It was shocking...vulgar emotionalism, self-pitying indulgence!

Mimi waded the paper into a crumple; then she unfolded it and tore it into tiny pieces. The bits floated down into the basket, and covered the wicker with disjointed fragments. Mimi returned to her chair to start the letter again. This time it would be something entirely appropriate.

Dear Dottie,

It was lovely to hear from you after all this time...

The story of John's fistfight is a direct quotation from Mimi Smith. She does say of her eight-year-old, "It was Lennon!" not "It was John!" Only Dottie is fictitious.

December 1948
Mendips
Woolton

Mimi could tell the house was empty before she even opened the door. The light inside the glass-enclosed vestibule was on, and the curtains were drawn. George and John always "secured the hold" that way just before leaving – overkill, as if closing up a summerhouse for the off-season.

Mimi shook her head. *Why not just hang out a "house vacant" sign for every burglar in town? Men!*

She struggled with her grocery bags and managed to get the key in the lock at the same time. Balancing one bag on an elevated knee, she wriggled her way into the house, almost spilling the produce from the green grocer's.

It had been one of *those* weeks – three phone calls from Dovedale Primary redundantly complaining of John's behaviour without offering any solutions. Mimi tired of the school's inability to cope with the child. She found him not the least bit difficult to manage, most days.

From the beginning, John had always determined to do exactly as he pleased, plopping down squarely in mud holes as a toddler or, a few years later, refusing to do chores if he could find a way out. But consistent supervision and unwavering authority had always produced positive results at home. Mimi failed to see why the school staff could not achieve the same result.

She thought them inept.

And then there had been the unnerving letter from Fred Lennon, inquiring about his son. Mimi had tossed it away, never mentioning a word of it to anyone except George. But it scared her nevertheless. She could never shake the fear that one day Fred would return to the doorstep. He had every right to claim his own child, just as he'd done once before.

Freddy had never stopped writing, had never stopped asking after John or wanting news of "his boy." He'd never let Mimi rest easy. A few months would pass without a word from Lennon, and Mimi would decide that they had, in fact, "heard the last of the man." And then, out of the blue, a letter would come in the post from halfway around the world, and Mimi's fears would be ignited once again. Fred had an uncanny way of rattling her just when Mimi thought the future was secure.

And now, *this*...so close to the holidays! Mimi wished she knew where John and George were.

She could only guess.

She knew they'd come home swearing they'd been in the Penny Lane roundabout bakery shop or the Woolworth's in Smithdown, Christmas shopping – but Mimi knew better. An adventure film, a holiday release, was playing at the picturedrome, and George had no doubt indulged the boy in an afternoon at the cinema.

The bitter pill was that her husband was acting in complete defiance of her rules. Such frivolous activities had always been off limits to John. And although George and John were both well aware of the guidelines, they had chosen to disobey. It was annoying, at best.

Mimi "hmphed" to herself, releasing the kitchen bags onto the table and reaching in the cupboard for a glass. *Perhaps an iced lemon will cure my ills*, she frowned. She doubted it, but poured a glass anyway.

Then she saw it – the note printed in a rigid, childish hand. Placed precisely on the middle of the kitchen counter, the message was left where Mimi was sure to find it. She picked it up, took a long sip of her drink, and began to read out loud to no one:

Dear Mim,
Don't be lonely or sad while I'm away. Read a good book.
Love,
John

Disciplinary phone calls and missives from Fred were at once forgotten. Dismissed was the inconvenience of having to unload the groceries all alone. Even the horrors of the picturedrome were wiped away. Mimi read the note again and smiled. *The boy should have a government post, that's what*, she decided. Then she pulled off her jacket, and settled into her work.

All events, including the note, are actual.

Autumn 1949
Woolton

Mimi had always clung tenaciously to ritual. It defined her in the post-war world of constant change. It gave her direction when she felt overwhelmed by society's threatening rush and precarious balance.

But just as Julia had predicted, John – the product of Fred's free spirit and Julia's brazen unpredictability – seemed ill at ease with artificial boundaries. The boy was particular, but he was creatively particular. He wanted perfection, but he wasn't compulsive.

John found routine senseless; he saw no logic in eating meals at prescribed times or labouring over homework simply for the satisfaction of paperwork completed. And chores he found completely useless. If the grass were clipped, why then it would only return thicker and stronger the next week! If he made his bed, he had only to unmake it later at bedtime. He regarded these practices as "totally wasteful."

Church, however, was one weekly ritual that the nine-year-old looked forward to with sincere glee. As predictable as it was, Sunday was never tedious. Once Mimi and George had released John into the good hands of his Sunday school teacher, John was essentially on his own for the span of two full hours. It was a freedom he relished, a recess he anticipated with growing enthusiasm.

Benevolent volunteers, John's Sunday school teachers were kind but always inexperienced. They were weekend saints, but not avenging angels. And try as they might to corral the collective energies of preadolescent John Lennon and his Shotton shadow, the boys frolicked ahead of any control at an alarming speed. In short, Shennon and Lotton did exactly what they wanted to do.

Loudly popping bubblegum and straggling into class with their pockets full of candy and toffees but devoid of their offering tuppence, John and Pete whispered and giggled to each other during the morning lectionary. They elbowed one another and snickered when others asked questions or offered answers.

On Harvest Sunday, particularly inspired by the festive occasion, John and Pete led a small band of revelers in a daring raid on the altar cornucopia. They filled their pockets with grapes, nuts, and dates. A heist of the Royal Jewels could not have been more celebrated. John called it "The Grand Caper," and the boys slapped one another on the back in congratulations. Pete divided the spoils among the crew.

At lunchtime, not one of them was hungry, but not one had the courage to "beg off" that day. The parish priest had already begun ringing up certain parents in search of the blasphemous thieves, and even a rebel like John had no desire to be caught. He ate his meal slowly and silently, while in Vale Road Pete listlessly endured pot roast and boiled potatoes without a bit of appetite. Such was the price of forbidden fruit.

To John, the whole concept of "the forbidden" was as attractive as it had been for "Mother Eve." It was the thrill of the caper that fueled him, not a desire to thumb his nose at the church or at any other authority, for that matter. He sincerely liked the church staff; he even tolerated Reverend, a whining Welshman with no apparent regard for children. John had no antagonism towards the Anglican Church in general or St. Peter's in particular. He felt no anger at all towards the God he spent little time worshipping there.

John was merely swept up in the thrill of getting away with something taboo. In a life that was stiflingly regimented, John's pranks and schemes became a "high," his antics an addiction.

By the time Reverend telephoned Mimi Smith with "the decision," the pranks had become practice. John and Pete had become miscreants. Their weekly escapades set the church on its ear, and gradually, the mischief had grown bolder.

"Perhaps another parish church might be better, as it were," Father's high-pitched voice falteringly suggested, "a larger church...one with a younger priest..."

"Are *you, sir,* not a capable man?" Mimi Smith returned curtly, her anger seething. "You should attend to your own discipline problems, not seek to pawn them off on the purported talents of others."

"Mrs. Smith," the agitated clergyman heaved a long sigh, "I *have* tried...honestly I have. I've ignored John as long as I dare. I've endeavoured to inspire him, but I'm not a Headmaster who can dole out punishments and demerits and make them stick. I'm only the pastor of a church, not a lieutenant, understand. And the truth is...well...frankly, I've come to the end of the road here."

"Are you saying, sir," Mimi's ordinarily even voice cracked a bit, "that St. Peter's – the church I have attended years upon end, the same church where John was baptized, the church where he learned his catechism – that *this* church is now off limits to my nephew, and thus to my husband and to me?"

"Mrs. Smith," the shrill voice rejoined, "we shall regret to lose you. You are well respected. Mr. Smith is a fine man. But we must ask you, at least for the time being, to take your nephew elsewhere. It is tremendously hard to say this, but at last, I must. John is no longer welcome in St. Peter's."

Mimi didn't say goodbye. She replaced the receiver in stunned silence. A warm, bitter bile rose in her throat, and she could feel her heart pounding away. Mimi was mortified. More than that, she was angry.

Could the church, in fact, turn you away? She scanned her memory for scriptural precedent. Could the venerable Church of England slam its doors on the youthful antics of a nine-year-old boy? Were the misdemeanours that John had committed valid justifications for "dismissal from the fold"? Mimi sank into her chair in the adjoining morning room and, in a rare moment of stillness, simply sat.

She thought of those who lived in unabashed sin, but who were cordially welcome in the church whenever they opted to attend. She thought of various drunkards, philanderers, swindlers, gossips, liars, gamblers, and adulterers who filled the pews, who thronged to St. Peter's Sunday after Sunday, year after guilty year without the slightest hand slap or priestly censure.

And then her gaze fell on John, busy in backyard play, absorbed in taunting his pup, Sally, who chased him round and round the enclosed garden. "The chief of all sinners," she whispered to herself. "The shunned of St. Peter's."

Mimi folded her hands and clenched her jaw in determined resolve. John Winston would have to be punished. As unfair as St. Peter's pronouncement seemed, it was a judgement. John would have to assume full culpability. Such was life.

Mimi rose from her chair, rapped sharply on the window, and motioned for her nephew to come inside.

He tumbled in, arms and legs everywhere. "What's up, Mim? What's the game?" Sally tried to squeeze through the door at his heels.

"No game, John. Come all the way in and close the door. We need to have to serious chat."

John's visage lost its playfulness. He cloaked himself in defensiveness as he walked across the room. He recognized the tone of his aunt's voice all too well; nothing good could come of this.

"John...St. Peter's has just rung me up."

"It wasn't me."

"Don't give me that. This is serious, John Winston. Would you like to venture a guess as to what they called to tell me?"

"Peace on earth, good will to men?" John tried humour. But Mimi didn't smile, not even a little.

"They said," she leaned forward accusingly, "that they've had quite enough of your shenanigans...your nonsense and mockery...your pranks. They're fed up with you, John...you and Peter Shotton as well! Because you see, even the church can finally reach the limit!"

"Ah, ole Father's just browned off about the Harvest grapes, Mim. That's all it is, y'know. He'll settle down once he..."

"So it *was* you after all!"

"Well...Pete'n me."

"Peter Shotton! The root of all evil, that one!" Mimi spat out. "He's been nothing but a detrimental influence on you ever since you met him! Just a scamp without..."

"It was *my idea*, Mim." John set the record straight. "It was me suggestin' the raid on the altar basket. It was me that talked Pete into the whole thing!"

"*You!*" She stood up, tight with anger. "*You?* It was *you*, then, who suggested mimicking the soloist as he sang last Sunday? It was you who suggested filching from the collection plates as well?"

"Right...well, just a handful here and there." John shrugged. "Just enough for the tuck shop...for a few Creamline toffees and a..."

"Toffees?" Mimi was incredulous. "For the want of toffees, your church standing was lost?"

"Lost? What'd'ya mean, *lost?*" John's nostrils flared slightly.

"You've been banned from St. Peter's, John. 'Booted out' as they say in *your* vernacular. Turned away! Disbarred is, I believe, the proper term."

"They can *do* that? It's allowed, then?" John squirmed uneasily for the first time since the interview began.

"They can, John," Mimi pronounced, falling back like a limp rag doll into her chair. "They can, and they have. And..." she paused melodramatically before saying it, "your uncle George and I have been asked to leave the church as well." Her voice fell. "After all our years at St. Peter's..."

"But *you* haven't done anything wrong!" John railed against the blindness of justice. "*I'm* the only one at fault here! I'm the one..."

"Well, it doesn't work that way, John."

"Look, I'll ring up the bleedin' reverend and get this sorted out for you, Mim. I'll tell him that it was all a..."

"You'll do nothing of the sort, John. You'll say nothing, do nothing. You'll learn to live by the rules of society. You'll learn that when you don't obey, you're chastised."

"But Ge'rge didn't act out! *You* didn't disobey!"

"But don't you see, John," Mimi's voice took on its lecture hall quality, "that when you choose your actions unwisely, you hurt others? Remember John Donne: 'No man is an island unto himself.' Remember that? Well, there you have it. Every action we take affects someone else. Every choice we make..."

Her voice trailed off into silence. John, apparently quite over his anger and indignation and bored by her harangue, had taken to making faces at his dog through the morning room window. Sally jumped up and down wildly and barked at him as John continued to egg her on from inside the glass.

"John Winston!" Mimi shrieked, "You're not paying one whit of attention to what I'm saying! Not even after all the trouble you've caused! Just exactly who do you think you are, young man? Tell me that!"

"Don't you knooooooooooow me?" he responded in a crackly, little voice. "A'im John Winston Lennon."

The little elf offered an impish grin.

It was a sputtered snort, a half-suppressed giggle. Mimi felt it rise unbidden and spill out without her permission. For a moment, she was afraid she would give way to laughter. John batted his eyes rapidly and pouted his lips as he moved towards her.

"Givvus a kiss, Auntie!" He grabbed her and hugged her hard.

Mimi pulled away and turned her head to hide the smile. *No one could discipline a child like this!* Just like Julia before him, John had the alchemy for turning chagrin into glee.

"Oh, go on and play, then." Mimi dismissed him abruptly. She would gather her thoughts and try to talk to John later that evening.

All that afternoon, John stayed close to the house. He made bizarre faces through the windows as Mimi worked. He pinched a rose from the rear garden and brought it in at teatime. He washed up for supper without being prodded and rattled off jokes over kidney pie.

"What's up with our John, this evening?" George asked in a hushed voice after John had gone off to his room to draw.

"What an odd question." Mimi looked puzzled. "He's been laughing with you for the last hour, hasn't he? He set the supper table for a change and even removed his own plate!"

"That's how I knew something was wrong." George pushed his own chair back from the table and stacked his glass and silverware on the china. "He's clearly upset."

"Ridiculous, George. We had a little set-to this afternoon, but John's been fine ever since. In fact, more than fine. He's been unusually agreeable.

"And *that's* the point." He lifted his plate and walked into the kitchen. "He's hurt, or angry, or both. You tell me."

"Sh-sh-sh-sh!" Mimi held up a hand. "You'll stir it up all over again – broadcasting it to the four corners of the world."

"Broadcasting what? So he *is* upset, then? Why?"

"No, no, no, no, no – it's all over and done with now, and John's fine." Mimi reached for her apron and turned the water on at the sink. "Really. John's perfectly happy."

"Is that right? Well," George placed his glass near the sudsy water that began to fill one side of the sink, " then you don't mind if I go up and have a chat with Mr. Jovial, do you? I think I'd like to witness this rare mood of elation all for m'self."

Mimi plunged her hands into the warm water and listened to George's heavy tread ascending the stairs. Now to her list of worries, she had to add the anticipation of George's heated reaction to the church fathers and their mandate. She knew her husband would never concede that "his Johnny" had been wrong. John never was – not in George's eyes.

She took the stemware first and placed it gently into the sink, her fingers shielding the delicate rims as they touched against the bottom. With slow and measured care, she washed each pedestal glass in a clockwise motion, rinsing it for twenty seconds in scalding water and placing each glass in the wooden bin to dry. Then she repeated the exact same process with her mum's favourite china from Newcastle Road, then the old silverware, and finally, the dented pots and pans. Mimi observed her time-honoured routine meticulously, especially on a night when things were in such a muddle.

As she washed, Mimi replayed the afternoon's conversation with John in her mind, wishing she had said this or done that, thinking how she might have handled the episode better. She played it over and over, wondering if John had learned a lesson at all or if, in fact, she was the one who had learned hers.

Why would a boy who had everything he wanted steal collection money for toffees? Why would a child whose plate was full of good food pilfer the Harvest grapes? Why would he torment his Sunday school teachers? Why would he pretend to be happy this evening if, as George asserts, he's really still upset or distressed over the matter?

Mimi had no answers.

In fact, the older John got, the less she knew him. The longer he lived with them, the less she recognized the child. She had tried to give him boundaries, rules, and guidelines to live by. She had tried to make "the right choices" obvious.

But all Mimi knew, as she folded the dishrag carefully into quarters and hung it on the metal rack above the sink, was that she *didn't* know. She didn't know anything at all.

John was increasingly a mystery.

All events in this chapter actually took place. Many of the quotes ("Don't you knooooow me?" for example) are also authentic. Only the "linking" conversations between documented quotes are conjecture.

May 1950
Mendips
Woolton

The sketch was eerie – one of those pictures that seem to follow you as you move. Mimi set it back on the tea table, took a step away from it, and then returned again. It drew her back.

John had completed the assignment in record time: a pencil sketch of a famous figure. It had, nevertheless, been drudgery for him. "A forced confinement indoors" he'd called it, a chore. Despite the fact that John regularly spent hours upon end sketching voluntarily, when he *wanted* to do so, he'd resented the recent assignment. He adored art, but homework John despised. He hated being *told* to paint.

Nevertheless, the sketch was good. It was the face of a young man with a strangely serious demeanour, ragged beard, and prominent, thin-pinched nose beneath the gentlest of eyes. Around the face, long hair cascaded to the shoulders, falling in almost imperceptible waves, framing mystical eyes with reflected curves of light that danced in a haloed effect. John's sketch was hypnotizing, inexplicably serene.

Mimi picked it up once again.

"Jesus," she whispered, and she looked dutifully pleased, remembering John's recent request to become confirmed in the church, despite his separation from St. Peter's the previous year. After all that had happened, she was amazed that the boy still felt God tugging on his naughty, preadolescent soul. The St. Peter's ordeal had been a bitter pill for them all, but obviously, John had simply forgotten. The sketch in her hand was proof of that.

God had long intrigued John. In fact, Mimi smiled remembering how the boy had actually "encountered" the Lord one dreary, winter afternoon several years ago. John had come upon Him quite by accident in, of all places, the parlour at Mendips. No one had anticipated such a prestigious visit.

"I've just spoken with God," John had announced importantly.

"Oh...really?" Mimi had bitten her lip. "And where did this chance encounter take place, if I may ask?"

"In the parlour," the child had spoken frankly as he climbed up in the ladder-backed chair to take tea. "He was warming himself by our fire."

Recalling it now, Mimi wondered. It was as possible as it was ludicrous. Anything was possible with God...and with John – anything.

Now she stared at the sketch again, studying it carefully.

The eyes in the drawing were vivid, real. They seemed rendered from experience, sketched from a model, as it were. Mimi shivered as she placed the artwork down again. She looked at it this way, that.

"Admirin' me sketch, then?" The artist's voice startled her. John swung his net pouch of marbles back and forth, and he, too, stared at the picture. He had grown tall in the last year, almost as tall as she, and every day, his face looked more like Fred Lennon's. Except the eyes, of course. Those were undeniably Judy's.

"Very nice work, John...lovely – if hastily done." Mimi never delivered a complete compliment. "Nice likeness, very accurate."

"And how d'you know that?" John was as direct as his aunt. "I mean, how can y'tell...about the accuracy 'n all?"

"Well...from other paintings, I suppose," Mimi struggled for logic. "From what we know...from tradition, from Biblical accounts..."

"*Biblical accounts*!" John's dark eyes danced. "Not bleedin' likely!"

"John Winston, don't say *bleedin'*; you're no Scouser; you're from Woolton, remember. And whatever in heaven's name are you going on about now?" His aunt was instantly frustrated. The boy was incorrigibly vague. He loved his little secrets and mysteries. He loved having the upper hand. It annoyed Mimi on the spot. "It *is* a portrait of Christ, is it not?" she barked.

"No, it's not." John took the sketch and held it up beside his cheek. "It's a portrait of a famous person in twenty years, a genius extraordinaire. Can't you see, Mim? Can't you guess who it is, then? Look closer," he sighed, as frustrated as she. "It's me!"

Mimi looked at the ethereal eyes in the sketch and then at the mischievous eyes of the boy beside her; she looked at the penciled face full of peace and resignation and then at John's own, full of lively contention.

"*You!* Impossible!" She poofed her lips at the ridiculous suggestion. "Utterly impossible, John. It's not you at all! Long hair? And a beard? And that sad, gaunt face with the crusader's eyes? That's not the boy I know. That's not John Lennon of Mendips, Woolton. Not in twenty years...not in thirty!"

John picked up his sketch and stared at it critically. He held it at arm's length and squinted.

"It's John Lennon," he pronounced flatly, placing the sketch back on the table. "That's who it is all right – end of subject, Mim." He swung his bag of marbles a couple of times and then took a step towards the door.

"People always think they know someone else," he called back over his shoulder, "but they hardly ever do. They only see what they want to see and hear what they want to hear."

"Well then, Mr. Philosopher," Mimi hissed, "we'll just have to wait to see if your prophecy comes true, won't we?"

"You're welcome to wait, Mim," he said. "I already know."

John exited as quickly as he'd entered, leaving Mimi alone staring at the drawing, looking far into the sketch for any hint of the aggravating boy who had just left the room.

This event and the meeting between God and young John are both reported by Ray Coleman. The conversation is conjecture.

Autumn 1952
Woolton

Quarry Bank School for Boys was two miles and a world away from Menlove Avenue. A brick bastion of education and decorum, the Victorian Gothic brick and stone edifice, casting long purple shadows from its towers and chimneys, rose majestically into the trees over Harthill Road. Quiet as its ivy-covered walls, reverent as the black-robed professors who swished through its corridors, Quarry Bank was serious, refined, and dedicated to the pursuit of knowledge.

Carved on the prominent oak Memorial Board and emblazoned on every student's coat of arms, was this engraved motto: "*Ex hoc metallo virtutem.*" "From this rough metal, we forge virtue."

It was a pledge, a commitment.

John and Pete saw the maxim as an outright challenge – and they tacitly vowed a brotherhood that would make the noble Quarry Bank's quest a struggle, if not an impossibility.

For years they had enjoyed only after-school fraternization and weekend camaraderie, but now the fantastic had come to pass: they were both attending the same school! What's more, they were grouped in the same "house" or scheduling cluster. All boys from their neighbourhood were in the "Woolton House" of Quarry Bank. Pete couldn't have been more elated; John couldn't have been more inspired.

Just the thought of the pranks they would pull at the helpless expense of dull others made them chuckle as they biked to school in their regulation black and gold ties and black blazers. John rode out ahead, standing on his pedals and pumping vigourously; he was sweating in the new tailor-made clothes that Mimi insisted Uncle Ge'rge pay for. Pete lolled behind, riding leisurely and taking in the scenery that his blind friend couldn't possibly see.

John had glasses – thick ones at that – but vanity prohibited his wearing them. He opted to squint instead and made Pete the designated lookout for obstacles. Generally, the arrangement worked fairly well, but at times Pete's interest seemed to wander.

"Fuggin' hell, Shotton, get it in gear!" John yelled from about fifty yards ahead. Pete picked up the pace a bit, just enough to satisfy.

"Y'know, a person's only given so many breaths in one lifetime, Shennon," Pete yelled at John's back, "and if y'fuggin' waste 'em on shite like pedalin', there'll be none left for the really good stuff, will there?"

Over his shoulder, John shouted, "We're already half-late, y'know, and old Taylor's threatened another in the long line of sordid tortures if we bungle it again. I'm barely over the bruises from yesterday. People are beginnin' to think I'm just naturally black 'n blue!"

E.R. Taylor, the tall, sophisticated, venerable Headmaster of Quarry Bank, was a man with an insurmountable task. He had assumed leadership of the faculty in 1947, with aspirations of instilling high ideals into willing young minds. Now, after five years of relative success, he was faced with the not-so-willing: John Lennon and Peter Shotton. Headmaster Taylor had tried every form of punishment at his disposal, yet he had found the two boys radically incorrigible.

At best, the duo did "not fit in with what we have set out to do," the weary man complained. At worst, the two were convicted of swearing, being tardy, "sagging off" school entirely, smoking, insulting professors, and, worst of all, gambling on school sporting events. Each day they met him with a new brand of defiance; each afternoon they concocted fresh deviltry. In no way were they making "positive contributions to the life of the school," Taylor fumed. And this was only their freshman term!

The bell rang loudly as John chained his bike to the only available post. Pete was still nowhere to be seen. *Shite! He's slow as Christmas!* John swore again silently, wiping his forehead on his sleeve and spitting on the sidewalk.

"Your name, sir!" It was one of the "black widow" professors John had not yet encountered. John squinted at him, trying to get a better look. The man repeated his demand of the silent, insolent-looking boy, "Your name, sir."

"Lennon," John returned evenly.

"Well, Mr. Lennon, I'm sure you're aware of our school regulations. I'm certain you're cognizant of the fact that spitting is specifically prohibited on Quarry Bank grounds."

Pete cycled up at this most unfortunate moment. He fiddled with his bike lock and tried to remain as inconspicuous as possible, eavesdropping on the conversation.

"It wasn't spitting, actually," John began toying with the man, "It was more in the category of catapulted drool, flyin' phlegm, what have ya. It was more..."

"That's quite enough!" The man exploded, gesturing with his black-robed arms. He looked like a ruffled crow.

John bit his lip hard, but smiled anyway. Pete, unfortunately, snickered.

"And you!" The professor turned in the direction of the sound. "You're tardy as well, are you not? You two should be in class as we speak. The bell sounded minutes ago."

"Well, then sir, we're off then, sir," John scooped up his books in mock seriousness, "posthaste and look sharp there, Shotton!"

"Shotton? Fine. Thank you." The teacher whipped out a small notebook from a hidden pocket and began to make notes. "Now I've *both* your names."

"You do, don't you?" John deadpanned. "Good work, then, sir."

Pete looked over with feigned interest, "And…awfully nice handwriting, as well." He nodded at John.

The man flipped the notebook closed with a "pop!" He glared at the pair with narrowed eyes and veins bulging in his neck. "Report to my office promptly after school," he threatened, "and be prepared to remain. I've a field of leaves and a couple of rakes just waiting for two apostates such as you. Quarry Bank is *not* the place for flippant answers and casual attitudes. It's a bastion of tradition and respect! And if you haven't any of your own, gentlemen, then perhaps I can instill some in you."

And with that, the educator lifted his chin and floated off. John and Pete mockingly lifted theirs and shoulder-to-shoulder glided straight in through the front door of the building, an entrance strictly forbidden to all students.

All incidents are documented; conversation is conjecture. However, the quotes from E. R. Taylor ("not fit in with what we have set out to do," and "not making positive contributions to the life of the school," are authentic.)

Summer 1954
Mendips
Woolton

"So you've survived yet another year at Ole Quarry Bank." George stood in his pajamas, robe, and slippers, stirring a glass of Ovaltine, John's favourite bedtime treat.

"I don't know how." John yawned as he talked. "It's awful – that place."

"You aren't learning anything at all, then?" His uncle handed him the glass and took a seat across from the teenager.

"It's more for those who want to get their names on the scholarship board, y'know. The rest of us can rot for all they care."

"All of them?"

"Yeah…well, there's this one history teacher. He advised Pete 'n me to become window washers, as it were."

"An interesting choice." George smiled.

"And then there's the chemist, Oldham. He hates me as much as I hate him."

"Ah…a symbiotic relationship!" George's eyes sparkled

"And not to forget the very joyous Yule, my math teacher." John took a long drink. "He's so fond of me, he lifted me clear off the ground by the lapels."

"Umm…rather close, you two." George shook his head.

"It's all about the elite, y'know," John leaned forward, "the professor pleasers."

"But it's that way in everything, John…in the dairy business, in the cotton industry, in upholstering, shipping, what have you. Those with 'brown noses' fare well in life. Young or old, that's the way of it."

"But *you* haven't lived that way, have you?"

"No," George rubbed his aching hands together, massaging the palms as he talked, "but then…I haven't done that well, now have I? Just ask your Auntie Mimi. She'll tell you straight up I've let her down. I mean, you know yourself we frequently have medical students boarding in to make ends meet, and we aren't off on holiday every few months as some are, are we? No, I'm no Andrew Carnegie, as it were, and it seems quite likely I never will be. I just get along, John…just get along…"

"Get off," John smirked. "Everyone likes ole Ge'rge." He raised his glass in a toast to his uncle.

"*You* like Ge'rge. That's what."

"And I've good taste," the boy grinned.

"But your mate, Rod…he gets on well at school, does he?"

"He's in on the whole effin' conspiracy – Rod!" John's voice came up a notch and George motioned for him to simmer down. Mimi was surely asleep by this time. "He's fuggin' head of the swim team…also known as Mr. Studious, y'know! He bleeds Woolton House pink, does Davis!"

"Well, Rod's all right. There's nothing wrong with fitting into the mould, once in a while, is there?"

"Oh no, a lecture." John swigged down the rest of his Ovaltine in one gulp. "She's sent you down to talk to me, to inspire me to do better next year."

"She wouldn't," George smiled.

"She would, and she has." John was to the point.

"Well," George rubbed his eyes sleepily, "consider it said then. I just want you to be happy, John. I want you to feel good about what you're doing in school *and* in life. I don't want you to end up like me…wishing you'd gone after your dream, wishing you hadn't spent your life reading the news and betting now and again on a lucky horse or working in a dairy and eating pot roast every single Sunday."

"Yeah, fuggin' awful, that," John smiled.

George reached over and ruffled his nephew's hair. "Right. Fuggin' awful," he chuckled.

"She'd cane you for talkin' like that, y'know." John mimicked Mimi's voice, "'It simply isn't done, George Smith. It's Woolton here, you realize.'"

"Well then, sounds to me as if you and me are due for a trip to City Centre where things are a bit more bohemian and a lot more relaxed. Must be something wonderful on at The Empire this summer. Why don't you investigate and get back to me on that, eh?"

"Done." John raised the empty glass. "We're off to see the wizard!"

"But considering how my lumbago's been actin' up lately," George rubbed his back gingerly, "let's not walk the length of the yellow brick road. If you don't mind, I'd just as soon take the bus."

"Y'er getting' old Ge'rge, ye old Ge'rge." John sniffed through one nostril derisively.

"Well, don't look now, but you're almost fourteen yourself, our John. *Now* who's getting on in years?"

John stood up slowly and carefully, holding onto the table for support. "Help me upstairs, sonny," he cackled in his old man's voice. "I'm tired and far too weary to walk."

"Let's go," George laughed. "You're makin' me ache just lookin' at you."

They flicked off the kitchen light and made their way through the dark parlour.

"Mind the cats," George whispered.

"Why not?" John whispered back, "I mind everyone else, don't I?"

"Right," George chuckled softly, "that'll be the day."

This chapter is purely conjecture. It is drawn from information provided in footnotes. However, the statements about John's teachers (the history teacher who advised his students to become window washers and the Joyous Yule, etc) are all accurate. And Rod Davis was a serious, successful student.

6 June 1955
Mendips
Woolton

She was peeling carrots at the sink when he returned. She heard the front door slam and the sound of hard-soled, dress shoes clattering down the hall. A bag, flung aside carelessly, skidded across the floor and collided with the oak quarter-rounds. Normally, Mimi would have cared. Normally she would have called out, "Mind the walls and floor, John! No need to be so helter-skelter!" But today she was silent.

"Ge'rge! Mim!" the boy's voice called, charged with the relief and the expectation of homecoming. "Mim! Ge'rge! It's me! I'm back! I'm here! I'm home!" He called up the stairs to sounds of nothing.

She kept her back to the kitchen door and continued peeling carrots.

"Mim!" His voice searched for her, reserved a bit now, laced with worry. But still she didn't respond to him. She pursed her lips tighter and stood up tall – a strong, invincible, Northern woman. He would find her soon enough.

"Mim?" The voice was right behind her now. "I'm back from Mater's." The words quavered.

Why didn't she turn around? Why didn't she look at him? He had left his room in order. He had written letters almost every day. He had behaved at her sister's with better than usual deportment, not having Pete or Nigel around to get into trouble with. What had he done to make her this angry? What had he done now? He backed up a step and clamped his jaw tightly.

Mimi looked straight ahead, through the window above the sink. She looked without blinking. She talked without feeling.

"John, your Uncle George...died...yesterday. I asked Mater to let me tell you. I wanted to be the one. The whole family will be coming over soon. Go wash up and get dressed."

"But...but he was just fine!" John wailed. "He wasn't even sick! He was *fine*, perfectly fine! Nothing was the matter with him! He was fine!"

John didn't budge. Mimi scraped the carrot she was holding three more times; then she turned to face the boy. His face was dangerously red; he looked as if he'd run a marathon. His eyes were wild.

"Go on up, now," she said flatly. "Julia's coming over with the girls, and Harrie and your cousin, Lelia, will be 'round at half three. I've got a thousand details to manage, John. Go on up. Go up and get yourself ready."

John clenched his jaw and turned on his heel. He didn't offer his condolences or attempt to touch the woman at the sink. He moved from the room without a scuffle, without a noise. Mimi returned to the carrots.

There. She had done it. John had been told. The carrot fell from her hand into the sink, but she scooped it up again, rinsing it off under the faucet before beginning the precise, diagonal chopping.

John was fifteen, almost sixteen. But John was her child. And children, Mimi told herself, are not as hurt by death as they are by the devastation it brings in its wake.

She had been thirty-seven – old enough to understand grief – when her mum, Annie, had passed away. But her father's tear-filled eyes and hollow moans still haunted Mimi. Her mother had gone quickly, but her father had drifted, until his death, into an interminable, living hell. His pain had become Mimi's pain; his emptiness, hers. Mimi had been desolated by his survivor's grief, and she had – at once – lost both a mother and a father.

And John's only fifteen, only a boy, only a child. I owe it to him to…

Mimi straightened her back, tightened her lips, and chopped another carrot. Her hands found an automatic rhythm. Her face was impassive.

A verse from Proverbs came to her for the sixteenth time in the last hour. This time she whispered it to herself, saying it in broken-record repetition. *"Strength and dignity are her clothing, and she laughs at the time to come…Strength and dignity are her clothing, and she laughs at the time to come…"*

Mimi began to chop the last carrot, putting the finishing touches on the salad she would serve. But her face would not stop collapsing, and she struggled for control.

****

John stood at the tiny rollout window upstairs. He looked down on Menlove Avenue and watched an inexperienced driver attempt to parallel park in an impossible space. He snorted at the twists and turns that got the driver nowhere. Then he hurled the shirt he was holding across the room and swore under his breath. The house was perfectly silent. John dared not make a noise.

He used one foot, then the other to slip out of his dress shoes without unlacing them, and he left them where they lay as he flopped back on the bed – on the forbidden bedspread – his face to the ceiling. John closed his eyes and held his breath as long as he could. Then he panted quickly and tried it again.

Dead. He could feel it. *Dead.*

"Dead," John whispered, balling his knees up to his chest and rocking, side to side.

"Let him go, let him tarry..." He could hear his uncle's voice softening the long-ago darkness. In those first few days when John had cried for his mother, George had offered him nursery rhymes at bedtime – a rhythmic, magical way of falling asleep.

Just before lunch on one long-vanished day, he and George had gone walking, off in search of adventures, off to "slay dragons and kick at stones." George had scribbled a note for the mistress of the household, offering no explanation for their absence, merely stating, "Will return for tea." And he'd taken John's hand as they crossed the busy Woolton streets in search of the vast unknown.

Later that evening, John had kissed him good night, inhaling a comforting wave of shaving astringent and newsprint. It was a wonderful aroma. John could smell it now.

Uncle George made a tradition of reading *The Liverpool Echo* just before bed, and John always sat with him, turning the pages slowly, squinting as his uncle squinted in the glare of the reading lamp light.

"Look under your pillow after she's gone," the spectacled man had whispered to the child.

"Right then!" John had winked and whispered back. Even now John could taste the contraband barley sweets he'd found sequestered there – their taste made even more delicious because Mimi never knew.

Mimi...

The sound of women's voices drifted up from the floor below. Soon they would all be here, the covey of Stanley women...Mater, Nanny, Harrie, and...(A knock came at the door. A voice called his name, "John?")...and Julia.

"Mum?" John sat up quickly, waiting for an answer.

"Yeah, can I come in, then?"

He shot up from the bed and unlocked the door. Julia was inside in an instant, clasping him in the hug he ached for. Her hair smelled like cinnamon, and when at last she held him at arm's length and studied his face, her shell-shaped eyes were outlined flawlessly in artistic brush strokes. She was beautiful.

"I'm sorry – really, truly sorry, John." She spoke softly, guardedly. "He was your best mate, wasn't he?"

John didn't know what to say. He looked down at a hole in his sock and offered a memory. "Remember when he got me the green Raleigh Lenton Sport...just like he said he would if I passed the eleven-plus exams?"

Julia grinned and nodded towards the floor below. "*She* was furious, wasn't she? '*Silly, extravagant waste of money!*'" Julia mimicked Mimi's voice.

"It's still the best fug–uh–bleedin' bike around," John met his mother's eyes. "Drop handle bars and derailleur gears. No one takes the Raleigh Sport on."

"How he ruined you!" Julia said softly. Then, after a second, she added fondly, "Our George always ruined you. I knew he would."

"Yeah." John put his hands in his pockets and stood awkwardly silent.

"Next week, John," Julia rubbed his bare shoulder softly, "come 'round and stay with us a few days. Mimi'll need the quiet, and we can work on those banjo chords you've been wantin' to learn. The girls can help make you Indian curry, and we'll all sit on the floor to eat, y'know. We'll burn incense and put veils over our faces and dots on our foreheads. And if worse comes to worst, I'll belly dance! We'll have a lark. I promise."

"Yeah, sure. Right." It was getting harder and harder to talk. John's throat had constricted, as if a noose were tightening around his Adam's apple. He tried to swallow. He tried to breathe. But John was suffocating, getting air in only as far as that soft spot on his neck. He needed oxygen.

Julia talked. She eased him over to the bed where they sat together. John concentrated on breathing in and breathing out. He listened to her cadence, the sound of her voice, her lilting, easy conversation – and he clung to it like a lifeline.

"I know it's not much consolation, but I see so much of your uncle in you, John...really...the way you love to draw and capture people just as they are, not as they want to be..." She waved an imaginary paintbrush in the air as she spoke. "Remember how George taught you to draw...to be observant of angles and perspective? Remember that watercolour set he bought you for no good reason at all, just for fun?"

John nodded solemnly.

"Well, *he* wanted to be an architect, you realize," Julia went on. "It was his big dream, his vision. And like you, with the things you truly care about, our George worked awfully hard to achieve it. He'd even won prizes for his artwork, y'know – lots of them! But then...well, he was expelled from school...for kickin' a ball after he'd been instructed not to..." Julia smiled wryly, "I guess even in *that* he was a bit like you...two cookies cut from the same mould, right?"

John made a small snorting noise, but said nothing. He simply continued to listen.

"And then...oh well, you know the rest of the story...*that* one moment of defiance was George's downfall. He had to give up his education and take over his father's dairy. But all of his relatives knew, John, that young George Smith was never a dairy man, not really."

John refused to meet her eyes. But he was hypnotized by her voice. He floated in it.

"And then there was the music, of course...our George's endless ditties. Was there ever a moment when George Smith was in this house that the radio wasn't on? I mean, you can't remember a silent night here at Mendips, can you? He was captivated by the sound of somethin' lovely, by any tune that was a bit unusual."

John wished to the center of his gut that he were three or four years younger. He wished he could cry. He wished he could collapse into his mother's arms and cry for the man who had taught him so much and now was no more. John longed for the comfort of tears.

But Mim must think it's improper, he told himself. *I mean, she hasn't given in, has she?*

Weakness was a tragic flaw in Mimi's book, a characteristic which would ultimately be one's certain undoing. Over the years, she'd pointed it out to John in several of Shakespeare's plays – in "King Lear," "Hamlet," and "Macbeth" – always stressing that weakness destroyed the most valiant and clever of heroes.

"Weakness topples monarchs and defeats tyrants," Mimi had often quoted. "One must not, under any circumstances, have an Achilles' heel, John. Once weakness buds, it flourishes."

So John didn't cry. His face grew sterner and sterner, and he listened to Julia's voice.

She talked about something and nothing. She talked of George's service during the Second World War, his employment at the aircraft factory in Speke. She talked of George's ten-year courtship of Mimi Stanley and of the desultory war George had waged to win her sister's hand.

"But what kept him spellbound that long, *I'll* never know!" Julia tried a gentle bit of humour. "She was sweet as a persimmon, our Mary Elizabeth, and twice as puckerin' green."

John lacked even the imitation of a smile. He didn't respond or participate in Julia's monologue. He merely absorbed what she offered as a kind of eulogy, not as conversation.

In truth, it was never intended to be conversation. What Julia was giving and what John heard was not consolation; they were both realistic enough to know there was no consolation to be had. Julia was offering a grand substitution: her presence for George's; her offbeat variety of humour for George's jokes and bawdy poems; her lack of discipline for George's million kindnesses.

Julia had been away too long. Now she was ready to return.

Countless times over the past ten years, John had lain awake, watching the car lights move across his bedroom walls and wondering why he had been sent to Mendips to live – why Jacqui and Julia, his half-sisters, were allowed to live with his mum when he was not, and why he alone was set apart from the happy family that lived at 1 Blomfield Road, only a few miles away. For years, John had wracked his brain for answers.

But now he welcomed Julia without reserve, clinging to the future she offered and never demanding an explanation. As long as he was with Julia, John lived in the moment. As long as she talked and smiled and smoothed his hair with her long, white hands, doubt, fear, anger, and bitterness were held at bay.

But when some time later, she left him alone in his room, emotion tracked him down again.

George the Gentle, gone. George the Slayer of Dragons, defeated. Defeated? John threw his eyes to the ceiling at the stupid word. *Fuggin' dead is what he is. Dead.*

A hemorrhage of sorts, a type of internal bleeding associated with liver disease. Cirrhosis it was called. Julia had told him.

John placed his hand on his own stomach and felt around gingerly. He was like George; she had said he was like George. Maybe he could get a hemorrhage, too.

Maybe I've got it already, he worried. *Maybe it's already growin' inside of me.*

John hated the thought of his unselfish, affectionate uncle's body lying alone in some dark, cold morgue – left alone to turn rigid and blue, left alone to decay. He hated death. He hated the ghoulishness of it all.

But most of all, he hated God for being so unfair, for taking Ge'rge away from him just when he needed his uncle most. He hated God for taking away the closest thing he'd ever had to a father, just when everything seemed so confusing.

George had been his sounding board, his counselor, his confidante, his comrade in arms. George had been his friend.

And now John would never get the chance to tell him so.

Never got to say good-bye! he raged, slamming his fists into his pillow. *Never even got to fuggin' say good-bye!*

Blurred memories of Fred Lennon faded in and out. John tried to blink them away as he did the threatening tears, but the memories were phantoms, living lives of their own. And the more he tried not to think of his father, the more he did so.

Where the hell is he anyway? Dead like George? How? Where? And why the fuggin' hell don't I know?

John pictured his father in shadow only, laughing above the sound of the shore. Freddy smelled of fish and chips, and he was bright, dapper, full of himself – blithe. He aimed a miniature gun at a row of painted ducks while carnival music encircled him. He cheered and laughed and sang as he strolled, clowning about foolishly. *Pater, Freddy, Daddy, Fred…*the vision wavered, then disappeared altogether.

And in his stead stood Uncle George, quiet and unassuming, dressed cautiously in worn, brown tweed. *"Come on then,"* he beckoned, *"we're off to the picturedrome, our John! No more fretting about your aunt's disfavour...I'll set it right with her somehow. It'll be worth all the piper I'll have to pay later on* if *I really, honestly think you're havin' fun!*" George bent down to help John with his coat and collar, and then George, too, disappeared.

Two weeks ago, in a huff to leave for Mater's in Sutherland, Scotland, John had fumbled about at the last minute looking for his hiking boots and hat. He adored casting for salmon, but had quickly and carelessly discarded the rod after the previous summer's adventure. No one had had a clue as to the rod's hiding place, and John had exploded when they suggested he leave without it.

Mimi had been justifiably frustrated; George had been unusually reserved and quiet.

"Damn, damn, bleedin'ell and damn!" John had raged a teenage rage at everyone in general, and Mimi had matched his irritation with ire. Voices had been raised; doors, slammed. And John had left for Scotland with nostrils flared.

But over the holiday, he'd written quick daily posts to George and Mim, one containing a clipping of a cartoon, "The Broons," that he was sure George would enjoy. "What a larf!" John had written in the margin, and he was certain that George would, indeed, "larf."

John had even learned several "questionable" new jokes that he'd planned to share with his uncle in private. And he'd photographed some "really spectacular ruins" that he knew George would find fascinating. He'd even memorized a little ditty that would challenge George's boldest, and John had planned to spring it on his uncle just before church on Sunday morning, when it was most forbidden and delicious. On the train home to Liverpool, John had chuckled to himself, imagining it all.

Now he had no one to tell.

"John." It was another woman's voice. The house was full of them.

"What?" He wasn't even cordial this time.

"It's me – Lelia."

His cousin, his cohort in "up-to-no-good." He walked over and unbolted the door.

"Lelia," he pulled her in with a strange look in his eyes, "Have y'heard the one about the dairymaid and the sailor?" He bolted the door behind him.

They tried to smother their giggles with pillows, but John laughed so hard that the sound was only muffled not muted. He laughed like a young child tickled unmercifully by an older brother. He cackled and howled like a madman, and Lelia withdrew.

She sat on the far corner of the bed and hugged a pillow to her stomach as she watched John roll over and over, flopping on the floor, shaking with delirium. Lelia watched as he laughed beyond merriment, beyond delight. She waited, but the laughter never ceased.

After a very long while, Lelia crept timidly down the stairs, shaken and afraid. But John couldn't stop laughing to call her back. He couldn't stop to follow her. He just laughed on and on, all by himself, up in his room, laughing as he had never done before – until finally, at last, some time later, all the laughter was gone, and John was asleep.

All events in this chapter, including Lelia's report of John's hysterical laughter, are documented. Only the conversations are conjecture.

Autumn 1955
Quarry Bank Grammar
Woolton

It was not easy to take Quarry Bank seriously. The antiquated rules under which the students lived dated back to the school's origin in 1922 and to its first headmaster, George Harrison. Very little had changed since that time.

Detailed books recording minor infractions of the school code of conduct were still carefully kept, penned in impeccable handwriting. One violation earned a "black mark." Two violations warranted detention. And detention involved forced manual labour, the raking of leaves or the sweeping of rubbish. John began to feel like the school custodian.

At length, when a boy appeared particularly unredeemable, detention gave way to corporal punishment. John had reached that stage. Generous to a fault, however, John never squandered his visits to Mr. Taylor's office on himself; he somehow always managed to involve his best mate in a tandem trip to "the Head." If he were scheduled to receive a caning, well, then, Pete might as well come along. The two were as striped as barbers' poles.

But far from discouraging their insurrections, the punishments and canings only served to fuel the boys' hostilities. Shennon 'n Lotton became school outlaws as well as self-appointed class clowns.

They hid alarm clocks timed to ring in the middle of a lesson; they unhinged blackboards so that the slightest touch from a professor would send them smashing to the floor. They filled their bicycle pumps with ink and decorated professors whose backs were turned. They tossed texts out of the second story window.

One Wednesday early in the 1955 term, upon discovering that the Liverpool Institute had a day's holiday, John and Pete persuaded two of their Woolton comrades from the Institute to attend school with them. Masquerading as new residents from abroad, Len Garry and Bill Turner followed John to class. Shining brilliantly in their roles as innocent, shy new foreigners, Turner and Garry boldly flirted with disaster by wearing their easily recognizable green and black Liverpool Institute scarves. But in the rush of early morning activities, no one noticed.

The day began unceremoniously in Mr. Martin's art class. Len and Bill fell into the Quarry Bank routine, sitting quietly across the aisle from John and sketching earnestly on borrowed sketchpads. John winked at them, and they exchanged knowing smiles, elated that the game was unfolding without incident.

Then the quiet was broken.

"What exactly are you doing here, Mr. Shotton?" Mr. Martin's booming voice sounded from the front of the room. John jerked around to see Pete craning his neck at them from the hallway. A partner in the diabolical plan, Pete had been unable to resist the urge to see the grand charade unfold. Now he was caught. John grinned widely as his friend squirmed.

Let's see y'edge outta this one, Shotton. See if curiosity doesn't kill the fuggin' cat, John laughed to himself. This scheme was getting better and better!

"Well?" Mr. Martin barked again. "What *is* your purpose here, Mr. Shotton?"

"Uh...sir..." Pete fumbled, "I've come 'round to get me pen off John Lennon. I lent it to him this mornin'."

Fanfuggin'tastic! John smiled. *Too bleedin' good to be true!*

As the class turned to stare at him, John gave in to temptation and let the chips fall where they may.

"What on earth are you talkin' about, Pete?" John summoned his most authoritative voice. "You know full well I haven't got your pen! I wish you wouldn't come 'round disturbin' me when you can see I'm hard at work here. And I'm sure I'm also speakin' on behalf of Mr. Martin. Right?"

Len Garry's face contorted with suppressed laughter. Bill Turner began to cough uncontrollably.

Mr. Martin took several steps towards the door where Pete stood helplessly, "Well, Mr. Shotton, for once I must agree with Mr. Lennon. You're missing your own class, and you're unquestionably a nuisance in mine. Therefore, you will bring me five hundred lines tomorrow morning stating, 'I must not disturb Mr. Martin's art class.' I'll have that from you first thing. Is that clear?"

"Yes sir," Pete monotoned, and he shot invisible bullets at John that whizzed uselessly past his head. Len was red with silent giggles. Bill had placed his head down on his desk, but his shoulders shook.

It wasn't until late that afternoon that John's charade collapsed under its own weight. Tiring of schoolwork on their holiday, Len and Bill had begged off at last. The sudden absence of the two "new students" raised questions, and the questions produced the obvious answers. The new students had not been students at all, and John Lennon was once again discovered, corralled, and headed for a meeting with Headmaster Taylor and his infamous cane.

John ached miserably as he pedaled home to Mendips, but bruised as he was, he was at least *"better off than Pete."*

Tough luck on Shotton, John chuckled, wheeling his Raleigh Lenton into the driveway. *No time on The Tip for him today...and probably no radio programme tonight as well. He's got a fuggin' lot of work to do – Pete. Five hundred lines! Five fuggin' hundred!*

And laughing to himself, John jumped off his bike and barreled in the house.

Pete Shotton, in his 1983 book, John Lennon In My Life, *tells the story of Len and Bill's visit to Quarry Bank as if it occurred during E. R Taylor's administration. In* Hunter Davies, The Quarrymen, *the incident is set in William Pobjoy's administration, which began in 1956. Len Garry, in* The Quarrymen, *says that he met John in the summer of 1955. As a compromise between Mr. Shotton's book and Mr. Davies' book and in keeping with Len Garry's date, I have set the incident in the autumn of 1955.*

A "must read" concerning this incident is Len Garry's book, John, Paul, and Me – Before the Beatles *(pages 104-106). There is even a photograph of the room in which this incident took place.*

In 1994, I was fortunate enough to visit Quarry Bank (then called Calderstones) and to review the "infraction book" mentioned at the beginning of this chapter. The incidents of misbehaviour involving John and Pete were taken directly from that book. All conversation, however, is conjecture.

August 1956
Quarry Bank Grammar
Woolton

Almost before he began, his enthusiasm was dampened.

Certainly, it was an honour to be named Headmaster of Quarry Bank School for Boys; the fact that he had captured this plum at only thirty-five years of age made William Pobjoy quietly self-congratulatory. He had initially approached the job with unchecked energy about the new concepts he would pioneer. Secretly he had sworn to bring in "a new day" at Quarry Bank, to issue in a new spirit. But now, only four weeks into the semester, he sat alone in his oak-paneled office, wrestling with possible solutions to an overwhelming problem.

For the last week, a steady stream of faculty members had trailed through his door, speaking to him in grim tones about "the dilemma." With clenched hands and tense, edge-of-the-seat postures, his faculty had begged him for help, implored him for a solution. Genuinely weary of trying to cope the situation that they bemoaned, they had petitioned their new protector for support.

"It's that...John Lennon!" one had blurted out, anger colouring his version of reality. The man's tales were long-winded and frightening, and Mr. Pobjoy took them with a grain of salt.

But later another, an experienced instructor with a haggard face, had echoed the initial lamentation.

"Mr. Pobjoy, I've come to speak with you about a student – of sorts – a monster if truth be told – a 'right layabout' to use the Scouse vernacular – the ignoble John Lennon." His soliloquy of horrors had filled most of the morning.

After lunch, a timid professor, a hump-shouldered veteran with a hushed demeanour had come quakingly forward to issue his own note of warning, "Mr. Pobjoy, I hope you'll forgive this intrusion so early in your superintendence, but...well...well sir, I feel that I've given my most earnest effort to deal with a certain situation...and I've found my skills inadequate for the task. In fact, I find it only fair to warn you that as Headmaster of Quarry Bank, this school has been grappling with the self-same problem for the last four years, and we've had very little success. I am speaking of the student, John Lennon."

Each tired voice had phrased it differently. Some spoke in terse sentences, citing only facts. Others shared intricate details in the most convoluted ways. But in essence, all of them had told the same story.

Now, William Pobjoy sat with his elbows resting on his desk, his face buried in his hands. He took a deep breath, puffed out his cheeks, and exhaled slowly. He rubbed his eyes, massaged the ridge just above his eyebrows and then looked up at the high shelves around him filled with books on psychology, curriculum development, adolescent education, and delivery systems. None of them excited him now.

"Mr. Pobjoy?"

Oh no, not another. "Yes, yes, do come in. Come in, please." Pobjoy was too deflated to stand, but he motioned for the professor to take a chair.

It was the young English master, Phillip Burnett, a man who exuded the charm that came with handling poetry and the classics. He walked with confidence, and his blue eyes met Pobjoy's without the shadow of desperation. Flashing a wry smile and settling amiably in the maroon leather sofa adjacent to Pobjoy's desk, Phillip Burnett leaned slightly forward as if divulging a confidence to a friend.

Burnett paused for a moment, setting the stage. It was apparent that the topic he'd come to discuss held great importance to him.

"Mr. Pobjoy," Burnett began, "you reminded us at the faculty meeting last week that your door is always open. Well, from the long line of faculty members I've seen filing in and out of here, it must *literally* be so."

Pobjoy smiled slightly and gave a single nod.

"Sir, I know," Phillip cleared his throat and continued, "I know I'm just adding to the interruptions and..."

"Not at all, Mr. Burnett. Conversing with my English Master is never an interruption."

"Well," Phillip shrugged, "I realize there're only so many hours in the day...nevertheless, I *had* to come in as well. In fact, I think what I have to say will surprise you."

Pobjoy gestured for the teacher to continue.

"I assume you've heard a great deal today about John Lennon and probably about Peter Shotton as well." Phillip took the bitter smile "the Head" gave him as an affirmative. "Well...I'm not sure if it's...as dreadful as my colleagues have made it sound."

"Go on."

"All right, then." Phillip took a breath, "Mr. Pobjoy, I'm somewhat well-acquainted with your background. You're an impressive scholar. Among other things, you know your history and literature. You know, as I do, that many great men through the ages have been 'tortured souls.' I mean, Coleridge was a ne'r-do-well in school and a drug addict in later years, wasn't he? And Byron – a cad and a scalawag! The American, Thoreau, was a blatant nonconformist, lauded – and jailed – for his refusal to pay taxes. Shakespeare was an atheist and a womanizer. Whitman was a shocking reprobate. Keats, Shelley, Poe, Williams, Shaw, Donne...far from being saints, they were all well-known for their 'colourful indiscretions.' Yet we revere them, don't we?"

William Pobjoy let him talk, and Phillip gathered momentum.

"Mr. Pobjoy, as a teacher, I deal daily with the *average*. I teach classes for the medium mind. My students wander in and out – names, faces, ordinary human beings. They and I are forgettable. But that isn't the case with John Lennon.

"John's different. In him – and I'm not being melodramatic here – in him I've glimpsed genius. You've heard he's disobedient, skips detention, and refuses to arrive at school on time. I tell you, he writes poetry that is biting but incredible.

"You've heard he's disrespectful. I say he has a proclivity towards satire that Jonathan Swift would have applauded. He is a modern-day Alexander Pope. Kindred spirits, those two. Their words sting.

"My colleagues have no doubt told you that John draws cruel caricatures of them, mocking their flaws, pointing out their failings. I've seen Lennon's sketches, and without a doubt they can make you squirm, but they're haunting and vivid. But while Toulouse Lautrec was applauded for his depiction of depravity and deformity, John is chastised...because *we* are the deformed!

"It's true...John bores easily. He mastered French and then tired of it. He wearied at the tediousness of mathematics. He withers under much repetition. And when he becomes bored, he becomes a problem. Either he absents himself and gets called on the carpet for truancy, or he comes to class and causes disruptions to keep himself amused. In either case, he's been caned repeatedly.

"But the canings have done absolutely no good! John can't be beaten into submission. If he could, life would've already done so."

For a moment, neither of them spoke. Then Burnett went on.

"I know you'll look at his file, Mr. Pobjoy, and you'll see the way it is. John's mother – so I've heard – lives close by...in Allerton, I believe. But for some reason John was reared by his aunt and uncle. If that weren't complicated enough, very recently – about a year ago – John lost his uncle as well. So now he lives alone with his aunt Mimi, who is a story all her own.

"If Duty with a capital 'D' were to take a human form, it would, no doubt, inhabit the frame of Mrs. Mimi Smith. Straight-backed, pinch-lipped, and no-nonsense, she makes her way to the school quite regularly, offering no solutions, but insisting that *we* nurture and develop John. 'It's *your* job to constrain him and to make something of his future,' she once told me.

'What exactly do you intend to do?'

"She never misses a conference, is never derelict in her performance as a parent, and never neglects John. But in all of her visits to the school, I've never seen her smile."

For a moment, both men were silent. Mr. Pobjoy waited. Then he asked, "All right, then. What would you have me do?"

"Would you really like to know?" Phillip was uncomfortable with this role reversal, telling "the Head" how to perform his duties.

"I would." Pobjoy's face showed no expression, but he continued to listen, eyes dartingly attentive though averted.

"Well, then," Phillip spelled it out, "I'd like you to 'wake John up,' to shock him into reality. Show him his future, as it were. Let him know that his school days are all but numbered and that soon he'll either go on to college on *your* recommendation, or he'll be forced into the workaday ranks of the dull drones he despises. Let him see what he might become."

"Hmmm, the old Charles Dickens routine," Pobjoy interjected.

"Yes, that's it...that's rather what I had in mind!" Burnett smiled. They both did.

"It's an interesting idea, Mr. Burnett. Interesting."

"Mr. Pobjoy, I *know* this is asking quite a lot...and I know it'll require some creative discipline and ingenuity. But sir, I'm almost certain that if we save this boy and set him on the right track, as it were, someday he'll make a name for himself and who knows? Perhaps he'll even manage to put Quarry Bank on the map as well."

Pobjoy removed his glasses and rubbed his eyes. "Your cohorts are convinced that Mr. Lennon'll make a name for himself in the annals of criminal activity."

"Well, they may be right, sir," Burnett moved even closer to the massive oak desk, "but in large part, I believe that's really up to us. It sounds rather trite and foolish, I know, but our school motto promises that we can forge virtue from rough metal. And there's none rougher than John, I can assure you...and there's also none concealing more precious potential."

"Right." Mr. Pobjoy pushed his chair back and stood to indicate the interview's end, "Well, I'll take it all under advisement, Mr. Burnett. But I want you to know...I must also carefully consider the other stories that I've been told ..."

"Yes, of course, I understand completely." Phillip stood and shook the Headmaster's hand. "And I want *you* to know that I didn't come here today to contradict my peers or to suggest that they were unfair or inaccurate. I'm sure that every word they've told you about John is true. I simply wanted to add another dimension."

With the formality of the unfamiliar, the two men said their good-byes, and Burnett left William Pobjoy alone. For several minutes the Headmaster stood looking out the window into the Memorial Garden, surveying the lush, grassy fields beyond. Trees lapped their heavy heads over one another; their branches newly tinged with colour from the pallet of early autumn. Every now and again, a leaf would let go and float erratically to the soft mound of grass below. Then a breeze would inspire a shower of leaves, and for a moment, they would dance. William Pobjoy wanted to watch them. He wanted to just stand and think.

But swinging around again, the Headmaster picked up the file he had been scanning just prior to Burnett's arrival. It was the educational history of John Lennon – the epitaph of a mind that Burnett swore was full of promise.

"Lennon has a simple lack of any wish to get on," Professor Eric Oldman had written in a terse but pointed appraisal. *"He seems determined not to conform to the rules."*

"Academic success matters not one whit," another had scribbled.

"He does not share in what we've set out to do," were the words of the former Headmaster, E.R. Taylor.

There wasn't a glowing – or even a neutral – report in the bunch.

Going back as far as the early days, John's reviews were bad. *"He's sharp as a needle. But he won't do anything he doesn't want to do,"* the Headmaster of Dovedale Primary had noted on the progress chart.

"Destined for failure," a final childhood account predicted. The portfolio was depressingly grim.

Pobjoy took a deep breath and let it out slowly. He tossed the manila folder back on his desk with a flip of frustration and then began to wind his watch mindlessly.

"A monster!"
"A right layabout!"
"A dilemma!"
"A genius!"

He wondered how could one adolescent create so much controversy. But more importantly, he wondered how one ingénue headmaster could stop the cataclysmic Mr. Lennon from destroying himself before his true colours were revealed.

All characters in this chapter are real and were actually on staff at Quarry Bank when John was enrolled. The comments from these professors at the end of the chapter are also authentic. Only the conversation is conjecture, but based on interviews with Dave Bennion and the Headmaster of Calderstones School in 1993. At this meeting, my husband and I were allowed to see the discipline book for the years that John and Pete were in school at Quarry Bank. A full roster of John's infractions and punishments was kept.

September 1956
Quarry Bank Grammar
Woolton

Several days passed uneventfully. Halls filled and emptied; the glistening, checkerboard floors grew scuffed; blackboards were cleaned and then scribbled on again. In the corridors, the black-robed pedagogues who were years his senior passed William Pobjoy shaking their heads and clucking pessimistically about the "shocking, hopeless" John Lennon and his henchman, Pete Shotton. But as yet, Mr. Pobjoy had not had to wrangle with the irreverent duo.

The closest that the Headmaster had come to a confrontation occurred when the Languages Master "appropriated" Lennon's sketch book, a collection of satirical jibes and illustrated poetry, most of which caricatured the Quarry Bank faculty. Entitled "The Daily Howl," this volume of tongue-in-cheek ditties and sketches infuriated the professors whom it ridiculed as much as it delighted the students. But Mr. Pobjoy could not find Lennon's "collected works" extremely offensive – nor could he deem it just cause for disciplining the boy.

In fact, the outlaw made him smile. The boy's humour was uniquely Liverpudlian, a blend of irony and pun. One Lennonesque weather report scribbled in "The Daily Howl" caught his eye: "Tomorrow will be Muggy...followed by Tuggy, Wuggy, and Thuggy."

It was Liverpool – the quick jab of wit and word play.

And though Lennon's parody of Davy Crockett entitled "The Story of Davy Crutch-Head" was a bit off-colour, it was cleverly acceptable nonetheless. The literature of "The Daily Howl" had a Jimmy Tarbuck, City Centre sting.

The pencil sketches, however, were a bit darker, outlined in deeper cynicism. One depicted a blind man in dark glasses being led in the street by a blind dog, wearing shaded spectacles as well. The two were drawn passing a street sign which read, "Bus Stop," and underneath the scene was scribbled a single word: "Why?"

In "The Daily Howl" art gallery, each Quarry Bank teacher was liberally lampooned, their black robes bulging with humps and deformities, faces riddled with warts, and hands, razor-sharp claws. The worst of the lot, the hypocrites, smiled from the pages of "The Howl" with two heads, sometimes three. Pobjoy even found himself grinning grotesquely from the sketchbook, a narrow-eyed monster with a pencil neck and lobster-clawed arms. "Popeye" the sketch was labeled. But it was unmistakably the Headmaster.

These shenanigans could be overlooked. They were mischievous but not disobedient. The author-artist had broken no rules.

So Pobjoy returned the controversial book to the confiscating professor without comment...and without censure for the inventive Mr. Lennon. *No use upsetting the apple cart without cause*, Pobjoy told himself. He would choose his battles judiciously.

But "cause" came at last, and Pete Shotton and John Lennon were issued into the office one Friday morning at half-ten. Lennon wore bandages on his arm while Shotton stood, red-faced and guilty.

"You gentlemen are quite tardy, now aren't you?" came the Head's obvious question. Pete began to stammer an excuse while John stood erect – stone-faced, defiant.

Pobjoy sized up his enemy as the Shotton boy rambled on, and John, with unflinching confidence, eyed him in return. Objectivity was absent; anticipation and rumour coloured their observations. The Headmaster saw a haughty and notorious rebel. And John saw only "a suit," a bastion antiquated injustice. The boy's nostrils flared.

"So sir, that's about it in a nutshell, then." Pete was tiptoe-animated. "That's how John smashed up his Raleigh Lenton good and proper and..." And when the blank expression on the Headmaster's face revealed he hadn't heard one single word Pete had said, Pete encapsulated for the now-listening audience, "and rode it slam into the back of an illegally-parked car. Hit it full force on, sir! You shoulda seen him go fug--- flyin'."

"I walked it back home," John offered. "The front wheel's buckled. The bike's dead useless now."

"Y' shoulda been there, sir...he was bleedin' somethin' awful!" Pete chimed in. "It was makin' me sick just lookin' at him."

"I see," William Pobjoy inspected John's wounds, refusing to play the dupe. John's eyes narrowed at the implications of such an action. He took a small backward step as the older man took hold of his arm.

"The bike's out in the lot now," John informed the doubter, staring down his nose at the Headmaster. "Y'can have a look, if that's what y'er after. It's obvious I've hammered the guard back and twisted the wheel, as it were. But it won't ever look the same again." The boy's voice fell almost imperceptibly.

Pobjoy ignored the challenge and turned to Peter Shotton instead. "Well then, what's *your* excuse, Mr. Shotton? Why are you similarly tardy?"

An accomplished actor, the red-cheeked, blond was incredulous, innocent, and wide-eyed. His head of curls bobbed as he gestured generously.

"Me, sir? Well sir...naturally I had to help John, y'know. His bike was a garble 'n all...and he needed me to help him carry it back home, y'see."

William Pobjoy stood up to his full height and looked at the fabled pair with all the ferocity he could muster. He folded his arms across his chest as he spoke, craning his neck out and looking a great deal like his caricature in "The Daily Howl."

"Gentlemen, I will not tolerate tardiness. It's disruptive, and it robs you of your complete day's education. It is also against the rules and encourages others to take deadlines and appointments lightly. Considering the circumstances, however, I'll let you off this time...*but* if there's any more trouble, you can be assured that I'll not be lenient again."

Pete nodded and smiled, a weak smile, an obligatory rather than grateful one, and John turned on his heel to leave, although no one had formally dismissed him. For one brief moment, William Pobjoy thought of calling him back and teaching the arrogant lad a lesson in respect. Lennon needed a severe tongue-lashing, if not an actual one. But as tempting as it sounded, *that* was the easy way out.

Pobjoy stood in restrained silence, recalling his well-planned strategy, letting the boys go. Lennon slammed the door a bit too loudly and once out in the vestibule, one of them snickered.

Bill Pobjoy gritted his teeth, jaw taut and clenched. Then without a word, he returned to his desk and to his work. The time was not yet right.

This exact event did not occur. Mr. Pobjoy did receive a copy of "The Daily Howl" from one of John's professors, and he did decide that it was harmless. He also disciplined John and Pete on several occasions for minor infractions, including tardiness for various reasons. This is just a typical example of one such meeting. The conversation is conjecture.

December 1956
1 Blomfield Road
Allerton

Julia stood centre stage in the kitchen floor, a sprig of holly in her hand, and a slightly yellowed mop head atop her own:

"So ends our Christmas pantomime, dear ladies, lords, and
   gents.
We hope you have enjoyed our show in all its full intent.
Come back next year, O patrons dear, and you'll have
   time well spent.
And if we have not pleased you sirs, we ask you to…"

"Get bent!" John yelled, concluding Julia's merry *speil*.
Jacqui and Ju rolled around the sofa with laughter. Pete applauded, and Julia pretended to be shocked, covering her mouth and blinking rapidly. When the girls and John joined in the applause, Julia curtseyed deeply, holding her mop-wig securely as she dipped her head.

"Bravo! Bravo!" Pete rose to his feet.
"Well done, Mum!" the girls joined him. "It was the best pantomime ever, wasn't it? The best ever!"
"It was that famous Julia Stanley Lennon, brilliantly portrayin' each and every character, bringin' the typically cynical Liverpool audience to its feet. Newsreel to follow." John did his best Fleet Street critic. Julia basked in the attention. She adored the limelight.
"Ta, luvs!" she waved her arm majestically. "But here's to the real star of the hour, our own Bard, Willy Shakespeare! His characters never dull, and his lines never lose their flavour."
"Which reminds us…" John raised an eyebrow, glancing towards the kitchen.
"Right! It's tarts and tea, clotted cream, raisin scones, and currant jam for the lot o' you!" Julia tossed the mop aside. "'Tis the season to be naughty!"
She fed the sweet tooth as well as the imagination; that was Julia's forté.

While the girls put a scratchy Christmas record on the player, Julia filled the teapot, set it on the stove, and motioned for John to get the cups and saucers from the cabinet above the sink.

"Well?" She struggled to pry open the lid of a dented metal cookie bin. Her scarlet fingernails were nuisances when managing practical things. "You've given it some thought, then, John Winston?"

John knew exactly what she was talking about. It was their favourite subject these days.

"Yeah, why not...we could do, me 'n Pete. But there's hurdles, y'know. I mean, we've got no instruments, as it were. And I as see it, a band without instruments would have to have a great deal more talent than we can muster up on short notice."

Julia swiped a dismissing hand at her son. "Tell him, Pete. Tell him that the two of you need your own skiffle band."

"He's got that mouth organ, y'know." Pete grinned at her.

"You've got that mouth organ, y'know," Julia echoed to her son.

"Right," John handed her the stack of tiny plates and china cups, "So I'll be dead fantastic as long as the fans only request, 'Walkin' M'Baby Back Home.'"

"Or 'Ain't That a Shame,'" Julia reminded him.

"You know 'Cumberland Gap' a thousand times over, Shennon." Pete took a seat at the kitchen table.

"Yeah, yeah! Play 'Cumberland Gap,' Johnny!" The girls jumped up and down, squealing their request. "C'mon. C'mon! Pleeeeese! We love it when you do that one. We love 'Cumberland Gap.'"

"You see? Fans already." Julia smiled. The teapot whistled as the thin line of steam began to rise.

"Eric Griffiths says he's gettin' this fug—uh, great guitar for the holidays." John began to make plans in spite of himself.

Pete let Jacqui climb into his lap. "And Rod Davis," he added, "already has a banjo or guitar, one; I can't remember which."

"Banjo," John said.

"So you *do* have instruments, then." Julia winked at her son as she handed him the first steaming cup of Earl Grey. She nodded towards the sugar and cream. "Don't stand on ceremony, luv. Dive in."

"Ta." John held the cup for a moment and let the steam rise to his face. It was easy to dream over tea, cakes, and pantomimes in Blomfield Road. At Julia's house, anything seemed possible. "I've been workin' on 'Wabash Cannonball,' y'know," he said almost to himself. "There's always that to add to the play list, and..."

"The play list!" Pete ran his hand through his thick, yellow curls and smirked. John could tell he wanted to laugh. "So it's 'the play list,' then, is it?"

"*I* want some tea as well!" Jacqui piped up.

"On the way, Little Miss Muffet," Julia grinned. "But next...one for our Pete here. He's the guest, y'know."

"Johnny's not our guest! And *he's* got tea!" Jacqui protested.

"No, but he's our only John." Julia gave him her son a wink and smile.

"Soon to be the famous skiffle star of the famous *play list*," Pete nudged his friend.

"Soon to be more famous than us all!" Ju added sincerely, always her brother's most ardent admirer.

"Soon to be the star of stage and silver screen," John pronounced in his deep announcer's voice.

"Go on. Laugh if you like!" Julia flounced back to the stove for Pete's cup. "But I wouldn't be a bit surprised. Music's your heritage, y'know." She motioned towards the banjo she played now and again at The Brookhaven Pub in Smithdown Road. "It's in me...it was in Fred as well. You can't help but be naturally inclined whether you like it or not. It's who you are! O'Leannon, Stanley...there's music in all of 'em. Music's a part of your Irish and Scottish ancestry."

Against this wealth of evidence, Pete silently resigned himself to inevitable membership in the "band to come." It was only a matter of time now. When Julia and John joined forces on anything, the outcome was a *fait accompli.*

If John's havin' a skiffle band, then I'd better decide straight off what instrument I'll play Pete thought. *John and Julia may "declare the war," but ready or not, I'll be the first fuggin' volunteer, as it were.*

"Cuppa, Pete?" Julia placed his tea on the table

"Ta," he smiled at her warmly. "And the cakes as well, if y'don't mind...we've only got biscuits or jam butties at home...what with me mum workin 'n all."

"Muck in, then – y'er at yer granny's!" Julia winked, using a favourite old Scouse phrase. Then she giggled and tossed her auburn hair back in a seductive motion that Pete believed was only for him.

"Who has drums, Shotton? Or who can we *talk into* drums?" John was in another world. "The holidays are just 'round the corner, y'know. I'm sure we could persuade *someone* to ask for drums from dear Old Father Christmas...that is, if we make it a *high priority,* as it were."

"What?" Pete surfaced, slightly embarrassed, from daydreams about Julia. "Drums? I dunno...I....are we ready for percussion at this stage of the proceedin's?"

"Well, we'll get nowhere without a drummer, won't we?" John shook his head in disgust.

The girls took their teacups from their mother and began ladling spoonfuls of sugar and inordinate amounts of cream into dark liquid. Julia gave them each a plate for scones, and then she poured herself the last cup of Earl Grey.

Instead of joining them at the kitchen table, Julia settled into the sofa, next to her banjo. She picked up the worn, fingerprinted instrument and began to tune it quietly while the others ate and drank. Julia began tentatively, but as she sang, her bravado increased.

Pete hummed quietly while the girls dangled their legs to the slow, mesmerizing rhythm. But John got up and walked over to the sofa, sitting on the arm next his mum. He never remembered all the words, even though he'd heard her songs hundreds of times. But he always hummed, providing high harmony and joining in when the lyrics struck him.

Julia loved it when he sang with her.

Without yoooou…
I'd be half what I could be,
Without yooooou…
I'd be lost eternally.

They sang "their song" with practiced perfection, never missing a note despite the fact that John felt the lump in his throat he always felt when they sang this way together. At the bridge, Julia paused. She smiled softly and nodded for her son to go on alone.

I'd miss you so forever
That life would cease to be,
Without you…
There'd be nothin' left for me-e.

Without you,
Every day would seem like night…
Without you,
There'd be nothin' wrong or right!
Without you,
There'd be moon'n stars in sight
But without you…
Not a hint of light…

Jacqui and Ju joined in the final chorus. And even Pete, who refrained from singing as much as possible, sort of mouthed the words for camaraderie's sake. Julia's banjo rose to the occasion, and they brought the ballad home with classic doo-wop schmaltz.

Without you, without you,
Ooooooooh, my lo-ove,
Without you-o-o-o-o!"

The girls loved it. They applauded, cheered their brother...jumped around, holding hands. Julia whistled and "bravoed" and gave them all, including Pete, quick, fierce hugs. Her eyes sparkled with great plans and exhileration. And before John's last note faded, she bubbled over.

"You see, John?" she motioned around the room, "Girls love you already, and you haven't even put a band together yet."

"I guess it's a mandate," John grinned. "No turnin' back now, Shotton."

Pete tossed his curls, a star already. "Anyone for autographs, then? Get them while they're available."

The girls scrambled for pens and paper as Julia handed her son the banjo. "Your turn," she winked. "Play somethin' for me...somethin' from 'the play list,' yeah?"

John began labouriously to pick out the chords to "Wabash Cannonball" while Pete imagined himself already in a skiffle band, playing the tea chest bass or strumming the washboard while waving to crowds of ogling girls.

"It might be worth a bash after all – this band thing," Pete shrugged, mischief in his eyes.

"Of course it is," Julia affirmed, reading his mind. "Women love handsome, charismatic singers, don't they?"

"All we really need now, y'know, is a name for the group."

"Work on it, then," John barked. As leader of the band, he delegated to his only recruit. "Work on it, and get back to me straight off."

"Yeah," Pete smiled. "Can do."

"And Shotton," John added as an afterthought, "you'll play washboard."

Many of the details of John's visit are found in John Lennon: My Brother *by Julia Baird. The conversations, however, are imagined.*

February 1957
Quarry Bank Grammar School
Woolton

Both sides had observed a temporary truce, but now the games were on again.

Late in the second half of a neck-in-neck Everton football match, one of the best games in months, an announcement blared over the loudspeaker system.

"Your attention please! William Earnest Pobjoy is summoned to the Goodison Park booth as soon as possible for an emergency telephone call. Once again, William Earnest Pobjoy, you have an emergency telephone call."

Despite the fact that Everton was pressing at goal and seemed just about to score, despite the fact that this was his own personal time away from the daily grind at Quarry Bank, and despite the fact that it was next to impossible to exit his inordinately packed row, William Pobjoy began the arduous trek to the booth.

Nothing could be more irritating, he stewed as he had wedged his way through the swaying, chanting crowd. *All I can say is, this had better be a near calamity*! He apologized as he climbed over legs, manoeuvered between sardined fans linked arm in arm, and threaded his way through irate, vocal spectators.

"A near calamity," he muttered, both to himself and as an apology.

And it was. The usually calm voice of the Deputy Headmaster was anything but calm. Pobjoy's associate had raged about "yet another Lennon debacle" which was "making a mockery of authority and dignity at Quarry Bank," and he had implored Mr. Pobjoy to take immediate, decisive action.

"Oh, suspend him!" It was Pobjoy's knee-jerk response to the cheers coming from the stadium. But almost immediately he checked himself.

"No, no, no…belay that. Forget I even said it. Just…just hold on until I return."

"But, Mr. Pobjoy, he's…:"

"Yes, I know." Another explosion of cheers filled the corridor, and the Headmaster was doubly irritated at Lennon for making him miss the match.

"I know what he is, and I know what he's done, and I know what he deserves and all that. But trust me. I've a plan. Just dismiss Lennon…and Shotton, too, if he's involved. Give them the standard reprimand, and I'll deal with the entire crisis as a whole tomorrow morning."

"Dismiss them, sir?'

"Tell him – or them – to be in my office first thing tomorrow morning. And while you're at it, please remind them exactly what time 'first thing' is."

****

Lennon and Shotton arrived almost a full hour late. They tumbled in, intoxicated with themselves, hardly recalcitrant.

Mr. Pobjoy let the reprobates wait in the Tower of London-like confines of his narrow, windowless, two-story outer office while he gathered his thoughts. He needed time to compose himself, to make certain that what he'd decided to do would be best for everyone. He remembered the many accounts of endless, useless punishments that the school had doled out to the two boys over the last four years. Detention, line writing, caning, humiliation – none of it had reached the two.

Nothing had ever successfully transformed John Lennon. Nothing had ever altered the innumerable reports of "wasted intelligence." John's insolent glare and unbowed demeanour were not diminished by assignments to collect garbage or rake leaves.

Up to this morning, nothing had ever worked.

Headmaster Pobjoy stood and straightened his tie. He let his hand rest at the base of his neck as his eyes studied the floor. *Lennon sketches me without a neck, but there it is after all*, he mused. *And it's a neck I'm about to risk on him, truth told. The legendary Mrs. Smith won't like this decision one bit. But it's a risk I'm willing to take.*

He walked to the massive oak door of his office resolutely, recalling Phillip Burnett's plea for creative disciplinary action in Lennon's case. Burnett had suggested shock treatment, "a wake-up call of sorts." Bill Pobjoy hoped that what he had planned would be the appropriate prescription.

"Mr. Shotton, Mr. Lennon, step inside, please." His voice was razor-sharp.

All three took their seats in utter silence. The Headmaster took an incredibly long time arranging his notes and settling in for the conference. He clicked a stack of papers into a neat pile; he clipped several together with an oversized clip. He let the silence hover.

"So…exactly what is the trouble this time?" he asked at long last, his tone betraying no emotion.

John gave Pete a sideways look before speaking. "The Prefect wasn't duly impressed with this remarkable new system we've set up, as it were," he shrugged.

"An entrepreneurial venture of sorts, sir," Pete began.

"Taking bets *against* Quarry Bank, as I understand it?" Mr. Pobjoy said.

John smiled slightly...not a bit ashamed of encouraging illicit wagers against his own team.

Mr. Pobjoy stared down at his desk, saying nothing for a moment, and John seized the opportunity to imitate "the Head's" stern expression. Pete couldn't suppress the snicker that spurted out without warning. It was a reaction, pure and simple.

Laughing in spite of himself, Pete was unable to hear the hushed words of the Headmaster, but John heard them. His stunned expression immediately silenced Pete. They both stared at the man behind the desk.

"Go home," William Pobjoy pronounced again.

"Home?" Pete mumbled, looking to John for answers.

"What exactly d'you mean by that, then?" John had lost his arrogance.

"I said, 'Go home.' Surely you boys understand *that* much English. We haven't been wasting our time altogether in this school, now have we?"

"No sir," Pete leaned forward, hoping beyond hope. "We know what *'go home'* means, sir, but..."

"Then go home *now*! I've had enough of both of you. I don't want either one of you to set foot on the school grounds again until I summon you to return."

And with that, the discussion was over.

The door had barely closed behind them before Pete launched into a hysterical soliloquy, "Fuggin' hell! Fuggin' h-e-double-l! How'll I explain this? Tell me *that*, why don't you? It's like we've committed some capital crime or what have you! It's like we've done the worst of the worst, y'know! I'll never be able to explain this! Me mum'll go fuggin' crackers when she hears it...I'm lousy *in* for it now!"

John slammed through the big, arched front doors that were strictly off limits to students, and he headed for his bike at record speed. His face was completely impassive, but over his shoulder, he tossed out the most terrifying concept yet, "Yeah, well, what'm *I* gonna tell fuggin' Mimi? Just tell me fuggin' that!!!"

Pete's stomach turned. His parents would be furious, would probably thrash him for this one. *But Mimi!* He was thankful beyond words it was John's lot, not his own. He didn't know quite *what* to say.

"Y'know what's happened, don't you, Shotton? Y'realize what's just happened, don't you, son?"

Pete just stared at him incredulously, saying nothing.

"We've been sus-pen-doooed, as they say. Utterly, bleedin' sus-pen-doooooed!" John crowed.

Pete began to grin. John's pretentious French accent at this most grim of all moments seemed riotously funny. Pete was suddenly giddy – hysterical, delirious in the wake of tragedy. He began to snicker all over again. And then both of them laughed together.

"And what, if I may inquire, are you two gentlemen doing out here at this inappropriate hour of the day?" It was Mr. McDermott, the Religious Instruction Master. "Are you not, in fact, scheduled for a class at this very moment, Mr. Lennon?"

"So you haven't heard, then?" John volunteered a Cheshire grin. "Me'n Pete – we've been recently sus-pen-doooed, haven't we?"

"What's this? What in heaven's name are you talking about, Lennon? Sus-pen-doooed? What's *that*?"

Pete and John exploded into laughter, shaking and letting their bikes wobble as they may. Covered in bewilderment and then in indignant anger, Mr. McDermott did his best to wrangle a satisfactory explanation out of them. Catch phrases like "permanently tardy," "let off," and "y'know, a vacation of sorts," began to paint a picture. The instructor began to understand.

*Why these two incorrigible sinners had been suspended! Sus-pen-dooed, indeed! Incredible! Why, they weren't even sorry, not even scared! They were **laughing**, larking about and laughing. Lennon! The boy made a mockery of everything! Everything! He hadn't a shred of scruples, nor a moral to his name!*

Shaking his head sadly, the mortified professor started to speak, but didn't. Instead, he "hmpfffed!" the "hmpff" of the righteous and walked on by.

"Sus-pen-dooed!" mimicked Pete, setting his bike in motion.

"Suspendooooooooed!" John yelled, like a Gaelic battle cry.

But as they wheeled down Menlove Avenue, closer and closer to Mendips, the cheering and insanity gave way to practical considerations. How would they tell their families? Or *should* they tell them at all?

"We've got to, y'know," Pete was never the dreamer. "I mean, they'll fuggin' sort it all out when come Monday, we're home, lyin' about the house at bleedin' midday."

"Yeah, well, that's three days off, now isn't it?" John was unusually quiet. "One day at a time, right? We'll work it out. I'll come up with a plan."

At the corner of Menlove and Vale, they usually waved good-bye and pedaled furiously home for teatime sandwiches and biscuits, but today they dawdled. John got off his bike and kicked a stone along the sidewalk, quietly plotting. Pete rolled his bike forward and backward, backward and forward – straddling it, but going nowhere.

"It'll get 'round, y'know, John." Pete was now the incessant voice of conscience. "They'll find out somehow, y'know. We've got to walk in and own up to it straight away. We've got to come clean and..."

"Lay fuggin' off, Pete! Y'er gettin' on me wick!" John snapped.

"Lay fuggin' off yourself, then!"

Dissension began to nibble though their unity, and unity was their only avenue for successful deception.

"Look, you heard the man," John quoted Pobjoy, "*Go home*, right? Well then, that's it...that's the instruction, then. Just go home. Don't suddenly 'see the light.' Don't turn yerself in. Don't come clean, as you put it. Just do exactly what you always do; act natural. Do nothin'...and leave the solution to me. We've got three days, y'know...three whole fuggin' days! In that length of time I could talk our way into the Vatican in Rome, as it were. Just be here Monday mornin' at the regular time – and be the usual Monday mornin' drag you always are. But most of all, needless to say, son...don't forget to come carryin' books and dressed for school."

With that, John sped off as if he had some grand plan to fine tune. But for the first time in ages, he was completely without a solution, and it was the longest, worst weekend John had ever spent.

When the shadows began to lengthen on Sunday afternoon, he still had no idea what to do. Pobjoy had outmanoeuvered him altogether. This time, John didn't know where to turn.

****

The answer was so obvious that John almost didn't think of it: Julia!

A very real port in all of his storms since George had passed away, his mother cared not a whit for schools or regulations or institutions or penalties. She considered them "perfectly trivial."

In near desperation to live, *really live*, Julia had little time for traditional values. She flung herself into experience, splashed in it, sensually delighted in every possible adventure. She lived life extemporaneously – exhilarated at the possibility of walking on thin ice. Only limits terrified her.

Julia would understand. Julia would be their shelter.

Monday morning, John and Pete rose at the usual hour, donned the customary groggy faces, and lolled about in their customary "school-is-drudgery" fashion. Pete's mum served up hot Semolina; Mimi dished up Kellogg's Corn Flakes. Both boys donned their black blazers and shouldered their book satchels. Both reluctantly pedaled off, as if en route to school.

At the intersection of Vale and Menlove, they met as always and then clandestinely cut back across the Allerton Golf Course towards Spring Wood, towards Julia's. Frost made their bicycles skittish – as skittish as they themselves – and they rode hunched over, like amateur spies setting out on a novice mission. Hearts and wheels raced as they cleared the quiet, manicured greens and emerged into the clamour of heavily trafficked Allerton Road.

"You're dead certain she won't let the cat out, then?" Pete panted, pedaling hard. He found it difficult to believe that any adult, even Julia, would condone such evasion.

John threw him a cutting look. "She's no *parent*, not that kind anyway. Julia thinks school's a waste of time, an uneven substitute for findin' things out on yer own and all that. She's not like Bess or Mimi; she's not like anyone, really."

"Thank goodfugginess!" Pete grinned from ear to ear. He had perfected Liverpool's Scouse tendency to insert expletives where least expected, and today the practise seemed even more useful and appropriate. It was a perfect day for swearing well and frequently, now that John and he had officially become renegades.

Feigning confidence, as if they knew exactly what they were doing, the boys quickly navigated the turn at Heath without raising eyebrows. No one even glanced in their direction. Only a terrier yipped his admonishment as they raced past.

In record speed, they were making the loop on Blomfield Road, peddling towards Julia's doorstep. The sleepy suburban street was completely empty, but the boys moved furtively anyway, looking over their shoulders, riding low. They grinned at one another, never relinquishing their pace until they skidded to a halt on the sidewalk at One Blomfield. Feeling heady and adventurous, they laughed and removed their gloves and hats. *This was the most fun they'd ever had!*

"Going in, then?" Pete had rolled his bike behind a bush, but he still hung back for John to lead the way.

"Where else would you have us go?" John rapped on the door with a bravado he didn't really feel.

"Boys!" Julia's early morning smile was sleepy but amiable. "Come in, come in, come in!" She stepped aside and closed the door on the frosty, nosy, outside world.

Pete could hardly believe his eyes. John's mother was not the least bit irritated with them; furthermore, she didn't seem suspicious or concerned about their early morning call. Instead she stood there, all drowsy, sunny, and eager to please.

"Cakes anyone?" the slim-hipped redhead led the way to the kitchen table.

John put on his best old man's crackly voice. "Why not, luv? Let's dine on cakes and ginger beer, me dear."

"And you shall have it, kind sir," Julia played along. "But first and always first, a song..." and they burst into a chorus of "My Bonnie Lies Over the Ocean" – mother and son singing harmony each time the chorus rolled round.

For a few moments, Pete battled jealousy. His mum rarely ever sang, but Julia was *always* singing. When she cleaned house, when she shopped or walked down the street, she sang. She sang, uninhibited, in front of total strangers, and she sang with zest around those she loved the most. She was, in fact, quite a bit like a song – lilting, happy-go-lucky, melodic. John was a lucky bastard.

"So what's up with Jacqui and Ju, then?" John asked after his half-sisters as the tune trailed off

"Same-same," Julia smiled, "You know girls, John – all fuss and bother...not at all like boys, who are fun in a common sense way." She cut her eyes coyly at both of them.

Pete grinned sheepishly. *Fuggin'ell, she's a looker!*

"And Twitchy?" John was condescendingly polite, inquiring after his step-father-of-sorts because it was the right thing to do. This much of Mimi he always carried with him; he found it impossible to eradicate duty entirely.

Julia set down a plate of sweet cakes and handed them dessert saucers. "Use your fingers, luvs," she instructed, "Much more fun that way, y'know!"

Then, stifling a yawn, she found an answer to her son's question, "You know Bobby, John...he's puttin' in so many hours now that things 're really lookin' up for me 'n the girls. And not that it's drudgery for him, either; Bobby honestly loves his work at the hotel, y'know. Not at all like me, I suppose, but then who is? You know my credo: 'What's best is play.'"

Almost as if to give credence to her speech, she reached for her banjo and settled into a plump armchair. As they ate, she serenaded them with "Be Bop A Lula."

Julia played and took requests. John and Pete swished down their gingers and gobbled cakes as if breakfast had never been served. Pete offered up a few immodest jokes, and John got up and cavorted, half-dancing, half parodying dancers while Julia cheered him on, an audience in herself. There was laughter and warmth and genuine celebration. It was actually half-ten before anyone ever mentioned the unspoken.

"So...how'd you beg off today, then?" Julia's eyes twinkled with a mischievous, knowing look.

"Sus-pen-doooed," John confessed without hesitation. "But you realize we're *at* school right now," John spilled the plan. "I mean as far as our Mary Elizabeth's concerned."

"Ah!" Julia nodded, "malice aforethought and treachery as well!"

"Duplicity in the highest," John grinned back, "and peace, goodwill to

Mim."

"Well," Julia tried to look stern. She paused for almost a minute before she said it. "You leave me no choice, John Winston; one simply must do what one must. You clearly leave me no choice but to...to sequester you both here!"

Pete let out a whoop, a cry of utter relief. John looked cocky and proud. He beamed at Pete with all the vanity of the victorious.

She's done it! he thought. *She's come through for me, just as I knew she would.* He'd relied on her, and she'd been there for him. Over and over in an unspoken prayer for the last two hours, he'd silently begged her: *Don't disappoint me; don't let me down.* Now he smiled as if he'd won a scholarship instead of a suspension.

The day passed too quickly for the truants. Julia played her gramophone, and they all sang, making up their own words when the real ones weren't quite clear. Bobby had wired extension speakers to every room, so music surrounded them wherever they moved. In a kind of teenager's heaven, rock'n'roll filled every minute of the morning and most of the afternoon. Julia's record collection awed and amused them, and her knowledge of rock'n'roll kept the conversation flowing.

But at 3 p.m., John suddenly announced their abrupt departure.

"Look, we can't make Mim suspicious. We've got to do everythin' by the book and accordin' to the plan," he insisted. "If we fuggin' screw this up today, there'll be no comin' back, will there?"

So over Pete's protest about one more Buddy Holly record, John switched the gramophone off and gathered up their book bags. The three exchanged hugs and hasty good-byes.

"Well then," Julia leaned against the doorframe as they wheeled their bicycles out of hiding, "I'll be lookin' forward to tomorrow, you know. We'll try those new chords again, John. I'm sure it'll come off easier on the second go. All you need's a little more practise. And listen both of you, relax! Don't worry; don't worry about a thing! Everythin's goin' to be absolutely fine."

This time they took the street route home, up Mather to Booker and right onto Menlove Avenue. They rode quickly and in silence. Now that the day was over, they were serious and quiet. Neither of them said it, but both of them wondered exactly the same thing. Had Pobjoy phoned their homes? Had they pulled it off successfully? Had they been found out? Was Fate waiting to strike?

Pete left John at the iron gate in front of Mendips, keeping a close eye on his watch as he moved on towards Vale Road. John had warned him to arrive at the usual time and to look exhausted and hungry. His mother owned a hairdresser's shop in Woolton and was rarely ever at home at this time of day, but the neighbours saw and repeated everything. Appearances had to be absolutely normal.

Incredibly enough, John had even demanded that Pete do homework, just to maintain their charade. "He's bleedin' worse than effin' Pobjoy," Pete muttered to himself, turning into the driveway. He could barely stand the burning tingle of fear in his gut.

When he spotted his mother's small car in the driveway, the hair on Pete's arms stood on end. *Why wasn't she at her shop? Why was she here? What did she know?*

Bess Shotton opened the front door, stood squarely in the doorway, and waited for her son to put his bike away.

"So...how was school then?" she asked in a noncommittal way.

"School," was the terse reply. It was all he usually said, and Pete was trying like hell to be normal. He scanned his mother's face for some hint of anger or disapproval, but he read nothing there. The guilt and anticipation were killing him.

"Take your shoes off, Petie." She walked back in to the kitchen. "And come have some tea, yeah? No dawdlin' now...I just popped 'round for the payroll papers; I need to be off straight 'way."

Perhaps that's the clue to relax, he told himself. *If she knew anything, she'd have spilled it by now...and besides, if she'd found me out, she'd hardly be callin' me 'Petie' or goin' back to work.*

Pete followed her obediently, looking at his mother, *really* looking at her for the first time in a long time. Bess Shotton was a remarkable woman; he realized that. In an era when most women were housewives and mothers, Bess had, through the years, owned a grocer's shop in Quarry Street, a wool shop, and now a hairdresser's. And even more remarkably, she had sat her driving test and then purchased her own personal car. For 1957, his mother was quite a pioneer.

But she's no Julia, Pete looked her over. In fact, the dress she wore was hardly new. Her blonde hair did not spill down over her shoulders. It was neatly pinned and coifed. And there were no stray locks to toss aside seductively. Her hair always behaved.

No one could call his mother large or overweight, but Bess was substantial, and her legs were good, sensible legs that took her about and did her bidding. Bess Shotton was *practically* made.

In the kitchen, his mother laid out a plate of digestive biscuits and shortbread fingers, and poured Pete a cup of English Breakfast Tea...no iced cakes and no ginger beer. There was no music competing with the conversation, and no one, especially not his mother, danced with a feather duster.

As she gathered her purse and her paperwork, she went on and on about ordinary things – fuming about the rising cost of Twinning's, doling out instructions for after-school chores, and reminding Pete to attend to his homework. Not once did she mention Bill Haley; not once did she fill him in on the latest chart toppers by Elvis Presley.

In a sudden rush of emotion, Pete interrupted her, blurting out the first thing that came to his head, "Hey...this shortbread's first-rate, Mum, really...first-rate!" and he smiled a generous, approving smile.

Bess Shotton acknowledged the praise, nodding and looking at her son rather inquisitively. He seemed a bit too effusive today, a bit too happy to be home. A cautioning voice whispered that something might possibly be wrong. But for the moment, she had no idea what it was.

Of course, it is documented that Pete and John spent their days during suspension at Julia's house. And the information about her banjo playing and performing is factual. All facts about Bess Shotton are accurate. And the route driven to Spring Wood is documented. Only the conversations are conjecture.

Late February 1957
Mendips
Woolton

For two uninterrupted weeks, Julia worked her magic. Eight hours a day, five days a week, she harboured the fugitives and distracted them. Strumming "Ramona" or "Wedding Bells Are Breaking Up that Old Gang of Mine" on her banjo, she urged the boys to enjoy life, to forgot Pobjoy and the consequences.

But John knew it wouldn't last, couldn't last.

He sensed trouble immediately when he saw Mimi standing in the cold at the brick and wrought iron Mendips gate. Her arms were folded tightly about her waist. Her face was as icy as the afternoon's impending snowstorm.

"Now there's an evil sight," he whispered to Pete.

"*Fuggin' hell!*" Pete's face drained of its colour, "They've called! She knows! I think she knows!"

"I *know* she fuggin' knows." John slowed his bike's pace down to a crawl. "Look at her lyin' in wait just like bleedin' Cerberus at the fuggin' gates of hell. Where's her boat and oarsman? Where's her other head?"

"Well it couldn't go on forever, could it?"

"No, but *this* bleedin' can. Just look at her. It's fuggin' awful."

John and Pete skidded to a halt at Mimi's feet. For a moment, their quick breathing was the only sound. No one said a word.

Mimi stared at them coldly. John was motionless, stilled by her eyes. The hunter and the hunted – they sized each other up, both resistant and rigid, too cautious to speak.

"Go home, Peter Shotton," Mimi pronounced suddenly, never taking her eyes off John. Pete was gone in an instant.

"Suspended." She said it. Somehow, the word had lost its merriment. "Suspended!" she spat out again. "And for two weeks, you haven't said a word!"

John tilted his chin up in arrogance. The old veil fell across his eyes.

"John, I'm at my wit's end with you – beyond that, I'm terrified. What will become of you ultimately? What will you do in the world, if you can't even manage to stay in school?

"You're sixteen years old, on the verge of deciding whether to go on to university or learn a trade of some sort. Sixteen – a crucial age where grades and good school reports and recommendations from your professors mean absolutely everything! In less than a year, you'll have to decide what it is you want to do with your life. But as far as I can see now, you're destined to be nothing...nothing but a common labourer – at best a cabby, at worst a staggering layabout. More than likely you'll drift like that flotsam father of yours before you – contributing nothing to society but balderdash and trouble.

"Your grades have fallen and fallen and fallen until there's nowhere left for them to go. Your antics have cast you amongst the worst of the worst. In fact, Mr. Pobjoy says he doesn't even *want* you back, but it's against the law to turn you away entirely. He's forced to let you back in.

"You're...*swimming* in indecency and in deceit!

"Why, if you'd only come to me, only *told me* you'd been suspended, told me *why* you'd been suspended...that would have been one thing! I might've been able to reason with the Headmaster, might've saved the loss of two whole weeks' work – work that you'll most assuredly be expected to complete. As it was, I knew nothing.

"I was totally humiliated when I received Mr. Pobjoy's call this morning. I was made a laughing-stock. I didn't even know where you've *been* for the last two weeks!

She turned and walked briskly towards the house. John followed at a slower pace, dreading the sequel to the tirade. Rolling his bike around towards the back door, he knew the sermonizing had just begun; Mimi had only delivered her opening.

His wiry mutt, Sally, twisted happily towards him, oblivious to censure and anger. She licked his hand. She whined as John bent down and roughed her a bit behind the ears. Yawning, stretching, comfortable now that her John was home, Sally offered silent devotion. She was always welcome, but especially today.

"Avoid Mrs. Smith at all costs, Sal," John whispered conspiratorially to the dog, "She's on a bleedin' tear, as it were. Could be rabies...more likely distemper. Whatever the malady, it's effin' dangerous 'round here! If I were you, little gerl, I'd dig me a hole out back and lay bleedin' low."

John only wished he could.

He gave Mimi a few minutes more to simmer down before approaching her again. He knelt beside the dog and patted her belly.

Ordinarily he would have retreated to his room for asylum, making Mimi come to him, but today he had something to say, something so important that it couldn't be tabled until later.

"Mim," he finally appeared in the kitchen, "there's one thing you're wrong about."

"Don't you *dare* tell me I'm wrong about anything, John Lennon!" she flared again. "You're in no position to judge anyone, are you?"

"You're dead wrong." His old spirit emerged. "You're wrong about me becomin' a cabby. I wouldn't have it. And I'm not 'fated' to be me dad or anyone else." He paused for a moment before announcing the big news. "In fact, I'm plannin' to have a skiffle band – me 'n Pete and a couple of others, maybe. And if things go as planned, we'll be famous some day...as famous as Lonnie Donegan, as famous as Elvis even."

"In a pig's eye!" Mimi was sick of his foolishness.

"It'll happen!" His voice leapt up with anger. "It'll happen because I *say* it'll happen. Music's in me bones! I mean there's Mum with her banjo 'n Pop Stanley with his! And I know me dad was..."

Mimi groaned a sick, hollow groan.

"I can effin' do it!" John was goaded into a furious outburst. "I've told you before that if there's such thing as genius, I am one! And if...."

"That's awfully lucky for you, John Winston, because come Monday morning you're going to *need* genius to get you back into school! You're going to need genius and *then some* to make up all the work you've missed while you were God knows where doing God knows what!"

"Who gives a f...fig about school? It's the group that's..."

"Enough! Enough idiocy about some ridiculous pipe dream that won't ever amount to anything! Enough dreaming and adolescent nonsense! *Grow up, John!* Grow up and think about who you are! Think about who you're going to be! Think about what matters in life!"

"*I am*!" he yelled back, gesturing wildly. "But maybe there's more to life than Quarry Bank and *ex hoc mettalico*! And maybe there's more to life than learnin' some trade and slavin' away at a job y'despise 'til half five drags around, day in and day out – sufferin' yer whole life 'til you fall down dead with effin' cirrhosis of the liver!"

Mimi gasped.

"I'll be famous one day!" John hissed, "I'll count for something! But what I won't be is someone who is what everyone else is! And I won't be who *you* want me to be! So if that's what y'er after, give over! I won't settle for it, Mrs. Smith!"

He stormed out of the room, and his bedroom door shook the house when it slammed. Mimi stood for a long time doing nothing – staring, thinking, reliving the scene.

Where would John conjure up such a ridiculous, outlandish notion? How had he ever latched on to this idea of a skiffle band to begin with? A skiffle band! He knows next to nothing about music, Mimi mused. Oh, she'd suggested piano lessons when he was young, but he'd never wanted to play, and as far as she knew, John couldn't read a single note. And aside from George's old mouth organ, she'd never seen him touch a musical instrument at all – that is, except Judy's old banjo.

Judy!

So that's where he's been hiding out! That's where all this poppycock originated! Stuff and nonsense, dreams and make believe! It's Judy! It's Judy all day long!

Mimi could hardly believe it, but she did believe it. Nowhere else in Liverpool could two very visible truants have spent two weeks unnoticed. And no one else would have hidden the culprits so willingly. This catastrophe bore Judy's signature. The skiffle band had given her away.

"I'm goin' to Julia's." John was back in the room, suitcase in hand, face stern and emotionless.

"No, you are not."

"T'rah, Mim." He walked towards the front door.

"John!" She followed him down the hall, "You are *not* going to Judy's, and that's final. Not tonight. You're going to stay right here in your own room in your own home and think about what you intend to do with your life! Before you go back to school on Monday morning, you're going to make your mind up about…"

"I'll be in Blomfield Road." He opened the front door.

"John!" Mimi's voice was cold. "You can't run away to Spring Wood every time things get too rough for you around here. Accepting responsibility is precisely what I'm talking about! Being accountable for your actions means facing up to consequences."

"I've faced them, and I'm off for the weekend."

"You're *not* going." Mimi put a hand on the door. "*This* is where you live. *This* is your home, John. You only go to Judy's as a privilege on weekends or when you deserve it or on occasions when you haven't been suspended from school! You go to Judy's when you're allowed to go! And this weekend, as I've said, you're not going."

John moved forward towards the arm that blocked his path, never slowing his pace or stopping the motion but moving as if Mimi were invisible. She dropped her arm from the doorjamb just in time, and John stepped out into the tiny enclosed porch.

"John," his aunt called after him, "if you go…you're in direct disobedience, and I'll not forget it. You needn't think I'll shrug it off and let you waltz back in here happy and contented as you please, brushing all this aside with a bit of larcenous humour. I'm telling you now for the last time: You are strictly forbidden to go."

John paused for a second at the end of the driveway, his back to his aunt. Then he turned his collar up and headed to his mother's house.

****

By Sunday afternoon John had all but forgotten the quarrel. The weekend had been so full of plans: names for the skiffle group, lists of half-learned songs, suggestions for possible members. And "Twitchy" had even pitched in a few pounds of his own "just to get the bleedin' thing rollin'."

John regularly took his stepfather's money, and Dykins was always generous, but no bond ever formed between the two that a long spell of poverty couldn't sever. Bobby Dykins' coffer of ready cash made him quite a hit with the Quarry Bank set; a handout meant the difference between a pack of Woodbines or Park Drive cigs. It meant Eccles cakes after classes. It meant sweets at the roundabout. And today, the money was John's nest egg for a real guitar. But it was the money John prized, not the relationship. Both he and Dykins knew the difference.

Now, home again, John set his bags down at the foot of the stairs and went to look for Mimi. Like as not, she'd be over their tiff by now. He'd tease her and pull funny faces at her. He'd refuse to take her seriously. And no matter how she lectured or threatened, he'd find a way to win her back. She never stayed mad at him very long, not even in the most serious cases. She just couldn't.

But the house was unusually empty and quiet, so Mimi was either at Harrie's or off on an important errand. She was always there when he returned home, always. Furthermore, her cardinal rule was observance of the Sabbath. Gardening and chores were strictly forbidden; no work that could possibly be postponed was ever done on Sunday.

John looked out back for Sally. It was all too quiet here after a weekend with Jacqui and Ju climbing all over him, goading him, giggling at his jokes. In contrast to Julia's red dresses and brighter laughter, Mendips was hushed indeed. John missed the topsy-turvy in Blomfield Road.

"Sally!" his voice seemed harsh in the quiet formality of Mendips. "C'mon, Sal!" It was strange.

"I'm surprised to see *you* here." Mimi's sarcasm scraped across him. She stood motionless in her hat and coat. "I thought you'd gone off to Julia's, as it were."

"That's right," he shuffled around a bit, "for the weekend."

"Ah, for the weekend. How convenient." She pushed aside the screen door that divided them and stepped out into the garden. John's eyes continued to search for his old, scruffy dog. "And now I suppose, conveniently as well, you're back." She didn't say "you're home," and the wording was noticeable.

"That's right." John's eyes were cool. He could feel a fight brewing.

"Well, how nice for you." She unbuttoned her coat and began to shed it. "How lovely to live in a world where one does exactly as one pleases, when one pleases, and where one pleases."

John glared at her, refusing to take up the bait.

"What's Sally up to?" He looked away.

"Gone," Mimi said, and she turned and walked back into the house, letting the door slam behind her.

John followed with his madman's walk – body bent forward, head down. He overtook her in several strides and grabbed her arm.

"What d'ya mean, 'gone'?" he demanded, eyes narrowed and cold. "What the fuggin'ell's *that* about?"

Mimi jerked her arm free and turned on him like a demon unleashed. "Gone, John. Gone! Gone the way I thought you were gone. Gone...and not ever coming back...just as I thought *you* were never coming back. Gone!

I forbade you to leave; I warned you not to go! And in spite of all of that, you turned your back and walked away! You made your choice."

"You knew I'd taken off only for the weekend!" John screamed. "I bleedin' told you that!"

"You took two suitcases. You took almost all your things. And you've been spending more and more time with Judy anyway, both with my knowledge and behind my back. Isn't that where you've been all day, every day, for the last two weeks? Haven't you been at Judy's all along, playing me for the fool, consorting with her, believing that *she's* the fairy godmother and *I'm* the evil stepmother? Haven't the roles been reversed a bit, John? Wasn't *I* the one who took you in, and isn't she the one you're running off to now, bags in hand, no matter what I say?" It was the closest John had ever seen his aunt to tears.

"I just had to have some time away." John's feelings tumbled over each other, clattering tinker toys scattering in all directions. "I had to...it's just that...look, Mim…Julia wanted to help me start this skiffle...where the hell *is* Sally anyway?"

"Gone." Mimi turned her back to him and folded her arms tightly, holding her waist as if she ached inside. "When I thought you'd moved away and weren't coming back, I...well, I just couldn't stand the sight of her around."

"But you knew I was comin' back..."

"I couldn't stand to see her so pitiful, missing you and looking for you. You just walked out on her, deserted her, and she was miserable, whining around for you with no one to look after her."

"I was only in Spring Wood for *two days*!"

"So I took her down to the clinic...she was old anyway, old and simply in the way."

"You did fuggin' *what*?"

"I had her put to sleep, John. It seemed the kindest thing to do, under the circumstances."

Not since that summer day when he had returned from Scotland to find his Uncle George gone had John been so numb. Words were being spoken, but they were far away and in another language. Fly words. Words spoken by a mouse. Words tiny and unintelligible.

Eventually, he found himself in his room, alone. Everything rang. Everything tingled.

John could make out the sounds of Mimi making supper downstairs. He was sitting in the window seat, playing the mouth organ, making some kind of music. But how he got there and what he played, John didn't know. He simply played a song, an old song, a meandering song, a song that leapt and rolled and curled around. He played a song of devotion – thinking nothing, thinking something, thinking only that he had loved his dog and that nothing could destroy the music in his bones.

Sadly, the events of this chapter are documented. Only the conversations are conjecture.

Spring 1957
Woolton

Despite Mimi's doomsday predictions, Pete and John were once again admitted to their classes. Some of their missed homework assignments were completed; others were ignored. Their final days at Quarry Bank drug on endlessly.

Only one thing had really changed. John now had something to live for.

He'd become infatuated with the American rock'n'roll music his mother loved. Ever since Julia had played Bill Haley's "Rock Around the Clock" for him on her brown tweed 45-rpm record player, John had thought of little else. He talked rock'n'roll; he daydreamed rock'n'roll; he often dreamt about it at night as well.

Against a heavy backbeat of Elvis tunes, John's life found direction. The music filled him. Its primitiveness seduced him; it spun round and round in his head all day long.

He carried his Uncle George's old mouth organ in his back pocket, and whenever the opportunity presented itself, John searched the tiny instrument for the sounds of Chuck Berry or Buddy Holly. Each day, he went through the motions of living – rushing through to the moments when he could sequester himself with rock'n'roll.

But being alone with the music wasn't really what John wanted.

John had always captained a group – instructed Indians or corralled cowboys. There had been moments when he'd cloistered himself away for intervals of inspiration or creativity, but those moments always culminated in interaction with others. John was a commander through and through, utterly dependent on interaction. John needed to lead. He needed a group.

Pete's participation in such a group was a given. He had, in fact, even come up with a name for the ingénue band, just as John had mandated. Pete suggested that they call themselves "The Quarry Men." Insisting it had a "sophisticated ring," Pete and classmate, Eric Griffiths, swore that the moniker would ingratiate them to the school, making The Quarry Men the obvious choice for Quarry Bank dances.

John was coolly indifferent to the title. As long as Eric supplied his guitar and Pete's mum gave the boys a place to practise, John didn't care *what* the group was christened or why. He just wanted to play his rock'n'roll.

Their long-time friend, Bill Smith, volunteered to man the homemade tea-chest bass that John and Pete had constructed using Bessie Shotton's hand-me-down broom and a ball of twine. And quiet, studious Rod Davis – the only real musician in the strangely assembled bunch – was coerced into joining the group because of his coveted banjo.

Pete was assigned the task of strumming an old washboard that John had uncovered in the Shotton's ramshackle garden shed while John wailed away passionately on Uncle George's mouth organ. The boys were not melodious. In fact, their version of "Blue Suede Shoes" limped along, laces dragging. But they were a band.

At first, John had taken the group on as a lark, promising Pete, "If it turns out to be a drag, well then, we can just doff it." But after only two hasty rehearsals in the Shotton's backyard air raid shelter, John was hooked. The concept of a band "just for laughs" immediately vanished, and the mirage of a legitimate group – a record-breaking group – shimmered before him.

"Where's Smith, then?" John barked as they assembled their makeshift instruments, crowding together in the corrugated iron shed, elbowing each other unavoidably.

"He had football practice, didn't he?" Rod Davis offered.

"Fuggin'ell!" John's face flushed. "Is he or *isn't* he in the bleedin' group, or what? He knows we can't bleedin' play without the fuggin' bass...he's screwin' us all, and he knows it! I say we boot' im! We can scrounge up any other tea chest player with an equal amount of invisible talent."

"I believe it's only the second practise he's missed, John." Rod was right.

"*Out of fuggin' four!*" John yelled. "This isn't kid's stuff, Davis, and if *you* think so, maybe *you* oughta get the bloody-two-shoes boot as well!"

"Look, John," Pete interceded, "We could ask Len Garry in instead of Bill. Len's like clockwork, y'know. He even sings a bit, and he's had as much experience on the bass as Smith has."

At that moment, Eric Griffiths swung clumsily through the rattletrap door, his face red from running. Gripped in one sweaty palm, he held his primary calling card, his own personal guitar, and although John threw him a dirty look, the bandleader held his tongue. Eric's guitar and Rod's banjo were precious commodities to the band.

"Sorry I'm late," Eric mumbled, catching his breath. He only glanced at John out of the corner of his eye. He knew there would be repercussions; John was so intense these days. "Me mum made me finish m'homework before I could leave, y'know...and as it is, well...I still have a bit of grammar left when I get home, though I told her it was all done."

John slammed things around, but he managed to say nothing. He needed Eric, and he knew it.

Pete adeptly filled the awkward silence with news of their latest collective decision. "We've decided t'boot Smith, Griffiths. He's saggin' off again today...football practise, y'know...other priorities. He's just not takin' the band seriously, as it were...and Len Garry wants to have a go at it…"

"Issthaso?" Eric settled down a bit, finding an old crate to sit on while attempting to tune his guitar, "Well, Nigel Whalley wants in as well."

"We already tried him out on bass, and he's got plugged lug holes has Nigel," John complained. "Whalley makes even Shennon here look like fuggin' Lawrence Welk!"

"Yeah well…he doesn't want to *play* exactly," Eric explained. "He wants to be our manager."

"Manager!" Pete and Rod roared.

"What's there to manage?" Pete gestured at the four of them, cramped into the tatty, echoing iron shelter.

"Whalley's right," John cut them off. "We need a bleedin' manager. If we're gonna be fuggin' different from all the hundreds, maybe thousands of other groups out there strummin' around in garages and plunkin' about in bathrooms, then we're gonna hafta come up with somethin' nobody else has."

"Well, I'll be willin' to bet *none* of 'em have managers!" Rod jeered.

"Yeah, and if *we* have one, maybe he can *manage* to teach us few songs," Pete jumped on the bandwagon.

"Well, if we get three wishes like they do in all the storybooks, then I'd like him to get us a fan club, if y'please," Rod raised an eyebrow.

They elbowed each other and snickered. The whole idea had them going.

"Right, well manage bloody *this*!" John gestured graphically, but he smiled anyway.

"As a matter of fact," Eric agreed with John, "Nige *does* have some rather fantastic ideas about a coupla things we could try...I mean, he even had this printed up as demonstration, John...just in case you wanted it."

It was a small, plain calling card, a professional card much like the ones used by larger, more affluent bands. In bold but dignified letters the inscription promised:

> County. Western. Rock'n'Roll. Skiffle.
> **The Quarry Men**
> OPEN FOR
> ENGAGEMENTS
> Nigel Whalley, Manager
> Gateacre 1715

"Open for *engagements*!" Pete sputtered. "We've got three bleedin' songs, one bit of a song, and one tad of another. It'd be a short engagement and a bad honeymoon - that!"

"Eric here can't even tune his lousy guitar!" Rod teased.

"Oh, like you're *that* much better on the banjo!" Eric tossed back.

"Whalley's in, then," was all John had to say. And he began to churn out a rudimentary version of "Rock Island Line." Halfway through the song's first progression though, he stopped and directed a final word to Eric Griffiths, a command that allowed no discussion. "Griffiths, be sure and tell that new manager of ours to *find* us a bleedin' drummer. Right?"

"Yeah, right John. All right. A new drummer....got it."

John began to play again, and The Quarry Men joined in. They pounded out the old folk song, missing more notes than they hit and struggling to find a beat, any beat.

But not even the echoing acoustics of the air raid shelter could enhance the performance. And not even the knowledge that they now had an official manager could transform the cluster of gangly fumbling teenagers into a real rock'n'roll group.

****

Nigel Whalley was as good as his word.

Using the mock-up calling card as an example, Nigel had signs painted for local merchants to display, advertising the expertise of the unknown and mysterious Quarry Men. Then pandering them on foot from shop to shop, the industrious young entrepreneur placed signs all over Woolton. In the plate glass windows ringing the Penny Lane roundabout and in Smithdown Road, the talents of The Quarry Men were heralded to all. Their names were everywhere. They became a local curiosity.

John saw the group's placard first in the window of The Old Dutch Cafe, and he goose bumped at the sight of it. Then reality stepped in.

What if we get an actual bookin'? He bit his lip. *What if someone really calls?*

Aside from "Cumberland Gap" and "Rock Island Line," The Quarry

Men's repertoire was pitifully handicapped. John was the sole vocalist, and he knew the words to only a few songs. Even those lyrics, he remembered only by writing them on the palm of his hand. He knew he couldn't give an evening's performance, even if one were offered.

It's about to get serious – this, he told himself. *We've got to decide if we want to make a go of it or chuck it in. We've either got to become a band like the signs say...or give it up. But we can't go around pretendin' to be a group if we're not.*

Lost in thought, John pedaled his bike furiously up Smithdown towards the turnoff at Queen's Drive, the path that would take him home. His legs worked mechanically, and he steered the familiar route without a bobble. But his mind was entirely on his band.

John knew that Pete was in the group only because he'd been forced to be, and Eric, whose parents were both employed, was using the band just to fill his afternoons alone. Rod loved music, but he wasn't in love with rock'n'roll. None of them were terribly enthusiastic about being Quarry Men.

But if they were going to advertise, John decided, things would have to change. And soon.

****

"All right then, let's try "Don't You Rock Me, Daddy-O," John instructed, one foot propped on George Shotton's dented, metal oil can.

"C'mon, Lennon," Eric complained. "That's too bleedin' hard for us! It's out of reach – that song. We told y'so last week."

"It isn't if you practise." John piped out the first chord with incredible force, the sound echoing off the air raid shelter walls.

"The chords are all too complicated for this group," Rod was practical. "It's Eric and me who're making the stretch here, y'know. If *you* had a bleedin' guitar, you'd realize what we're talkin' about."

"Well, we'll see about that, son," John puffed up a bit, "because I'm orderin' one, as it were...from the *Daily Mail*."

"You? With what money?" Pete was the only one brave enough to question John's facts.

"With what I saved from mowin' Mim's lawn."

"Sod that!" Pete grinned sardonically, "You've never earned a fuggin' thing in yer life, and you know it! You just cut half the grass and then run in for a bleedin' handout, as it were! It's just that ole Mim's a soft touch, y'slacker!"

"Piss off, Shotton," John countered playfully. "I'm gettin' the new guitar, aren't I?"

"How much was it, then?" Eric knew the cost of guitars.

John polished his mouth organ on his shirt and mumbled softly, "Five pounds, all right?"

"What?" Eric seized the rare opportunity to give John a bit of what he always got. "Five pounds, is it? Five pounds! What good can *that* be? That's a bleedin' box with a hole...and no strings attached!"

"That's how much you fuggin' know, Griffiths! It's a regular 10s model, guaranteed not to split." John was riled now. "You'll be laughin' out the other side of your fuggin' mouth when it comes in as bleedin' good as anythin' *you've* ever owned!" John began playing "Don't You Rock Me, Daddy-O" again, his lips tight and his nostrils flared.

"I don't like that song." Rod tried one more protest over the mouth organ intro. "Besides it bein' too difficult, it's too much like rock'n'roll."

"Yeah, that's the idea, son," John barked back.

"Don't 'son' me, Lennon," Rod squared off. "And that *isn't* the idea at all, y'know! We're supposed to be *skiffle* band, not a rock'n'roll group. We're supposed to be playin' *skiffle*, remember? That's why we bleedin' got together in the first place!"

"Things change." John said.

"Well, no one ran the changes past me!" Rod blurted out in a huff.

"That's because no one gives a bleedin' red meg what *you* think, Davis!" John glared. "Just play the lousy song or get the hell out!"

Within three sessions, The Quarry Men had added "Don't You Rock Me, Daddy-O" to their play list. And in the weeks to come, The Quarry Men's repertoire of rock'n'roll tunes continued to grow.

****

As a drummer, Colin Hanton was no dynamo. But he was regular, steady, and dependable. Eric Griffiths's mate, Colin had been referred to Nigel for an "audition" of sorts, but the audition was only a formality. No one expected a drummer, *any* drummer, to be turned away. Few boys in Liverpool had their own drum sets, and on top of that – in Nigel's cool appraisal – Colin wasn't "half bad."

John had as few complaints with Hanton as he had compliments for him. He accepted the new drummer with a modicum of fuss and bother.

Now the band was complete. John's three-quarter sized Gallotone Champion guitar had arrived, and as Eric had anticipated, it was a paltry excuse for an instrument.

Ivan Vaughn, known fondly as "Ivy," had stepped in to man the tea chest bass on occasions when Len Garry was temporarily out of pocket, and things were, as John put it, "comin' together."

Only Mimi Smith was coming apart. From her station in the Mendips parlour, John's constant strumming and toe tapping in his room above sounded like a barrage of thunder. Over and over and over he practised one chord or one series of chords. Time after time he rehearsed one tiny bit of a single song.

"Play something else!" She shouted up the stairs.

John emerged from his lair, looking down on her from the top step, "I can't just 'play somethin' else,' Mim!" His voice showered down in frustration. "It's called *practising*, y'know. That's what's it's all about...doin' it over and over again."

"Well, you'll have to do it somewhere else then, John. Go out to the porch. Get out of the house for a while. You're absolutely driving me to madness with all that noise!"

"It isn't noise, and I'll wager Elvis Presley isn't shunted out to a bleedin' vestibule," John muttered, walking back into his room for his instrument.

"Well, Mr. Presley you are *not*," Mimi snapped, "a fact for which I thank God daily, you can be sure!" She watched the teenager gallop down the stairs. "All this obsession with rock'n'roll simply has to have limits, John Winston. You're not Elvis Presley – and if I have anything to say about it, you never will be."

John's face hardened.

"The guitar's all very well, John," Mimi wagged a finger, "but you'll never make a living out of it!"

John eyed his aunt with a blend of disappointment and anger. "Well," he offered icily, "I'll have a bash at it anyway, ta. And someday, Mimi Smith, you'll find you have to eat those words."

And having had the last word as usual, John retreated to the tiny, enclosed porch where the air was biting with a late spring chill.

There is some disagreement about whether the band name is The Quarrymen or The Quarry Men. Hunter Davies opts for the former. Pete Shotton, in his 1983 book, writes the group names as The Quarry Men, and he was in the group. Bill Harry and Phillip Norman also use Quarry Men. However, written as one word or as two, the name is still the same.

In Porter's excellent and very accurate book on this era, he mentions that John rarely ever referred to The Quarry Men as "the band." He always said, "the group." Although I have used the term "the band" in several places in the chapter, I've tried to stay true to stay true to that as often as possible, especially when John is speaking.

Another note from Alan Porter – he says that John's guitar was ordered from "Reveille Magazine."

Although it was not used directly in documenting this chapter, another excellent source of information on The Quarry Men is The Walrus was Ringo *by Alan Clayson and and Spencer Leigh (pages 22-27).*

All conversations in the chapter are conjecture. The quote, "The guitar s all very well, John, but you ll never make a living out of it!" is, of course, quite actual. Many years later, John had the quote framed for Mimi's parlour. And the calling card is quite accurate - to the fonts.

May 1957
Quarry Bank Grammar
Woolton

A splat of spit landed at Dave Bennion's feet. It had been a calculated miss, fired as a warning shot. Dave stopped and slowly lifted his eyes to the second floor landing, but no one was there. Lennon was too clever for that.

The attack wasn't surprising to Dave, and it wasn't amusing. He had long since grown weary of Lennon's escapades, his constant digs and verbal lacerations; John was "an absolute salt," no getting round it – salt in any open wound.

Stepping over the small glistening spot, Dave moved with unruffled determination towards the massive staircase. He moved with a quiet calm that fit the atmosphere of the place. Dave Bennion was Quarry Bank: traditional, unshakable, serene. He was, in fact, everything John Lennon detested.

Dave was the Prefect, the Head Boy, the supreme symbol of ornately carved oak stairways, arching mirrors, lush rolling lawns, and formal reception rooms. Dave was tea and biscuits; he was assignments completed well and on time. He was the class leader.

That, in itself, made Dave a prime target for Lennon's dark humour. John had the unique knack of "getting at you," of finding a vulnerable spot and then sinking his teeth in. He sleuthed out weaknesses, found deformities, and tormented the vulnerable. Lennon was not a bully, per se, but he was a bitter pill. Dave had found that out through experience.

Generally, John left Dave alone. Dave was imperturbable. Agitating Dave was as useless as hurling paper airplanes at a real, flesh-and-blood enemy. John would rather win.

But lately, their paths had crossed unpleasantly on several occasions, and John had had just about enough of "the staunch Mr. Bennion." He was tired of the punishments Dave meted out on behalf of the faculty. He was fed up with the ridiculous futility Dave represented.

John's sixth form year had "iced the cake." He had come to despise school entirely. And while John believed that he resented Quarry Bank in particular, it was the whole of formal education he rejected.

He resented being told where he could and could not eat his lunch – so he routinely left the campus in mutiny, "skivin' off" for protest as well as pleasure. He rejected all forms of organized sports, defiantly opting out of physical education, to the destruction of his grade in that area. But most of all, John resented the daily grind. *Nothing* interested him anymore, and as he withered, no one seemed to care. Drowning in utter ennui, John was purposely and openly failing.

As staff-selected Head Boy, it was Dave's job to ensure that John's self-destructive tactics didn't intrude on others around him. In this last year of school, John had obviously decided to create his own brand of excitement by needling the meek, rousing the rabble, and excelling in disobedience. And Dave had been appointed to stop this.

On the second floor landing, there were no signs of Lennon. The large hall with its gallery overlooking the entrance foyer below was completely empty. Dave stood in silence.

From the hallway to the left, Mr. Burroughs, John's house teacher, emerged scanning a long list of examination ratings. He nodded to the Perfect and smiled a faint smile.

Dave returned the nod with a question. "Excuse me, sir, but John Lennon...he *is* in class?"

"Rarely," the tall, distinguished man admitted, "but this particular morning, yes."

"I see," Dave folded his hands behind his back in a thoughtful sort of parade-rest. "Well then, could you please tell him, sir, that when it's convenient, I've something to discuss with him?"

"Trouble again?" The professor's bushy eyebrows arched. Burroughs had crossed swords with Lennon on several occasions at his beloved cricket matches. Lennon had jeered and teased his players relentlessly until Burroughs had finally banned "the wretch" from sporting events. He knew the boy's vexatious nature firsthand.

"Not really." Dave's cool, blue eyes told the man nothing. "Not this time, anyway."

"Well," Burroughs was skeptical, "in any case, I'll pass the word along for you. Good morning, Mr. Bennion."

"Sir." Dave nodded and walked on towards Mr. McDermott's class where he had been asked to administer a handful of make-up examinations. He consulted his watch and quickened his step. Only two minutes to spare – it wouldn't do to be late.

****

"You wanted to see me, Bennion?" Lennon's nasal tone sounded behind him in the narrow, student coat closet.

Dave turned casually, glad he hadn't shown how startled he'd just been. His steel-blue eyes were expressionless.

"What is it, then? Speak up, son." John gathered his own aura and looked down his nose at the goody-goody boy.

"Your band." Dave offered the information in tidbits.

"Yeah, what of it? Go on. I don't have time to be muckin' about in coat closets with Head Boys, y'know. It's not good for me reputation."

Dave ignored the jab. "Mr. Pobjoy has graciously agreed to your proposal that The Quarry Men perform at the end of term dance...that is, if you're not incredibly booked up by now." Dave had an acerbity all his own.

"Yeah sure, all right," John shrugged nonchalantly, although The Quarry Men would be overjoyed to play for the dance – delighted to play anywhere at all. Dave Bennion aside, it would be an opportunity to perform, a chance to be heard, a gig. But John turned his back on the Head Boy in feigned indifference and started to walk away.

"Oh, and Lennon..." Dave called from behind John, almost as an afterthought.

"Yeah?"

"You'll be staying after school again this evening, if you don't mind." Dave moved across the second floor lobby to stand purposely beside the circular overlook to the floor below. "You see, perhaps you're not aware of this regulation, but there's no spitting allowed in Quarry Bank – not anywhere...and most especially not over the banister."

****

In the days that followed, Dave Bennion secretly questioned Headmaster Pobjoy's decision to allow The Quarry Men to perform for the sixth form dance. Energized and empowered by the privilege of being chosen, John and his first-mate, Shotton, arrogantly lorded it over everyone. They were in rare form.

Only Dave's utter faith in Mr. Pobjoy's perceptive administrative abilities kept Dave from pleading with the Headmaster to ban the two teen-aged pirates from the dance altogether.

Now at lunchtimes, Shennon 'n Lotton blatantly bolted out the side door and paraded across the grassy lawn toward All Hallows Church, or boldly exited through the front entrance to "picnic" in Calderstones Park across the street. They hid in the teachers' staff room and carved their names on the small, wooden desks. They lurked about on the school playing fields while class was still in session.

More than once Dave watched the unscrupulous pair saunter across the school's Memorial Garden as casually as if they were walking into a classroom. From the wide windows in the second floor staff room, he could see them lighting up cigs and chucking their books as they headed for the old, gnarled Calderstone trees. Like infants who assume that when they cover their eyes you can't see them, John and Pete felt invisible beyond the high brick wall that encompassed Quarry Bank.

Eating their lunches and tossing the remnants to the birds, the truants watched the old, hunchbacked gardener refurbishing the mortar in the stone wall around the park, and they jeered at his creeping, arthritic gait. They purposely trampled through his prized flowerbeds, did what they pleased, and returned only at their leisure, elated at having escaped the limits of authority.

But of course, they hadn't. Not really.

Dave Bennion passed John late in the day and spoke to him from across the hall.

"Detention, Lennon," was all he said. "And Peter Shotton, too. You know why."

"Naturally – I'm bleedin' clairvoyant, aren't I just?" John pulled himself up to his full height.

"Saggin' off, Calderstones, lunchtime today." Dave rattled off the offense without a moment's pause. Then he stopped walking and looked John in the eye, his voice quiet and controlled, "Look Lennon, you *do* want to play the end-of-term dance, right? You do want to *attend* the sixth form bash at all? Well, cut the shenanigans, then...before Mr. Pobjoy turns you out for good. It can happen, y'know. You're not invisible, and you're not invincible, either."

"And neither are you, Head Boy." John brushed past him with a dangerous, hollow laugh. "Think of that."

But at detention time that afternoon, both John and Pete were there, and the veiled threats of physical violence never matured past angry, embryonic thoughts.

****

They had made it. They had behaved just long enough to avoid punishment or expulsion. And now, as The Quarry Men arranged their ratty tea chest bass and washboard band up on the auditorium stage, Dave Bennion watched and shook his head in frustration.

How Lennon finagled events to perform tonight, I'll never understand. But here he is – against all odds – setting up, as if he deserves the gig! And the word is...the so-called Quarry Men aren't even all that talented.

John, for his part, was less philosophical. He was busy working, sweating, and moving equipment around.

"It's bleedin' ovenish in here, isn't it?" he yelled across the room to Bennion. "Douse the radiators, Prefect! Try makin' yerself useful for once!"

Under each of the thirteen-foot windows clothed in gold velvet draperies, painted radiators pumped out waves of frost-withering heat. It was chilly outside, a stinging day in a lingering spring that gave no hint of summer. Inside, however, the room pulsated. It was smotheringly warm.

Everyone felt it. Three of the professors' wives who were putting the finishing touches on a trellis threaded with satin ribbons, greenery, and sweetheart roses, wiped their temples now and again with tiny white tea napkins. And the mothers' committee, busy placing white wicker baskets of peonies and laurel blossoms about the room, fanned themselves with old Christmas programmes, found in the storage area.

John, pushing several heavy oak chairs towards the stage and wrestling with the cumbersome brown velvet accent curtains, dripped sweat. He wiped it with the back of his hand and swore under his breath as he dragged the straight-backs into position.

"Hey, Bennion," he barked again, "at least come up and open the bleedin' curtains, right? It's impossible all this, y'know. It's..."

"Hey John. I'm here! I'll lend a hand!" It was Nigel Whalley, the band's manager. Dave sighed with relief and left John's barked demands to Nigel – though he certainly pitied Whalley at this moment. Dave had never seen John Lennon satisfied or happy about anything in his entire life; he doubted that even the best of managers could change that.

"Hey, the place looks fantastic, eh?" Nigel hopped up on the stage and began searching for the curtain pull.

"Yeah, lovely...jolly festive," John smirked.

"Gerroff, Lennon – look at it all...the bunting, the decorations..."

"The Liverpool Lou's in their lurid loveliness lurkin' and learin' lasciviously at the lonely lyricists luridly learin' at them!"

Nigel shook his head and smiled.

But John was right. Already a cluster of girls had formed to watch The Quarry Men work; whispers and giggles mingled with perfume and the smell of fresh flowers. Wearing soft pastels for the final dance of the final year, the girls huddled together under the old oak Memorial Board at the far end of the room. They helped themselves to tiny cups of Orange Squash from the silver punch bowl and nibbled on delicate finger sandwiches and biscuits.

But despite his alliterative pun, John hardly noticed the girls. He was focused on the arrangement of equipment on the stage and insistent that Eric tune his guitar...again. John ordered Pete to help Colin arrange his drum set, and he hissed at Rod and Len to "quit larkin' about and get to work." It was less than an hour until show time, and John was all earnest.

From the rear doorway, Headmaster Pobjoy watched The Quarry Men rush about, and his piercing grey eyes lingered on the scene. *This* is what he had wanted. It was enough to see Lennon so involved, so interested in something. Merited or unmerited, it was the kind of opportunity every student deserved – even the rascals, especially the rascals. Every child, every teenager deserved a niche, a place to belong. This evidently was Lennon's. The boy was in his element.

"Hello, Mr. Pobjoy...good to see you, sir." It was one of the mothers coming from the kitchen, her tiny shoulders drooping cautiously over another tray of sweets. He smiled at her and nodded.

"And to you, too, Mrs. Lallande. Thank you so much for being here. Your loyalty is always noticed...and always appreciated." Then his focus drifted back to the stage again.

To watch John Lennon at work tonight, one could only call him "industrious." The boy was everywhere at once, making things happen and taking charge. John gathered the other band members around him and reviewed a small slip of paper, gesturing to this one and that, talking over incidentals. They nodded and followed his lead, alert and mesmerized. Several asked questions, and John answered quickly, directly, wasting no time.

Then checking his watch, John sent Nigel Whalley on an errand and directed two other Quarry Men to close the curtains on their assembled gear so that the band "could make an entrance" when the dance began. Colin licked his palm and slicked the back of his hair. Pete turned his collar up and urged John to do the same.

"Mr. Pobjoy." Dave Bennion stood quietly at his side.

"Bennion, Bennion," The Headmaster took a deep, slow breath, "what do you see, Mr. Bennion?"

"Sir?" Dave wasn't at all sure he understood.

"On stage, front and center." Mr. Pobjoy folded his arms in satisfaction. "Right there...take a look."

Dave saw The Quarry Men, nothing more. He shrugged and looked at Mr. Pobjoy for elucidation, for something he'd missed.

"There, Mr. Bennion, right in front of Queen and country, you see an indolent soul who has found industry. There, Mr. Bennion – as incredulous as it may seem – the venerable John Winston Lennon is actually checking his watch!"

"Not tardy tonight, is he, sir?" Dave offered.

"No," the progressive educator smiled, "not tonight. Tonight truancy and tardiness are the last things on John Lennon's mind. In fact," he paused to watch John wave Pete Shotton urgently to the stage, "tonight, he is us."

In his book, In My Life*, Pete Shotton says that although he and John were frequently* *in Mr. Pobjoy's office that Mr. Pobjoy would not have recognized them if he had passed them on the street. He says that Mr. Pobjoy had no interest whatsoever in helping John.*

Dave Bennion, who was also there, indicates that Mr. Pobjoy was a progressive educator who did take an interest in John. Ray Coleman, who interviewed William Pobjoy, also asserts that the Headmaster was thrilled that John was interested in music and encouraged that interest.

These facts remain: William Pobjoy permitted The Quarry Men to perform at the Sixth Form Dance. Furthermore, in the months that followed, Pobjoy was instrumental in getting John into Liverpool College of Art, even though John's grades and performance at Quarry Bank did not merit such a recommendation.

Mid-May 1957
Quarry Bank Grammar
Woolton

William Pobjoy removed his glasses and rubbed his eyes for a moment. His head ached, right in the deepest crease between his eyebrows. It hammered away miserably, though he tried to massage it into submission. It was an unfortunate, untimely distraction; today he needed to be completely alert.

Any moment now, she would be here. Mrs. Smith was always punctual and as sobering as a dose of vinegar. He reviewed the speech he planned to give the formidable woman. He whispered his opening to himself.

All around him, ceiling high, were his orderly shelves of books on adolescent psychology, methods, administration, curriculum development, and discipline. He had read them all, and none of them addressed the problems he faced this afternoon. Not one volume offered a solution to John Lennon's anger and misdirection.

The boy was disturbing. In five years at Quarry Bank, John had delighted in little and responded to less. He had failed his O-level examinations when he clearly could have excelled. He had regressed from "exceptional" in English and French to out-and-out failure. And though the Sixth Form Dance had demonstrated John's organizational and leadership skills – and his initiative to achieve when placed in the right environment – the rest of the year had established John's refusal to perform under ordinary circumstances.

Life would not offer John only scenarios in which he was inspired or interested. In Bill Pobjoy's opinion, the prospects for the teenager's future were limited indeed.

Keeping an eye on the clock, the Headmaster sighed and replaced his glasses. Like it or not, it was time. Mrs. Smith would be waiting.

He straightened his tie and then walked briskly from his office through the small anteroom and into the formal reception foyer, where Mimi Smith stood waiting, her purse and umbrella in hand. She stood primly at attention, all decision-and-business, and she extended her right hand as he approached.

"Mr. Pobjoy," she nodded without a smile. She never referred to him as "Headmaster." To do so would confer upon him a certain amount of leverage – leverage that would put her at a bargaining disadvantage. Mimi preferred a level playing field or, if possible, the upper hand.

"Mrs. Smith, good to see you again." His smile offered what her visage did not. "Please walk this way," he gestured towards his office and hurried to open the door for her.

"Thank you," she responded formally, never using the colloquial Scouse, "ta."

"Tea?" Pobjoy queried.

"No…thank you." She waved him off as she settled onto the edge of the large leather sofa adjacent to the Headmaster's desk. Her bird eyes roamed the octagonal room as if she had never been there before. She took in every detail, evaluating it, just as she always did.

Inwardly, William Pobjoy smiled at the intent, little woman before him. She was observant, clever, and shrewd – more than a bit like her infamous nephew. She had been one of Mr. Pobjoy's toughest customers, just as John had been. Both had had agendas of their own.

Mimi "ahemed" impatiently, and the Headmaster took a seat behind his desk.

Generally, he assumed a chair in front of the sofa, talking to parents from a relaxed, concerned posture. But *this* meeting called for all the distance and authority he could muster. He needed to "pull rank," to retain control of this interview; it was no secret that Mimi Smith harboured resentment towards him

In the uncomfortable silence that hovered, Mr. Pobjoy reached for John's folder and handed it to the boy's guardian. She took it, thumbing through the pages without expression and saying nothing to ease the tension. The Headmaster waited.

"As you can see, Mrs. Smith," he began as soon as her eyes lifted from the last page, "John has reached an educational impasse. He's failed his O-level examinations, so it is virtually impossible to consider him for university. He's failed most of his courses, so even a local institution is quite out of the question. With graduation so imminent, we're limited in our options for John's future. The fact of the matter is, the avenues still open to John can be counted on one hand."

He paused, waiting for her to speak. Instead, Mimi folded her hands tightly in her lap, straightened her posture, and said nothing.

The Headmaster continued. "Well, Mrs. Smith, tell me, then…what are *your* thoughts? What do you think should be considered?"

Her body tensed slightly; her chin lifted even higher. "I believe the appropriate consideration is what *you* think, Mr. Pobjoy, and more to the point, what you are going to do. You…well more accurately, *this school* has had John for exactly five years. His future should have already been clearly mapped out at this point."

The headache throbbed just over the rim of the Headmaster's glasses. He wrinkled his brow tightly, then tried to relax. Gathering his thoughts before answering, Pobjoy got up from his chair and walked to the large picture window overlooking Memorial Garden. He stood and stared, buying time. Then he turned to the wiry woman.

"Mrs. Smith, I have, of course, given this matter a great deal of thought. Had I not done so, this meeting never would have occurred. Your nephew matters to me…as does each and every one of the students in this institution."

Mimi stared back at him with the same indignation he'd often read in John's eyes. He wondered if the boy realized how very much he resembled his aunt.

"John," he continued, "is a lively, intelligent young man – an originator, not a follower – one who deserves a chance for something more than menial labor." Pobjoy took a step forward. "And as you can see from his marks," he indicated the folder, "he is far above average in literature and in poetry…"

"Poetry! Surely you're not suggesting…"

"Not at all, Mrs. Smith. Rest assured your nephew is not destined to be the next T.S. Eliot." Pobjoy sat down in the curved wooden chair closest to the window. "But I am underscoring the boy's aptitude for the fine arts, his natural tendency to excel in literature, music, drama…that general vein."

Mimi said nothing.

"In particular, John seems to have an innate ability for artistic creation – for caricatures and indeed for more serious character studies…for unique sketches which spring from his keen observation." He reached over to the desktop and produced a small, brown spiral notebook, the latest purloined version of John's "Daily Howl." He handed it to Mimi Smith.

As she flipped through the pages, the Headmaster continued. "As you can see, the boy has talent – not the sort that's always been applauded in a structured environment such as this – but talent nevertheless."

They stared at each other.

"I believe, therefore," Pobjoy spelled it out, "that John's a prime candidate for an art college."

Mimi studied the sketches, without offering an opinion.

"Mrs. Smith, if I could somehow manage acceptance for John at Liverpool College of Art – and I'm not promising that I'll be able to do so – would you agree to finance his first year? After that, I'm sure he could successfully make application for a grant."

Mimi lifted her chin proudly, resenting the discussion of finances with so casual an acquaintance. She answered with dignity. "Any port in a storm, Mr. Pobjoy, any port in a storm."

"Fine then." He moved to his desk again. "I'll make the necessary arrangements, and I'll schedule an appointment with the powers that be within the next two weeks." He scribbled something on a desk reference calendar. "In the interim, John needs to assemble a portfolio of his best works, and he needs to be prepared for a formal interview with several professors on staff. He will be asked to delineate his reasons for attending art college and so forth, and he needs to have convincing answers."

"Yes, of course, I understand all of that; I'll discuss it with him, naturally." Mimi returned the notebook of John's sketches to the Headmaster's desk.

"No, please." He handed "The Daily Howl" back to her. "Take the sketches with you. They're John's property, not mine. And even as derisive as many of the uh, representations are, they're magnificent, don't you think?" He paused. "Mrs. Smith, I...I sincerely wish your nephew all the best. I hope you realize that."

"Thank you very much, Mr. Pobjoy." She rose to leave. "I'll speak to John about this prospect straight away."

"Believe me, no thanks are necessary. As you've indicated, it is *my duty*, and moreover, my pleasure to send my students on. John is no exception to that rule." He walked her to the door and opened it. Mimi Smith exited without a backward glance.

William Pobjoy returned to his office, exhausted but relieved. The headache he had been battling seemed to have eased a little, even without the usual Lucozade to diminish it. Instead of requesting a glass for his medicine, the Headmaster splurged and rang for a cup of Earl Grey.

Now the monumental task of convincing Liverpool College of Art to open its doors to yet another spirited nonconformist was about to begin. Pobjoy picked up his personal phone list, scanned for the number of College Principal Stevenson, and began mentally rehearsing the speech he'd deliver...lauding the merits of the renegade who'd been Quarry Bank's greatest tribulation.

Every student deserves a chance, Pobjoy reminded himself. *Even the undeserving deserve a chance. But John Lennon? How can I, in good faith, create an opportunity for such a miscreant?*

As the phone began to ring in the Headmaster's ear, his conscience waited in the wings, eavesdropping. It would be no small task, transforming Lennon into a desirable commodity. But at least one hurdle had been successfully crossed. He had, at least, appeased Mimi Smith.

All events in this chapter (including the name of the Principal of Liverpool College of Art) are documented. Only the words used in the exchange between Mimi Smith and Headmaster Pobjoy are imagined

Late May 1957
1 Blomfield Road
Allerton

He took turns hounding them. First Julia, then Mimi. Then Mimi. Then Julia. One of them had to "give way" at last. One of them had to buy John a real guitar.

Eric's and Pete's predictions had, of course, come true; the five-pound Gallotone from *The Daily Mail* was only worth five pounds. It was a hollow, twangy kid's toy, not the sort of thing one needed for a band, and John, who'd championed it in the beginning, now despised it. He enviously strummed Rod's classic banjo or filched Eric's guitar. More and more, he dreamed of owning "the real thing." It became his only topic of conversation.

"Nigel's gotten us a gig, y'know," he informed his mother after an afternoon rehearsal in her bathroom, where the acoustics were just right for a small band.

"You don't say?" Julia's carefully plucked eyebrows arched in interest.

"Yeah…the Roseberry Street Carnival in Liverpool 8," John explained. "Not America's Carnegie Hall or what have you, but a gig…more or less."

"Just think!" Julia envisioned, *"The Quarry Men, Live on Stage!"*

"The Quarry Men live from the back of a lorry's more like it!" he corrected. They both smiled.

"But it *is* a legitimate booking, John."

"Without a legitimate guitar." John came around to the issue at hand.

"Oh no, not that again!" Julia began to tidy up, skirting the threadbare discussion.

"Yeah, *that* again...and again and again and again and again and again!" John persisted. "Look, I bleedin' *need* a guitar! A real one! It's like playin' with me hands in me pockets – this!" He gave the odd, little instrument a thump.

"But I haven't the money, John. You know that," Julia squirmed. "And besides, even if I did, I couldn't override Mim's decision. She made it quite clear when you had that mail order thing shipped here to my house and not to hers that I was not to interfere further. I didn't make a fuss of it at the time, y'understand, but I realize you told her *I* bought it for you! I didn't want to contradict you, but I did catch bleedin' hell for it though, John! Mim spelled out explicitly that *she's* the one who's to have the final say-so in all matters re: John Lennon. No exceptions, no excuses."

"But *she* isn't budgin'!" John flared.

"Oh, you can do better that that." Julia lovingly poked her son in the ribs. "You've always done better than that, John. You know how to get 'round Mary Elizabeth, if you give it a try. You've always wound her 'round your little finger, haven't you? Even the moment you were born, you did."

"Well, she's come undone, then," John grumbled, hoisting his rank guitar. "She's havin' none of it...and I think knowin' this so-called guitar is dead useless gives her some sort of perverted pleasure."

Julia snickered, even though she tried not to. She walked with him to the door. "Mary Elizabeth's just good and sensible. 'Waste not, want not.' That's her motto. If you'll only appeal to her reason and intellect, you'll get exactly what you want. Somewhere inside of you, John...there's a bit of the barrister, isn't there? Use it, and you'll find a way to succeed."

****

Mendips
Woolton

That is precisely what John did. That evening over supper, he broached the issue of the guitar once again, employing logic as his secret weapon.

"I need a new guitar, Mim," he stated bluntly while carelessly buttering an iced cross-bun, "Not just that five pound mail-order special, but a *real* guitar. The old one's not effective, and it won't measure up. We're playin' too often these days...and now publicly. The thing's become an embarrassment...and won't hold up much longer."

"John," his aunt sighed, "if you'd put half as much energy into your lessons as you do..."

"That's off the subject," John interrupted like a seasoned solicitor. "I need a new guitar."

"You need to study," Mimi insisted, putting her fork down to do battle. "Another guitar will only distract you further. No good can come of it, as I see it, and for the last time, I'll not be a party to such tomfoolery."

"If I have to earn the money to buy a new guitar, I'll study even less," John began. Julia's plan was working. John was winning with logic.

"Impossible!" Mimi stood firm.

"I'll have to take on a job as well as the band," John said. "I'll be dead creased and distracted...too bleedin' fagged out to wrestle with dead borin' subjects that'll do me no good in the long run essentially."

Mimi said nothing but resumed eating in silence.

"Just let me get it out of my system, Mim!" John finally resorted to emotion, using the phrase he'd often heard her use. "Just let me get it over and done with! I've tried to think of other things! I've tried to forget about music – to forget about gettin' a new guitar...but it's not bleedin' workin', Mim! It's really not."

Mimi placed her napkin on the table beside her plate, a small white flag signaling surrender.

"All right, John," she sighed. "Get it out of your system, then. I give up; that's it. You win. Reserve Saturday morning, and we'll go in to City Centre and see what we can find at Hessey's. But I'll only agree if we can locate something reasonable..."

"We can."

"....and *if* we can locate something reasonable, then you may have a new guitar. But this is the last I'll hear of it. Understand?"

"Hear of what?" John smiled. His eyes wore the glint of victory.

****

Hessey's Music Store
Whitechapel Road
Liverpool

Three days later, Mary Elizabeth Smith and an unknown musician named John Winston Lennon walked through the narrow glass door at Hessey's off Whitechapel in Liverpool. For a moment, they stood stock still, staring in wonderment at the hundreds of guitars hanging like colourful gourds all around them. Folk guitars, six-string and twelve-string guitars, Spanish guitars, bass guitars, semi-solids...all sorts. John was too elated to move. This was the ultimate candy shop, and he was the lad with a pocketful of change.

"May I help you, then?" Frank Hessey's top salesman, Jim Gretty, approached the pair. An established Liverpool musician in his own right, Gretty had seen more than his share of young musicians who only wanted "to browse a bit" and then retreat. It was reassuring to see a mother accompanying her son. It hinted at the possibility of an actual sale. Gretty smiled directly at the mother.

"No thank you. My nephew will be doing the shopping today," Mimi Smith declared haughtily. "He's the expert here."

"Indeed?" Gretty raised an eyebrow at John. He wondered if the boy even knew the meaning of the word.

John spoke for the first time since boarding the bus for Whitechapel. "I'll have that one down, if y'please." He pointed directly to a Spanish guitar with steel strings, a rather regular sort of instrument with a light, honey-coloured body.

"Right, all right." Gretty hurried to hoist it down, gently placing it in John's cradling arms. John turned it in his hands, sighting down the bridge, running his hand along the neck. Then without asking permission or speaking at all, he rested his foot atop a three-legged stool and strummed the new instrument. No one said a word.

Gretty put a hand over his mouth, as if in deep thought, to hide his smile. The boy was far from "an expert." In fact, he was a beginner. But the lad seemed to know what he wanted, and Jim had learned not to offer suggestions unless he was asked.

In mid-song John stopped the tune and tried another melody. Mimi smiled to herself, thinking this couldn't possibly take long; John only knew a smattering of songs.

At that moment, the music ceased.

Mimi tilted her head to one side and raised an eyebrow in the silent question. John nodded and gave consent. Without further ado, the aunt who had long resisted this moment stepped forward.

"We'll take it, then," was all Mimi said.

"Of course." Jim reached over to grab a complimentary plectrum for the boy.

As Mimi followed the clerk to the register, she opened her weathered leather wallet and quickly produced the seventeen pounds he requested. Then the pocket book snapped shut, and Mimi silently swore it would be *"the last good money I'll send after bad,"* the last time she would contribute to this lunacy – this preoccupation with American rock and roll music.

"Thank you, and good day," she nodded to the salesman as he handed her his business card.

"Good-day, Madam...and thank *you*! And please come again, both of you!"

John was already in the street, guitar in hand. As Mimi approached him, he swung around exuberantly, his eyes full of laughter, his customary touch-me-not reserve completely vanished. He even wore a smile, a broad one; Mimi hardly knew how to react. It had been such a long time since she'd seen him this way.

"Someday when I'm bleedin' famous," he hugged his bony aunt

spontaneously, "I'll make it all up to you, Mim."

It was a crushing hug, and she resisted as best she could. Judy always called her a "bag o' bones." Right now, every one of them seemed about to break. The guitar clunked gently against her as she tried to shrug them both away.

"All right, all right, all right then." She wriggled free. "Just do what you promised and get it all out of your system. That's all I ask, John; just get it out of your system."

But as she watched his face on the bus ride back to Woolton, Mimi realised her request was a pipe dream. John tapped his foot and hummed a tune, his fingers drumming out a familiar beat on the edge of his prized purchase. His head rocked to the rhythm, and his eyes looked to something miraculously imagined.

The galumphing bus crawled laboriously along the Saturday morning streets towards Menlove Avenue, but John careened ahead in another dimension. He was listening to a song that Mimi's ears could never hear and dreaming of a future she would never understand. And although Mimi wanted to protect the boy from himself, she was powerless to call him back.

My description of Hessey's comes from frequent visits to Hessey's between 1993-2000. (In fact, my husband was fortunate enough to acquire an Epiphone Casino originally purchased at Hessey's and formerly owned by Colin Fallows, Head of the Art Department at John Moores University – formerly Liverpool College of Art.) All events in the story are accurate including the fact that Mr. James Gretty sold the guitar to John. The conversations are conjecture.

Sunday, 2 June 1957
Mendips
Woolton

John was learning rapidly. While appearing to "muddle about," he was observing, reacting, and adapting. Every time Julia played a rock'n'roll number on her record player, John listened intently. Every time Radio Luxembourg, "Luxy," offered up faded moments of "Tutti Frutti" or "Giddy-Up-a-Ding-Dong," John lunged for his guitar and strained to memorize what he heard. The energy that other students reserved for academics or athletics, John expended on music.

He played his treasured 78-rpm of "Rock Island Line" endlessly until it scratched more than it sang; then he sold it for 2 shillings, 6 pence – ready cash for more music. John stalked Quarry Bank students such as Mike Hill, who had extensive collections of American rock'n'roll, hounding them for lunchtime or after-school listening sessions.

John became his new guitar's slender shadow. In fact, he was rarely seen without the instrument slung over his shoulder, the strap rumpling his disheveled Quarry Bank blazer. Like a ruffled crow with a precious morsel tucked jealously under his wing, John flew awkwardly through all other experiences, bird's-eye focused on music and oblivious to the bigger world around him.

If Mimi had even faintly hoped that the guitar would exorcise the demon of rock'n'roll as John had suggested it would, her hopes were miserably dashed. Far from performing an exorcism, the music machine acted as a catalyst. Far from "getting it out of his system," the instrument only encouraged John's visions of fame and fortune, and he began to practice his "play list" to the exclusion of everything else.

"*It's just like heaven, bein' here with you,*" John sang, pausing briefly and then beginning again. "*It's just like heaven, bein' here with you...*"

"John!" Mimi screeched. "Out to the porch, *now*!"

"It's humid out, y'know! Glance out the window, Mim. It's rainin'." He didn't budge.

Silence. John took it as a reprieve.

"*It's just like heaven, bein' here with you...*"

"John, out! Out! Out! Out!"

He bolted down the stairs, guitar in hand, as always. "Give over, Mim. It's bleedin' wet and miserable out there. M'fingers won't work in the damp, y'know. And it's not good for the guitar, as it were." But he moved, nevertheless, towards the doorway.

"Out!" She stood resolute, "and..."

John moved more quickly, his shoulders hunched against "the homework and industry lecture" that was sure to follow.

"...and please close the door tightly behind you, if you don't mind."

John's shoulders relaxed as he reached for the doorknob. *A narrow escape!* He couldn't believe his good fortune! The "importance of homework" exposition was a Sunday afternoon tradition. He called it the Mary Elizabeth Apocalyptic Creed.

"One more thing, John," her voice curled around the half-closed door.

"Yeah?" He poked his head back in again.

"You've got a marvelous brain, you know. It's a pity you've chosen not to use it."

For a single moment he thought of arguing with her, of reminding his aunt of the countless afternoons he'd spent reading his old encyclopedias cover to cover, of days spent sketching or writing short stories, poems, and satires. He started to remind her of the hundreds of books he'd devoured that no other teenager had ever read, much less understood. But in a flash of inspiration, John pulled a funny face at her, defying serious conversation, deflecting debate.

"Save *that* for the music hall!" she snapped, turning her back on him, supplanting ostracism for the usual tirade.

John sighed. He laid his guitar down gently against the enclosed porch wall and came back to the place where his aunt stood sulking. Treading cautiously, he leaned over and planted a "squeaker" kiss on her bony cheek. She stiffened.

"Don't soft soap me, John Winston." She moved away, folding her arms about her. "I'm serious, and you know it. Sideburns, skin-tight jeans, and guitar music morning, noon, and night...a travesty, John. A complete waste of time."

"Well, you'll be changing your tune in a few weeks, won't you?" John let the cat out of the bag.

"Because?"

"Because we've an audition, that's why."

"An audition?" His aunt turned to face him, her expression incredulous.

"Yeah, that's right." It was John's turn to be laconic.

"An audition with *whom*?" Mimi's voice said a thousand times over that she didn't believe him. So for a moment longer, John prolonged the suspense.

"An audition with whom, John?"

"Levis," was the terse reply.

"Levis?"

"Yeah, that's right." He tilted back his head and looked down his nose at her. "Carroll Levis. Mr. Star Maker Levis, Levis of London, Levis of television's *Search* programme, Levis of England, Levis of practically everywhere in the known 'n charted world. He's comin' here…in person…to the Empire…for a Discovery Night or what have you – a talent search of sorts for Northern genius.'"

"*Our* Empire Theatre, City Centre? When?"

John resented her disbelief. "Six June, nine June, somethin' like that. I have it all written down if it's details you're after."

"During the school week?"

"A Sunday, Mim."

"And what exactly would you win, anyway, if indeed you won this Discovery whatever-it-is?"

"An opportunity." John glared, all desire to explain or impress her now vanished under the third degree.

"An opportunity to do what, John? Must I drag this out of you, bit by bit?"

"Must you?"

"Spell it out, John Winston! Enough falderal."

"All right, then, it's an audition for one Levis's television programmes on ATV, a chance to be showcased performin' live somewhere other 'n that sarcophagus of a porch you've got out there," he shot back at her.

"Well…Levis…" she dismissed him with a wave of her hand. "It's certainly a long shot, isn't it?"

"It's a shot."

She picked up the *The Echo* and took her chair by the fire.

"So as I've said before," John went on, "there's an actual need for all this practisin', y'see – porch or no porch, rain or no rain, homework or no homework and all that academia aside." And he closed the door tightly behind him before she could respond.

Mimi shook her head in disgust. Once again, they had reached stalemate. Their arguments never budged either of them an inch. In truth, no amount of arguing was going to dissuade John, and nothing was going to convince her he was right about a future in rock'n'roll. They could find no middle ground.

That night for the first time Mimi Smith turned her radio down a bit. Curious, she eavesdropped on the concert fading in through the thick oak front door. She listened to her nephew strumming one pitiful little song over and over again. She listened to his young voice straining for the notes, his unskilled fingers blundering over the basic chords.

Mimi tried to imagine herself seated high in the Empire Theatre balcony, a principal at the June audition, perhaps one of Levis's assistants or even the powerful Levis himself. She tried to hear what Levis would hear, to appraise with critical ears, ears that had no emotion or bias of any sort. She listened for any sound of star potential, for any shred of talent in John's music.

But Mimi heard nothing past mediocrity, nothing more than the rudimentary music of a high school boy possessing little talent and big dreams.

"Well," she sighed to herself after a fashion, reaching for the volume knob on her radio, "good, then. Perhaps after this 'Star-Maker audition,' life will return to normal after all. Perhaps then John'll get on with the business at hand and find himself a career instead of wasting every evening obsessed with this futile, unhinged music."

Out on the porch, John continued to strum.

Mimi's desultory war with John over rock'n'roll is a matter of record. The fact that John was relegated to the porch for his practices is also legend/fact. The Levis audition is factual as is all information about Levis. Only the conversation is conjecture.

Sunday, 9 June 1957
Empire Theater, City Centre
Liverpool

Pete missed "lurkin' about" Calderstones Park and daring the Rose Lane School scruffs to set foot on their turf. He missed hiding with John in the Woolton bushes and shooting pedestrians with pea bullets. He missed "chattin' up" girls at the Penny Lane Abbey Cinema or mastering the Three S's: "swearin', skivin' off, and smokin' cigs." Pete missed the old days.

Only a few months ago, Shennon and Lotton had been the terror of Quarry Bank athletic events, the sultans of jeers and catcalls, the bane of local merchants who'd routinely chased them off for filching Cadburys or lifting toffees. Now they stood – John and Pete – groomed and polished, outside the majestic, white stone Empire Theatre in the heart of City Centre, Liverpool. They stood waiting nervously for Eric Griffiths to join them. Pacing, marking time, intent and impatient, they were young men waiting for an incredible audition, waiting in the shadow of government buildings and museums for the chance at a grown-up job.

Lime Street was "the big time." It was Liverpool's "Main Street," the very centre-pulse of the city. All around them towered ornate, imposing structures, all granite and columned. The immense Walker Museum of Art, the Greco-Roman St. George's Hall, and circular Picton Library stood shoulder to shoulder to shoulder – massive, dignified, and serious. The Washington Hotel with its hundreds of chimneys, bevy of bright windows, and immense archways peered down at them, reminding the suburban lads they were no longer carefree boys out on a lark. This was the adult world.

Suited businessmen shoved past The Quarry Men; vendors offered them wares. And even now, at noontime, prostitutes strolled casually up and down the wide promenade, calling out to sailors fresh from the sea and to the young slicked-back boys from Woolton who clustered together nervously.

In the old days, Pete smiled to himself, John would have winked at a "judy" or two, would have called back a bawdy line of his own – might even have engaged one of "the Liverpool Lou's" in a quick cat-and-mouse conversation. But today, John was preoccupied, checking his watch every minute-and-a-half and cursing Eric Griffiths's very existence.

"There! Look! *There* he is…over there!"

Eric rounded the corner, guitar in hand, his face flushed. Holding his guitar out to the side with one hand and smoothing his hair back with the other, Eric pounded towards them at a pace that proved his sincerity. "Sorry, John…sorry," he stammered.

"No fuggin' excuses!" John barked back. "Just get it together, Griffiths."

"But I…"

"Not fuggin' interested." John gave his lead guitarist no quarter. "Whatever the reason, it doesn't fly today. Levis doesn't care if the dog ate yer homework or the sun was in yer eyes."

Eric re-coiffed his hair with his fingers; his breathing began to regulate. Pete laid a hand on Eric's shoulder in support, and Nigel took his guitar case with a quick nod of understanding.

"Right, then." John looked them over. "We're all here. Let's go."

"No time like the present, eh?" Nigel threw in a bit of managerial patter. John gave him a quick glance that silenced anything further.

They followed John's lead, one by one, into the Empire lobby. Like schoolboys on a holiday outing, they gawked, drinking it all in. The gilt trim, the high mirrors, the ornate carving – the Empire was nothing short of fantastic. Built in an era of plush, extravagantly decorated theatres, no detail had been left to chance. Every inch of the lobby was larger than life and lovely.

John had seen it all before with George or Mimi, on outings to Christmas Extravaganzas. But secretly, the place never failed to amaze him. He loved the balconies and velvet curtains, the parapets and colour. It was a remarkable place, washed lavishly in mauve, burgundy, and gold. The Empire, he was sure, was as impressive as anything London had to offer.

"Carroll Levis's '*Search for the Stars*,'" a large banner spelled out boldly.

"The stars! That's us!" Pete grinned.

But the lobby was filled with stars. The long stream of young, Northern musicians was being corralled by a uniformed usher and directed towards the tall swinging doors straight ahead. They opened to the orchestra level of Liverpool's finest theatre.

"Fall in with the pack," John directed.

"Hey John, they're handin' out somethin' over there," Pete nudged him.

"Looks like some appropriate paperwork…forms of some sort." Rod could see what the nearsighted John could not.

"All right. Just stay here then. I'll go sort it out." John began to thread his way through the crowd.

In about ten minutes, he was back.

"Well, we're conscripted, lads." He managed a bit of humour. "Registered…ready for assignment." John retracted his hand inside his sleeve and limped. "And to think it only cost me an arm and a leg, mates!"

"Price o' victory!" Pete tugged at the empty sleeve. "It was all well worth it, wasn't it?"

For a moment, it almost felt like old times.

Suddenly, the line began to move. The Quarry Men were funneled though the doorway, given a number and a stall to sit in. Rod waved to some skifflers he knew from The Liverpool Institute, and Pete recognized even more faces…chaps John hounded about records and music, Liverpool hopefuls who dreamed of becoming Bill Haley and the Comets, Cliff Richards, or Lonnie Donegan. Pete nodded, saluted, and smiled his cocky, Shotton smirk while John pushed forward blindly in the dim light, unable to see anyone at all.

But even without his glasses and clear vision, John knew he'd never experienced anything remotely similar to this. The room was filled to capacity with skiffle groups from Liverpool, Litherland, Chester, Blackpool, Garston, Toxteth, Brighton – even as far away as Manchester. There were teenage boys from every neighbouring town – boys in leather jackets, chaps in matching suits with individually coloured ties, groups with monogrammed shirts and dark dress slacks, groups in drainpipe jeans. Rod groaned at the length of the waiting list, but John smiled for the first time all afternoon. This was Nirvana; they were in for an afternoon of music.

"We won't be on 'til three at least with all this lot," Rod grumbled, falling into the folding velvet theatre chair.

"Rambullon, son. No one's listenin'." John sat forward, squinting to see.

On stage, a group from Rhyl introduced themselves and began their audition; they were Elvis-inspired and ready. Belting out more rock'n'roll than skiffle, they performed with relentless energy and elicited wild applause from the other waiting hopefuls. One rowdy bunch from Aigburth even stood in their seats to cheer before a stern usher hauled them back down. It was a room electric, and John was on cloud nine. He cupped his hands and yelled, "Good on yer!" as the Rhyl band took a second bow.

Then a band from Speke called The Sunnyside Skiffle Group took the stage. From the outset, they were incredible. Their lead singer and tea chest bass player was a ball of uncontained enthusiasm. Standing only 4 feet, 6 inches tall, Nicky Cuff was the smallest nineteen-year-old John had ever seen, but size was Nicky's secret weapon. Like a sprite riding unpredictable air currents, Cuff leapt all over the stage, delivering a *show* instead of a song. Wearing a top hat and tails, pounding out the beat with his heels, and leaping atop his tea chest bass as a grand finale, Cuff used every second of the five minutes allotted to his band.

The Quarry Men, in comparison, were tin-soldier lifeless. They stood stiffly at their designated microphones and droned out their practised tunes, generally in sync, but rigid – obviously nervous. John managed a smile towards the end of the set. Pete looked rather green. Rod merely looked out of place.

And so it was no surprise to anyone that although they qualified in the first heat, The Quarry Men failed to make the final cut. Head to head with Sunnyside Skiffle, The Quarry Men were little competition, and at last, they found themselves free to go.

Scuffling out through the lobby to the street, none of them said a word. No one complained; no one argued the point. The Quarry Men had been out-classed, and they knew it. They lacked "that certain something" that Cuff's group had had. What it was and how it was obtained, though, none of them could say.

"We're no bleedin' good, are we?" Once on the street, Pete found his voice.

"Dead lousy, that's what." Eric summed it up.

"Look, it's not *that* really," Nigel began. "It's just that we don't have a…gimmick, as it were."

"You've got to *put it over* to do rock'n'roll," John cut in. "You've got to dig in…not just stand there like a cluster of rhythmical hand puppets whose strings're barely bein' pulled!"

"He's right." Rod backed him up. "Did y'see that Nicky Cuff up there balancin' on his tea chest and not singin' a whit better 'n John? He outdid us, didn't he?"

"It was the antics," Pete admitted.

"It was the *show*!" Rod spelled it out. "The jumps, the leaps, the high jinks…the extras…they were all part 'n parcel of the song."

John pulled out a Woodbine and lit it. He offered Pete a drag, and Pete handed it on to Nigel.

"Havin' a group isn't bein' a group," John pronounced, reaching over and taking the cig back. He took a long drag and stared blankly towards the Walker Art Gallery. "It's more than just playin' the instruments. It's more than just mouthin' the fuggin' words and gettin' the chords right."

"They were unified – Sunnyside Skiffle," Eric observed.

"Yeah…bleedin' fantastic," Pete said to the sidewalk.

"All right, then," John had had enough. "Enough dissection. Practise – tomorrow, four o'clock."

"Tomorrow? Bollocks to that!" Rod stepped forward. "Look John, we need a day off – how's *that* for a change? We've given up all Sunday bein' here, and all day yesterday rehearsin' and…"

"Couldn't we give it a rest, then, John?" Nigel spoke in his official manager's capacity.

Pete glanced uneasily at Eric, and they waited for the other shoe to fall.

"So that's what you want – a rest?" John's nostrils flared. Pete took a step back from the circle.

"Yeah, if it's all right with you, that is." Nigel cleared his throat and glanced nervously at Eric.

"We've other lives, John." Eric ran his hand through his thick, dark pompadour. "We can't just practice seemingly unendingly."

"Yeah, it's just a lark, John, remember?" Nigel tried a bit of a smile. "Just a way to chat up girls 'n get a couppla free pints, right?"

"We've bleedin' given all we have lately." Eric took the "give'n go" from the others.

"*More*, really," Pete echoed quietly. "That's the truth, John."

John glared at each of them individually, demanding a roll-call vote of loyalty. His eyes met theirs slowly, and he held each gaze a full second.

"Yeah…but I'm not doin' all that much tomorrow, am I," Eric mumbled, " it bein' Monday 'n all."

"Yeah, slow day – Monday," Pete shrugged.

"Right. Me, too," Rod nodded. "Nothin' on, really."

John took one last draw on his Woodbine before flicking it onto the sidewalk and crushing it out, "We'll practice right after school then. Nigel, get to work on some gimmicks. Find us a hook."

"Can do."

"And the rest o'you, y'er borin' me. Work on doin' somethin' besides just standin' there, as it were."

"Yerokkay, John."

"Yeah."

"Right."

"And keep in mind," John hissed, "we've a *real* gig comin' up…"

"One week," Nigel reminded them. "Roseberry Street."

Pete cleared his throat and tried to look agreeable. Eric stared at his feet. Rod watched a black cab whiz by and spray water, just shy of where they were standing. No one answered.

They walked back towards the bus queue in absolute silence. None of them had the courage to clash with John. None of them had the nerve to say, "Y'er fuggin' crazy, Lennon," but they all thought it.

They had no desire to spend every waking minute practising and becoming a band. But John did. And until The Quarry Men found replacements for themselves, they were in it for the duration.

Bill Harry quotes Colin Hanton as saying that he was not at this Sunday audition. His mother, he explained, would not permit it. Therefore, I have not included him in the chapter.

Furthermore, in Len Garry's book, John, Paul, and Me, *there is no mention of this incident. Since Len covers all incidents in 1957 carefully, one must assume that he was not present at this audition even though he was a member of The Quarry Men* at the time.

Traditionally Beatles' experts have agreed that the Sunnyside Skiffle Group defeated the Quarry Men at this audition, and a conversation that I had with Nicky Cuff in August 2005 confirmed this. However, current sources have new information.

In Bill Harry's The John Lennon Encyclopedia, (p. 178-179) Rod Davis is quoted as saying that The Quarrymen were bested at this audition not by The Sunnyside Skiffle Group but by a group from Colwyn Bay, North Wales. Davis is quoted as saying that the Welsh group performed all sorts of antics, including lying on the stage while auditioning, and that The Quarry Men realized that they would have to stop "standing around like wooden figures" and begin putting on a show.

Whether a Welsh group won or Sunnyside Skiffle bested The Quarry Men or both, the result was the same. The importance of charisma on stage was the lesson of the day, and John Lennon took it very seriously

One note of interest: I had a great deal of difficulty getting information for this chapter (and a later one) about The Sunnyside Skiffle Group. I tried hundreds of reference books and the Internet. I even wrote to experts and asked other Beatles authors at New York's Beatlefest about them. Nicky Cuff was the only member of the group that any of the experts could recall. A friend in Liverpool, Jean Beck, called Radio Merseyside for me and asked them to help. They ran a contest to see if listeners could recall any information about The Sunnyside Skiffle Group. One listener could; it was Nicky Cuff. He gave the radio station his telephone number and told me to call him. In August of 2005, I talked to him from my home in West Grove, Pennsylvania. He was extremely helpful, gave me wonderful information, and answered the questions raised above. My gratitude to Nicky Cuff; ta!

Saturday, 22 June 1957
Roseberry Street
Liverpool 8

Marjorie Roberts had high hopes for the day. It was the 750th anniversary of King John's charter giving "willing and adventurous settlers" parcels of land in Liverpool and promising them "all the privileges enjoyed by free boroughs on the sea." It was Liverpool's birthday celebration, a Founders' Day of sorts.

To raise community awareness and commemorate the auspicious occasion, the *Liverpool Post* and *Echo* newspaper group was sponsoring a contest offering "a fabulous grand prize" to the neighbourhood most gloriously fêting the day. Marjorie was the illustrious chairman of Liverpool 8's Roseberry Street festivities.

An evening street dance featuring the popular Merseysippi Jazz Band was to be the highlight of the Roseberry celebration, and all the preparations for the big event had been completed. A string of flags – tossing up and down in a volley of colour – crisscrossed the street directly above the spot where the jazz group would perform. Fresh flowers poured from window boxes, adorning the narrow brick row homes. Buntings cascaded over doorways. And about midway down the street, at 76 Roseberry, Mrs. Roberts had arranged for a lorry to be parked half on the street, half on the sidewalk; it would serve as a stage for the local skiffle bands who would entertain the crowds throughout the afternoon.

A perfect flatbed platform, the lorry was draped with drippy, hand-painted banners, multi-coloured crepe paper twists, and clusters of crepe paper flowers. A primitive microphone stood wired and ready, its cord snaking across the wooden platform and into the front window of the Roberts's home. And up on the "stage," young Charles Roberts was frantically touching up the logo on his best friend's, Colin Hanton's, drum set.

Supervising the primitive calligraphy work, Colin crouched down beside Charles nervously. While Charles worked on hands and knees, perspiring and doing his best to keep an unsupported hand steady, Colin prodded him with alternate choruses of "Great, great, all right," and "Hurry up, then. C'mon. That'll do."

"Look, I'm doin' the bleedin' best I can, aren't I?" Charles bit his lower lip and tried to concentrate on the capital "M" in *Quarry Men*.

"Right, well – all I know is, you'd better dot the last effin' 'i' and cross the last effin' 't' before John arrives. You don't know 'im, but trust me; he's a bleedin' maniac! Ever since our Carroll Levis audition, he's got this bizarre notion that we're supposed to be – no *destined* to be – more than just an air raid shelter band."

Charles stood up, wiped his hands on his pants, and surveyed the lettering critically. Colin glanced over his shoulder for any sign of John and then turned to appraise the artistic rendering on the bass drum himself.

It isn't half bad, he thought. *The stencilin's not all that terrific – certainly far from perfect – but at least now we've got that "identity" John's been demandin'. At least now the so-called fans'll know who we are.*

"Bleedin' swelterin' out, isn't it?" Charles squinted. For the last several days, the arrival of summer had declared itself all at once.

"Yeah, crackin' the flags," Colin wiped his forehead. "And just think of *us*...up here performin'...all bleedin' trussed-up, coifed hair and maybe even a jacket or two."

"Shirrup, Hanton! Give it a rest." John had appeared out of nowhere. He jumped up on the lorry, walked over to the drum kit, and put his face down close to the new lettering. "Not bad – this." He put a finger out to test the paint that smelled rather wet.

"Ta," Charles smiled.

"You're the artist, then?"

"Yeah – Charles Roberts." He offered John his hand. "Me mum's in charge of all this whole to-do."

"Right...John Lennon." John shook his hand with a genuine smile. "Quarry Man. Lead vocals, harmonica, guitar, and buffoonery...no extra charge."

"Didn't think you were with the Merseysippi Jazz Band," Charles chuckled.

"Jazz!" John gave him a look that would wilt flowers, "It's subversive – jazz. Corrodes the brain – jazz."

They stepped back from the drums. Colin checked the sun's angle and then adjusted his kit a mite. He thumped the microphone and bent to give attention to the hook-up.

Pete, his fair cheeks already blotching red, arrived in a plaid shirt and a dark jacket that were sure to prove unbearable before the day was over. His blonde curls were carefully styled and piled high, and he smelled of his dad's cologne. His performance on the washboard might not measure up, but he would look the part of a rocker. John wouldn't be able to accuse him of being unprofessional today.

Nigel, swathed in managerial reserve, checked in – reminding John that they needed a few minutes for a quick "meeting of the minds" before the first song. Then he excused himself to speak with Mrs. Roberts about last-minute details. He was properly self-important, as any manager of a destined-to-be-famous band would be.

Fifteen minutes ahead of schedule and dressed to the nines, Eric and Len hustled in together. Eric had plastered his curly, dark locks into a James Dean swoop, and he wore a black and white plaid long-sleeved shirt, thick and suffocating. When he saw John's rolled-up sleeves, he quickly followed suit.

Rod was the last to arrive, but he was still there well before the appointed hour. John checked Pete's watch and seemed satisfied. All the Quarry Men were there, perspiring in their finery and ready a full ten minutes before the performance was slated to begin.

As groups of children, prammed infants, gossiping mothers, and celebrating fathers began filling the street, Nigel and John called the group together.

"Look, there'll be lots of people out today – a crowd, no less," Nigel reminded them, "so sing to the last person in the last row. Sing for the bleedin' end of the street, as it were. That's showbiz talk."

"Just fuggin' belt it out!" John summarized.

"And," Pete held up a finger, mimicking John, "remember Sunnyside Skiffle, lads!"

"Just resurrect yourselves from the fuggin' dead, right?" John gave them all the eye. They knew they had to perform.

Hot sun, free lager, and a double dose of attitude went straight to John's head. Halfway through the set, Julia arrived with Jacqui and Ju in tow, and John became invincible. He was arrogant and full of rock'n'roll. He was all over the stage – Nicky Cuff and then some. He'd adopted the best of every act he'd seen the previous week at The Empire, and now he put each gimmick to work.

The Quarry Men were a bit too much for the older crowd. They nodded politely for a song or two, but gradually they filtered away, talking behind their hands, as if the band could hear them. But Jacqui and Ju, seated on the edge of the lorry, clapped, sang along, and beamed from ear to ear. Julia winked at Pete and John; she even danced a bit where she stood. The beautiful redhead was in her element. She moved and felt the music.

Julia watched with amusement as a covey of pony-tailed girls with wide eyes pushed past her to stand right beside the stage. They ribbed each other – giggling, staring at the lead singer in the blue-plaid shirt. *John,* Julia smiled, *is a boy no longer. Today he's the stuff of fantasies and dreams.*

It was Colin who first recognized the danger John was putting them all in with his "high voltage" charisma. Because Colin's drums were set back away from the group, he was less able to view the rapt audience and more able to peruse backstage business – more able to overhear a group of angry "toughs" who'd gathered behind the lorry, Teddy Boys infuriated at "the wack centre stage" who had their girls ogling openly. It was a jealous mob, a gang set on revenge.

Two, five, eight....no, nine of them outnumbered and outsized The Quarry Men significantly. They were older than the band and hell-bent. This was trouble.

Less and less able to hold a steady beat, Colin kept an eye on the nasty coalition forming beside him, and between songs, he strained to catch bits and pieces of their conversation.

From what he could gather, they were from Hatherley Street, a block known for its fisticuffs and action-before-words decisions. They were all "well into their cups" and aching for a fight, particularly on a scorching day like today. The high-spirited festival only charged their determination to "get that checkered sod up there as soon as the set's over." Colin suspected they had knives, and God only knew what else. And with every song, John was making the situation worse.

Without drawing attention to himself, Colin smiled and passed the word along to Rod. He figured that as the brains of the group, Rod could use their last few songs to formulate a plan. But Rod only flushed and quickly relayed the message to Pete.

Pete, using the smile he saved for "the Head's" office and whispered the conspiracy to Nigel. And Nigel, in turn, relayed the sentence to the condemned man.

John blanched. He shot a quick look over his shoulder and evaluated his chances in an instant. Here, out of his territory and four lagers into oblivion, he was on shaky ground. Stalling, searching for a solution, John wiped the sweat off his forehead and took his time tuning up for the final song. His eyes met Julia's, and he gave her a sheepish grin.

Instantly, his mother stopped smiling. Her eyes scanned the crowd in search of something amiss, trying to decipher the look she'd seen in John's eyes, but all the fans around her seemed happy enough. They applauded, called out requests, and pushed towards the stage, edging her back another notch or two. Nothing seemed unusual.

Julia shrugged and brushed it off. Besides, John had already turned away and seemed preoccupied with something else. He had his head together with Nigel Whalley.

"It's not that I'm out to avoid trouble, y'know." John talked and Nigel listened, nodding. "But there's no sense in fightin', Nige, if we can't win. And odds bein' as they are..." Nigel glanced at the Hatherley gang, one of whom was now leaning on the back of the lorry. "Don't *look at them*!" John hissed. "Odds bein' as they are, there's no fuggin' chance of winnin' this one, is there? Not here. Not in Roseberry Street."

Nigel picked up an electrical cord and pretended to examine it, then motioned to Charles Roberts, who'd been standing on the sidelines, eager to be part of the popular band. Smiling and waving to the crowd, Charles hopped up on the lorry and took a leisurely stroll towards centre stage.

John spoke to him evenly. "Look Roberts, we're fuggin' in trouble here…and don't change yer fuggin' expression! Just look at this electrical cord and pretend to be concerned. Listen and nod."

Charles's smile was a mannequin's now.

"There's a group o' scruffs back there from Hatherley…*don't look at them*!" he warned. "And it seems they're eager to smash us up as encore for the afternoon's entertainment."

"Fuggin'ell! Shite!" Charles swallowed hard.

"Just keep on examinin' the cord." Nigel jumped in. "That's it. All right. After John introduces this next song, you fade off into the crowd – then run like hell to get yer mum. Tell her we've got to wait it out inside yer house until they've good and gone, right? Tell her it's an ambush… tell her it's life or death, right?"

John kicked the cord in mock frustration. "It appears we're in need of political asylum, Roberts. It appears we need to be sequestered away for the rest of the afternoon, as it were."

"Yerrokay," Charles gulped. "I'll go 'n get me mum straight away."

"No fiddle-arsin' about, right?" John said. "Get on with it."

Charles nodded and tried to smile. He hoped he could even find his mother in all this mayhem. *No telling where she is right now!* But he had no choice. The Quarry Men were slated to vacate the stage in five minutes. Five minutes was all Charles had.

"All right then," John turned to the others with a knowing look, "This'll be the last song of the day, as it were – so make it the best. Ad lib, jam, and do whatever it takes, but don't stop the effin' song 'til I give you the signal, right?"

Pete nodded. He and John were used to close scrapes and uneasy moments.

"And Shotton," John stepped in a bit closer, lowering his voice, "if this doesn't work, and if Roberts doesn't make it back with his mum in the nick o' time, and if the fuggin' bastards do set on us after all…well then, let's give'em one to remember, right! Let's fuggin' take care of ourselves, son."

"Rip off their legs and hit'em with the soggy ends!" Pete revived a favourite Liverpool football cheer. Then he smiled his first genuine smile in months.

"Right," John grinned back, "fuggin' marmalise'em, son!"

And when, at the end of the last song, The Quarry Men were escorted from the stage by the entire carnival committee led by the stalwart Marjorie Roberts, Pete felt a sharp pang of homesickness and a kind of loneliness.

He missed the undaunted deeds of Shennon and Lotton. Pete missed the old days. It all boiled down to that.

Julia Baird (the Ju in this chapter) claims that she remembers the group being announced as "Johnny and the Rainbows" that day because they all wore different coloured checked shirts. Lewisohn, however, credits Charles Roberts with painting Colin's drums for the event and says that Roberts got the group the gig that day. One look at the photo of the group on that date (on page 14 of Lewisohn's book) shows that Roberts had indeed painted the drums with the words, "The Quarry Men." It seems safe to assume, then, that they were still The Quarry Men for this performance.

All other facts are documented. Only the conversations are conjecture.

Saturday, 6 July 1957
Mendips
Woolton

Saturday's no day for brooding, Mimi told herself, folding the last load of laundry and collecting the newly ironed shirts from the door handle. A quick glance at the mantle clock told her that in less than an hour Nanny would arrive to accompany her to the annual Garden Fête at St. Peter's. And it couldn't be soon enough. The way John had been grumbling and grousing about, Mimi needed an afternoon away – an afternoon of parade watching and socializing.

For years now, the Stanley girls had made the Woolton Garden Fête a family tradition, and most years Judy had joined them. She hadn't, however, mentioned going today.

But John was going. He'd been upstairs grooming for well over an hour now.

Truth is, he probably spends more time in the bathroom these days than Judy's two girls put together, Mimi fussed.

She set the laundry basket next to the stairs and thought of the mess she'd have to rectify later. John was recklessly untidy. Everywhere he went he left a trail: wet towels, discarded socks, rumpled shirts, combs, hair oil, and brushes. Mimi sighed.

She'd hoped that the anticipation of attending art college in the city would change John somewhat. She didn't know exactly what she'd expected of "a college man," but it wasn't the harum-scarum of the teenager upstairs who seemed to have no apparent schedule or agenda other than rock'n'roll.

If anything, the fact that John was headed for Liverpool College of Art in September had made him more difficult and defiant. Though Mimi would be financing virtually everything from tuition to books and John would still be living under her roof, the boy had walked away from his art college interview with a picture of himself as self-sufficient, an adult.

It had made the last few weeks miserable.

"I'm off, Mim!" John's voice startled her back to the moment.

"Not so quickly," she called out, moving in the direction of his clanging and bumping. "Stop right where you are, John. I want to have a look at you first!"

John turned towards his aunt with challenging eyes. He pulled himself upright and looked down his nose at her. Mimi gasped. It could have been Julia glaring back at her. The expression was identical; the defiance the same.

What she saw before her was nothing short of repulsive. John was regaled in a checkered shirt and dark, smoky jeans – jeans that seemed to have sprouted from his skin. They were tight-legged, nearly elastic, and every inch rebellious. Mimi had no idea where he'd gotten them.

"What in God's name..." she began.

"Don't start, Mim," he warned, his face stern, his nostrils flaring. He lowered his eyelids.

"*Don't start*, is it? You're the one who needn't start...out the door, that is. You're *not* going to the Fête dressed like that, John – not while you're living under my roof, anyway!" Mimi hissed. "Now get upstairs and wash that grease out of your hair...and put some decent clothes on before I dress you myself! This is a *church* affair, John, not a gathering of hooligans. All my friends will be there...Nanny...perhaps even Judy and the girls. Practically everyone we know will be there. I can't imagine your dressing like that!"

"Well, imagine it, then." He held his ground coolly.

John sauntered casually towards his guitar, which was resting against Mimi's overstuffed ottoman, and he shouldered the instrument without a word.

"And put *that* thing down." Mimi blocked his path.

John moved into her space. "Listen, Mim, I'm out of school now. I'm not some toddler in sun suits – some fat-cheeked chappie in knee socks and blazers, as it were. I'm after makin' m'own decisions these days."

"Fine then!" She threw up her arms in disgust. "Just fine! Because I've spent practically all morning stewing over the decisions I've made lately – wondering if the art college really is the right place for you – if I'm truly helping you discover what to do with your life. And *now*...now I'm hearing it's not my problem anymore, not my 'teapot tempest,' as it were. Well, thank God for that, John! Thank God!"

"Cut the melodrama, Mim," John snorted, taking a furtive glimpse at the grandfather clock in the hallway. "You know exactly what I'm talkin' about. And I'm not shovin' you off or walkin' out on you or any bleedin' rubbish like that. It's just I'm old enough to pick me own clothes and hairstyles and friends and music and all that. You can't dictate things forever. I've got to be able to choose the basics without runnin' to me Auntie Mimi for her bleedin' Good Houskeepin' seal of bleedin' approval!"

"You can make me sound as tyrannical as you like," she made a strange sniffling sound, "but as long as what *you* choose to wear comes out looking like *that*, you obviously still need my guidance."

"When will you realize it's not the bleedin' Thirties anymore?" John exploded. "Wake up and face it, Mim...it's 1957, y'know! Chuck Berry, Little Richard, Elvis, and Bill Haley...."

"Don't say, "bleeding" and don't cite rock and rollers to me as role models."

"Rock'n'rollers?" John returned dryly. "That's where *I'm* headed, Mim."

He picked up some sketches he'd completed the previous evening and waved them in her face. "And y'see these? Well, you'd better tuck 'em away carefully and guard 'em with yer *bleedin'* life, as it were...because one day, Mim, believe it or not, *this* rock'n'roller's gonna be *bleedin'* famous! That's right. Famous! All this stuff you're tossin' out's gonna be *bleedin'* worth thousands more than you ever realized, woman!"

"That's completely beside the point!" Mimi grabbed the doodlings from his hand and flung them furiously into the wastebasket. "It has nothing to do with the subject at hand."

"It has everything to do with the subject *in* hand," John brandished his Gallotone at her.

And without waiting to hear the next lecture, John and his guitar, co-conspirators in one dream, slammed out the front door. Silent, angry instruments, full of gall, ire, and cynicism waiting to become music, they moved rapidly through the Liverpool morning, barreling down Menlove Avenue towards Church Street with a tenaciousness born of imagined destiny.

****

St. Peter's Church Grounds
Woolton

Reverend Maurice Pryce-Jones strolled about the parish-owned fields adjacent to his church like an American politician on the campaign trail. He stopped to kiss rosy-cheeked infants, to shake hands with the men assembling the "shilling-in-the-bucket" tent, and to chat with the well-endowed ladies at the fruit and vegetable stalls. He laughed over the bumbling attempts of several Boy Scouts who were "helping" to assemble the airborne kiddy ride, and he accepted a cup of tea and a plate of fruitcake from the parish mums in the sweets booth. Reverend Pryce-Jones was full of good humour.

No day in the year was as much fun as the annual Garden Fête, and no other church activity – not even Easter Sunday – brought as lively a turnout. There were people from all denominations everywhere...burly gentlemen setting up a hardware booth, elderly ladies overseeing the loading of parade floats, and toddlers tumbling about, rubbing grass stains into their pale, gauzy frocks. Everyone was in a festive mood, especially since the weather was cooperating splendidly.

A slight breeze rustled the crepe paper skirts around the carts and lorries that had been donated for the parade. It moved gently through the cascading hair of Sally Wright, the Rose Queen, seated on her motorized cardboard throne. Reverend Pryce-Jones smiled and waved to her, giving an appreciative nod.

Lovely, lovely, truly lovely, he breathed deeply. *All is as it should be.*

Everything seemed special today. The just-mown fields were brilliantly green; the old, claret sandstone church lifted its spires against the kind of sky that promised rain, but never delivered. Silk handkerchiefs, hanging on the accessory stall display rack, waved seductively to strangers. And the aromas of jam butties, homemade cakes, shortbreads, cigarette smoke, cologne, and ale mingled congenially.

Reverend Pryce-Jones felt good about the whole event. *Today will be,* he told himself, *a wonderful day in Woolton...a day for all parishioners to enjoy.* He had intentionally planned something for every age group this year.

He'd even agreed to Bess Shotton's suggestion that her son's skiffle group – led by the infamous Lennon – take part in the event. It was an opportunity for healing old wounds with Mimi Smith and for involving the dwindling population of teenagers in the life of the parish church.

An excellent strategy on many fronts, he beamed.

Of course, since the Band of Cheshire Yeomanry had been selected to provide the parade's primary musical entertainment, the little skiffle group had been given only a small spot at the end of the parade. But it was enough to let young people of Woolton know that they mattered to the church.

Later in the day, Lennon's group had been asked to perform two concerts of sorts – one on the parish grounds at 4:15 p.m. and one at intermission during the evening church hall dance. It was a generous gesture, one that made Reverend Pryce-Jones proud.

He saw a couple of Lennon's lads already assembling around the coal-merchant's cart – their float for the two o'clock parade. They were animated, and their voices yelped in high-pitched anticipation.

Some of the youngsters, he knew well. *Tow-headed Peter Shotton, of course, who's grown a foot since I've last seen him...the young Hanton chap with that pitiful, little drum set, and the serious Davis boy...a rather atypical character for a Lennon band.*

They were ribbing each other and clowning about. Dressed like grown men in skiffle costumes, the thin, adult veneer failed to cover the frivolity beneath.

"Good afternoon, gentlemen," he greeted them.

"Reverend," Pete offered his hand.

"You have everything you need here, as it were? No problems, then?"

"No sir, no problems, really. We're all set," Pete returned, rubbing the back of his neck where his crisp white shirt was already irritating.

"And Mr. Lennon? He's here?" The Reverend looked around as if expecting to see John materialize on the spot.

"Um…no, not yet, sir." Rod Davis stepped forward. "But it's all right, though. John's never absent…and especially not today. He's been up about this thing for weeks. Y'needn't worry about John, sir."

A lanky youth, all arms and legs, joined the group with anticipation in his eyes. His red and black plaid shirt was an obvious contrast to the others in their "uniform" white short-sleeves, but the lads slapped him on the back when he gingerly lifted a crude tea chest bass onto the stage. Once the bass was secure, Rod Davis gave the newcomer a "hand up."

"Reverend, this's our tea-chest player, Len Garry. He fills in with us now and again as does Ivy Vaughn…but Len's just as good really, so don't think we're second ratin' you or anythin' like that. I mean, we'll all be top notch today, sir."

"Quite…yes, I'm sure." The pastor smiled at the primitive instrument and shook hands with Len before turning to Pete. "Peter, when you mother offered your band's services for the Fête, I'd mentioned to her about your performing this evening as well…at the dance intermission."

"Right," Pete nodded. "John's got it all planned out. We'll be there with bells on!"

"Bells…yes, well," the pastor smiled, "I know you lads'll be a tremendous 'hit' as they say, and I'm sure all the young people of the parish will thoroughly…" he looked at his watch. "Oh dear, we're just about to get underway. Let me tell you one last thing before I'm off to check the other floats, then. We've set up a stage of sorts for you in the far field behind the church…adjacent to the Boy Scout hut. So immediately after the parade, you'll need to manoeuvre your equipment over there as quickly as soon as possible. The parade'll leave here at two o'clock, go up Allerton Road, then onto Woolton Street, down King's Drive turning right onto Hunt's Cross Avenue, then up Manor Road, onto Speke Road, then back again onto Woolton, Allerton, and Church. Since you're at the absolute *end* of the parade, you probably won't return to the field until after half three…and you go on at 4:15. What I'm getting at is, you'll have to hustle to make it on time, you understand. Can you do that?"

"No problem, sir," Eric Griffiths stepped up and made his presence known. "John'll see to it, y'know. He's like that, is John."

"Hmmm, well, I just hope he *gets* here." The Reverend looked at his watch again. "It's almost parade time now." And he left the boys with a half-hearted wave.

"This *is* a bit uncanny, y'know," Rod muttered after the clergyman had wandered out of earshot. "John's usually here barkin' out orders and crackin' ye olde whip by now. He's usually..."

"Cor! Wudja you look at that!" Len nudged Colin and pointed to a figure cutting his way through the crowd.

"It's John!" Colin gasped. "And I think he's bevvied up!"

"Yeah, I think he's had a few...a coupla few...and then some." Len chuckled.

"Nah," Pete took a step forward and watched carefully as John approached the stage. "It's not that. He's *more* 'n just lushed. He's browned off, that's what. Somethin's set him off."

They'd never seen John this way. Arrogant they'd seen. Domineering they'd seen. But the John approaching now was swaggering conceit personified. He wore jeans tighter than conservative Woolton had ever witnessed, and his upswept pompadour was a rooster's coxcomb of sexual prowess.

Pete whispered warning to the others, his face serious, "Today's *not* the day to give John 'what for.' Odds are he's had a row with Mim; that's my prediction. I mean, I know for a fact he didn't tell her we were playin' here today. Maybe she found out and...well, whatever's wrong, it appears he's put back a few at the off-license, and..."

"Fuggin'ell!" John leaned heavily on the lorry, spewing lager vapors liberally, "We're effin' *last* in the fuggin' parade. Did y'know that...fuggin' *last*, Shotton...behind some fuggin' trained police dogs! What a stench that'll be! Right?"

All eyes shifted uncomfortably to the ground.

Pete rescued them, slowly turning John around towards the audience behind him, the street full of on-lookers. "Well, with the flock o' bairds you just decoyed in that strut across the lawn, Lotton, I don't think our bleedin' position in the parade matters all that much. I mean, looks as if *they'll find us*. Just take a gander, Johnny! It's a virtual covey of females out there."

True enough, a crowd of teenage girls had gathered a few feet away from the float...girls in wispy whipped cream summer dresses, girls in pastel hair ribbons flipping coquettishly in the breeze. They rubbed their lipsticked lips together and tossed sideways glances at the "tough" with the Elvis aura – the boy in the checkered shirt. But when John wavered on his feet and stared back at them through a fog, refusing to smile or look politely away, the girls blushed and averted their eyes.

"John – you filthy, little Ted," Colin teased from up on the float, "Come on up here, wack, and give 'em a better view."

"Yeah," Len Garry tossed in, "You're already puttin' on a show, as it were, and we haven't even tuned up yet!" Len offered John a hand.

With all eyes on him, John batted Len's hand away and swung up on the makeshift float unaided. Giggles and ooooh's rose in tiny waves. John bowed to the audience, a flashy, mock-serious bow, and a couple of the braver girls applauded. He did a wobbly soft shoe step, and they applauded again.

"There'll be quite a performance *here* today, won't there just?" Len mumbled to Pete.

"Yeah, y'er only right." Pete winked at the bass player. "John's good when he's sober, but he's fuggin' unbeatable when he's drunk and angry!"

Len raised an invisible glass and saluted softly, "Well – to Auntie Mimi, then."

"To the beloved – the one and only Auntie Mimi!"

And the parade began to roll.

****

He ordered a kidney pie, offering a cherubic, "Ta, mum," to the woman who manned the booth. She grinned at his innocent charm and handed him the largest of the lot, a pie big enough for two. Dipping his head, the lad acknowledged the favour with a shy, sweet smile, and a small tip, appropriate for his youthful means. It was all too lovely; the woman was enchanted.

Then the polished teenager nodded and pedaled away towards the crude stage where The Quarry Men were assembled, ready to perform. He balanced himself in a half-sitting, half-standing position, using his bicycle seat for support, leisurely unwrapping the steaming pie and making himself comfortable. With an air of detached interest and cool reserve, the boy waited for the show to begin.

"Ladies and gentlemen," Reverend Pryce-Jones's voice reached him over the heads of the crowd, "I hope you all enjoyed the annual parade this afternoon," he waited on the applause, "and all of the day's festivities thus far. Let me remind you about our dance this evening in the hall…tickets two shillings, with all proceeds going to the church repair fund – my favourite charity, as it were." He paused and smiled at the smattering of polite chuckles. "I know we're all tremendously excited about hearing the George Edwards Band there once again this year…and with me on stage right now is the other band who'll be performing with the Edwards combo tonight. They're some of our very own local lads from the parish who've graciously agreed to entertain us with a bit of skiffle this afternoon. The skiffle craze, which has swept over our young people, is personified in these young men from Quarry Bank School for Boys. Ladies and gentlemen, I proudly give you The Quarry Men!"

Polite applause arose, and John signaled the first chord. The opening strains of the familiar "Cumberland Gap" fanned out over the crowd. Ladies selling tickets to the bagatelle tapped their toes; members of the Church Committee smiled at each other and nodded in approval.

The lad on the sidelines bit into his pie. He chewed slowly, watching the band, watching the immature banjo chords that the lead singer and another boy were using on their guitars. He watched the clumsy transitions between chords and winced at the squeaky, tinny sound their fingers made sliding on the fingerboards.

He watched the blonde, ringleted washboard player who seemed to be only "going through the motions" and the drummer whose beats never quite zeroed in on the downbeat. The youth on the bicycle tried not to frown at what he saw on the stage, but he involuntarily shook his head.

"Railroad Bill" was the next selection, and the doe-eyed lad in the crowd tried to see the magic that his friend, Ivan Vaughn, had insisted was there.

Technically, the song's a train wreck, no pun intended, the boy smiled to himself. *Each instrument's off on its own – and they never seem to reach a junction, as it were. But although, note for note, it's a disaster, it's got...energy.* He wiped the back of his hand across his chin as he stared at the band. *If these Quarry Men had a coupla real musicians, they mightn't be half bad.*

As he carefully brushed the pie crumbs from his pristine jacket, the discerning lad heard the charisma above the clamour. Glancing up with one dark eye, he caught the lead singer with his head tilted back contemptuously and his wet hair flopping recklessly over one brow.

Yeah, all right, there's a bit of the Elvis there, the doe-eyed observer thought to himself. *But not just Elvis really, somethin' else...somethin' ad-lib and off the cuff.*

"Come Go With Me" was one of John's favourite songs. In private, he always modified the words to amuse his mates, but in public he obligingly sang it as a safe, little ditty. Now, in an effusion of alcohol, anger, and defiance, even the most innocent had to question John's intent as he sang with a sardonic smile.

His eyes sent unveiled messages to the handful of mesmerized girls beneath the lorry, and the tension between the music-maker and his audience wound tighter and tighter.

Rolling his three-speed, drop-head Raleigh a bit closer to the stage, the curious boy in the crowd studied the singer's sweat-streaked face. The boy couldn't tell how old the musician was, really...older than he obviously – but two years or three, it was hard to say.

Instead of trying to please his fans, the performer seemed to challenge them, almost to disdain those who stood adoring him. He looked out over his audience with authority and aloofness.

Then abruptly – halfway through the song – the lead singer began falling part. His hard-shelled reserve dissolved, and his self-confidence vanished. Moments before, the singer had been a flesh-and-blood performer in a cardboard band. But now he waxed two-dimensional. Whatever charm he had once exuded was gone.

Even the words to the song had changed. The soft-cheeked boy in the audience knew the lyrics to "Come Go with Me" well. Indeed, he knew words to hundreds of rock'n'roll songs, and *these* words he'd never heard before. Something about "Mimi comin' down the trail…" It was extremely odd.

A small, wiry woman had joined the adult crowd, and she advanced towards the stage. Eyes narrowed and purse clutched tightly to her ribs, she stared at the lead singer and he at her in a quiet contest of wills. Each one's expression mirrored the other's, and neither gave a mite.

Then just as quickly as she had arrived, the woman turned with a flounce and trotted away. From his bicycle vantage point, the dark-eyed boy watched her exit, digging her heels in and making tiny divots on the soft, rolling lawn. And the lad noticed that the singer was watching her, too – watching until she disappeared into the crowd at the far end of the field.

Shrugging off the curious scene, the boy below wheeled his bike slowly away from the band, waiting now for his friend, Ivy Vaughn. There was nothing left to see here – nothing in the mediocre concert on stage that could teach him anything about skiffle or rock'n'roll. James Paul McCartney was decades ahead of these chaps, even on his most unremarkable day.

****

St. Peter's Church Hall
Woolton

Ivan Vaughn had known John most of his life. He knew the band leader, the class scalawag, and the Teddy Boy imitator. After years in school together, he was sure he knew John as well as anyone.

And he'd been convinced that John would be delighted to meet Paul McCartney, a form mate of his from The Liverpool Institute – a lad who knew as much about music and guitars as anyone Ivy'd ever encountered. Why, Paul could even tune his own guitar! He knew legitimate chords; he knew the lyrics to almost every song they'd ever dreamed of learning. Moreover, Paul McCartney had done the ultimate; he had written some original compositions! Ivy was sure that John would be impressed.

"John! Hey, John!" Ivan tugged at Paul's white sport coat sleeve, pulling the newcomer into the church hall where John and The Quarry Men were busy setting up for the evening's big dance. "John, this is me mate from The Institute, as it were...the one I've been goin' on about. Paul...Paul McCartney...the guitarist." He nudged Paul forward. "Paul, this is our group leader...John Lennon."

"Hullo, then." Paul offered nonchalantly.

"Oh, hi." John barely acknowledged the kid as he moved Pete's washboard and the tea chest bass back a bit, out of the way.

"Paul's effin' great on guitar!" Ivy bubbled. "His *Dad* was even in a band once, the Jim Mac Jazz Band or whatever it was. Right, Paul?" Paul nodded slightly. "And as I've been sayin', Paul knows absolutely everythin', and I mean *everythin'* about guitars. And songs, he knows songs, too – I mean *words*, chords, the bleedin' works! You should hear him play, John. He's fuggin' great!"

"Well, have at it then." John offered a challenge rather than an opportunity. He nodded to a folding chair, and without a word, Paul walked over and made himself at home, strumming the guitar he'd pedaled home to get, making adjustments to the tuning screws.

Not until Eddie Cochran's "Twenty Flight Rock" came rolling off the frets did John turn to look at the stranger. He stopped what he was doing to watch Paul's nimble fingers fly over the fingerboard with the agility of a pianist. John walked over for a closer look, squinting to see McCartney's easy movements. And closer still, John hovered, fascinated with the way the kid played without error, without effort.

Paul wrinkled his face against a fog of lager fumes that enveloped him. It made him cough a little, but he kept on playing. The closer Lennon came, the more the smell filled the room.

Unbelievable! He's bleedin' drunk! McCartney thought, glancing up at John who was now only inches from his head. *So that's why he put on such a show thisavvy! I should've known!* But Paul kept on playing, determined to impress anyone and everyone.

When the song ended, John launched into a rapid-fire interrogation, never delaying his curiosity with praise, "How'd you finger that run again?" he asked.

And Paul ran it slowly.

"And how d'you finger those bar chords...E, G, and A? I only know'em on banjo 'n the sounds not the same, y'know."

Without fanfare, Paul demonstrated.

"Do you know the words – all of 'em – to 'Be Bop A Lula' then?

"Yeah, sure," the younger boy smiled. "If you'd like, I'll write 'em down for you when I've got the chance. You'd have 'em then, wouldn't you?"

"Sure, why not?" Even John's pride couldn't refuse such a gift. "And 'Twenty Flight Rock' as well...that is, if you know the words to that."

Paul did.

By the time the eager couples began arriving for the first set of the Garden Fête dance, Paul had performed his entire repertoire. He had strummed, sang...even ended with a real rocker's version of Little Richard's "Long Tall Sally," gyrations and all.

Eric and Len were flabbergasted. *McCartney's bleedin' fantastic!*

And Ivy, like some two-bit tent promoter, went about repeating over and over, "Didn't I tell you or what? Isn't he great, then?"

Rod didn't say a lot. Typically analytical and thoughtful, he rarely passed judgement on anyone or anything at first glance. *Merit comes in the long run*, Rod thought to himself. *Anyone can be a flash in the pan...a star for a day.*

Pete, too, was quiet, but not for any reservations of his own. He was thinking about what would happen next, concentrating on John and wondering what *he* would do.

Unlike Ivy, Pete *knew* the Lennon clockworks; he knew the springs and coils that made John tick. And he knew that John was now in a dilemma for which there was no easy answer. The new boy, Pete realized, posed a problem.

Paul McCartney was undeniably talented; he was knowledgeable, appealing – a first-rate musician. He was, in short, everything The Quarry Men needed and unfortunately, everything John could not allow.

It was *John's* band. He called the shots. To admit Paul McCartney, for whatever reason, would be to relinquish some bit of control, to allow another leader to share in the balance of power. It would, in fact, *create* a balance of power, dividing it among two where once there had been only one.

Pete realized that the others would, naturally, press John to accept the younger musician. (And the fact that McCartney *was* younger was perhaps a saving grace.)

But younger or not, The Institute kid meant trouble. He was suave and smooth, and already Pete could sense tension between Paul and John – a tug-of-war unseen and unspoken. A struggle had already begun, and Pete believed it was dangerous.

But Pete knew his friend well enough to know what he would do. Pete knew where John's priorities were placed. John had only one avenue to take, and he would take it. Whatever the long-range, consequences, whatever the future might hold, John would ask McCartney to join the band. There was no "perhaps" about it. It was already a done deal.

Ah, the Beatle controversies! Paul McCartney is quoted as remembering the audition in St. Peter's Hall this way: "...this beery old man getting nearer and breathing down my neck as I was playing. It was John. I showed him a few more chords he didn't know, then I left. I felt I'd made a good impression."

But Pete Shotton (in Porter's book) denies that John was drunk that day and points out that they didn't have enough money to get drunk. I have opted for a middle road in the chapter, stating that John had probably been drinking, but that his attitude was also closely linked to his argument with Mimi.

Even the Beatles themselves have fuzzy memories about the events of that day. In Miles' book, John Lennon: In His Own Words, *John says, "So one day when we [The Quarry Men] were playing at Woolton he [Ivan] brought him [Paul] along. We can both remember it quite well. We've even got the date down. It was June 15th 1955." Sorry, John.*

The definitive authority on this subject is Jim O'Donnell whose elegant book, The Day John Met Paul, *is the end-all, be-all on this date in history. In fact, I would not have attempted to write this chapter at all since Mr. O'Donnell has covered it so thoroughly, if it were not for the fact that the story is crucial to plot development and cannot be omitted from the narrative. I highly recommend that the reader take some extra time to read Mr. O'Donnell's book or to listen to his audiotape of the book, read by none other than Rod Davis!*

Tuesday, 9 July 1957
Mendips
Woolton

John sprawled across his bedspread and picked at the wall with his fingernail. Hunched over the rumpled pile of pillows under his belly, he stared at the floor while the Radio Luxembourg crackled out its static-wrapped tunes.

Paul whomever. Paul of the expert guitar! Paul of The Quarry Men bow-down-and-worship him – Paul!

John was sick of hearing Ivy and the rest of them rave on about McCartney and his expertise. He was sick of thinking about the wack as well.

"They dream of Paulie with the big brown eyes," John muttered to himself. He rolled over, hugging the pillows to his chest, staring at the ceiling. But this position was no better than the last. He was miserable. He had to decide what to do.

The pool-eyed kid could, no doubt, be an asset to the band.

We could expand the play list, class up the act for performances 'n the like, and change our sound – and McWack would help me break away from skiffle once and for all. He'd stand shoulder-to-shoulder with me for rock'n'roll; I can tell that already.

Together they'd mount the offensive. They'd change The Quarry Men from skifflers into bona fide ravers.

One thing was certain; the audacious stranger was talented. Paul could, very feasibly, grow into a star; he had all the looks, stage appeal, musical ability, and apparent ease of a rocker. Paul McCartney had the earmarks of "a bleedin' phenomenon," as Ivy had phrased it.

But "phenomenon" meant competition. And if Paul captured the loyalty of the others with his musical prowess, John could, quite possibly, lose control of his own band.

Already, the others're convinced this wack's some sage 'n savvy genius, instead of just a bloke from Allerton repeatin' memorized lyrics. They fuggin' fawn all over him...just because he knows a few words to a few lousy songs. Just because he can tune his own fuggin' guitar!

John sat up, digging in his jeans pockets for a sequestered cig. He plodded over to the window to steal a smoke.

It was a brown summer night, cheerless and doleful, a darker rendition of a dull day, mottled and masquerading as nightfall. The smoke John exhaled floated off and dissolved into the umber. Everything was stale.

So, what now? John stared at the murky sky. *Do I risk or do I play it safe? Which?*

A large Luna moth tried to bat its laboured way into the lighted window, but John brushed it back into the thick, ochre silence. He doffed his Woodbine in a teacup and tossed the cigarette butt into the shrubbery. Then waving away the last bit of smoke and pulling the window closed, John quietly secured the latch and stared out into the shadows.

In the silent dialogue that always accompanied his decisions, John began to wrestle with the illogic of his own insecurity.

All right, then, face it. The Quarry Men – what are they anyway? Short-timers – mates out for a laugh, lads with washboards and tea chests that've seen better days. To see 'em as more than that is not to see. Any day now they'll be returnin' to their own amusements; they'll chuck it all in for somethin' they really care about.

Truth is, they've played the game much longer than I'd expected...none of 'em really wants to be in a band.

But with McCartney...with McCartney I could form a group. We could start over, as it were...start over and get it right from scratch...we could work together and form our own band. We could actually be somethin' – "make it big," as it were.

John wandered back to the bed and sat down hard.

Without him, there'll eventually be no group to be the leader of. The Quarry Men'll drift away. Mother'll call and off they'll toddle, like good little Liddypool lads – takin' their little toys home with little them. And that's the way it'll go, won't it?

Glaring at himself in the bureau mirror with a grimace that came from the gut, John signaled defeat. He had no choice in the matter really. He'd known from the very beginning that he would have to gamble to win.

"I'm two years older 'n McCartney," he muttered aloud to his reflection, "and though I'm not the guitarist he is, *I'm* the bleedin' genius behind this collection of two-bit rockers! I'm the one who makes it all work, aren't I? So...right, then. I'll have Mister Paul McCartney join us. But that's where it ends, y'understand? He'll *join* us, not fuggin' lead. That job," he threatened his own image with a wagging finger, "that job is already taken."

John's dilemma over whether or not to invite Paul McCartney to join his band is well-documented...for example, Barry Miles in John Lennon: In His Own Words, *quotes*

John as saying, "I'd been the kingpin up to then. Now, I thought, if I take him on, what will happen? But he was good. He also looked like Elvis. I had a group, I was the singer and the leader; I met Paul and I made a decision whether to...have him in the group; was it better to have guy who was better than the people I had in, obviously, or not? To make the group stronger or to let me be stronger?"

However, the words used in this chapter are conjecture.

Late July 1957
Woolton

Nigel Whalley was the proverbial cat who'd swallowed the canary. In his six or seven months of managerial experience, nothing had topped this! He'd gotten The Quarry Men a booking – not a third-rate beer bash, not an end-of-term hop – but a serious gig in a City Centre jazz club owned by the son of a golfing acquaintance.

Nigel, recently hired as "Apprentice Golf Professional" at the Lee Park Golf Club, had made it his business to befriend Dr. Joe Sytner, a physician whose son, Alan, had lately acquired a trendy nightspot in Mathew Street, Liverpool. In-vogue and fashionable, this dark, cellar club in an alleyway just off the St. John business district catered to the upper class, to Sytner's friends and associates.

Here the sons of barristers and physicians met to hobnob against the backdrop of smooth, mellow jazz. Glasses clinked; voices fraternized; music oozed from saxophones and clarinets. The Cavern Club was soft and easy, the "in" place to mingle and unwind, and in its dark corridors, young Alan Sytner kept the Lee Park golf crowd lazily entertained.

The Merseysippi Jazz Band, The Ralph Watmough Jazz Band, and the Wall City Jazzmen had opened The Cavern to a crowd of six hundred plus on 16 January. They had filled every chair and packed fans to the walls – standing room only. "The Social Centre with a Swing," as The Cavern was advertised, had quickly become a Mecca for jazz aficionados.

But lately another sort of rhythm had pervaded the thick, stone walls of the Cavern: improvisational music – part jazz, part blues, part folk – music played on jugs, washboards, tea chests, and crates. Skiffle – a rather renegade genre born in New Orleans, Chicago, and Kansas City – had seeped down from the streets above and found its way into Sytner's club.

In the upstart music, Sytner heard deep jazz roots. He felt the untutored lure of raw skiffle despite its bloodline to American rock and roll. In its dramatic downbeats and primitive sound, Sytner glimpsed something rather remarkable.

And so, in spite of strict supervision by the National Jazz Union to whom Sytner paid monthly dues, Liverpool bands such as The Gin Mill

Skiffle Group or The Dark Town Skiffle Group were invited to The Cavern Club to perform. They came for the "Wednesday Skiffle Nights" that Sytner courageously created. They came to sing "Down By the Riverside," "Red River Valley," and "Cumberland Gap."

And it was just this kind of performance that Nigel Whalley boasted The Quarry Men could deliver.

When he'd intentionally shot well over par on eighteen holes just two days ago, Whalley had given Joe Sytner the lead on the ninth. Nigel was as talented with a putter as John Lennon was with a sketchpad. But instead of dropping the ball easily into the cup, Nigel had given his attention to a sales pitch for The Quarry Men, "a first-rate Woolton band that's just performed at the St. Peter's Garden Fête and the Roseberry Street Carnival." The sales pitch drew Joe Sytner's interest, and when Nigel's putt missed just slightly and had to be bumped in, Sytner was even more amicable.

"That's all right, son," the Liverpool dockside practitioner had patted the lad's shoulder sympathetically. "Just havin' an off day, what? We all do. Relax and enjoy. You're usually a prodigy at this."

Sytner had putted out with ease.

"Ta," Nigel had grinned, picking up his ball and dropping it into his pocket. "But I'm afraid m'game's all smoke and mirrors, actually. Today, it's the real me."

As they laughed and moved on to the next hole, Nigel continued his speech about the local skiffle group who'd recently auditioned for Star Maker, Carroll Levis, and who'd been selected by Headmaster William Pobjoy to perform at the Quarry Bank Grammar Sixth Form Dance. In fact, Nigel had vowed as they teed up on the tenth, The Quarry Men were tremendously in demand all over the city.

Flourishing a business card at Sytner and praising the lads' versatility, Nigel hinted that it would be prudent to book the band early. He couldn't vouch for The Quarry Men's availability now that they were "all the rage."

By the eighteenth hole, Dr. Sytner had cinched the game. Pleased and in good spirits, he agreed to hear the Woolton lads perform at the golf club as an audition of sorts. And he further promised to arrange things with his son's jazz club – unless, of course, the group was not as stellar in person as Nigel made them sound.

And so it had happened; Alan Sytner, on his father's recommendation, had indeed tentatively booked The Quarry Men at The Cavern Club for Wednesday, 7 August, promptly at 10 p.m. Nigel was thrilled! At last The Quarry Men would play in Liverpool proper, in an honest-to-goodness club, earning a meagre but tangible salary, and possibly establishing a name for themselves. This was one time when they wouldn't kill the messenger!

****

"'ullo, Nige!" Pete reached out to cuff his ear, missing intentionally.

"What's up, Whalloggs? What'd ya summon us here for, then?" John was curious, but a bit irritated. He liked to call all band meetings.

Nigel smiled mysteriously, shook his head, and refused to say a thing. The news wouldn't be as spectacular announced piecemeal. He wanted to tell The Quarry Men as a group. He believed he deserved that bit of melodrama.

Eric and Rod sauntered up, Eric giving Pete a playful shove. Pete shoved back, delivering a mock knee to the groin, complete with sound effects.

Colin Hanton careened in on his bike, glancing meaningfully at his watch as if to highlight the fact that he was on time.

Only Len was absent, but Nigel couldn't wait.

"Well then," Nigel began to pace as he envisioned a manager would pace, his hands folded ceremoniously behind his back, "let's hear it for the Manager, then! Three huzzahs for me, as it were!"

"And why is that exactly?" Pete took the bait. "What's the griff?"

"Well, I ask ya," Nigel stopped and looked at them, his eyes twinkling, "what wudja say to a real bookin', then? A real, on stage, money-in-hand gig? How'd that be for starters?"

"It's a joke, right?" They refused to believe it.

"Go on wit'ya."

"Bushwa!"

"Oh ye of little faith!" Nigel threw up his hands in exaggerated frustration. "You're on for Wednesday evening, seven August, City Centre, Mathew Street, Liverpool! You're on...at the one and only Cavern Club!"

"Crawl back in yer hole, Whalley." John waved him off.

"You're not serious, then!" Eric Griffiths laughed, skeptical.

"You're havin' us on, aren't you, wack?" Pete brushed his blonde curls and tried to read Nigel's eyes. "The *Quarry Men* at City Centre...for actual pay? A real gig?"

"Yeah," Nigel nodded, assuring him, "The Quarry Men at the Cavern Club; it's all set...signed, sealed 'n delivered. You're in the big time, lads!"

"Look Whalley, you're sure they understand what it is we do?" John's face was grim. "I mean The Cavern's an effin' jazz club, chock full of elitist swine...scarves and ties and all that ilk."

"Yeah," Nigel began uncertainly, "but we're booked for a *Wednesday* gig, John...skiffle night. Sytner's a big fan of Lonnie Donegan. He's willin' to compromise on the jazz thing."

Colin Hanton interrupted with more direct logic, "Hey, it's a bookin', John! You're always pressin' us to play, play, play! Well, all right, then. Here's our chance! Let's take it, y'know..."

"I need the fuggin' money," Eric threw in.

"And if you don't want to perform for the jazz crowd, John, well then, just ignore'em then!" Nigel cajoled. "Just think of it as a fuggin' *paid* rehearsal."

"At rehearsals," John stood firm, "we play rock'n'roll."

"Yeah, but they don't *listen* to rock'n'roll in Mathew Street, as it were!" Nigel was angry now. *Damn John Lennon! The ungrateful bastard!* "They want skiffle in Mathew Street. Skiffle, that's all! And on seven August, that's what we'll be singin'! Because *they're* the ones payin' our bleedin' quid, John."

John walked closer to Nigel, his eyes squinting perilously, his nose pinched in, "Yeah? Well, in case you're forgotten, Whalley, I'm the only effin' singer in this whole effin' group, so *I'm* the one earnin' the actual quid here, as it were. You're all backup, aren't you? And if I'm out, the band's out. So whether we play the vacancy in Old Mother Hubbard's cupboard or a packed-out concert at the fuggin' Albert Hall, *I'll* fuggin' say what we sing and what we don't sing. Got that?"

Each one of them secretly wanted to mutiny, but none of them had the nerve. John had more than control on his side. He had logic.

"Right well, we'll play The Cavern, then," John relented, "but we'll open with 'Come Go with Me,' and we'll follow up with 'Hound Dog.' And next practise, we'll start workin' on 'Blue Suede Shoes.'"

Some nodded; some by silence gave consent.

"And Shotton," John gave the final edict, "find that fuggin' guitarist Ivy brought to the Garden Fête and tell him I said he'll be bleedin' joinin' the band."

"Paul McCartney, y'mean? That one?"

"Yeah…McCartney," John nodded. "Find 'im. Find 'im and tell him he's in the group."

It was clearer every day that John would need an ally in the struggle for rock'n'roll.

****

The last thing on Paul McCartney's mind was The Quarry Men. It was the height of summer. Boy Scout Camp at Hathersage in Derbyshire was only a few days away, and after that, the family vacation at Butlin's Holiday Resort was slated to begin. Paul and his brother, Michael, were only half-packed for Hathersage; there were still a million things to do.

But Auntie Jin had made a time schedule and a list, and methodically, she kept things moving forward. Even now, as Paul returned from a visit to Ivy Vaughn's house, he knew he was on the clock. Auntie Jin entertained no apologies.

The shortest route between Ivy's house on Vale and Paul's just off Mather was to cut down Menlove Avenue, then zip across the Allerton Golf Course. One could pick up speed there, and according to Paul's watch, speed was demanded right now.

Paul zoomed over the Allerton greens, standing and pedaling as he wheeled around the last lap of an imaginary race. The invisible competition was hot on his heels, but he pressed on past them all, puffing as he pedaled, pulling into the lead.

"Hey, you...hey, McCartney!" It wasn't an imagined voice after all. Someone was actually hailing him; Paul slowed down.

"McCartney! Hey! Wait up. Wait up a minute then!"

The voice got closer, and Paul stepped down, turning to glimpse a real, flesh-and-blood pursuer. It was that chap from the Garden Fête...the blonde one, the washboard player...Peter someone-or-other.

"Oh, hi Peter!" Paul offered a smile of recognition.

"'ullo yourself." Pete pulled alongside, wiping his flushed forehead with his hand, "Who the hell's after you, McCartney? The ghost of bleedin' Windsor or fuggin' what?"

Paul grinned, shrugging his shoulders, trying to breathe without showing fatigue. "Just ridin' as usual. What's up, then?"

"Well, I've been talkin' with John about it and...well, we thought you might like to join the group 'n all."

Paul looked down at his handlebars in thoughtful silence.

"The *band*, y'know." Pete thought perhaps his offer needed some clarification. "Our group...The Quarry Men."

Paul continued to think and hold off.

Then his eyes met Pete's with no hint of expression, no trace of elation or distaste. They were only eyes meeting eyes, telling nothing, revealing nothing.

"That sounds all right – I suppose. But I'm off to Scout Camp on the weekend...and then to Butlin's on holiday after that. You'd have to 'make do' for several weeks at least."

"Yeah...a-all right." Pete was totally disconcerted by the lad's lack of enthusiasm. "Sure," he muttered, "can do...I'll tell John."

"Okay, t'sarahh, then," Paul said, mounting his bike.

"Yeah, t'rah."

And before Paul's imaginary adversaries could narrow the gap between them, the meeting was over, his bike was in motion, and he was quickly on his way.

The definitive work on the Cavern Club is The Best of Cellars by Phil Thompson. I highly recommend reading the entire book. It is an excellent source of information on skiffle, the Beatles, and the beginning of the Mersey Beat in Liverpool. All events are documented. Only the conversations are conjecture.

Wednesday, 7 August 1957
The Cavern Club
Mathew Street
Liverpool

The Cavern Club had only been open since 16 January, but it didn't feel new or look new. It looked like a dungeon.

Down a dark flight of eighteen concrete stairs into a sweltering, brick catacomb beneath the street, the club waited, musty and oppressive. The atmosphere was part water, part air, part ammonia, and part perspiration. John struggled to breathe beneath the low barrel vault ceilings; humidity conspired with pre-performance "jitters" to make respiration a chore.

Although he managed an unruffled façade, John was ill at ease with the posh clientele, the jazz crowd. He knew what they expected: smooth Ken Colyer or Chris Barber tunes. They expected a band like The Coney Island Skiffle Group who dipped into skiffle for a lark, but were schooled musicians. They expected a combo whose kits contained sheet music and a variety of specialty plectrums.

John snorted derisively; he was lucky to even *own a guitar*!

Braceleted princesses smiled at him as he helped drag Colin's inexpensive drums into the place; John glared in return, hoping to set the record straight before the set ever began. He had no business being here, and he knew it.

Damn Nigel to fuggin'ell! He swore. Nigel had forced him into a corner; he'd *made* him do this. Rarely, almost never, did John ever do anything he didn't want to do. Now his face burned with paranoia.

"So this's The Cavern Club, then." Pete set his washboard and the tea chest bass in place and tried to put John at ease.

"Yeah, what's a nice group like us doin' in a place like this?" John hitched his guitar strap up over his head and around his neck. He frowned.

"Y'know, that McCartney's really missin' it all." Pete scanned the room, fascinated with the City Centre atmosphere. "Scout camp's nothin' like this, I'm thinkin'."

"I'm thinkin' we've finally gone legit!" Rod Davis smiled as he tuned his banjo. "I mean, *The Cavern Club*, lads! Look at it…The Cavern Club!

Just take it all in – the atmosphere, the number of people in this room!"

John's stomach did flip-flops. He looked away from the crowd and strummed a few strings, hoping Rod's tuning job had held during the bus ride into town.

The long and narrow center vault room was packed with chairs, shoulder to shoulder and front to back, with rows upon rows of patrons waiting for the show to begin. The painted, black brick walls – wet and dripping – compressed towards one focal point: the low, primitive wooden stage front and center.

Onto this platform, Sytner now stepped. He issued the usual greeting, made some announcements of upcoming events, and then cleared his throat for the big moment.

"In keeping with our tradition of Wednesday Evening Skiffle here at The Cavern, we have with us tonight several talented area groups. They are The Demon Five, the Deltones, Ron McKay, and the gentlemen you see on stage with me right now. So first off, I'd like to introduce to you a combo from Woolton, as it were, who's performed locally with the George Edwards Band at the Woolton Garden Fête, with the Merseysippi Jazz Band at the Roseberry Street Carnival, and most recently at the Allerton Golf Club. With no further ado, I give you Liverpool's own, Quarry Men."

Polite applause rose in the cloud of expensive cigarette smoke.

This'll be one dead audience, John sulked, hurling Nigel a dagger of a look. Awkwardly, he chewed his gum, tapped his foot, and then began the intro to "Come Go with Me."

When a high-pitched, feminine laugh punctuated the first chorus, John actually blushed. He glared at Nigel again and sang less confidently.

But the laughter wasn't directed at the band. In fact, no one really noticed The Quarry Men. The borderline skiffle-rock'n'roll tune filtered through the room without opposition. Many in the crowd had lapsed into their own conversations, concentrating on ventures and deals rather than the evening's performance. The Cavern clientele were relaxing, talking, and making connections. They were preoccupied.

But when John began "Hound Dog," faces turned. Babble trailed off into silence. Alan Sytner straightened to attention.

And when John followed the initial insult with "Blue Suede Shoes," Sytner stared incredulously at the tiny platform stage. Waitresses paused with soft drink trays still elevated; coat check clerks stood slack-jawed. Everyone froze.

What was happening now was strictly taboo. It was rock'n'roll. Up on stage, in the heart of straight-laced Liverpool, some upstart boy with a rakish drake was belting out Elvis Presley. It couldn't have been more inappropriate.

Sytner grabbed a scrap of paper from behind the bar and scribbled out a terse but demonstrative note. "Cut out the bloody rock!" it read, and he sent it to the stage by the closest available lackey. At the song's end, he watched the lead singer receive and read the mandate, throw him a look, and then fold the note, placing it slowly into his pants pocket.

Sytner relaxed and breathed a bit easier now, feeling sure he had allayed disaster. He could just imagine what the National Jazz Union would have to say to him if they heard about the incident. Although Sytner was, on paper, the owner and manager of the club, the purist Jazz Union presided over its operation. It was a union that tolerated no nonsense and sanctioned no rock'n'roll.

But no matter, Alan sighed, *no harm's been done. It was obviously just an honest mistake. We're all in accord now.*

On stage, Rod Davis wasn't as optimistic. He saw, close-up, the way John looked at Sytner, and it worried him. Rod scanned the faces in the audience, and that worried him, too.

"We shouldn't be playin' rock'n'roll," Rod mumbled, just loud enough for John to hear. "Not here. We agreed."

John ignored him and popped a fresh piece of chewing gum into his mouth. Rod took a step closer, forcing himself to say it one more time. "We shouldn't be playin' rock'n'roll on the Cavern stage. It's *skiffle* they're after and…well…we're here to entertain *them* not ourselves, as it were."

John raised his head inch-by-inch the way dragons or hydras do in epic movies. If he could have breathed fire or turned bodies into stone, he would've done so at that very moment; he would've worked his worst. Instead, he focused on Rod with a lethal glare, daring his opponent to meet his eyes.

But Rod was far too savvy to glance John's way; he'd seen enough adventure films to know the score. He knew he stood unguarded and alone – without a talisman or magic potion to protect him, facing a terrible danger. Rod stared intently at the floor.

"Rock Around the Clock," John imagined himself announcing, in a raspy, unnatural voice. And his band, without further hesitation, would follow him into "Rock Around the Clock."

But John was seventeen, not twenty-seven. He was only a boy enrolled at Quarry Bank Grammar who rode a Raleigh Lenton wherever he wanted to go. He was too young and too inexperienced to stage a revolution in City Centre, a mere eighteen steps below the heart of the business district.

"Red fuggin' River Boogie," he spat out hoarsely, with invective. And much against his will, the unhappy song began.

But although John had acquiesced, he swore that The Cavern Club in Mathew had seen the last of him and his. John vowed that he and The Quarry Men would never return this awful place…not until jazz was shelved and rock'n'roll was all they played.

Was Rod Davis really present at the gig or not? And who, exactly, performed with The Quarry Men? No one has "the answer."

Alan Porter states, "John was itching to play rock 'n' roll. Something, according to [Rod] Davis that he'd tried to do on previous occasions and been prevented by arguments from the banjo player [Rod]. However, on this occasion The Quarry Men were without Rod as he was on a family vacation in France."

However, Lewisohn's, Griffith's, and Davies's accounts in this chapter do not exclude Rod from the evening. And In Hunter Davies' book, Rod Davis is quoted as saying that the groups who appeared with them that evening were The Deltones, Ron McKay's skiffle group, and The Demon Five. If Rod were not present at this gig, then how would he be qualified to state who performed? (Barry Miles, however, says that it was The Deltones, Ron McKay's skiffle group, and The Dark Town Skiffle Group.) My interview with Cavern Compêre, Bob Wooler, in March 1996 was a great source for this chapter and for all others involving The Cavern Club. Bob was not only a Cavern compère and expert, but a true gentleman, beloved by everyone in Liverpool.

Pete Frame's Rock Trees was also invaluable. It is out of print now, but if you're interested in the history of the Mersey Beat groups, it is well worth locating and adding to your library.

September 1957
Woolton

Mimi watched him leave for Liverpool College of Art as if he were hopping the bus for nearby Wavertree or scooting off to Speke for the afternoon. Wearing George's old, brown tweed, John barely mumbled, "T'rah, Mim," before slipping out the front door. Mimi bit her lip, her arms folded across her waist. *John wants no fuss,* she told herself. And with Mimi, he got none. He was off to college. That was that.

"Shennon and Lotton" had exchanged parting quips and digs a few days earlier – John deriding Pete's decision to enroll as a cadet in the Liverpool Police College and Pete roaring loudly, "John Lennon, boy artist!" Neither of them knew why they were doing what they were doing, and neither of them cared. They were just marking time, really – waiting for something else to happen, waiting for something better.

At seventeen, they'd reached an end. The days of chucking dirt clods off the West Allerton Bridge were over. They were going off to life instead of the haunted house at the end of Vale Road. The frog pond near Strawberry Field would become the unwritten property of some other gang, and mischief on The Tip would be left to younger adventurers.

"Friday, 18 October, then," John had reminded Pete at their last meeting.

"Yeah, yeah, Clubmoor Hall, Norris Green…I've got it, Winnie. I'll be the first one in the door. Count on it."

"Good on yer, lad," John cackled in his old man's voice. "Y'er a good boy, you are."

"Yeah, well I wouldn't miss seeing *McCartney* perform for all the tea in fuggin' China!" Pete grinned widely, "He'll be great – McCartney!"

"Don't get eggy, son." John pulled a face. "It's not becomin', y'know."

"See ya, Lotton."

"T'rah yerself."

That had been over a week ago. Now John sat on the Number 72 Canning Street bus watching the lanes and avenues of Woolton whiz past him…the old, brick bakery; the antique shop with its white china-dotted windows; the sidewalk florist; the red, arched Woolworth's awning in

Smithdown. Everything customary was slipping away.

At the Penny Lane roundabout, they stopped for a moment to pick up passengers; then the bus doddered on. The last familiar landmark was the expansive, Tudor, Brook House Pub where Julia performed now and again. Beyond it, undiscovered territory.

John settled back in the torn leather bus seat and watched the leaves falling on the lawn of Sefton General Hospital; others were building into small piles around the weather-chiseled graves in Toxteth Park Cemetery. Even this early in September, John could feel the change of seasons. The wind off the Mersey had a premature bite – a hint of winter to come.

Bicyclists had donned jackets and hats; mothers had pulled pram tops up over their babies as they hurried from shop to shop. John shivered and patted his coat pocket in search of an errant Woodbine. He needed something to chase the chill.

Julia was forever singing, "Wedding Bells Are Breaking Up that Old Gang of Mine," and it seemed to John that this had become his theme song lately. The Cavern Club gig had marked Rod Davis's last night with the group. No words had been exchanged; no "line in the sand" had been drawn. But it had become apparent that Rod's and John's attitudes were "180 out," as Rod had always put it, and no compromise could weld their polar differences.

John glanced around the bus now for a recognizable face or two, but found none. He found no cigarettes either. He tucked his hands under his armpits and snuggled down into his uncle's familiar tweed for warmth.

The bus veered left into Ullet Road where traffic hummed and scurried, thickening into downtown Liverpool. Horns gave rapid fire; motorists offered epithets to one another. Vendors sing-songed from their markets or stalls. Children hailed each other on the way to school. John held his breath and narrowed his eyes as a taxi squeezed past in a space far too tight for manoeuvring.

At the Toxteth stop, a handful of groggy day labourers plodded on, moving past him – lunch pails dangling from fat, gloved hands, eyes downcast. And on the fringe of Liverpool proper, City Centre clerks edged into the mix, carrying folded posts and wearing suits or smart black skirts with buttoned sweaters.

Many were headed for the city's international markets or for the shops on Renshaw or Ranelagh. It was all routine to them – this trip into the city. Only John saw it with new eyes that took nothing for granted.

In St. James Street, the immense Anglican Cathedral came into view. *Almost there, then,* John thought, and he leaned forward. He craned his neck, trying to see the top scaffolding emerging, but the tallest spire had grown past his line of vision. Only the enormous base of the Cathedral could be seen. It obliterated the Mersey River and its docks entirely and filled all the windows on John's side of the bus. Even partially completed, the church was enormous.

Then just as Mimi had predicted, it started to rain. She had made John, against much protest, carry her bedraggled, once-black umbrella, a ragged source of embarrassment. But now, as the construction site around the Cathedral pooled in muddy water, John was glad he'd given in to her demands.

The rain hammered the bus roof ferociously, and after a few minutes, it grew difficult to see anything outside the window. As the overloaded bus plowed painfully up steep Parliament and then slowly turned left into Hope Street, John drew the hideous "bumbershoot" from beneath his seat and began to loosen the ribboned snap. Lightning flashed, and thunder answered. It had become a full-fledged autumn storm.

"Oh nice," a bug-eyed Lime Street Station porter groaned.

"Yes, lovely weather, isn't it?" his seat companion used a crisp London accent and threw her eyes to the ceiling.

"For them what has feathers," a young secretary from Bootle across the aisle commiserated.

"Fuggin'ell!" another spat.

"Yeah, fuggin' inconvenient," a raspy voice from the back agreed.

"Canning Street!" the bus driver announced as the last stop approached. The passengers struggled to their feet slowly, straggling and trying to wait out the downpour now that it was slackening a bit. "All out! All out, then," the driver opened the door and urged them into the weather. "All out for Canning Street."

"If y'er here for the art college – this is it, luv," a buxom lady who smelled of inexpensive perfume and mothballs informed John. She patted his shoulder and smiled a smile devoid of several teeth. John nodded and looked away. He felt a little queasy.

Outside the rain had diminished for a moment, but drizzle persisted. The air was heavy – full of dock smells, car exhausts, and tobacco. A hint of Chinese cookery drifted over from somewhere, and the overpowering mould of brown gutter water sat in the back of John's throat.

Moving without hesitation, as if he knew the place, John headed up Hope towards Hardman Street. Leaning into the walk, he kept his shoulders hunched against the wind and the residual rain that skittered underneath Mimi's umbrella, and he squinted at the buildings on either side of him, trying not to gawk. John hadn't spent a lot of time in this part of town, but Mimi had given him detailed directions. He watched the buildings and navigated by her landmarks.

Out of nowhere, music drifted down from some open window. It was "That'll Be the Day," the new hit tune from the American, Buddy Holly. John tilted the umbrella to one side and tried to find the sound, but every window, as far as he could see, was "buttoned up."

Nevertheless, the song continued. It was one of Julia's favourites these days, one of his favourites, too. The tune was simple; the lyrics, catchy and easy to remember.

"'Cause that'll be the da-a-a-y when I die," John sang along. "That'll be the day, ooh-hoo, that'll be the day…"

As he sang, John picked up the pace. He could see the art college now. *Only a coupla blocks to go,* he encouraged himself. Unconsciously, he swung his arms to the beat.

A clap of thunder threatened. John glanced up nervously and then jogged the last twenty paces or so to the college, bolting up the wide, concrete steps just as the rain found momentum again. John elbowed inside the front archway and awkwardly managed his umbrella, shaking it out in the marble lobby and brushing the water off his coat as well.

"Welcome to Liverpool College of Art," a secretarial type in a slim, olive suit greeted him. "Would you need a map, then? Your first day, perhaps?"

"No thanks. I'm on staff here, luv." John eyed her coolly.

"Oh really?" the woman smiled. "Well, you're over an hour late then. Faculty meeting's well underway…in there," she pointed.

"Right," John grinned back. "But I'm optin' out today, as it were."

"I wouldn't make a habit of that, if I were you," she clucked.

"Wouldn't you?" John sniffed.

"Regular attendance is tantamount to success, y'know," she quoted Principal Stevenson.

"That's overkill, gerl," he called back over his shoulder as he walked away.

That one, she thought, *will be nothing but trouble.* But John was down the hall in the wrong direction before she could offer any more advice.

Moving left towards the main office and then backtracking to the foyer again, John took it all in – the enormously high ceilings, the fat crown moulding, the large central stairway that wrapped itself around a wire-caged elevator. John began to hum – primarily whistling in the dark – but there was some sincere joy in the song as well, some satisfaction in the moment.

For months, all he'd thought about was getting away from Woolton, leaving Quarry Bank behind him and going out on his own. He'd longed for the independence that college would provide – a taste of adult life without constant supervision. Now, emancipated, free of all family ties, he was finally here in the city.

Wearing George's coat, carrying Mimi's umbrella, and singing Julia's favourite song, John swaggered in the direction of Room 22. It felt good to be self-sufficient. John was a man on his own at last.

An excellent guidebook to Liverpool (with pictures of the places mentioned in the book) is The Beatles Liverpool *by Ron Jones.*

I could not have written the chapters on Liverpool College of Art without the tremendous assistance of Colin Fallows, Head of the College of Art for John Moore's University, Liverpool (formerly Liverpool College of Art). He answered all my questions, gave me several tours of the buildings, and helped me meet so many people in Liverpool who were crucial to this book. Besides being an acclaimed artist and excellent administrator, Colin is one of the nicest people you'll ever meet.

19 October 1957
1 Blomfield Road
Allerton

"Good *and* bad." Julia read the critic's terse evaluation of her son's band's performance at The Clubmoor in Norris Green. She threw her eyes to the ceiling and handed the paper back to John.

"Eloquent isn't he?" she smirked. "I mean, I've heard of 'less is more,' but 'good and bad'? What kind of commentary is that, I ask? Why'd this so-called critic bother makin' a statement at all if that's what he had to say?"

"It was generous, that." John folded the appraisal and jammed it back into his coat pocket. He flopped on his mother's sofa and threw his legs over the armrest. "We were shite. Worse than shite. We were chronic."

"Then why didn't he say so, John? What's this 'good and bad,' then? What was good? What was bad? He could've spelled it out for you, y'know."

"Well here y'have it, ladies and gents, the bad..." John used his announcer's voice.

Julia wedged in next to her son and playfully elbowed him over to make room. "Go on," she gestured.

"First off...no Pete...it's strange not havin' him up there on washboard, even though Shotton never was any effin' good to begin with. And no Rod Davis on the banjo as well...despite Rod's bent toward skiffle, he was one of us...confident in his...whatever he's got."

"His *je ne sais quoi*," Julia suggested, picking up her own banjo and strumming it absently.

"I wouldn't use that kind of language on a bet," John deadpanned.

Julia nudged him in the ribs. "So...what else, then?" she prodded. "What else was wrong?"

"How does white sport coats and string bow ties sound?" John let the concept sink in.

Julia fell out laughing.

"*White sport coats*?!?" she shrieked. "You're not serious, are you? *You* wore a white sport? You must've looked like Bobby serving Sunday brunch at the Adelphi." Julia couldn't stop giggling.

"I looked fuggin' ridiculous, that's what."

"And who's idea was that, then? Nigel's?"

"Nah, the new guitarist…McCartney of Allerton…he says he's tryin' to 'up the ante,' as it were."

"Oh, well…yer Auntie *definitely would be up* for white sport coats," Julia strummed a vaudeville chord at her pun. "It's right up her alley, that sort of gear."

"Well, it wasn't up mine." John pulled a rumpled package of Woodbines from his pants pocket and offered one to Julia. She took the cigarette in her long, manicured fingers and leaned over to her son for a light. He obliged and then lit his own.

"So let me understand, then." Julia leaned back against the sofa, letting her head rest as she envisioned the scene. "There you all were…regaled in these crisp, white sport coats and brandishin' these long, bootlace bow ties."

"And Len was wearin' two pairs of pants to plump him up, and Colin was well into the Guinness and cider."

"Where'd you get them anyway, the sport coats?" Julia backtracked.

"The golf club where Nigel works."

"Oh, lovely," she snickered, tossing her hair. "Maybe he could find me a dress for Sunday next. I didn't realize Nigel was a fashion consultant, as it were."

"But that's not the worst of 'the bad.'" John took Julia's banjo from her and settled it onto his lap.

"There's *more*?"

"McCartney." John strummed lightly as he talked.

"Yeah?"

"He effin' froze."

"Froze? What d'ya mean?"

"Well, he started off bonzers…I mean, he's all right on the Little Richard stuff, isn't he?"

"And then?"

"And then we decided to let him do another number straight off since he'd done so well on the first one, y'know. We moved the play list around a bit, as it were."

"And?"

"And on that one…"

"He was a dead flop?" Julia closed her eyes, imagining the fiasco.

"No, on that one he was great."

Julia's eyes popped open again. "So *where's the bad* then, John Winston? So far, I fail to see the difficulty."

"Well, after McCartney's second one," John took a drag on his cig, "I did 'All Shook Up'…and made the inevitable jokes about me Elvis wig."

"Um-hm…yeah. Go on."

"Then we launched into McCartney's big number – his famous guitar solo, his famous rendition of the famous 'Guitar Boogie.'"

"You're not jealous of this Paul, are you? I mean, it sounds a little harsh – this retellin' of the story."

"As I was sayin'," John ignored the psychoanalysis, "right there in front of God and everyone…"

"*God* was at Clubmoor in Norris Green? That's remarkable, even for that end of town! It should've been in *The Echo*, y'know." Julia sat up and reached for the post, pretending to search for an article on the subject. John batted the newspaper down and went on.

"As I was sayin'," he repeated.

"As you were sayin'," Julia teased, "God was there and…"

"And then he froze."

"God?"

"McCartney."

"Froze?"

"Unraveled's more like it." John played one dissonant chord and then another. "I had to call the whole thing to a halt before he actually hurt someone."

"You *didn't*!"

"I fuggin' did. I just stepped up and said, 'He's our new boy. He'll be all right, given time.' And then I moved right on to the next song with record-breakin' speed."

"And the crowd? How'd they take *that*?"

"They laughed. They thought it was all rigged. They thought it was all part of the fuggin' act."

"And McCartney? How'd he handle it?"

"All right, I suppose. He knows he's dead talented. We all do. It was just first night nerves and all that."

"And the rest of the night, then?"

"*That* was the aforementioned 'good.'" Now it was John's turn to lean back and relax. "We did about sixteen more songs, what have you. All rock'n'roll…all fairly fantastic."

"If you do say so yourself." Julia edged her arm around her son and gave him a squeeze.

"Yeah, well if y'don't believe me," John fetched from his pocket the tiny slip of paper that promoter Charlie McBain had given The Quarry Men at the end of the evening. He held the review up close to Julia's face, "then don yer glasses, woman, and read this. It's all here in black and white."

"Oh?" Julia pretended to read the review for the very first time, "Oh I see, 'Good and Bad.' How perceptive! How extremely informative! What an *excellent* critique this is!"

"It was generous, that." John repeated himself. "But next time…next time we'll bring down the effin' house."

"There's always next time," Julia smiled.

"That's what I've heard."

All events, including the note from Charlie McBain, the facts about Paul's performance, and the description of the clothes that The Quarry Men wore (including Len's double pair of pants) are true. Even the term "he was bonzers" is a quote from John. Only the conversation between mother and son is conjecture.

Once again, let me recommend Alan Porter's book Before They Were the Beatles *for more information about this event. His Beatle scholarship is impeccable. You'll be impressed.*

24 January 1958
The Cavern Club
Mathew Street
Liverpool

"A bleedin' Happy New Year, everyone!" John hailed The Cavern Club. "Seems a few resolutions have been made here, now doesn't it? Seems a few *changes*'ve taken place at the once-jazzed Cavern!" He smirked and then turned to the newest member of The Quarry Men. "So...what exactly is it that we've come to play, Mr. McCartney?"

"You know, it's on the tip of me tongue, Mr. Lennon. What *have* we come here to play?" Paul grinned.

"Could it be?" John widened his eyes in mock-astonishment. "Might it be...*rock'n'roll*!" He strummed a chord that set an exclamation mark right where it belonged.

Pete, sitting in the second row, started the cheer of approval, but the crowd wasn't far behind. They were clapping their hands and stomping their feet before Colin could even find the beat. They were shaking their heads to the sound before John even hit his stride.

Though still billed as The Quarry Men Skiffle Group, John, Eric, Paul, Colin, and Len played only rock'n'roll. And although the chords were raspy and the percussion, less than par, the Friday evening Cavern dwellers devoured it.

Paul, eager to give up lead guitar as soon as possible, plodded through "Guitar Boogie" with only a few less blunders than he'd made at The Clubmoor in Norris Green. John forgot the words to almost every song they played, and Len manipulated the tea chest bass that had no place in rock'n'roll.

But somehow, it worked. Rock'n'roll pounded The Cavern walls. The sound ricocheted around the room, and volley followed volley. As if darting protectively from the artillery-sound, the sea of bodies in front of the band weaved and moved. They ducked and bounced in an unpredictable, chaotic rhythm. Not a soul sat still.

Midway through "Worried Man Blues," something bizarre began to happen. The lights, shining directly on the stage, made it almost impossible to see beyond the first three or four rows of the audience, but John – whose vision was limited in the best of circumstances – realized that the audience was leaving, a couple at a time.

Between "Come Go With Me" and "Blue Suede Shoes," John walked back casually towards Colin as if they were fine-tuning the next number. He leaned in to the drummer and nodded towards the diminishing audience, "What the fuggin'ell's up, Hanton? Why're they all leavin', then?"

"I don't know, John. I can't really see. But you're right."

John shielded his eyes from the lights and tried to distinguish forms. There were a few people here and there. Pete was still smiling from his chair. But the centre hall appeared virtually empty. John's throat tightened, and he launched into "Hound Dog" without any introduction at all. He didn't feel that an audience of ten or so warranted all the bells and whistles.

Fortunately, it was the last song before their break. The Merseysippi Jazz Band was waiting to perform, and The Quarry Men were slated to retreat to the tiny, humid, concrete band room. They would have a full half hour to regroup and then try again.

Pete was the bearer of the tidings. He burst through the backstage door as if he'd won the Irish lottery and won it big.

"Fanfuggin'tastic!" His arms were thrown open as if he wanted to hug them all.

"Sod that!" Colin was furious. "They all left!"

"Like rats off a sinkin' ship!" Eric slapped his hands against his thighs.

"You were the last, great survivor, Pete." Paul gave him a nod and quick, clicking sound with his cheek.

"What?" Pete was incredulous. "Have you all gone fuggin' mad? What's all this? They bleedin' *loved* it!"

"What d'y'think we are, Shotton…deaf, dumb, *and fuggin' blind?*" John nursed a Woodbine moodily.

"What're y'talkin' about? The place was packed…" Pete began.

"Right," Paul shrugged. "For the first few numbers."

"Before the Exodus, Leviticus, and Deuteronomy began." John was bitter.

"Before the…whaaa? You're not too brilliant, now are you, Lennon?" Pete was gloating.

The five Quarry Men looked at him with faces devoid of understanding. They were hurt and embarrassed. Pete thought he'd better spell it out for them. "All right, yew." He put one foot up on a guitar case, "Listen up and listen good. You didn't *lose* the fuggin' audience! You had them on their feet!"

"How's that, then?" Paul walked over closer.

"They were all in the side wings…the vaults, y'know." Pete gestured largely. "They were all *up*, jivin' like mad. You got them off their seats! You had them in a near frenzy!"

"Us?" Eric was grinning from ear to ear. He nudged Colin, and Colin nudged back.

"Ennit smashin'? *Us!*" they chuckled.

"Up dancin', then?" Paul gave John the "thumbs up." "Must've been 'Guitar Boogie Shuffle'!"

"Nah," John tried not to smile at the news. "They were all sittin' down then, weren't they?"

"It was me incredible backbeat that put us over, if you'd like to know!" Colin winked.

"Or perhaps it was the bass," Len added quietly.

"Right, the bass."

"Oh yeah, the bass, of course."

"I've always said it's the bass."

"Good on yer, Len! The bass!"

They all laughed, toasting each other with their Coca-Colas.

"Here's to rock'n'roll," John shouted. "Long may she rave!"

"Here, here!" Paul seconded the motion.

"To rock'n'roll!"

"Yeah, right. Let's hear it for rock'n'roll!"

"Time for the second set, lads." Pete tapped his watch. "If I'm not mistaken, you lot are all wanted back up on the stage. Back – believe it or not – by popular demand."

In Before They Were the Beatles, *Alan Porter states that, "In January, the group returned to The Cavern for yet another skiffle appearance. After their last encounter with the club owner Alan Sytner, they stuck firmly to their skiffle repertoire. Sytner had gone beyond sending notes on stage to bands that broke the play list rules. He was now fining anyone who played rock numbers..." This would lead us to believe that The Quarry Men avoided rock'n'roll numbers...*

But...in Hunter Davies' The Quarrymen, *he quotes Colin Hanton as saying that The Quarry Men played "All Shook Up" upon their return to the Cavern. Furthermore, on page 72, the exact story that I have recounted above is told.*

All conversation, however, is conjecture.

Thursday, 13 March 1958
The Morgue Skiffle Cellar
25 Oakhill
Broadgreen

They'd been getting gigs. Oh, not the kind that would make headlines. But gigs, nevertheless – places to play on a Saturday night, trips that required dragging the tea chest bass onto and off of a bus and then onto and off of another.

The Quarry Men had no "roadies," no assistance of any kind. So they straggled to their assignments, set up their crude equipment, sang their hearts out, and then straggled home again. They were busy, and that made it seem as if they were making headway. Nigel swore that they were. "Beyond all doubt, we're on the road to success!" he promised.

But looking around tonight, John wondered if Nigel was unrealistically optimistic.

The Morgue Skiffle Cellar in Broadgreen was aptly named. It made The Cavern Club look elegant. In fact, it made any place – a holding cell, a sewer line – look elegant. It was hardly "on the road" to anywhere.

"A corpse wouldn't have it here." John sniffed the infected air.

Paul shrugged carelessly, happy to have a venue.

"There're no loos, y'know!" Colin walked up, agitated. "Nothin' at all! Not even a lousy, effin' drain!"

"And what's this?" John fingered a single, bare light bulb hanging from the ceiling, the only source of light in the dingy, basement dungeon.

"A bulb," Paul deadpanned. He winked and headed across stage where The Texans, Alan Caldwell's skiffle group, were tuning up.

Caldwell was in charge here. He'd located the old, abandoned building – once a home for retired nurses – at 25 Oakhill Park and had, with his parents' assistance, obtained the decaying Victorian to use as a dance venue. Tired of dealing with Merseyside's staid promoters whom Caldwell said had no enthusiasm for the emerging rock'n'roll scene, Alan had persuaded his mother, to help him invest in a new kind of club – a club primarily for teenagers. Now operating under the business name, Downbeat Promotions, he had done just that. And it had seemed like a brilliant idea at the time.

But now, with bands arriving from all over the city and couples lining up on the once manicured lawn of the fairly friable house, Caldwell was rubber band tight. His bony, lanky form darted this way and that, directing traffic and issuing orders. He kept exhorting, "Bugger it all, just make it work! We can't deal in details, y'know. Doors open at half seven and no later, regardless! So just get yer gear stowed and get the show on, right?"

It was opening night.

John herded The Quarry Men into position, laughing at Caldwell, ribbing him generously whenever he came into earshot. The Texans' blond lead singer gave John a bit of his own in return, and the two bandied razored witticisms as only Liverpudlians could.

"What's cheeky boy doin' here?" John asked Paul, John's good humour vanishing as he gestured towards a recent hanger-on – a gangly, fourteen-year-old named George Harrison who'd snaked his way into the shadows just behind the band.

Paul shrugged and acknowledged George with a nod. "I asked him in," Paul cocked his ear toward his guitar, listening as he tuned. "I mean, we've been talkin' music, George 'n me, on the bus to The Institute, and we've played a bit together now and again." He plucked another string repeatedly listening and tuning, "I invited him up," he paused, "as one of us, as a part of the group, as it were."

"As a part of the *group*?" John looked scalded. "Sod that! Whose effin' idea was that?!"

Paul moved on to the next string.

"And what part of the group," John raved, "would he be exactly, then? Our kid?"

"Get stuffed, John." Paul flashed a quick smile in George's direction in an attempt to convince the quiet lad that John's obvious anger was about something else entirely. The timid Harrison half-smiled in return and shifted nervously.

"He's *twelve* if he's a fuggin' day!" John glared.

"Actually, he's just turned fifteen." Paul finished his tuning and hoisted the strap over his head, ready to perform. "And what's more, he's talented, is George. We play a bit between classes, y'know, and he's incredible on guitar. I mean it. Really fantastic."

"Well trefuggin'mendous, McCartney! Let him sign on for Mickey Mouse, then. I've no use for child prodigies."

"C'mon, John. Why not include him? He's easy to get along with, and he thinks we're bleedin' perfect."

"He's barely out of knickers, isn't he? Just tie his little Buster Browns, wipe his nosey on a hankie, and trundle him back home before we're all fuggin' nursemaids around here!"

"Ah, he's not a half bad – George – and he's only come 'round to hear us play." Paul turned his back so that George couldn't read his lips. "Truth is, the Texans turned him down at audition…"

"Good on them!"

"…and he's been playin' in this little group with his brother – but he really wants to be part of a real band, a more experienced band. I mean, he's got this Futurama guitar with a really incredible sound…and…I told him he might be able to play a number or two later – that is, as the night goes on."

John groaned and threw his eyes to the ceiling. The last thing he wanted to do tonight was audition some "Boy Wonder" when the room was filled with spectators hungry for rock'n'roll. Despite the bleak setting – the singular entrance, singular light bulb, and singular electric fan – teens were pouring in, stacking up like boxed dominoes.

But before John could argue further, The Texans woke up the neighbourhood with the opening set. Then soloist Paul Rogers stepped up to the microphone and kept the momentum going. And when Rogers left the stage in a madness of applause, The Quarry Men were hot on his heels, performing "Jailhouse Rock," "Baby Let's Play House," and "Come Go with Me."

When The Quarry Men began to sing, George Harrison placed his Futurama carefully on the floor next to him and leaned against the wall. He folded his arms, crossed his ankles, and settled in to watch the band perform.

When Paul, left-handed, soloed a ballad, George studied the unusual right-handed chords with a scrutinizing eye. When John screamed out "Blue Suede Shoes," George memorized his compact tension and powerful release. The boy absorbed every move The Quarry Men made. He chewed his thumbnail and took it all in with an almost reverent expression.

In truth, the older boys were his heroes. They could mimic Elvis. They could pile their hair high into rockers' pompadours. Paul could prance like Little Richard, and John had all the gusto of Chuck Berry. But while the American rockers were vague – an ocean away, and remote – John and Paul were "here and now." Here and now, they were George's idols.

In the dim, blue stench of the Morgue Skiffle Cellar, George waited nervously to audition. He'd decided to play "Raunchy" for John. Or maybe "Guitar Boogie." He only hoped that whatever he played, he wouldn't forget everything he'd learned when Paul called his name and brought him to the stage.

All events in this chapter are documented. However, I found no record of the songs performed by The Quarry Men that evening. This list was taken from Len Garry's record of the songs played by the Quarry Men at the 6 July 1957 Garden Fête. All conversations are conjecture.

There is a huge amount of controversy about when George auditioned for John and what he played when he did audition. Many sources say that George auditioned for John after The Quarry Men's 6 February gig at Wilson Hall. According to legend, George played "Raunchy" for John on the bus after the performance. Other Beatleographers list the evening above as the correct date. Even John showed some humourous doubt about the exact details surrounding George's audition for the group when he commented, "I listened to George play, and I said, 'Play Raunchy or whatever the old story is….." (Miles, p. 25)

In The John Lennon Encyclopedia *(p. 307), Colin Hanton told Bill Harry that "contrary to what people have said, George did not meet the group for the first time at Wilson Hall, Garston…George met them at the Morgue Club in Old Swan, a small place run by Rory Storm."*

Morgue Skiffle Cellar or Morgue Club? Caldwell or Storm? "Raunchy" or "Guitar Boogie" as the audition song? We may never know.

What is certain is that George began "standing in" with the group in the spring of 1958. He was never officially "invited" to join the band. He just gradually became a member. Eric Griffiths, whose place George took, was never told that he was "out" of the group. Read on…

April 1958
1 Blomfield Road
Allerton

"Ah-one, two...ah-one, two, three, four!"

It was elbow-to-elbow music, chords echoing off the bathtub tiles, lyrics slipping through the shower curtain.

On this number Paul sang lead, his foot atop the loo lid, his guitar balanced at a painful angle on his left thigh. Len, leaning stiffly against the lavatory, was suffocated by the primitive tea chest bass that filled most of the tiny room while John utilized the bathtub acoustics, singing harmony into the porcelain tiles and strumming his Gallotone Champion with all his might.

Even little George Harrison, the newest member of the band, had found a roost, his back to the bathroom door, one winklepicker boot hoisted up on the bathtub rim. He played lead guitar with an earnestness that left no space for tomfoolery; the bathroom rehearsal was as serious to George as a studio set.

But Julia compensated for the boy's reserve with impishness. Sitting in a cramped corner with her legs folded yoga-style, she crashed two makeshift cymbals – saucepan lids – smashing them at odd moments just to watch George jump. She laughed and pulled a pink shower cap down over one eye. Employing various voices and accents, she called out requests as each song drew near its end or filled the air with "huzzah's" or "bravo's." None of them could be serious with Julia around. She was reality's antidote.

"Givvus 'Raunchy,' then!" she put on the Scouse, winking at George. It was the song that the boy had first played for John in a "catch-as-catch-can" audition. It was, in effect, the Harrison boy's signature song, and Julia knew it.

"Sorry, luv." John played along. "It's a bleedin' instrumental, that...and our kid, Georgie here, can't quite manage the thing."

"Yeah, John's right." Paul ducked his head to one side. "Sad to say, the lad's no talent for it, y'know."

"It's a shame," Colin piped up, "...the obvious lack of skills...in spite of Georgie bein' such a nice boy 'n all." Positioned halfway in the bathroom, halfway in the hall, Colin sniffed and wiped an imaginary tear from his cheek.

"Get off!" George grinned a bit, using only one corner of his mouth, "You're all daft, aren't ya? And ta for askin', Mrs. – I mean, Julia. Quite naturally, I wooden say no."

The boy's heavy Scouse accent charmed Julia every time he spoke. The Stanley girls had never been allowed to indulge in Liverpudlian Scouse, and it fascinated her to hear it delivered so thickly and well.

Scouse was almost a language all its own – a language of catch phrases and similes, a language full of imagery. It was Liverpool at its best, a friendly porridge of slang, brim-full with tasty, colourful expressions. Julia loved to hear George serve it up.

Without asking permission, George launched into the requested song with expertise and energy. The others listened politely for a moment, then joined in as well.

Julia had to admit that Harrison had real talent, enough to quell the issue of his age. She knew John had struggled between ambition and embarrassment, weighing the benefits of Harrison's strong lead guitar against the detriments of including such a stripling in his band. *It's socially dangerous,* he'd told her, *hangin' about with children.* And it *was* a distinct disadvantage to a gig-seeking rock'n'roll group who needed to be able to play in locals and dance halls.

But in John's eyes, talent conquered all, and George had earned his "birrova corner" against the bathroom wall. The reserved boy from Speke was, these days, a valuable member of the lavatory group. Age be hanged, George contributed.

And so, here they were – the ones who'd endured over the last year...John, Paul, George, Len, and Colin.

They'd only recently lost Eric. When George had come on board in March, Eric had been given notice. John had demanded that Eric switch to bass guitar or leave the group entirely. There'd been no room for negotiations.

"Put John on the bleedin' telly and let him fuggin' talk for himself!" Eric had demanded, infuriated that John was booting him without a face-to-face explanation.

"Well..." Nigel had paused for a moment, "he's not here actually."

"Yeah, right. And I'm not here as well."

"Besides, Eric," Nigel had felt his cheeks growing warm, "*I'm* the manager here, right? I'm the one to say who goes and stays, and who plays what in this band."

"Right! In a pig's eye, Whalley! You're John's effin' puppet, that's what! *You* wouldn't do me this way, left to yer own devices."

Goaded by the insult, Nigel had blurted out that Eric had only "half the talent of Harrison" and wasn't "half the match that George was" for the evolving Quarry Men. He'd raved a bit to ease his guilty conscience and then had issued the final edict: Eric could either elect to play bass guitar or choose to play nothing at all. That was the only option.

"Look Nige, I'm not buying a fuggin' bass!" Eric had exploded. "It's too much money – that! I'd never earn that kind of money back playin' with the lousy Quarry Men. And besides, John's no better 'n me on guitar. Why doesn't *he* play the fuggin' bass, as it were? Why *me*? Answer me that!"

But the only answer Nigel could offer was the repeated ultimatum. And Eric Griffiths had opted for early retirement.

Now Julia watched the fledgling group closely as they launched into the chorus of "That'll Be the Day." Paul tapped his toe as he played and rhythmically rocked his head from side to side. He was performing for an admiring audience, however invisible his public might be right now. Paul was busy fine-tuning his charisma as well as his music; for him, it was a package deal.

George, on the other hand, hovered over his guitar, rarely glancing up from his fingers. Lips half-parted and dark eyes glassy-wide, he was listening to what he played.

Then, of course, there was John, almost a man now, no hint of the incorrigible little boy left. Far from incorrigible these days, John was Julia's friend. They spoke the same language; they saw life from the same vantage point. They loved the hustle of the city and the depth of expression in a single line sketch. They loved the sound of an electric guitar. They loved to laugh, even when it was inappropriate to do so. And most of all, they loved to flout convention.

John would never be what Mimi wanted him to be. Julia was sure of it. John was destined to be a rocker.

Julia had fed him the rhetoric about "music in his bones," and she couldn't deny her own modicum of musical talent or Fred's. But that wasn't what convinced her of her son's innate ability. She saw it in his eyes. In them Julia read passion – passion for the music.

She could see it in those moments when John, "the real John" – open, vulnerable, and completely genuine – emerged; when he sang, when he cradled his guitar high against his chest, just the way she held her banjo. When John performed, it was hardly a performance at all. It was the time when John was most alive.

Len glanced at his watch for the third or fourth time in the last hour, and Julia saw him do it. Had she been a betting person, Julia would've put her money on the fact that Len wouldn't last the summer. He and his awkward skiffle instrument were becoming superfluous to the group, and Len knew it. He was the "odd man out" now no matter how friendly he was with the others. Len and the tea chest bass were simply becoming obsolete in a band of rock'n'roll.

It was all coming down to four – this group...John, Paul, George, and

Colin. They were the only four still infatuated with the music, the only four who still believed in this mirage of a shoestring band.

"*Alleycat*," John announced, and the music began. Julia rocked back and forth and snapped in time, but the jaunty little tune begged for something more.

"Wait one!" She waved her hand and pulled herself up using the lavatory as a handhold. Climbing over the pig nose amplifier that filled the floor and edging by the ungainly bass, Julia clamoured over cords and legs; she squeezed past elbows pushed in tightly. She giggled and threaded her way to the door. "Right back, then. Don't even *hum* a tune without me, lads!" And she was off.

John shrugged as all heads turned in his direction. But Julia was Julia. He could never second-guess or explain her.

In a few minutes, she returned with her own rather well used washboard and a serving spoon, ready to play. The pink shower cap had vanished, and in its place Julia wore a straw hat – a wide, black one with a gathered net at the brim and a large sequined flower dangling off the back.

"All right, then," she winked at her son. "*Now* I believe we're ready, as it were. It's the Quarry Men and Woman, Live from the Loo. *Alleycat* on four. John?"

" Ah one, two… ah one, two, three, four…"

The Quarry Men and Woman played all afternoon and well into the night. They played until Bobby returned from work. They played past teatime and suppertime, too. They played as Jacqui and Ju danced raucously around Colin in the hallway. They played until someone finally had to use the loo for its intended purpose.

"One last one," Julia begged as they started to pack their things away. "One for the road, as it were."

"Right." Paul threw a wink her way. "One for the lovely Julia!"

"And for this lot as well," John nodded affectionately at his half-sisters.

"Yeah, why not?" George smiled. "Just name the tune, and we'll givit a try."

"How about…" Julia strained to reach her banjo. "How about 'I Remember You'?" It was a tune she could play blindfolded.

"Uh…it's not rock'n'roll, y'know," Len warned, nodding meaningfully towards John.

"Pfft! I think he'll make an exception…just this once," Julia smiled, meeing her son's eyes with a look they all longer for.

"I remember you. You're the one who made my dreams come true,"* John announced without hesitation as he hoisted his guitar.

"And when the angels ask me to recall," Julia answered him, "the thrill of it all…" She touched her nose and then pointed to her son. "I'll tell them I remember you."*

And for Julia, The Quarry Men played one more.

Again, the experts are at odds. Alan Porter in Before They Were the Beatles *claims that John forced Eric Griffith's best friend, Colin Hanton, to call Eric and release him from the Quarry Men.*

And Barry Miles, who notes that Nigel Whalley resigned as manager of the Quarry Men in late 1957 because he had developed tuberculosis, seems to support this theory.

But Eric Griffiths himself, in Hunter Davies' The Quarrymen, *tells a great many details about Nigel's (not Colin's) phone call to him, releasing him from the Quarry Men. (This happened because George Harrison had joined the band.) Furthermore, it is Len Garry who developed tubercular meningitis and left the band, not Nigel Whalley. (Len left the Quarry Men due to illness in August of 1958.)*

Barry Miles dates George's audition with John as February 6, 1958, and Ray Coleman dates George's audition as March of 1958, so it is clear that George did not join until spring of 1958. Therefore, Nigel was still acting as manager in the spring of 1958, and was therefore, probably the logical choice to call Eric and release him.

Julia Baird paints a very vivid picture of the bathroom rehearsals in Blomfield Road in her book, John Lennon, My Brother, *and this chapter is modeled on her descriptions. All information is accurate; only the conversations are imagined.*

*A few lines from "I Remember You" by Schertzinger and Mercer

15 July 1958
Mendips
Menlove Avenue
Woolton

It was a wolf whistle, but unlike most women who would have ignored or resented it, Julia drank it in, tossing her shoulder-length auburn hair and smiling widely, generously.

"Not so bad yourself, luv!" she laughed and called to the upstart.

The walk to Mimi's house was always eventful. Weary men on their way home from work turned to stare at the five-foot-two bombshell prissing by on her six-inch heels. Others, driving down the wide boulevard of Menlove Avenue – what Liverpudlians called a "dual carriageway" – beeped their horns at her while she grinned and waved flamboyantly. The walk from the bus queue became a parade of sorts with Julia the main attraction.

At least three or four times a week, she popped 'round for tea at Mendips. Mimi always half-expected her and never seemed surprised, especially when John was at home. Julia was almost addicted to him now, grabbing any chance to rub shoulders with her cocky, music-crazed teenager. They traded barbs, new songs, and the latest gossip; Mimi couldn't help but realize that it was John whom Julia really came to see.

But the two sisters shared much as well, including the same obsession. It bound them together and pressed them apart in a tangle of mutual understanding and jealousy. John was both their doing and their undoing.

There was Mimi. There was Julia. Neither was "Mother," yet both were. One was guidance, discipline, and direction; the other was tenderness, inspiration, and possibility. They were two orbs in a gravitational spin around one planet, one cooled and permanent, the other hot-glowing, unstable, and unpredictable. And as their orbits decayed around their son, they spun closer and closer. Tragedy seemed almost inevitable.

"Well, you've certainly done it now." Mimi's lips pursed in disapproval as she greeted Julia at the door.

"Oh nice!" Julia teased, "I've only just arrived, Mary Elizabeth. Try 'hullo,' why don't you? Or better yet, ask me in, y'ole fret! What've I done this time?"

"Don't 'hullo' me, Judy...and you know *exactly* what I mean." Mimi took Julia's parasol and placed it in the corner of the small glassed-in porch before ushering her sister inside. "That...that *shirt!*"

"That shirt? What shirt? What are you on about now? Oh...that? Really, Mim."

"Yes, really Judy. It's entirely inappropriate, you know. Entirely..."

"Why? Because it has a bit of colour to it? Boys do colour these days." Julia plopped onto the sofa, pushed a pillow behind her back, and poured herself a cup of tea from the waiting silver tea set. "Don't be such a dinosaur, Mary Elizabeth; it's just a..."

"Oh, now you sound like John: 'Be reasonable, Mim. Get with the times, Mim.' Well, I am reasonable. It's *the two of you* who're out of control! A coloured shirt! Ostentatious! What's *next*, Judy? Those hideously vulgar drainpipe jeans? Those so-called 'winkle picker' shoes the Harrison boy wears?"

"And what'd be wrong with that?" Julia poured a cup for her sister, too. "They're all the rage, you know. The Teddy Boys look smashin' in 'em!"

"Perhaps you haven't noticed, but you're no longer a teenager, Judy. We're supposed to be the..."

"Pfff on that! I'll never grow up." Julia kicked her shoes off and wiggled her toes. Mimi pursed her lips even tighter.

"And telling John *not* to wear his glasses!" Mimi marched onto a new field of combat.

"Mmmm, right." Julia slurped her tea loudly. "Our John's too pretty to wear those ugly glasses!" She smiled the smile of the emancipated.

"But he's virtually blind! You know that!" Mimi fumed.

"Well? So'm I! So's Ju! But we don't wear our glasses either, you'll notice. We're too glamorous for that, our Mim. Mustn't let the practical interfere with the beautiful. That's what I always say. *That's* the maxim to live 'n die by."

"No, that's the *problem!*" Mimi stood up, pacing like one of her wizened cats. "You've not a practical bone in your body, Judy, and whether I like it or not, *you're* setting the rules for my household."

"Oh, you're free to wear glasses if you like," Julia teased. "Your eyes aren't nearly as pretty as our John's."

"Julia!"

"Mary Elizabeth!" Judy made a face at her sister, crossing her eyes and sticking out her tongue. "Oh, pooh on the glasses, now. It's all up to John, anyway; he's grown, Mimi. He's already in college for heaven's sake!"

"Grown? Hmphf! Not really."

"Yes, *yes he is*...but that's not what I came by to tell you anyway. Guess what? You'll never guess, not in a million years."

Mimi pouted and didn't even try.

"I'm playin' again…" Julia ignored it. "They're havin' me back at The Brook House this weekend. The regular banjo player's under the weather, as it were, and well…they rang me up to step in for a day or two."

"I thought you were bored with that sort of thing." Mimi sat back down to sip her Earl Grey before it cooled completely.

"I was, and would be again for any length of time, but a coupla nights and a coupla bob? That's right up my alley." Julia set her cup and saucer on the tea tray, leaned back, and flounced one leg over the other. "I was thinkin' I'd have John come 'round with me for a couple of sets, what have you."

"You certainly will not!" Mimi straightened up and frowned. "What would a boy of eighteen be doing down at The Brook House Pub at half-eleven?"

"Oh, I can only imagine!" Julia laughed naughtily. "Mimi, Mimi. Dear, dear Mimi, when will you face it? Your little boy is all grown up. He's a man now, no way around it. No cloisterin' him away. No reinin' him in, as it were."

"He's a lost child," Mimi's voice trembled, "lost and going nowhere…with only that nasty, two-bit little band of his on his mind."

"Then let him, Mimi. Just let him." Julia tenderly put a hand on her sister's hand. She searched the older woman's eyes. "Don't you remember?" Julia almost whispered, "Don't you remember how we planned it all lyin' side by side in that one wee bed in Newcastle, whispering in the shadows, talking in the dark? You were goin' to be a professional nurse, the new Florence Nightingale, the inventor of somethin' earthshakin' – some painless, miracle cure, as I recall. And I was goin' to get a manager and travel 'round the world performin' my songs on banjo. Remember how I'd sing to invisible audiences, until Pop – unable to hear the literally millions who cheered me on – would come rushin' in and bring the curtain down? I had quite a followin' for a season, didn't I? I was the bleedin' toast of London back in those days."

"We were just silly, little girls." Mimi's voice softened.

"We were visionaries," Julia corrected, "prophets, conjurers, spinners of the dream. For a while, way back then, we had it, Mim. We had what our John has now."

"But that's why we must *stop* him!" Mimi exploded. "We've learned, Judy! We know better; we've lived long enough to see illusion for what it is. It's our job to direct John away from the pitfalls. And a rock'n'roll band? It's ludicrous, Judy! Absolutely hopeless…one in a million."

"Is it really?" Julia drew a cigarette from her pocket and lit it in silence. "D'you really think so, Mim?"

"Yes, of course it is. The band's no good! I've heard them perform… and so've you."

"Right." Julia took a long drag, holding the cigarette with her shaped, polished fingernails, exhaling slowly. "I've heard them. But I'm fairly sure I heard somethin' you've yet to hear, sister mine...because I listened with my heart."

"I'm sure you did." Mimi's eyes were grave. "And that's the crux of the matter entirely. Emotion. Fantasy. Building up the boy's hopes of 'what might be' in that make-believe world of yours! Ginning up tales of greatness and London and Florence Nightingale – unabashed possibility that allows no hint of impossibility! It's all well and good for you, Judy, this happy-go-lucky lark-about. But where will *you* be when John's house of cards comes crashing down around him?"

"And where will you be, Mary Elizabeth, when the stage lights *really* go up? You think our dreams were *pitfalls*? I think they were our salvation. To me, life – real life – isn't about countless, repetitive days filled with routine – the same thing over and over. That's the fate of the living dead. I worry all the time that John might have to live like that. I don't want him to stop dreaming...not now, not ever. When the dream is over, life is over." She took another drag on her cigarette and held it for a moment before releasing the smoke in a thin line.

It was no use arguing with her. Mimi removed the teacups and walked to the kitchen in resigned silence, realizing that it didn't matter what she thought, anyway. John refused to wear his glasses now, and the coloured shirt was his prized possession. His mother had his loyalty. He would always follow Julia's lead.

"So...how is he this weekend, then?" Mimi called out from the sink. John had gone directly from the art college to Spring Wood earlier that afternoon. He'd rung Mimi up to say he was staying the weekend "with the girls." Mimi hoped her angst didn't show in her voice.

Julia sauntered in from the sunroom and leaned lazily against the doorjamb, "John's John," she reported, "cheeky, impertinent, always the court jester. Same-same."

"No doubt." Mimi wanted to say that she hadn't had the luxury of studying John's actions much in the past few weeks. Between school and and the infernal band and his new friends in City Centre and his weekends at Judy's, John was always otherwise preoccupied.

Mimi dried the cups, folded her drying towel neatly into fourths, and hung it on the towel rack. She straightened her shoulders and kept her back to Julia as she stared out the window into the garden.

The summer roses were crawling everywhere, blood-red velvet and almost as large as winter kale. And back by the fence, George's beloved fruit trees hung heavy and low, unpicked and badgered by the evening birds. Mimi watched a scavenger squirrel digging up her lawn. She listened as a harsh, unvaried cricket concert rose over the silence.

"I left Ju ridin' her bicycle, waitin' for John to come out and play catch with her," Julia said softly, "but he was completely absorbed in this new tune he's just about mastered on the mouth organ, somethin' he and Paul've been workin' on."

"Paul McCartney." Mimi bristled.

"Um," Julia joined her at the window, watching the faint darkness fall over the garden. "He has lovely eyes hasn't he?"

"When he comes by here, I send him home."

"Like as not, Jim McCartney feels exactly the same about our John, y'know. John's not the most sought after companion for the sons and daughters of Allerton, Mim."

"Well, I certainly don't know why not!" Mimi flared. "John's as honest as a copper – that's what. There's not an ounce of shilly-shally in him, not for anyone! And as much as I'd like it sometimes, he's never up to acting like something he's not. There's no pretense in that boy! None at all!"

"Soothe those ruffled feathers, Mother Hen!" Julia smiled, putting her arm around her older sister and squeezing her close. Mimi "hmpfed" and stiffened against the hug. She hated to be teased.

"It's simply an honest evaluation, that's all," Mimi protested as she squirmed to a safe distance.

"No…it's a defence of your boy." Julia followed her to the kitchen table and took a seat. She rested her chin in her hands and looked at her sister with admiring eyes. For a moment, only the sound of the crickets and water dripping from the faucet continued the dialogue.

"You know *you're* his real defender…and heroine," Mimi said quietly.

"No…in his own way, John loves you as much as he loves me. C'mon, you old bag of bones, you know he does." Julia reached across and covered her sister's thin, blue-veined hand. "He loves us both, and he needs us both to lead him in the paths of righteousness for his name's sake."

"Don't be sacrilegious, Judy," Mimi frowned.

"Oh, not that, never that!" Julia tossed her hair. "Not Julia Stanley. Not me!"

Julia offered a huge stage wink, and in spite of herself, Mimi snickered.

And instantly they were girls again – girls with politics and current events and opinions to hash over, sisters with family stories and rumours to share. With Mimi carrying the shears and Julia, the basket, they decided to walk in the evening air and snip flowers from the garden. Julia giggled over her own outlandish stories, and Mimi doled out the rare, occasional smile. Stars filled the sky quietly and it grew late, without notice.

Before either of them realized it, the clock sounded ten.

"Good heavens, they'll be sortin' me out in Spring Wood!" Julia laughed. "And think of it…those two capricious, little girls at home all this time with John Winston! He'll be crackers by the time I trek back."

"Oh, nonsense. It's good for him to have the responsibility of minding the girls once and a while." Mimi walked her sister to the door. "He's had far too much of his own way here – you know, being an only child of sorts."

"Well, I'm sure an evening with those two ragamuffins has supplied him with a lifetime of experience!" Julia smiled, "It's lucky they're infatuated with their big brother or they'd be his undoing for sure and certain."

She stopped at the door and stared at her sister for a moment. Then she leaned over and gave Mary Elizabeth a long, tight hug. "Look Mim, about John..." Julia held Mimi close, refusing to let go. "We're oil n' vinegar, you and I...but taken together...well, it's a rather wonderful blend, don't you think?"

"All right, all right...enough mush. Off you go, then." Mimi returned the hug. "I won't walk you to the bus tonight. You're late enough as it is already."

"See you tomorrow, then." Julia let her go with a final squeeze. "And don't worry, Mim. It'll all..."

"'Ullo. 'S John here?" A familiar voice behind them edged into the conversation. It was Nigel Whalley.

"Nigel, Nigel, nefarious Nigel!" Julia teased. "What a treat to see you, luv...and lookin' so brilliant, as it were." She brushed a bit of lint off his shoulder and straightened a lock of his hair. "John's in Spring Wood tonight – mindin' the girls, if you can imagine me takin' such a risk."

"John? Our John?" Nigel grinned. "Nursery sitting?

"The very one," Julia winked. "And if I don't get back straight off, he'll be eggy, that's for sure."

"John? Eggy?" Nigel rolled his eyes. "Are you sure we're speakin' of the same pleasant and even-tempered John?"

They both laughed. Even Mimi raised an amused eyebrow.

"Well, I'm off," Julia blew them a kiss. "T'rah luvs!" She clipped across the curved walkway to the drive like a tiny, wind-up doll, and she threw them a parting wave at the end of the driveway. For a moment, Mimi looked after her, envying Julia's endless youth and feeling very tired and leaden, as if she moved in slow motion, weighed down by duties and cares that Julia knew nothing about.

Mimi sighed. She bid Nigel good evening and stepped inside the house, pushing the thick, arched, oak door shut, snapping the lock into place. She picked up the evening *Echo*, switched on her reading light, and settled into George's old wingback chair for a rest and a read.

That was when she heard it.

The sound was terrifying; it was Emily Dickinson's "zero-at-the-bone." A screech of tires, a horn blast that never ended, a scream of terror, a young male voice crying out in the summer night. Mimi rushed to the window, stumbled to the door. Something in her throat ached; her arms and legs trembled.

Nigel Whalley came running up the sidewalk, his arms flailing madly, his eyes irrational. He tried to talk but couldn't find words. He looked at Mimi with raw, quivering pain and collapsed on the walkway in front of her. Nothing else had to be said; nothing could be said. In the irrevocable fate of a silent instant, Mimi knew all she needed to know about the unspeakable horror.

****

One Blomfield Road
Allerton

"Is this One Blomfield Road, son? The sign's down, y'know."

John eyed the aging Irish policeman coolly. He tilted his head back a bit, squinting at the man in the glare of the front porch light.

"Yeah, that's right."

"And are you John Lennon, son of Julia Stanley Lennon, of this address?"

"Yeah..." John was wary now. The fish and chips he'd had for supper turned rancid.

"It's your mother, lad," the policeman hesitated before letting it spill forth. "She's been knocked down by hit-and-run driver...in the carriageway...about a half hour ago." He took a breath. "Her body's at Sefton General, as it were. Yer auntie's there with her now, lad."

"What's this? What's going on, Officer?" John heard Bobby's voice behind him. It came through a fog, through the clamour of ringing bells.

"It's the boy's mother, sir." The policeman wasn't at all sure of this man's relationship to the deceased woman. "Sorry sir, but the fact is, well...she's dead. Hit and run...drunk driver, as it were."

"Oh, no! God, no!" Bobby Dykins crumbled in a heap.

"Hey now...hang on, there. Steady there. Steady. Could you lend a hand, lad? Take an arm, if y'don't mind. C'mon, then. Are you with me, lad? Lad? Can y'hear what I'm sayin' to ya, son?" The policeman's voice floated in on waves.

Waves upon waves.
Bells upon bells.
Waves.

The policeman's voice droned on above the noise, "All right then.

Right. Lift him up. That's it. Gently...good, good. That's right. Hold him there."

After some moments, the voice was heard again.

"C'mon, son. Walk this way. We need to get you both to hospital and let you say yer goodbyes'n'all that. Can y'manage it, lad? Are you with me, son? D'you know what you're doin', then?"

John knew, but he couldn't say. His tongue had turned to stone, and soon his brain would harden, too. He was dying. He was being slowly asphyxiated. Bobby Dykins screamed in agony beside him, but John's screams were smothered, swallowed. There was no way to breathe or speak.

I've no one left now, the fragment that was John repeated over and over.

>*No one left!*
>*No one left.*
>*No one on earth.*
>*Nowhere to belong.*

They arrived at Sefton General in record time. Bobby told Mimi that John had arranged for the cab. Bobby said that John "rabbited hysterically" all the way over, going on about this and that to the cabbie as if nothing had happened.

John didn't know what anyone had said. His brain had petrified. He was a statue. *Can't they see I'm only stone?*

"John! John!"

Voices.

"The nurse wants to know if you want to see Judy, John."

"Answer her, John."

>*Voices,*
>*Voices,*
>*Bells and voices.*
>*Waves and voices.*
>*Stone.*

"Please, *I* need to be with her!" It was Dykins's voice – pleading, crying. And there were the other voices, too.

"Hit and run driver...tossed some forty feet they say..."

"Yes, she just stepped out of the tall hedge in the middle of the carriageway...crossing over to the other half of Menlove..."

"Only forty-four she was...probably never knew what hit her...died instantly."

"Drunk driver, I believe...some boy saw it...a friend of the son's...said he'd just spoken with her...10 P.M. it was."

"Rather late to be out alone, wasn't it?"

> *Voices, voices, pounding voices.*
> *Music screaming over bells.*
> *Voices hammering.*
> *Stone unyielding.*
> *Voices hammering at the stone.*

"John, John. Oh God, John!" Bobby fell into his arms, sobbing, trembling. John couldn't feel the man's body as it rested against him. "She's gone, Johnny! Gone and left us! That's what she's done!"

The voices sobbed and talked and wept and shrieked for the incomparable Julia Stanley Lennon. But John said nothing at all. He stared straight ahead, unable to speak – stared with unblinking eyes, unable to acknowledge those who clutched and moaned.

He stared as his blood congealed, as his limbs froze in the rigor mortis of living death.

"Who'll tell the girls?" someone asked, grateful that a neighbour had taken them for the evening.

"No one at all," John heard Mimi say. "We mustn't say a word to either one of them until we consider what to do."

"Will they not attend the funeral then?"

"Where'll they think their mother's gone off to in the meantime?"

"I can't go on," Bobby wept. "I can't…" He tried to lean on John, but the boy was rigid.

> *Screams and bells and waves and bells.*
> *No pain, no breath, no thought at all.*
> *Music – foreign, sinister, old,*
> *Stone encroaching. Suffocation.*

John's left eyelid twitched. His fingernails dug into his hands.

> *Voices, bells, wails and groans.*
> *Ancient whispers 'round the stone:*
> *"Julia Lennon's dead and gone.*
> *And you're alone. You're all alone."*

****

19 July 1958
Allerton Cemetery

It always rains at funerals, Mimi thought, her heels squishing down the soft turf, penetrating the wet soil. A more poetic soul might have seen the light shower as heaven's tears, but Mimi only shouldered her umbrella as yet another burden on this day of many burdens.

The girls were conspicuously absent. As planned, no one had told Jacqui and Ju. The family, Mimi decided, had plenty of time to "orient them" later on. And since it was summer anyway, they'd just pack the girls off to Harrie's for several weeks – off to the moors of Scotland where John had been when George had died.

George. She hardly thought of him anymore. But Allerton Cemetery and the umbrellas and the rain brought back memories. How she wished he'd lived just a bit longer, long enough to see John through all this misery and pain. The boy was strange now – withdrawn, stoic, aloof. Mimi didn't think John had shed a single tear since Judy's accident. He'd hardly spoken to anyone.

John refused to stand with the family. The arms that entwined Mimi, Mater, Harrie, Nanny, and the pitiful Bobby Dykins could not hold him. John stood out in the rain without an umbrella. He stood letting the weather pelt his face and drizzle down his clothes.

Lelia watched her cousin with gooseflesh alarm. John had changed. This wasn't the same John who had lapsed into hysteria in his upstairs room when George had died. This boy was different ...dangerous, malicious.

Lelia had tried to talk to him, but he'd looked at her with "nothing eyes." It seemed dramatic to say, but it was as if John's soul were gone. *All those weird films about zombies!* Lelia shivered. *What if they're really true?*

There were strangers everywhere. The lawn of the cemetery was trampled by their feet, coming here on the most inclement of days to toss a rose on Julia's grave. Lelia resented them. She gave them her worst, angry stares. *Who were they anyway, all these people, all these strangers on a family day?*

Had John been able to speak, he could have told her who they were.

They were Julia's masses...her fawning public, the people who had loved her all the years of her life: the butcher from Smithdown Road who was infatuated with "sweet Julie's" smile, the Penny Lane businessmen who used to flirt with her at the roundabout where John caught the bus. There were shop girls she had teased and complimented and the bakery workers who always saved their best for the happy, cheery sprite. "Isn't she lovely?" they used to whisper after she left their businesses. "And isn't she always in just a ducky mood?" Julia had never let them down.

And so today they came with red-rimmed eyes and flowers. Many of them wept openly. They hugged the family as if they were old friends, and they gladly shared their stories of the girl with the auburn hair. They tried to say the right things. They spoke from their hearts.

But John never saw them. He just stood and stared at the muddy, gaping hole in the earth, and blinded by the rain, he hardly blinked. The roses of strangers and his family's tears were equally invisible. Their fumbling embraces were never felt. Only once, when they threw wet clods of dirt on the casket, did John move at all. He flinched and turned away.

Later, at Mendips, John lay with his head on Lelia's lap as she ran her fingers through his hair and told him a story. The sound of her voice was the sound of bees around a hive. Low and monotonous, it droned on, never rising above the malevolent chants that haunted him constantly now.

> *All alone,*
> *All alone,*
> *All, all, all alone.*
> *John Lennon, all alone.*
> *Dead and gone, all alone.*

****

City Centre
Liverpool

John sat in the courtroom with his jaw set, his eyes straightforward.

The coroner's inquest had revealed that his mother's murderer had been an off-duty policeman, drunk and afraid to stop, afraid to help the dying woman. John clinched his jaw in a solitary show of emotion. He left hatred and revenge to Mimi now. He left fury and threats to Bobby Dykins. He left action to the living. John was a void, present but always absent. John had ceased to exist.

Each day, when the coroner closed to the proceedings, John was led back to Mendips, to his room above the porch – his old, quiet room. He shut the door and sat on the bed, but he didn't listen to music anymore. He didn't draw or read or play guitar. He did nothing.

Downstairs, Mimi paced back and forth, creaking the floor, missing Judy's evening drop-ins, her jokes and puns, the way Judy always egged her out of gravity into mirth. She missed the arguments that Judy always won and the idiotic songs her sister sang to a twangy banjo.

But most of all, Mimi missed John. She had lost them both – Julia and John – and she knew it. Julia was dead and buried, and John, the old John, was no more.

His voracious appetite had vanished. His rebuttals to her every word were hushed. The radio hadn't hummed in days, and his guitar lay in a pile of dirty clothes. Aside from the creaking of the floor, the house on Menlove Avenue was utterly silent.

Mimi stood at the bottom of the stairs and listened for something, anything. It was quiet. The stone had sealed the tomb, and even iron-willed Mary Elizabeth could not roll it away. Mimi knew that with each passing day there was greater danger. If something miraculous didn't happen soon, she feared there would be no resurrection for John.

Mimi had never imagined that she would miss the sound of rock'n'roll, but she did. She never dreamed that she would welcome John's arrogance, but she longed for it now. Something at all was better than this. Anything would do.

Mimi sat on the stairs and rubbed her aching hands.

None of this should ever have happened! None of it! she raged. She covered her eyes with her hands. It was hard not to cry.

****

"Murderer! Murderer! Filthy, lousy murderer!" Mimi screamed violently, shrieking like a banshee. The plaintiff's face was chalk-white, full of guilty pain. "Murderer!" With very real malice, she waved her walking stick at the man. "Drunken slime, filthy slime!"

Lelia took one arm and Nanny the other. They pulled Mimi back, holding the weeping woman to them, shaking with their own tears, sharing her agony. The walking stick clattered to the floor, and the Stanley family wept.

John never moved.

A voice of authority was heard. The crowd rumbled. Someone rapped a gavel sharply, over and over.

John jumped a bit at the sound of the gavel…a shoulder shrug, an eye blink. His reaction was almost imperceptible. No one saw it.

Bobby was wailing again…still. His friends muttered muffled curses, and the brave issued low threats. But none of it mattered. The inquest was over.

Nigel Whalley's testimony, coming as it did from a minor, was inconsequential. And the policeman – off-duty or not, inebriated or not – had mournfully confessed to being an inexperienced driver, to pressing the accelerator instead of the brake in his confused haste to avoid the woman who'd essentially "stepped out of nowhere."

A verdict, not of manslaughter but of misadventure, had been returned. And that was the end of it.

The room emptied slowly, clusters of heartsick relatives shouldering each other along. The great, paneled doors swung open and shut, open and shut to the sound of cries. Nowhere was there justice or balm for pain. Nothing had been accomplished here.

Summer was almost over along the Mersey. Soon the bitter breezes would come again to sweep away the memories and the ignominy. Winter snow would cover all, and not even icicles would slow the hands of the Liver Building clock. Then spring would return, a brigand of narcissus overtaking Sefton Park without warning – fat, bright yellow daffodils nodding vigorously over the Allerton graves. Life would go on. The wounded would gradually learn to cope with the loss of their vibrant Julia, and the angry – pulling away from the courthouse now in long, black taxis – would eventually learn to forget.

All facts concerning the tragic death of Julia Lennon have been documented hundreds of times, as they are here. I have purposely not included the name of the driver, however. And any conversation in this chapter is pure conjecture.

August 1958
Mendips
Woolton

When the Phoenix emerged, it was hideous. Reborn with wails of rock'n'roll, it lived again, but violently, horribly, cruelly. Bearing the scars of his demise – wearing them like a badge – John was back.

He cranked up the volume on his radio and announced himself with sound. He pushed open the stained glass panels above his window and smoked cigs, one after another. He littered the bedroom floor and trampled through the debris.

Mimi pounded on the locked door. "Turn it down, John! Turn it down and put out those cigarettes as well." There was no response. "Do you hear me, John Winston? You're not the only one living in this house, you know – and you're not the only one suffering."

She heard movement but nothing else.

"John!" she pounded again. "John Lennon!"

"Gerroff." It seemed like John's voice, in a way.

"Not likely!" she exploded, pounding even harder. "This is my house, and in my house…"

The door flew open.

"*Your* house, is it?" John glared at her, seething.

She folded her arms and returned the look.

"Well, then," he looked around as if seeing his surroundings for the very first time. "What the hell am *I* doin' here, then?" And without even stopping to turn his music off or to grab up a jacket, John stormed down the stairs and slammed his way out into the late August evening.

****

Ye Cracke Pub
Rice Street
Liverpool 8

He began and continued to drink. At unexpected hours, John was drunk. Pouring depressant over depression, he enhanced his torment. Lager was the medication John self-prescribed, and without realizing it, he was highly allergic to the drug.

No one had seen this John before. He swore, not expressively now, but in anger. He pummeled walls. He lacerated those around him with a sabre tongue, striking without reason. Old friends began to avoid him, and new acquaintances sought out the deviant character he'd become. They didn't realize John had ever been someone else; they liked "the mad offender."

Moody, inebriated, volatile, and angry, John roamed from pub to pub, punching holes in the summer nights. He became a fixture at the tiny Ye Cracke in Rice Street or the majestic Philharmonic Pub in Hope. And with him were his fellow art college merry makers: the handsome, swarthy Geoff Mohammed, whose penchant for mischief distinguished him; Scouser Tony Carricker, who never stopped laughing at John's antics; and Dave Davies, who gladly joined John a season of demented indulgence.

But it wasn't enough. Fury wasn't enough. Lager never worked lasting magic, and John's bizarre escapades only amused him temporarily.

Plodding through the days of August in a fog, searching for "the next big thing" to diminish his misery, John ached for the mother he'd lost a second time.

And he desperately searched for someone to blame.

****

Mendips
Woolton

The door slammed shut.

"John?" Mimi looked over her glasses.

"Not here!" was the only reply.

"Well, if you happen to see him, tell him the Harrison boy's been 'round asking after him again – decked out ridiculously, as always."

John leaned against the kitchen doorframe. Mimi threw him a look as she sat trimming, de-leafing, and arranging the last of the hydrangeas. John enjoyed seeing her exasperated, and George's attire never failed to do just that.

"What was it this time?" he egged her on. "The boots, the trousers, or the shirt?"

Mimi refused to give details. "He's just outlandish – that boy."

"Right," John folded his arms, "he's a rebel if ever there was one. Subversive. A threat to all that's holy – George Harrison."

"You can laugh, John, but he's definitely not the sort you should be rubbing shoulders with. I mean, he's clearly…different…"

"And Pete's rotten to the core, and Paul's this, and Ivan's that, and you're immensely suspicious of everyone you haven't met yet." John counted the score off on his fingers. "So who the hell *is* good enough for the 'Marvelous Me,' Mim?"

She put her kitchen shears on the Formica-topped table and wiped her hands. She refused to respond.

"Who?!" John barked again. "I'd like to hear you answer that, if you've an ounce of honesty left in you!"

"It's just that…"

"It's just that you don't like George; you don't like Paul; you don't like Ivy, Pete, Len, or Eric…and, truth told, Mary Elizabeth, even me own mum wasn't good enough for you, was she?"

"That's ludicrous! Ridiculous!"

"It's the truth, isn't it?" He squinted at his aunt with phoenix eyes. "She never could make the grade, could she? But no worries now, Auntie Mimi. She's gone, isn't she? You can cross her off yer list of ne'er-do-wells!"

"John!" Mimi began, but he didn't give her a chance to speak.

"And as for the rest of 'em, you can breathe easy as it were. Because I don't bleedin' care what they wear or what they believe or what they say, drink, think – what they do or don't do! Whatever influence it is you think they're havin' on me, whatever you think they're out to get from me – I don't care about any of it…or any of *them*! No one has anythin' to do with me anymore! And that includes you!"

"John Winston!"

The Phoenix wheeled around and mounted the stairs to his cell. He had wounded his victim as he'd intended, and for at least a little while, he had expended his anger. But the calm wouldn't last long. John would need another victim.

Mimi knew the boy was still in shock, still hurting. She knew he was venting and would go on venting for some time. She knew he was lashing out.

But the truth was, his words had hit too close to home.

She *had* disapproved of Judy.

She'd loved her sister dearly, but Mimi never had condoned Judy's unconventional association with Dykins or Judy's refusal to fit into the mainstream. Mimi had taken umbrage at Judy's insistence that John form a band, and hardly a week had passed when she and Judy hadn't squabbled about what John should or shouldn't do. They had always been polar opposites of permissiveness.

But to imply that I'm glad Judy's gone! Mimi bit her lip against the tears. *To say that about me! I'll never be glad one day without her. Not one minute. John knows that. He...*

And suddenly, the music began again. John banged out a song that had every intention of irritating – a Chuck Berry number that Mimi especially disliked. He played it and sang it as loudly as he could.

But tonight Mimi chose to ignore the performance. She decided to let him play. She walked to the farthest end of the house and closed the door. She tried to busy herself with other things.

At 9 P.M., John emerged from his room, dressed for the haunts of Liverpool 8, eager to water down his bitterness with inexpensive, lukewarm ale. He was headed for the city – for crowds, for laughter loud enough to drown out his thoughts. He didn't bother to ask his aunt's permission or say when he'd be home. John slammed out the door without the courtesy of an agenda or a goodbye.

The creature that had become John Lennon slinked off to Liverpool, hungry and unaccompanied and on a rampage.

John's drunkenness and anger after Julia's death are a matter of record. In fact, John is quite candid about his actions and feeling in the days following his mother's death in The Anthology *(p. 14-15). The information John provided formed the basis for this chapter. However, all conversation is conjecture.*

September 1958
Liverpool College of Art
Liverpool

That autumn John's life was as blurred and hazy as his myopic vision. "Pissed to the gills" on lager or Black and Tans, John moved in a waxed-lens world. Swathed in a noxious, grey cloud from Woodbines, Embassys, or any other cig he could "cadge off an easy touch," John struggled to get on with life.

"Hey John!" a girl called to him across the registration room. It was the first day back at Liverpool College of Art, and there were hopefuls everywhere – meeting with advisors, grabbing up the best classes, inquiring about professors' reputations. John was disinterested. He was merely going through the motions and doing so without his glasses. He had no earthly idea who had hailed him.

"Hey, John! John Lennon!" The voice came again, this time closer. John could make out a female form without having to deal with the details.

"Yeah," he mumbled back, unenthusiastically.

"Hey, I believe your mother was killed, wasn't she?" The girl's voice was too loud, too shrill. "Wasn't it an off-duty policeman, then? At least that's what we all heard."

John felt all motion cease. The hum of the registration room suspended; the crowd was holding its collective breath, waiting for him to reply. He could hear the blood singing in his ears with its piercing, high-pitched squeal. He could hear his heart.

"Yeah, right," he shrugged nonchalantly. "It was her."

Then the room began to buzz again, and the world moved on to someone else.

John picked up a brochure from the Walker Art Gallery and looked it over…something about a one-man show that would open in two weeks. He grinned at an overheard joke and quickly threw a quick retort of his own into the mix. Then he moved off casually, walking self-confidently towards the front exit.

Tilting his head back slightly and shoving through the large, arched entry doors, John made it to the other side. Three steps down to the street and a short walk around the corner, he finally collapsed against the cool, brick wall. He closed his eyes and fought off a wave of nausea.

"You all right?" A voice sounded at his elbow. He startled, not realizing anyone had followed him.

It was, surprisingly enough, a somewhat quiet and reserved girl he he'd met last session, a girl from near Woolton – Thelma Pickles. But timid or not, she'd obviously been bold enough to follow him outside and lean against the wall next to him. She crossed her arms and stared at him. And when he stared back, she didn't try to get away.

"That girl's a regular bleedin' heart, isn't she?" Thelma hissed, nodding towards the registration hall, her eyes full of feminine indignation.

"Right. She's one-off the Sisters of Mercy," John spoke slowly, his strength returning.

Thelma smiled. She'd come out to champion John, to cheer him up, and here he had *her* going! He was all right – John Lennon. She leaned closer, drinking in his dark, almond eyes, the Romanesque nose, the smell of fish and chips mingled with cigarette smoke and ale.

During the spring term, Thelma had watched John carouse with his infamous cronies in the Castle Street bus terminus, but he'd never noticed her, not really. Oh, on a few, rare occasions, he'd gone so far as to walk with her to the terminus and exchange a few words with her, but Thelma doubted if John could even recall it now. She had always been "just an acquaintance," and a very casual one at that. But now, today…

"You done in there, then?" John motioned to the registration room behind them.

"As I'll ever be," Thelma said softly. "Most of the good classes were taken long before I got here."

"Right. Me, too." John pushed off from the wall with newfound arrogance. "But who effin' cares, right? I mean, in the end, they'll only pigeonhole me someplace where I'll do the least damage."

"Right," Thelma grinned. "So why bother?" She would have agreed with almost anything John said.

"Well…c'mon then." He reached for her hand and headed towards anywhere other than school. "Let's go do something worthwhile for a change. Let's go kill time, and come sundown, we'll drink to those better 'n us."

"*Are* there those better 'n us?" She raised an eyebrow.

"There's Morecambe and Wise." John glanced at her sideways.

"And the Queen Mother, I suppose," Thelma shrugged.

"Not to mention good ole Lonnie Donegan. There's always Lon."

"*He's* not better 'n us!" Thelma made a face.

"Isn't he?"

"Never has been."

"Well then," John smiled a little, "I suppose it all comes down to

Reginald Duffy Hughes, as it were."

"Who?" Thelma giggled.

"If you don't know Reginald…never mind, gerl. We're off to somewhere where your lack of namedroppin' won't be noticed."

John led, and Thelma followed.

And in the weeks that passed, he directed her to all his favourite haunts: the Odeon Cinema in London Road, the Palais Deluxe Cinema, and the ornate Philharmonic on Hope Street. Recreation became their mutual interest, and whatever classes the administration had in fact pigeonholed John into, they were attended only occasionally.

****

"That Lennon boy's absolutely destroying you, Thelma!" One concerned professor cornered her after class. "You *do* realize this is only the third time you've been here all month? *The third*?"

Thelma shrugged.

"And I know you've been well enough. I mean, you've been well enough to take in Jimmy Tarbuck a time or two, haven't you? And that new Elvis film, *King Creole,* down at the Odeon. Right?"

Thelma nodded sheepishly.

"Word is you've been out and about with the irreverent John Lennon and his ilk…cavorting through City Centre during class hours instead of buckling down to your studies!"

"But I've only…" Thelma began.

"You've only what?" The professor wasn't in a listening mood. "What good will come of all this nonsense when John Lennon gets bored and decides to throw you over for some other, more intriguing companion? What then, Thelma? What of your grades and your future? What will you do when Lennon walks away?"

But Thelma didn't care. She was completely infatuated with the second-year art student from Woolton who said and did exactly as he pleased.

Thelma was mesmerized by John's commanding presence. Wherever they went, John was the ringleader. When he entered a room, the focus of attention shifted in his direction. Though he was only 5'11", he spoke and moved with a confidence that made others seem small in comparison. In the classroom, pub, or coffee house, John dominated, and Thelma found it invigourating, exciting. Power was part of his appeal.

Likewise, John respected Thel's quiet pluck and spirit. People wilted when he accosted them. They were afraid of him for the most part. But Thelma could stand toe to toe with him and give back what he offered. She was one of the few who could withstand one of his verbal attacks and then retaliate with one of her own. She wasn't as outgoing as he, but "Thel" was durable and strong. Theirs was a level playing field.

"John?" Thelma ventured quietly.

"Yeah?" He leaned back on the steps of the Victoria Monument, his eyes closed, his voice drowsy.

"Y'know, we've talked about your Mum'n all," she began. John's eyes opened. He focused his attention on her, and Thelma faltered. "Well, I mean…well, you've never said…where'd you say…is your Dad still around, then?"

John jerked his head away from her and watched the cars of City Centre dart past in helter-skelter fashion. Red and green double-decker buses lumbered along in herds, rumbling to each other as they moved awkwardly down circuitous city paths. Humped-back taxis shoved ahead obnoxiously, edging through the crowd with agile superiority. Motorcars shifted gears this way and that. The city jittered around them.

John concentrated on the traffic – the smells, the sounds, the speed of it all – and he tried to find a way to tell her. Thelma bit her lip and prayed that she hadn't "put him off" once and for all. For several minutes, nothing was said, and neither one of them had the courage to look at the other.

Then John faced her full on.

"He pissed off and left when I was a toddler, all right?" John spit it out. There was no preamble to the facts, no sugar coating. He simply admitted it.

"Well…welcome to the crowd, then." Thelma spoke softly. "So did mine."

Flat out honesty – it was a turning point in their relationship.

Broken homes were taboo in middle-class Liverpool. They were an embarrassment that one glossed over with lies, conditions, and "someday-things-will-be-all-right" optimism. One could say that a parent was "away" or "overseas" or "on assignment." But to admit the truth of separation or divorce was to reveal something intensely private.

John's candour about his mother's death had been one level of intimacy, but this was something deeper. It was the beginning of a camaraderie that went beyond the superficiality of common interests or physical attraction. John had admitted Thelma into his inner sanctum, and she, him. They had each permitted the other the intimacy of things as they really were. It was a measure of trust neither had quite counted on.

That night they didn't go to a performance at the Philharmonic Hall or sit for hours with Geoff and Dave at Ye Cracke. Instead, they spent the entire evening alone, discovering passions that seemed impossible to quench. They gave each other what they themselves needed, what they most longed for.

It wasn't something with a future or promise attached, but it was wonderful – warm and comforting. And for a while, it seemed as if this panacea would work; it seemed as if John and Thel together might somehow summon a courage neither of them had apart.

For the moment, it seemed that way.

This "Beatle legend" is well documented, as are John's happy days with Thelma Pickles. Barry Miles talks about John's being pigeonholed into classes where he would be the least disruptive. Coleman tells the Pickles-Lennon story. The conversation between John and Thelma is conjecture.

Mid-September 1958
20 Forthlin Road
Allerton

John didn't suffer fools lightly; he respected only the talented, the intelligent, the unique. Without meaning to be, John was intolerant.

But Paul McCartney made the grade. Paul was undeniably talented – brilliantly so. In fact, he wore his attractive intelligence like a club emblem. He wasn't embarrassed about being capable – he capitalized on it. And in John's eyes, that aura of self-confidence covered a multitude of sins.

It helped him overlook Paul's happy-go-lucky command of The Quarry Men that itched to edge out John's often-dictatorial leadership. It helped John transform his jealousy of Paul into a wary respect. John never forgot that Paul was a *coup* waiting to happen. John never relaxed against the threat that Paul imposed.

But in spite of himself, he liked McCartney. He liked him even though Paul tended to be all things to all people. While John was alternately hostile, hilarious, or bitter, Paul was generally – day after day, in all situations – well adjusted and quite agreeable.

Paul had lost his mother, too, when he was fourteen, but John found no resentment in him, no anger or deep, throbbing loneliness. Instead Paul had fond memories of Mary McCartney and the ability to go on. While John stumbled through each day, barely coping and earning a reputation as a "mad lad" bent on destruction, Paul was busy establishing himself at The Liverpool Institute as polite, charming, and most likely to succeed.

Theoretically, the lad from Allerton and the boy from Woolton seemed antithetical. But their great minds, poles apart, pulled them together in an attraction that their differences could not destroy. They complemented each other, spurred each other on. Each challenged the other to be better than either could possibly be alone. Each served as the other's critic, teacher, and muse.

In the McCartney's compact front room in Forthlin Road or upstairs sprawled on Paul's narrow bed, John scribbled lyrics and picked out tunes. Paul sat cross-legged on the round braided rug and doodled lyrics on a notepad, picking his guitar up every few minutes to rework his creations.

Every now and again, they would say something to another – ask a question or listen to each other's compositions. Making a note change here or a phrase alteration there, they practised compromise. John would suggest a lyric line with an ambiguous double entendre. Paul would insist on an artistic change that would set a string of chords right. Without agreeing to do so, the two fell into a pattern of editing one another – erasing the worst and adding better – enhancing and amplifying their music.

Equally as often, they argued.

When Paul sang their latest composition for the eleventh time – a faced-paced ditty set in a train station – John rebelled.

"You've changed the tempo again," he snarled.

"Right," Paul didn't even look at him. "Better, isn't it?"

"Look, you're bleedin' worryin' the bit to death!" John slapped his thigh in frustration. "Why do and do and redo the thing once it's been fuggin' done? Just move on, son. It's enough."

Paul ignored him, fiddling with the sound. "Well, it isn't enough if it isn't right, now is it, John?" he shot back. "I mean, the truth is you're just tired of rehearsin', really."

"I'm gettin' that way with your redun-da-dundancy."

"What's the rush?" Paul shrugged. "Where's the hurry up, after all?"

John got up and slung his guitar into its scarred and ragged case. "The rush is…" he repeated with finality, "it's bleedin' *done enough*! You'll ruin a perfectly good thing if y'keep plunderin' it. It's all in the spontaneity – rock'n'roll."

"Not when spontaneity means ragged, right?" Paul kept experimenting.

"It's not ragged. *It's done!*" John snapped his case shut.

"Right, yeah, but…we've nowhere else to go, have we?"

"That's not the point."

"And the point is?"

"The same as it was a half hour ago." John's nostrils flared. "It's *rock'n'roll* – this! It's not some slick jazz creation for the light of feet or the airy-fairy! That's not what it's all about – rock'n'roll. It's a spur of the moment thing."

"Right, well…whatever you think." Paul's calloused fingers never left the fingerboard. He hummed the tune again and ran the bit one more time.

"Ah, buggeroff!" John grabbed his guitar and pounded down the stairs towards the snug foyer below, being careful not to nick the walls with his guitar case. John was well aware of the unseen presence of Jim McCartney, "the ever-watchful eye" as John called him, so he checked the urge to slam the front door in a final exclamation point. Paul's father might be a musician himself, but Jim McCartney had made it clear that he would not tolerate vulgarity or "nonsense" within his walls. John had learned to control his temper in Forthlin Road. He had to.

It was after all, with Julia gone, one of the few places left for them to really work on their songs. George was allowed to volunteer his tiny Arnold Grove living room only sporadically, and the lunchtime jam sessions at the art college were not conducive to writing and creating. The catch-as-catch-can rehearsals at school were poor substitutes for the long, relaxed sessions they'd once enjoyed in Julia's loo. Nothing matched the sounds they'd mastered in that box of pure acoustics.

Nothing was as good anymore.

John stormed up Forthlin Road, carrying his guitar in one hand and shielding his eyes from the late afternoon sun with the other. He could still hear Paul reworking the same tune at the second floor window. Paul would play, stop, and then play it all over again. Hurtling towards the bus queue, John shook his head and swore quietly.

John missed Julia. He missed her chicanery, her thumbed nose at convention. He missed her ability to temper him with pure nonsense, to cut his hostility with laughter. His missed her lifelong commitment to taking nothing seriously. He missed her "fly by the seat of the pants" way of doing everything.

Most of all, John missed the way she listened when he talked.

The truth was that no one knew or understood John the way Julia had. Although constantly surrounded by acquaintances – the "odd sods and bods" from the art college who occupied his hours – John was an extremely popular recluse. He was rarely but always alone. In the pubs, in the classrooms, in the theatres and on busses, John was ringed with hangers-on, but no one – not Thelma, not even Paul – could fill the void Julia had left behind.

Although the facts in this chapter are well documented (especially in Giuliano's The Two of Us *which goes into more detail), all conversations are conjecture.*

October 1958
Ye Cracke Pub
Rice Street
Liverpool 8

John needed little incentive to miss class. In fact, he was highly motivated in the other direction. But the advantageous location of the elegant Philharmonic Pub – with its tall, gilded mirrors and ornate marble loo – made truancy convenient. And the art crowd's haunt of choice, the Tudor-themed Ye Cracke, was equally close. John began to acquire an advanced degree in off campus pursuits. He became a fixture at one pub or the other.

Only the faces around him changed. For an hour or so, John would laugh with Thel. Then Geoff Mohammed, Ann Mason, and Dave Davies would sit in for a spell. Rod Murray and his girlfriend, Diz, would keep John company for a while, and the gregarious, handsome Bill Harry would entertain John as the evening wore on.

When the regulars and the swarms of tired businessmen began to fill the pub, Bill and John usually adjourned to the smaller, quieter room at Ye Cracke, to the nook just across from the fireplace, just under the portrait of "The Death of Nelson." They settled in the pocket of warmth and relaxed over pints of liquid inspiration.

"I'm still kickin' around that idea of doin' a newspaper or somethin' of that nature – about all of us, about the ins and outs of dear, old Liddypool, as it were," Bill Harry confided over a bitter and cig. "Have y'given it some thought, Johnny? Would it fly, d'ya think?"

"If y'give it wings," John returned, blowing a thin line of smoke just above Bill's head.

Bill smiled his charismatic Tony Curtis smile, "Give it wings! Yeah. Good – that." He took a drag on the cig and leaned back in his chair. "But what's it mean exactly? What d'ya see in a publication like that? What would make it work?"

"You'd want to print good stuff. Print what's *real*."

"Define 'real.'" Bill ran a hand through his thick mop of dark hair.

"Creative pieces…original works – unique, one-of-a-fuggin'-kind,"

John explained.

"More artistic than observationist, then?"

"Well, we have newspapers, don't we?"

"Exactly what I've been thinkin'." Bill hunkered over his bitter. "And I do have this one friend who could do some fantastic illustrations for me, if he would. Incredible…"

"That bein'?" John had little doubt that Bill was referring to him. His caricatures were legendary.

"Sutcliffe. Stuart Sutcliffe. You've heard of him?"

"Here and there." John didn't show his disappointment. He completed the series of concentric circles he'd been making with his wet glass on the tabletop. Then he shoved the almost empty pint in Bill's direction without subtlety.

Bill pushed the glass back again. "Gerroff, Lennon! You know you've heard of him. *I* know you've heard of him! He's all the rage Merseyside. Everyone's goin' on about how Stu Sutcliffe's fuggin' great!"

"So they've said. So they would say." John sniffed and batted his glass again like one of Mimi's impatient cats. Bill grabbed it and headed to the bar.

"It appears Mr. Lennon here's havin' another." Bill smiled at the overworked barmaid.

"And it appears you're payin' once again, luv." She brought John's mixture of dark ale and cider up to and above the rim, decorating the floor.

Bill tossed a few coins onto the polished bar and gave her a quick wink. "Ta." He found another coin for a tip and pushed it in her direction.

"Ta yerself." She grinned and pocketed the money. "You're all right, Bill Harry."

"Tell *him* that!" Bill pointed towards John.

"Ah, he's all Mutt and Jeff – John Lennon!" she scowled.

"Cheers to y'both!" John gave her a look that would wilt daisies.

"And yerself, cadge."

Bill handed the pint to John; they toasted and drank. He wiped his mouth with the back of his hand and barely took a breath before continuing with his plans. "Y'know John, if somehow I do get a publication goin', I think I'd ring up Sutcliffe and ask 'im to do the sketches for the premiere issue, as it were."

"I'll be holdin' my breath for his reply," John deadpanned.

Bill nudged his friend. "Cumoffit. Stu's great. And he's not in competition with you! I already asked *you* if you'd contribute some of that gibberish you call poetry."

"So now it's gibberish now, is it?"

"What would *you* call the literary 'concoction' you scramble up – one part irreverence, one part humour, one part – let's be honest – crap!"

"I call it rhymed and rhythmical rubbish, assorted quips and whips, verbal recreation, literary layaboutness!" And John pulled several mangled, dirty sheets of folded paper out of his pants pocket and tossed them at the would-be editor.

"Ah, here they are at last!" Bill held up the crumpled, soiled poems with two fingers. "Ugh! Disgustin' – this! What'd you do with these, Lennon? Wrap yer lunch in 'em?"

Bill unfolded the abused creations carefully, keeping them at arm's length. He shot John a look, as if to chastise him. But John, having polishing off his Black and Tan, downed the remainder of Bill's bitter and then looked away, disinterested.

Ye Cracke – liberally doused in smoke, ale, and laughter – wasn't exactly the place for poetry. But what Bill read on those scribbled sheets needed no backdrop. In fact, the words John had jumbled together seemed quite at home in an art college pub.

Bill had long acknowledged John's bizarre artistry with words. But *this* poetry was different altogether. It was playful word leapfrog that cavorted in and out of seriousness. One moment, Bill was chuckling; the next, he was barbed, but consistently he was fascinated with the world according to Lennon.

Bill cleared his throat and read aloud.

> Owl George 'ee be a farmer's lad
> With mucklekak and cow,
> "Ee be the son of 'is owl dad
> But why I don't know how
>
> 'Ee tak a fork and bale the hay
> And stacking-stook he stock
> And lived his loaf from day to day
> Dressed in a sweaty smock.

Bill raised his eyes to John in amazement, "This is fuggin' Lewis Carroll, Lennon! What're y'doin' wastin' yer time in *art* college? Y'er a bleedin' writer, son!"

> One day he marry be
> To Nellie Nack the lass
> And we shall see what we shall se
> A fookin' in the grass.

Rod Murray, a mutual friend of Bill's and John's, chuckled, "I couldn't help overhearin'. It's demented – that. Go on!"

Rod took a vacant chair and motioned over another student John had never seen before, a "death-warmed-over" chap – a pale, thin, ethereal ghost of a man. In exaggerated drainpipe jeans, pink shirt, fawn coloured corduroy jacket, and leather boots, the stranger smiled as Rod repeated, "Go on, Harry. Read the rest."

Bill sat up and began to read with more emphasis now that he had an audience:

> Our Nellie be a gal so fine
> All dimpled wart and blue
> She herds the pigs, the rotten swine,
> It mak me wanna spew!
>
> Somehaps, perchance, 'ee'll be a man,
> But now I will unfurl,
> Owl George is out of the frying pan,
> 'Cos ee's a little girl.

Rod and Bill smiled, but the mysterious stranger chuckled warmly, a sound that erased any doubts about his mortality.

"Brav-fuggin'-o!" he applauded.

John eyed him appraisingly. The man wore sunglasses inside the darkened pub, and he had an ostentatious scarf tossed around his neck. Either he was "light on his feet" or remarkable. John wasn't sure which.

"'Ullo." The pink shirt and scarf extended a hand to John. "I'm Stu – Stu Sutcliffe."

"That's John Lennon, poet *extraordinaire*," Bill answered before John could form his own words.

"Yeah right, what he said." John shook Stu's hand. "Always good to meet a fan of me work."

Bill reached out and grabbed an ashtray off the nearest table while Stu dragged an oak pub chair over next to John's.

"Well, if y'er such a fan," John segued, "how's about a round then, Sutcliffe?" John offered up his glass. He slid Bill's over, as well.

"Stu's been warned about you, y'know," Rod growled. "And on top of that, he's one of those starvin' artists y'hear so much about. He hasn't two of anythin' to rub together, John – much less coins. So this time y'er out of luck, mate – spittin' feathers, as it were."

"And what's *yer* excuse, Murray?" John turned on him and pushed the glasses to Rod.

"Would that I had one," Rod sighed and shook his head. He headed for the bar.

"Fantastic stuff – your poetry." Stu offered cigs all around. "It's impertinent, unexpected."

"And deeply symbolic as well." John fluttered his eyelashes and talked with a lisp. They all laughed.

"Stu's the one I was just tellin' you about, John," Bill chimed in. "A real genius…graduated early from grammar, went right on into art college…is even bein' considered for his own one-man show…"

John leaned forward on one elbow, "So, you're a *real* artist, are ya? Didn't know we had any of those here. I thought we were all just messin' about until the army called us up or until our 'evil step-some ones' forced us into drivin' busses."

Rod returned with the drinks and doled them out – John's last of all. "Ta, Murray," Rod said to himself, looking pointedly in John's direction.

"Couldn't have said it better meself, could I?" John raised his glass. "Cheers."

They all toasted, sloshing on the table. Settling in, they rested their elbows in the goo and went on with the conversation.

"What is it you do, Sutcliffe?" John zeroed in. "And if it's nudes, you'll have to meet a friend of mine. She's fantastically, incredibly arranged."

"One can never know too many nudes," Stu smiled, "but actually, m'work's rather expressionistic. Like your Owl George, it has its dark side. It's…I dunno, it's hard to describe it in words. I guess you'd just have to see it and categorize it for yerself." He took a long drink.

"Yeah…that'd be great." John was unusually receptive.

"Well, when y'er free, Rod here can direct you over. He just moved in as well. It's Percy Street, number eleven. Come by any time."

John nodded, sincerely interested.

"We're two floors up right now," Rod winked at Stu and lifted his lager, "but rumour has it Stu and I're about to acquire the ground floor apartment as well. Isn't that right?"

"Yeah, that's what I heard." Stu nodded. "It appears the tenants below us don't care a great deal for the 'frequent showers' that've been dousing their motorbikes."

"It rains a lot in England these days," Rod shrugged.

"And especially from our window, as it were."

They chuckled and raised eyebrows.

"But right now, if you don't mind," Rod gestured towards the door where his girl, Diz, stood waving, "I'll be excusin' m'self from your service, King John, and I'll be about the biddin' of others more enticin' than you'll ever be."

"Be off!" John gestured royally.

"T'rah," Rod grinned, grabbing his Guinness and heading in Diz's direction.

"So what about you, John?" Stu turned to his new acquaintance, "What's *your* medium, then? Besides poetry, I mean."

"Rock'n'roll," John seemed entirely serious.

"John's got his own band, The Quarry Men," Bill edged in closer to the table. "They've been together quite a while now – since grammar school days, actually."

"Is that right?" Stu was intrigued.

"Yeah." John relaxed back against the back of the tall wooden bench as the third or fourth Black and Tan of the evening worked its magic. "We're all right...as groups go. We've a fair lead guitarist, and this mate of mine from The Institute picks up rhythm. I play rhythm as well – and all of us do vocals now and again."

"I love rock'n'roll," Stu leaned across the table. "Me best work's done to Buddy Holly's stuff. As a matter of fact, m'art's a sort of rock'n'roll that you can see. Visual rock..."

John sat up again. "Have y'ever considered bein' in a band, then?"

"No, not really, not more than any other son of Liverpool," Stu laughed and shrugged. "The strings'd wreak havoc with me fingers, y'know. I've got artist's hands. And besides that, I've got no earthly idea how to play guitar...or drums. There isn't one musical phrase or one lead lick in this whole paint-splotched canvas of a brain up here."

"You could learn." John's eyes were intense. "We need a bass player."

"Moreover," Stu volleyed back, "As Rod said earlier, I'm continually dead skint. You don't get an instrument or even instruction without money – now do you?"

"He lives in utter 'squaverty,' John," Bill attested for Stu. "He hardly ever eats anythin' that's not free."

"Well, that's the Sutcliffe myth anyway," Stu grinned.

"Fuggin' great...just the ticket!" John loved it. "That's what every bleedin' rock'n'roll group needs...a scroungin', true-to-life artist who lives in an effin' hovel and shits mystery and romance! Fans would bleedin' make you their cause! They'd wring their hands and sympathize with you. You'd add the insanity we need – the missin' ingredient, as it were."

"But I *don't* play!" Stu looked to Bill for support.

John dismissed the hurdle, "You'd learn."

"But I'm an artist, John...I don't have the time. I..."

"It's not all that difficult, truth told, once you have the basic chords down. I mean, look – I learned all I needed in just one fuggin' afternoon! You'd see how it goes. You'd pick it up."

"Nah. I couldn't. Ta, but not me."

"You'd be great. Fuggin' great."

"I…" Stu gave up arguing. He could see that John's mind was made up, and John was not going to budge. He could only hope that the dervish Lennon had conjured would blow over as quickly as it had brewed. Stu figured that tomorrow in the light of day, the flamboyant John Lennon would just go his own way.

But Bill Harry, who knew John well, realized this was only the beginning of Stu's entanglement. Stu was in for it now.

****

John became Stu's shadow.

With a kinship that amazed even Mimi, who'd seen acquaintances come and go in John's life, the two art students became constant companions. And in a matter of only a few weeks, they'd changed each other. With John around, Stu was less intense, and with Stu, John found life less hopeless.

He began painting more seriously, and under Stu's tutelage, he began opting for large canvases rather than quick cartoon sketches.

"Not so much detail, John." Stu would move an invisible brush over John's canvas to suggest a line that he would delete or improve. "Think larger, freer. Remember the adage: 'Less is more.' Right?"

John's careless caricatures now emerged into free-flowing, single line sketches that adeptly captured complex expressions, actions, and emotions.

"*Concentrate*!" Stu instructed. "Feel the movement of the line. Don't give the canvas so much. Hold back a bit of what you've got."

And John, not as patiently, began to tutor Stu on guitar.

"Fuggin'ell!" John screamed as Stu hit the wrong chord for the fifteenth time in so many minutes. "Look, it's *this, not that*!" John grabbed the guitar from Stu and showed him one more time. "*Think* about what y'er doin', Sutcliffe! Y'er actin' the village idiot, son! Keep it up, and they'll give you a corner, a cup, 'n a seein'-eye dog to get you there."

John was a slave driver. He never tired where music was concerned, and he couldn't imagine anyone feeling differently.

"Listen, John, that's it. I'm chuckin' it in for the night," Stu would finally say, dark circles under his eyes. "I'm done."

"Y'er not done. Y'haven't got it down yet, have ya?" John pushed the guitar in his direction.

"No, but I've got work to do, real work as it were."

"*This is* real work!" John was offended.

"Right, yeah…but *your* work, not mine." Stu rubbed his sore fingers. "I'm the local artist, remember? You're the local musician. Keep our bleedin' nightmares sorted out. It's easier to scream at the right moments that way."

John smiled. Stu made him smile when most couldn't. These days almost everyone browned him off. Mimi, professors, other students, people on the streets…all of them were gallery ducks; targets for the angry, dark sarcasm John randomly fired at the innocent.

"How'd you lose yer legs, old chap?" John would scream out to handicapped veterans on the Liverpool streets. "How's that? Chasin' the wife, eh? Lousy excuse for desertin' the war if you ask me, wack! I'd be ashamed if I were you.'

His cronies dissolved into gales of laughter and approval, but they laughed only because they were afraid of becoming the next victims. John raved on, unchecked and uncensored. He insulted anyone who wandered within his range. He terrified people.

But Stu was not afraid.

He realized that beneath the cruelty that John meted out lay aching insecurity. He knew that John despised hurting people – hated himself for the things he said…but would do whatever was necessary to keep spectators at a safe, protective distance. Afraid that the world around him would discover his deformities and weaknesses, John pushed them away with both hands. John shielded himself so that no one, almost no one, knew him.

But Stu knew. Stu knew that whatever John *pretended* to be, he felt deeply and cared immensely. In that, they were alike; both of them had artists' souls.

But while John was outwardly hard and inwardly soft, Stu was tender throughout. He was quiet, soft-spoken, reserved, artistic, easily wounded, deep thinking, and gentle. But his gentleness wasn't a weakness on which John could prey. Instead, it became John's greatest source of strength.

****

They sat on the crumbling concrete steps outside Stu's new flat in Gambier Terrace and watched the sun drop against the steel scaffolding of the Anglican Cathedral. Their cigarette butts glowed amber in the early darkness as a rattletrap taxi grinded its gears and spun towards the docks. Otherwise, the street was unusually quiet for a Wednesday evening.

"Hey John." Stu's voice was diminished by the immensity of the sunset and the long view of the Mersey below. "How long will it be, d'ya think?'

"Spit it out, Sutcliffe." John exhaled smoke slowly. He let the aroma and silence linger.

"How long 'til we're famous, d'ya think? Until we've made it big?"

"Arthur Ballard says you'll be immortalized any day now," John grinned. Stu's tutor had the highest praise for everything Sutcliffe.

"Ah, that's just the Scotch talkin', isn't it?" Stu smiled back.

"Nah, he's Liverpudlian, son," John punned.

"And prejudiced as well," Stu sighed. "He thinks I'm fuggin' fantastic."

"He's right."

"So…how long d'ya think? How long…"

"'Til we're bigger'n Elvis?" John used his favourite catch phrase.

"Yeah, that." Stu leaned back against the cracked concrete landing and plucked at a determined weed growing through a fissure. "How long will it be, would you say?"

"Sometimes…" John tossed the last stub of his cig onto the sidewalk, "Sometimes I'm convinced I'm a ravin' madman obsessed with a dream of fame and fortune that'll never actually happen…that I'm livin' a fuggin' fantasy as it were, every Liverpool son's dream of escapin' to the world outside. And then," John hardly moved, "sometimes the vision's so fuggin' real I can almost touch it…can almost feel it comin' about." He leaned forward, elbows on his knees. "As strange as it seems in the light of day and as mad as it sounds to anyone else, Stu, I believe I've got this fate, this kismet, what have you – this predestination to make it big."

Stu watched the streetlights ignite, dotting the sunset sky. He drew on his cig and listened.

"There's nights, Stu," John went on, "when I fall asleep listenin' to rock'n'roll, and somehow it becomes *my* rock'n'roll, not Roy Orbison's, not Gene Vincent's, not Cliff Richard's, not anyone else's. It's *me* I hear performin' – and I'm great…fuggin' famous…the conquerin' hero, what have you. I'm up there…and I'm there for no other reason than I've just *made up me mind* to be there, y'know!"

"Yeah…right…I believe it." Stu gestured towards the world beyond the Mersey, beyond the Wirral Peninsula, beyond the Irish Sea. "I believe you, John. I believe you'll be right out there with Elvis Presley and Buddy Holly and Chuck Berry, and all the rest of 'em someday."

"And you'll be there as well, Sutcliffe…the two of us."

"The artist and the poet?" Stu smiled.

"The rocker and the painter. Get the order right, son."

"Well, what say we drink to that, then…before we're too fuggin' famous to frequent the Liddypool pubs?"

"Yeah," John hoisted himself up and then gave Stu a hand, "*Carpe diem* and all that crap."

And pulling their coats around them, the dream spinners set out towards Rice Street, each telling the other most incredible tales and believing in a holy quest whose ramifications neither of them fully understood.

Invaluable information about Stu Sutcliffe was given to me at a 1996 interview with Bryan Biggs, Director of The Bluecoat School in Liverpool. I appreciate the insights, articles, and letters. It was extremely helpful in portraying Stu accurately.

All information about Bill Harry and Mersey Beat is documented from Harry's three remarkable books, found in the footnotes, and from information graciously supplied to me by Bill via e-mail in August 2007. John's poem is also courtesy of Bill Harry and can be found with other wonderful information on his website, merseybeat.com.

The description of Stu is accurate as is all information about Stu's and Rod's flat. My gratitude to Rod Murray for supplying that information so graciously.

We know that John and Stu met during the autumn of 1958, but whether they met in this exact setting is unknown. All conversation is conjecture.

Mid-October 1958
Mendips
Woolton

Something was happening, something over which Mimi had no control. And it was not something good.

"Ahhh, Mrs. Smith?" The heavily accented voice on the other end of the phone began.

"Yes?" Mimi stood to talk as she always did.

"Charles Burton, here. Liverpool College of Art."

"Indeed, Mr. Burton. I've heard John speak of you." Mimi hoped the professor couldn't read minds. John had only referred to "Burtie" in the most disparaging terms.

"Well, Mrs. Smith, I must say that surprises me somewhat, because you see, we're having a bit of a problem here with John." He paused, waiting for the boy's aunt to catch her breath in shock or dismay. Mimi Smith did neither.

"Go on, Mr. Burton."

"Well...that is...your nephew does *not* seem to be taking our curriculum very seriously. In fact, if I may be blunt, he's throwing his college career to the wind."

"Indeed?" Mimi remained calm.

"Yes, quite." Burton wound up for the big pitch. "You see, Mrs. Smith, John is extremely disrespectful to our staff. He makes a farce of all we do. He refuses to complete his projects or assignments on time, and when he does, I'm convinced that some – if not all – of the work he submits is crafted by one of several young women who seem to've 'fallen under his spell,' if you will. Of his own accord, John seems to have no initiative that I can detect."

"So you're saying, in essence, that John is lazy as well as rude?" Mimi summarized.

"More aptly put, Mrs. Smith, he is dangerous." Burton gave a dramatic pause. "John, you see, is *influential*. He virtually 'holds court' on campus. He has a devoted band of hangers-on who mimic and applaud his every word. Geoff Mohammed, Helen Anderson, David Davies, Thelma Pickles,

Tony Carricker...and lately, even the dependable Cynthia Powell has been hypnotized by John's charisma. And believe me, there are others. In one way or another, John infects everyone with whom he comes into contact."

"And exactly what would you have me do, Mr. Burton – about John's charisma, that is?" Mimi's voice was unreadable. If she were angry, concerned, or insulted, Charles Burton could not ascertain it from her inflection.

"That, madam, is entirely your dilemma," he huffed in his grandest Welsh accent. "But I *will* tell you this much. If young John does not alter his actions, he will *not* have a future at Liverpool College of Art. I'll personally see to that. In fact, I would've done so already were it not for the blind affection that Professor Arthur Ballard has for your nephew. Professor Ballard sees John's behaviour as the manifestation of 'the noble spirit,' as he puts it, and he likens John to Thoreau's marcher to a different drummer. I, however, have never held with the American concept of 'rugged individualism,' nor will I tolerate uncontrolled behaviour in my classroom. Ballard or no Ballard, I cannot view John as gifted or even forgivably Bohemian. I see him as undisciplined. And that, I believe, is *your* department."

"Well, thank you very much for sharing your views with me, Mr. Burton. And good afternoon." Mimi ended the soliloquy. The receiver hit the cradle long before Charles Burton had had a chance to say good-bye.

But it was not this phone call alone that had awakened Mimi's sixth sense. She had already anticipated the worst. The stains on John's fingers – stains that had grown darker since Julia's death – indicated advanced addiction to nicotine. Stains of that nature came from two, three packs of cigarettes per day.

Where's John getting the money for such an expensive habit? she fretted. Mimi provided him only with bus fare, lunch money, and a stipend for art supplies. *How's he affording to smoke on such a limited budget?* She'd been afraid to ask.

Nor had Mimi overlooked the lager-saturated breath that accompanied John into a room. His clothes reeked of lager. His room emanated lager. His eyes were always glazed and bloodshot.

More than once, she'd found matchbooks in John's pockets from a club called "The Jacaranda" at 23 Slater Street, Liverpool 8. It was, she was told, an artsy coffee bar like so many others that had recently mushroomed in downtown Liverpool....places like Streates, The Studio, and The Zodiac. Mimi wondered how John could afford forays to these art school hangouts and who forayed there with him.

John's friends had changed. Peter Shotton still came around every now and again, and Paul McCartney and George Harrison were still permanent fixtures. But so many other friends had fallen by the wayside: Ivan Vaughn, Bill Turner, Nigel Whalley, and Len Garry. John never saw them anymore and rarely even mentioned their names. Instead, he had new associates sprinkled into the tales he sparingly divulged.

"There's this girl in my letterin' class who's buyin' me chocolate biscuits and coffee, Mim," John bragged over an early supper one Monday evening, not long after Burton's 'gloom and doom' telephone call.

"At least you were *in* lettering class." Mimi rinsed off her large, lamb stew pot while John ate alone.

"Powell...Cynthia Powell. She's from the Wirral...Hoylake."

Hoylake lay across the Mersey River from Liverpool on the Cheshire Wirral Peninsula. It was the home of the posh class of Liverpudlians whose well-maintained gardens and pristine middle-class homes set them apart from the Scousers of Merseyside.

Hoylakers wore sweater sets, sipped Darjeeling from Royal Doulton teacups, and transported their families in sensible motorcars or on bicycles built for two. Liverpudlians donned leather, downed pints, and prided themselves on knowing the ins and outs of bus and pedestrian travel. While Hoylake children learned to fly kites on sunny, spring afternoons, Liverpudlian mites discovered the best alleyways for football and the most secluded schoolyard walls to scale for "clandestine" adventures. More than a river divided the two distinct communities.

"Hoylake?" Mimi raised an eyebrow. She couldn't blame the little filly. Her boy was undeniably handsome with his mother's almond eyes and his father's reckless, charming smile. "What's in it for her? That's what I'd like to know."

"I think she wants me, Mim!" His eyes danced for the first time in a great while.

"Hmmm, well that may be, but just remember the old saying John..." She removed John's stew bowl and turned towards the sink.

"A baird in the hand's better 'n two in the bush?" John suggested, leaning back in his chair and grinning.

"No," Mimi bristled. "'Beware of Greeks bearing gifts.' Beware of people who want to give you something for nothing, John. In fact, I don't believe I'd accept those biscuits, if I were you."

"Well, you're not me, now are you?" John's smile faded. "And Powell's all right. I mean, she's a bit Hoity-lake – not the sort to take bacon butties with her tea, as it were – but aside from the fact that she does all her assignments before they're due, she's not as despicable as you make her sound...and not a bit Greek to the naked eye."

"I'm glad you broached the subject, John Winston."

"Greeks? Eyes? Or nakedness? And if it's nakedness, I'd rather avoid the discussion, if y'don't mind."

"Assignments." Mimi ignored his humour and took a seat across the tiny table from her nephew. "One of your professors rang me up to commend you on your 'remarkable' schoolwork, John." Mimi shot him a meaningful look.

"Yeah, really? Which one's that?" John wasn't surprised.

"Professor Charles Burton."

"Ah, Burtie!"

"And as a matter of fact, he mentioned your Miss Powell in that conversation as well."

"She isn't *my* Miss Powell. And what's *he* got against Miss Prim?"

"He claims you're leading her astray, John."

"Oh, right. And Burton's the authority we all set our clocks by, now isn't he?" John folded his arms.

"Well?" Mimi wanted more of an explanation.

"Well? Yes, I'm feeling brilliant. Ta for asking."

"Be serious, John. What about it, then? *Are* you having an adverse effect on this young woman?"

"Don't believe it!" He acted mortified. "It's *her* havin' the adverse on me! Y'know the type...always offerin' me cigs when I don't really want them. Destroyin' me health since I can't just turn her down flat, y'know! It'd drive her around the bend, eventually – that sort of rejection!"

"So *she's* the one giving you the cigarettes!" Mimi was relieved to discover the source.

"Well," John shrugged and grinned, "Powell and a couple others. I try to be as agreeable as possible, Mim. It's just part of me nature, y'know."

Mimi stood up, tossed him a dishtowel, and began washing his dinner bowl and bread and butter plate. "Be a little less agreeable, John, and a little more careful about what you do. Do your own homework and stop flirting with girls from across the water who've no idea how to deal with a Northern man. You know as well as I do that you'll only break her heart in the long run. Hoylake and Liverpool just won't work."

"I never said it bleedin' would." John dried the small plate she handed him. "Cynthia Powell's just one of the bunch who come up to Room 21 – Arthur Ballard's room – to hear Paul 'n George 'n me play of a lunchtime. Other 'n that, we've only got letterin' class together – me and Powell. That's the long and the short it."

Mimi eyed him sharply.

"That's it!" John tossed the dishtowel on the counter and swaggered into the living room to dispute the evening news.

Mimi worked on alone in silence, filling the coffee pot for later. She worried about the phone call from the college. She worried about the lager on John's breath. She worried about the fancy coffee shops he was frequenting. She worried about the homework John never seemed to do. She worried about the cigarettes he smoked and John's dark, stained fingers. But most of all, she worried about the girl from the Wirral named Cynthia Powell who was buying John chocolate biscuits.

None of it boded well.

Most of the events in this chapter are real...the fact that Cynthia was giving John biscuits and cigarettes, the fact that John, Paul and George were practising in Arthur Ballard's room at school, the fact that Charles Burton called Mimi to complain about John, and the fact that Mimi found a matchbook from The Jacaranda. All conversation, however, is conjecture.

Late October 1958
Liverpool College of Art
Liverpool

"Givvus a fag, luv?'

Even before she turned her head, Cynthia Powell blushed with recognition. The slightly acid, nasal tone could belong to no one else. And although it was clichaic and ridiculous, her stomach did strange things. Her breathing shallowed into inadequate mouse-breaths. But all John saw was her long brown hair flipping casually as she turned to face him.

"All out. Sorry." She smiled nervously. "Don't you ever have any of your own?"

"They're unhealthy, y'know." He eyed her coolly. "They'll kill you eventually – cigs."

"Perhaps so," Cynthia teased, "but *that* doesn't seem to stop you from pinching off everyone else, does it?"

She looked back down at her lettering exercise, pretending to study it carefully, trying to avoid his penetrating gaze. John continued to stare.

"Besides," she glanced back up at him briefly, "I don't really smoke, you know."

"Right." John rested his elbows on his desk top and leaned even closer to her, "It's a known fact that you don't. But it's also known that I'm always skint, and you've always got cigs on hand… Embassys…me favourites, luv. Makes a person wonder what you're up to."

Cynthia blushed again, this time visibly. John pressed on.

"What's that, Powell?" He nodded towards the lettering assignment on her desk, letting his arm brush hers as he pointed.

"Uh, our assignment." His touch distracted Cynthia. She had to focus to talk normally. "You know…the *semester project*? The one you've been labouring over, no doubt, hours-on-end at home?"

"Oh, that one. Right." John looked her squarely in the eye. "I've been thinkin' me cat ate it."

Cynthia sputtered a tiny laugh.

"But wait, what's this?" John pulled a crumpled piece of paper from his jacket pocket and unfolded it for closer examination. "I think I've discovered it after all, and it's amazin'ly like yours, isn't it?'

Cynthia took the assignment and the bait. She looked down slowly, half-expecting to see a blank sheet of paper or, at best, something sloppy and incomplete. But the composition that met her eyes was shocking.

It was a collage of imperfection…spastics on street corners, diseased sailors on rotten wharves, ugly couples casting romantic glances at one another, withered matrons sporting protruding warts. Cynthia grimaced involuntarily.

"Now *this* is art!" They were startled by the voice of Arthur Ballard, the lettering professor. Ballard took the collage from Cynthia and held it at arm's length, studying the creased page like a Rembrandt. Without asking John's permission, Ballard marched to the front of the room and held it aloft for all to see – proudly displaying John's deviates to the class. "Now *this*, ladies and gentlemen, is the kind of creativity for which art colleges are searching…the kind of originality that separates the artist from the draftsmen and craftsmen."

A low mumble-rumble followed…some in agreement and some with skepticism. Most of the girls looked away in disgust, but Cynthia's eyes never left the sketch until John's voice broke the spell. He spoke close to her ear, his nose almost touching her hair, "What couldn't you see thisavvy, Powell?"

John had lost interest in Ballard's praise, and as the teacher went on, highlighting the finer points of Lennon's artistry, Lennon himself had moved on to more intriguing territory.

"Shhhhh!" Cynthia tried to pay attention.

"What couldn't you see thisavvy?" John repeated, ignoring her reprimand.

It was a game they'd begun lately. Discovering that they both were terribly near-sighted, they had initiated a competition of sorts…comparing notes to find out which one of them had committed the biggest blunder due to blindness. Cynthia generally wore her glasses, and John refused to, so more often than not, he won the competition. But lately, Cynthia had stopped wearing her specs as well, and now the game was afoot.

"Miss Powell, Miss Powell, what couldn't you see?' John persisted in singsong fashion.

Whispering behind her hand very discreetly, Cynthia tried to answer him without being disrespectful to her professor. "Couldn't see the bus number and almost boarded the wrong…"

"Right." John cut in, "Well, I couldn't see the bleedin' bus at all – which explains why I dragged in a half-hour late."

Cynthia smiled at the exaggeration, but said nothing as Ballard continued to lecture.

"And instead of me sketchpad, luv," John went on, "I somehow wound up with yesterday's *Echo,* as it were. It's much more entertainin' than me sketchpad, as it were, but it leaves little room for design, y'know. How'd you like to lend a blind man a paper 'r two?"

"All right, but shhhhh!" Cynthia handed him her whole sketchpad and let him take what he liked. She knew she was a pushover, but she'd never been happier.

"Ta, luv." John tore several sheets out and handed the pad back to Cynthia, leaning in close. The all-pervading smell of scallops washed over her.

So! He was able to see well enough to stop at the fry shoppe on Mount Street. And he could see well enough to quif that hair of his to detailed perfection! What an out-and-out con artist this Woolton boy is! Cynthia smiled. *What a scammer!*

Cynthia turned ever so slightly in her chair so that she could see John out of the corner of her eye and still pretend to listen to the lecture Ballard was giving. *Keeping a watchful eye on John Lennon's good advice for any girl,* she mused. And she did so as he began to work, his back hunched, his eyes squinting at the chalkboard.

Good heavens, he's just beginning the semester project! she realized. *And it's due in three days!*

John pressed his lips together tightly as he worked, making a thin line of determination paralleled by his squinted eyes. His ugly, calloused fingers worked rapidly and well, making the exacting lettering exercise that Cynthia had struggled with seem almost elementary. But within minutes his face glazed over with boredom and his progress slowed. Once the newness of the task wore off and repetitiveness settled in, John lost interest altogether.

Cynthia wondered why John had selected lettering as a course of study at all. *Surely illustration or even graphic design would've been more his bailiwick. But lettering? That's for regimented, structured...mathematical students.* It just didn't make sense.

What Cynthia couldn't know was that John had had no choice in the matter. After his first year at Liverpool College of Art in the general painting curriculum, his reputation had limited his sophomore year's selection. No professors had wanted him in their classes; no one would have him at all. Only Arthur Ballard, the lettering instructor, continued to admit John, though he knew John was not cut out for his discipline.

John was scribbling now, the prescribed lesson abandoned. Cynthia watched hideous, deformed creatures leap from his pen and crawl across the pad.

God, what must be in his mind! Who could concoct such horrors? Who is this man, really? John terrified her almost as much as he intrigued her. He was taboo and utterly enticing.

"Miss Powell?" She heard her name in the distance. Cynthia snapped her head around to a sea of staring faces. Some snickered. Others merely looked smug and amused. "The answer, Miss Powell?" Arthur Ballard asked again.

"I-I'm terribly sorry. I didn't hear the question," Cynthia stammered. She washed deep red as the class muffled laughter.

Damn you, John Lennon, she thought as Ballard moved on to someone else. *Why am I wasting my time even thinking about you anyway? You're a Ted, a Scouser, a troublemaker, and a moocher! And besides that, I've got no business even looking in your direction. I'm engaged, for Pete's sake! I'm in love!*

But annoyingly and quietly a small voice posed the critical question: "In love are you, Cynthia Powell? With whom?"

Cynthia stared straight at Arthur Ballard and tried to concentrate. And she tried not to think about the question of "true love" and what the answer to that question might be.

This chapter is somewhat fictional. John and Cynthia did have lettering class together. She did lend him paper quite frequently. They did play the "what couldn't you see" game. John did stop at the fry shop in Mount Street frequently and did come to class quite tardy. Ballard did praise John's bizarre sketches. And the autumn of 1958 did find Cynthia falling in love with John. But the above scenario is only representative of those facts, not an exact detailing of a literal day.

November 1958
Liverpool College of Art
Liverpool

Cynthia had been envious before – envious of girls whose fathers hadn't died – girls who had two parents, traditional lives. She had envied girls who didn't "give a whit" about propriety, whose caution-to-the-wind attitudes gave them license. She had envied her Liverpool classmates their artistic freedom that came from growing up on the "wrong" side of the Mersey – far from conventional Hoylake with its dull, somewhat pretentious decency.

But although she'd been envious, until today Cynthia had never been jealous.

The college lecture theater was packed to capacity, a cricket box of noise, motion, and restless activity. A few students were still filing in, searching almost hopelessly for a vacant spot, but most of the battered seats were already occupied. The professors hovered together, the leftovers of their just-past-noon pub talk winding to a close.

Bruce Sabine fiddled with the podium microphone, toying with the height a bit and adjusting the O-ring while the designated lecturer accepted a small glass of water from the staff secretary. One of the intermediate students called out to another just entering the room to join him, and the friend returned, "Right, then!" as he climbed over already settled classmates en route to his destination. Notebooks snapped and paper rustled. Laughter punctuated everything.

All this was lost on Cynthia. It was distraction, activity on her periphery. She focused narrowly on John Lennon, five rows ahead, and several seats over. She tipped her head from one side to another, circumventing the bobbing obstacles in her line of vision, keeping John in her sight. No one else in the room even existed.

Everything was blurred except John…John and the dark, lovely Helen Anderson. Helen was hard to miss. She sat directly behind John, dead centre in Cynthia's view. Helen sat forward – on the edge of the worn, leather theatre seat – close to John. *Shamelessly close*, Cynthia thought.

Laughing spontaneously and claiming John's full attention with her flirtatious, "I-like-men" sparkle, Helen was all casual confidence and ease. She moved, and as she moved, John's eyes followed her. She whispered in his ear. Helen leaned back, then forward, rubbing John's shoulder with her long, elegant fingers. She rested her arm on his arm and then edged away adeptly. Helen was relaxed and in her element; she was relishing the moment.

Cynthia grew increasingly uneasy.

As the microphone on the podium squealed into action and the lecturer thumped it for effect, Helen's audible tones diminished to whispers. Cynthia watched as John turned sideways in his chair, propped one plimsoled foot up in the empty seat beside him, and listened to Helen quietly continuing a story that he was obviously enjoying. His left elbow rested on the top of his chair, and Helen's hands fell on the worn pad of his over-large, brown tweed jacket.

Gesturing, pausing, giving her friend's arm a playful squeeze, Helen continued to amuse him. They were completely oblivious to the serious business of the lecture hall – the more-than-routine assembly announcements. John and Helen had better things to do.

Cynthia ears and cheeks grew warm. She watched Helen's hands fall on John's back, carelessly touching his shoulders through the thick, soft fabric. And when he laughed with the girl, Cynthia could almost smell the scallops-and-ale breath washing over Helen's face.

Suddenly, unexpectedly, Cynthia hated Helen Anderson for her aplomb, for the ease with which she spoke to men and specifically to John. Cynthia hated Helen's boldness born of familiarity. She hated Helen's beauty. She hated the fact that John even had a nickname for the dark-haired girl. "Heloon," he fondly called her.

Cynthia was just "Miss Powell" – not Cynthia, not Cyndy, not anything intimate. In fact, the truth was that John spoke to her only occasionally. He barely knew her, at least not in the way she wanted him to.

And Cynthia barely knew John. Although she'd exchanged homework favours and small tokens with friends for a seat right next to him in lettering class, she still hardly knew him. His infamous tardiness precluded any chance to chat him up before class, and his maddened hurry to meet Paul McCartney, his mate from the Institute, for their lunchtime jam sessions prohibited any dialogue after class.

Of course, John wasn't opposed to conversation *during* the professor's lecture and he frequently initiated those, but Cynthia hadn't his rebel's spirit. She was as goody-goody as the conservative, matched sweater sets she always wore, as reserved as her Hoylake vocabulary. She reluctantly resisted his tempting nudges, notes, and far-too-vocal whispers inside the classroom confines. But Helen didn't.

Heloon fell in with John without any twinge of guilt. She encouraged his joyful rampages; she delighted in prompting him with, "John, be funny!" And when, at the end of every class, he rushed headlong from the room, his guitar slung madly over one shoulder and books left carelessly behind, Helen generally picked up the abandoned texts, joined Geoff Mohammed, and followed her pied piper gladly along.

The sound of half-hearted applause brought Cynthia back to the moment. The announcements concluded, the guest lecturer had now stepped to the podium. All second-year students were advised to take copious notes, and a brief moment was provided for the necessary preparations. Cynthia opened her notebook and fished in her purse for a pen, but her concentration was minimal. She couldn't take her eyes from the cozy couple five rows up.

Cynthia's throat cinched. It pulsed with anger she didn't have a right to feel, with a sense of betrayal that made no sense at all.

Cynthia even envisioned herself walking forward, taking a stance between John and Helen, and putting an end to the *tête a tête*. She imagined taking the slender brunette's place and sitting with John – captivating him and amusing him the way the confident, Liverpool girl always did. Cynthia fantasized about laughing and flirting and commanding John's attention.

A brash, familiar, nasal voice interrupted everything in the room. Cynthia heard the voice rise above her daydreams, above the speaker's voice – calling out over the crowd as the distinguished professor paused, stunned into mid-sentence silence.

"All this talk of Art ..." the voice said, "and yet we don't know him that well, do we? Oughtn't we refer to him as Arthur, then?"

It was a typical Lennonism.

John's loyal subjects howled their appreciation. They applauded, as the rest of the room slowly absorbed the pun almost by osmosis. Even the befuddled art lecturer himself finally lowered his head and suppressed a wry smile. One had to admire the Scouse-Lennon humour. It was simply funny, even when it was inappropriate.

Cynthia was one of the few who didn't enjoy John's joke. She didn't laugh; she didn't even smile. She was jealous, furious. Cynthia was seething.

As Cynthia watched, Helen nudged John playfully, ruffling his hair a bit for all his irreverent nonsense, mussing the coifed DA that John so carefully guarded. Helen sifted his hair through her fingers, separating the strands and letting them fall, sculpting them once again. It was a private moment, the intimate interaction of two very comfortable friends for whom touch is not seduction.

Cynthia folded her arms and hated...hated Helen for being unconsciously beautiful, hated herself for being irrationally drawn to a total stranger – for being inexplicably "head over heels" with the school madman.

John Lennon smoked. He drank. He cackled in class. He crept up on people and shouted in their ears. He challenged the assembly lecturer. He ridiculed everything and everyone.

But he was Cynthia's fantasy – her own James Dean in tight, black drainpipe trousers and greased-back hair. John's dark brown eyes were the essence of her daydreams, and his arrogant stare haunted her at night. She imagined his stained fingers caressing her artist's hands. She imagined his brittle callouses brushing across the soft nape of her neck. It was all incredibly sensuous, but it was all make-believe.

Only Helen Anderson was lucky enough to experience the real thing.

Over the past few months, Cynthia had tried to reason away the attraction she felt to John. She had tried reminding herself that John was nothing like her, that he was totally foreign to everything she'd been reared to understand. He was unpredictable while she was routine. He was music; she was decorous silence. John was wild laughter; Cynthia was a quiet smile. But in spite of the incongruity of it all, Cynthia thought of him constantly.

She studied Helen Anderson now; she watched the girl move and speak and fall silent. She examined Helen's body language, her self-assured posture, the way she tossed her long, brunette hair and angled her shoulders. Cynthia watched carefully, took it all in, and realized what she had to do.

She would have to become more like the girl…or some very close facsimile. She would have to be less "Miss Prim" and more "Heloon."

No "demure miss" from the Wirral would ever lure John away from his colourful friends. No reserved girl who had been labeled "very conscientious, but lacking in confidence" would have a prayer with John Lennon. To take Helen's place, Cynthia Powell would have to change. And the change would have to be a dramatic one.

My husband and I were invited to Helen's home in Chester in March of 1994, and I was thrilled to meet "Heloon." It never occurred to me that this beauty, who went on to become a famous designer (designing the award winning costumes for TV's "Dallas") would still be the girl from this chapter. But she was. With a half hour, she had made fast friends with my husband and was showing him her new line of clothing and letting him hold John's "Daily Howl." That afternoon, I found myself in Cynthia's shoes. And never was a chapter so easy to write. Helen is just as charming as she was in 1958.

Late November 1958
Room 21
Liverpool College of Art
Liverpool

"We'll be startin' off today with one from the late, great Buddy Holly," John announced ceremoniously. "Hope you bohemian masses enjoy it as much as we do. Feel free to toss in a harmony here'n there, or a pound or two…whatever it is you've got to toss."

"No crackers, please," Paul winked.

And the jam session began. Twenty or so students ate lunch, tapped their feet, flirted over the music. First, it was "That'll Be the Day" and then "Maybe Baby." John did a spoof on "Johnny B. Goode," inserting tidbits of gossip about art college faculty into the lyrics. The crowd loved it.

Paul crooned "Searchin'," looking soulfully romantic for three girls who dangled their legs off the design table and whispered behind cupped hands. He winked and wagged his head while George offered one shy and unaffected grin.

Traditional chords and old-time favourites filled the room. And gradually, one cluster at a time, the onlookers stopped doing whatever it was they were doing to join in the familiar lyrics. Michael Isaacson, walking down the hall towards his next class, popped his head in and joined the pub-like sing-along.

When you're smilin'
When you're smilin',
The whole world smiles with you,
When you're laughin',
When you're laughin',
The sun comes shinin' through,

But when you're cryin'
You bring down the rain,
So stop your cryin',
Be happy again!
'Cause when you're smilin',

When you're smilin',
The whole world smiles at you!

John played a nifty lick he'd devised, and then the whole thing began again, John singing lead and Paul harmonizing with tight, high harmony. They stood close together, necks craning forward, shoulders hunched as if their bodies were cupping around the notes, amplifying them.

Standing shyly in the doorway, Cynthia was transfixed. She stared without blinking at a John she'd never seen before. The Ted with the cigarette breath had virtually disappeared inside this man with the sad, vulnerable face and sentimental eyes.

John was singing unabashedly – oblivious to scrutiny, oblivious to anything except the joy of singing. He was singing of family and tradition and days past. He was singing more for himself than for anyone else.

Watching him, Cynthia remembered something she'd overheard June Furlong, the art college's famous life model, say a couple of weeks back. Now the phrase echoed as John lost himself in his song.

"He hasn't gotten it all together quite yet, but there's this originality…yes, yes, originality is the word, don't you think…there's this originality about him that won't quit!"

June was right. Cynthia found him…extraordinary.

Then the song ended and with it the set, and motion began again. People ambled out down one hall or another, making plans for the afternoon. Paul began to wipe his guitar with a soft, shoeshine cloth while George ran a few licks in solo. And John promptly resumed his accustomed persona.

"Money, money for the poor!" He hobbled around the room like a crippled hunchback, carrying an empty coffee cup and begging for pocket change. Cynthia exchanged glances with Michael Isaacson, who seemed to be watching her, and she gave him a quick wave. Michael only half-smiled, raising an eyebrow in greeting, and looking pointedly at John and Cynthia once again. His message was loud and clear.

"Money for the poor, gerl?" John's face looked up into hers from his pitiful, withered posture.

"I've contributed quite enough to your cause this morning, Sir Beggar, don't you think?" Cynthia pretended to be hard. "I mean, two pencils and a new paintbrush later – I'll have to stop at the supply shop just to make it through the rest of the day! What else could you possibly expect me to give?"

"Anythin' you'd care to dish out, luv," the hunchback answered, but his voice had taken on a new tone. John stood up to his full height and looked down on her with an intimidating smirk, "Out with it, Powell. What is it you've got to give?"

Cynthia blushed ten times over and stammered something – anything –

to escape. "I uh...enjoyed your recital 'n all. Got to run...next class, you know. Tatty bye." She almost tripped over her own feet in a mad dash for the hall.

"It's *not* a recital, Powell!" John called after her. "It's commonly known as a jam session among us bourgeoisie. We don't subscribe to recitals in this part of town, luv. But call it what you will, and as always, come back again, eh? We never seem to tire of the aristocracy here Merseyside, y'know!"

Then he turned to Paul and made an obscene gesture that was one part machismo and three parts conspicuous lust. Paul gave a "thumbs up" and a quick nod, but he doubted that John's interest in Cynthia Powell was as casual as it seemed. For some time, Paul had had another theory, and this seemed the perfect time to test it out.

"She's very mature, now isn't she – this Cynthia of the Wirral?" Paul goaded his friend.

"Powell? I hadn't given 'er much thought." John strode over and began gathering his things.

"Very bright...very different, Cynthia," Paul teased. "The sort of girl me dad would take to."

"Grow up McCartney, she's not your type." John's voice was low and gravelly.

"Still," Paul placed his hand on his chin, "it gives one pause, as it were."

"Yeah," John shot back, "menopause or some such malady. She'd never go for you."

"I don't know," Paul smiled and winked, "She came here today, didn't she? And if I do say so meself, she was watchin' me quite a bit. In fact, it put me off at moments...I nearly missed a note near the end of the second verse, y'know."

"Get off."

"No, really." Paul looked serious. "I've been thinkin' about asking her out 'n all. I mean, she's quite pretty – Cynthia. I quite fancy her...what do y'think?"

"I think you're fuggin' daft!" John hoisted his guitar to his shoulder. Just as Paul had suspected, John was "browned off." It was written all over his face.

Paul feigned shock and hurt as John glared at him. For several seconds there was a very uncomfortable silence. Then Paul glanced at George, and George began to smile. It was Paul who snickered first.

"Fuggin' hilarious – the both o'ya!" John realized the joke was on him. "Remind me to chuck you a bob after the next performance, McClown. Everyone loves your ilk, son." Then he turned on George, "And what are *you* laughin' at, Sonny Jim?"

"I hadn't realized I was laughin'...not actually." George turned his back and began to roll his guitar cord in a careful figure eight. He bit his lip and tried not to smile.

"It was more of a…pleasant visage, I believe," Paul wouldn't relent.

"Go on. Knock yerselves out." John was furious.

"It wasn't me, John…it was me brother!" Paul protested his innocence, thoroughly enjoying John's outburst.

"I was only an innocent bystander here!" George called as John stormed out of the room.

"T'rah, then!" Paul yelled out.

"T'rah John! We're right behind you, all right?" George shouted after him, trying to smooth things over. But John never looked back. He slammed the tall, frosted-glass paneled door and clacked his boots down the marble hallway.

"It appears that Mr. Lennon's after a Black and Tan," Paul grinned, undaunted. "And it appears he's *not* invitin' us."

"Yeah – it appears we've been left behind," George agreed, a little crestfallen. John was his hero; it was uncomfortable to take anyone else's side, even for the sake of a joke.

Paul smiled, shrugged, and began to put his equipment away at his own pace. There was no need to rush about in fear of missing a rendezvous at Ye Cracke with John. John would be there all evening. These days he always was.

But George worked double time to make the assignation. He hadn't realized that teasing John about Cynthia Powell would make him quite so angry. He'd assumed John was still dating Thelma Pickles and would just play along. But John had clearly been offended. It was strange.

"There's more to this than meets the eye, isn't there?" Paul grinned from across the room.

"Yeah, seemin'ly," George pouted.

"Ah, give it the half hour, and John'll be all right," Paul assured him.

George picked up his guitar case and headed for the door. "Yeah, maybe so. I hope," he shrugged. "But will Thel?"

"Actually," Paul raised an eyebrow. "From what I've just seen, it's a bit too late to worry about Thel. Whether she knows it or not, Miss Pickles is already one for the memory books, isn't she?"

The boys did practice at noon in Room 21, and a crowd did gather to listen to them. Coleman tells us in Lennon *that they often sang "When You're Smiling," and Cynthia did attend several of these practise sessions. Toward the end of November 1958, John was becoming interested in Cynthia Powell and less involved with Thelma. However, this specific incident did not occur. All conversation is conjecture.*

Many thanks to Alfred Music Publishing for permission to reprint "When You're Smiling." Would that all music production companies were as kind as you are!

Early January 1959
Ye Cracke Pub
Rice Street
Liverpool 8

Smoke settled low over the tables of Ye Cracke, obscuring the crazed, yellowed stucco walls. Gossiping, speculating, debating – the college crowd celebrated the Christmas holidays just past and drank to the beginning of the new term ahead. Dave Davies, Tony Carricker, Ann Mason, Geoff Mohammed, Helen Anderson, and John Lennon hunched around "their table" in the small back room and made merry. After weeks away from school, they had stories to tell; they had adventures to bring back to the collective.

For once, John merely listened, swilling his Black and Tan mixture of Guinness and cider. Although it was oppressive in the tiny Tudor pub, John sat perspiring in his jacket. He hadn't the energy to remove it or the motivation step outside and clear his head. A clear head, in fact, was the last thing he wanted, this close to the holidays.

What he wanted was amnesia. He took another long drink towards oblivion.

"Yer girl's glancin' meaningfully this way once again," Tony elbowed John. "She's waitin' for you to make the first move, y'know."

"She's not *my* fuggin' anything," John snarled.

"Go on!" Geoff grinned, reaching across the stout oak table with a fake jab, "She's yer girl – Thelma. She's yer girl, and half of everyone knows it! It's been that way for months, hasn't it? It's a known fact."

John's nostrils flared.

"Bugger off, Mohammed!" he growled. "She's…a diversion, a bit of a diversion…an acquaintance, that's what."

"Right." Helen smirked. "Tell us more, John."

Tony cut his eyes at Geoff, "Well, I'm thinkin' it's Lady Muck o' Muck Hall that Mr. Lennon here fancies these days…" He raised his voice. "The celebrated Cynthia Powell, y'know."

"Pffft! Not in a million years!" Helen snickered. "Miss Prim's blood's too thin for a man like our Johnny."

"Besides which," Geoff said loudly, "He's thold on Thel, aren't you?" Ye Cracke turned the volume a notch down to listen.

John blew smoke in Geoff's face, but there was no reply.

It was ominous silence. One couple got up to leave. Others averted their eyes. But Geoff leered at John without an ounce of caution.

Across the room, Thelma swallowed hard. She felt her ears and cheeks stinging, her neck tingling. She felt warm bile rising in her throat. Any minute now, John would explode.

"C'mon. Tell us how it is, Johnny," Helen cooed.

"Explain it to us, lad!" Tony Carricker teased.

John downed a large gulp of his Black and Tan and stared across the rim. He narrowed his eyes and waited.

"I'll explain fuggin' nothin' to you," John finally answered, just above a whisper.

"You say she's like *fuggin' nothin'* to you?" Geoff smirked, twisting John's words. He had his stage voice on now. "Thasso? 'S that how it is, then?"

A few brave souls laughed. John whipped his head around and stared at the onlookers. His eyes met Thelma's.

Up-ending his pint, John polished it off in a single gulp. But instead of slamming the empty glass down with a warning force, John raised it and flashed a charismatic smile. "Yeah," he laughed hollowly, "that's about the sum of it, son! But then again...aren't they all, Mohammed? Aren't they fuggin' all?"

Tony slapped him on the back. Geoff reached across the table and shook John's hand. The "boys' club" guffawed fraternal approval. While their girlfriends threw their eyes to the ceiling, they toasted each other and John.

John had gained control of the room again. No longer was he the brunt of the joke – the "odd boy out" – the kid whose mum lived 'cross town but whose auntie had reared him. No longer was he the strange lad whose dad had run off to places unknown, the "poor little boy" whose Uncle George had died while he'd been off on holiday. He had vindicated himself. All the whispering had been squelched. John had them under his spell again.

"Givvus another round, Carricker!" John leaned back, victorious and smug. "Because it appears *I'm* not goin' anywhere, and it appears me glass is a pessimist at its prime."

Thelma sighed. She knew John better than almost anyone. She knew that John had only one life jacket, and tonight he'd saved himself. But Thelma was tired of treading water in the rough seas in which John swam. John was a sole survivor; he would never be the one to rescue her.

Thelma gathered up her books, her navy cloth coat, and scarf. She checked the jacket pocket for her bus ticket and then pulled on her thick, hand-knitted gloves. Since her dad's disappearance, goodbyes had become extremely difficult, so Thelma moved inconspicuously along the wall – keeping her eyes down, trying to exit without a scene.

At the black, diamond-paned door, she heard his voice rise above the din of laughter and holiday music: "So Miss Pickles is leavin' us then! It appears she's shunnin' our company, as it were! It appears she's walkin' out on the well-known odd sods and bods…the Ye of the Cracke."

John's faithful "ooohed" at the challenge, and John stuck his tongue between his gum and lower lip, grinning mockingly. Even when he read the hurt in Thelma's eyes, he continued to act the fool.

Six months ago, Thelma had defended him from the same cruelty he now dished out to her. As she watched him preen and clown at her expense, Thelma's entrance became her exit.

"John!" she yelled above the fracas, "don't blame me…just because your mother's dead!"

And with a nod, she walked out.

Tony motioned for another round of drinks while Geoff signaled the crowd to raise the glasses they had.

They toasted John with warm, cheap lager and celebrated his newfound independence. They grumbled over the possessiveness of women and amazed themselves with tales of sexual prowess. They lied, swore, and laughed. They talked too loudly.

But that night, John left the pub alone and fell onto a bus bound for somewhere. Even before he collapsed against the window, John felt the queasy blur of blackout. After that, he remembered nothing of his jagged snores and drool. When the bus reached the end of the line, the driver hauled him out – tossing him into the street to retch.

And that night, John walked home by himself, stumbling and weaving in the icy, deserted Liverpool blackness…drunk, blind, and almost unable to find his way alone.

The quote, "Don't blame me just because your mother's dead" is a well-documented quote from Thelma, spoken to John at Ye Cracke after he had been verbally abusive of her. It was the end of their relationship. The other bits of conversation in this chapter are conjecture.

Mid-January 1959
Mendips
Woolton

She'd been almost impossible to placate. In fact, Mimi was livid.

"But I'm fuggin' eighteen, Mim! And in *second* year art school!" he shouted at her.

"Don't use vulgarities, John. It's not appealing."

"I can't go on livin' here forever, can I?"

"No one said you should. No one even suggested it."

"Then why can't you understand why I'm movin' in with Stu?" John pressed on.

"Because you've no business out on your own, John," she lifted her chin defiantly. "Or have you somehow learned to manage your own laundry without my knowing about it? Have you learned to cook overnight?"

"I can always bring the laundry back here, can't I?"

"No, thank you."

"You could cook for me on weekends now and again."

"Not really interested."

"It's only three kilometres away, Mim. I'm not leavin' for bleedin' America, as it were!"

"It's your decision, John. If you think you're ready to leave home, then by all means don't let me stand in your way." She tried to brush past him.

"Look," he grabbed her bony shoulders and stared into her eyes, "Stu's flat's closer to m'classes. It's cheap. It's where m'friends are. There's plenty of room for me there….and it's within walkin' distance of the Chinese take-aways…"

"Which you cannot afford."

"…and it's with Stu, y'know. You like Stu, right?"

"That's neither here nor there, John. It's completely beside the point."

"I wasn't aware there was a point."

The debate waged on. It was the bittersweet moment of independence. Mimi fought to hang on, and John, to walk away.

In spite of his rebellion, anger, and all too frequent intoxication, John was Mimi's boy. And she knew that once he left, he would be gone for good. Their volatile friendship would become a polite, distant relationship. Their points of interaction would be infrequent. The days of "mother and son" would end.

Since George's death, John's world had been, albeit tumultuous, her world. His rock'n'roll, jokes, sarcasm, friends, clandestine girlfriends, Quarry Men plans and dreams, strange stories, stranger caricatures, vacillating moods – even the pungent smell of greasy scallops permeating his room – they were all she had. Since that first day, back in October 1940, she'd chosen John as her destiny.

If she'd been an emotional woman, she would have told him so.

She would have told him that he was her best friend, that her heart was broken to see him go. But Mimi was who she was, so she convinced herself that her objections to John's moving out were simply rooted in "John's own good."

"It's just…I…I can't see how this will work." Mimi walked over to the windowsill and took down the small bottle of American, almond-scented hand lotion – Jergen's, her favourite. It was her one and only indulgence after a day of cleaning, gardening, and cooking. She squirted a dab into her palm and then rubbed her hands together. "You've no money for rent, John. You've no money for food. As it is now, you're constantly plying me for extra cash…even though you live *here* where everything's free! How will you possibly be able to afford the extra demands upon your finances once you're no longer under this roof?"

"I'm workin' on gigs for the band, 'n things are shapin' up," he shrugged. "There's this coffeehouse in Liverpool 8 – The Jacaranda – where the owner's all but signed on the dotted line to let us play in the basement now and again. And we just played Garston…and Saturday next, there's the Village Club thingy."

"Um," Mimi grunted. "Holiday parties."

"Yeah."

"And what will you do in February, John? Bar Mitzvahs?"

"Top o' the list, Mim."

"That's your plan?"

"There *isn't* a plan, Mimi! Why does there always have to be a bleedin' plan?!"

"Because prudent people don't like nasty surprises, John. Because wise people like to anticipate the down side. By planning for failure, people succeed."

"Prepare yerselves lads!" John yelled to the cats, "The Queen Mary Elizabeth is about to launch on her less-than-maiden voyage into the Sea of Lectures, as it were. Come one, come all! She's just about to…"

"Enough, John." Mimi turned and walked into the parlour, but he was hot on her heels, not about to give in.

"Listen, Mim…Pete's been on his own for two bleedin' years now!"

"Peter Shotton has a job." She grabbed *The Echo* and searched for her reading glasses.

"Well, what about Rod Murray then...and what about Stu?"

"I'm not responsible for Rod Murray and Stu."

"And y'er not responsible for me as well!" John's pressed his palms against his forehead in frustration. "That's the crux of it, y'know! I'm in art school, Mim. I'm in a band! I have a..."

"Incredible accomplishments, John." Mimi stared him down. "But are you financially independent? Isn't that what you're asking to be?"

"I'm not askin', Mim. I'm puttin' it out as a fact," he glared back. "I'm movin' out, and I'm movin' in with Stu! I'm movin' in with Stu at the end of this week. So let that be an end to it."

"Quite interesting, John – especially in light of the fact that I am the one paying your tuition, financing your books and supplies. I'm purchasing your clothing, your guitar strings, your bus fare...and I'm the one providing your transport to and from these gigs of yours." Mimi took a step forward. "But what I'm *not doing,* however, is paying for a flat, John. I'm not backing the free and easy lifestyle of Liverpool 8...no matter what your friends and associates choose to do."

"Right." He lifted his chin in his typical defiant posture. "So it all comes down to a question of money, then?"

"That has a great deal to do with it, yes." Mimi lifted the paper in front of her face.

More than anything, she wanted to tell him the truth. She wanted to say, *The fact is, I'll have no family after you're gone, John...only boarders who come and go. And...I'll miss you. I'll miss your inane, funny faces, your constant puns, your dry wit, your silly poems at odd times. I'll miss our discussions about the latest books and radio programmes and Stanley family gossip. I'll miss our tea times together.*

She wanted to lower her paper and ask him to stay – because she wasn't ready to let him go. Instead she cleared her throat and pretended to read the entertainment page.

"Right, well...I'll earn the money then," he said.

Mimi could tell John was hurt.

But she also knew that he was going, no matter what. To state her case would only postpone the inevitable, would only incur his pity. It was only a matter of packing now; in a few days, John would move on.

He stood there for a moment, waiting. He chewed his gum, rubbed a finger over one eyebrow, and shifted his weight back and forth. He stared at the back of *The Echo* and waited for some word from the face behind the headlines. But Mimi was silent, almost motionless.

What he expected her to say, wanted her to say, John didn't know. He wanted her to approve his decision, but he wanted her to ask him to stay. He wanted to leave, but he wanted to know he'd be missed. He wanted to be a part of the college scene, but he still wanted to be a part of Mendips. Nothing Mimi could have said or done would have been right. Even her silence was painful.

As John turned and climbed the stairs, Mimi pushed her glasses back up on the bridge of her nose and crossed her legs. She fluffed the paper authoritatively and resisted the temptation to glance over the top of the newsprint and watch him go.

When she heard his radio come on upstairs, she lowered the paper, sat with her eyes closed, and listened. She listened to him slam around as he always did, from "pillar to post," as she put it. She smelled the faint hint of cigarette smoke drifting down the stairs, and she heard John swearing as usual, just loud enough to be heard.

By this weekend, she thought, *this house will be changed. By Saturday evening, everything will be completely different. There's nothing I can say to change his mind or delay it all. I'm just lucky to have had him as long as I did.*

And switching off her reading lamp, Mimi sat in the dark and listened for a long time to the sounds that were John.

Information about the Percy Street flat and later the Gambier Terrace flat was provided to me by Rod Murray, May 2002. Rod acquired the Gambier Terrace flat in 1960…prior to that date, he and Stu lived in Percy Street. The flat referred to in this chapter, therefore, had to have been the Percy flat. John lived in Percy Street for only a short time before returning home to Mendips, but he did eventually move out for good when Rod and Stu acquired the Gambier Terrace apartment. Only the conversation in this chapter is conjecture

April 1959
Ye Cracke Pub
Rice Street
Liverpool 8

Stu had no respect for the unholy alliance of Geoff Mohammed and John Lennon. In fact, Stu thought Geoff brought out the worst in John, at the worst times and in the worst places.

Five years John's senior, Geoff was nevertheless John's contemporary in school – because although he was incredibly intelligent, Geoff waged a desultory war against authority that he was too outnumbered to win. "Sagging off" classes and always playing the clown, Geoff used his keen mind to concoct illicit schemes that amused his classmates and infuriated the faculty – schemes that were carried out with finesse. And lately, with John by his side, the two school fools had combined forces to spin up extraordinarily imaginative improprieties.

It saddened Stu. He thought John destined for better things.

Just when Stu managed to find some small panacea to John's frightening chaos, Geoff would foment it all over again. Geoff encouraged John's most erratic behaviour and applauded John's mania. He unearthed John's dark side. He egged John on.

Over the last six months, as John had fluctuated between ennui and despair, it had taken all the magic Stu could conjure just to get his friend to pick up a paintbrush and work. It was so much easier for John simply to wander down to Ye Cracke and "get smashed." Mayhem was a tremendous temptation, and John had little resistance to it. The last thing John needed, as far as Stu was concerned, was a cohort in crime. But Geoff was all too ready to be just that.

****

"'ullo!" It was a raven-haired Dublin girl – a first year student – drawn to John's tight, black jeans and steely glare. "Anna," she smiled, tossing her hair and offering her hand. "What yours, then?"

John's nostrils flared. Anna was "in for it."

"Simply Simple Pimple John Wimple Lennon," he said, looking completely serious. Geoff snickered beside him.

The girl blinked her heavy lashes rapidly, laughing nervously. But John said nothing. He continued to stare at her.

"I-I'm first year..." Anna shrugged, "still in me paintin' classes, of course. But you...you must be..."

"A genius," John finished her sentence. "A genius or a madman! You decide." He pulled a spastic face, and lurched towards her.

Anna bolted.

Geoff and Tony roared. And John laughed, too. But the laugh that came from him chased after the girl with the rattle of old, dry paper.

Stu watched without expression from the bar. He watched as Geoff ordered another round of Black and Tans and suggested a midnight raid on the streets around the art college. Stu watched as the sloshed trio finalized their plans and left Ye Cracke together, singing, "Anna, Anna, give me yer answer, do! I'm half crazy, all fer the luv of you!" Their "whoops" could be heard, even after the door slammed behind them.

The next morning when the Liverpool College of Art canteen opened for business, its stock was strangely enhanced. Tucked among the standard tablets, bottles of ink, fat erasers, and artists' brushes were street signs, shop shingles, one bulky traffic light, and quite a few expensive, collectable doorknobs. The purloined goods lay neatly displayed on the canteen shelves and artfully hung on the canteen walls. But how the assorted trinkets got there was a mystery. No one seemed to know.

Of course, Stu knew. He knew, but never offered comment. He accepted John as John...a package deal.

Stu accepted the days when John was tight-lipped and monosyllabic and the late evenings when, blind drunk, John tripped over himself, lashing out in dark anger. He accepted the moments when John ran in, berserk with excitement – animated over some "big break" The Quarry Men had on the burner. And Stu accepted the times when John sat quietly and smoked and talked about the future.

For years, Mimi had tried to reform John. George had worked to emulate him. Paul had attempted to polish him up a bit. Arthur Ballard had longed to inspire him. Thelma Pickles had tried to forget him. And most people had scrambled to avoid him.

But Stu simply accepted him.

John was hard to love. Tirelessly self-destructive and relationship-suicidal, he fought his way out of friendships.

But Stu wouldn't permit it. He was John's friend.

And he thought that perhaps the quiet, sincere Cynthia Powell might be John's friend as well. She had all the earmarks.

The raid on the Liverpool shops that added new produce to the art college canteen actually occurred. This information was given to me in detail by Helen Andersen. Many thanks, Helen! This evaluation of Stu's friendship parallels both Ray Coleman's account and Pauline Sutcliffe's. All conversations are conjecture.

Early May 1959
Liverpool College of Art
Liverpool

June Furlong clipped down Falkner Street. If anyone, living in the fastidious line of Liverpool 8 brick row houses, had at that moment glanced outside his front window, he would have paused to admire her, to enjoy her natural elegance, her unconscious arrogance. He would have smiled to himself as the young model swayed along the sidewalk; June Furlong was smile-worthy. Poised, purpose-filled, and unusually, strikingly lovely, she was an amazing woman. All heads turned when she passed.

The willful gusts off the Queen's Dock wisped her dark hair loose from its French twist, but June didn't mind. *"No matter that, no matter,"* she would have said, *"It's all better free and natural, isn't it? I mean, it's got character, hasn't it?"* Others were completely disheveled by the Mersey blasts; June found the wind's styling artistic. Nothing about her ever looked amiss; she turned circumstance into fashion.

Almost as if she knew this – and she did – the twenty-nine year old let a Mona Lisa curl taunt her lips, and she lifted her head a little higher against the bluster. She checked her watch. *Half-one...perfect.* She was right on schedule. Life Class began at two. She still had a half-hour to spare.

June disliked tardiness. She disliked anything haphazard. One thing that her time in London had taught her was the importance of conducting oneself professionally. And just because she'd reluctantly returned to Liverpool to assist her aging parents did not mean that June had relinquished her cosmopolitan outlook. She was still a sought-after, big city model with a keen eye on success. Her standards were high and would not be compromised or provincialised, even for a moment.

Besides, this stint in Liverpool was only temporary. In three months, she would resume to her modeling career in London and on the Continent. Things would return to normal. She would be petitioned by the masters to pose for them again. Frank Auerbach, Lucian Foy, Francis Bacon...they hadn't forgotten June. They were simply waiting for June's life to get back on track, for her family business to be settled.

But for now, June found herself in Liverpool, the place where she'd learned to skate and move gracefully against a battling wind. She was home again living in the shadow of the art college and posing for artists she'd known for years.

It was icy yet in Liverpool. Though the daffs that June had planted in her parents' small courtyard garden were in full bloom, it was still winter. As she hurried across Hope Street, the wind rushed up to meet her, swirls curling around her legs, playing havoc with her skirt and her model's walk. But June pretended not to notice, disciplining herself to cross effortlessly towards the imposing, grey stone building that was Liverpool College of Art. She raised her chin and strengthened her stride.

"A bit more than exhilarating, this! Yes!" she thought to herself. Never once in the months she had spent in London or abroad had she missed the chilling blasts of her old hometown. Liverpudlians were warm and friendly, but the Mersey winds could be breathtakingly cruel. And although June lived only three blocks from the college, her daily walks were lessons in self-control and dignity.

"Junie-June! Hail, fellow-well-met, though fellow thou never wert!"

It's that madman, John Lennon, June thought, smiling, waving him off. She was intent on her destination and had no time for Lennon's shenanigans. But his headlong, fire engine stride soon put him abreast of her as they approached the college's front entrance arch.

"Hullo, John! Hullo!"

"Glad you got to see me, luv," he teased, opening the door for the famous model, "especially since I've just completed it, y'know."

"Yes, yes...what?" She threw him a glance. She had no idea what on earth the boy was "on about" this time.

"It's a bleedin' masterpiece of dramatic craft, Junie June."

"Did you say, *craft?*" she teased, raising one perfectly plucked eyebrow as she removed her scarf and wrapper with swift, efficient movements.

"That's what all the critics claim." He sniffed as if offended.

John followed June upstairs like an excited pup. He dashed this way and that as they climbed to the second floor, his narrative never slowing down. June only deciphered key phrases in the babble: terms like "literary greatness," "George Bernard Shaw" and "standin' ovation." He raved on about costumes and scripts and curtain calls.

"Oh, I'm on to it now! A play, *a play*! You've done a dramatization! Yes, yes, lovely." She caught on at last. "Finished it, you say? Well, all right, then, great. That's lovely. You got it done. Good job."

John stopped and looked down his nose. "You've a lousy lack of curiosity, y'know." He acted wounded. "You'd think you'd want to be the first to read the script, as it were...to say you saw it 'before it was'...before it becomes legend 'n all that."

"Well all right, yes, yes," she laughed softly. "But we all know you'll show it to me anyway, right? Yes, yes, there's little chance of escapin' that. Little chance of that. We all know you, John Lennon."

"I don't show me work to just anyone," he lied. "You'd have to be part of the production, as it were...a part of the insider's group and all that rigmarole, Junie-June."

June "pffed' through her lips in a Liverpudlian scoff. "Well then, not likely I'll ever see it, then. No, no, I'm no actress, John. No, no, certainly not. Not me. No."

"Costume mistress, then." Determination was written all over his face. "It's a revamp of Cinderella, y'know – and as such, we're in need of a manager of bustles, bangles, beads, and braids...a manager with a sense of style and fashion in all things thespian."

"Go on!" She brushed past him into the classroom, hanging her wrapper on the rickety, oak coat stand. "I'll not be mistress to anyone, will I? No, no, of course not. No."

"Such pathetic purity in one so 'well-thought-out,'" John cluckingly teased.

June smiled in spite of herself.

Without warning, John collapsed to his knees dramatically, clasping his hands together and yelling at the top of his lungs, "Lady of the Wardrobe, Queen of Ceremonious Costumes, Duchess of Fancy Dress...be what you will, pick yer own title, call it what you want, famous model. Only say you'll help us out! Say you'll favour us with a bauble or two and a bit of your own style of the Continent, as it were."

"Costumes, is it?" she smiled. "And for Cinderella, y'say? Right, all right. Not a terrible idea, not bad, not bad..." She considered it.

"No one else is as perfectly modeled for it as you, are they?" John punned.

"Well, all right...could do...might find some things here and there."

"Or there and here."

"Yes, all right, yes, could do. And besides, I'd hate to stand in the way of dramatic invention, right? Yes, yes, dramatic invention! Because it's good – this play? It's great, isn't it?"

"It's one of a kind, luv." John tapped the hand-written script inside his coat. "It's 'the thing in which to catch the conscience of the king.'"

"Oh, the king, the king...well, all right then, yes! And no wonder it's so great, this play." June began to arrange her hair a bit in the small oval mirror on the wall. She held the silver hairpins in her teeth and reshaped the French twist, leaving one dark wisp loosely curling along her long, graceful neckline.

"So, you're in, are ya?" John eyed her with interest.

"All right, then. I mean, why not? What with the king and all. And it's great – this play. First rate. Can't miss."

"Ah, you're comparable June!" John jumped to his feet. "Priceful, that's what you've always been!"

"Go on, John Lennon." She always pronounced his name as one word. "Get back to Ye Cracke with your odd sods and bods. I've no time for you. Work to do, you know. Always work. Go on! Go on, then. I'm in."

June entered the small dressing room just off the Life Class, and closed the door firmly in the boy's face. She secured the brass lock with a flip of her wrist, but John's voice still echoed on the other side. "You'll absolutely love workin' with us, Junie-June! We're a quality act, y'know…the chance of a lifetime, as it were!"

June smiled and shook her head. John Lennon always amused her. In some ways, he was a lot like her. He swaggered through life, doing exactly as he pleased, insisting on making the slightest fantasies into reality and doing it "all-out." John never gave an inch when he wanted something, and neither did June. They were kindred spirits.

She empathized with his brashness and envied his boyish joy in "playing make believe." John still had one foot in innocence. He was a one part Peter Pan, one part Lost Boy, and one part sinister Captain James Hook. John was imaginative, uncompromising, improbable, and always determined.

June slipped on the soft blue belted robe that she always wore for Life Class and took one last check in the mirror beside her. June was not vain, but she was not blind to her own beauty, either. The high cheekbones, the classic, oval face, the soft, expressive eyes all conspired to make her remarkable. June flashed a quick smile at her reflection, and then turned, looking back over her shoulder in her signature pose. *Yes, yes, great. All right, then. That'll do, that'll do,* she told herself. *Enough of this Cinderella nonsense and make-believe. Time to be serious. Time to be about work, then.*

And checking her watch, June unsnapped the lock and opened the door. She stepped into the Life studio. It was exactly two o'clock.

****

Life Class was the one and perhaps only place in which John was absolutely serious. Under Stu's influence, John bubbled down to a simmer. He sketched with intensity, saving the wisecracks and cackles for Nicolas Horsefield's art history lectures.

Tweed jacket tossed aside, John rolled up his sleeves, hiked one jeaned leg onto the stool's second rung, and went to work. With back hunched, eyes squinted, and neck craned forward, his head weaved up and down as he hovered over his sketchpad. John was atypically quiet.

Everyone was quiet: the ordinarily bubbly June Harry; the ever-talkative Ann Mason; rakish Tony Carricker; John Hague, and of course, Stu. With an artist's bitten bottom lip, Stu sketched June Furlong with fervour, capturing the inherent motion of her life-energy in quick, broken lines.

Professor Teddy Griffiths moved slowly, a marshal reviewing his troops. He suggested an amendment here, an addition there. Sometimes he merely cleared his throat in vague disapproval or stood and watched an ingénue artist stumbling onto something rather fantastic. But it all happened in silence. The sounds of pencils scritching and the low mumble of Griffiths's terse comments were the only undercurrents in the stillness.

It was an atmosphere John respected. The uselessness of art history and things past or art theory and things yet to come were forgotten. Here, surrounded by other artists, John found creative expression not superfluous but necessary. In the quiet of Room 71, something was being accomplished – something that mattered.

June Furlong indulged in the imperceptible movement of a hinted smile. It was satisfying to watch the fourteen aspiring masters at work. Some, like Stu, would no doubt take their rightful places in history, remembered for paintings that haunted dreams. Others, the hopeful bourgeoisie, would find commercial pursuits that paid their mortgages. Their art would become furtive – scribbled on memo pads while answering long-distance telephone calls or doodled in margins during long-winded committee meetings. Art school veterans, they would "do a bit" now and again for some charity benefit, but for them, art would become frivolity.

June stared at the squinting Lennon. *What will his fate be – John Lennon? How will he fare in the 'when-I-grow-up-world'? Right now,* June mused, *he seems hell-bent on being an artist, but how much of that is actually John, and how much is Stuart Sutcliffe?*

June's body rested on the powerful ball of her right foot. She held her body completely motionless while her brain raced ahead endlessly. *Besides,* she thought, *John Lennon's quite good at a great many things these days...puns and poetry and music – even this Cinderella concoction he's cooked up. Art's far from the lad's sole obsession. He's got irons in every fire, has John.*

June knew almost everything that happened on the art school campus; nothing slipped past her critical eye, and she was well aware of John's lunchtime jam sessions in Room 21. She knew the boy was mad about rock'n'roll and was wildly immersed in the Merseyside music scene, but her practical nature saw little future in it. Skiffle or rock'n'roll bands in Liverpool were as common as football fans and catarrh. It wasn't something to build a life on.

Yes, yes, he's all absorbed in that group of his, June never moved a muscle, *but it's hopeless – that band. Hundreds of bands fill the streets these days. I mean, you literally can't go anywhere without hearing a drum* pounding or a guitar tuning up from some window. They're everywhere – these bands! Absolutely everywhere!

The chill in the room turned June's fingers to ice, but her mind wandered to warmer places – the warmth of southern France, the dry, hot summer of 1951. Her memories of Perpignan and its tall, golden, European grasses ran freely into the watercolour aquamarine of the Mediterranean, a mind-sketch, a lifeline to her now. They insulated her against the ever-present cold, the wind that permitted Northern seagulls to spread their wings and simply float between the Mersey buildings.

June's eyes wandered over the room and her train of thought returned to John Lennon. *A lad hungry for fame, desperate for fame, for some big hit song. All right, then. But what would John do with fame if he got it? How would he handle it – this thing he craves? It's not easy – fame...not easy at all,* June mused. *Not a bit what John Lennon imagines it to be.*

June knew, first-hand, the pressures that the famous shouldered. Her days posing for Frank Auerbach were vivid still. Though they'd remained friends, Auerbach and she had quarreled endlessly. *Great artists, great sacrifices,* June thought. *I wonder if John Lennon could handle a life like that. It's no easy road, is it?*

"Two hours," Teddy Griffiths announced, and half the room jumped. The students blinked rapidly, rolled their heads side to side, and shrugged their shoulders. "Pencils down; heads up, please. Let's see what it is you've been up to."

June wrapped herself demurely once again in her welcome blue robe, watching with amusement as she began to appear in odd shapes and at varying angles on the assorted sketchpads all around her. Her likeness was recognizable, but the renderings were, for the most part, amateurish. In a few, she could clearly recognize herself as the artist's model, but none of her personality was there. Other drawings were passionate and expressive, but technically inaccurate.

"And this, Mr. Lennon," Teddy Griffiths barked, "exactly what is *this,* then?"

The class collectively held its breath. Lennon's sketches could be bawdy, a Northern man's vision of the female form. Or his drawing might hold brutality, a quick glimpse into the dark disillusionment through which he viewed humanity.

Griffiths turned the sketchpad for all to see. Stu smiled. Someone coughed nervously. June quickly covered her mouth with her long, elegant fingers, and stared out the window.

John's creation was precise, accurate, and almost life-like. It was artistic, yet exact in form. Under Stu's influence – his insistence on simple, expressive lines – John had captured the subject poised in motion. He had created, in realistic detail, a close-up view of June Furlong's watch, the only article of clothing she had been wearing. The timepiece was so real; they could almost hear it tick. And the room was so quiet, they almost did.

It was a Liverpudlian work, straightforward and candid, swaddled in humour. It defied and yet fulfilled the letter of the law. John had indeed, as assigned, sketched June Furlong…one arm, one wrist, one tiny watch.

"Mr. Lennon," Terry Griffiths sighed, "you wouldn't be wasting our time, now would you?"

John looked slowly at his picture and then back at the man who stood challenging his intentions. "I think we can all see," he said flatly to the instructor, "that I haven't wasted it. I've reproduced it – down to the last second, as it were."

Someone suppressed a giggle. Someone cleared a throat. Bodies squirmed uncomfortably in the absence of laughter. Only Stu smiled openly while John grinned his Cheshire grin.

"Well then," Teddy Griffiths tossed the sketchpad back on John's desk and walked briskly to the front of the room, "according to Mr. Lennon's watch, it's long past four. Class dismissed."

The room emptied instantly, a clattering mob forming around John, vying for position. Teddy Griffiths and June watched the boy retreat, all wisecracks and sharp retorts to those who challenged him, all banter and wit to those he favoured. As John rallied his troops for another ale-soaked evening in Rice Street, the controversial sketch fluttered to rest in a tall, mesh trash bin. And the room hushed again.

Teddy Griffiths walked over and snatched up sketch, holding it at arm's length.

"Great pity, isn't it?" He turned to June. "Just look at this, Miss Furlong. Sorry to say, the boy's work's not half bad, is it?"

June smiled noncommittally, ever the diplomat in controversial moments. She liked John, but she worked for the college. Tact was needed here – tact or silence.

"Oh well, then," Griffiths let it go. "What a waste of a life…what an utter waste of life that boy is! He may call himself an artist and fancy himself like his friend, Mr. Sutcliffe, but Lennon's little more than a clown, playing daily to the masses, seeking the fleeting applause of the crowd. I'd like to see him try to make a living off that, for what it's worth! I seriously doubt his dog-and-pony panache will ever pay the bills."

"Oh, I don't know," June said softly, "he has this wonderful powerhouse of confidence, has John Lennon."

"Hmpfff!" Teddy Griffiths tossed the sketch back into the trash. "John Lennon isn't a bit as great as he thinks he is."

And June gave a slight nod that could mean anything.

****

Ye Cracke was not just convenient; it was conducive to everything a college student might want "to conduce." Warm – almost over-warm – sleepy, and ale drowsy, it was a haven of lotus-like forgetfulness where deadlines, exams, and projects could be obliterated.

The pub was tiny and close: a stand-up bar of dark, battered wood and a second room lined with chiseled oak benches to which pub tables had been introduced. One barley twist leg table almost touched the next, and privacy was at a minimum. Camaraderie was the whole object of the place. Everything and everyone overflowed.

John liked the immediacy of the pub. Only what happened in Ye Cracke mattered. Nothing "out there" seeped in through the thick, plastered, mustard-coloured walls. In Ye Cracke, the world was on hold.

It might have been a tavern straight out of Chaucer, a gathering place for tellers of tales. A tired artist, straight off four days' work on a hand-sewn, cloth banner, nodded off against the far wall, and no one appeared to see him there. Several old plates on the high decorative chair rail had been knocked off and broken, but no one scolded or wept over them. It was of little consequence. No one was anxious about anything.

Here, on an ordinary day, a student could indolently sweep over a newspaper – reading the headlines and ignoring the details – while his girl leaned against his shoulder, her legs stretched the length of the bench, her boots spilling tiny piles of crusted mud onto the weathered oak. A cluster of competitors pitching darts in the small centre room could insult each other without disturbing a table full of businessmen, bickering over quick lagers between meetings. Ordinarily, the room was shared with "one-for-all" ambiance. But not today.

It was opening day – opening day and closing night – for the one-time only production of John Lennon's irreverent "Cinderella," a farcical comedy in three buffoon-filled acts. Today Ye Cracke was more than a pub. It had been commandeered as a "green room."

A dozen or so "actors and actresses" had converged for some rounds of liquid confidence to slake the pre-show jitters. Their costumes alone, provided as promised by costume mistress June Furlong, were enough to set the pub on its ear. No one could politely ignore them.

Geoff Mohammed paraded about in a hot-pink corset, his "muscles" protruding though every diamond-shaped, ribboned opening. Trimmed in a bevy of yellowed lace, Geoff had, indeed, become an unusual stepsister. But in spite of the ribbons and frills, he was still handsome. There was no denying it.

John was loud and leading the fray. Decked out in June's grandmother's blue silk gown, he was a garden of outrageous pink and red blossoms on the move. Skirts swishing through the pub, John wobbled on heels and tossed his shoulder-length hair back with dramatic effect, accosting everyone with his falsetto query, "Seen the prince, have you, luv? Where's that cad when you least reject him?"

Only the prince himself, John Chase, sat quietly on a pub stool, looking as green as his emerald silk breeches. He gingerly nursed one, singular ale as John and Geoff downed a dozen. Chase hardly moved, and he spoke in one-word sentences while Lennon and Mohammed larked about as if they were on Spanish holiday. Wishing he were even a little like them, the prince took deep breaths and wiped his palms dry.

How'd I let John Lennon talk me into bein' in this drama at all – much less playing the role of Prince Charming? It's past all understanding – this. It's lunacy.

Chase had never done anything theatrical before; singing aloud in church was the boldest "performance" he'd ever attempted. He wished he were anywhere else but here; he wished he were anyone but himself.

"And how's charmin' Prince Charmin' then?" John batted his false eyelashes in true, ugly stepsister fashion and leaned on his elbows next to Chase.

"Go on, Lennon. I've enough on my mind, thanks to you."

"You're welcome," John flagged down the barmaid and raised his falsetto voice a notch, "What we have here, dearie, is a man all green. Have you noticed it, then?"

The girl hardly reacted. There was no love lost between John and her. And drunk and in drag, he was even less likeable.

"So why not givvus a bevy, eh luv?" The ugly stepsister voice whined on. "It'd do him a world of good, y'know. It'd…"

"No, no, *no*, definitely not! I've had enough." John Chase swung around, his back to the bar, his green silk costume gathering and wrinkling as he turned. "What's more *you've* had enough, too, Lennon!" He watched John knock back yet another lager that someone had paid for. "You 'n Mohammed won't be able to gin up a single line! And June Harry? She's teeterin' like the bleedin' tower of Pisa over there. One shove, and she's over! Your whole cast is up to the gills! And look!" He tapped his wristwatch. "The play's in less than an hour!"

"How's that?" John pretended to be shocked. "Last call, then! Last call, one and all!" he shouted to his cast. "Drink up, mine thespians! Drink up! We're down to the wire, jadies and lents! One fer the road, and all that break-a-leg shite."

"Ugh! How'd I get dragged into this?" Chase mumbled.

"Drink up, son." John had no sympathy for the fidgety, fretful prince, but he silently applauded his selection of Chase for the role. It had been a brilliant bit of character casting. While the other actors would, no doubt, bumble through what they could remember of the Lennonesque script, Prince Charming would emerge stuffy and arrogant – a disapproving royal in an overdressed, rented costume. Stone sober and stoic with stage fright,

Chase would be anything but suave. He would be hilariously ludicrous.

Julia would've fuggin' loved this! John smiled.

The thought came quick and unbidden. It jabbed and retreated, taking John's breath away.

He raised his eyes to the mirror in front of him, looking into the face of the ugly stepsister he was supposed to be. But he wasn't ugly at all. The auburn hair, the dangling earrings, the impish smile – he was Julia.

There was no escaping it. Even in disguise, even in Ye Cracke, even in the most jovial of moods, the pain had somehow found him.

John slammed down his empty mug and ordered another. Then he cancelled that, and instead, ordered two.

****

Cinderella was smashed. In a sooty dust cap and apron, she tottered around backstage collapsing into the makeshift backdrops, giggling as if she'd already been to the ball. Her breath was distilled. June Harry was drunk.

Her ugly stepsisters were perfect companions. Muttering obscenities and extemporaneous variations on their lines, Geoff and John snickered and waited for the curtain to go up. Only John Chase stood apart, trying to endure them as he quietly rehearsed his lines.

The show began – with most of the cast swimming in bravado and impromptu. Their lines were off the cuff; their actions, surprises. John Chase hardly knew when to speak or what to say, so altered was the script. Nothing could be anticipated. It was all up for grabs.

About the middle of the first act, the last thread of control frayed, and what happened happened so quickly that no one saw it coming.

Dead centre, three or four rows back, sat June Harry's former boyfriend – a boyfriend who'd "vanished more or less" just after Easter, some five weeks ago. In all that time, he'd never rung her up, never offered an explanation. Yet there he was – right in the middle of the art school auditorium.

Cinderella spotted him, just as her fairy godmother entered, prepared to make magic with words and wands. But the magic was quickly tabled.

June Harry stepped boldly out of character and stumbled to the front of the stage. She pointed an accusing finger and bellowed, "Yeeeeeewwww!" Her eyes were blazing. "Y'pathetic, rotten, fuggin' louse, yew!"

"H-Hi, June," the cad stammered. "Um…good to see you…I mean…you're lookin' awfully…"

With a quick leap from the tiny stage and a mad rush that no one expected, June was on him. She shrieked and delivered a walloping blow, a jaw punch that sounded as painful as it felt. The shocked, Canadian lover reached for his face and wobbled unsteadily; Cinderella had a powerful right hook.

Up on stage, the ugly stepsisters began to cackle uncontrollably, stamping their feet – whistling and applauding, and motioning for the audience to cheer as well. Delighted with this bit of real-life drama, the crowd rumbled with catcalls and whoops.

But Cinderella had no ear for the audience. In an angry whisk of skirts and graphic language, she was out the door, out of the building – retreating with not a look over her shoulder. She left no parting lines to end the play, and this time, no glass slipper.

On stage, Prince Charming stood gaping after her, his face and neck hived in various shades – his lines forgotten, his eyes wide and horrified. Just glancing at him, John and Geoff were beside themselves all over again. They doubled with laughter. Geoff collapsed to his knees. John yelled, "Go after her, lad! She's yer dream come true, isn't she?"

And the audience began to heckle the stunned prince as well. It was a good five minutes before the crowd fell to a murmur, before John stepped forward to offer the final soliloquy, albeit a brief one.

"And...as y'can see...they all *lived*..." John pronounced, taking a sweeping bow in his borrowed ball gown, "ever after." He shuffled a little dance step and offered a toothy grin.

The crowd sprang to its feet, this time cheering spontaneously for the man of the moment, the organizer of it all, John Lennon. John cavorted and pulled faces as they applauded. He grabbed Geoff for a quick waltz around the stage and almost tumbling over, the two exited, stage left.

"Fantastic, that!" A second year student from Litherland was still laughing.

"Who would've fuggin' believed it?"

"Incredible!"

"June Harry! She's all right, isn't she?"

"Was that real...or was it planned?"

"Couldn't have been staged...the wack toppled, didn't he?"

They began to file out in double lines toward the rear exit. Purses, umbrellas, and book bags nudged. Progress was slow.

"And what about Geoff Mohammed, then...he was dead good, wasn't he?"

"As usual."

"He's a natural – Geoff."

"Right! In that satin corset! Cor!"

"Yeah, and John Lennon...he wrote the whole fuggin' thing, y'know! Dreamed it all up, did Lennon."

"Borrowed the costumes..."

"Choreographed it all, if y'can call it that."

"He's mad, I believe."

"Yeah, mad."

"Everyone says that."

"Nah, you're wrong," another Woolton student piped up. "He's just…a clown, that's all. Just a clown."

The sobering voice cut into their cheerful praise. It was Thelma Pickles. The recent and public separation from John was still fresh for her; it still hurt a bit to be in the same room with him, to see him guffawing and pretending to be jovial when she knew he wasn't.

"Oh, Lennon's a natural," she went on, "and you're right, he's the 'supreme jester.' But you're wrong to laugh at him – even though he goads you to…If y'ask me, he's the ultimate Pagliacci – John. The only difference between the two of them is, John never wipes off the disguise."

"That's awfully dark, isn't it?" A demure girl in a taupe matched sweater set cut her eyes at Thelma.

"It's brighter than it could be," Thelma answered the girl she knew as Cynthia Powell. "In fact, it's generous."

"Well…I've talked to him now and again," Cynthia mustered her courage, "and I've always found him…genuinely amusing."

"Why don't you get to know him a bit better, luv?" Thelma smiled sadly. "And then get back to me."

"I might do." Cynthia bit her lip and filed out with the others. But she wasn't quite sure how to go about that, really. The group surrounding him now, congratulating him on the stage, constantly insulated John. And Cynthia didn't know how to get past his barriers.

June Furlong has told me this story many times in great detail, and Helen Anderson validated the details repeated here. The only element imagined is Cynthia's and Thelma's presence at the play. No one has ever mentioned that they attended the event. Since Cynthia "had a crush" on John, it's very likely that she did. But I simply don't know if that's true.

June has read this chapter and made any corrections necessary. She assures me that this is exactly how the event transpired. The conversations, of course, are conjecture.

Late May 1959
Liverpool College of Art
Liverpool

Cynthia thumbed slowly through a stack of 45's, looking for something to play. She was sick of "someday songs," of "what if – dream songs." Dreaming was the last thing she wanted to do right now.

This was it – the end of the term, the end of the school year. But despite her efforts to the contrary, John Lennon was still just a dream, and the illusion was becoming depressing. Cynthia craved a shot of reality.

The "End of the Term Bash" had been organized rather spontaneously, and the lack of decorations or proper refreshments attested to the students' hurried neglect. Crammed into a classroom with only a scuffed-up, portable record player and several stacks of discs bearing the names of their owners, the party-goers furnished their own Cokes or gingers and supplanted enthusiasm for party trappings. Determined to celebrate somehow, they had pushed back desks, shoved easels aside, opened a few windows, and set a turntable in motion.

Cynthia was similarly determined. This was it...the last day of the term, the last – very last – chance she'd have to let John know.

She walked towards the paint-splotched table where an Everly Brothers' tune was spinning to a finale, and she lifted the needle from the record. She picked up another stack of discs.

What to play? What to play? What would send the message? What would work? Cynthia tucked her chestnut hair nervously back behind her ears and began screening the new 45's, holding them close to her nose.

"She's dead obvious, isn't she?" Geoff elbowed John, nodding in Cynthia's direction, "Look at her, wack! She's been lookin' at *you* all afternoon, y'know!"

"Give yer chin a rest, son." John was not above Scouse.

"Go on, Lennon. Give'er a tumble! She's ripe for the...pluckin', so t'speak."

Ann Mason frowned at her boyfriend, but Geoff only laughed her off, giving John a playful shove towards the shy Miss Powell. "Go on," he repeated. What's keepin' ya, mate? Why're y'still over here when she's over there?"

Cynthia could feel John's eyes on her. As crowded as they were in this room-meant-for-forty, she could feel his stare. Cynthia stood tall, tummy in, breasts pressed against her blouse, and she licked her lips as she'd see Marilyn Monroe do in those movies Mum despised.

"This is it," she whispered to herself, selecting a record.

But the sound of her heart pounding was all she could really hear. She wasn't sure if the Victrola ground out The Teddy Bears' hit love ballad or Chuck Berry's latest rocker. Turning the volume up a notch, Cynthia let the needle work its magic.

"D'ya wanna dance this one, then?" John's nasal voice sounded at her left shoulder. Cynthia turned very slowly, afraid to break the spell and turn the coach into a pumpkin. Blushing hot, then sweeping cold to blush again, she nodded without saying a thing. They moved onto the dance floor.

Geoff pinched Ann, smirking over John's success. Ann huffed and smacked him, both of them staring at the dancing anomaly in amazement. Helen Anderson stopped telling the story she was telling to gape openly.

Folding her arms protectively beneath her breast, Thelma Pickles looked down and then looked away. *Poor little fool*, she thought. *Poor innocent, little fool. She's up against it now. Well, I wish her only the best – Cynthia Powell. She'll need it.*

Cynthia saw none of this. She closed her eyes and melted into the smell of scallops, chips, and cigs. She edged her hand a little tighter around John's shoulder and barely touched the back of his neck, the spot where she'd seen Helen touching him a few weeks ago. She breathed in waves, almost as if she'd been crying. And never once did her eyes open.

But John saw it all – the looks of incredulity and disapproval. *Miss Powell and Lennon! Hoylake and Merseyside!* He could feel the room gawking. He pulled Cynthia even tighter to his chest, wrapping his arms around her back in a way that was far too familiar. But Cynthia never squirmed. In fact, she seemed to relax, and it gave him confidence.

"Not much of a gatherin', is it?" John searched for even stilted conversation to break the current that raced through them both. He pulled away a bit and looked down the length of his nose at her.

Cynthia smiled, but couldn't think of anything clever to say. She just stared and waited for him to go on.

"Would y'fancy goin' out with me then?" John fumbled for words. *What the fuggin'ell?* He'd never found words a problem before. Now nothing sounded right.

"I-I'm awfully sorry," Cynthia couldn't believe she was saying this. *How stupid to be saying this*! "I'm actually…engaged…to-to an old school chum of mine from Hoylake."

What?! John was completely floored. And moreover, he was

humiliated. He immediately released her with an imperceptible shove that he meant and she felt, but no one else observed. Then he raised his voice for dramatic projection and barked, "I didn't ask you to fuggin' marry me, now did I?"

The noise he made as he walked away was supposed to be laughter. And he was across the room so quickly that Cynthia had no chance to reply.

It was almost as if it had never happened at all. Except, of course, that it had.

And calling out to Helen, John was gone.

Still rooted to the dance floor, blinking back tears, and trying to find something to do with her arms, Cynthia couldn't move, even to save face. She stood alone, wanting to call it all back, wanting to amend the last five minutes, wanting to make it right with John.

But the record – whatever it was – scritched in the playout grooves and sounded to Cynthia like a chorus of mocking tongues clucking disapproval. Phyllis McKenzie lifted the needle and looked at her friend.

"C'mon Cynthia," Phyllis commanded. "Don't just stand there."

"Why not?" Cynthia's voice cracked.

"Because we're goin' after him. That's why not."

Cynthia's face was slack with bewilderment. *Follow him? To a pub? Unaccompanied? Tag alongs?* She blinked a few times. She looked at Phyl through a haze.

"Don't look so rattled. You heard me."

"To Ye Cracke?" Cynthia took the hand Phyllis offered.

"That's where *he's* gone, hasn't he?" Phyllis had Cynthia in tow. It was almost a tug of war.

Cynthia pulled to a stop. "I can't do it, Phyl. I simply can't."

"You can, and you will. Look Cynthia, we've been good girls all year, haven't we? We lived by the rules and played by the book – Grade A and all that. And what's it gotten us? No someone for me. No John for you. Time to change the strategy, then – time to do an about face, luv."

She gave Cynthia's arm a yank and began moving her towards the hallway. This time Cynthia was coerced.

The nippy evening air of late spring cut into their thin party clothes. Cynthia wished she had her jacket. She shivered as Phyllis tightened her grip and moved along quickly, eager to reach the warmth of the tiny pub just ahead.

A cluster of giggling Liverpool 8 school children, still in their uniforms, filled the sidewalk, engaging in some blend of hopscotch and marbles on the corner of Hope and Rice. They hardly noticed when the girls passed. But two older boys with slingshots saw them and paused in their pursuit of a streetlight, waiting until Phyllis and Cynthia navigated out of sight.

A group of professors, on their way to an evening session in School

Lane, moved past them, deep in conversation, shoulder to shoulder, sketch pads under their arms, and the scent of vanilla drifting from their pipes. Phyllis smiled and nodded, but hardly got a murmur in return.

Cynthia was equally quiet.

Even in the fading light, Phyllis could see that Cynthia was completely expressionless, perhaps stunned, gathering courage for her entrance into the pub. *Perhaps,* Phyllis surmised, *she's manufacturing clever things to say.* But it was none of those things.

Cynthia was reliving the last half hour, rewinding and replaying the muddle of events. She was seeing it all again, and hating herself for running from what she wanted most.

"What *happened* back there, then?" Phyllis had tried to respect Cynthia's privacy, but what were friends for anyway?

"I..." Cynthia's voice quavered, "I told him I was engaged, Phyl!"

"You're not serious? You're not bleedin' serious, are you? After waitin' all this time for a bit of His Majesty's attention – you *never*?"

"I did. He asked me out, and I said I was engaged."

"Unbelievable!" Phyllis shook her head. "Well, you've got a lot of makin' up to do, then – a lot of lovely ground to cover and not nearly enough time to do it!"

"I can't, Phyl. I'm just not up to it. I...I say all the wrong things when he's around. I become an ostrich. I hide my head in the sand when he's there. John Lennon trips me up."

Ye Cracke was only a few steps away. Its Tudor walls caught the last glint of late evening sun. In a few minutes, it would be dark. Phyllis dropped her grip on Cynthia's arm and turned to fluff her friend's hair.

"Well, you *can't* be an ostrich tonight," Phyllis gave Cynthia's cheeks a playful squeeze. "Whatever it takes...if you need a drink, if you need to pretend you're someone else, if you need a swift kick in the rear – whatever it takes, now's the time. You *have* to do it, Cynthia."

"But it's just that..."

Phyllis gave her a quick hug. "He's just a man – a Northern man at that. He's not a mystic, and he's not a monster. He's just a chap. Normal through and through. And that's the truth of it, Cynthia. That's all there is to it."

"And how would *you* know, anyway?" Cynthia pouted a bit. She resented the inference that Phyllis knew John better than she did.

"Bus." Phyllis pulled her towards the door. "We ride the same bus – John and I."

"So," Cynthia shrugged.

"So I'm tellin' you," Phyllis opened the heavy, black, lacquered portal, "John's just a bloke and not a bad one at that." She motioned Cynthia in. "As me mum always says on occasions like this, 'Time and tide wait for no man.' And they wait for no woman, either. Get in there, girl."

The publicans were all huddled inside as expected. They'd entrenched themselves at a corner table near the rear wall, and John was sitting astride the back of a chair in an impenetrable posture. He glanced at Cynthia briefly and then looked away. But he knew she was there, and she knew he knew.

Smoke flooded the room in dry-ice surrealism, and the last thin vestiges of sunlight illuminated hundreds of dust specks dancing wildly. Cynthia shielded her eyes and followed Phyllis to a table across from John's. Phyllis directed her to sit. After a quick word of whispered confidence, Phyl walked over to the bar to order, leaving Cynthia alone to fend for herself.

"Relax. It's all right, y'know." It was Michael Isaacson. He patted Cynthia's folded hands. They were sheer ice.

"Hmmm? Oh, sorry, Michael. What'd you say? I'm off in another world it seems."

"I said, relax," he smiled. "Relax! He's not worth it, is he?"

"Who?"

"You know who." He offered her a cigarette, and Cynthia took it in spite of herself. Phyllis returned with her hands full and quickly lowered two heavy pints to the table.

"Get you somethin', then, Michael?" she offered.

"Got one. Ta." He raised the glass, then took a sip. "Y'know, I was just tellin' Cynthia here that he's not worth it." Michael flashed his warm, friends-forever smile.

"But that's not entirely true, Michael," Phyllis said.

"You're kiddin', of course."

"No," Phyllis settled into her chair. "I'm not. I think John Lennon's...all right."

His brow furrowed.

"I truly do," she said, with gathering conviction. "He's genuine, is John...and when he wants to be, generous to a fault."

"*Generous!* Lennon's never a bleedin' pound to his name! He's a known beggar from here to Chester and back!"

Phyllis took a sip of her lager, then lowered her voice, "As you may or may not know, Michael, things have been rather... uh, meager lately...I mean, I haven't exactly had millions to squander, as it were."

"Oh...sorry."

Phyllis waved it off and went on. "But this one day John sees me sittin' in the canteen havin' a smoke, and I wasn't havin' lunch. I couldn't afford it, that's all. So he sits down and says, 'Where's yer brown baggie, Phillip?' He calls me that now and then – Phillip."

"Right. What then?" It was Cynthia who was interested now.

"So," Phyllis smiled, "I flipped him an answer that put him off a bit."

Michael smiled.

"But a coupla days later, John sees me again, and he starts sortin' me out...askin' why I'm not havin' lunch 'n all that."

"Um-hum." Cynthia leaned forward.

"So," Phyllis took a deep breath, "so just to hush him up, I had to tell him I was usin' all my money for bus fare, to and from school. I mean, you can skip a meal, can't you? But you can't really walk from Woolton to Mount Street and get here in any reasonable length of time."

"Well? What happened then?" Cynthia's eyes were fixed on Phyllis's.

"That's it." Phyllis leaned back. "That's all of it...except that from then on when the bus picked me up, my bus fare was already paid. Driver never would say...but if I had my guess, I'd say it was taken care of by John Lennon over there."

"C'mon!" Michael shook his head. "It's all wild conjecture – that!"

"Is it?" Phyllis raised an eyebrow. And a lively debate began.

Three lagers and two cigs later, Cynthia had listened to Phyllis and Michael debate John and a wide range of other topics, but nothing else had happened. Cynthia hadn't budged, and John hadn't budged. Despite a few covert glances and the incessant butterflies her stomach, Cynthia hadn't made a bit of progress, and John seemed reluctant to disentangle himself from his "Liverpool Irish," his merry band of thieves. It was a standoff.

Only Michael moved. He packed up and headed home, wishing Cynthia good sense and failing that, good luck. It worked.

"Look!" Phyllis grabbed Cynthia's arm. "John's movin' to the bar! And...what d'you know...he's finally glancin' over here!"

Cynthia held her breath, waiting. *God, please. I'll never lie to Mum about staying late at school again. I'll try to mind my tongue when she sets me off. I'll go to church more regularly. I'll do better, truly I will. Just please let him try one more time. Please.*

John joined Tony Carricker at the bar and turned his back to the girls.

"Enough of yer beggin', son," John announced loudly, cuffing Tony on the shoulder. "I'm here to let you buy me a round."

Tony shook his head and ordered a Black and Tan for his parasitic friend. The two fell into mumbled conversation, heads close together, backs forming a wall of indifference.

Cynthia sighed, "This is goin' nowhere, isn't it?" Her eyes threatened tears, and she let them form, knowing she could always blame it on cigarette smoke.

Phyllis patted her hand and squeezed it gently. "Don't give up. He gave you a chance back there, and you virtually shoved him off. Now you give him one, right? Just wait it out a bit longer, then."

Cynthia stared at John's back – his hunched shoulders, his hair feathering the nape of his neck. She stared and drank in his every move.

"Phyl, I-I have to ask...I mean, has it ever occurred to you that this whole thing – his askin' me out 'n all – might've been just one grand set-up, as it were? Just another of John's elaborate, practical jokes?"

Phyllis listened with an open mind. Cynthia might be right. John and Geoff were known for "having people on."

"In fact," Cynthia became more animated, "I can just hear Geoff Mohammed saying to John, 'Ask her to dance, son. Ask her, and I'll wager Miss Prim'll practically fall apart!' And I did!"

Phyllis could see the logic in it. John and Geoff had been known to execute some pretty heartless jokes on the vulnerable and unsuspecting. "Well, I…" she hesitated, "I guess we can't be sure of anythin', now can we?"

Cynthia grabbed her purse and began to rummage through it for bus money to the train station. "At first – when he asked me to dance – I was too shocked to think anything at all. Then, I was too furious at *myself* to analyze the reason for…but over the last hour, I've gradually come to think…I might've dodged a bullet, so to speak. I mean, they say if something's too good to be true, it probably is. And I've just about decided it probably was."

Cynthia dumped a pile of change on the table and began counting it out slowly. The lagers had made her light-headed. It was hard to think.

"All right, then," Phyllis conceded, "but bear in mind that there's still the possibility you might be paranoid. I mean, if it were a joke 'n all, wouldn't John have just kept on dancin' with you – no matter what you said? Even after you turned him down? Wouldn't he have just shrugged it off instead of walkin' away in anger? Don't you think it's possible you might *really*'ve hurt him? Isn't that a possibility?"

"I dunno," Cynthia swept the coins into her palm and snapped her purse shut. She pushed her glass away. "All I know for certain is, I'm tired, I'm dizzy, I've a bit of a headache, and I should be going home, Phyl."

"All right, then. Go on. I'm right behind you."

Threading their way through storytellers, office mates, and couples edged up against each other, Cynthia and Phyllis slowly made their way towards the back door. Cynthia was sour and defeated.

"Didn't you know Miss Powell's a nun, then?" John's voice rose obnoxiously from the bar. He still had his back to her, but he challenged her in the large mirror in front of him.

Damn him to bloody hell! Cynthia saw it all in one glance. *He's been able to see me in that mirror all along! And I've been staring at him for God knows how long…*

"There it is!" Phyllis whispered, squeezing Cynthia's elbow. "There's your chance. Pick up the gauntlet."

Cynthia couldn't believe it. Her pulse raced.

"Go on!" Phyllis urged. "Answer him!"

"Nun, you say?" Cynthia pretended to be offended. John turned his head and offered her the once-over. Cynthia took a couple of steps towards him as Phyllis exited. "Nun, is it?" She took another step forward.

"Yeah, that's right, luv," Tony Carricker wiped his mouth with the back of his hand and grinned. "John here's been tellin' me there's 'nun' like you, Miss Powell!" And John's troop of troublemakers exploded at the pun.

Cynthia now stood in front of John who had turned to face her, his back against the bar, his elbows supporting him in a casual semi-recline.

"Perhaps so, Mr. Carricker," Cynthia smiled bravely, "but the question is, 'Is Mr. Lennon man enough to actually find out?'"

The room went wild.

"All right, then!"

"She's got you, there, Johnny!"

"Good on yer, Powell!"

"Take her up on it, John."

"Yeah, go on then!"

Each retort was more suggestive than the last, and Cynthia felt herself blushing in spite of her conjured courage.

John pretended not to hear any of them as he stood up and took Cynthia's hand. He led her back to the table she'd just abandoned and took her purse from her, placing it on the chair. "You might as well sit down, luv," he gestured. "I never run from a challenge. Especially when it comes from a nun."

Cynthia smiled and took a seat.

****

"You're one hundred per cent wrong." Cynthia parted her bangs slightly with her fingertips. Those who knew her well could read her mood by the quick, agitated motion. "We're not all silver spoons and caviar on the Wirral. In fact, far from it."

"Yeah, well y'er not chasing pups up Upper Parly, are y'now?" The old Liverpool tongue twister came in handy.

"We have good times…and bad ones, like everyone else. Mostly bad over the last few years, in my case."

"Go on." He took a sip of Cynthia's half-pint. She had nursed it for the better part of an hour. Someone had to drink it.

"My father…" It was still hard for Cynthia to talk about it. "My father died three years ago next month. Cancer. Very quick, very unexpected. Not that death ever is – expected – not even when you've had time to prepare for it. But in six months, he was just skin 'n bones, emaciated…and all the drugs in the world couldn't shut out what he suffered."

"Look," John blanched. "I never knew…I mean, when I was poppin' off…I had no way of…y'er always so Mary Sunshine, as it were."

Cynthia shrugged. "It's all right. I mean, I'm over it...as over it I'll ever be. And my mum, well... it's life, right? We go on somehow."

John flicked an empty matchbox to the floor. He had no response.

"After a while," Cynthia went on, "Mum received the insurance money Dad left – actually quite a good bit...enough for us to live on comfortably for some time, I suppose. But she'd have none of it."

"And why's that?" John's eyes met hers.

"She put it into an account for me and told me to apply to art college. I knew from the way she said it that 'no' wasn't an option. According to her, I was going to college – come what may, no matter what. So straight off, I came here as the obvious choice...closest to home, easiest to access, best for all concerned."

John nodded, his eyes never leaving hers.

"And, well... I know I look different with my Hoylake way of doing things and my Hoylake clothes, but none of the clothes are new John, and no matter what people say, I've no silver spoons sequestered anywhere. Really."

John snorted and shook his head. "Just when I thought I was above fuggin' snobbery, it appears I've misjudged the book by the fuggin' cover, haven't I, Cyn?"

Cyn!!! A nickname at last! Finally a pet name – something endearing...

She smiled at him. "I'm more than used to the 'over the water' judgements and jibes from everyone around here. I mean, I know full well that the Wirral's famous for hoity-toity. But...you and I have more in common than we do in difference, John, don't we?"

John smoothed one eyebrow with his finger, then looked at her straight on. He couldn't think of anything clever or witty to say. So for a while, they sat without talking.

John knew she'd heard about his mother. Everyone had. And he didn't have the strength to go into the stories about Fred Lennon – Julia's version, his Uncle Stanley's version, Mimi's version, or any version in between. He didn't feel up to a narrative about George or Mimi yet. It all seemed too much too soon.

"Up for a walk, then?" he asked instead.

"Sure. Why not? It's a bit stuffy in here, isn't it?"

"Yeah, right. C'mon."

Cynthia and John had been all but forgotten in the last hour, and not even Geoff chose to notice when they slipped out the back door around half ten. The Liverpool night was amazingly changed. A warm front from Ireland had blown in – balmy, almost spring-like – and the once-brisk air was now moist, smelling of peat and rains to come.

They walked in silence, holding hands, John helping Cyn maneouver the cobbles on Rice until they reached the sidewalk on Hope Street. But even then, he held on to her hand, their fingers interlocked.

"That song you were playing back there..." John looked straight ahead.

"Song?" It was the last thing on her mind.

"That last song at the bash."

"Oh, that one." Cynthia played along.

"It isn't true, y'know."

"True?" Cynthia wrinkled her brow. She couldn't remember the song to save her. "What d'you mean?"

"It isn't true...about me, that is. To know me isn't to love me. You can ask almost anyone."

She stopped walking. "All right," she said. "I'll ask Stuart Sutcliffe then."

"That's different." John pulled her along. "He's fuggin' blind – Stu."

"He sees well enough to paint better than anyone in school."

"Yeah, well he's a visionary, not a realist – Stu. He sees things in a different light, as it were."

"So? I'm a visionary as well. I have my own credentials, and they're just as valid as Stu Sutcliffe's."

John stopped without warning and grabbed Cynthia by the elbow, turning her to him. He tilted her chin up to his.

"Look Cyn, you don't fuggin' know what you're gettin' yerself into." His eyes were narrowed, serious. "You've created somethin' in yer head that's really not there. I mean, I'm not that man they're singin' about in that song. I can't be anyone's version of a dream come true."

"Too late for the lecture, John. You already are."

He slid his arm round her waist and held her for a moment. Then he guided her across Canning Street and into the shadow of the cathedral, its scaffoldings silver in the moonlight. The seagulls, losing their loft in the calm, called to one another as they flapped to the docks and back. Muffled music drifted over from some club nearby. And the sounds of arguing from an open window mixed with the staccato of John's shoes hitting the sidewalk.

Cynthia memorized each moment as if it would never happen again. She memorized the warmth of his body close to hers, the smell of his jacket, the feel of his callouses rough on her blouse. She memorized the feeling of joy racing through her every time he talked.

John stopped in front of the tall, late-Georgian row houses in Percy Street, and he touched Cynthia's bangs gently, just as he'd seen her do. "This's Stu's place." He nodded towards the building. "D'ya want to come in, then?"

Cynthia nodded, following John's lead. It was the easiest decision she'd ever made. In fact, it wasn't a decision at all.

John was her existence. Apart from him, there was no logic, no imagination, no happiness, no sorrow, no concrete, no abstract. Being with him wasn't something she could choose. It was something that had chosen her.

Somewhere in the distance a dog barked at its shadow. Cab tires screeched on the pavement. A horn honked, and another answered angrily.

John found the key that Stu always sequestered, unlocked the door, and nudged it open. He fumbled for the light, and failing to find it, took Cynthia's hand and pulled her into the darkness.

Entangling his fingers in her hair, he hesitated. Breathing in her perfume, he prayed she wouldn't pull away. And when she reached up to touch his neck, he booted the door closed, shutting out the moonlight, the city sounds, the Irish breeze, and the wisp of gentle rain that had just begun to fall on Liverpool.

Cynthia and John did attend the End of the Term Bash at the Art College, and John did ask her to dance and did ask her out while they were dancing. Cynthia did say that she was engaged to someone else and John did reply, "I didn't ask you to fuggin' marry me, did I?" and walked out. Cynthia and Phyllis did go over to Ye Cracke, and John did make the comment about Cynthia being a nun. Cynthia did reply to him and did end up spending the rest of the evening with him and going with him to Stu's flat. Some sources say that flat was in Gambier Terrace, but Rod Murray says that he and Stu were still living in Percy Street at this point.

There is some controversy about what song was playing on the record player when John and Cynthia danced that first dance. Ray Coleman says it was "To Know Him is to Love Him" by the Teddy Bears. In her 1978 book, A Twist of Lennon, *Cynthia says the song was "slow and smoochy" as Coleman indicated. However, in her 2006 book,* John, *Cynthia says it was a Chuck Berry tune, and she says that John had to "shout" the question at her, indicating that it was a fast dance, and they were dancing apart.*

But, whatvever the song, all accounts of this event have John asking Cynthia out. I have him propose a date to her on the dance floor for dramatic effect, but in actuality, it occurred later, at the end of the party.

Obviously, the conversations that Cynthia has in this chapter with Phyllis, Michael Isaacson, and John are all conjecture.

June 1959
The Jacaranda
23 Slater Street
Liverpool 1

The upper end of Liverpool 1 was Merseyside's business district. Dignified addresses such as Whitechapel Road where Rex Makin had established his law office or North John where investment firms and exclusive men's clubs put down roots gave the district its square shouldered reputation. But the outskirts of the district, the lower corner touching the more colourful Liverpool 8, had a flavour all its own.

Once glorious as the residential quarter for aristocratic cotton merchants and ship owners, lower Liverpool 1 had evolved into a haven for radicals and creative souls – forward thinkers. In dark coffeehouses that would have failed a daylight inspection, customers nursed espressos and cappuccinos while listening to poets such as Adrian Henri – poets with quirky, extraordinary visions.

Throughout the narrow streets of Seel, Colquitt, Parr, and Slater, artists set up easels and sketched Indian restaurateurs hurrying off to market or Buddhist groups gathered beneath neon take-away signs. And art college students, full of fresh ideas and strong coffee, ventured down from Hope Street to mix with trendy shopkeepers.

In this offbeat world, bright-eyed, exuberant Liverpool-born Welshman, Allan Williams, had invested a borrowed one hundred pounds in a capitalist's dream. Hungry for a slice of "the Big Apple," as he put it, he had tapped his relatives for the investment capital needed to open a coffeehouse. He'd planned to name his exotic venture, "The Samurai," but his mate, Bill Coward, who'd just finished reading the popular novel, "The Jacaranda Tree," suggested that Allan dub the place, "The Jacaranda." And he did.

Known for its bacon sandwiches or bacon "butties," its dropped trelliswork ceiling splashed with fishnets and brightly coloured glass balls, and its bizarre Royal Caribbean West Indian Steel band, The Jacaranda fit neatly into its arcane surroundings.

On narrow, padded benches that lined the walls, the college set sat around kidney shaped tables and gawked at the "in crowd" of older artists who debated the evenings away. Munching on jam butties – or bacon butties if they had a few coins to spare – the eager-to-be-not-so-innocent clientele slipped flasks of liquor from their jackets and spiked the Cokes that Williams was licensed to sell. The coffee became Irish; the conversation became fluid, and the evenings slipped into mornings. The Jac, as it became known, quickly grew into a Liverpool institution for those who despised institutions.

John loved it. He loved the wide wall of windows with copper kettles artfully arranged on the ledges. He loved the dark basement room beneath the coffeehouse and the recessed corners where couples necked. He loved the uneven brick dance floor and the narrow tables where anything might be said or overheard. He loved the extremity of it all.

Never entirely abandoning Ye Cracke and its convenient proximity to the art college, John nevertheless found himself drawn more and more frequently to the musty recesses of Williams' hideaway. Herding his crowd along with him, John found it exciting to rub elbows with "the elements" – to wind his way down the basement steps to the syncopated sound of West Indian music.

Mimi'd bleedin' despise this, he smiled to himself, imagining her standing in the room. *What's more, she'd forbid it if she knew!* "Not the sort of place for you, John," she'd say. "All these unorthodox people…and that music…completely beyond the pale."

So John made it his Mecca. And Allan Williams was quickly getting to know the cantankerous art student from Woolton.

"You – Lennon! How's it *you're* back again?" the ruddy faced entrepreneur almost skidded to a halt. "You were all but dead skint after last night's adventures, weren't you? Who's footin' the fffffuggin' bill tonight, then?"

John scanned the room for a likely pigeon. Someone would come to his rescue; someone always did. John would clown about, say extraordinary things, and entangle his marks with humour and insight. He'd lean on the bar, talk in hushed, clipped sentences, and mesmerize his bait into favouring him with cigs, drinks, and food.

And tonight it would be especially easy.

John pointed to a small group seated at a side table. He grinned, and Allan shook his head. John's chums, George Harrison and Paul McCartney, were already seated there and had already ordered the boy a coffee. The rest, for John, would be child's play.

"So *they're* yer front men, are they?" The compact, handsome Welshman had little patience with Lennon. He considered the boy "a fuggin' layabout."

"Right," John flashed a grin and brushed past the owner with just enough insolence to get by without "gettin' the boot." "If they've got the money, I've got the time,"

Allan watched him stride off, full of audacity. But Al knew that had the boy and the rest of the so-called Quarry Men would be on their best behaviour in The Jac. In fact, Al had them right where he wanted them. For weeks they'd been begging for a chance to perform in the basement – and Lennon had been the most persistent of the group. Al knew that as long as John thought he had a chance – albeit a slim one – to take The Jac "stage," he'd toe the line.

"Hey Al," Paul McCartney called out as the owner passed by their table, "you'll be givin' us that break any day now, right?"

John had pulled up a scuffed captain's chair and was seated with his friends.

"You've let others play downstairs, not just The Steel Band, y'know." George Harrison was usually reserved, but when it came to business, he was all courage and practicality. "We've heard them, Al."

"We've all heard them, Al." John leaned his chair back at a dangerous angle.

"Right the fuggin' chair, Lennon –you'll break the legs off!" Al gave him a swift nudge.

"We're a great band, y'know." It was McCartney's turn to heckle.

"No lads," Allan pointed to the members of the Royal Caribbean Steel band who'd gathered outside The Jac for a smoke and a bit of cool, summer air. *"They're a great band.* You lot....pfffft! You've no drummer; you've no songs! You haven't even a fuggin' fan to speak of."

"We've got fans." John seemed to believe it.

"Pfff! I'm not talkin' about those randy judies whom you promise the world to for a night's bar tab, Lennon. I'm talkin' about *real* fans that'd come here for *real* music. Rory Storm? Now he's got fans, and he's damned good, too! That's why I..."

"We can play as well as Rory." John was single-minded.

"Pfffff! Right!" Allan scoffed. "Y'er fuggin' miserable – all of ya. You and yer 'Red Sails in the Sunset' and all that crap..."

"Y'er behind the times, Mr. Jacaranda." John folded his arms. "That was months ago. We've got a play list these days."

"And fans as well," Paul insisted. "Loads."

"Furthermore," John jumped in, "we told 'em to look for us here. We told 'em you'd be givin' us a fuggin' break, as it were."

"Well, you were dreamin' then, weren't you? But very good – that. Nice try – that. It never hurts to try, now does it?" Al stood firm.

"Say Al," Paul tried his saddest, puppy dog eyes. "You let Derry and the Seniors play here, didn't you?"

"Derry Wilkie's band's made a name for itself, McCartney."

"We've got a name, and you know it, son." John leaned forward, shoulder to shoulder with Paul. "Quarry Men...Q-u-a-double r-y. You know the rest. Write it down. It'll be important someday…you'll want to have it. That is…if we remember who you are."

"Pffft!!!!"

"But, listen Al," George always had a solution, "if it's a name y'er after…we could always *change* our name…I mean, if that's what's standin' in the way of your givin' us a chance 'n all."

"In fact," Paul picked up the ball and ran with it, "we were already thinkin' of changin' it – weren't we, lads?"

"Right," John shrugged, "Johnny and the Moondogs…that was the latest iteration, wasn't it?"

"You can call yerselves the fuggin' Prince of Wales for all I care," Allan waved them off, "and I'm still not lettin' you play…not in the basement, not at the bar, not on the sidewalk – not anywhere where I can hear the three o'you mewlin' like tomcats."

John folded his arms and sniffed. "He's offended your sensibilities, hasn't he, George?"

George nodded. "Yeah, he's dead rude, seemingly."

"You've all but hurt the lad's feelings, haven't you?" John looked at Al accusingly.

Paul pretended to wipe away a tear, "And trampled on mine."

"Pfffft! Sod off, all o' you!" Allan snipped, but he smiled at their nonsense anyway. "You haven't half a band! You haven't half of fuggin' anythin'!"

"So out of sympathy, you'll be sendin' over a plate of bacon butties, then?" John suggested.

Allan threw his eyes to the ceiling and scurried away before the four of them could begin negotiating with him all over again.

"So…where's Stu?" John looked around, dismissing Allan as soon as he was out of sight. "He was supposed to've been here by now."

"I dunno," Paul bit his lip, "My guess is he's doin' high jumps to reach the very top corner of the very last easel."

"You're the same kind of perfectionist he is," John spat back. "and this John Moores competition is the fuggin' end o' the world to him…bigger 'n any gig we've ever had…"

"He's right, y'know." The voice came from behind them. "It's life-changin' – John Moores." It was Stu, or what was left of him. Colour drained from his face, hands paint-splotched, hair disheveled and dotted with paint, he looked as molten as candle tallow.

For weeks he'd worked virtually non-stop on his entry into the prestigious John Moores Biennial Art Competition at Liverpool's Walker Art Gallery. And even though the event was still a good four months away, Stu devoted every second of every day to his work. The immense oil painting sprawled across two canvases was truly one of the best Stu had ever undertaken – but it had taken its toll on his body. His eyes were sunken and dark. His hands shook, and he collapsed into the seat John offered him.

"How's it goin', then?" John offered Stu one of Paul's cigs.

"It's goin'." Stu hated to "rabbit on" about his creations. He knew that not everyone at the table shared John's interest in his art.

"So...what's the prize money in a thing like that, Stu?" George offered him a light.

Stu took a long drag and then slumped back into his chair again. "Around four thousand pounds. But not just to one artist, y'realize." He took another drag. "It's all divvied up."

"Four thousand pounds?" George smiled widely. "That could motivate me, as it were!"

"Oh, I'm motivated," Stu nodded, running a hand through his hair over and over. "I'm motivated just bein' asked to compete! Too motivated, perhaps. 'Intimidated' is the better word. 'Terrified' might work as well."

"And what'll you do with the money, then," Paul gave Stu a quick grin, "that is, if you win, place, or show – whatever?"

"I dunno," Stu sighed as if he were on the verge of collapse at any moment, "buy supplies; dream of private lessons; rent a good night's sleep for once. I haven't given it much thought since the money isn't what I'm after anyway."

"And what is it you're after exactly?" John looked back over his shoulder at his friend, who was now almost reclining in the chair behind him.

"To compete, John. Y'know – *really* compete." Stu held the cigarette out and watched the smoke curl towards the ceiling, following its bends and turns. "To be worthy of my peers – to be worthy of bein' judged."

"Next thing y'know," Paul chuckled, "we'll be losin' Stuart here to some London gallery or some studio garret on the Continent."

Stu laughed through his nose, a quiet breath of amusement.

"Stu's goin' fuggin' nowhere." John's voice was low. "He'll be usin' the prize money to join the band."

Allan interrupted, returning with plates of bacon butties, steaming coffees and silverware. "All right, all right," he clattered the plates onto the table, "here!"

"Ta, Al!"

"You're all right, aren't ya!"

"Hullo, Al." Stu gingerly passed the cups around, and John divvied up the plates.

"Mr. Sutcliffe." Allan nodded. "You look like fuggin'ell."

"Ta." Stu attempted a smile.

"*De nada.*" Allan dragged a chair over, wedging his way in between Paul and George. "Muck in, lads – y'er at yer granny's!" His eyes danced as he laid the Scouse on thick. "And while you're devourin' your *free* repast like the lousy scavengers I know you are...I think you might be interested in an earth-shatterin' idea I've come up with."

"Let's have it." John wasn't letting anything earth-shattering slip by him.

"Well, imagine this," Allan began. He held his hands in the air. His eyes danced. "Imagine an arrangement of sorts, a trade-off, a tit for tat, as it were…"

"We're all for tit. Go on." John stared straight at him.

"I'd reluctantly agree – *reluctantly* mind you – to let you bunch o' layabouts practise here at The Jac, down in the basement…in the *afternoons* when business isn't as…demandin', shall we say."

"When there's nofuggin'one here, you mean." John cut to the chase.

"When there's a smaller crowd around." Allan gave him the eye. "And…I'd graciously leave the door open to the upstairs, so that you can provide, let's say, 'background music' for the afternoon patrons…"

"Great. Right." Paul clicked his cheek and gave Allan a quick nod.

"Not bad," George shrugged.

"…in return for…" Allan paused.

"In return for," John rolled his hand.

"In return for the completion of a few odd jobs here and there – for a few small favours of a compensatory nature."

"Spell it out, Al." Stu had mustered the energy to lean forward.

"Well, let's see…" Allan combed his fingers through the thick tangle of dark curls falling onto his forehead. He pretended to search for an idea. "Well, for example, you've no doubt heard of the fantastic Chelsea Arts Ball – the highlight of the social season?"

"Yeah, we've heard of it." Stu nodded, well aware of the celebration. Many of his cohorts at the college had been recruited to paint backdrops, make floats, and plan elaborate decorations for the dance.

"Well, as it pans out, I'm plannin' a gigantic event of my own…of the exact same caliber, if not fuggin' better – a Merseyside Arts Ball, right down in St. George's Hall. And of course, I'll be needin' decorations…balloons, floats, extravagant amounts of sparkle and panache – just the sort of thing you art college boys should well be able to do."

"That leaves me out, then." Paul lost interest and winked at a pretty brunette who'd just come in on the arm of a rather miserable looking bloke. She wrinkled her nose in a bunny smile and winked back.

"I wouldn't know a paintbrush from a spanner, would I?" George protested.

"But we could do," Stu committed them all. "I mean, John 'n I could direct, and we could delegate jobs to everyone else…"

John was wolfing down the last bacon butty as if he hadn't eaten in months. He thumped his empty coffee cup with his fingernail, asking for more. "Yeah," he mumbled between bites. "We c'always find a way to make it work."

"And you'd have to," Allan winked mischievously, "because *this*, Quarry-boys, is yer once and future offer, as it were."

"Well...we need a practise studio, don't we?" George pointed out.

"And free publicity as well," Paul agreed.

"John and I *could* design the floats..." Stu began to plan.

"And we could always hammer in a nail or two." Paul nodded towards George.

"Lennon?" Allan wanted confirmation from all of them.

"Allan?" John refused to play along.

"Are you fuggin' in or not, Lennon?" Allan demanded.

"Like Flynn," was the terse reply.

****

"Bloody fuggin' hell, there's cats *dyin'* down there!"

"Yeah, turn it off, Al!"

"It's horrible, that!"

"They're fuggin awful, aren't they?"*

The Quarry Men were not a hit with The Jacaranda's afternoon set.

"Ah, it's Chuck Berry stuff, y'know – from the States." Allan tried to be cheerful in the face of disaster. "American rock'n'roll!"

"Chuck Berry, me arse."

"Chuck, bury *me*, if they keep that up!"

"Givvus some aspero, luv!" Two ladies by the window made faces and held their ears. "Aspero or earmuffs – your choice, Al."

"We're not up to this!"

Cheniston Roland, an afternoon regular, had the best solution of all. He walked over, stood at the door to the basement, and yelled at the top of his lungs, "What's the bleedin' racket down there? Take a break, why don't you? God knows *we* need one! We never done nothin' to you!"

The room cheered the Liverpool photographer – laughed and applauded with vigour.

In a couple of minutes, the "music-makers" and Stu appeared – aromatic, hungry, and as usual, skint. They ignored the barbs and insults from the customers and huddled around one wobbly table, as if they expected service.

"How's about a jam butty or two, Al?" George summoned his most disarming smile.

"Coffee and butties 'til times get better, mister!"* John clasped his hands together, pleading like a corner beggar.

"Pffft! It's not in yer fuggin' contract!" Allan's Welsh jaw was firmly set.

"Beryl! Beryl! We want Beryl!" It was George who started the chant, but the others joined in quickly.

Allan tried to shush them with his hands, saying, "No! No! No!" but they got louder and louder, calling with urgency for Allan's tenderhearted, Chinese wife.

Beryl Chang Williams came out of the kitchen, grinning from ear to ear, brandishing a large ladle in a display of mock anger. It was the standard game they always played, a ritual reenacted each afternoon.

John fell to his knees in the middle of the room, wringing his hands and pleading dramatically, "Have mercy on the starvin' poor, lady! Have mercy on the poor!"

Paul reached out to her from his chair, "Weak…weak from hunger…" His hands trembled with authenticity

George looked sheepish and innocent, but extremely hungry as well. It was the same every time. And every time, Beryl gave in. She laughed out loud and turned back to the kitchen to get The Moondogs, The Quarry Men – or whomever they were this week – something to eat.

"Hey, thanks for your warmhearted generosity, Al," George teased.

"Yeah, it's real pearl in your crown, y'know," Paul winked.

"We'll be mentionin' it to Father Christmas and to all the saints as well." John got up off the floor and wagged a finger in Al's face.

"Pffffft, all o'you!" Allan blustered as he always did. But he took a seat beside them companionably, waiting for Beryl to return. "So…how's the progress on the arts ball, lads?"

"Not bad," Paul shrugged.

"We're makin' the floats in stages," John began.

"Small enough to be transported easily and slipped inside the doors of St. George's," Stu explained. "But then, once inside, they'll all fit back together again, puzzle-like."

"It was all Paul's idea," George teased, pointing at him.

"Right. It's kept me up nights – this decor," Paul wiped his brow. "I've got watercolour in me veins these days."

Beryl reappeared with a stack of small, white ceramic plates, a rack of buttered bread, and a generous plate of bacon. She had also included assorted jellies in a tiny, glass bowl, some cream and sugar, four white coffee cups, and a stack of spoons.

"Coffee coming up!" she beamed.

"Ta!" George dug in without delay.

"Thanks, Beryl. You know we love only you." Paul dipped his head.

"Here's a toast to the donor of the feast!" John lifted a symbolic slice of browned bread in her direction. The others followed suit. "To Beryl, then!"

"To Beryl!"

"A toast!"

"A toast to the lovely Beryl!" Paul smiled disarmingly.

"Enjoy!" she grinned. "Compliments of the house!"

"Oh nice!' Allan shook his head and waved her off. But he didn't contradict her, and he sat with Johnny and the Moondogs as they finished the gratis meal. "So…you're sayin' it'll all work, then – the floats, the decorations, the whole rigmarole?"

"We're sayin' it works on paper." John was direct.

"But we've never done anythin' like this before, y'understand," Stu admitted.

"And we're not engineers or anythin' of that nature." George made it clear. "I was only an electrician's apprentice, y'understand, not a full fledged electrician, as it were."

"And he was only that for one day," Paul grinned.

"Just make it work! Just make it fuggin' work!" Allan laid it on the line. "I've a small fortune invested in this venue, lads, and it has to go off like clockwork or else…"

"We're doin' our best, Al." Stu was sincere.

"But we're better at bein' musicians, y'know," John said.

"*Better*?" Al snapped his head around.

"Yeah, we are a rock'n'roll band, aren't we?" John sniffed.

"The ones from the basement," Paul bowed from his chair.

"And y'er better at *that* than makin' floats and decorations?" Allan's face was white.

"Seventy times seven, son." John nodded.

"Fuggin'ell!" Allan slumped over the table like a rag doll. "I'm done for then! If y'er seventy times better at makin' music than makin' floats, I might as well…"

"Four hundred and ninety," George corrected.

"What?"

"It's seventy *times seven*," George pointed out. "That's four hundred and ninety to be exact."

"Ah, great." Allan groaned, leaning back in his chair, defeated. "How did it all come to this?"

"Multiplication," John said. And he smiled.

I first saw The Jac in its dilapidated state in the early 1990's, when a group of homeless people had set up "camp" there and had utterly destroyed the place. Then, in the late 90's, I attended the reopened Jac, a commercial success that paid tribute to the tribute to the Beatles and Allan Williams…and a great venue for local bands.

I must add that it has been my pleasure to share several memorable evenings with Allan Williams and his lovely friend, Beryl Adams, who was Brian Epstein's office manager and Bob Wooler's ex-wife. Beryl is completely charming, and Allan is one of of the most colourful characters I've ever met. Energetic, vivacious, and animated, he helped me with all the chapters on The Beatles at the Jac and in Hamburg. I owe both

Al and Beryl a great deal of gratitude.

*All the events in this chapter took place just as recorded. The two sentences that are highlighted by the asterisk are quoted from Allan Williams book The Man Who Gave The Beatles Away. *Roland Cheniston's act of closing the door is fictitious, although he was a regular afternoon customer in The Jac.*

Late June 1959
The Jacaranda
23 Slater Street
Liverpool 1

Although John was now a Wooltoner twice removed – by art and rock 'n' roll – he knew that Pete Shotton was never more than a phone call away. A couple of weeks would go by, and then Lotton would ring Shennon or vice versa, and immediately the distance between the two would dissolve.

Pete had just completed his training as a Cadet Apprentice at the Liverpool Police Academy by doing a horrific year's stint in Vice Squad. And now more comfortably stationed at the Records Office – learning "the ins and outs of almighty, effin' paperwork," as he put it – Pete found it easier to traipse down to Hope Street in search of John. Bringing with him sordid stories about the underside of Liverpool life, he treated Rod Murray, Stu, and John to raunchy details about prostitutes, the Garston "blood baths," the Toxteth gang wars, and drug trafficking throughout the city. And reciprocally, they amused Pete with fantastic tales of Ye Cracke, The Philharmonic, and The Jac – outlandish scenarios studded with embellishments.

"Right!" Pete laughed, shaking his head as Rod recounted the day they'd brought traffic to a standstill by sweeping the zebra crossing at Hope and Mount Streets. "I can see you'll be the very ones I'm sent to lock up next."

"Yeah," Rod grinned, "Vice is my middle name, y'know!"

"Rod Vice?" John raised an eyebrow. "A bit pornographic, isn't it?"

"Speakin' of pornographic," Pete slapped John on the back, "who's 'the girl' in yer life these days, son?"

"Careful, Shotton." Rod wagged a warning finger. "Y'er on dangerous ground there."

"John's in love, y'know." Stu used both hands around his coffee cup, taking a long slurp.

"That's right. *In love!*" Rod gave John a shove.

"Get stuck, Murray." John failed to see the humour in it all.

"And yerself, Mr. Lennon." Rod toasted.

"Don't be holdin' out on me, Johnny boy," Pete said. "C'mon. Who is she?"

"Cig?" John patted his pockets as if there were an ounce of hope anything there.

"A cig..." Pete held one out, "for a confession." He pulled it away as John reached for it.

"Ah, you've gone completely copper, haven't you?" John frowned.

"It's Cynthia Powell." Stu filled in the blanks.

John jerked the cigarette from Pete's hand and began the ritual of patting for a light.

Pete flipped him a matchbook. "Cynthia Powell, eh! Cynthia Powell! Blonde? Short? Tall? Tits? Bum? What's the griff, son?"

"You're off the fuggin' clock, aren't ya, Officer Shotton?" John took a drag.

"She's from the Wirral, Pete." Rod leaned forward and cupped a hand to his mouth, divulging the secret.

"A *posher*?" Pete gave John's arm a whack. "From over the water, then! Y'er shittin' me, Winnie! Say it isn't so! From the Wirral! She must be Mary Elizabeth's fondest dream come true."

"Yeah, right." John gave Pete a look that spoke volumes. "You know Mim."

"Oh...so now even a posher's not good enough for her little Johnny, eh?"

"No one ever has been, have they?" John snarled.

"I know *I* wasn't."

"And a fuggin' shame, too." John batted his eyelashes. "Just when I was thinkin' of askin' you to marry me."

Tensions eased, and they all chuckled. Rod got up to order a plate of butties, and Stu wandered off to the loo, giving the two old friends time to talk.

"Go on," Pete rested his elbows on the table. "Tell me more."

"Y'can see her for yerself. She's on her way over right now," John glanced at the clock that Allan had hung at the rear of the room. "And look...don't pull any of that Winnie crap around her, right?"

"You like her that much?" Pete leaned in closer.

"Cyn's all right."

"She must be more than 'all right' if you're so fuggin' particular."

"There," John nodded towards the front door. "Have a look-see."

Negotiating the tall, concrete Jac steps slowly in her tight, black skirt, dark hose, and high heels, the newly bleached platinum blonde stepped into the coffeehouse and immediately began scanning for John. Her heart-shaped face was fringed with bangs, and she looked for all the world like John's beloved Bridget Bardot.

A fuggin' knockout! Pete thought, *Fuggin' phenomenal!*

Cynthia moved towards the table with her eyes locked on John's. She smiled and blushed, and Pete doubted she knew he was even there.

John reached for her hand and pulled her over to him as he turned in Pete's direction. "Cyn, this is me old chum from Quarry Bank – and even before that, right Pete?"

Pete stood up. "Yeah, that's right. Hullo. I'm Pete…Peter Shotton." A formal introduction. He felt he owed it to this girl.

"Oh the *famous* Peter Shotton!" Cynthia shook his hand. "I've heard quite a lot about you, y'know. Lovely to meet you, Pete."

"A-and pleased to meet you as well." He fumbled a bit.

"Right…fuggin' lovely to meet y' fuggin'both and sit down." John commanded.

"You were in The Quarry Men, right?" Cynthia deposited her purse under the table and scooted her chair beside John's. "Percussion, I believe?"

"Yeah, washboard." It was Pete's turn to blush. *Washboard!*

"Washboard?" she giggled, cutting her eyes at John.

"Oh, he was talented, actually – our Pete. Strum a little, clean a little, strum a little, clean a little."

"It was like a tambourine of sorts," Pete explained.

"And handy as well. Me socks haven't been the same since." John pulled his pants' cuffs up to check. Cynthia loved it.

"So," Cynthia laid a hand on John's, tossing her hair back seductively, "what happened, then? Why no washboard? Why no Pete?"

"Oh that," Pete rubbed his head, giving John a meaningful glance. "Well, I almost lost me head over that instrument, didn't I, John?"

"It was a rather heady experience," John grinned.

"Y'see Cynthia," Pete explained, "it was after this gig in Toxteth, and well…Johnny here had had a bit of the brew, as it were…"

"And rather than offer the traditional critique, bashin' his washboard skills…" John added.

"Which he always did…"

"I decided to make it a bit more literal that night."

"So he bashed the board right over me head!" Pete rubbed his skull and grimaced.

"You *never*?" Cynthia laughed lightly, nervously.

"He did." Pete vouched. "He absolutely did."

"I was only doin' him a fuggin' favour," John said. "Shotton never wanted to be in the group anyway. He only wanted the pints, bairds, and worldwide acclaim."

"But as John knows," Pete agreed, "what I really wanted…was out."

"So I just took matters into m'own hands," John nudged him.

"As it were!" Cynthia laughed.

"Right. As it were." Pete nodded.

They exchanged the warm, knowing smile that two only strangers with a close, mutual friend can share, even early on in a relationship. Pete found her bright but not pretentious, as Hoylake girls were rumoured to be. Cynthia found Pete potentially mischievous, but open and genuine, much like John himself.

It'll be easy to be friends with this Pete Shotton, Cynthia mused.

I can see exactly why John's so taken with this one, Pete smiled wider.

"But unfortunately for us all," John interrupted their smiles and unspoken appraisals, "Peter here has to be leavin' us straight off. Isn't that right, Shotton?"

Pete stole a quick look at his friend. He could tell from John's expression that he wasn't kidding and that Pete was required to play along. "Uh-yeah. Right. Sorry, Cynthia. Prior engagement, y'know." He tripped over the words.

Cynthia could tell that something wasn't quite right. But she wasn't sure what it was. John seemed agitated. Pete seemed confused.

"Great meetin' you then, Cynthia Powell." Pete stood and tossed a few coins on the table for his coffee.

"And you, Mr. Shotton." She offered with a slight wave.

"T'rah John. See ya, then."

"Yeah, t'rah."

There was complete silence, uneasy silence, as Pete walked to the door. It was almost a full minute before John turned on her.

"You fuggin' *like* him!" John's face was sharp and angry.

"Of course, I like him. He seems lovely. He..."

"You're completely taken by him! It's all over your fuggin' face!"

"What? John, I..."

"No excuses! No fuggin' pretense! You were all smiles when he was here."

For the first time, Cynthia understood. John was jealous. She took a slow breath and swallowed, hard.

"John," she began quietly, "it isn't like that at all."

But her reticent demeanour only fueled his hostility. John read it as guilt.

"I don't want to hear it!" he said, and one hand flew up to fend her off. But Cynthia instinctively ducked, and as she flinched, John's ire increased. "Fuggin'ell, Cynthia! I wasn't out to fuggin' strike ya, y'know!"

"And I wasn't out to hurt *you*, John." She felt a bit of strength returning in the quick rush of adrenaline.

"Yeah, right." His eyes narrowed. "So y'er sayin' I'm *imaginin'* it, then? That I'm only a thick, fuggin' Scouser, right?'

"No! No, you're the man I love." There, she'd said it. She knew John knew. But until that moment, it had been an unspoken pledge.

John said nothing. He took a drag on his cigarette and looked away from her. He looked out the window towards the street.

"I love you, John," she repeated, a bit more boldly. "And yes, you're right, I like your friend, Pete. He was up-beat, not moody-broody like Geoff and some of the others." John relented and glanced in her direction. "He seemed a real friend to you, not a hanger-on."

John took another drag.

"But," Cynthia grabbed his arm with both her hands, "but it's *you* I come all the way to Liverpool for. It's *you* that I take the last train home for – with all the drunks and bums. It's you I've changed my hair, my dress, my entire look for. It's you I'm in love with. No one else – just you."

John lowered his head, but said nothing in return.

"D'you want me to leave, then?" Cynthia's voice quavered. John's eyes quickly met hers.

He held her glance, scrutinizing, measuring the sincerity in her expression against the apprehension in his own.

Then without a word, John pulled her close and wrapped her in his arms. His mouth met hers with intensity and desperation, and he kissed her, almost violently, while tears tumbled down her cheeks, and they both tasted salt.

****

"So naturally, Stu's worried." John held her hand as they walked down Lime Street towards City Centre. Half-six and Liverpool was almost a ghost town. Shopkeepers had flipped over "Closed" signs for the night, and metal security screens were double-latched. Only the last, straggling vendors were left in the open-air market. Everyone else had gone home for tea and rest before returning at half-eight or nine for late evening revels in the pubs. John and Cyn had the town virtually to themselves.

"Worried? Again?" Cynthia smiled wryly. "Or still?"

"Yeah," John nodded, "it's the perfect name for him, isn't it? 'Stew'?"

They both snickered lightly.

"And…what's he on about this time?" Cynthia paused in front of the picture window at Lewis's to admire a black sheath that was really too formal for any event she was planning to attend. It was the kind of dress that required pearls.

"Allan's arts ball… or rather, the *crowd* at Allan's arts ball."

"The attendance, you mean?" She imagined herself in the sleek dress. She knew it would take John's breath away.

"No, the caliber of clientele…and the amount of destruction they might wield. You know how it gets at these things."

"But," Cynthia strolled to the next window, "that's the point, isn't it? I mean, the floats are supposed to be destroyed at midnight, aren't they? Isn't that the tradition?'

"I've told him that. Paul's told him that. Allan's even fuggin' told him that." John nudged her to move on. "But he's got it in his head that this is some Stuart Sutcliffe Exhibition instead of the riotous revel it's supposed to be. He's gone all motherly about the backdrops and details of each float. He's worried sick that it's all goin' to come down in a riotous mêlée."

Cynthia picked up her pace as they neared the front entrance of Lewis's Department Store, and she kept her eyes averted from the larger-than-life statue above the front doors. The gigantic, bronze Jacob Epstein sculpture – the symbolic "Liverpool Resurgent" – was the brunt of many off-colour jokes and risqué quips with the art college set. The well-endowed, nude male figure, lifting his arms to the skies, was known colloquially as "Dickie Liverpool," and whatever Epstein had originally intended the significance of the sculpture to be, the sexually explicit landmark always made Cynthia blush.

"'Ullo there, Dickie!" John saluted the bronze man. Cynthia turned her back towards the statue and faced the Adelphi Hotel instead – white-columned, elegant, and quiet in the early evening streetlights.

As the traffic signal changed, John guided her across the zebra towards the hotel, and Cynthia manoeuvered John's attention back to the arts ball. "So...how's Allan holding up in the midst of all these preparations, then?"

"Al? He's a madman – fuggin' obsessed, that's what. He keeps pushin' us to make everythin' e-fuggin'-normous!" They turned towards City Center. "He wants this gig to come off without a single hitch, y'know – but *everyone* knows what the chances of that are. I mean, it's not even one in a fuggin' million, is it?" John complained.

Cynthia smiled. Allan was Allan. He was alternately enthusiastic, irritable, furious, thrilled, and despondent – on an ordinary day. This arts ball was important to him, and that meant trouble.

"Speakin' of madmen," John smiled weakly, "about this afternoon at The Jac..."

"Forgotten, John."

His calloused fingers squeezed hers. "Y'have to let me say this."

She glanced at him from under heavily mascaraed lashes.

"I'm not a fuggin' lunatic, Cyn."

"I know, I..."

"And I'm..." He swallowed. His voice grew husky with emotion. "Look... it's like...it's like I've been sick all m'life...wonderin' who gives a shit and who doesn't...wonderin' when the fuggin' rug's goin' to be jerked out from under me all over again. This one says they love me, and then they're gone. And that one says they're family, and then they're gone. And now you're here...and you seem this miracle cure to make it all right. But I'm only just recoverin', y'know. And it's one day at a time, isn't it? I mean, I can't be healed overnight. I have to take it by fuggin' degrees, don't

I?"

"We both do." Cynthia ducked her head. "I mean...look John, before I met you I was perfectly content measuring and etching out letters for advertisements. But these days, strange and bizarre line sketches interest me somehow."

John smiled a little.

"And what's more," she went on, "I used to adore Tchaikovsky and Frank Sinatra – but now I live and breathe rock'n'roll."

"Good gerl."

"Before I met you...you know it...I was painfully shy. And well, look at me! Black hose and leather!" she smiled.

"Minx!"

"I guess what I'm saying is...I'm changing as well, John...one day at a time. We both are."

Cynthia wished she had more time to explain – that she didn't have to go home. She wished she hadn't promised her mum she'd be back on the Wirral at a reasonable hour. Most of all, Cynthia wished she had an apartment right here in Liverpool. But at the sound of a low train whistle, they both picked up the pace.

Besides, this wasn't something that could be solved by one long heart-to-heart, anyway. Their pasts would always tug at them. Their jealousies and insecurities would shadow their future. Finding their way out of the shadows would be a life's work, not just a conversation.

Many sources tell us that John was jealous of everyone all the time and frequently accused Cynthia of flirting and not loving him. In fact, Cynthia, in her book, John, *(p. 37) tells of an incident when John became furious with Cynthia and Stu because they danced together at a party. According to her, he even hit her in the face over this incident. And in* A Twist of Lennon *(p. 25-26) Cynthia talks in detail about John's jealousy and anger. But there is, however, no recorded story of him becoming jealous of Pete Shotton in the Jacaranda per se.*

Cynthia did change her hair, her clothes, her music preferences, and many other things for John, and she did long for an apartment in Liverpool. Cynthia did frequently take the last train back to the Wirral, and Mrs. Powell was constantly irritated with John because Cynthia stayed in town too late. And I'm sure that John and Cynthia had many conversations about the upcoming arts ball.

So all the ingredients of this chapter are true and documented. However, this exact unfolding of events is not actual, and the conversation, of course, is imagined.

20-27 August 1959
8 Hayman's Green
West Derby

Mona Best, her sons – Pete and Rory – and Mona's invalid mother, lived in a sprawling, drooping-a-bit-at-the-corners, Victorian home in Hayman's Green, a sleepy backyard stick ball sort of neighbourhood on a quiet, curved, treed street. Miles from City Centre, it was all garden swings and walkways, a residential nook for families who motored into town for work. It was a long established neighbourhood, just past elegance – a completely unlikely place for a nightclub. But the Best family was about to change all that.

Fresh off an unhappy separation from her husband, Johnny, the lovely, whey-skinned Mona now found herself in an uncomfortable and untenable financial situation. With two teenagers and a bedridden mother to care for, Mona had evaluated her opportunities and acknowledged they were slim. She couldn't accept a position in the city and leave her mother unattended all day long, but she couldn't afford a professional nurse or caretaker, either. Her sons' needs were, as were all adolescents', never-ending, and no matter how frugal the exotic, dark-eyed Mona tried to be, she simply couldn't make funds stretch as far as the demands placed upon them.

Her marriage to Johnny Best had not been without its redeeming qualities, however. Mona had learned a great deal from the talented, smooth-talking, handsome boxing promoter known for his grand events at the 6,000-seat Liverpool stadium. He'd taught Mona how to make something from nothing and how to find the one element for success in even the most hopeless predicaments. Johnny Best had taught her how to market herself and others successfully – how to recognize, Tom Sawyer-like, the inherent, albeit hidden, value of an unpainted fence.

The extensive, seven-room cellar system that lay beneath Mona's rambling Victorian home was such an "unpainted fence." Until recently, it had been a dank and leaky storage area, perfect for boxes of Christmas decorations, discarded clothes, and once-treasured toys. But now, the huge basement looked for all the world to Mona like a real moneymaker. She stood in the cellar doorway and let her imagination run wild.

In their former married life, Johnny and Mona had rubbed shoulders with other Merseyside entrepreneurs and business owners, and they'd frequented the fashionable coffeehouses of lower Liverpool 1. She'd visited basement clubs such as The Lowlands and Streates and had watched the growing market for establishments that featured jukeboxes replete with skiffle and rock'n'roll. Mona knew that a large room – any large room – could be converted into a gathering spot for the espresso and music crowd. And now as she swished her flashlight from corner to corner across the massive Hayman's Green cellar, her mind raced with possibilities.

Almost a year ago Pete and Rory, bored on summer holiday, had approached her about converting their subterranean "catacombs" into a clubhouse for their friends. Mo, as they called her, had indulged the boys' whims, but only half-heartedly, with only a grain of interest.

It wasn't until lately that Mona had seen in her sons' idea the glint of a greater vision, and she'd joined wholeheartedly in their enthusiasm, agreeing to knock down several walls to open up space – and to finance the construction of a fireplace. Mona had invested the little money she had left in her sons' plans.

She had footed the bill for a Dansette record player. She had hauled in endless sacks of plaster and buckets and buckets of paint. As the cool Liverpool summer crept on towards autumn, Mona, Pete, Rory, and a whole host of assorted friends had gradually transformed the dank basement into something interesting, even amazing.

Now the strong, Anglo-Irish woman who'd spent her childhood abroad in India stood leaning against the doorway, shining her flashlight on the ceiling beams and down the carefully patched walls into the recesses of each wider, broader compartment. After months of repair and restoration, Mona was beginning to envision the kind of club she and her sons were going to create. There would be one smaller room with tables and chairs, a cozy fireplace, and an espresso machine; there would be a larger room for dancing – a space big enough for a live band. Bit by bit the plan was unfolding. It was all coming together.

"Great. Looks great." Mona spoke quietly to herself. "We'll sell the coffee and Cokes over there, and perhaps a few sweets, who knows? And over in that area, the local bands can set up and have a go at it..."

"And we'll have really fantastic decorations as well, won't we?"

Mona jumped at the sound. It was her oldest son, Pete. He smiled and put a hand on her shoulder.

"Hullo, luv." She gave him a hug and quick kiss. Her handsome boys, Pete and Rory, were the joys of her life.

"Y'know, we need somethin' on the wall over there, Mo," he pointed, "somethin' to...erase the space, as it were." He always called her by her pet name.

"Right. But what?"

"Well, I thought about it, and Rory thought about it...and then we turned around and had this great idea."

"Yeah?" She was interested.

"A mural." Pete smiled his gorgeous Bobby Darin smile.

"A mural? Where'd we get one of those?" Johnny Best had taught her to be practical as well as creative.

"Well, as luck would have it, I've several connections that might just pay off," Pete winked. "Y'see, Ken Brown's friend, George Harrison – you know him – well, he's in a band with these lads from Liverpool College of Art, and quite naturally they'd love to play here sometime after we open, as it were. So..."

"So you're your father's son, Peter," Mona beamed. "You've seized the opportunity, haven't you?'

"They'll be over tomorrow mornin' to begin paintin'."

"Don't I love you!" Mona gave his arm a squeeze.

"Rory says we ought to do spider webs on the wall as well," Pete grinned, borrowing her flashlight to trace out the plan, "silvery white ones against the black background...highlighted with spotlights here and there for an eerie sheen."

"Good for hiding the plaster patches as well," his mother agreed.

"Creative camouflage," Pete nodded.

"And up there," Mona lifted his arm so that his flashlight yellowed the dark ceiling, "we'll have a magnificent dragon...a dragon big and bright and vivid...a dragon dramatic enough for a place known as 'The Casbah.'"

Pete smiled. "We'll give y'one even Charles Boyer would be proud of!"

Mona ruffled her son's thick, wavy hair. "I've got complete confidence in you, luv. After all, it's really *your* dream, isn't it – this place? Yours and Rory's. I'm just the foreman, so to speak."

"More like the CEO-Manager-Chief-Cook'n-Bottle-Washer all rolled into one," Pete laughed, following her upstairs.

"Well, as long as we're all in it together somehow." Mona heaved open the door to the ground floor. Pete followed her into the kitchen.

At her makeshift desk, the breakfast table, Mona scratched a few more notes on a clipboard tablet and then stuck the pencil back in her French twist. Tomorrow she'd purchase the business license while her sons supervised the painting and decorating, and with a little luck, the dream born of summertime ennui would become a "corporate" reality by teatime.

Mona only hoped that Pete and Rory would never realize how significant their pet project really was. She hoped they would see it as only a lark and remember it as one of the happiest times of their lives.

****

West Derby was the last place Cynthia had planned to spend her summer vacation. Renovating a musty, cobwebbed basement was the last thing she'd planned to tackle. But John had coerced her into doing so many things she'd never anticipated, and transforming Mona Best's suburban cellar into a teen nightclub was just another way of proving her devotion.

Cynthia's shoulder-length pageboy was splattered with paint. Her arms and shoulders ached, and she was grateful that John had insisted she wear old clothes.

But her delicate spider webs were intricate and well crafted. The smallest ones glistened from the corners and detailed, larger ones crawled across the main walls. *Quite wonderful if I say so myself!* Cynthia smiled. *Not bad for a lettering student, is it?*

John was equally exhausted. In the last few days, he'd virtually moved into the Best's home – running errands, attaching the hand-made wall benches, and moving scads of cardboard boxes into a rear, locked storage room. John had spared nothing ingratiating himself to Mona and her sons. From the moment George had hinted to him that a new club was opening in West Derby – a club that needed a headliner band – John had become the Best's primary volunteer.

What he didn't realize was that Pete had spent a great deal of time over the last week trying to keep John *away* from the murals being carefully crafted all around him. The little work that John had done on the Casbah's spider webs had been just shy of devastating.

Blind as a mole, John had, nevertheless, tried to paint enthusiastically alongside the others. But whereas Cynthia had worked meticulously, John had smeared and smudged. He'd applied black oil paint liberally on the ceiling without undercoat as a base, and now it stubbornly refused to dry in the moist, subterranean atmosphere. He'd touched up the mural work from one room to the next, and now glistening blotches of wet oil paint stood out, unsightly patchwork in the spotlights. It was all Pete and Cynthia could do to keep John otherwise engaged until the mural was finished.

They sent him out for electrical wiring, asked him to place telephone orders, and busied him with the final installation of the refreshment counter. And when John was spotted with a paintbrush in his hand, his coworkers intervened with a laundry list of odd jobs that needed doing right away.

"John, John, come talk to me, luv!" Mona patted the seat beside her on the wall bench. She moved over a bit for the boy and smiled. Mona had a plan, and John Lennon was the first pawn in the strategy.

The band she'd slated for opening night – The Les Stewart Quartet – had recently quarreled with their rhythm guitarist, Ken Brown, over the many hours he'd spent renovating the Best's basement, and in a defensive fit, Ken had left the group entirely. Ken was still The Casbah's most devoted volunteer, but he was a man without a band, and Mona was left to suffer the consequences. She now had to fall back on "Plan B."

"Right, Mo!" John genuinely liked Mona Best. She was like Julia in many ways – unconventional, brash, beautiful, and interesting to talk to; she was what John called "the genuine article." "How's the lovely Mona, then? Ready for openin' night, as it were?"

"Well…just look around!" Mona waved her hand at the room. "I think we're more than halfway there, don't you? I mean, I've even put in an extra order for crisps and hot dogs. We're expectin' quite a crowd, young John."

John smiled a little and nodded. "I'm sure you've thought of everythin'…you 'n Pete 'n Rory."

"Let's hope." Mona crossed her fingers. "At least, it *looks* great. Unusual…exotic. Reminds me a little of India, as it were."

They sat in silence for a moment watching the others scurry around with last minute touches and changes.

"Georgie tells me he plays in a band of yours when he's not playing with The Les Stewart Quartet," Mona broached the subject.

"That's right. The Quarry Men…sometimes we're Johnny and the Moondogs." John hoisted his guard. This was the moment he'd been waiting for. "Pete knows about us." Chewing gum and leaning forward a bit, he looked around the room nonchalantly. "We've played some dances at Quarry Bank Grammar…and the Woolton Fête as well. We've even done a coupla gigs for Allan Williams down at The Jacaranda, y'know."

"Really? Not bad." Mona was guarded, too. She knew John's group had been virtually out of work for the last few months, but she didn't show her hand.

"We've even played The Cavern Club," John went on. "On occasion."

Mona bit her lip to hide a smile. *So, the boy knows a bit about promoting as well. I'll have to watch this one! He's savvy – John Lennon.*

"Right, well, sounds as if you're all very busy then." She put out the bait.

"Yeah, right. Here and there, there and here." John held his ground. He turned and looked her squarely in the eye. Mona liked that.

"Actually, *here* is exactly what I had in mind," Mona smiled. The mountain came to Mohammed. "I'd actually like to have you boys play at the opening of the club on the 29th. We've lots of local publicity, and it promises to be a sensation if all goes as planned – a blockbuster event as West Derby events go. But I need a group that'll live up to that kind of expectation…that level of excitement. I need a band that'll be as spectacular as these incredible decorations…"

"Right then, we'll take it." John snapped up the deal. Mona suppressed a giggle.

"But there *are* some stipulations, John." She held up her hand, reining in the boy's enthusiasm. "I can only offer you a small fee since we're just settin' out…three pounds a night for the group – divvy it up as you will."

John nodded, less exuberant now.

"And," Mona went on, "I've already promised Ken Brown that he can play as well, so you'd have to take him on for all the gigs you do here."

"Ken Brown?" John cut his eyes at the skinny, hollow-cheeked lad. Mona could see that John wasn't at all thrilled.

"That's right. Ken's been here helpin' us all summer long – well before Georgie brought you lot over. He even separated from The Les Stewart Quartet, y'know, when they criticised him for workin' for us. As I see it, Ken deserves a chance to share in whatever so-called glory there may be…"

Mona paused for a moment, and John looked away. He stared at Cynthia, squatting to touch up a corner spider web. He waited. John, too, played his cards close to his vest.

"And of course," Mona pitched in the trump, "you do realize that Ken's got a ten-watt amplifier you could use as long as he's part of your group. I know you boys need one, especially in a dungeon like this." She paused again. "In fact, you might be entirely surprised, John, to discover how much Ken could add to your…presentation, as it were."

"Right…but…well," he chewed his gum vigorously, "it's just that we've got guitarists, y'know. It's a drummer we haven't got." John was up-front with the entrepreneurial woman. Mo respected that and nodded. "And Ken Brown – he's never played with us, not even once, has he? It'd all be new to him – the play list, the style 'n all."

"Well," Mona Best looked at her watch as if every second counted, "then I'd say, you'd better get to practising then. You've only a few days remainin' if you Quarry Men plus Ken want to be The Casbah's resident band, and 'time is money' as they say. Isn't that how it goes?"

"I wudden know." John smiled. "Is that how it goes?"

"Exactly," Mona stood up and patted John perfunctorily on the shoulder. Then, without another word, she hurried off to greet the fire inspector who'd just appeared, stern and businesslike, clipboard in hand.

Pete Best says there were seven rooms in the basement and draws a map of them in his book, Beatle! The Pete Best Story. *The Casbah was large enough to hold 2,000 teens as a record in one evening.*

Without a doubt, the best source for information on Mona Best and The Casbah may be Roag Best's book, The Beatles: The True Beginnings, *written in conjunction with Rory and Pete Best. Maps, photos, interviews, and an excellent narrative tell The Casbah story in great detail. For example, all other books refer to Mona Best as an "Anglo-Indian woman," and her jet-black hair may have given credence to that legend. But Mona's parents were Irish (see p. 10). Her father, Thomas Shaw, had been educated at Cambridge and then sent to India as a major in the British army. And although Mona was often mistaken for "an Indian princess" when she returned to Liverpool with her British husband, Johnny Best, she, according to her sons, had not an ounce of Indian blood in her.*

In 2006, the Liverpool City Council voted to place The Casbah on the list of historically important places in England. This means that the building will be kept intact for future generations. The paintings described in this chapter will be well preserved.

Saturday, 29 August 1959
The Casbah Club
West Derby

Liverpool was never steamy in August, particularly late August, but it was tonight. Streams of perspiration trickled down between Mona's ample breasts and pooled at the beltline of her dress as she doled out Casbah membership cards to the noisy swell of teenagers. It was a few minutes shy of eight, and The Quarry Men were tuning up, twanging out sour notes and finding better ones.

"Ouch! Watch fuggin' out!" a girl yapped as someone crushed her toe.

"Watch out yerself, gerl!" came the sharp retort.

A boy with particularly unpleasant acne inadvertently elbowed the boy beside him for room, and the injured swung around, ready for a fight. No one had an ounce of patience in the heat, and Mona was working as furiously as she could to herd them all inside before something awful began.

Around half-seven, Mona had decided to open the upstairs kitchen doors as well as the basement entranceway to help expedite matters, to help get the crowds in off the quiet, residential street. But teenagers were arriving faster than Pete and she could process the membership fees, faster than they could fill out the official club cards. No matter how efficiently they worked, there was still a backlog – a steady stream of teens trampling her early chrysanthemums into fragrant mush.

"Cynthia!" she called out to John Lennon's girlfriend, who had come up from the basement for a momentary breath of fresh air, "Be a luv and run back downstairs and tell the boys to hold off for a while, all right? We'll need at least another half hour to get these Johnny-come-latelys off the street and in the door."

"Half-eight, then?" Cynthia queried.

"No…I'll signal when ready. There's still a steady stream of taxis out here."

It was busier than Pete, Rory, or Mona had ever anticipated.

But Rory had had little chance to notice, to take in the big picture. Head down, sweat running from his forearms and over his fingers, he stood at the downstairs entrance to the muggy basement and sold sweets and cold drinks – pulling change from a metal divider box and counting it out carefully as his mother had instructed. He waded in sticky, syrupy pools of Coke as he worked, and every few minutes, he would grab a handful of paper napkins to daub the sweat dripping from his chin.

The place was packed. With school only a week away – summer dangerously near demise – the desperate teens wanted to party. They squealed to each other, waving their arms wildly above the mass of bodies. They yelled out messages that couldn't be heard and tried to signal with hand gestures and over-exaggerated expressions.

Finally, at 8:45 pm, Mona gave Cynthia Powell the nod, and The Quarry Men struck the opening chord. Applause rippled through the room. Everyone standing began to dance – some voluntarily, some by unavoidable motion.

John, in black skin-tight jeans and a black, short-sleeved shirt, his collar upturned like Elvis's, placed his mouth against the microphone. He took a deep breath, held it for a second, and then exhaled song.

Sweat poured off his face. His shirt was thoroughly soaked. John's hands slipped across the frets, and his thoughts raced. *This is it! This is fuggin' it!* he repeated to himself over and over as he sang. His hands tingled, and he shivered with goose bumps. He'd only had a couple of pints before arriving at The Casbah, but he was thoroughly intoxicated – drunk with the mania of it all. Everything was a blur.

Cynthia was mesmerized. She'd seen John practice many times at the college or The Jacaranda. She'd seen him play for friends. But he'd never looked or performed like this. This was revel! This was something primitive, something sexual. This was an energy she'd never seen. Cynthia couldn't take her eyes off him.

Other girls felt it, too. They danced with their faces to the band – staring, absorbing not so much the music as the magnetism. And strangely enough, although their dates acknowledged the attraction, they seemed to like the band as well.

Paul laughed and winked at the crowd, rocking back and forth, picking out girls in the crowd to sing to. George played with a satisfied smirk, glancing up at Ken Brown now and again to share a knowing look. The four boys on the stage were having fun.

As the first song ended, the crowd roared, hands in the air, bodies pressed together, breathless. John made a face at the audience while Paul consulted with George. Ken Brown waved to a friend. Someone whooped. John did a quick dance step and a lunge, and the audience laughed.

"Hi everyone!" John shouted above the rumble of the room, "Welcome to The Casbah!" The cheers went on for what seemed like minutes. "We're The Quarrymen, and we're goin' to play y'some rock'n'roll!"

Stomps, shouts, applause, cheers!

The infectious rhythm of Little Richard's "Long Tall Sally" set the gel of bodies in motion again, and John squinted at the blur of faces while Paul belted out lyrics, sparing nothing. George concentrated, making almost no mistakes in the complicated lead line, while Ken followed adeptly on rhythm in spite of a dearth of practises. Everyone knew "Long Tall Sally."

It was George's turn next. "Three Cool Cats" was his one big vocal solo, and he doled out deep-dish Scouse. John and Paul sang the harmony and hammed it up. The crowd devoured it.

From the back of the room, Pete Best watched, resting a second from the non-stop ticket sales that had been going on since seven o'clock. He was dead sick of saying, "Annual club membership two shillings, six p – and five p for entrance tonight." He'd literally said it hundreds of times.

Pete watched with envy as John Lennon stepped up and launched into the Del Vikings' hit, "Come Go with Me," while a girl in the back of the room cupped her hands and screamed, "Good on yer, luv!" at the band.

Cynthia heard it, too. She popped her head around towards the sound and issued an icy glare. But the cry could have come from anyone in the room. Every girl she could see was brazenly staring at John.

John was singing as he'd never sung. The old Quarry Men standard – one they'd sung myriad times – had new life in the packed room. Adrenalin high, John found a power in performing that he'd never felt until tonight.

It came, in part, from the empowering anonymity of this venue. No one knew his name in West Derby. They weren't his cronies, his relatives, or his professors. They owed him nothing. They had no allegiance of any kind to John Lennon. To them, he was just "the rocker," the throaty, nasal rebel with the puckish grin. "Good on yer!" was all the girl had yelled. But it had instantaneously made him the one adored. He basked in the feeling.

The pace quickened now. John stepped forward to sing. He swallowed, squinted his eyes, and snaked his neck towards the microphone. Ken's amplifier screamed, and John winced automatically, but he went right on:

I know a girl, a friend o' mine,
Sixteen years of age!
Every day in the book of men,
She turns another page.
Innocent and sweet...
Hearts fall at her feet...
Her soft replies capture eyes
No matter what she says -
Or where they meet!

His raspy, rock'n'roll voice sent the crowd into delirium. They waved their arms erratically – their bodies spinning and gyrating, their hips moving to the music. Even Mona, now handing out Cokes and Fantas in assembly line fashion, bobbed her head to the beat as she worked.

The lads are unpolished, no doubt about it, she admitted, *but they're also brash in a catchy sort of way. Not bad – not bad at all.*

She shot a quick glance in the direction of the small, raised platform they'd devised as a stage, and she smiled at her choice of opening night band. There was John Lennon, hips thrust forward in those "born in them" jeans, singing his gut out to a throng of elated females.

He's in his element here, Mona mused, wiping her sweat-streaked cheek on her shoulder, *not unlike Johnny Best himself...powder kegs both of them...energetic, handsome, sexy, and talented. But very dangerous – those two.*

"Hey mum! Coke *please!*"

Mona snapped back to the moment. The line of demanding customers was never-ending. It wound back into the narrow hallway.

On the crude wooden stage, Paul fanned the fury in the room. "Are you all enjoyin' yourselves, then?" He wagged his head from side to side as the crowd roared. "I can't hear you. Do you really want some more?" He laughed and winked and lapped up the cheers.

George seized the moment to launch full-throttle into "Roll Over Beethoven." Ken Brown chugged along behind them good naturedly, and John cavorted madly across the platform, entertaining the crowd even though it was not his song.

All eyes were on The Quarry Men from Woolton. The West Derby newspaper had billed the group as "Kenneth Brown and some boys from south of town," but now that billing seemed ludicrous. The "boys from south of town" were clearly running the show while Ken was all background scenery. Every eye in the room was on The Quarry Men.

As they paused for a short break, Mona's hired d.j. Bob Stuart, set the tiny Dansette record player in motion. Pete and his friends, Chas Newby and Bill Barton, seized the chance to make their way through the crowd towards the refreshment booth. Slowly weaving and squeezing this way and that, they edged closer and closer to the counter. When Bill found a former girlfriend to reconnect with and Chas begged off for a breath of fresh air, Pete wedged inside the tiny wooden refreshment stand and nudged his mother playfully.

"Come with me to the Caaaasssbaaah!" he said in her ear, delivering his finest Charles Boyer impression.

"Not bloody likely...not anytime soon, that is. Look at that line of bodies, would you? Where'd they all come from – this crowd? Pitch in, Pete luv. I'm all but buried here." She pushed a Coke bottle, a thick, nickel bottle opener, and a tall stack of cups towards him.

"Not buried, Mo," Pete grinned, lifting the heavy moneybox beside her. "Rescued! In fact, I think tonight we're all witnessin' the beginnin' of something really big here!"

"I'll drink to that!" Mona toasted, and she downed the small Coke she'd just poured for someone else.

"Hey, miss...Coke *please*!"

"Yeah, we're all blindin' parched here, y'know!" another complained.

"It's several hundred degrees in this room, as it were!"

Mona nodded at the Scouse teens and returned to work with Pete beside her. There was no chance to reflect further. Within the half hour, the band began again, but the line of teenagers never diminished until closing time, and in her sleep that night Mona was still selling and pouring Cokes to the sound of John Lennon singing "Blue Suede Shoes."

The events and characters are documented. The song John is singing in this chapter is not the one he actually sang. He really sang "Sweet Little Sixteen" by Chuck Berry. The song in this chapter is "Sweet Sixteen Lisa" by Rande Kessler. The conversations between Mo and Cynthia, and later Mo and Pete are imagined.

September 1959
Canteen
Liverpool College of Art campus
Liverpool

Cynthia had somewhat lost touch with the outside world. John was her world these days. They were constantly together, meeting for lunch behind the curtain on the art college canteen stage and parting only reluctantly at Cyn's classroom doors. On the weekends, Cynthia went with him to The Casbah and in the evenings, the couple closeted themselves away in Stu's flat.

Today they sat in the school canteen, leaning in, almost touching, forming an arc of interest. Their eyes fixed on each other, their conversation intimate – whispered words – Cyn and John were oblivious to the hurried noon scramble around them.

"Yeah, well the best part was when she'd reach through those open glass frames to rub her eye." John smiled a little. "Up to that point, it'd never occurred to the store clerk, or whoever, that her glasses were bogus. And Julia'd act like it wasn't a bit out of the ordinary to be wearin' empty frames. She'd just go right on with her conversation – never smilin' or breakin' character."

Cynthia squeezed his hand. "I would've loved her, wouldn't I?"

He went on. "I remember the two of us walkin' a bit after school or on days when I was saggin' off...me mum'd do all sorts of things to make me laugh. She'd say to me, 'Watch this, John!' and she'd then drag out this old pair of knickers from her handbag...and she'd arrange them on her head like some ridiculous hat!"

"She wouldn't!"

"She would. And people'd stare at us as if we'd both gone completely daft. One grocer in Mossley Hill even ordered us out of his establishment altogether...as if we were interruptin' the decorum of his radishes and Weetabix."

"So what'd Julia do then?"

"She gave him this long, haughty, down-the-nose glare...and then turned to me and said, 'As one green vegetable said to the other, lettuce leaf!' And we did."

Cynthia's laughter was contagious. People at other tables in the canteen smiled along, even though they couldn't hear a word John was saying.

"And when Twitchy was workin' late," John paused his narrative to take a slurp of tea, "we'd sit up at their house in Spring Wood, listenin' to one Elvis record after another – 'Jailhouse Rock,' 'Heartbreak Hotel,' 'Hound Dog,' and all the rest. She had the complete collection, y'know."

Cynthia rubbed his hand with her thumb.

"Then we'd all dance around the front room…me and Jacqui and Ju and Julia…goin' on for what seemed like forever. I mean, she was never tired – especially when m'cousin, Lelia, was there to egg her on. We'd all 'rock around the clock' for hours. We'd have Chuck Berry and Little Richard and Buddy Holly on the player, and always Elvis. It was always Elvis in those days."

"Did she look like you?" Cynthia's face was serious now.

"I've got her eyes. I've got her blindness." John half chuckled. "And Mim says I've got her smile as well."

"I feel as if I almost know her. I wish I had."

They were silent for a moment. Cynthia poured John a bit more Earl Grey from the small, white ceramic pot between them. "You know, I never had the joy of having sisters as you do," she said, "I mean, having two older, much bigger brothers is no comparison. There's no teasing or pulling pranks on them, you can imagine."

"Yeah, Jacqui and Ju were always easy targets when it came to shenanigans." John rubbed a finger across his thick, unruly eyebrows. "They believed just about anythin' – hook, line and fuggin' sinker…in fact, Julia and I once convinced them that there were giant fish and sea monsters swimmin' about the Wirral Tunnel."

"You're joking now."

"Nah, every time we'd cross over to Cheshire to see me mum's older sister, Nanny, we'd have the girls convinced we could see mermaids and sharks movin' around, all about us. Jacqui was too young to question our authority, and Ju had too much fun with it all to admit she wasn't really taken in. We'd string'em along mercilessly the whole three and a half miles to the Wirral."

"There was never anything like that in my family."

"Well, we cornered the market on fun, I suppose. Life was all games and stories and music and paintings to Julia – all imagination. She was just out to have a good laugh, y'know. Just out to…" John looked away.

Cynthia rubbed his hand and waited.

"One afternoon, she spent hours paintin' a daffodil on the wall of her bathroom," he went on. "She took a lot of care with it, and it turned out great. But when it was done, she painted underneath: 'Do you want your teeth to look like a spring daffodil? Then brush them!' That's how she was. There was this current of humour underlyin' everythin' she did."

"Just like someone else." Cynthia said. "Although you've a serious side, too."

"Well in a way, she did as well," John nodded. "I mean, she was all about independence and the power of women and the rights of the person – Julia. She was the rebel of the family. 'A real eyebrow raiser,' as Pop Stanley used to put it."

"Because she refused to follow the norm?"

"Because she bleedin' thumbed her nose at society – at its rules and authority and all that. She did whatever she fuggin' pleased – Julia. She played the banjo in the local pubs, danced 'til all hours, never had a regular job for too long, and lived by her own fuggin' instincts instead of by the book. Mimi and Mater and Nanny and Harrie – they all had spunk and plenty of it, y'know. The Stanley sisters, strong and determined! But Julia, she was *passionate* about life. She was…" His voice trailed off.

"I know you miss her." Cynthia spoke with tightness in her own throat. "I miss my father, too, John…his quietness, his gentleness, the way he softened our family. My mum is much too strong these days. Too…joyless."

"Right," John snorted indignantly. "That's Mim in a nutshell – joyless."

Cynthia nodded.

"I asked Mim once," John bit his bottom lip, "why she made it this rule to be home every day when I arrived back from school. She always told everyone she was there for me, always made it a point to say that 'John never arrives home to an empty house.'"

"And? What did she say to that?"

"She said, 'Because it's my duty to be here, John.' *That* was her fuggin' answer."

"But I'm sure in her own way she actually meant…"

"I told her she didn't have to be there," John interrupted. "I told her there was no need for her to be there and that if she was only there for duty then she could be excused from it…that I would be fine from then on, as it were. But all she ever said was, 'Someday when you grow up, John, you'll understand.' And now that I am – grown-up, that is – I do. And that's the worst part of it, Cyn… the understandin'."

Cynthia reached out and pulled John to her and kissed him with a tenderness that disregarded time, place, or convention. John didn't resist, and Cynthia pulled him gently closer, enveloping him, past pain, past memory, past understanding, past the agony he lived in. She kissed him.

Cynthia was rarely funny. John's cohorts were eager to point that out to him at every opportunity. She wasn't a risk-taker or a rebel…and seldom a merry-maker. She didn't really fit into his circle of friends. She wasn't bohemian. She wasn't a rocker or a raver. And she was blatantly uncomfortable breaking rules or even stepping a bit out of the norm.

But Cynthia listened with quiet empathy, spoke with love, and was always there. And most importantly, nothing that she said to John was ever said out of pity. And nothing that Cynthia ever did for John was done for duty's sake.

All the stories about John and his mother and sisters are lovingly told by his sister, Julia Baird, in her book, John Lennon: My Brother. *It is a quick read and a good one. And the information about Cynthia's father is found in* Twist of Lennon, *also an excellent book. Even John and Cynthia's habit of meeting on the canteen stage at noon is documented. Very little in this chapter is imagined.*

November 1959
Liverpool College of Art
Liverpool

John's return to Liverpool College of Art in September had been reluctant at best. In fact, drudgery. He viewed school now primarily as a convenient rendezvous spot for moments with Cyn. Without her as a draw, he mightn't have bothered to return at all.

Exhilarated from weekly Saturday evening performances at the Best's ragingly popular Casbah Club, John was obsessed more than ever with rock'n'roll. Everything else was extraneous. School was less than that. It was useless.

He no longer turned in half-completed homework exercises; he ignored them entirely. Devoting every afternoon to the composition of hopeful hits, every evening to practise and performance, every spare moment to some new tune or lyric, John dismissed school completely. Only Cynthia fretted over his academic standing...fretted *and* intervened.

Forging John's name, she submitted lettering exercises on his behalf while John spent his hours "half-pissed" at Ye Cracke or The Jac. Jotting lyrics on envelopes or beer mats and swapping ideas with Paul, John remembered the art college only peripherally. Cynthia completed his art projects and handed in his papers, and John attended college *in absentia*.

In truth, John no longer even considered himself a student at Liverpool College of Art. He was eager to end the charade.

But the art college had not forgotten John. They were insulted over his absence, infuriated. And they saw absolutely no reason to give the boy a spot that some other more deserving young artist might fill. After ten weeks of John's noncompliance with the rules, George Jardine spearheaded a faculty group calling for the boy's dismissal.

"Yes, yes, yes, I see your point, George. I understand," Arthur Ballard, John's only proponent, admitted. "But at the risk of being redundant...let me remind you again that John is...strangely brilliant...outstanding in a thousand different ways...though, all right, a rebel."

"Understatement," Jardine lightly stroked his dark goatee.

"Yes, we all know John's off focus now. No doubt about it. I'll give you that."

"Nice of you, Ballard," Nicholas Horsefield cut his eyes subtly at the others.

"But all of you know his circumstances," Ballard leaned in, "and they're…overwhelming."

"We *all* have circumstances of some sort, Arthur." Jardine drummed his fingers on the faculty table.

"Right, right. But Lennon," Ballard reached out, trying to capture some shred of empathy, "John Lennon's shell-shocked, really…still in mourning over his mother's death, y'know."

"That happened well over a year ago, Arthur," Charles Burton stepped in.

"Right. True…." Arthur took a long drag on his cigarette and stared out the tremendous, floor-to-ceiling Palladian window at the end of the room. The slate November sky offered no inspiration, no wisp of encouragement as he searched for something to say. "But, y'must understand, that John's…"

"Give it up, Arthur," Horsefield chided.

George Jardine cleared his throat.

Ballard sighed with puffed cheeks. But he tried again. "Let me take another tack, then, if you won't have that. And this, I believe, is more pertinent to the situation." Arthur pushed his heavy chair back from the table and stood up, as if addressing Parliament. "Lettering, gentlemen, is simply not John Lennon's medium. Never was. Never will be. And so if there's blame to be had for his boredom and non-attendance, it's ours entirely. Mine, more specifically. Mine…for forcing him into a curriculum for which he's completely ill-suited and thoroughly disinterested."

"You didn't force him! You rescued him!" Horsefield insisted.

"I'll not have him back in graphics, if that's what you're implying!" Jardine took a firm stance. John had disrupted his *last* drawing class.

"Force him?" Charles Burton chortled. "I'd like to see someone force John Lennon to do *anything* he didn't want to do!"

"But regardless," Ballard wouldn't relent, "you know John's far too creative for the strictures of lettering, far too design-oriented…"

"Don't go in that direction either, Arthur! He's no appeal for me." The voice came from the far end of the table.

"That's right, Ballard," came another. "We're *all* done with him. Absolutely done."

"I firmly believe," Arthur paced, undaunted, "that John Lennon belongs in the new Faculty of Design."

"He'd be lost, Arthur." Charles Burton rose as well, getting up with great difficulty, stabilizing himself with an iron grip on the large, oblong table. "John Lennon would be lost," he repeated in his deep, Welsh brogue. "And why you ask? Because Arthur, in the School of Design *you* would no longer be his mentor. There'd be no Arthur Ballard there to forgive the man's tardiness, profanities, thinly veiled threats, cynicism, and hell-bent, destructive nature. You'd not be there, Arthur...and thus ultimately, Lennon would fail."

"It's not like you to be so fatalistic, Charles." Arthur leaned against the wall, "Or to give up without a fight."

"Without a *fight*?" Burton snapped back. He rubbed his thick hand across his forehead, stopping to squeeze the bridge of his nose. "Arthur, for two and a half years now we've *all* served as the butt of Lennon's sick jokes. We've argued with him, pleaded with him, reprimanded him, and despised him more and more with every apathetic response we've received. He's disrupted our classes and infected our more serious students – including your Stuart Sutcliffe! He's frittered away his college years. He's hardly attended a class since the beginning of this term. But ironically, that absence has been nothing short of a holiday for us all! Listen, I could go on and on, Arthur. We all could. We simply can't rehabilitate your genius or serve as his personal team of psychiatrists. We're artists here, Arthur, not clinical physicians. And what you're asking us to do is simply undoable."

Arthur slumped back in his chair. This was defeat, and he knew it. They had summarily dismissed Geoff Mohammed. Now John was next in line.

"I believe," he said, "the appropriate quote here is, 'The only thing necessary for the perpetuation of evil is for good people to do nothing,'" He looked around the room. "Is that it, then? Will we do nothing to save this young man's career?"

But there was no response. Arthur hadn't anticipated one.

"Well," he took a deep breath, "suppose we table this discussion of the indubitable Mr. Lennon for a while...until we can mull it over, give it some thought...roll it around, as it were." Arthur employed the last trick in his bag. "Who knows? Perhaps over the next week or so, things'll improve. And if not, then you have my promise: I'll relent in this crusade. I'll relent *under protest*, of course... but if things don't improve soon, then I give you my word, I'll concede."

"We all live in hope, Arthur. We all live in hope."

This entire conversation is conjecture based upon interviews with George Jardine and June Furlong, and upon information found in Sutcliffe-Clayson and Coleman.

Saturday, 14 November 1959
Mendips
Woolton

Mimi despised the cold.

But there was no tuna for the cats and nothing for tea, and last night she'd used the last two eggs for a Stilton and canned mushroom omelet. If she didn't force herself to walk to the grocer's in Penny Lane, she'd have nothing at all on the weekend.

Her reflection in the hallway mirror was dour as she dug out her wool coat with its outdated buttons and epaulets and pulled it on. She wrangled with a mohair wrapper that an American pen pal had sent her last Christmas, winding it securely around her head and neck, crushing her set-and-style hairdo. Mimi patted the thick scarf down well into her collar.

The day was miserable. A dark wind howled and shoved the last of the leaves right up against her iron fence and stucco walls and wedged them into the crevices. Mimi had tried to rake them all as they fell, but without John's assistance – although he'd been precious little help when he *was* living at home – the leaf removal had been exhausting.

Mimi shook her head. She stepped out and locked the door behind her.

In the many novels she'd read in her book-of-the-month club, heroines frequently took long walks in the brisk winter air to clear their heads, and American essayists, such Walt Whitman, recommended such constitutionals as invigourating, therapeutic. Mimi vehemently disagreed. She found the persistent wind and chill annoying.

Nothing made her happy these days, really. Not her books, her cats, her boarders, her plans for the spring garden, her holiday shopping, or even her sisters. Everything was depressing.

John was hardly ever home. Even though he lived less than half an hour away and the bus system was inexpensive and excellent, he rarely came back to Mendips. Yesterday he'd rung her up to tell her that his band was headed to Manchester for yet another audition with that Carroll Levis, the "Star Maker" they'd attempted to impress several years ago. John had bragged that the group had already made it into the final round of competition, and he felt confident they'd win. But his voice had negated his words. Mimi knew that John had never been more unsure of anything.

Mimi knew the score. She realized that John had probably needed money for his bus trip – fare for the train excursion into Manchester. But she didn't volunteer. She didn't say much.

She didn't tell him that she'd seen articles in the various local papers about his band's appearances at The Casbah Club. She didn't mention the phone calls she'd been getting from disgruntled professors, and she didn't ask about his new friend, Cynthia Powell. Mimi had been quiet and stoic on the line.

"How's Nanny and Harrie, then?" John had tried to gin up conversation.

"Well," she'd answered.

"And Lelia?" He'd tried to sound interested.

"She drops by quite regularly," came the pointed reply.

"How's Tim, then?" John knew she loved to talk about her cats.

"Fine."

"Read any good books, Mim?" He'd grasped at straws.

"I didn't realize you'd be interested," she had pouted.

And because he really wasn't interested, John gave up. He slammed down the phone with a pledge to call her less frequently – to distance himself from the sour woman who prided herself on being impenetrable.

Now Mimi walked down Menlove Avenue with her chin tucked into her coat and her arms crossed over her waistline. She took purposeful strides to keep her temperature up, and she tried not to think about John. She wondered how he'd afford the trip to Manchester, how he'd afford lodging if the band had to stay over. She wondered if he'd have anything to eat. And she wondered how in the world she'd come to deserve this cruel separation from the boy she loved so much.

Information about John's relationship with Mimi was provided by interviews with June Furlong, Helen Anderson, Allan Williams, Beryl Adams, Eddie Porter, Charlie Lennon, and Joe Flannery.

The Manchester Levis audition, calls from professors, and infrequency of John's visits to Mendips are all documented. However, this particular incident is conjecture.

Sunday, 15 November 1959
The Manchester Hippodrome
Manchester

"Unfuggin'believable! Sunnyside Skiffle's done it to us all over again!" Colin Hanton slapped his thighs with his drumsticks. "Look at that, would you? It's *déjà vu*! They're bringin' down the house again… just like they did at The Empire two years back!"

Paul was equally frustrated. "There's no accountin' for taste these days, is there?"

The unruly crowd of Manchester fans who'd gathered in Ardwick Green for Carroll Levis's "Search for the Stars" was applauding madly – stomping and shouting for The Connaughts, formerly The Sunnyside Skiffle group.

"Is *that* what the masses want, then?" John snarled. "A side show, as it were?"

"Apparently so," Paul grumbled.

"Ah, give it up," George shook his head. "The Connaught's'er just better'n us, that's all."

"Listen laddie," John put on his pensioner's persona, "we were bleedin' good back in our day, weren't we, son? We can't help it if we're all washed up now, can we?"

George smiled and shook his head. "The Connaughts have won it, fair and square."

Nicky Cuff's Liverpool's Connaughts came bouncing into the stage wings, laughing and ribbing each other over their obvious victory, cheering for their diminutive leader. Nicky grinned and clasped his hands together, swinging them from shoulder to shoulder in anticipation of their obvious victory. His band mates whooped and talked over one another.

"Ugh!" John waved them off. "Disgustin' – that."

"Cuff one – Johnny and the Moondogs, zip," Paul muttered, aggravated.

"Actually that's Cuff *two*, Moondogs zip," George reminded him. "Don't forget Sunnyside defeated The Quarry Men at the '57 Empire audition as well…. back in the day…before you and me came along. Isn't that right, John?"

"He's only right – he is." The old, hunchbacked John cackled, patting George's shoulder.

The roar in The Manchester Hippodrome increased. The crowd was still cheering and chanting for The Connaughts to return to the stage. Since Carroll Levis had empowered the audience to pick tonight's winner in the "Search for the Stars" finalist round, the rambunctious masses were taking the selection seriously.

"Great show, lads!" The Connaughts congratulated each other, shaking hands.

"Took'em by storm, didn't we?" Les Conway shook a fist in the air.

"Yeah, what a rave-up, eh?" Martin King laughed.

"We love you, Manchester! We fuggin' love you!" Billy Jevons did a little dance and collided into Cuff with a shout.

"Yeah, Manchester! We effin' love you!" drummer Art Knowleson agreed.

They were oblivious to the frustrated Moondogs standing beside them.

"Good on yer, Cuff. Good to see all yer work hasn't been for con-naught!" John slapped Nicky on the back, a slap just past congratulatory.

"Ta Lennon," Nicky grinned. "Say, how'd we sound from back here, then?"

"Paul was moved to tears," John straight-faced. "And George is seriously considerin' leavin' us and joinin' you straight'way. We all so want to be like you, Cuff. That's the long and *short* of it, son."

"Buggeroff, Lennon." Nicky hardly flinched at yet another joke at his expense. "I should've known better'n to ask you. McCartney?"

"Loved it Nicky," Paul offered a thumbs-up and a smile. "You were right on tonight, weren't you?"

"Not bad, not bad." Nicky raked in the laurels. "And you weren't so bad yerself. Our groups are sure to go head to head in the final clap-o-meter, as it were."

"I'll see your applause and raise you three cheers," John muttered.

"We're not sure if we'll even *be here* for the final clap-o-meter," George informed Nicky. "I mean, it's gettin' rather late, isn't it?"

"Only half ten," Nicky consulted his watch. "You Moondogs *are* lodgin' in – here in Manchester, aren't you?"

"Couldn't afford it," George shrugged. "We've got to catch the last train back to Liverpool. We've only an hour to go."

"Yer mum's expectin' you then, Lennon?" Nicky saw his chance to give back a little of what he'd received. "Standin' at the gate, is she?"

Paul intervened before John could react. Everyone who knew John sucked in breath.

"Actually," Paul rattled on in a hurried, buffering banter, "it's me dad throwin' a spanner in the works, as it were. He's not too keen on

Manchester, y'know – bein' an Everton man' n all that…and naturally, he's especially leery of venues where I'm laggin' about with the likes of you!"

Nicky chuckled. That sort of "mickey-talk" would have irritated the leader of The Connaughts if it had come from John Lennon, but it only amused him when it came from the amicable McCartney. Nicky grinned and pointed a finger at Paul. "Well, yer dear old dad's wishes aside, McCartney, here's hopin' you'll be around for the final applause-o-meter, anyway. I never like to win without at least a birrova fight!"

"Right," John lifted his nose, arrogantly. "That would be *little* of you, wouldn't it? And you Connaughts aren't accustomed to doin' things in a *small* way, are you Cuff?"

"Bollocks to you, Lennon."

"And also to you."

"You're a fuggin' sod, y'know!" Nicky shouted as he headed for the alley exit, a cigarette already in his hand.

"What Nicky said!" guitarist Johnny State echoed.

"Rambullon!" John grinned widely.

Obscenities mingled with the slamming of the stage door.

"How much time d'we have left before we have to leave?" George whined, glancing around for a clock.

"Five minutes less than the last time y'asked." John took a seat on the old, scarred floor and leaned against the wall.

Paul had begun to pace. "We have to leave within the hour, y'know." "We've got to catch that last train back, or we're stuck here all night. And if we don't leave soon…I mean, it's a bit of a hike from here to the station – especially with all our gear in tow."

"They're takin' forever to set up between acts, aren't they?" George craned his neck to see how much progress had been made on stage.

"At this rate," John sniffed, "they'll be judgin' the final round come tea time tomorrow."

"I really wanted to win this time," George protested.

"Well…we've got the hour." Paul tapped his wrist where a watch should be. "Maybe the last group'll perform straight off, and then they'll wind it all up rapidly. Could be. You never know."

"We deserve to be in that final clap-o-meter," George kept mumbling.

"Yeah, we had a blindin' chance to win this time around," Colin agreed.

But The Hurricanes, also Liverpool finalists, were called to the stage next, and they had a full set of equipment to assemble. Their drummer, Richard Starkey, nicknamed Ringo Starr, was an experienced musician, and he was meticulous about arranging his drum kit "just so." No getting around it; the next half hour would easily go to The Hurricanes, and there were still several groups on the docket, slated to perform.

"Well," Paul looked at the others, "that about does it for us then, doesn't it?"

"Right." John picked up his Hofner Club 40 and headed for the door. "Let's chuck it in."

"I really wanted to win this audition." George shouldered his Hofner Futurama and tagged along behind him. "I mean, I think we would've done all right this time, Connaughts or no Connaughts."

"Yeah," John said, "they're a little too off the cuff for my tastes."

George chuckled in spite of himself.

"Oh well," Paul muttered, "better luck next time, right?"

"Yeah, yeah…next time." John kicked the back door open.

"One of these days," George was helping Colin with his gear, "*we're gonna be the ones the audiences ask for!*"

"Yeah, we'll show Levis yet," Colin pledged.

"Next time we'll give the fuggin' Connaughts what for!"

"We'll show 'em."

"That's the spirit."

"Next time!"

Just after 1 a.m., The Hippodrome's weary emcee announced, "And now, ladies and gentlemen, put your hands together for yet another group of finalists from Merseyside…let's hear it for Liverpool's one and only Johnny and the Moondogs!"

"Ah, they've fuggin' gone!" someone shouted from the audience.

"Na, they're just invisible – the Moondogs!" yelled another.

The crowd wasn't too exhausted for laughter and a bit of fun. But an absent group failed to inspire the audience's appreciation, and The Moondogs hardly registered on the clap-o-meter at all.

"Move on," Carroll Levis calmly instructed. "It appears The Moondogs've taken their exit."

"Right," his assistant nodded. "Scratch Johnny and the Moondogs, then. Completely out o'the runnin' – that lot."

I had a difficult time finding any information about The Sunnyside Skiffle group until a friend from Liverpool, Jean Beck, enlisted the aid of Radio Merseyside. She asked them to help me with my research for this book, and Radio Merseyside ran a contest to locate any members of the band. Nicky Cuff himself called in to the station and gave them his telephone number and invited me to contact him directly. I interviewed Nicky in August of 2006, and he was very kind and generous with quotes, names of members of the band, and information about this event.

As to the other facts in this chapter…In Phillip Norman's book Shout, *he writes, "Colin Hanton was still playing with them when a second chance arrived to become Carroll Levis' "Discoveries." Norman even quotes Hanton explaining: "We hadn't worked out in advance how much it would cost us to get there by train and bus. When we got on the bus in Manchester, Paul discovered he hadn't enough money to get home again." Therefore, Norman places Hanton at the Levis audition.*

But Hunter Davies in The Quarrymen *says, "Sometime in mid 1959, The Quarrymen cut their first record in the back room of a house in Liverpool owned by Percy Phillips. Some time later, Colin Hanton left the group." And no mention of Colin being at the Hippodrome audition is offered, although Colin Hanton offers this exact same story about Paul not having the proper bus fare in conjunction with an audition that the group had in Didsbury, Manchester at ABC TV studios. And Davies goes on to say that the disc cut at Percy Phillips house was cut "in mid-1958." (p. 72-73)*

Salewicz first says, "On November 15, 1959 Paul McCartney, John Lennon, and George Harrison auditioned at the Liverpool Empire Theater for a national TV talent contest, 'Carroll Levis Discoveries." He does not directly mention Colin Hanton being present at the audition. However, he says, "Paul was increasingly critical of Colin Hanton's drumming" which seems to imply that Colin was indeed at that audition. Due to preponderance of evidence, I have included Colin in this chapter.

One final note: Rory Storm's group was known as Jett Storm and the Hurricanes at this point.

Christmas Eve, 1959
Mendips
Woolton

John slumped on the corner of his bed and listened to the muffled sounds of Christmas carols rising from the room below. Obviously, one of Mimi's boarders had switched the radio on in hopes of rallying some holiday spirit, but it was, in John's opinion, a bleak effort. Outside colourless rain fell from a colourless sky. John flopped backwards and stared at a large crack snaking across the ceiling.

"Home for the holidays," he muttered to himself. "Happy fuggin' Christmas to me. The whole thing's a drizzle 'round here."

The fact was, he missed Cyn. Hoylake, less than an hour's bus and train ride away, seemed remote and unavailable. *She might as well be in fuggin' America*, he thought.

John realized that Cyn's mum wanted her home, at least past Boxing Day, but he needed Cyn more than anyone else…and needed her in a way that mattered more.

To compensate, he'd been up in his room all afternoon working on a Christmas card for her. The sketch on the front panel depicted the two of them standing face-to-face and forehead-to-forehead – John uncharacteristically wearing a suit and glasses, and Cynthia wearing a checkered mini skirt and a fat, fur jacket. Above their portraits John had scrawled in dark letters, "Our First Christmas!" And though the sketch was not "art college quality," the clearly recognizable figures conveyed powerful feelings.

The back of the card showed the couple again, this time standing with arms around each other – their backs to the viewer, their heads nestled together. Cyn rested her head against John's shoulder, and John rested his atop Cynthia's while a bevy of assorted hearts rose from their shoulders and flew around their heads, vaulting to a cluster of words that read, "I hope it won't be the last!"

John picked the card up and looked at it again, then tossed it down on the bedspread. He'd spent hours creating it. But it wasn't what he wanted to say at all.

"I hope it won't be the last!" he scoffed. "Now there's a fuggin' cheery thought."

The enclosed sentiment was no more optimistic. Along with the traditional pierced heart bearing the lovers' names, John had also included a letter. It read:

> DEAR CYN, ~~ xxxxxx
> I love you I love you I love you I love you I love you I love you I love UIIIII love I love U I love you LIKE MAD I DO I DO LOVE YOU yes YES YES I do love you Cyn. You I love, I love you Cynthia Powell. John Winston loves C. Powell Cynthia, Cynthia, Cynthia I love you, I love you I love you forever and ever isn't it great? I love you like guitars. I love you like anything lovely lovely lovely lovely Cyn lovely Cyn I love lovely Cynthyia Cynthia I LOVE you. You are wonderful I adore you I want you I love you I need you. Don't go...I love you, HAPPY X.MAS MERRY CHRIMBO I love you I love you I love you Cynthia CYN CYN CYN CYN CYN CYN CYN is loved by JOHN JOHN JOHN JOHN JOHN I L O V E YOU X X x x x x x   Love, John xxx*

John closed his eyes, trying to imagine Cynthia reading the card, trying to guess how she'd react. It scared him to be this entangled with anyone, this vulnerable. It scared him to be happy. Happy was dangerous; happy was tempting fate.

"Don't go....I love you." It had been the central request of his letter. "I want you. I need you. Don't go."

He meant it.

Lately everything seemed too tenuous. The Fifties were coming to a close. Ten months ago, Buddy Holly had been tragically killed in a plane crash; in only an instant, an icon of an age was gone. The Beatniks were passé now, and even the unmovable Teddy Boys had vanished, taking their skiffle with them. Everything sure, comfortable, and constant seemed to be changing.

All afternoon, The BBC had been broadcasting listeners' predictions for the decade to come – predictions of household computers, smaller cars, a worldwide end to polio, and colour televisions in every home. But John didn't want to imagine what would happen in the 1960's. The uncertainty of it all was nerve-wracking.

For a week, the airwaves had been deluged with programmes predicting the next ten years, talk shows discussing the long-term implications of the Cold War, and radio broadcasts discussing Elvis Presley and his impact on the loss of teenage innocence. There had been news specials depicting the emerging of the Civil Rights Movement in America. And in the U.K., Harold McMillan's name was on every tongue.

Informed historians and uninformed commentators were busy this last Christmas Eve of the decade speculating about what "big trends" might emerge in the Sixties – who the leaders and most influential personalities might be. It was all too much for John. He didn't care who the icons of the Sixties would be. He rolled onto his side and tried not to think about it at all.

Paul'll be graduatin' this spring, and his dad'll want him to take some regulation job straight off. And George is still goin' on about becomin' a fuggin' electrician's mate. But how'll we tour if they do that? How'll we ever be great if the two of them go on with these unimaginative, shortsighted plans?

John flopped to his other side and tried to shut out the worries.

And art school…if I go back there I'll wither on the fuggin' vine! I'm not cut out for art college…especially a local venue. I'm a fuggin' genius…for good or for bad.

"Supper, John!" It was Mimi. "You'll have to come out of seclusion long enough to eat."

"Right. All right," he muttered, not sitting up, not budging.

"Not next year, *now*!" she harped. He could visualize her pursed lips and folded arms.

"I'm not really up to it tonight, Mim." He told the truth

"Don't be melodramatic, John. Pull yourself together and be civilized. Come downstairs this instant!"

"Aye, aye, Cap'n," he bellowed back.

Mimi trotted off in a huff.

If only we'd gotten a fuggin' shot at the Levis thing…then at least I'd have that in my hip pocket to convince George and Paul that…

"Now, John!" the sharp voice demanded.

He sat up, but made no attempt to leave the bed.

I mean, we've got a fuggin' sound! I know we've got a sound. But how can it ever come through over cheap amps and borrowed equipment? And how can we afford to buy our own equipment if we never get a shot? Money makes money…it's a fuggin' merry-go-round, but the ones on *the ride won't slow it down and tell us how to get on the bastard thing!*

And Al – what's he done for us…besides stringin' us along with promises of gigs, just so we'll paint his fuggin' loo?

"John, come down at once." The voice was just outside the door now. It was calm but stern.

John puffed out his cheeks and exhaled, but he didn't respond.

"John Winston!"

He threw the door open with a bang that raised the boarders' eyebrows. One of them coughed nervously downstairs. The fire popped. Someone quickly flipped the record over, and Bing Crosby began crooning "Faith of our Fathers" in soft, soothing tones.

"Pull yourself together," Mimi hissed. "You've no reason to be antisocial this evening. It's inappropriate. It's embarrassing."

"No reason, is it?" John's eyes told the story of the last nineteen years at a glance. "No reason?"

Mimi looked away.

"We've Beef Wellington," she made herself say, dismissing the unusual lump in her throat, "And there's Yorkshire pudding with a holly sprig, hot fruit compote, and even though it's not seasonal, I've made your Irish soda bread, John...the one with the currants in it. Lelia came by and polished up the silver this week, so there's that. And I've made all your favourites for dessert."

"Yerrokay." He looked at the floor and motioned for her to lead the way. John was tired of fighting, even with himself.

"We were all talking," she tried to ease him into a better mood as they entered the dining room, "about who the most famous person of the 1960's will be. Mrs. Grange here holds with McMillan, of course, and Professor Fallows has opted for America's Eisenhower. I've given the nod to a man of medicine...Jonas Salk, perhaps. And we were guessing that your vote would go to the beloved Elvis Presley."

"Mim," John took his place at the far end of the table, the place Mimi had set for him since George's death. "I'd rather not discuss it, if y'don't mind."

"But surely you've an opinion," the lean, good-looking Fallows passed John the Royal Doulton gravy boat.

"Yeah, that's right." John was tight-lipped.

"Of course he does," The myriad bracelets on Mrs. Grange's arm dangled and clinked as she took the lovely dish from John. " It's just that he'd rather be congenial and agree with us all? Isn't that right, John?"

"It's just that I'd rather be private about it is what I'd rather be," he said.

"John thinks *he's* going to be more famous than Elvis Presley," Mimi commented, using the silver cranberry spoon to ladle out a generous portion.

"Oh, really?" Fallows raised an eyebrow. "The man of the decade, then...at our own Christmas table, eh?" They all smiled and chuckled.

"Well, I say...what a way to begin a new age!" Beryl Grange toasted with her almost empty glass of port, "Christmas Eve dinner here at Mendips with the most famous man of the 1960's!"

"Right. Good, yes!" Fallows raised his own glass good-naturedly.

"Quite a privilege, I'm sure!"

John's eyes narrowed as he raised his own glass in return. "And from the one destined to be the most famous man of the Sixties, many happy returns of the day! Cheers!"

He downed the glass in one long gulp.

This is my best attempt to describe John's Christmas card to Cynthia in December 1959. You may view the actual card in Coleman's Lennon, *in the photo/picture collection between pages 240 and 241.*

All descriptions of Mendips were wonderfully supplied to me by a letter from the owner of the residence in the 1990's. That letter can be found in the appendix.

The conversation in this chapter is only imagined, except John's comment that he was "a genius…for good or for bad."

**17 January 1960
The Jacaranda
23 Slater Street
Liverpool 1**

"You'll never guess!" Stu rushed in, tossing gloves, scarves, and hat aside.

"You've done it, haven't you? You've fuggin' done it!" John smiled, really smiled. "You've *won* the bastard thing, haven't you? You fuggin', artsy pseud!"

"Pseud yerself!" Stu laughed. His grin was ear to ear; his face, flushed.

"You *really* pulled it off, didn't ya, son!"

"Well, you were a great part of it, y'know." Stu pumped John's hand vigorously, as if reuniting after a long separation.

"Like fuggin'ell I was!"

"Y'were, John. You know it; admit it! You were the only one who believed I could actually do it!"

"Gerroff, Sutcliffe. Yer mother believed."

"They always do, don't they?" Stu chuckled, dragging over one of The Jacaranda's walnut captain's chairs. "But *you* were the one ravin' on about never givin' up – about puttin' in nights and days 'for the dream' and all that never-say-die Quarry Men mantra."

"Badgerin's me specialty," John admitted, "inherited from Mim – direct descent. But palaver's fuggin' cheap, and it doesn't win art competitions, Sutcliffe. It takes talent, *real* talent to win a thing like the alfuggin'mighty John Moores Contest!"

"Talent, is it?" Stu laughed softly.

"I knew it meself as soon as I'd finished the rounds with Mim at the Walker the other day. A gallery full of paintings there, but yours…*that* was art. Nothin' in the competition held a fuggin' candle to it, y'know."

"Ta," Stu clapped John on the shoulder. "Comin' from you, I know it's sincere. And so," he held out his arms expansively, "because we're in the midst of a grand celebration…"

"The grandest," John eyed the virtually empty coffeehouse with a smirk.

"...the coffee's on me today," Stu finished, "and real bacon butties as well! Today I can afford it...at least for a while."

"Right." John leaned back in his seat at the sun dappled window table. "You do have the prize money, right?" he asked.

"Yeah and it's fantastic!" Stu patted his coat pocket. "Much more convenient to be rich, y'know."

John leaned across the table, as if waiting to hear a secret divulged. "And?"

"And what?"

"And how much'd you win, then?"

"Almost too much to believe." Stu glanced over his shoulder to see if any of the other early afternoon patrons could hear. He'd finally warmed up enough to tug off his heavy jacket, and he scooted closer to his friend. "Listen John, believe it or not, the great Moores himself turned around and bought the fuggin' thing!"

"Don't mess with me, son."

"Really," Stu nodded. "He bought it! He actually bought it!"

"*Summer Painting?*" John's eyes narrowed. "The one with the sand and the wax and the fuggin' kitchen sink thrown in as well?"

"I thought you said you liked it!" Stu's face fell. "I thought you said it was real art – true talent and all that crap."

"John Moores, the real John Moores, paid real cash in real life for *Summer Painting?*"

"Sixty-five pounds, no less." Stu reached in his pocket. "Look, here it is."

John took the small cluster of bills that Stu handed him and fanned it out like a deck of cards. He glanced at Stu, then back at the money.

"Two thousand entries...and John fuggin' Moores bought yours!" John lifted up the bills and shook them at Stu. "You're tellin' me that not only did you win the thing over seasoned artists like Arthur Ballard and the entire art college set – that you won over everyfuggin'one down there, even though we only took *half* your canvas to the fuggin' Walker! And now on top of that...there's this!" He wagged the money at Stu again.

"Right." Stu chuckled. "If they'd seen the painting in its entirety, it mightn't have fared so well, y'know. But lucky for me, you and Rod were too effin' lazy to haul the other half of the work to the gallery. And *I* was too exhausted to force you into doin' it!"

"Well, happy birthday to us!" John jumped to his feet, waving the money around his head. "We're on our way then! We've got it now!"

"Yeah, right." Stu's eyes shone. "No more burnin' the furniture to keep us warm; no more stealin' from the art college coal bin or cadgin' meals as cadge can or pickin' Chinese take-away boxes out of the rubbish. No more stubs for sketch pencils; no more debts for paint. No more jam butty banquets when what I really want is a thick lamb chop with mint and boiled potatoes and a real cup of coffee with real cream."

"Sod that!" John was still holding the money. "Y'er spendin' this money on a Hofner President bass."

"Not again, John." Stu groaned, reaching for his prize. But John held on firmly.

"Y'er gettin' a bass guitar, and y'er gettin' a black polo from Mark and Spenser's just like the rest of the group. White plimsoles as well, if we negotiate right. But the guitar's a given. You're in the band, Stu! It's done."

"Spend *all* of it?" Stu grabbed the money, "On one, single bass guitar? I could live for months on this, y'know!" He stared at the notes as if they were life-long friends from whom he would soon be parted.

"You're buyin' the guitar," John repeated.

Stu rubbed his forehead. "Look John, I've got expenses, y'know! I've other canvases half-way done, waitin' back at Gambier for the rest of their paint."

"And you'll need black jeans." John grabbed a napkin and began making notes and adding up numbers. "Unless you've got those already?"

Stu nodded.

"And the white plims – d'ya need them?"

"I…I think I've got some somewhere." Stu's voice was hushed.

"I haven't seen'em." John looked down his nose at his friend.

"Well, they're…somewhere," Stu looked around distractedly as if he thought they would make themselves known. The prize money was rapidly dwindling, and he had no way to stop it.

"All right, then. All we need's the Hofner and the polo, then. That'll do for starters. At least that'll get you in the group."

"But John," Stu mustered his courage, "you don't really need me in the band. Not really. I can't play, y'know. And I'd have to work to learn. And the truth of the matter is, I don't have *time* to work to learn…especially now that I've earned some measure of success in the art world – especially now that the time's right for 'strikin' while the iron is hot,' as they always say."

"Bugger it, Sutcliffe. You're always pressurin' me to work at sketchin' and paintin' and doin' all the things *you* love," John snapped, irritated at any hint of dissent. "Now it's my turn to call the shots, as it were."

"But that's different, and you know it!" Stu's voice was loud enough to turn heads at the surrounding tables. "I'm pressurin' you to do what you're *supposed* to be doin' anyway…what you're enrolled in art college to be doin'!"

"Sod that!" John shouted back. "Don't fool yerself into believin' that art school's *anythin' for me* other than a fuggin' way to keep fuggin' Mim from makin' me punch a clock. It's a dodge, y'know… a way to keep the band goin' – a way to muck about the city and make contacts. It's only somethin' to do while I wait for somethin' to happen."

"And *that's* how I feel about rock'n'roll." Stu stuffed the money in his pocket and pulled out a crumpled pack of Embassys. He tossed it over to John along with a small matchbox. "Here, have one."

For a few moments neither of them spoke.

"Look John," Stu tried again. "Rock'n'roll's tremendous. I love it. I do. But for me, it's tremendous as a *backdrop*, tremendous as an inspiration for what I put on the canvas...the best muse I could ever ask for. It's the rhythm of art, the pulse that beats in the best of m'creations. But it's not *the creation* itself, y'know. It's only what I hear and feel and respond to – not what I do."

"You think that now," John took a long drag on his cig, "because you haven't played rock'n'roll, because you're a virgin to it, as it were. You can't really *want* rock'n'roll because you haven't had it yet."

"It'd ruin me." Stu stared helplessly at his hands, the instruments of his art.

"Bushwa! There're only four strings on a bass, and you only play one fuggin' note at a time, not a even chord." John was growing more exasperated by the moment. "Yer hands'll toughen in time, Sutcliffe. Grow up."

"But that's just it, John!" Stu leaned in, his elbow on the table, his cigarette punctuating every word. "I don't have time!" He took a drag and blew the smoke over John's head. "I paint. It's what I do. That's my expression! That's *my* rock'n'roll!"

John reached around the back of his chair and hoisted up his tweed jacket. "C'mon," he said. "Let's go."

"Go?" Stu sat transfixed. "I'm starved. We haven't even ordered yet! We haven't had a thing to eat!"

"Hessey's'll only be open another half hour," John pointed to the clock behind the bar. "We can still make it if y'get up now."

"Hessey's? In Whitechapel?"

John grabbed Stu's coat and pushed it towards him.

"Where else? You'll not get a guitar in this neck'o the woods, will ya?"

"So," Stu slowly put his jacket, scarf, hat, and gloves back on, "so we're off to get the Hofner, then...no matter what I've told you...no matter what I've said?"

"Right." John announced flatly. "You're in, son! Welcome to Johnny and the Moondogs, Sutcliffe!"

"Yeah, welcome," Stu muttered. And he slammed the weathered captain's chair back under Allan's pub table.

All details in this chapter including the amount of prize money, the location where Stu told John about his victory, the items John wanted Stu to purchase for the band, John's insistence that Stu join, and Stu's reluctance to join are true. Only the actual conversation between John and Stu is imagined, given the facts. The quote, "You'll never guess!" however, is a documented direct quote from Stu. See Norman's account.

Phillip Norman asserts that Stu was looking forward to joining the band and did so much to his mother's chagrin. But Pete Shotton states, "John bamboozled his new soul-mate into spending every penny on an electric bass guitar...it never occurred to him that anyone to whom he felt especially close could not also participate [in the band]. By all accounts, Stu's experience in the group...was as painful as mine had been."

Stu told many details about this day to Rod Murray, and Rod passed them on to me.

24 January 1960
20 Forthlin Road
Allerton

"What's *he* up to, then?" Paul nodded towards Stu who'd perched on Paul's bedroom windowsill and was struggling with the tuning screws on his new bass.

"Tuning, it would seem." John knew exactly what Paul meant, but he refused to play the game.

"C'mon John, straight up. Why's he here?"

"It appears he's playin' bass guitar, McCartney. It appears he's joinin' the band."

"Now look, John," Paul abandoned the set up work he'd been doing for their practise session, "what's the use, eh? He can't play a note – Stu. We're all light years ahead of him on guitar."

"He'll manage, given a few days."

"With art, Stu's a quick study. Right. Good. Fantastic. But this is isn't art, John. This is rock'n'roll!"

"He's in the fuggin' group."

"Why?" Paul's voice went up a notch. "Even if he were bleedin' great, even if he knew how to play, even if he had a smidgen of talent – we don't need him. We've got more guitars than we can use right now, don't we?"

"We don't have a bass, do we?" John sniffed, agitated.

"Well, here's a news item, John," Paul leaned closer, lowering his voice although everything could be heard by everyone in the tiny bedroom, "Stu doesn't play bass! So we're no better off than we were before, are we?"

"He'll add depth."

"I can turn up the *amps* if it's depth you're after!" Paul threw up his hands. "Why didn't you have Stuart buy a set of bleedin' *drums* if y'really wanted to add somethin' significant to the band?"

"And why don't you and yer negativity drum yerself right out of here?" John shot back. "Stu's in the group. End of subject."

"Right. Great. Okay. But what does George think about it, then?"

"I didn't ask." John stood up, making the most of his five-feet-eleven.

"It's not his group."

"And you don't intend to? Is that what you're sayin'?"

"Now you're with the plan, son."

"I wouldn't say that's exactly democratic or exactly friendly on your part. In fact, I'd be more inclined to classify it as completely dictatorial and unfair."

"Welcome to life." John flashed a toothy grin.

Then he turned and walked to the window where he edged in beside Stu on the sill and began a conversation that didn't include Paul.

There are so many sources that document Paul's logical stand that Stu was not right for the band. But perhaps the simplest documentation is Paul's own explanation from The Anthology *(p. 62). He says, "There's something I'd like to get straight because it is kind of historical – someone a few years ago said how it was my relentless ambition that pushed Stu out of the group. We did have some arguments, me and Stu, but actually I just wanted us to be a really cracking band, and Stu – being a really cracking artist – held us back a little bit, not too much. If it ever came to the push, and there was someone in there watching us, I'd feel, 'Oh, I hope Stu doesn't blow it. I could trust the rest of us; that was it.'"*

Late January, 1960
The Jacaranda
23 Slater Street
Liverpool 1

What he lacked in skill, Stu made up for in style. As George observed, he looked "fuggin' fabulous" in the Moondog Regalia. The black polo sweater and black jeans posed a perfect contrast to his pale skin and distinctive cheekbones. As a finishing touch, Stu chose a pair of dark glasses – à la Zbigniew Cybulski, the Polish James Dean – and he strategically positioned himself at the rear of the group…apart and intriguing.

Despite many lessons from bassist David May and from Paul and George, Stuart still couldn't play well. In fact, his playing was rudimentary. John had expected Stu to learn by simply "havin' a go at it," but Stu was, as he'd always insisted, an artist not a musician. His thin, delicate fingers stumbled into position. He blundered through the easiest songs. He lost his place during rehearsals, and because The Moondogs weren't into compassion, Stu never caught up.

"Just turn your back to the audience now and again – when you reach an impasse – and leave the playin' to us, right?" Paul winked with a quick nod of the head. "Look over your shoulder and all that, if y'like. Y'know…go through the motions, Stu."

"Yeah, right." Stuart took it hard. It was unusual for him to experience failure. As the eldest child and the only boy in his family, he'd always been the "chosen one." And as an artist, he'd always garnered praise and acclaim. At only sixteen, he'd been accepted into Liverpool College of Art, a full two years' earlier than most students. Stu wasn't used to falling short of expectations. He cared too much about what others thought.

And that, in itself, was Stu's undoing. It presented, for the first time, an Achilles' heel for John to assault. It exposed a weakness in Stu that frightened and irritated the friend who so closely identified with him. John wanted no part of Stu's vulnerability, and he began to lash out at Stu with his old, childhood cruelty.

"What's the matter, Sutcliffe? Chastised once again?" John found Stu sitting near The Jacaranda's thick fish-eye front window, basking in the sun and self-pity. The hurt on Stu's face made John's skin crawl.

"It's not that I don't deserve it." Stu shook his head. "Paul's absolutely right, John. I'm no good at bass. Paul knows it. David May knows it – he's tried to teach me, but can't. And George doesn't say it, but he knows it as well." He shook his head. "And believe me, when we perform, the fans'll know it – glasses or no glasses, stance or no stance."

"So…it's a regular pity party you're havin', is it?" John narrowed his eyes. "Sendin' out invitations or just askin' in the neighbours, as it were?"

"It's *not* pity," Stu bristled. "It's frustration. I just can't play the way you 'n Paul 'n George can."

"Can't or won't?" John refused to accept failure in anyone he had imbued with trust.

"Look," Stu dug the heel of his winklepicker boot into The Jacaranda's concrete floor. "I've got no talent in that vein, John."

"And how much time are you givin' it, son? As much as y'er givin' to yer canvases and paints and life models, as it were?"

Stu's shoulders squared. He looked John in the eye. "You fuggin' know the answer to that, John! Art's m'life. It's who I am! It's to me what music is to the rest of ya."

"Well, you'll never be great if you're not obsessed, son. Greatness, any *real*, fuggin' greatness is born of obsession. As long as y'er only givin' bits and pieces, y'er doomed to stand at the back of the band. That's how it is, isn't it?"

"But that's exactly the problem!" Stu was angry now. "I *am* obsessed! I have a passion! But it's never been rock'n'roll…it's art!" Stu picked up the Hofner and tried to hand it to John. "Here! Here, have it. Find someone else! Do whatever you want with it! Just let me outta the effin' band! Let me get back to doin' what it is *I* do best and regain a bit of self-respect for a change!"

When John refused to take the bass, Stu plunked it against the chair next to John and started searching for his coat. The Jacaranda basement, where they'd been practising for the last hour and a half, had been dank and cold, but perspiration had soaked Stu's shirt anyway. And now, even though the late afternoon sun spread thin and weak, sweat ran from Stu's sideburns.

"Pick it up." John eyed the Hofner. "Pick it up, Stu! Y'er not walkin' off. And y'er not givin' up – not after all you've fuggin' preached to me!"

Stu continued to gather his things. He didn't acknowledge John or offer rebuttal.

"Y'er in the fuggin' band, Sutcliffe. You can't just walk away whenever you want to! It doesn't work like that. Instead of ginnin' up a string of lame excuses, why not have the fuggin' courage to give us somethin' to remember you by, then?"

Stu refused to answer, but turned and called, "T'rah Beryl! T'rah

Allan!" He glared at John, then hit the door.

John picked Stu's Hofner up carefully and placed it in its new, unscratched case. Then he sat alone in Stu's vacated sunshine, fishing the last cig out of a pack Stu had left behind.

After a few minutes, Paul and George ambled upstairs to beg coffee and butties off Beryl as usual. A couple of art students straggled in from the cold, stamping their feet and choosing a table in the far corner. But other than that, the place was quiet. John cupped his shoulders around his cigarette and bit the cuticle of his thumbnail. He waited.

He knew that by the time he walked over to Stu's place, Stu would have already forgiven him. But he was sick of needing to be forgiven. He was tired of being venomous at the drop of a hat. Anger was the only emotion he genuinely felt anymore, and it was monotonous – always there, always seething, always a second from daylight.

John stood up and flicked the cig away, and then headed downstairs to pack up his gear. Paul and George watched him cross the room without a word, and John said nothing to them, either. The whole room was pregnant with violence.

In the basement darkness, John swung around, booted over a chair and knocked the table beside it across the room. In domino effect, furniture clattered and echoed, ringing loudly in the empty room.

"What the fuggin'ell, Lennon?" Allan yelled. "Don't make me come down there and turn you out!"

"Knock yerself out. I'll be here."

But the empty challenges were just that, and John began packing his gear as if nothing had ever happened.

He wasn't looking forward to the frigid January walk from The Jacaranda to Percy Street, and he wasn't looking forward to the reparations he'd have to make once he got there. He never knew what to say to make things right – not with Mimi, Cyn, or Stu. But he trudged upstairs anyway.

"Wait one –we'll go along." Paul swallowed the last of his tea as John crossed towards the door. George quickly slipped into his heavy pea coat.

"I'm headed to Stu's, y'know," John explained, not sure that Paul would want to tag along.

"Yeah, we figured." George smiled.

"He's quit the band," John said. "Strange as it seems, I've actually browned him off."

"Not you?" Paul grinned.

"You've got that certain knack, haven't you?" George teased.

John picked up Stu's guitar and tried to think of something to say, but he was fresh out of clever.

"Let's go and get him back, then." George clapped John on the shoulder.

"Right." Paul wrapped the heavy scarf that had once belonged to his mother around his neck. "We'll offer him fame and millions, John. He can't refuse that, now can he?"

"Millions...and us," John smiled sadly. "Who could refuse?"

"I couldn't," George chuckled.

"Thousands couldn't," Paul said.

The late afternoon sun splashed the sky in deep, oyster pink – a shade that seemed ostentatious, gaudy against winter's grey. It rose above the slate roofs that snaggletoothed the skyline and offered them hues that had long since drained away. The city lit up like a movie set, like an inexpensive painting of a weathered seaport town.

Allan Williams stood at the window of The Jac and watched The Moondogs zig and zag until they turned the corner and disappeared in the direction of the art college. Then he threw up his hands and shook his head.

"Put McCartney's and Harrison's guitars in the back room, Beryl, and hold'em for fuggin' ransom 'til they come back and ante up for the jam butties they just nabbed!" he yelled. "If I know that sod, John Lennon, the way I think I do, they'll all be back with Sutcliffe in tow within the hour. Cadges...mutts, every last one o' them."

"Well, I like them." Beryl picked up the guitars and moved them to a safe location. "I like them all."

"Like them a little less," Allan massaged the back of his neck. "And fuggin' *charge* 'em a little more!"

"But they might go somewhere else, then," Beryl grinned.

"Great!" Allan fumed. "I'd love to give'em away – part, parcel, and postage due. But the truth is...who'd have a lousy bunch like that? They're no good to man nor beast."

In The John Lennon Encyclopedia, *Bill Harry (page 878) states, "Stuart's playing was nowhere near as bad as people have been led to believe from writers who have used Williams' book as the source. Stuart was only an adequate musician, It's true, but he had presence and charisma on stage."*

However, if we go to The Beatles' own words in The Anthology, *we find:*

"Stuart was in the band now. He wasn't really a very good musician. In fact, he wasn't a musician at all until we talked him into buying a bass. We taught him how to play twelve-bars...he picked up a few things and he practiced a bit until he could get through a couple of other tunes as well. It was a bit ropey..." George Harrison (p. 41).

"And Stu couldn't play bass, so he had to turn his back." John Lennon (p. 44).

"We had to tell Stuart to turn the other way: 'Do a moody – do a big Elvis pose.' If anyone had been taking notice, they would have seen that when we were all in A, Stu would be in another key." Paul McCartney (p. 44).

Furthermore, in Backbeat, Alan Clayson and Pauline Sutcliffe (Stuart's sister) write: "…[Stu's] fingertips became calloused but not particularly supple with daily practice that dwindled to merely when he felt like it, partly because his finger-lacerating effort was having a detrimental effect on his painting."

Bill Harry's case for Stuart is very good. He states that Klaus Voormann was inspired by Stu to become a bass player and that of all the Liverpool bassists, Voormann thought Stu the best.

To be fair to all viewpoints – and to Stuart – he may not have been as bad as legend would have it, but most likely was not as good as his band mates wanted him to be…or as he wanted himself to be.

The events in this chapter are conjecture based upon information in the sources above. All conversation is conjecture.

3 February 1960
The Jacaranda
23 Slater Street
Liverpool 1

It had been a year exactly.

"I remember I was just up," Stu reminisced, "millin' about, dressin' for class when the word came." He strolled to The Jac window and stared outside. "It was all over Radio Luxembourg, unclear – ghostly in all that static."

"I wasn't even sure I'd heard it right," their friend, Bill Harry added. "I *hoped* I hadn't heard it right."

"Yeah, they're playin' his songs all day today, as a tribute," George nodded.

"And what good's that?" John sipped the "before hours" tea that Beryl Williams had brewed for him, savouring every swallow against a ragged throat. "I mean, what's *he* bleedin' care if we're all down here waxin' sentimental? He's fuggin' dead! Done! Finished. And that's all there is to it, isn't it?"

"Nah, not really." Stu folded his arms against his chest. "Not if the music lives. Not if he started somethin' that's buildin' even now to epidemic proportions."

"Buddy Holly's rock'n'roll's still out there, y'know," Bill agreed, "still alive, even after the year, isn't it?"

"That's all shite," John sneered.

"Ah, but it isn't, and y'know it isn't," Bill smiled.

"It is and *you* know that it is," John insisted, joining Stu in the sunlight of the bay window, "I won't give a fuggin'ell what people think of me or even *if* they think of me, once I'm gone."

The two friends stood together, watching the first, feeble trickle of city-goers plodding lifelessly towards unimaginative destinations. John slurped his tea and felt the acrid lemon sting his tonsils. He took large gulps and let it work.

Beryl had brought The Moondogs and their affable journalist friend in out of the cold despite the fact that it was her time for cleaning and restocking. The Jac didn't officially open for hours – until almost noon – and she never admitted customers early. But "her boys" had been shivering and hungry, and John Lennon had claimed to be half sick. That, for Beryl, was reason enough to bend the rules.

"Well," Stu refused to relent, "I want to be remembered. In fact, it's crucial as I see it. For an artist it's all that matters, if y'think of it. It's eternal life. It's the artist's 'hereafter' – fame."

"Oh no, it's ole Van Gogh again, George!" John shouted over his shoulder. "Lend him your ears."

"What's here and now," Stu went on, unfazed, "it's just the construction phase, y'know. But what comes *after* life, that's the appraisal, the critique – the chance for immortality."

"It's the chance for immorality I'm after," John muttered to no one.

"Here's where we do the work," Stu continued, "but only the years'll tell if we made it count…if it changes things."

"That's all mystical hype, Sutcliffe!" John strolled to the rear counter and began nosing underneath in search of cigs – reaching into the far recesses and shoving saucers this way and that. "I mean, face it – other'n a day like this or perhaps his birthday, who goes around memorializin' Buddy fuggin' Holly?"

"I do, for one." Stu was earnest. "I think about him a lot, really. I listen to him as I paint, and I wonder if he knows – wherever he is – that he was one of the greats, right up there with Chuck Berry and Little Richard and Elvis – not just a rocker, in for a moment and out after a season – but a *pioneer*, a creator of a movement."

"A dead man," John said. Finding a half-pack of Embassys, he lit one and straddled a chair.

"Well, be that as it may," Stu went on, "I was thinkin' that since it *was* a year ago today that he died, and since we've been kickin' around the idea of a new name for the band 'n all…I was thinkin' we might give 'im a nod and rename the band after him."

"The Hollies?" John made a face at George who snickered. He laughed at anything John said. "Fuggin' lame!"

"The Buddies, then?" George chimed in.

"That's very public school," Bill teased.

Stu hardly smiled. "I was thinkin' more along the lines of Buddy Holly and the Crickets, y'know, except with a twist…like…well…what I'd come up with is "The Beetles " – a tribute and a double entendre…a wordplay on the *beat* of the band."

"Not bad. Right, John?" George raised an eyebrow.

"Beetles, is it?" John hunkered over his tea and cig. "But to get the meanin' over to the ordinary man, it would have to be Beetles spelled B-e-a-."

Stu quickly sat down next to John. "Right," he nodded, "B-e-a-t for the beat rhythm and all of that. The Beatals."

John had to buy into this name, or it wouldn't have a chance.

"Yeah," George's hand traced an invisible marquee, "I can see it now: The Beatals, live from Liverpool!"

"Except for the fact," John pointed his cigarette at Stu, "that Al's dead set on that Long John Silver nomenclature of his. Especially since his 'worshipped golden Cass' suggested it."

"Let Brian Casser name his own group!" Stu snubbed The Cassanova's leader and grabbed John's cig for a long draw. "We can manage for ourselves in the creativity department, ta."

"Yeah, we can manage for ourselves." George sat on the tabletop next to them.

"There's only one hitch in that philosophy, son." John took his Embassy back. "Al's our actual manager now. And he's not much for tribute crap. He hasn't a single sentimental bone in his entire Welsh frame – has Al."

"If something's not razzmatazz, it's no fuggin' good where Allan's concerned," Bill agreed, "and if it's not his idea, it's all shite."

"Yeah, okay," Stu conceded, "but we could use his name…and just shorten it, right? I mean, how about…The *Silver Beatals* then? Spelled B-e-a-t-*a*-l-s? Unique spellin'…even a bit of the quirky tossed in as well."

"Silver Beatals," George smiled. "Paul'll go for it. He's a great one for names these days, isn't he?"

They laughed at Paul's recent suggestion that they all assume "stage names" for performances. Paul wanted to be Paul Ramon. Stuart had chosen Stu de Stael in homage to his favourite artist, Nicholas de Stael, and in honor of American country singer, Carl Perkins, George had selected Carl Harrison. Only John had flatly refused to participate in the pseudonym game. It annoyed Paul and disappointed George that John wouldn't join in the fun. But Stu looked past John's stubbornness to his friend's need for validation.

Despite what John said about the futility of fame and notoriety, Stu knew that John ached to prove his worth. Becoming famous anonymously or under some assumed identity had no appeal, no meaning for John at all.

Suddenly, without a word of explanation, George jumped up and flipped the laminated cardboard sign on The Jac to "Open." An attractive blonde shop girl in a crisp white blouse and charcoal pencil skirt clipped by on Slater Street, and when the motion caught her eye, George smiled, waved, and motioned her inside. She pinched in a grin and hurried on, but at the corner, she hesitated for a moment, indulging in a furtive backward glance.

"Jilted again," George shrugged, wandering back to his perch.

"I've told you a thousand times," John put his feet up on one of Allan's tiny tables, "drummers get all the girls, son. You'd be great as a drummer, y'know. You ought to give it some consideration, oughtn't you?"

"I'm a guitarist, John." George plopped back down, weary of the drummer discussion, "A lead guitarist."

"I thought Al was workin' on that – gettin' you lot a drummer." Bill settled into a chair with the rest. Stu tossed his cigarette stub into the last of John's tea.

"Yeah, right," John grumbled. "He's always just about to close the deal, just about to sign some fanfuggin'tastic one or the other."

"But he never does." George threw his eyes to the ceiling.

Right on cue, as if the old adage of speaking of the devil actually held potency, Allan Williams burst through the front door, his cheeks red from the February cold, his dark eyes sparkling.

"What the hell are you lot doin' here before openin'?" he sputtered, flipping the sign back to "Closed" and pushing the front door shut with his heel. "Why are you here, Harry? And get yer filthy feet of the fuggin' table, Lennon…"

"'Ullo, Al," George beamed.

"Always a pleasure," Stu teased.

"Mr. Williams," Bill's eyes were full of mischief.

"Yeah, yeah, yeah." Al removed his gloves and coat and joined them, pulling up a chair for once – leaning in with a grin, as if he actually liked them for a moment. "Helluva way to start a mornin', but since you're here, albeit uninvited…there is a bit of news, lads."

"Go on," John was guarded.

"Whether y'deserve it or not – and I personally hold with the 'or not,'" Allan licked his lips, his eyes bright, "you Quarry Men or Moondogs or whoever the hell you are this week are in for a fuggin' fabulous treat, as it were!"

"Please say it's a drummer, Mr. Manager. Please!" John batted his eyelashes rapidly.

"Yeah," George agreed, "we could use one of those. My future depends upon one of those."

"Well, you'll have to settle for tickets this go-round." Allan brandished a handful of yellow, paper squares.

"Naturally. We love tickets as well." George was immediately interested.

"To what?" Stu reached in for a look-see, but Allan held back, dramatically setting the stage.

"Tickets…to "The Greatest Show Ever to be Staged," to a ffffuggin' production you'll never forget…to the show of shows, the night of nights, the one and only extravaganza at The Liverpool Empire, featurin' none other than Eddie Cochran and Gene Vincent themselves – in person, in life, and in Liverpool! 14 March! Be there!"

"And exactly what do they have to do in order to deserve this night of nights?" Bill narrowed his eyes at the entrepreneur. Allan feigned a hurt expression.

"That's cold-blooded thanks, Harry, when here I am...strivin' to show the lads my unabated appreciation for all they've done around here...for fixin' up the loo and for being so fuggin' patient about waitin' for just the right drummer to come along, as it were."

"And," John flashed a caustic grin that lasted only half a second, "for waitin' so patiently for a decent gig as well. You forgot that one, didn't ya?"

"Pffffft!" Allan waved him off. "Concentrate on the here and now, Lennon. This show – this Vincent-Cochran thing – is goin' to be my biggest production to date...I'm dottin' every 'i' and crossin' every fuggin' 't' to make sure it's as first-rate as first rate goes. And for you, it's the rarest of chances to see professional bands up close...to learn techniques, study showmanship – to pick up a few things you've never even dreamed of!"

"I've dreamed of a drummer," John said. "Have they got any of those at the show?"

"I'd like to see what one looks like," George added. "We haven't any 'round these parts, y'know."

"Bugger off." Allan went on, unfazed. "Now..." his cheeks flushed with the drama of a pregnant pause, "without a doubt, the very biggest advantage of this whole entire production's the incredible chance if offers to rub shoulders with the *other* promoter of the event."

"Who is?" John squinted, skeptical.

"Who is only..." Allan waved his hand in a flourish, "Larry Parnes himself! Larry Parnes! *The* top impresario around England today – creator of Tommy Steele and the 'Oh Boy' television programme...a man, for your purposes, Lennon, even more fuggin' powerful than the Prime Minister himself! If ever a man could get you a string of top-rate gigs, it's Parnes! He could kick-start yer career without so much as a wink and a nudge."

"Isthasso?" John grabbed a ticket and examined it closely. "But we've been down this yellow-brick road before, haven't we, Manager? And yet, no one's winked, and no one's nudged."

"It only takes the once." Allan took the ticket back and wrapped all four of them together with a rubber band, handing the bundle back to John. "And who knows? This might be that once! This *could be* the start of The Moondogs...or better yet, Long John Silver and his Band of Brigands. It could..."

"We haven't had a chance to bring you up to speed, Al," George interrupted. "We're The Silver Beatals now."

"*The...pffft...what?*" Allan snapped his head around. "Not fffuggin' likely!"

"No, we are, Al." Stu glanced at John, looking for unity. "We're callin' ourselves The Silver Beatals...as a tribute to Buddy Holly – this bein' the day he died 'n all."

"Beetles!" Allan sputtered. "Sounds as if y'need to be fuggin' exterminated! And despite the fact that The Jac patrons have suggested exactly that, more than a time or two, I'll not have any band of mine goin' about with a dickhead name like Beetles!"

"Look Al," John spat out in double time, "it's symbolic – this name – with a symbolic double entendre in a symbolic sort of symbolic sense, y'know." He liked the name even better now that Allan had rejected it.

"It's crap, that's what it is!" Allan barked. "And it isn't even in vogue, y'realize! Every band around puts their leader in the headliner...Cass and the Cassanovas, Rory Storm and the Hurricanes, Derry and the Seniors, Gerry and the Pacemakers and so forth and so on. Tell them, Harry!" He looked to Bill for support. "I thought we had the whole Long John Silver thing worked out days ago."

"Well, it's The Silver Beatals now." John's nostrils flared. "Get with the iteration, Al. We lead; we don't follow. Tell the other groups to try and mimic us."

"No one laughed at The Crickets, did they, Al?" George insisted.

"No...and d'ya know why, Sonny Jim?" Allan stood with his hands on his hips and waited for a moment. "Because, y'lousy sod, they were *Buddy Holly and* the Crickets!"

"But if we don't have a leader, what then? What if we're a group?" John asked.

Without dignifying such a ridiculous question, Allan turned and headed to the kitchen, letting the door swing back and forth furiously behind him. With thousands of details to work out before mid-March and with the well-heeled Larry Parnes to woo, Allan had far more important fish to fry than this obstinate bunch of mediocre musicians with a ridiculous stage name.

"You're the journalist, Harry!" he yelled over his shoulder. "*You* sort them out! Tell them what's what in the world of publicity these days!"

Allan sighed and shook his head. Every day, so it seemed, The Quarry Men, The Moondogs, the idiotic Silver Beatals grew more and more annoying.

The leader of Cass and the Cassanovas was either Brian Casser (Bill Harry) or Brian Cassar (Buskin, Pawlowski, Williams). Buskin says that Cassar, upon hearing the band name, The Beatles, told John Lennon that the name was ridiculous and that John should rename the group "Long John and the Silver Beetles."

According to Allan, the events in this chapter are exactly as they occurred. On the anniversary of Buddy Holly's death, The Beatles were meeting in the Jacaranda. Paul had not yet arrived. As they discussed Holly, Stu suggested a new name for the band. They presented it to Allan that day, and he rejected it 100%.

All conversation is conjecture

In August of 2007, just as this book was going into print, I received an e-mail from Bill Harry, graciously giving me details that I used for this chapter. He wrote, "I was in Gambier Terrace flat when John and Stuart actually tried to find a name for the group. Stuart suggested that they should have something similar to Buddy Holly's band, The Crickets – they played a lot of Holly numbers – and they begin to think of insects and came up with the Silver Beats, The Silver Beatles, and finally, The Beatles." Although I set the chapter in the Jacaranda instead of Gambier Terrace, I did include Mr. Harry in this chapter, and I thank him for sharing his first-hand knowledge with me.

Saturday, 16 April 1960
Gambier Terrace
Liverpool 8

It wasn't the haven John had envisioned. Sure, Stu's new flat in Gambier Terrace offered ultimate freedom, but it was difficult being "recklessly radical" when you were starving. It was hard being Bohemian when your fingers were frozen numb. For the past few days, John'd been thinking of giving up the liberal lifestyle. In fact, though he'd never said it out loud, he'd been thinking of going home to Mendips.

At first, sleeping on Stu's makeshift camp bed had been somewhat of an adventure. Now it was merely cramped and uncomfortable. And living off the least expensive items from Liverpool 8's Chinese take-aways was causing John's sides to rub together. In the ice-bath of Liverpool spring, John was constantly hungry, constantly cold, and constantly uncomfortable

Besides, he told himself, he had a legitimate excuse for going home. He had news to tell Mim.

Allan's recent alliance with "the great man from London," the legendary Larry Parnes, had created a tangible opportunity for John's music to be heard, for his group finally – finally! – to make a name for themselves. Allan had courted the influential Parnes, and in doing so, had made great strides for them all.

At the 14 March Liverpool Empire programme, Williams had gained Parnes' respect, assisting him expertly with the Vincent-Cochran Show, playing "Johnny-on-the-Spot," and insinuating himself gingerly into Parnes' good graces. Then over drinks and dinner following the performance, Williams had cleverly proposed a collaboration, a joint venture from which both men could profit – a second Liverpool concert for Parnes' stars in which Williams would serve as "leg-man," handling all the promotions and arrangements. Parnes would simply garner the glory and net most of the profits. It was a deal that had no downside for Larry Parnes. It was a partnership from which Allan's bands would clearly benefit.

It was news Mimi had to know.

John was sure that the newly christened Silver Beatals were, for the first time, on the brink of fame and fortune. At last they now knew someone who knew someone, and incredible things could happen quickly.

But in spite this, John been struggling with a loneliness he couldn't shake. It seemed like nostalgia; it seemed like homesickness. John wondered if a good meal and a night under his old roof might do him good.

"Tell Stu I've gone 'round to Mim's," he scribbled a note to Rod Murray. "Back in a coupla days…sooner if she's in a snit. T'rah to all this luxury! John!"

And in search of happiness, he was off.

****

Mendips
Woolton

The Canning Street bus retraced the familiar carriageways home. Nothing had changed. First the smoky Toxteth row houses, the grey Dingle cemetery, the roundabouts mad with traffic, and then further down the line, the gardens of Woolton. It was all the same as last year and the year before that.

The "daffs" were blooming by the thousands in Sefton Park, and tiny, tightly packed gardens were brilliantly arranged in front of the suburban, gated homes of John's childhood. Woolton was still intent on uniformity. Each semi-detached Tudor dwelling gleamed from a recent window washing or a new coat of paint. Each iron rail fence shone, scoured and varnished. John had taken it all for granted once, but now, in contrast to the irregular sidewalks of Rice and Falkner and the broken-windowed buildings hovering together down on the docks, he saw dignity in the treed and landscaped Woolton neighbourhoods.

When the bus stopped at Menlove and Vale, John hopped off, looking around half-expectantly, as if some of his former neighbours might hail him. He imagined them viewing him from behind their café curtains or shutters. He could hear their conversations.

"Look it's that Lennon lad from over in Mendips, home from City Centre, luv!"

"Yes, right…Mimi Smith's boy! Just look at him!"

"He's quite the man about town these days, isn't he?"

"Oh yes…in art school, y'know."

"And in that band as well…the group that performed at The Garden Fête a few summers ago…the one managed by the owner of The Jacaranda coffee house, I believe it is."

"Right, yeah...the manager who's just recently linked up with Larry Parnes – that music mogul from London, y'know."

"The influential Larry Parnes?"

"The same one. Silk pockets – Parnes."

"Well, then the Lennon lad's off to a great start, isn't he? Off to fame and fortune, I'd imagine."

"From Woolton to the world. That's what I always say."

John walked with a hint of arrogance, acknowledging the imagined kudos in his head.

At the end of the walkway, he stopped for a minute and stared at Mendips, seeing it through the rose-coloured glasses of absence. He saw the sunset reflected in the stained glass transom, not the widening cracks in the stucco walls. He saw the bed of fat yellow and red tulips but never noticed the first brown tinges of disease in the cedar by the front door. John stood for a long minute and reminisced. He thought of Uncle Ge'rge – of Len, Rod, Eric, and Ivy. He thought of Quarry Bank and days he'd spent roaming The Tip. He thought of Pete. And of Julia. Then he turned the doorknob quietly and tiptoed down the hall into the kitchen without creaking a single board.

In a way, he wanted to surprise Mim, just as he used to in the old days...to pop out of nowhere and grab her for an unexpected kiss on her bony cheeks. But more importantly, he wanted to get firmly, completely into the house before unleashing the sinewy woman's wrath. He hadn't come all this way just to have the door slammed in his face. And since he hadn't phoned or visited in weeks, he was sure Mim was absolutely furious with him.

But Mimi showed no emotion at all. Although she jumped and yelped when John grabbed her, she managed an astonishing calm, almost as if she'd anticipated this moment for a long time and had rehearsed her response.

"Hello, John," she monotoned, pulling away, her eyes registering no hint of anger or joy. She turned back to the stove where she was grilling up a marinated flank steak and fat mushrooms for supper. "So...you've run out of money - then?"

"That's the reason you think I've come 'round?" He dropped his grip on her arms.

"Isn't it?' Mimi glanced over her bony shoulder, sizing him up with a look. "I know you're not here to give me a progress report on your grades. The art college keeps me well posted on your many lapses, delinquencies – failures."

John pulled out a chair and settled uneasily at the tiny table where he'd always taken his breakfast. He breathed in the heavy aroma of food and cut, fresh flowers. His stomach growled audibly. It had been almost two days since he'd really eaten.

"You can't believe half of what you hear these days." John fingered the arrangement of crocuses in the tiny flow-blue vase.

"Well, even if *half* of what they say is true, it's shocking enough," Mimi shot back.

"All right. We'll give 'em that." John leaned forward, ready with his *piece de resistance*, "But how about some good news for a change?"

"Good news? *What* good news?"

"We've made a connection, Mim…an association with a real name in rock'n'roll."

Mimi rested her long cooking fork against the black, iron skillet and turned to face her nephew. Wiping her hands methodically on her apron, she stared at him with the look of one who carries a grudge. "We?" she spat out. "We, who?"

"We, the band…we've started calling ourselves The Silver Beatals now. Y'know, like Buddy Holly and The Crickets, only with a hidden meaning. Beatals, y'know…rhythm and beat…y'get the drift."

"So, that again," she said with real invective.

John met her glare. "*Still*."

"Then I suppose nothing's changed in all these months."

"Didn't you hear what I just told you, woman?" John's volume rose. "I told you we've made a connection, or rather our manager's made one. He's sealed a partnership, as it were, with this famous entrepreneur in the music industry, Larry Parnes. Even *you've* heard of Parnes, Mim! He's all the rage in London; he has commercially backed television programmes and venues everywhere…from Bath to bleedin' Birmingham."

Mimi's eyes showed no recognition or interest. Her lips remained in the same, straight line.

"Look," John's nose hardened as he condescended to explain, "he's a promoter…and a powerful one at that. He was the one responsible for the Gene Vincent-Eddie Cochran show at The Empire. You must've read about it in *The Echo*. It was unbelievably huge."

"Good for him." Mimi folded her arms around her waist.

"And now…he's linked up with our manager, Allan Williams, to stage another event, a one-night only show on 3 May at the Boxing Stadium. It's designed to feature Merseyside bands as well…Cass and the Cassanovas, Rory Storm and the Hurricanes…"

"And *you're* going to be included?" For one brief moment, Mimi's eyes hinted enthusiasm.

"Not this time," John took the long way around to the point. "We weren't able to get a drummer, but…"

"I see." Mimi turned back to the stove.

"But," John ignored her, "we'll be there anyway – makin' contacts, makin' ourselves visible, settin' the stage for future…"

"So what exactly *is* your good news, John?" Mimi jabbed and flipped the steak. It sizzled and popped in the heavy pan. "Oh wait, I think I've got it now. You'll *not* be one of the groups performing at this Boxing Stadium event, and you *don't* have the slightest offer of an audition with this Parnes fellow, and he's never actually heard of your group, *but*...and this is important...you'll have the rare opportunity to hang around backstage and hear the others in action! How fortunate for you, John! How very lucky indeed!"

"Bleedin' hilarious." Now John folded his arms and leaned back in the chair. "You really ought to take it on the stage, Mim."

She shrugged and heaped a bowl of raw onions into the skillet, stirring them around and pushing them to the edges of the pan.

John stood up and moved towards the stove, "Look, *this* is how it's done in the music business, Mim. This is how you set yourself up."

"Oh, you've been set up all right." Mimi looked at him briefly. "Because I'm sure Allan Williams has been kind enough to let your group do more than simply observe. I'll wager he's permitted you to work backstage as well, to set up equipment, to clean, and to do his errands, what have you."

"Right. That's all part of the game."

"John Winston Lennon," she shook her head. "You're a fool."

"The foolishness of the wise!" He leaned on the counter next to her. "The foolishness that's strategy. The foolishness that'll make me rich and famous someday, and then you'll have a pink fit to say you knew me when and you were once privileged to feed me steak and onions – right here in this very room."

"I thought you hated my cooking." Mimi began filling a plate with her own private feast, a generous portion of steak - thick and nicely done - a side of hot buttered rolls, and a dollop of cooked cabbage. "That's what you said when you moved out, if memory serves."

"That's before I'd tasted cardboard," John grabbed a roll from the pan and bit off more than half of it, talking with his mouth full. "That was before the unspeakable horrors concocted by Stu and Rod. Before I learned to stomach rancid leftovers from the deadliest of delis."

"So," Mimi eyed him coolly, without surrendering her plate of food, "it's not what you'd thought it'd be – living on your own?"

John stuffed the rest of the roll greedily in his mouth and reached for another, but Mimi grabbed his wrist, and their eyes met in a standoff.

"Answer me, John," she insisted. "This so-called independence – it isn't what you thought it'd be, now is it?"

"What do you think?" His voice became dangerously husky. "*Nothing's* ever what *I* think it'll be, now is it?"

Mimi released her grip and shoved the plate of food at him without another word. She filled another plate for herself in silence, and poured them both a cup of tea. Then she joined her nephew at the small kitchen table.

Flatware clinked now and again, but no one said a word. Parnes, auditions, grades, school failures, delinquencies, and dreams...after weeks apart, they discussed nothing. And when the plates were empty, John cleared the dishes without comment, just as he'd always done.

That night John sat on the braided rug and tossed a ball of yarn to his lethargic stray, Tim. He fed Mimi's persnickety Persian from his palm. He asked after Ivy Vaughn. He even amused himself for a while with the harmonica before scanning the pages of *The Echo*, just for old times' sake, just for "Uncle Ge'rge."

At bedtime, John dug out his thick white beaker with the Kellogg's rooster on it and took his traditional Ovaltine up to his room. He flopped about in the torn, frayed bedroom slippers that Mimi hadn't been able to throw away and washed up with familiar lavender soap. After an hour or so of Radio Luxembourg, John slipped into the old, sun-dried sheets and stared at the patterned cracks in the ceiling.

But the loneliness he'd felt at Gambier Terrace was still with him.

The hours dragged on. The clock made too much noise. The blankets itched. John found sleep impossible. He wondered what band was playing at The Jacaranda while Woolton slept, huddled under eiderdown comforters. He wondered if the group tonight was better than his, if the room was packed, if Paul and George were there.

And he wondered what Cyn was doing in Hoylake tonight. Would she understand why he'd left for Woolton? Would she ring him up? Would she be worried? How would he explain that he had needed to come home for a while? And *why* had he needed to come home...to this?

He imagined the icy apartment at Gambier and wondered what Rod and Stu were burning tonight to keep warm...and if they'd had anything to eat. He wondered if Stu knew why he'd had to leave. If he did, he hoped Stu would explain it to him, because John had no idea at all.

He turned this way and that, folded his pillow and unfolded it, watched the car lights travel across the walls and then shut his eyes, trying to force himself to sleep.

He tried to remember what it had been like living in this room when he'd had no responsibilities, no worries, no decisions to make. But as far back as he could go, John couldn't remember a time when he'd ever been peaceful.

He opened his eyes and stared at the ceiling again, remembering the first days in Mendips, those first nights without his mother – those first nights he'd sung himself to sleep. He remembered Uncle George's stories...his pipe, his chuckle...the crackle of the radio, the sound of book pages turning in an empty room. And every thought John had was laced with sadness.

He remembered the wiry fabric of Sally's fur, the unwilling smiles

Mimi eked out at his antics, the weary look on her face when he pretended to be The Famous Eccles. He remembered the lectures she'd given him when he came home scuffed from a fight and the nights she'd helped him with his homework. But not one memory was without melancholy.

And now, his world was more complicated but no happier. In Gambier, in Mendips, in Slater, in the universe, there seemed to be no place where he could "just be."

Returning to Mendips hadn't been the answer. Going home hadn't solved the problem. It had only created new ones and emphasized the old.

John's future glory with the sure-to-be-famous Silver Beatals was as doubtful to him as it was to Mimi, and lately he'd begun to worry that if they made it – no, *when* they made it – happiness might fail to show itself.

Blanketed in faded, pebbled cabbage roses, John flipped about in his bed uncomfortably. Every half hour or so, he looked at the clock. As soon as it was morning, he would go back to Gambier again.

But he wasn't sure that Gambier was right for him, that any place was the right place for him. John seemed destined to be discontent.

This incident in Mimi's kitchen is related by Tremlett in his book, The John Lennon Story. *The conversations are imagined.*

Wednesday, 4 May 1960
The Jacaranda
23 Slater Street
Liverpool 1

London, England
4 May 1960

Mr. Allan Williams
Jacaranda Club
23 Slater Street
Liverpool, England

Dear Allan,

    Enjoyed our venture at the Boxing Stadium last night immensely. Thank God for Rory's all-pervasive charisma; he worked wonders on the "over energetic" audience. I thought for a time we might have a "situation" on our hands!
    But "all's well that ends well," and Mr. Parnes will be returning to Liverpool on business within the week. We are in the process of fanning the North in search of prominent, local bands to serve as touring groups for headliners, Duffy Power and Johnny Gentle (formerly of Liverpool).
    Power will be touring Scotland from 2 June to 11 June, and Gentle will be touring Scotland from 16 June to 25 June. We are willing to pay a touring group one hundred and twenty pounds (£120), plus the fares from Liverpool. Should you have some groups under your management that you feel would be suitable and would be agreeable to these terms, please let me know as soon as possible.
    Please select four or five of your most promising groups for an audition date of Tuesday, 10 May. Secure an audition hall, and ring me with your decision as soon as possible. We will then make arrangements for Mr. Parnes to come and audition your groups to select the most suitable ones.
    He will also bring Billy Fury, as Billy will want one of these

groups for his own personal use. Incidentally, the idea of Billy wanting a group from his own hometown will provide several interesting press stories and publicity tie-ins.

As you can see, your groups will be afforded a wealth of opportunities, if you should decide to participate. I look forward to hearing from you and hopefully, to working with you once again.

All the best,

Mark Forrester

Assistant to Larry Parnes

Williams let the textured, ivory stationery float to the floor.

"'*If* you should decide to participate!' '*Hopefully,* to working with you!' Ffffuggin'ell!" Allan shouted to the empty Jac, "What else *but* interested? What fuggin' else *but*?" He threw up his hands and roared with laughter. "I've ensnared the fuggin' lion at last! Mouse I may be," Allan bent down and picked the letter up again, "but I've got the lion right where I want him, don't I!"

"Al?" Beryl emerged from the back room, one wisp of dark, silky hair falling across her gently slanting eyes. "What is it? What has you talking to yourself this time?"

"Parnes!" He wagged the letter in front of her face. "Larry fuggin' Parnes, that's what! He wants to audition *my* groups! He wants to come back to Liverpool and hear *my* boys play…for tourin' opportunities, as it were! *Tourin'* opportunities!"

"You're serious?"

"Would I ffffuggin' lie about *that*?"

"Let's see." She reached for the letter.

"Back off, woman!" He pulled it in.

"Well, read it to me then. Word for word."

Allan complied, adding a dramatic Welsh flourish to his rendition, adding special emphasis on the words, "need your assistance" and "your groups" and "hopefully working with you again." Allan's naturally red-veined cheeks flushed deeply, and his mischievous eyes danced.

"Four top-notch groups…" Beryl repeated at the end of the reading. "Four groups…"

"Well," Allan walked behind the bar and poured himself a cup of coffee, leaving room for a liberal shot of whiskey from the flask he kept hidden behind the stack of banded napkins, "there's Gerry Marsden and his bunch, right off the bat."

"Of course, The Pacemakers." Beryl handed her husband the sugar bowl and a spoon.

"Yeah, they're Parnes material all the way." Allan stirred the liquor and sugar in.

"And Cass," Beryl leaned on the counter, running one hand through her fine hair. "Cass and his boys without a doubt."

"True professionals!" Allan agreed. "The Cassanovas're sure to make the grade."

"And The Rockers?" Beryl raised an eyebrow.

"I'd have them in the wink of an eye, but…they're heavily engaged these days, y'know. Hard to say what they could do on such brief notice."

"Well," Beryl swallowed hard. "There's always The Silver Beatles, Allan."

"Pffffft! Right. The Silver Beatles! When pigs fly!" Allan threw his eyes to the ceiling and took a sip of his coffee. "Derry and the seniors…now *they'll* work."

"They do have a very Northern sound," Beryl nodded.

"The kind of sound Parnes is sure to go for." Allan grabbed the notepad and pen next to the telephone and began to make notes.

"But…what's wrong with John's band, Al? He's been after you for months now to 'do something for him' as he puts it. What's the harm in giving the boy a shot - since it's so readily available?"

"Listen Beryl, Lennon's lads'd never cut it with the likes of Larry Parnes. They haven't a look *or* a sound. They haven't even a fuggin' drummer, have they?"

"But whose fault is that?" She gently laid one hand on her husband's arm.

"Bugger off!" He jerked his arm away. "I've easily got a thousand more important things to do than run about the city knockin' on doors and drummin' up drummers for the fuggin' Silver Beatals or whatever it is they're callin' themselves this week! I'm runnin' one of the most successful clubs Merseyside…just about to purchase another, and for weeks I've been involved with Forrester and Parnes on all these promotions, what have you! So when, in God's name, did I have time for trivial crap like sleuthin' out drummers for The Silver Beatals? And while we're at it, why is it up to *me* – a prominent businessman and entrepreneur – to scout the fuggin' woods for a drummer for John fuggin' Lennon and his ilk?"

"You're their manager," Beryl smiled. "And besides that – you said you would. You gave your word. You promised." She paused and looked him in the eye. "And this, Al, is the perfect opportunity to make good on your promises without a great deal of effort either way."

Allan took another long drink of the Irish coffee. The warmth was almost as soothing as the whiskey itself. He drank and let the liquid mellow his mood.

I could do, he mulled. *I could give the lads a break…give them the single biggest thrill of their young lives.*

"You'd be a hero, y'know," Beryl said, almost as if she could read his mind. "And it'd do the boys good, just to have the experience. Whether they were selected or not, it would count for something, wouldn't it?"

"Larry Parnes meets The Silver Beatals!" Allan snorted. "Now there's a fuggin' image!" He took another swig. "Little Stu sweatin' out a decent performance…John Lennon tradin' his soul to succeed…McCartney with those doe eyes sweepin' the room, and Georgie Harrison, one serious Scouser. But I'd have to find them a drummer somehow, somewhere…someone who could at least get them through the afternoon."

"You know everyone Merseyside," Beryl encouraged.

"Perhaps ole Tommy Moore from the Garston Bottleworks would consider it…for a fair fee and the promise of a coupla favours now and again."

Beryl nodded.

"Can you see the pitiful Silver Beatles, as it were, stragglin' into the room, all optimistic and clumsy, wearing those scuffed-up, ratty plimsoles they always wear and carryin' that god-awful gear of theirs?"

"I'm sure Mr. Parnes has seen worse."

"And better as well." Allan shook his head. "Nah, I'd worry that Parnes'd think we're all like that around here. Liverpool's best represented by Gerry and Cass and Derry and…"

"I suppose." Beryl words agreed, but her voice did not.

Allan stared at her with eyes that tried to be cold and shrewd. Then he rubbed his hand across his mouth and sighed heavily. "But with the better groups as alternatives," he conceded, "I suppose yer fuggin' Beatals won't totally degrade the whole of Merseyside in one fell swoop."

"How could it hurt to give them a chance?" Beryl shrugged. Allan sipped his coffee and looked out the window. "What's the worst that could happen?" his wife whispered.

"All right! All right! All fuggin' right, then! What's Lennon's line…GAT 1696? That's it, isn't it?" Allan confirmed the number with the listing on the wall and dialed as he spoke.

"That's his aunt's line," Beryl nodded. "But I believe he's there, now and again. Or if not, try Stu's…his number's posted as well."

Allan tapped his foot impatiently as the phone rang, but his mouth hinted a smile. It was oddly refreshing to be, for once, the bearer of good tidings; it was rather fun to offer a bit of hope instead of excuses. Allan rubbed his thick, dark beard and hummed. Four times the phone rang before John answered, his distinctively nasal voice sounding rather sleepy.

"John – Al here…" the entrepreneur began with a smile. "Listen, y'lousy sod, I've a bit of good news."

Allan winked at Beryl, and she smiled.

All events are documented, including John Lennon's telephone number. The letter from Mark Forrester is not an original. The conversation between Allan and Beryl is imagined, though Allan's invaluable input helped to recreate the events in this chapter.

Friday, 6 May 1960
The Jacaranda
23 Slater Street
Liverpool 1

It was Thursday before Al had secured Tommy Moore as their drummer and Friday before they'd decided on a band name. Stu still favoured the Holly hat-tip that "The Beatals" implied, but the odd designation was ridiculed by experienced showman, Brian Casser, and influenced by Cass, Allan put his foot down. "It's fuggin' lunacy – this Silver Beatals! Give it up! Beatals is out!"

Among John, Paul, George, and Stu, there was general grumbling and a string of half-hearted suggestions that inspired no one, and while they were divided, Allan resurrected the Long John Silver tag again. This time he insisted on it.

"Look, Lennon," he raged, "I haven't time to argue about this. I've scads to do before Tuesday mornin', so listen up. It's Gerry and the Pacemakers, as I've said before, Colin Green and the Beat Boys, Cliff Roberts and the Rockers, Bob Evans and his Five Shillings, Derry and the Seniors…"

"Cass and the Caskets," John snarled.

Allan ignored him. "To select some anonymous band name without delineating group leadership is flagrantly swimmin' upstream, and you know it! In fact, from Manchester to Doncaster – in all the fuggin' musical North – not one fuggin' name like the fuggin' Beatals has ever been heard of!"

"Right." John's nostrils flared. "Now you're catching on, son."

Paul shouldered in, standing beside John without one hint of his usual cheery disposition. "John's not a solo virtuoso 'shoo-bopped' by some insignificant chorus, y'know," Paul said. "We're *all* in the group, Al. It's all of us, y'know."

"It's a hand-selected band of individual players," John agreed, tactfully re-establishing his leadership without saying so.

"No one sings all the songs," George tossed in.

"Sod that!" Allan stood his ground. "It's Long John Silver and the whatever else you want to call it…or it's nothin' at all."

John stood up. "We'll not be a name and a conjunction, Al… and I won't be Long John anythin' – not for you, Parnes, or the Queen Mother herself – gig or no gig, tour or no tour, audition or the obvious fuggin' alternative!"

"Look," Allan stepped up, equally irate and stubborn, "I don't give a fuggin' rat's ass what you say, Lennon. I've no time for your shenanigans at this point." He pushed a finger in John's chest. "You're *not* gettin' up there in front of Billy fuggin' Fury and Larry fuggin' Parnes with some hare-brained insect name spelled in some jimmied up, ludicrous fashion! It's bad enough you've never even practiced with yer bleedin' drummer yet…"

"And who exactly do we have to thank for that?" John hissed.

"…but at least you'll look legit and act legit and have a name that sounds like an honest-to-goodness musical group!"

"Gerroff, Al," John sneered. "We've work to do."

"Understand me?" Allan tried Paul first for confirmation, but Paul only shrugged and looked away. "Got it, Harrison?" George whistled and twiddled his thumbs. Only John continued to make eye contact, and his rebellious glare promised only defiance. Allan raised his voice in one final threat, "I'm tellin' you lot right here and now…don't fuggin' cross me on this! Don't come into the fuggin' Blue Angel as the bloody Silver, Bronze, Gold, or Iron Beatals, or y'er out on yer bleedin' ears before you even darken the door. Dress professionally! Don't be late! And *don't* bring this crap up again! You'll not give my management a bad name just because you're all too fuggin' green to know what's what in the music world!"

"And you make sure," John returned, not the least bit intimidated, "that *yer* fuggin' drummer shows up. You do your job, Manager…and we'll do ours."

"You'd better hope so," Allan turned to leave, "because if any of you so much as *begins* to embarrass me in front of Larry Parnes…"

"Out!" John pointed towards the door, dismissing Allan from his own coffee bar, and turning to George in the same breath. "One, two…one, two, three, four…"

"Bollocks to you, Lennon!" Allan mouthed while John flashed a malicious Cheshire grin and began to play. Paul smiled and waved goodbye. George gave a slight nod, then turned away.

Quickly glancing at his watch, Allan pulled his "final-final checklist" from his pocket and hurried to the street, shaking his head in disgust.

They need a fuggin' warden, not a manager, Allan swore. *And John Lennon needs a zookeeper with a muzzle and a cudgel.*

Al unlocked the sleek, navy blue Jaguar parked in front of The Jacaranda and piled in, his heavy cloth coat rumpling about him. He flipped on the radio and pushed the cigarette lighter in with one quick, simultaneous motion. He inhaled deeply. Holding it for a second, Al let the air out slowly with puffed cheeks. He closed his eyes.

Radio Merseyside was playing Rosemary Clooney's '56 hit, "Come Rain or Come Shine." It was a musical martini for the nerves. It soothed. Allan inhaled deeply again, and turned up the volume a notch.

Not my favourite – Rosemary Clooney, he thought, *but I'll take a bit of a lullaby after that lot inside! Sing, Rosemary, sing! Work yer magic, girl!*

Allan turned on the ignition and revved it three times.

Beatals! he frowned. *Idiotic! Silver Beatals! Who's ever heard of shite like that?*

Adjusting his mirrors, settling into the cushy leather, and popping into gear, Allan screamed away from the curb, foot to the floor. A group of pedestrians scattered out of his way as Allan flew down the street at twice the speed limit. And another crowd jumped as he cut the corner short at Slater and Seel. Allan had been warned several times about aggressive driving on the M-6, but no one, he reasoned, could fault him for this. Having to wrangle with the Silver Beatals was, in his opinion, adequate justification for a little vehicular recklessness.

"In fact," he snarled to his reflection in the rear view mirror, "it's far and away the perfect excuse for just about any crime."

All events are actual, including the make and colour of Allan's car (which, by the way, he lost the license to drive a year or so later...you can read the story in The Man Who Gave The Beatles Away. *Priceless!) All conversation is conjecture.*

Tuesday, 10 May 1960
The Blue Angel (formerly The Wyvern Social Club)
108 Seel Street
Liverpool 1

The Wyvern Social Club, in the unforgiving light of day, was of all places, least likely to succeed. Like any nightclub, it depended heavily on deceit – a dense screen of cigarette smoke, reflected neon, layers of perfume, and giddy laughter – for effect. Allan Williams had just purchased the club for a song, and it whimpered for a facelift. The Blue Angel, as Allan had decided to christen the place, was an old girl.

Bare bulbs hung from frayed cords that swayed in the Mersey drafts, and wallpaper drooped from the ceiling and slumped at the corners dejectedly, wrinkled and decaying. The divoted floor was gritty and strewn with trash. The whole building ran mouldy and foul.

On a brisk Tuesday morning with the sun full on, Williams' garish acquisition in Seel Street was rank with dust and urine. The Blue Angel was hardly ideal as an audition hall.

It was only 10 a.m., but everything that could possibly go wrong had. Wall heaters refused to heat. Outlets refused to work. Amplifiers, power cords, and guitars in their stands littered the floor, waiting for the resumption of "the juice," but nothing worked in the cold, dingy room.

"What's the problem now, Al?" Rory Storm gave the entrepreneur a playful nudge as he walked by. Rory's group had declined the offer to audition for Parnes, but they'd come along for the ride anyway. Rory was decked out in his best Italianate suit and his usual easy smile and suntan. He'd come primarily to get his picture made with Billy Fury for publicity purposes. But that didn't stop him from needling Al, since the opportunity presented itself.

"I'm doin' the ffffuggin' best I can, Storm!" Allan hissed, waving his arms in frustration before the host of accusing eyes. "It's just a fuse, surely a fuse – though why the fuggin'ell it happened today of all days is beyond me! I mean, it has to absofffuggginlutely be up and runnin' by the time

Parnes arrives!" He jabbered to himself as he clattered up the stairs again. "And if it isn't...well...well, we'll have to move lock, stock, and fuggin' barrel back to The Jac somehow, though God knows how I'd cram you lot in over there."

"It's on, Al!" a voice called from somewhere above them. "Tell someone to plug 'er in and give 'er a test, then."

"You heard the man!" Allan, thumped his watch with rediscovered confidence, barking commands to Brian Casser, "Get off yer duff and get on with it! Get your group up on the fuggin' stage, Casser! It's after ten now, isn't it?"

"The *stage*?" Brian glanced at the grimy corner of the room that Allan had set aside for their performances. He exchanged looks with his drummer – handsome, burly Johnny Hutchinson – and they both grinned. "Yeah, right Allan. The 'stage.' Whatever you say, then."

"I don't know as I can lift me drums onto that *stage*," Johnny Hutchinson – "Hutch" to most – teased, pretending to strain. "It's a giant of a thing, now isn't it?"

"Bugger off, Hutchinson," Allan scurried like a Liverpool wharf rat. He took the stairs in double-time, calling back over his shoulder, "I can pummel you, y'know. Every last one o' ya!"

"But you wouldn't dare," Hutch shot back, laughing. "I mean, who'd black yer boots for y'then?"

Everyone laughed, nervous laughter. Some paced; some smoked cigarettes. Some milled about in absolute silence, shivering in the cold, rehearsing lyrics in their heads. George ran a few riffs lightly. Every couple of seconds, Stu scratched his ear or nose, and John flipped a coin he had borrowed from Paul, tossing it up and down, up and down, over and over and over again – each time pitching it a little higher than the last.

Allan darted back again, his hands full of extension cords, his forehead dripping sweat. He was a cyclone among them, intent and everywhere at once.

"Hey Al," Cliff Roberts voiced what everyone was thinking, "What's he really like – Larry Parnes?"

"And how much does he pay again?" Johnny Gustafson piped up.

"And what's he mean exactly, 'includin' fares'?"

"Yeah...tell us what's he lookin' for, as it were."

"Look Al," John caught the coin one last time and then pocketed it, "if this Parnes thinks he's fuggin' comin' up here to take advantage of some legendary workin' man-Northern naiveté, we're not havin' it, y'know. We're wise to the ways of the worldly wicked. We're on to that game, son."

"Right, Lennon," Allan shook his head. "You're all so fuggin' cosmopolitan – the lot o'you!"

"Yeah well," Howie Casey, the Seniors' sax player sniffed, "Parnes'd better not try 'n swindle us, anyrate. We may be provincial 'n all that, but we're not blind stupid, y'know. We know when we're bein' had, don't we, mates?"

"C'mon, lads," Allan stopped and scanned the roomful of scowls and frowns. "Would I let that happen to you after all we've been through? I mean, I got you this chance, didn't I? And I found *you* a fuggin' drummer, didn't I, Lennon? Look, I set this up for *all* o' you, with nothin' but your good fortunes clearly in mind when I could've..."

"Abbreviate it, Al!" Paul McCartney grinned. "We know y'er all right."

"Yeah!" Gerry Marsden called out from his perch on the stairway. "And besides that – we all know where you live as well, don't we?"

The crowd dissolved into laughter.

Allan waved them all off and returned to work, smiling in spite of the slurs and innuendo all around him. He knew it was to be expected – this was Mersey talk. Ribbing, teasing, "mickey talk" to Liverpudlians – it was all part of the game.

Tough as nails, these lads, Allan thought, taping Cass's extension cord into place. *Tough, savvy, hungry for success, excited, eager, but not starved blind. Not yet, anyway. They're still comfortable enough to be wary and suspicious of strangers – still young enough to evaluate each opportunity with eyes wide open. They're a good bunch, these boys. Good as...*

"Rock Around the Clock" suddenly filled the room. The power was working, at least for the time being, and The Cassanovas had seized the chance for one last rehearsal before "the big moment."

Allan hacked nervously and stirred the air with his hands. The proliferation of cigarette smoke was beginning to choke them all as one butt after another burned away and was ground out on the floor. But no one could stop smoking. It was a lifeline right now.

Every few seconds, someone asked the time or trudged upstairs to check the front door. Only John remained motionless, leaning against the wall, inhaling a Woodbine, and talking to no one.

Around him stood his partisans: Stu, wriggling his fingers to keep them warm; Paul, chatting and laughing with the Seniors' bass player, Lu Walters; and George tuning his guitar, ear low to the instrument. Beside them, John hardly moved, staring with arctic eyes at Allan's strained smile.

"You look fffuggin' lousy, Lennon!" Al joined the cluster and patted Stu affectionately on the shoulder.

"Where's this so-called drummer, Manager?" John had no time for small talk. "He isn't here, now is he? We haven't got one, now have we?"

Allan checked his watch. "You've got one, and he's a good man – Tommy Moore." Allan coughed again and waved the smoke away. "If Tommy said he'll be here, he'll be here! Give the man a fuggin' chance!"

"Well, he *isn't* here." John threw the Woodbine down and crushed it out. He gestured towards The Cassanovas, who were coming to the end of their song. "How d'ya expect us to compete with *that* when we've no backbeat, Al? What d'ya want us to do...stomp our fuggin' feet? Clap our hands?"

"They're here, Allan!" a lookout called from upstairs. It was half-ten exactly. "Gettin' out of the car right now...Parnes and someone else in a silk jacket...and Billy fuggin' Fury himself!"

"Dear God!" Someone sounded sick.

"Where's a place to piss around here?" Another panicked voice sounded from the far end of the room.

"Listen, lads," Allan took control. "I know you're all in dry heaves right now, but stop'n'think. This Parnes' just another fuggin' wack...Jesus Christ he ain't, right? So go through yer show, do yer best, and put everything you've got into it. But don't let it rattle your cage."

Lennon's complaints about the missing drummer were quickly forgotten in the hubbub that followed. Parnes' assistant, Mark Forrester, descended the stairway first, and Allan rushed to shake his hand and make apologies for the audition hall as Forrester's eyes took in the obvious.

"I've only just secured the place, y'know," Allan explained, sweeping his hand panoramically. "It's got great potential and all that, but we've hardly had the chance to sweep the cobwebs away yet, and well, this is how the previous owners left it to me. My other club, The Jacaranda, is completely refitted and upscale, but not quite large enough to accommodate all this." He indicated the six groups, with their assorted equipment and paraphernalia, waiting around the room.

"Well, here we are, then." Forrester sniffed as if he smelled something odd. "I'm sure this'll work just fine. We've seen it all these past few days. That's the nature of the job, is it not?"

But to himself Forrester thought, *Liverpool! It's a long way from London, a tremendously long way!* "O, what a falling off was there," he mentally quoted Shakespeare.

"Where would you like us to sit?" was all he said aloud.

Allan indicated four wooden pub chairs and a long, paint-splattered table. Wiping the table perfunctorily with his hand, Forrester set his briefcase down and opened it.

"As a matter of fact," Forrester lied, smiling his businessman's smile, "we're all looking forward to this morning quite a bit. Billy, especially, is delighted to be back in his hometown for a day. He always says great things about Liverpool."

Almost on cue, Billy Fury appeared in the room. Dazzling in a pale, hand-tailored jacket with an upturned Elvis collar and a wide-lapelled, white shirt, Billy stood for a moment, drinking in the scene. He smiled, one corner of his mouth doing all the work. And with a patterned showbiz wave, one that barely escaped the wrist, he acknowledged the room full of hopefuls before making his way deliberately over to Forrester.

As all eyes followed Fury across the room, Larry Parnes slipped in quietly, descending the stairs. His hand brushed lightly over the guardrail; his eyes looked through and above them all, seeing everything at once, evaluating those beneath him without once making eye contact or involving himself. Only his cologne touched them. It was expensive, as impressive as the silk tie he wore knotted tightly at the neck, its ebony pattern the exact colour of his thick, curly dark hair. He was quietly fantastic.

"Larry! Larry! Welcome back to Liverpool!" Allan was all around him, shaking his hand, telling him the story of The Blue Angel, making excuses, and running through the line-up for the day.

Parnes was as reserved as Allan was gregarious. Parnes smiled, nodded, listened, and asked all the right questions. But he only looked interested when Allan began the preliminary introductions of the young musicians.

As he walked among them, shaking hands and learning names, Parnes made what he called his "first impression notes." Mentally, he took stock of them all and filed it away for reference against their practised performances.

Gerry Marsden...his boys are Fury look-alikes...light jackets, dark shirts, upturned collars. Nothing out of the ordinary.

Roberts...the country and western tack...boleros, jackets with suede shoulder panels and rough western slacks.

Derry Wilkie...end-of-the-term dance band...neat, shiny jackets, black ties, patent shoes, handkerchiefs...they need only carnations to complete the cliché. Electric keyboard, saxophone: nice touch.

Casser...sequined drum kit, matching shirts, look of experience and confidence.

And this last bunch...no leader perceptible. Old, faded jeans, black and white baseball boots...less careful. One in a black dress shirt, topstitched. One in a Marks and Spencer polo. Economical attire at best...perhaps even contemptuous. If the audition means anything to them, they've failed to demonstrate it.

"I believe we're ready, then," he said quietly, nodding to Allan.
"Right. Great. Just have a seat over here, then."
And the session began.

****

For the most part, Allan Williams' stable of performers seemed prepared and proficient. Cass and the Cassanovas had Johnny Hutchinson's drumming as their trump card. Derry and the Seniors banked on Derry

Wilkie's stylized vocals and Howie Casey's sax runs to impress. Marsden's group was smooth and melodic, and Roberts's group, interesting. But none of them bowled Billy Fury over. The morning vanished; the afternoon was disappearing, and Parnes had found nothing remarkable.

Then the scruffs in the faded jeans and two-toned plimsoles walked towards the performance area, to the spot that Williams kept referring to as "the stage."

"And the name of your group?" Mark Forrester was filling out he necessary paperwork.

John glanced at Allan for a second before leaning in to the microphone and announcing a little too loudly, "Silver Beatals… that's B-e-a-t-a-l-s."

Forrester looked at John point-blank. "And The Silver Beatals' drummer – where is he this afternoon?"

John and Allan glared at one another openly.

Allan glanced at his watch and turned to Parnes. "I'm dead sorry about this, Larry," Allan schmoozed, "I'd hand-picked a man, a good drummer, a mature chap named Tommy Moore who'd promised to sit in with the boys today. He's a bit older, quite experienced, and he seemed more'n'happy to do it. Can't imagine where he's…"

"Someone *will* be filling in, however, I presume?" Parnes folded his hands and leaned back against the worn pub chair.

"Absolutely, absolutely – all in hand, as it were." Allan motioned Johnny Hutchison over to the table, turned his back to Parnes, and whispered, "As you can see, I'm in a bit of Dutch here, Hutch. Parnes is threatenin' to walk away entirely if we can't get the, uh, Silver Beatals - or whoever they are - a temporary drummer," he lied, "and Lennon over there – he'll string me up and leave me for fuggin' dead if that transpires, won't he? I'm as good as dead now. Just look at him!"

Hutch barely cut his eyes at John. "I don't give a crap about Lennon," he whispered back, "but all right – I'll do it for you, Al. If y'ask me, it's a bleedin' waste of time – drummin' for The Silver whoever. It's only tossin' pearls before swine, isn't it? They're dead last here. No amount of backbeat can change that."

"Just do it this one time, Johnny, and I'll be in your debt forfuggin'ever," Allan pleaded.

"Yerrokay," Hutch threw his eyes to the ceiling, but gave in.

"Great!" Allan patted him on the back. And in just a matter of minutes, it was all a go.

Johnny looked bored and coerced when The Silver Beatals struck their opening chord, but in spite of Hutch's lack of enthusiasm, John and Paul careened into the first song. George leaned over his guitar and let his fingers convey his excitement. And John sang raw rock'n'roll.

Only Stu, his palms wet, his hands quivering, despised the experience. Now and again, as instructed, he turned his back to the judges, his head bowed in the stance Paul had devised for him. But when he could, Stu faced Parnes and forced his hands to make music on the thick bass strings. Behind a pair of dark glasses, Stu prayed it would all end soon.

Parnes leaned forward in his chair, his right hand on his thigh, his left ear turned slightly towards the band. He glanced at Billy with eyebrows briefly raised, and Billy rubbed his chin before answering behind a cupped hand. They whispered, paused, and whispered again. Mark Forrester took a quick drag on his cigarette, jotted a note, and slid it down the table. The three men nodded.

After a couple of numbers, Parnes motioned Allan closer, and the decision makers huddled. Allan held up a hand to suspend the performance, and the room fell silent. No one moved.

Only a commotion on the stairs interrupted the powwow at Parnes' table.

"It's Moore!" Allan muttered. "A day late and a dollar short, as luck would have it, but here at last. I knew he wouldn't leave the lads high and dry!"

Tommy Moore had indeed arrived, drum kit in tow, face sheepish and aggravated – his embarrassment as thick as his Scouse.

"Was collectin' me gear cross-town," he growled to Allan awkwardly, glancing now and then at the boys in the performing area. "Browned off as hell, y'know…fuggin' traffic, y'know. Knew I'd miss the fuggin' kick-off, as it were, but came 'round anyway. Still…if you'd like to use that other drummer over there instead of me…y'can do."

Allan patted the befuddled forklift driver on the arm and smiled his reassuring best. "Just glad you're here, Tommy boy. Relax! No use gettin' yer knickers in a wad, eh?"

Tommy smiled a bit and wiped his forehead on his sleeve.

"Yeah…that's it, then." Allan smiled back. "Just join the lads over there and give it year best, yeah? They've been hopin' you'd make it in time. Go on," Allan guided Tommy over towards The Silver Beatals with a gentle shove. "That's it."

Then he turned back to Parnes and Forrester with a quick whisper, "Just give him a moment, if y'don't mind, and I'm sure it'll all be worth it. The boys'll do well with Tommy backin' them. Hutch is great – as you've seen, of course – but, well…it's not his band, is it? No vested interest, as it were."

Parnes was impassive. Forrester nodded and sat back in his chair.

Allan's beard glistened with sweat, and his left eye had developed a twitch. *Now if only Lennon won't out and out refuse to let Tommy play,* Allan worried. *If he won't belt the lad for been' so late. If he won't upbraid him in front of God and country and make a gigantic issue of it all…*

There was shuffling, muttering, and general confusion in the performing area as Johnny Hutchinson got up and began to slide his gear out. Tommy was conferring with Paul, who had the play list in his hand. John's eyes were narrowed, his head tipped back, his nostrils flared. Allan braced for the worst.

But John refused to let anything, even gross ineptitude, stand in the way of his title bout. He rested his hands on the top of his guitar, looked away, saying nothing as Moore clumsily inserted his drums where Johnny Hutchinson's had been. Clenching his jaw and concentrating on the business of the next song, John ignored the older drummer entirely.

"Ready, then," Tommy hoarsely signified after a couple of minutes, "But...what's the next song again?"

Paul handed the drummer the play list and told him to keep it, and they were off. With Tommy back-beating expertly, typically heavy-handed as Mersey drummers were, the audition began again. Half on the drum, half on the rim, Tommy gave them a solid, strong, hard-pounding percussion that had its roots in the marching bands of the Scottish highlands. And even without the luxury of a rehearsal, the songs and the rhythm gelled. The Silver Beatals' performance was as good as could be expected.

At the end of the offering, Parnes leaned across to Allan with a single request, "Have them play the next song without the bass, please."

"Without the bass?" Allan hoped he'd misunderstood.

"That's right." Parnes didn't look up from the notes he was scribbling. "Without the bass player. If you don't mind."

"Yeah, all right. Will do," Allan swallowed. *Poor little Stu*, he thought. *I'd rather eat nails. This'll fuggin' kill him, this kind of shame.*

It was the longest thirteen seconds of Allan's life. He swallowed and racked his brain for a way out. *But the only fuggin' way out is through*, he thought, standing to speak.

"Okay lads, we'll have one more number then," Al began, forcing a weak smile.

John tapped out a quick time step and ended with a lunge. "How's that?" he asked with a genuine grin.

But Paul was all business. "Another number, is it? Right. No problem, Al."

"Just a minute," Allan fidgeted. "There's something else, lads..."

John stopped smiling to listen.

"For the next one..." Allan glanced at Parnes who nodded unflinchingly, "for the next one, Mr. Parnes would like to hear the group...without...without the bass. He's just curious, y'understand. All right?"

No one else got a chance to answer. The decision was made, and it was final. John took a step forward, his eyes slanting dangerously.

"No, it's not all right." John's voice was the only sound in the deeply silent room.

"Not even one song?" Allan despised himself. "Not even a..."

"Sorry, Al," George added his voice to John's, "We can't do that."

John spoke to Parnes now, sidestepping Allan entirely. "We're a group – all or none. That's the way it is."

"Come on boys – for me?" Allan whined.

"Forget it, Allan." Parnes spoke softly, folding the papers on which he had been taking notes. "They're good boys. They want to stay together." His smile hinted sarcasm.

"That's right." John's nostrils flared. "We're a group."

"But John, I..." Stu began.

"That's the way it is." John cut him off, ending any further discussion.

"Well then, there you have it." Parnes spoke directly to John now. "I think you boys have potential, and I'd love to give you the opportunity to prove it."

The two men stared at each other, neither compromising, neither backing down.

"If you change your minds," Parnes appealed to the others, especially to the handsome lad with the large eyes who hadn't spoken once during the exchange, "please have Mr. Williams let me know as soon as possible."

"Thank you, gentlemen." Mark Forrester dismissed The Silver Beatals with a nod.

And without further ado, they were finished for the day.

****

"I'm fuggin' sorry, John." Stu's voice was almost a whisper. "I'm sorry. I really am."

"He's a sod." John slung an amp cord loop over his shoulder and shoved the front door to The Blue Angel open with his foot.

"Yeah, what's he know? Right?" George agreed. "It's all bushwa, that."

"You gave it yer best, didn't you?" Paul said.

"I wouldn't go ter bits over someone like him, Stu." George walked down Seel Street with one foot on the sidewalk, one foot in the gutter. He carried his guitar over his shoulder, his amp in the other hand.

"Lads! Stu!" Allan was suddenly behind them. "Wait up, lads! Wait one!" His face was genuinely stressed. "Look...don't go off in a huff...not like this, right? I mean, it's only fuggin' showbiz, y'know. That's the way of it. Once in a blue moon, it's glorious'n all that...but most days, it's a bitter pill – showbiz."

"Just let it be, Al." Paul warned him away. He knew John was ready to explode.

"Yeah, thanks Al...but no thanks." George began to walk again, still half-on, half-off the curb.

"Sorry, Al." Stu ducked his head. "Sorry I let y'down. Sorry I…"

It was the match John's short fuse needed. "Shirrup, Sutcliffe! You're fuggin' pathetic, aren't you! If anyone should have apologies, it's Mr. Manager here. Where's his, 'Sorry I didn't have you the fuggin' drummer I'd promised, and sorry I betrayed your fuggin' trust, and sorry I asked you to break up your fuggin' group!" Or how about, 'Sorry I humiliated Stu in front of a room full of his peers, and sorry I didn't have the fuggin' guts to tell fuggin' Parnes to fuggin' stuff it!'" John spewed molten invective.

"Look John," Allan began, holding up a hand, "just give me a chance to explain, right?"

"Geroff!" John shoved past him, walking away. "You've done enough for one day, haven't you? Crawl back under yer rock. We're done here."

Allan looked quickly around, stammering quick excuses to the others. But they turned away to follow John, leaving Allan calling after them – furious at everyone involved, including himself.

****

Hours later, dockside, over a blur of Black and Tans, Allan relived the scene again. John had been livid; they'd all been. They'd assumed he'd sold them out.

But nothing, Allan encouraged himself, *nothing could be fuggin' further from the truth*!

He liked Stu. He really did. Stu was the one of the only guileless souls he'd ever known. But as Billy Fury himself had phrased it at the end of the day, "That guy'll never play guitar, Al. Not as long as he lives, will he?"

For the life of him, Al couldn't imagine why he was so focused on this one incident with the so-called Beatals. The rest of the day had gone reasonably well.

Parnes had selected Cass and the Cassanovas as a backing group for Duffy Power's upcoming Scottish tour. And Allan's friend, Roland Cheniston, had photographed Fury, Parnes, and Al's bands for press releases in the Northern newspapers. After the audition, Parnes, Forrester, and Fury had retired to The Jacaranda for drinks, and Allan's alliance with them had grown even stronger. It hadn't been a bad day, all things considered.

But Allan was miserable.

He tried to think of something other than The Beatals. He mulled over Rory Storm's refusal to sign The Hurricanes as one of Larry Parnes' backing groups. In Rory's mind, The Hurricanes already *were* a backing group. They backed *him*. If they agreed to sing back up for Billy Fury or for any other of Parnes' stars, what would he do? Where would he fit into the picture? It wasn't an avenue the tall, blonde lead singer wanted his band to take.

Rory's decision to deny his band the opportunity to audition was, in a strange way, the exact opposite of Lennon's refusal to "play without the bass." Rory was a savvy businessman – cautious, wise…careful to preserve his front-man image – whereas Lennon had refused to acknowledge *his* leadership at all, had refused to do anything that meant surrendering the least of his band members.

It makes no fuggin' sense, does it? Al downed another gulp. *On most days, Rory Storm's a real prince and John fuggin' Lennon's a real bastard. He's razor-tongued and rarely ever a delight to be around; he's sullen and mean and caustic to the core.*

But then, Allan muttered, shaking his head, *suddenly and without fuggin' warnin', it's fuggin'* Lennon *who refuses to play even one lousy song without Stu! It's Lennon who won't compromise for a man as influential as Larry Parnes, who won't compromise his fuggin' "group" as it were. Hard man. Big, tough guy – John Lennon – chip on his shoulder and all that shite.*

He had a chance! He had a break! He had the inroad of all inroads – a way out of Scousedom and Merseyside altogether. But "we're a group," he says, and he walks away from it all. "We're a group," he tells Larry fuggin' Parnes! A group! Shite.

Allan lifted his glass in the corner of the pub. *Well, John Lennon,* he said to the invisible boy, *here's to ya, y'fuggin' swine! Here's to the man who walked away from the chance of a lifetime – the man who gave his fuggin' dream away – all for the sake of a friend."*

Allan snorted, swilling the cider and ale round and round in his glass, watching the tiny maelstrom of dark amber liquid swirl. Then Alan tipped the glass and drank it down quickly, slamming it down as hard as he could on the table, almost shattering the glass in the transaction.

One never forgot the accusing eyes of John Lennon. But Black and Tans certainly helped, and Allan stumbled to the bar to order another.

The "facts" about what happened on this day are probably lost forever. Allan Williams swears to the truth of this story. But Larry Parnes says it was Tommy Moore that he objected to, not Stu. Johnny Gentle in the book Johnny Gentle and the Beatles' First Ever Tour *says that no decisions were made that day and that Allan was notified of all decisions by mail. (Johnny was not present at the audition.)*

Salewicz affirms the Stu story. Gareth Pawlowski also confirms Parnes' request to hear the band without Stu, and his story corroborates Williams' almost word for word. Peter Brown affirms it as well.

Bill Harry denies the story emphatically as does Alan Clayson who wrote Stuart's biography with Pauline Sutcliffe. Hunter Davies, in the early "authorized" biography of The Beatles, ignores the issue entirely, as does Ray Coleman.

Mark Lewisohn acknowledges all accounts of the afternoon.

Interestingly enough, Albert Goldman interviewed Billy Fury in 1982, and Billy said that John's confrontational attitude over Stu steered Fury away from the Beatles. Fury is quoted as saying, "Lennon was a troublemaker as far as I was concerned. I turned them down."

The Beatles themselves talk extensively in The Anthology about that day. Both John and Paul specifically state that Stu could not play and turned his back to Parnes. But none of them mention the confrontation with Parnes over Stu.

At this point, years after the fact, who knows what was said at the table where Allan sat? But what we do know is that Stu was an artist first and a musician reluctantly. We do know that John was fiercely loyal to his friend and for years rejected Paul's logical observation that Stu was not an attribute to the group.

The ingredients for truth reside in the tale you have just read, and the concept of "group" rather than "self" became a watchword for the Beatles in the years to come.

19 May 1960
Ye Cracke Pub
Rice Street
Liverpool 8

"To Inverness!"

"Galasheils!"

"Fraserburgh!"

"Alloa!"

George let out a "Yippee!" and Paul clanked glasses with John. Then Paul raised his pint to the rest of the pub and took a seated bow.

A concession from Larry Parnes, any concession, was reason to rejoice.

"Look, y'bunch of layabouts," Allan leaned across the tiny oak table, giving his best manager's glare, "I expect seriousness from the four o'you. I expect industry."

"We're nothing if not industrious," Paul shrugged, smiling,

"I have serious every mornin'," John rapped his glass sharply on the table to re-head his lager.

"I mean it, Lennon!" Allan pointed a finger. "Despite the shite you pulled last week...you landed a tour, right? And a tour with your whole bleedin' group *in tact*, just like you wanted, right?"

"Get to the point." John looked down his nose.

"The point bein'," Allan snarled, "Johnny Gentle's a star, a real star. And if you so much as halfway muck up this tour, trust me, it'll be a cold day in the fuggin'ell before I send you out on anythin' ever again! Parnes isn't paying you lot eighteen ffffuggin' pounds a week to "yippee it up." I expect you play music, think music, and dream music. Right?"

"At eighteen pounds a week," George pointed out, "we won't be able to afford anythin' but."

"Well," Allan's cheeks flushed with aggravation, "you're not exactly rollin' in dough around here, are you?"

"I wouldn't say that exactly," George sniffed. "We apprentice electrician's mates don't do so badly, y'know."

"Speakin' of that, Harrison," Allan tossed a pocketful of coins on the table for the round, "I told Parnes you'd bring yer electrical kit along – to repair amps and whatnot. You're the appointed 'Sparks' on the tour."

"But I'm only an apprentice, Al!" George's eyes widened.

"Do it." Allan smacked his hand on the table. "And you, Lennon," Allan leaned in, "you *have* actually talked with Tommy Moore, right? He has the dates and specifics? And he's no problem gettin' away from the Bottle Works?"

"That's the rumour." John was unenthusiastic. He had little use for the older drummer. The meld of simplicity and innocence that made Tommy Tommy rubbed him the wrong way.

"Is he on board or is he not?" Allan snapped.

"He'll meet us at The Punch and Judy tomorrow mornin'." John spelled it out. "He knows what time the train is, and he knows to bring his gear along...let's hope."

"And you'll be on time as well?" Allan scanned each one of them.

"With bells on!" George smiled.

"Wouldn't miss it for the world," John admitted.

"I told me Dad we had a two-week holiday from school to 'clear our minds' before exams," Paul winked, "So there's no turnin' back now, is there?"

"Stu and I are outright saggin' off," John confessed. "The only difference is, *he* fuggin' cares. He's out goin' 'round today givin' notice to the entire fuggin' college staff! Like it's the end of world, as it were. I'm just packin' me gear and slippin' silently away to the west."

"That would be the north actually," Paul nudged him.

"Check your compass, son," John argued. "I think you'll find I'm half right."

Allan was almost afraid to ask the next question. "And how'd *you* manage a holiday break from the job, Harrison?" The Silver Beatals had given up so much for this one pitiful, measly Parnes-sponsored tour with Johnny Gentle, a tour that would last only eight days. He hoped they weren't "cutting off the nose to spite the face."

"Well, I called me big brother," George explained, "and I asked him, 'Would you pack it all in and have a go at it...that is, if you were me?'" George blushed a little at the admission. "And he says to me...he says, 'You might as well, George. You never know what might happen.'"

"So?" Allan rolled his hand for George to continue.

"So, I packed it all in then. I quit. John says we'll all be rich and famous in no time anyway, so I didn't want some apprentice electrician's job standin' in the way of a certain and lucrative future."

Allan took a deep breath. "You lot *do* realize this tour is only from 20 to 28 May – not fuggin' forever, right? And it's only eighteen pounds per group, not eighteen pounds per man? And you have to *live* on that as well...no expenses provided, as it were?"

"And *you* realize," John shot back, "that it's a professional tour with a nationally known star who's asked for *us* to open and close his fuggin' show? A chance to have our names on printed posters, a chance to stand on a stage outside of Liverpool, out of Merseyside – a chance to give it a fuggin' shot!"

"As long as you understand the finances..." Allan began.

But John interrupted him with the group's familiar mantra, "Where are we goin' lads?" he asked.

"To the toppermost, Johnny!" Paul and George chanted with gigantic smiles.

"And where's that, then?" John called, almost in cadence.

"To the toppermost of the poppermost!" they called back.

"Oh, buggeroff!" Allan rubbed his hand across his thick, black beard and shook his head. There was clearly no reasoning with the enthusiasm of youth, but he hoped that the four of them would feel the same way when they returned home a fortnight from now

****

The Following Morning
The Punch and Judy Cafe
Liverpool 1

Guitars and cases, Tommy Moore's drum kit, George's electrical repair box, amplifiers, cords, patched duffle bags jam-packed with "stage clothes" and street clothes...it was mania. How the lads ever expected to load all this onto the train to Glasgow, then transfer it all onto the Stirling-bound train, and then finally, onto the train to Alloa, Allan had no idea.

"How, I'd like to know, d'you expect to carry all this crap through the Glasgow terminal?" Allan kicked one of the duffel bags.

"Hey, lay off!" Paul gasped. "That's John's teddy in there."

"Well," John answered the question, "we've got old Tommy here, haven't we? He's a strappin' mule of a man – Tommy. You'll carry all this gear, won't you, Tommy, mate?"

Tommy Moore stared at John warily. He didn't know how to take The Silver Beatals' rhythm guitarist. He thought John had a nasty overtone, but he wasn't exactly sure. He thought John was making fun of him, but it often sounded like compliments.

"I say we let Paul *Ramon* handle the baggage," George winked. "He sounds very swashbucklin', doesn't he?"

"Yeah?" Paul gave it right back. "Well, if y'ask me, Carl Harrison sounds every bit the porter, doesn't it, John?"

"All right, all right! *Efuggin'nough* all o'ya!" Allan held up his watch. "Look, it's already half eleven, and your train leaves Lime Street at 12:25 precisely. Let's get over there. Chop-chop! Load it all up! C'mon. Get with it, John."

Without the characteristic Silver Beatal groans and arguments, each of them shouldered more than he could carry, and looking somewhat like a Moroccan caravan, they limped out of The Punch and Judy towards the City Centre station. Stu lagged behind – carrying his bass, amplifier, cords, suitcase, and a large wooden artist's box. John fell back to match his stride.

"Look Stu, you're gonna have to let Al take some of that back," he said. "We don't have room for it, son. Once we get to Alloa, we're gonna be cramped into a ramshackle road van, eatin' our knees all the way through fuggin' Scotland! We've barely got room for necessities, understand? The art paraphernalia has to go."

Stu pulled the box tighter to his chest. "Well I'll just have to hold it, then, won't I?"

"And what's more," John went on, "you'll have no fuggin' *time* for it, either, Stu!"

"I will. I'll make time."

"You *won't* make time!" John jerked the box from Stu's grip. "Any free time you have'll be spent practisin'! We're not on art holiday here. This is a job, a real job – not some fuggin' boondoggle!"

"Look Stu," Paul had fallen back beside them and joined in the discussion as well, "we've barely got room for a packet of fags, mate. You can see what we're all up against. You have to be reasonable, then."

"I *am* being reasonable," Stu returned, now with an edge to his voice. "I said I'll carry the fuggin' kit, and I'll carry it! I'll sleep with it if that's what y'er after. You won't even see it. It won't even touch you." He turned to John. "And as for practisin', look at this!" He held one hand out for inspection. "I've practised 'til me hands are bloody, and I'm no fuggin' better than I was before! You might as well let me stay behind, y'know. I'm never gonna be an asset to the band!"

"Right!" John slammed the kit back into Stu's chest. "Not with that attitude, you won't!" And he stormed off towards the station, far ahead of the others.

"Aggh!" Paul was clearly irritated, "Now you've gone and browned him off, even before we leave Lime Street, mate." He shook his head. "C'mon Stu! Get with the programme, right? This is serious – this tour. It means a lot to John 'n George 'n me."

"I've got that." Stu stared him straight in the eye. "But what does it mean to *me*? Have you or John ever thought about that, then?"

Paul bit his lip a moment, trying to find tactful words to say. Then he shrugged and walked away. Stu watched the others move ahead of him.

He thought, strangely enough, of Pete Shotton, John's childhood mate. Stu wondered what Pete had finally done to escape the band, to earn a reprieve. He'd often heard the tale of John's smashing Pete's washboard over his head and setting the hapless Quarry Man free. But what Pete had done to secure pardon and release, Stu wished he knew.

For a moment, he considered turning back. It was almost the end of the term, and he had important projects to finish. And what was there for him in Scotland, anyway? Why should he waste his time?

But that would be it with John, he mulled. *John'd never forgive me for walkin' out on him, and he'd never forget it, either. He'd see it as another desertion in a long line of desertions and take it as a personal affront – a fuggin' line in the sand for our friendship, as it were.*

Stu sighed and kicked at a pebble on the sidewalk. Then he readjusted his shoulder strap and picked up the pace again, following the others up the wide concrete steps and into the busy downtown train station.

Stu jogged for a second, trying to catch up – but his gear was too heavy, and he lost sight of the group entirely. The huge station clock ticked away, and perspiring, Stu gulped down panic. Ten minutes to go, nine minutes, eight…he was certain the others had boarded without him. But what train they'd boarded, he wasn't sure.

But then, at end of the walkway, Stu caught a glimpse of John standing alone, waiting with his gear in hand – waiting for Stu on the far platform.

"All right," Stu muttered just under his breath, "that seals it. For the next two weeks, I'll do what John wants. I'll say goodbye to Stuart Sutcliffe and hello to Stu de Stael. Just until 28 May, just for the next eight days, it's all about rock'n'roll."

The Beatals were in fact awarded an eight-day tour of Scotland with Johnny Gentle after the 10 May audition with Billy Fury and Larry Parnes at The Blue Angel. And all of the details of this tour are given in an excellent book written by Johnny Gentle and Ian Forsyth entitled, Johnny Gentle and The Beatles First Ever Tour. *It's a fast and fun read. I highly recommend it.*

The boys did meet at Ye Cracke the night before the Scotland trip to review the details of the tour. Stu did resist the tour, coming as it did at the end of the college term. The Silver Beatals did walk from The Punch and Judy Café on 20 May to the Lime Street Station, and the train agenda given in the chapter is correct, as are the contractual agreements with Larry Parnes for the tour. In his book, Johnny Gentle does mention Stu having his artist's kit with him on the trip, and he indicates that the others were not always happy with Stu sketching in his spare time. Only the conversations in this chapter, therefore, are imagined.

23 May 1960
A96 Highway
Scotland

"Bloody fuggin'ell!"

The scream of brakes, the crunch of metal on metal, the sickening thud of bone slapping glass – the tiny road van careened into confusion while objects of every sort assaulted the boys inside, adding pain to danger.

Johnny Gentle had been driving, relieving the tired and hung-over Gerry Scott, and for some time Gentle had been manoeuvering, in fog and a drenching rain, the eighty winding miles of the A96 from Inverness to Fraserburgh. They were all exhausted – "fagged out" from wet, windy days on road after road, drained from back-to-back performances in which Gentle would perform twenty minutes and The Beatles, as they now called themselves, would carry the rest of the show. They were hungry and significantly thinner than they'd been on that first night at Alloa when Scottish promoter, Duncan McKinnon, called them a "motley, skinny bunch o' scruffs." They were ragged.

"Get effin' off me!" Gerry Scott had awakened when George catapulted into his lap. Irritated, he pushed the kid away.

"It wasn't me; it was him!" George pointed at Johnny Gentle.

"What the fuggin'ell happened?" John barked from the floor of the front seat. He'd hit the windshield but didn't appear seriously injured.

"Well done, driver!" Paul dislodged himself from the barrage of duffel bags that had been flung forward. "We'll all be calling you Johnny Rough from now on, I believe."

"Save it, McCartney! Look!" Johnny ignored their complaints as he watched the passengers emerge from the Ford Popular in front of them. "What rotten, lousy luck! We've hit old ladies...*old ladies*! Helpless old ladies, parked at a crossroads – pensioners who weren't even movin' their bleedin' car!"

"You're done for, aren't you, son?" John rubbed it in. "Larry Parnes'll have you swingin' from the fuggin' yardarm for this one."

"Shut up, Lennon!" Gentle was in a sweat. He laid his head down on the steering wheel, his neck and back aching from the force of the impact.

Paul hopped out of the van and was standing with the victims before anyone even realized he'd even slipped out.

"I...I shouldn't'a let you drive." Gerry Scott was fully awake now and remorseful. "What were y'doin', man?"

"I-I don't remember...I don't know." Johnny's head was still down, "I must've dozed off..."

"It'll be all right." Stu spoke up for the first time. "Paul'll sort it all out in no time. He's good at that, y'know. See? Look up. They're already startin' to chat 'n smile. Look, he's makin' friends with 'em, as it were."

Johnny raised his head and took a peek.

"You smashed up old ladies, Gentle." John nudged him. "You're a smasher, that's what you are. A ruthless man. There'll be posters 'n rewards on you – from here to Birmingham and all the way back."

"Maybe we could collect a tidy sum for him!" George rubbed his hands together, and they laughed nervously.

"Hey, there's blood back here!" It was Tommy Moore. His speech sounded slurred and dazed. "I'm fuggin' bleedin'!"

"Crap!" Gerry Scott turned to look. "Shite! Moore's lost his fuggin' teeth!"

"Someone tell Paul! Tell 'im to come on!" Stu was examining Tommy closer. "We've got to get to a medic fast! This doesn't look good at all."

"Watch out, Moore," John complained. "Y'er bleedin' all over me fuggin' guitar case, son!"

"Well, it struck *me* in the mouth, not the other way 'round!" Tommy said as best he could. He held his hands to his lips. Blood had saturated his shirt entirely.

"I'll go get Paul." George hopped out of the van.

Tommy groaned, turning his face away. "Quit fuggin' starin' at me, Lennon!" he tried to say.

"Great," John snarled back. "Now he's witless and toothless."

Paul and George returned within seconds.

"Are the ladies all right, then?" Gentle was still rattled – worried about the long-term consequences.

"Middlin' to dreadful," Paul teased. "And the worst part is, they'll never be able to sit at a crossroads again."

"Can we leave, then?" Stu was all business. He held a cloth to Tommy's mouth. "I mean, we've a bit of a situation here, as y'can see."

"Yeah, right. Go on," Paul closed the door behind him. "We exchanged numbers and names, and I've assured them that the eminent Larry Parnes of London'll be ringin' 'em up. That seemed to settle 'em down a bit, as y'can well imagine."

"Wait, wait!" Gerry Scott scrambled out to the right side of the vehicle, "*I'll* drive. I'll drive! I only hope the effin' van still motors under her own steam."

"I gave her a quick once over," Paul shoved John's guitar case back where it belonged, "and it doesn't look that bad. The bonnet's smashed up a bit, but it's minimal, as far as I could see."

Gerry Scott revved the motor successfully, and they slowly backed away from the injured Ford Poplar.

"Isthasso?" John cut his eyes mischievously at Tommy. "A smashed bonnet, is it? Sounds like this drummer I once knew. His bonnet was smashed as well, and that's the God's tooth, it is."

"Geroff, Lennon!" Tommy mumbled. But he was too weak to do or say anything more. And besides, everyone else was laughing.

Only the sound of a police siren sobered the group. In the rearview mirror, Gerry Scott could see an ambulance heading towards them with lights blinking. He stopped the van and pulled over to the side of the road.

"Oh God, someone must've notified the authorities!" Johnny Gentle bit his lip.

"Prepare to be shackled, son," John teased, "and you Moore – prepare to treated like the famous drummer you are, mate…because if I'm not mistaken, your bloody limousine, and I do mean bloody, has just arrived."

****

Dalrymple Hall
Fraserburgh
Scotland

They had planned to be in Fraserburgh early. Duncan McKinnon had instructed them that Johnny Gentle's gig at Dalrymple Hall was to begin at ten, and he had mandated a 7:00 p.m. arrival. But the Beatles were late.

"Where the hell have you been?" The wiry, balding promoter met the van as they drove up. He waved his arms as if signaling a landing plane. One of The Beatles snickered at the melodrama while Gerry Scott put the van in park. The others piled out, elated to have reached their destination.

"You're as late as Alice's rabbit!" McKinnon eyed The Beatles' wrinkled clothes, "And you *look* as if you'd been down the very rabbit hole as well – worse for wear."

"He doesn't like our shirts, George," John sniffed, pretending to be hurt.

"Hmmm," George brushed himself off. "I'm not that fond of 'em either."

Paul stepped up and faced the music straight off. "Sorry to say, but we've got no drummer, as it were."

"*What*?!" the man exploded.

"Did have one," George added cryptically. "Damaged."

"Bunged up," John echoed. "Scrapped, smashed up, marred, mutilated…"

"I *know* what 'damaged' means!" Parnes' promoter screamed. "How? Why? What in God's name happened to the lot of you?"

"Actually," John pressed on with his joke, "it's more like *defaced,* if you want to get technical about it."

"Look, you bunch o'…." The man's frantic growl began, but Johnny Gentle stepped in.

"It's like this…we had an accident on the A96, near Banff. Not serious, mind you, but serious enough. And well, Tommy Moore…to be honest about it, he lost his front teeth in the process."

"My God!" the man rubbed his head, helplessly. "My God," he said again. "Well, that's it then! You've no bloody drummer, and that's all she wrote. The audience won't take well to that. We're done for. It's serious trouble here, lads!"

"Paul here plays drums now and again," John volunteered.

"Not for somethin' like this!" Paul gave him a look. "Volunteer yerself."

"There's always the *one* option, y'know," John muttered, as if harbouring a great solution.

"What? What option's that?" The promoter looked at John, almost as if he were seeing him for the very first time. And John looked back into the eyes of a desperate man – a man who realized the full fury of Scottish audiences disappointed at the eleventh hour.

"Well, he *is* still breathin', as it were," John began. Only those who knew John best guessed what was coming next. "And he is a good man, Tommy Moore…the sort of man who'd want to be here tonight, fulfillin' his obligations – bravely carryin' on in the face of adversity."

"Is that right? McKinnon was interested.

John looked at the ground for a moment, working to suppress a smile. "It's only the physicians, y'know. Conservative lot. Y'know how they are." He let the information sink in.

"Right." The promoter agreed. "Overcautious – do-gooders."

"Look," John put a hand on the man's shoulder, "Why don't you just go to Banff and drag ole Tommy out…rescue him, as it were? He'd love to be here, doin' what he does best, pleasin' the crowds and all that. That's what Parnes contracted for, and that's what you deserve, isn't it?"

"Not that badly hurt then, is he?" The man raised an eyebrow to John.

"His injuries won't take a bite out of his future, if that's what you mean," John punned.

"Just go get him, then? Drag him out, you say?"

"Go get him, Promoter!"

And to the amazement of the rest of them, that is exactly what McKinnon turned on his heels to do.

****

Ten minutes to curtain. John squirmed into his tight black jeans, still damp from last night's sweatbox. He bent over as best he could and pulled on the legs to ease out the wrinkles. The jeans smelled of cigarette smoke, sweat, and mildew. And they were as uncomfortable as they were foul.

"Well, he's not here yet." Stu pronounced from his perch four rungs up the backstage lighting ladder.

"Brilliant, de Stael," John straightened and stretched, "Keep that up, and you'll be pegged a fuggin' savant, son."

George peeked through a hole in the curtains before scuffing over, buttoning the black stage shirt they'd adopted as their official touring costume. "It's a house full of down-and-outs out there," he complained.

"Yeah," Paul was at his heels, "he's right...a mixed bunch of scruffs, if ever there was one. Welcome to Fraserburgh, fishin' capitol of Scotland."

John's eyes narrowed as he reached for his guitar, "Just the sort to smash us up royally if Moore doesn't make it."

"We'd have a blood bath on our hands," Stu nodded.

"In that case," Paul started towards the rear exit, "I'm entitled to one last smoke."

But just at that moment, the door banged open and McKinnon scrambled in, escorting a dazed and stumbling Tommy Moore.

"You made it! Fantastic!" George cheered them on, but he was drowned out by hysterical laughter. It was John.

Paul and George turned away to hide their smiles, but John laughed uncontrollably. Even Stu bit back a grin and hung his head over his drawing. Gerry Scott snickered as well.

Tommy Moore waddled forward slowly like a clumsy blue-billed duck. His lips, enormously swollen, formed a perfect bill where his mouth once had been. His eyes, tiny slits in a strangely contorted face, were almost birdlike...tiny, beady eyes that were diminished by the bill's protrusion.

"Buggeroff, Lennon," Tommy struggled to say, but his mouth – anesthetized – sounded full of cotton. The words clumped together.

"Shut up, the both o'you!" McKinnon physically pushed them towards their places, "There's no time for fisticuffs now. Curtain's up in three! Get on the stage! Gear up!"

He grabbed Tommy by the shoulders and walked him over to the rostrum, steadying the drummer's wobbling gait. "Now listen, lad," he instructed, "keep yer head down as much as possible and concentrate on the job at hand. You've only six songs to do before Gentle comes on. So hang in there and don't frighten off the locals with that mutilated mug o' yours."

Tommy nodded, and he didn't try to speak again. He clung to the promoter's arm and let his drugged, heavy body fall into place. Reaching for his drumsticks like an automaton, he sat there with his head down, almost lifeless.

Paul was reviewing the customary play list with George, while John patted his pocket to make sure he'd remembered his mouth organ. He could see Gerry Scott in the wings brushing Johnny Gentle's white jacket and giving the star all the attention a headliner deserved.

"Hey, Stu," John called out over the house-shaking stamping of feet, "go tell Gerry and Johnny we're all ready to roll here."

Stu nodded and exited quickly. It was John's only chance.

While everyone was busy and preoccupied, John edged over to the electrical outlet on the pretense of grabbing an extra plectrum from his traveling case. In one quick motion, he unplugged Stu's amplifier and kicked the cord inconspicuously under a dragging curtain.

No use makin' things worse than they are, John slipped back to his spot. *He's doin' the best that he can.*

Stu hurried back, slid into place, and gave a nod. Paul smiled and shook his Elvis pompadour, and George began to tap his foot. With adrenalin pumping, John swallowed hard and then initiated the familiar countdown.

"Ah-one, two, ah-one, two, three, four..."

The Beatles gave Fraserburgh Merseyside's version of American rock'n'roll.

Again, discrepancies everywhere!! Gerry Scott or Jerry Scott? Beetles or Beatles? Was the tour nine days (Lewisohn) or two weeks (Norman)? Was Parnes' Scottish promoter Douglas McKenna (Goldman's name) or Duncan McKinnon (name used by other sources)? Did the Beatles (Beetles) hit a Ford Popular (as Lewisohn states) or a Ford Coronal (as Goldman claims)? Did an elderly couple get out of the Ford (as Goldman asserts) or a couple of elderly ladies (as other sources state)? Did McKinnon go get Tommy Moore out of the hospital himself or did John go with him (as Gentle remembers) or did all the Beatles retrieve him from the hospital, as Norman states? Did Tommy ride to the hospital in an ambulance, as Norman states, or did the Beatles (Beetles) take him there (as other sources say)?

The only things we know for sure are: the Liverpool group of John Lennon, Paul McCartney, George Harrison, Stuart Sutcliffe and Tommy Moore went on Scottish Tour with Johnny Gentle in late May, 1960. They played intro songs each night and then played another set after Johnny performed. John terrorized Tommy Moore as much as humanly possible, and he picked on Stu as well. On May 23, they had an automobile wreck at the Banff crossroads. Tommy's teeth and mouth were badly injured. Somehow, Tommy ended up playing the gig that night anyway, and all sources indicate that John was involved in that decision. The Beatles came home broke. They ended the tour on great terms with Johnny Gentle. But Tommy Moore never wanted to have anything to do with them again. The rest is all debatable.

The most comprehensive source for information on the tour is Ian Forsyth's and Johnny Gentle's book, Johnny Gentle and the Beatles, First Ever Tour.

29 May 1960
Lime Street Station
Liverpool

They'd elected to come home by train. Although Gerry Scott had offered them free transport to Liverpool, they'd all agreed that one more night in the "rattlin', stinkin' van" would spell disaster.

They'd scraped together what little funds they had left and bought tickets to the Lime Street station. But this final "extravagance" bankrupted them entirely. The Beatles were coming home empty-handed.

Only Tommy Moore returned to Liverpool with pocket change. He had a full five pounds to show for his nine-day jaunt into Scotland. Early on, Tommy had discovered that Larry Parnes had refused to pay Stu's wages and that John had coerced the others into giving Stu part of the cut. Tommy had nothing against the slender artist with the silent amplifier, but he had no reason to split his earnings with the wack either.

When Lennon had confronted him, Tommy had flat-out refused to dole out any part of his money to anyone. And it had proved to be a wise financial decision. Tommy, at least, had a few coins to rub together at tour's end.

"Welcome home, lads!" A bleary-eyed Allan Williams had been at the station since half-four, waiting on their five a.m. arrival. He shook hands with each of them, slapping them on the backs and shoving John around a bit. "And how were the Scottish moors this time of year?"

John made a face in Tommy's direction. "Irritable and off his beat, if y'ask me."

But the pun never registered with the weary drummer who continued unloading his gear without a backwards glance.

"We're all dead skint, Al!" George said accusingly. "Is that the way a successful tour's supposed to end, then?"

"Only if you travel with John Lennon here," Allan teased, well aware of John's appetite. "In fact, if you're not all deeply in debt, I'd say you came out fairly well, all things considered."

"Speakin' of that, I'm fuggin' famished!" John played along.

"I'm quite sure," Allan grinned behind his beard. "As a matter of fact,

I've become amazingly well-to-do with you Silver Beatals away. No one's cadged bacon butties off Beryl even once. That fuggin' tour was the best thing I ever did for m'self!"

"Hey Al," George corrected him, "It's just *The Beatles* these days. B-e-a-t-l-e-s."

"It's always you, isn't it?" Allan pointed at George.

"Me?" George imitated the motion.

"Right. You're always the one givin' me some dickhead name on the spur of the moment, aren't you?"

"It was Beatles the whole trip," George shrugged.

"We didn't feel all that silver." John backed him up. "It was more like iron…corroded and ready for a smelt down."

"Well, regardless," Allan shook his head, "it's officially The Silver Beatals until after Grosvenor Ballroom." He motioned for them to follow him to the exit. "I've already booked you for June, and the posters've gone up."

"Grosvenor Ballroom, eh?" John picked up his guitar case and sniffed haughtily. "Our reputation must've preceded us, lads!"

"Grosvenor?" George followed, dragging his duffel bag on the ground.

"On the Wirral…Wallasey." Al gave Tommy a hand with his drums. "It's a municipal dance hall. And you're booked for 11 June with Brian Kelly Promotions."

"For beans and toast…or free pints?" Paul questioned.

"Real money," Allan beamed. "Two pounds each,"

"You're not bad, are you, Manager?" John smiled a hundred per cent real smile. It was a rarity, and Allan smiled back. Both men had agendas and for once, they coincided.

Shouldering bags and cases and amps and Stu's art box, they filed underneath Lime Street station's gigantic clock just as the hands pegged half-five. Stu yawned and followed along, half asleep, and Tommy lagged far behind, quiet and distracted.

When they reached the sidewalk and turned towards Allan's car, Tommy stopped and dropped his gear near the curb. "Hey, Al," he called out, "I'll have that other drum if y'don't mind. I'm gettin' off here."

"Come on, son!" Allan walked back over, trying to read Tommy's eyes. He'd heard all about the drummer's calamity, and he tried not to stare at the gap in the wack's front teeth. "Let's all have beans and toast and reminisce over the gory-glory details. My treat, eh?"

"No, go on though," the drummer shrugged, taking his drum and setting it next to the other equipment. "I've had enough for one stint, if y'don't mind me sayin' so."

"But I'm carryin'!" Allan patted his wallet. "And y'look as though you need a square meal right about now. Java as well. The works!"

"Ta, mate," Tommy lowered his head in appreciation, "but I think I'll just go home and have a jam butty, as it were. I've had me bellyful o' John Lennon, and I'm just not up for another round with that rotten sod."

Allan didn't know what to say. He patted the drummer's arm and nodded, trying to be reassuring. "Right then. All right. I know John can put the boot in when he wants. But don't take it to heart, son. He's got his own problems, and they're more 'n he can carry sometimes."

Tommy shrugged and raised an arm for a cab. "Sure, Al. Whatever you say. Maybe I'm just too damned old, or maybe I'm just too dead creased to try to figure him out. Truth is, I don't really fuggin' care. He's not werth a light to me – John Lennon."

Allan's empathy went only so far. "Yeah, I understand. But...you'll still meet us at The Jac next Monday night to play Grosvenor with the lads, right?"

"I wouldn't let *you* down, Al." Tommy promised

"You're a good man, Tommy," Allan smiled and patted him on the arm again. "Have a cuppa and a long sit down, and we'll see y'then. Rest up."

"T'rah," Tommy's still bruised lips attempted a smile, but it hurt to grin.

Tommy glanced for a moment at the others waiting for Allan on the next block. John was recounting their misadventures and acting out all the parts while Paul and George interrupted every few seconds to add their own details. Stu was leaning against the wall, but he chuckled now and again. None of them even looked in Tommy's direction or questioned why he hadn't joined the group. And none of them yelled goodbyes.

"Next Monday – The Jac, then!" Allan called back over his shoulder as he walked away towards The Beatles.

"Right. Next Monday," Tommy repeated, bending over to pick up his duffel bag.

But they were only words. Right now, Tommy only cared about reuniting with his "baird," sleeping in his own bed, taking a hot shower, and having a pint or two with his mates from The Garston Bottle Works. He thanked God that the tour of Scotland was over and that he was rid of John Lennon. And he never intended to travel with The Beatles – Silver or otherwise – ever again.

****

Tommy had the cabbie take him straight to Smithdown Lane. He had no trinkets, flowers, or money to speak of. He had nothing to offer his girl in the way of homecoming...only himself – a tired, disgusted 36-year-old drummer with two puffed and partially swollen lips and a gap of missing teeth.

"What in gawd's name happened to you?" his girl shrieked, horrified by Tommy's changed appearance.

"Smash-up," Tommy mumbled, pulling her to him. "C'mon, givvus a kiss and make it all better, then…"

"Right! Like I would! It's bleedin' awful – that!" She squirmed away and peered at him with eyes squinted. "It's worse than awful, Tommy. Grotty!"

"Nice." He sighed. *First John Lennon, now this.*

She patted his arm in quick consolation. "What you got for me, luv, after all this time?" She held out her hand, expectantly.

Tommy just stared, playing the fool.

"You know exactly what I'm after, Tommy Moore." She didn't flinch. "Don't stand there gawkin' like you can't tell Paddy's Market from St. George's 'All. How much've you brought back, luv?"

"A coupla quid, that's all." Tommy hung his head.

"*A coupla quid*? A fuggin' coupla quid!" She backed up as if she'd discovered he had leprosy. "After nine fuggin' days trompin' about with the likes o' Johnny fuggin' Gentle hisself? A coupla quid after you was so chuffed about bein' asked to go along!"

This time it was Tommy who retreated, his hands raised against the tirade. The angry woman followed him, her voice shrill and loud. Tommy hung his head and backed down the hallway.

"A grand paycheck, *I don't think*!" She spit the words out as he ducked into the kitchen.

Tommy emptied his pockets and tossed it all on the kitchen table. His five pounds had dwindled to almost nothing, considering the extravagance of a cab ride from City Center.

"That's the whole of it," he stated. "Take it or fuggin' leave it then."

"Cor, wudja look at that!" She picked up the money and held it out for him to see. "Ennit smashin'? Ennit lovely!"

"I did better 'n the others," Tommy shrugged. "They was fuggin' starvin' halfway through the tour."

"Yeah, well think o' what you coulda made at The Bottle Works in nine days' time, Tommy Moore! Think what you coulda earned if you hadn't gone off on some wild fuggin' goose chase – chasin' after some fantasy y'er already well past yer prime to achieve!"

She folded her arms and glared. Tommy slumped into a chair and rubbed his eyebrows. Despite the pain medication the doctor had given him, the headache was returning.

"Sorry, luv," was all he had to offer. What else could he say?

"Look Tommy," she crouched down and looked him in the eye, "I don't wanna argify w'ya, luv." She patted his knee, "But this is how it is, y'know. Tell them lousy Beatles to piss off, then! They're no bleedin' good to man nor beast! And while y'er at it, tell their shortarsed manager to sod off as well! You've no business w' the likes of them – none at all. A coupla quid for nine days' work? That's not enough for a thimble full o' gnat's piss, is it? I'm tellin' ya, if you hang about with the likes o' the fuggin' Beatles, Tommy Moore, then we're done – the two of us. Mark me well, Tommy, I fuggin' know this…. them Beatles is no good."

Again, Beatle scholars disagree about another Stu myth linked to the Scottish tour. According to Williams (who arranged all the details of the tour) and Goldman, Parnes refused to pay Stuart for his bass playing, and the others agreed to give him part of their money. Lewisohn doesn't mention this. Neither does Norman, Davies, Pawlowski, or Forsyth. The Beatles make no reference to this in The Anthology.

June 1960
Liverpool

It had only been with his brother's, Michael's, assistance that Paul had been able to convince his father to let him go on the Scotland jaunt in the first place. Jim McCartney wanted nothing – especially John Lennon – to interfere with the fine education Paul was receiving at The Liverpool Institute.

Eldest son, talented son…Jim was justly proud of all Paul had achieved. Respected professors Jack Sweeney and Alan Durband had only accolades for Paul's academic achievements.

"Intellectually clever!"

"Born communicator!"

"Natural leader," they'd said of the boy.

"He'll make a very imaginative teacher," they assured Jim McCartney. And if, instead of education, Paul decided to pursue his second interest, architecture, his professors were certain that the boy's artistic bent would serve him handily there as well. Paul succeeded in all things with his magical Irish charm.

And so, after nine days' absence, the handsome McCartney strolled back to The Institute, full of apologies and energetic promises to score commendably on the impending term exams. Dingy hotels, meagre meals, foul back-stage sack suppers, and auto fiascos behind him, Paul resumed his accustomed seat in the front row – his wide eyes riveted to the professor's, and his intentions unquestionably good.

****

With Scotland and all its colourful mishaps now past, George had a decision to make. Both of his brothers were electricians, and they did rather well – maintaining nice, secure jobs with stable incomes. As sons of a Liverpool bus driver, the opportunity to be an electrician meant a "rung up" in society. It was a job with a future.

Scotland had been amazing – a chance to spend time with John and Paul, a chance to see things George had never seen before. John had visited Scotland regularly as a boy, spending whole weeks with his Auntie Elizabeth or "Mater," as John called her, but George had never been far out of Liverpool. The sixteen-year-old had relished the new vistas – the freedom and excitement of it all.

The last two weeks had been "a regular lark." But now the gig was over, and George needed a future. Only months earlier, he'd received his report card from The Liverpool Institute, marking him a failure in every subject except art. George had burned the report immediately, deciding then and there not to waste another second on academia. But now, as he stared in his mother's full-length mirror, he wondered what he should do.

He knew he was an excellent lead guitarist for his age, and he knew that he had the drive to work hard and to get even better. But he also knew that there were hundreds – rumour had it six hundred – local bands in Liverpool alone, and a warning voice told him that in such an orgy of talent, he had little chance of emerging as the singular star.

George sighed and studied his reflection critically. He was skinny, gangly, and hardly as good-looking as Paul. He hadn't John's swagger and confidence. He hadn't Stu's mystery. He didn't see "star potential" reflected in the looking glass – no matter how he angled himself, grinned, or turned up his collar.

But he didn't feel comfortable holding his electrician's box anymore. It didn't feel right in his hands. His guitar did. Somehow it suited him.

George sat on his mother's bed and rested his head in his hands. He had to decide what to do. In the Harrison family, "being on the dole" was not an option. George had to have a job.

****

John had gone back to Mendips. Rod Murray didn't ask why, and Stuart was as tight-lipped as always. Rod wondered if the two friends had had some sort of falling out along the "high-roads and low-roads" of Scotland – if Stu had finally had his fill of the infamous Lennon bollocking. But Stuart wasn't volunteering any information, so Rod left it at that.

Stu was working feverishly on a canvas bigger than any he'd attempted so far, a work of staccato colour – colour patched on colour – swatches of layered emotion and rich texture. Half the time, he was incommunicado, immersed in intense passion that congealed as creativity. He nodded and muttered to Rod's inquiries about food or appointments, but little else was willingly offered. Stu was in a world of his own.

He had missed his art in the nonsense that was Scotland. The hasty, guilty sketches he'd dashed off on the road hadn't been enough. The less Stu had painted, the more he'd yearned to, and now all that he'd seen and experienced and endured was transmuted by his artist's brush into orgasmic expression. The restraint of the last two weeks exploded onto his canvas.

Stu hardly wondered what had happened to John – John and the rest. Instead, he ran a tiny, paint-soaked hand through his baby fine hair and chewed on the end of his long, detail brush – studying his canvas critically, squatting low to get another angle or standing on a stool to get a better perspective. He worked and reworked and improved and changed. Stu painted for hours on end, and as he painted, Scotland became not a memory but a resource bank. He used the anger, resentment, laughter, excitement, frustration, hunger, and exhaustion of the tour as a catalyst for his work. Stu used what he felt. He transformed the last two weeks into something that, at last, really mattered.

****

It was an extra-large bowl of cornflakes. John had become almost gluttonous since Scotland, hovering jealously over his food, eating to excess. He poured the milk on liberally, reaching for the sugar bowl and grabbing another banana while he was at it. He wolfed down a bite on his way to the table, dripping milk onto the floor.

"So…up at last." Mimi startled him.

"Its only half-ten, Mim."

"I've already been to the market at the roundabout and back." She dropped the paper sack on the table in front of him as if to validate her statement. A jar of Branston Pickle rolled out and across the table. John grabbed it, hardly looking up from the bowl of floating flakes.

"Bravo," was his only reply. "Good on yer."

"And speaking of 'bravo,'" Mimi pulled a tri-folded document and a ripped enveloped from her coat pocket and tossed them onto the table, "here's some wonderful news from the collegiate world that got my day off to a brilliant start, as it were."

"What's this?" John jabbed at the paper with his spoon. A fat splotch of milk stained the envelope.

"You tell me. The explanation's all yours."

"As y'can see, I haven't got m'specs, Mim. Read it. What's it say?"

Mimi picked the letter up and unfolded it. She held it at arms' length and peered at John over the top of the letterhead. "It says," her voice was razor sharp, "that you've failed lettering, John. Failed lettering entirely! Lettering – the last hope, the last curriculum, the last discipline that would even have you! Failed…after all the bother it took to get you into school!

After three years of college tuition and supplies."

John got up and clattered his empty bowl into the sink. He turned, folded his arms, and leaned on the counter, waiting for the rest of the lecture.

"You're going nowhere at record speed, John," was all she said. Her voice was full of resignation and futility. Anger had given way to hopelessness.

"Nine days we were in Scotland," John said slowly. "Nine days for eighteen pounds split five ways. And out of that – expenses."

"My point exactly…" she sighed.

"Nine days," John interrupted her, "and all of us came home dead skint. But two days from now, we're off to Grosvenor Ballroom for a regular 10-pound gig with our names printed large on public posters that say *we're* the headliners, not backup men. And in one night, I'll make more than I did on the entire tour, Mim! Two pounds at Grosvenor…and for only two hours of work! And what's more, I'll be makin' the two pounds for two hours of playin' *rock'n'roll*!"

"Oh, two pounds…" she threw her eyes to the ceiling. "Quite a bankroll!"

"And after that," John went on, "there's The Neston Institute and then The Jacaranda…all real venues for real money and real audiences."

John grabbed the letter from his aunt's hand. "I don't need a piece of paper to tell me where I'm goin', Mim! Ask Allan Williams where I'm headed, *not* Nicholas Horsefield or George Jardine! Ask promoter Les Dodd. Ask Grosvenor's Brian Kelly. Ask Larry Parnes."

Mimi groaned and shook her head.

"Look, it doesn't matter what you believe!" John pushed away from the sink and stood tall. "I'm right, and time'll prove me right! Wait around and see what happens. Wait and…"

"It appears I have no alternative." Mimi pursed her lips. "I've never had a choice where you're concerned."

"Right," John barked back. Then he crumpled letter, tossed it in the trash, and pushed through the swinging door into the parlour.

****

Allan was giddy with success. According to Larry Parnes, The Silver Beatals had been even more popular than headliner Johnny Gentle on the Scottish tour. Except for the many annoying phone calls from John Lennon requesting more money, The Silver Beatals had lived up to all of Parnes' expectations, and Parnes intimated that he'd be calling Allan about the group again.

The Silver Beatals, Beatles, or whatever they're callin' themselves at the fuggin' moment, are in and of themselves enough to crow about, Allan mused as he walked towards The Jacaranda. And word of their successful Scottish tour was just beginning to get around town. There would be more calls for The Beatles in short order.

All of Allan's groups – doing backup stints for hit-paraders like Duffy Power, Dickie Pride, and Georgie Fame – were, in fact, out-singing, out-performing, and out-acting the stars themselves. The tough little Liverpool bands were achieving a certain "diamond in the rough" acclaim. These days, Allan walked with a cockerel's strut.

Lately, he'd been considering yet another entrepreneurial investment that would have been cost-prohibitive only six months ago. He was contemplating a partnership with a recent acquaintance, a West Indian chap nicknamed "Lord Woodbine."

Woodbine was a freethinker and a devil-may-care dabbler into all pleasures of the flesh, and Woody, as Allan called him, had the ready income with which to do these things. It was this income, coupled with Woody's seamy side, that enticed Allan to enter into a joint business venture that would be "a first" in Liverpool history. Woody wanted to open a strip club instead of a traditional pub – a strip club that would rock the foundations of the stolid City Council, a club that would be shocking, outrageous, and immoral.

Allan liked that.

He liked being the talk of the town. He liked being the manager everyone knew and gossiped about. And he liked the income that was firmly attached to such success. He grinned his impish grin and chuckled to himself.

Al reached The Jac in record time and propped the front door open wide, allowing the June breezes to sweep out the odours left souvenir from the night before. The place needed a good top-to-board scrubbing down.

Too bad The Silver Beatles are so in vogue these days, Allan laughed to himself, pouring a cup of coffee that Beryl had brewed earlier. *They were the best fuggin' loo cleaners this place ever had!*

And speakin' of that...where the hell are they anyway?

It dawned on Al he hadn't seen them once since he'd treated them to breakfast four days ago. For Stu, that wasn't unusual. Sometimes Stu was absent for a week or more, depending on his workload at the art college. But the others rarely missed a chance for beans and toast or any delicacy Beryl would generously toss their way. And Lennon was always, as Tommy Moore called him, "an absolute gannet" when it came to free meals. It was generally Allan's curse that The Jacaranda was in walking distance of Gambier Terrace.

But even Lennon hasn't been 'round once, not even at mealtime! Did Scotland cure his itch for fame and rock'n'roll? Don't tell me The Beatles have had enough of backstage life and van transports! Or have they had some kind of fallin' out that I'm not aware of? Are they cheesed off amongst themselves or just restin' up?

Balancing a cigarette and coffee cup in one hand, Allan wedged the phone receiver between his ear and shoulder and dialed John Lennon's aunt's number.

"I'll have this sorted out straight away," he pledged. "I'm not about to lose a potential gold mine – not at this fuggin' stage o' the game!"

The Beatles owed him a fortune in bacon butties alone. And Allan Williams intended to see that over the next year or so, they paid off in spades.

Each vignette is documented. Only the conversation between John and Mimi is imagined.

6 June 1960
The Jacaranda
23 Slater Street
Liverpool 1

Allan's phone call had been the nudge John needed. But ringing his mates up – as Al had done him – produced little results.

Stu was immersed in his work and refused to even lift a receiver. George had taken a new apprentice's job and claimed he couldn't afford to be docked a day's pay to practise. And Paul – his nose in the books – was reluctant to "off-track" again so soon. So John went door to door, pulling his band back together.

He had to. Grosvenor Ballroom was by far the most important venue they'd ever booked. It was Paramount's "21 Plus Night," and promoter Les Dodd, advertising the event as complete with "Jive and Rock Specialists," had splashed posters all over Merseyside. An experienced dance promoter on the Wirral since 1936, Dodd realized the importance of eye-level advertising, and this week every available space in Liverpool and over the water in the Wirral had been filled with a Grosvenor advert.

"The Silver Beetles" – as the bright yellow, cardboard posters proclaimed – were scheduled sometime between 9:00 p.m. and 11:30 p.m. But John had insisted they all arrive at their designated meeting place, The Jac, at seven. Before George had even finished changing his work clothes to have tea, John was pacing in his front room and clearing his throat impatiently. George knew that if his mum hadn't been home, John would've been much more demonstrative.

Over the last week and a half, Tommy Moore had refused to return John's or Al's telephone calls, although Allan kept insisting that the drummer's word was "as good as gold." And at 6:55 p.m. – when Paul, Stu, George, and John tumbled into The Jac – there, sure enough, was Tommy's kit, waiting at the ready. The tightness in John's chest eased a bit. He tried to tell himself that Allan was right. Whatever bad blood they'd had between them, Moore was still planning to live up to his commitment.

"Hey, look at these, wudja!" George handed John the small stack of yellow admission tickets he'd found next to the telephone. "Tickets...to see us!" he grinned.

"Grosvenor Ballroom…Paramount's 21 Plus Night!" John read in his announcer's voice. "Whit Monday, 6th June, Gerry and the Pacemakers…"

"We know them," George smiled softly.

"And…" Paul pointed to John.

"And direct from their Tour with Johnny Gentle, The Fabulous Silver Beetles!"

"Fabulous, is it?" Paul looked at George. "Is that what *you've* heard, then?"

"Right," George bandied back. "Word has it we're fab.'"

"I've heard it repeated a time or two." Stu lit a cigarette and passed the pack around to the others. "And *I've* been in total seclusion, y'know."

"Ah! But there's more! Read on!" Paul pointed to John again.

"Every Tuesday, Dancer's Night. Come early."

"We're *extremely* early, aren't we, Stu?" George called across the room.

"Actually 25 hours early for Tuesday Dancer's Night. This is Monday, y'know…hereafter to be known as Monday Fabulous Night," Stu corrected from his post at the front door. He prayed that Tommy Moore would arrive. John had been so tense about it all.

"I wouldn't be caught dead at Tuesday Dancer's Night!" John held out the ticket for them all to read. "Look, it says, 'Tuesday, Dancer's Night. No Jiving! No Rock'n'Roll! No Teenagers!'"

"No jivin'? No rock'n'roll?" Paul threw his eyes to the ceiling. "Would that be *dancer's* night or *dosser's* night?"

"If they can't jive to rock'n'roll, what are they showin' up for, exactly?" George wrinkled his brow.

"For tranquility, son." John folded his hands in prayer. "It's all the rage on the Wirral, y'know. Money for rope, that's their spec-i-al-ity."

"Speakin' of tranquility," Paul tapped his watch, "where's Tommy, then?"

"I thought we were all supposed to be here by now." George looked worried.

"Right." John had never expected the drummer to show in the first place. He joined Stu in the doorway. "It's all a sham, isn't it – this kit? He's not turnin' up, is he? I *knew* he fuggin' wouldn't!"

"Right. Well, he said he would…" Stu began.

"He said he had his own teeth as well," John snapped, "and look how that turned out in the end!"

"Hadn't we better call Al, then?" Paul began to share John's paranoia.

"We'll wait another half hour." John mandated, pulling a rickety captain's chair up to the large, front, picture window and plunking down, his feet on the sill. "But that's fuggin' it! If the sod's not here by half-seven, we're goin' 'round to sort him out. Al knows where he lives."

"It doesn't bode well, does it?" George took a seat next to John. "I mean, they'd spit us out at Grosvenor without a drummer, wouldn't they?"

John took a deep breath and blew the air out of his bottom lip in a gust that moved even the greased curl hanging over his forehead.

"Yeah," he said, "Y'er only right." And his face was grim.

All events are documented. Only the conversation is conjecture.

July 1960
The New Cabaret Artists
Liverpool 8

"So, we've come down to this have we?" John stared at the three-story Victorian on Upper Parliament Street, taking in the chipped, flaking paint, the unsteady porch pillars, and the rusted iron fence that swayed, whining in the Mersey up-drafts.

"It's a train wreck – this place," George said.

"The New Cabaret Artists. Doesn't look a bit new…or artistic, does it?" Paul sniffed.

"It's a fuggin' dive," John frowned.

The place looked deserted, bleak, condemned. It was impossible to believe that this was Allan's latest business investment. The building was hopeless.

"What's Al gettin' us into *this* time?" George moved forward carefully, edging through the dilapidated gate. The others followed. "I mean, it doesn't look even a little like a club, does it? We'll be playing to no one here – just echoes."

"I wouldn't come here, would you?" Paul made a face.

"Well, I *am* here, aren't I?" John shrugged, searching for an entrance into Allan's "nightspot."

He followed the broken, weedy sidewalk around the right side of the house, and Stu tagged along, taking it all in with an artist's perusal, seeing the details that the others missed: the faded platter-blue shutters with snaggletoothed slats; the overgrown hedges that tugged their rusted, ornate espaliers to the ground; and the geometrically lovely wormwood spirals in the exposed, rotting siding. The once-handsome Liverpool 8 home was dangerously close to ruin.

"Open, Sesame!" John found an entrance and gave it a shove. The Beatles followed him down an uneven flight of concrete stairs to a warped and chipped basement door.

"Who'd've imagined we'd be headlinin'…in a ruin?" Stu shook his head.

"A strip club, as it were." Paul said.

"I'm too young and clean for all this, y'know." George was right behind him.

"Not for long, son." John pushed the inner door open and stepped inside.

The interior of The New Cabaret Artists Club was no more elegant than the front. In fact, the basement was rank with stench. Allan Williams was nowhere to be seen, but the dark and pungent room was clearly some kind of nightclub. They were undoubtedly in the right place.

Six or seven anemic tables huddled around a jimmy-rigged box-and-carton bar, and as the boys threaded their way through a maze of wobbly chairs towards the stage, the furniture waggled back and forth like pendulums. John reached out and quieted the chair closest to him, then squinted in the red, glowing lights, looking for Allan or his new partner, the notorious Lord Woodbine.

"It's filthy – this." George swiped one finger across a tabletop.

"I dunno…it's quite stunning in its own way, isn't it?" Paul kicked at the tiny stage with the toe of his plimsole.

"Purgatory," Stu pronounced.

"And we're stuck here for only ten bob a night," George raised his old complaint, "not countin' the bob deducted for Al and the one for the bouncer as well."

"It's bound to be unhealthy – this place." Paul wrinkled his face at the putrid air.

"Do we *have* to take this one, John?" Stu rarely dissented these days after the round he and John had had just before Scotland, but The New Cabaret Artists was straining even his loyalty.

"We could go back to *talkin'* about bein' a band instead of actually bein' a band," John tucked his hands under his armpits. His body language spoke volumes.

"Right," Paul shrugged.

"Yeah, there's always that." George got the message.

John grabbed Stu's wrist and checked his watch. Then he pulled one of the bamboo-like chairs over and sat down to wait for Allan to materialize.

"One day," he kicked a chair out for Stu as well, "when we're all rich and fuggin' famous and performin' for the Queen, we'll use this, y'know."

"How's that?" Stu flipped the chair around, straddling it.

"We'll look back and say, 'Remember when we played that Liverpool 8 dive? Remember when we backed that stripper whose name we can't even recall? Remember how we did it all…and for only ten bob? Remember that?' we'll say."

"I'll remember," George said. "I'll have had nightmares about it for years."

"And we'll remind each other," John went on, waving a hand at his surroundings, "about how success wasn't easy or undeserved – some overnight thing handed to us on a fuggin' platter."

"He's right," Paul nodded. "We'll be able to say we weren't just some good luck story. We'll be able to say we paid the piper to get to the top."

"Right," Stu laughed. "We'll have…legitimacy, won't we?"

"Besides," George grinned his lopsided grin, "worse things have happened at sea, y'know." The timeworn Scouse motto made them all chuckle. But on an afternoon like this, it was very much like laughing in the dark.

****

It was, John supposed, as low as they could go. Grinding out "Begin the Beguine" or "Ain't She Sweet" while Shirley from Manchester swung her ample tassels and Paul beat out an inconstant rhythm on Tommy Moore's deserted drum kit was as close as The Beatles had come to disaster. Night after night, as Shirley undulated her enticing hips to The Beatles' repertoire of Buddy Holly hits, John tried to remind himself that "this too shall pass."

But it couldn't happen soon enough.

Nothing had been going right lately. Allan had been unable to find a replacement drummer for Moore, and while John wasn't sorry to lose him, he was desperately sorry to lose the drumming. The band needed a backbeat.

John's extemporaneous decision to try recruiting a fill-in drummer from the audience had almost cost them all their lives at Grosvenor Ballroom. Only Allan's rapid-fire double talk had convinced an audience volunteer – a ganger named Ronnie – to surrender his perch on the rostrum without a full-fledged gang war. Since then, John had refrained from asking for substitutes from the crowd.

When Shirley, however, had insisted upon a "real heavy drumbeat, yeah?" to accentuate her bumps and grinds, Paul had smiled and volunteered. But Johnny Hutchison he wasn't, and all of them knew it. In fact, the only saving grace in the whole unusual arrangement was that literally no one was listening to them.

The slimy, rain-coated clientele of The New Cabaret Artistes audience hated The Beatles. Every night they shook their heads, yelled obscenities at the lads, and begged Allan to boot them. They complained that the band "put them completely off their game."

And things weren't much better at the other gigs The Beatles had had lately. Either they performed at "blood baths" like the Neston Institute where rock'n'roll was just a backdrop for fisticuffs, or they played afternoons at The Jacaranda – unappreciated - prophets not accepted in their own land.

Instead of things getting better or easier, things only seemed to be getting worse. John looked back on gigs like The Cavern Club in Mathew Street or Mona Best's Casbah with fond memories. The Beatles had absolutely hit rock bottom.

Fame was too long delayed.

All incidents are documented. Only the conversations are imagined.

Mid-July 1960
The Jacaranda
23 Slater Street
Liverpool 1

"Where's the fuggin' Steel Band off to, Al?" John tilted back in one of The Jac's heavy, wooden chairs.

"Take a gander at this, Lennon." Allan righted John's chair, handing him a newspaper clipping and ignoring the question. "It's a press review. You Beatles've been critiqued in *The Heswell and Neston News and Advertiser*, as it were."

"Ah, the press, eh?" John took the clipping and scanned it.

"That's right," Allan smirked. "The layabout Beatles've actually made the grade, as it were."

"Mumble, mumble jumble, jumble," John scanned the column. "Yeah, all right. An article. Great. But they failed to say a single fuggin' word in there about us gettin' a new drummer in the near and impendin' future."

"Balls to that!" Allan grabbed the news clipping and stuffed it back in his coat pocket again. "My conscience is one hundred and eighty per cent clear on that issue! I *got* you a drummer, didn't I? I got you Tommy fffuggin' Moore, and *you* fuggin' ran him off, as it were! I've done all I can do for you in the way of a drummer."

"Well," John deadpanned, "try doin' it in the way of a manager, then."

"Look, John," Allan ignored the pun, "As I told you before, there's supposedly a drummer right here 'round The Jac."

"And what d'we know about this purported percussionist?"

"Only that he's supposedly great. And a busy man – a decorator by day and a drummer by night."

"A drummin' decorator?" John sniffed. "Sounds queerly suspect, doesn't it?"

"His name's Norm Chapman," Allan went on, "and word has it he's available."

John batted his eyelashes. "But for what, we ask?"

"Look Lennon," Allan's voice went up a notch, "none of that! *If* I can locate this Chapman and *if* he agrees to give The Beatles a go, you'll *not* fuggin' terrorize him like you did good ole Tommy!"

John traced a line with his finger from his eye down his cheek. "Tears for Tommy – a fellow of infinite jest."

"I mean it, John!" Allan's face instantly flushed. "This Chapman supposed to be talented, and he's…"

"Light on his feet?" John suggested.

"Fuggin' hilarious, aren't you?" Allan began to fluster. "Well, laugh on, but understand that a drummer's a necessary ingredient for you four pathetic, undeservin' scruffs…that is if you want to play the three new gigs I just got you at Grosvenor."

"Where's The Steel Band these days?" John came back to his original question, his purpose never circumvented. "They haven't been 'round The Jac once this last week. Are they playin' Grosvenor as well? Where've you booked *them* that you should have booked *us*?"

"You haven't even thanked me for the new gigs…and yet you're on about where the fuggin' Steel Band's off to?"

"Where are they?"

"How should I know?" Allan exploded. "The twisted bastards! They just up and left me. No notice, no explanation! The Jac just opened one night, and they didn't! Overnight! They were gone without a trace – takin' their fuggin' kettle drums, Caribbean strings, and assorted noisemakers with them – never sayin' one fuggin' word of goodbye!"

"West Indians!" John sniffed. "Who can trust'em?"

"They didn't ask for even so much as a by-your-leave!" Allan raged on, "They just chucked it all – packed up and took the first transport to the filthy brothels of fuggin' Hamburg, as it were."

"Hamburg?" John perked up.

"Right, yeah. Hamburg. Four black-as-night West Indians and their forty gallon steel drums bangin' their way through Germany without one single shred o'remorse for leavin' me in the lurch!"

"Hamburg, Germany?" John repeated, leaning in. Allan never noticed the subtle change on John's face.

"Here, read this!" Allan pulled another folded piece of paper from the same coat pocket where *The Neston News and Advertiser* clipping had been. He smoothed the document out and handed it to John. "The sunshine bastards had the fuggin' gall to post me this note a coupla days ago. Not one effin' shred o'guilt in the entire missive, mind you. Not a shred!"

Allan Man!
This town was meant for you, man…money flowing in the gutters, yes…and women doin' everything and everywhere…no holds barred, man. Anything goes! This is the place to make some real money, not England. Come on, man. Come have a looksee. Come over and bring some

groups. We've met lots and lots of influential people. We'll help set you up. This is where the loot is. Don't blow it, Al. Take the chance! Come over!
Everett, Otto, Bones, and Slim

The blood raced in John's ears as he read the words. *"Come on over! Come have a looksee."* They seemed to be speaking directly to him.

Allan grabbed the letter back and smacked it with the back of his hand, "Can you believe the effin' nerve o'this? Not a single, 'Sorry we deserted you, Al." Not one sliver of shame in those feel-good bastards! Just eternal sunshine in their lousy, opportunistic, fuggin' little hearts!"

"How'd they strike on Hamburg?" John was all business now. He had no time for Allan's crises or crushed vanity.

Allan refolded the letter and tucked it neatly away for future reference. "Some fuggin' Kraut promoter, as I understand it, weaseled in here one night when I was up to my fuggin' ass in complications – battlin' the Vice Squad down at New Cabaret Artistes, as well as jugglin' the demands of a celeb party over at The Angel. Anyrate, the promoter snaked in, liked their sound – and the hungry crowd of women that The Steel Band was always attractin' – and he seized the fuggin' opportunity to fill their heads with propaganda about the thrills and spills of dear, old Hamburgy, as it were."

"Doesn't seem as if it turned out to be propaganda, does it?" John walked towards the bar and grabbed a coffee cup. "Sounds like a regular rave-up – the filthy brothels of Hamburg." He poured himself the last dregs of coffee and put the empty pot back on the warmer.

"Well…we'll see how it goes as it goes." Allan began to get cautious. He'd heard that tone in John's voice before. "As it is, they've only been over there a few days." Allan walked over and flipped off the warmer, then removed the empty coffee pot to the counter top. "Let's wait until the boys've experienced life on The Reeperbahn for more than a week. Let's see if the fascination's the same once the new's worn off."

"And what then?" John slurped his coffee loudly. "Are you goin' over to check it out, then?"

It was the beginning of a campaign that Allan knew would never end.

Allan groaned. "I never shoulda said a word to you, should I? I should never've…look, don't start with me, Lennon! I mean it! I've only just found you a drummer, and I've only just booked you *three more gigs* over at Grosvenor…"

"So who's playin' The Jacaranda – now that The Steel Band's stolen silently to The Reep?" John never relented.

Allan thrust his short, wide hand through his mop of dark curls and let it rest there. He closed his eyes.

Of all the Merseyside rockers that Allan represented, John Lennon was the only hopeful who never rested, who never appreciated the moment, who bulldozed his way ahead without taking a breath to enjoy the present.

Successful lads like Derry Wilkie or Gerry Marsden, whose careers had real promise, waited for Allan's lead and took his advice and leadership. But Lennon blazed on without control, never tempering his pace one iota, never finding satisfaction in the status quo. Over the past year, Allan had discovered that the only way to achieve any semblance of peace in life was to acquiesce to John's demands as quickly as possible. Now he looked at John and slowly emitted an exaggerated sigh.

"Live at The Jac..." Allan said begrudgingly. "The Beatles, I suppose. That is...on one condition..."

"Spell it out." John listened.

"Not another effin' word out of you about fuggin' Hamburg, understand? I'm serious, John! Not my scene – The Reeperbahn. Liverpool Eight'll do me just fine. Got it? Not another word about Hamburg. Zilch."

"Right." John swallowed the last of the coffee and wiped his mouth on his sleeve. "Y'can count on me. *Sieg Heil!*"

All incidents are documented. The letter from The Royal Caribbean Steel Band is not original. The conversations are conjecture.

Late July 1960
Gambier Terrace
Liverpool 8

John slammed the door, rattling a stack of teacups balanced precariously on a teapot lid. Cynthia – doing Stu's, Rod's, and John's dishes at the sink – jumped and instinctively reached out to steady the leaning tower. She was unnerved, even before she saw John's face.

He was flushed – his nostrils flared, eyes narrowed. He was as agitated as Cynthia had ever seen him.

"What is it?" She'd learned to remain calm when John was angry – to minimize the tragedies.

"Smug, self-righteous, self-servin' sods!" He waved his hands and paced around the room, his heels slamming into the floorboards. He kicked at a pile of dirty tarps. "Fuggin' bastards!" He kicked it again.

"Al didn't get the loan for Hamburg, then." Cynthia's heart broke for John.

Obviously, no one had seen fit to finance, on a hope and a whim, some unknown band's passage to Germany. No bank – on the optimistic promises made by some itinerant group called The Caribbean Steel Band – had been willing to risk travel fare for Williams' five young musicians.

"Great observation, Miss Powell! Astute, Miss Powell!" John spat out. "Very observant…"

"Look John…"

"Yeah, all yer prayers have been answered, haven't they?"

"That's not true…"

"Isn't it?" he barked. "Isn't it exactly what you want, truth be told?"

"No…I-I want you to go." She took a deep breath and wracked her brain for the right words to say. "I want you to go…and…all right…I don't want you to go as well."

"And it's thinkin' like *that* that's jinxed the entire venture, hasn't it? Ta, very much, Cynthia!"

"It's the financiers you're angry with, John, not me."

"Don't psychoanalyze me, Powell. I'm way beyond all that." John found an abandoned pint partially filled with flat, warm ale, and he swigged it down in a long gulp, spitting to erase the aftertaste. "You don't want me to go any more than the fuggin' bankers do, admit it. You never have...not once since I first brought the idea up!"

Cynthia had never voiced her opinion, but John was absolutely right. She had no desire to see him run off to Hamburg, doing God knows what with God knows whom. She didn't want him "chaperoned" by the likes of Allan Williams or the lecherous Lord Woodbine – a man whom she seriously doubted was nobility of any sort. She didn't want John performing in a city well known for its lascivious living. She didn't want him to have the "opportunities" Hamburg afforded.

Even here in Liverpool, "well-meaning friends" (who only wanted her own good!) constantly informed her that John was "steppin' out" with this girl or that. They even broadly hinted that John brought girls right here to Gambier Terrace. Cynthia had enough to worry about without adding the temptations that a place like Hamburg could provide.

But she'd never said so.

"John," she stepped towards him, "you're not being fair."

"Who's bein' unfair when you get right down to it, Powell?" John's razored voice began to slice. "Who's puttin' their own selfish needs in front of the needs an entire group? Who'd be much happier if I took some nine-to-five stint – hunchin' over some desk in the back room of a small-time advert agency?"

"You're dead wrong."

"Like fuggin'ell I'm wrong!" He was on a rampage now. "You don't want me to play Hamburg at all, do ya?"

"It's just...I'd...I'd miss you."

"You don't *want* the band to succeed, to get bigger 'n bigger with audiences and managers and agents lookin' on, do you? You don't want me to have the chances that are out there, outside the confines of this...nowhere land."

Cynthia bit her lip. *A soft answer turneth away wrath.* She had memorised the scripture back in Sunday school, and now it served her well. Honing the delicate balance between passive resistance and cowardice, Cynthia forced her voice to be firm.

"I can't honestly say that I want you to go, John, but I don't..."

"Forget the pipe and slippers, home for tea, and out to the local once a week just for old times' sake, Cynthia. That's not me, and it never will be." He began to tear through Stu's scattered belongings looking for another discarded lager, for anything to drink. He tossed clothes, paintbrushes, old newspapers, and canvases everywhere. "I'm not yer fuggin' father, Cynthia...no matter how much you fuggin' miss him!"

"That's ridiculous!" She felt control slipping away.

"I'm me and only me! I'm John fuggin' Lennon, and that's not about to change!" He stopped and faced her, his eyes bits of amber glass. "The *music's* who I am! It's *all* I am! It's the most important thing in the whole fuggin' world to me! It's fuggin' crucial, comprehend?"

Cynthia nodded slightly and shrugged her shoulders. Even though her heart was pounding in her chest, she walked indifferently to the window and stood there, hardly moving – waiting for some inspiration to tell her what, if anything, to say.

The room was filled with anger, silence.

Across the street, the unfinished Liverpool Anglican Cathedral rose and rose into the air, unbelievably huge, unbelievably beautiful. Few Liverpudlians traveled extensively, but every Scouser knew the Anglican was going to be one of the most magnificent cathedrals in the world, second only to the Vatican in Rome. Cynthia studied it, looking at the immense castle-like structure carefully, really seeing it for the first time.

Spires, towers, thousands and thousands of stained glass windows, mountains of stone, scaffolding rising incredibly high. "Incredibly high," she whispered.

John turned and made uneasy eye contact with her.

"Incredibly high," she pointed to the church. "Just look at it John. It's a phenomenon – a work of art." She ventured a trembling smile. "We don't deserve it here all to ourselves, y'know. It's too lovely, isn't it? The world should see it."

John joined her at the window, and she reached for him, taking his hand.

"You're that cathedral, John." She squeezed his hand three times, their code for "I love you." "Too wonderful for Liverpool." She paused a moment. "Selfishly, I'd like to keep you here…always and forever…but it wouldn't be right, would it? And it wouldn't be possible."

He made a funny sound that might have been a laugh or a sob.

"Look John," she went on without glancing at him, "there're other banks…other financiers, y'know. And Allan…well, he's always coming up with his own brand of godmother magic, isn't he? Whether it be skill, finesse, or just pure luck, Allan Williams always manages to land on his feet. He'll get you to Hamburg by hook or by crook – you and Paul and George and Stu and your new drummer…you'll get there, for all the world to see."

"I didn't mean it, y'know," he said quietly. "Sorry, Cyn."

She nuzzled into his shoulder, resting her body slowly into his and letting her closeness tell him how she felt.

A tight cluster of birds lifted off the ground with incredible grace, swooping over the cathedral and turning towards the docks. They flew in formation as if their destination had been charted, their path discussed among them, and they employed the following winds of the Mersey, setting course for the Irish Sea. John watched them until they vanished altogether, leaving Liverpool far behind them. Then he turned to Cyn. "I thought we'd agreed to meet here for reasons other 'n conversation," John said, quietly.

"I hadn't forgotten," Cyn moved closer. "I only thought *you* had."

"Did you, now?" he whispered, pulling her to him. "Did you really, Miss Powell?"

****

They laughed and kissed and talked simultaneously, sharing news from The Jac, the Art College, and mutual friends. John raved about Norman Chapman's "fuggin' incredible" ability as a drummer and gave a blow-by-blow recap of the latest gig at Neston Hall, including graphic details of a ganger he'd seen "really puttin' the boot in." Cynthia grabbed a calendar and counted the days until the college started again and she could be back in Liverpool full time. John related the latest news from The Steel Band, and Cyn divulged her Mum's recent yen to move to Canada.

Suddenly Cynthia inhaled sharply.

"That pain again?" John blanched.

"Wait." Cynthia held up her hand. She took tiny breaths and concentrated.

"Y'need to get that looked at, y'know. We…"

"Shhhhh!" Cynthia doubled over.

"Look Cyn, I'm takin' you 'round to a medic. It could be serious – this."

"No, just let me wait it out. It may be something I ate."

John fumbled for his shirt. "Yeah, but it might be something worse. You've no idea, have you? It's only a guess."

"I don't *know* any physicians Merseyside, John." The pain toyed with her again. She fought the urge to vomit while John asked a hundred questions. "I've *got* to get home," she whispered at last. "Mum'll sort it all out. Trust me, John. She's the champion of champions where emergencies are concerned."

Cynthia pulled herself to her feet as the jabbing pain painted the room in light and dark. She took a slow breath and concentrated on standing.

"I can get to the train, John. I can make it. Truly." She reached out and took his hand. "I *have to*, y'know," she breathed. "If you accompany me home or take me to doctor here in Liverpool, then Mum'll know I was with you this afternoon. I assured her you weren't even in town! I said you were off in Liscard – on a gig, well out of harm's way."

"You can't ride the fuggin' train all the way to the fuggin' Wirral!"

"I have to." She held on tight as John guided her slowly towards the door.

"I wish we could afford taxi fare or even a bus to Lime Street," John was crushed.

"Us?" Cynthia tried to smile. "We can't afford tea."

On good days, the walk from Gambier Terrace to Lime Street Station was a lengthy one. Today it was excruciating – a struggle. Block by block, John supported Cynthia, while pedestrians stared at her with concerned and curious eyes.

Cynthia saw nothing but the pavement. She counted the dividers in the concrete, and at every corner said a little prayer for strength. Cynthia kept her eyes down and her fears well hidden from John. She knew that hospitals and illnesses were his greatest fear.

****

Lime Street Station
City Center, Liverpool

"We've made it." John had said almost nothing on the long trek across town. His mouth was a tight line of agony. He was suffering along with Cyn, fearing the worst. "Sit here a moment." He indicated the slatted wooden bench just inside the station door. "And don't try to 'manage,' Cyn. Just sit back or double over…or do whatever feels best. I'll be right back with yer ticket."

Within the quarter hour, John had made all the necessary arrangements, and he released Cyn to the afternoon shuttle bound for the Wirral. Businessmen, dangling expensive briefcases, bumped and jolted her heedlessly as they wedged against the narrow train doors and threaded into the first passenger coach. Others, already intent on newspapers, hardly looked up. Only sheer good fortune provided her with an aisle seat just as a balding accountant lunged for it as well. Cynthia collapsed onto the rigid, leather bench with a muffled cry.

A jerk and shudder set the wheels in motion, and Cynthia, lifting her head from her hands, strained to find John, to wave goodbye with a brave face that said things weren't half as bad as they seemed. But the train had its own rumbling agenda, and before she'd found him, she was well on the way to Hoylake.

John stood motionless on the platform, his arms and legs trembling. His palms were wet. He wiped his nose with the back of his thumb and stood for quite a while, looking down the track at nothing.

He didn't remember the next half hour or how he threaded his way through the interlocked streets to Ye Cracke, but he found it instinctively –

the old, comfortable, college haven. John ordered a pint, then another, then a third – and he lurched unsteadily to the only available table.

The chanting voices had started again, the same ones he'd heard the day Julia died. They badgered him. They made it difficult to breathe.

Whatever Cynthia had, John knew he was to blame. He was full of recriminations, full of guilt.

How will I know if she's all right? How will I know if she's in hospital? Who'll ring me up? Who'll even know where I am? How'll I know where to call? How'll I find her?

There were few answers tonight.

"Hey, John! How's it goin', then?" It was George. "You look fuggin' awful. Mind if I sit down?"

"Cyn's come down with somethin' serious." John blurted it out without preamble.

"How's that?" George pulled up a chair and loudly slurped on his Black and Tan.

"For all I know," John raged, "she might be in hospital by now!"

"So…" George looked around, trying to determine some motivation for John's presence in the pub, "what are y'doin' here, then? Shouldn't you be with her…or checkin' on her or somethin' of that nature, as it were?"

"I don't *know* where she is…I mean, she's only just gone. She took the train back to the Wirral an hour ago."

"Well," George pointed with his pint to the pay phone stationed between the two rooms, "there's a phone on that wall, y'know, and I've a pocketful of change, if that's what y'need."

John held out his hand for the money. "Ta."

"Y'remember the number, right?" George was worried about him.

"Yeah," John nodded. "Right. The number."

George watched him stumble towards the phone and stand there a full minute before picking up the receiver. Even then, John dialed in slow motion. He looked at the receiver curiously, moving it slowly to his ear.

John's not right, George shook his head.

George knew nothing of the chanting voices, their whispered predictions of loss and hisses of desertion. John was the only one who heard the raging – and he told no one. He'd been indefensible against the evil warnings two summers ago and now…when the phone rang and rang and rang without answer, John felt nauseated.

****

A Local Cottage Hospital
The Wirral

"A grumbling appendix." That had been the doctor's considered diagnosis. But the inflammation had called for an extended hospital visit and complete bed rest. Cynthia was monitored closely, even through the night. And just in case the situation took a nasty turn, Lillian Powell slept in the chair next to Cynthia's bed, forcing her daughter to take fluids as often as possible.

Over the next forty-eight hours, flowers, fruit baskets, and a parade of nurses filled the room. But no John. Between his gig at The Jacaranda and The New Cabaret Artistes and a recording session that Allan had mandated, John hadn't been able to leave Liverpool for the half-day's trek over the water.

He'd rung Cyn up daily with passionate proposals that made her blush in the sterile environment around her, but he hadn't been able to visit. That he'd promised to do on Sunday afternoon.

****

John slipped on his glasses long enough to identify the room number. Then, swiping them away, he knocked on the door.

"Come in!"

Wagging a small bouquet swathed in layers of printed tissue paper, John grinned devilishly at Cyn. "'Ullo, Powell!" he swaggered in.

"John!" Cynthia beamed. "It's you! And...flowers as well!" It was a sentiment she hadn't anticipated. She took the flowers and inhaled deeply. Then she reached for John as a familiar voice called from the doorway.

"Hi Cyn! Hope you're all better, then!"

"Oh no!" The words were out before Cynthia could censor them.

"Uh...ideal weather, isn't it?" George blushed, looking down at his feet. He hadn't expected Cynthia to be angry. He'd thought she'd be thrilled to see him.

"John, how *could* you?" Tears welled in Cynthia's eyes.

George stared at her, dumbfounded. Even John seemed unprepared for her reaction.

"Here, Georgie," John fumbled in his pocket, "how's about goin' for a packet o' fags? Or a coupla toffees for Cyn here? I'm sure you'll find a palm shop or chemist's...or somethin' of that nature 'round the block, as it were. Take yer time, George. Look around a bit."

"Yerrokay," George shrugged, nodding compliantly, moving towards the door. He found this difficult to believe. He and Cyn were great friends. In fact, they were best friends.

He went everywhere with Cyn and John. If John and Cynthia went to the movies, he was there. If they met in Ye Cracke for a drink, George almost always came along. Cynthia had never objected to him before. His shoulders sagged as the door closed behind him.

"John, how *could* you?" Cyn hardly waited until George's footsteps had faded down the hall. "I've been so lonely for you. I've…"

"Georgie Porgie, Scouser aye, came to Powell and made her cry," John recited. "When her ire came out to stay…" He made a face at Cyn, and she smiled a little in spite of herself. "Georgie Porgie ran away."

"It's a good thing he did, too!" Cynthia sniffed and wiped her eyes. "The last thing I wanted, today of all days, was a chaperone! I've missed you so terribly, John. It seems ages since…"

"You're all right, then?" John sat gingerly on the side of the bed.

"I'm wonderful *now*."

"I'm serious. You're tellin' me all there is to tell?"

"I'm telling you all there is to tell. It was just appendicitis. Well, actually a grumbling appendix. Nothing more."

"Not Arabian Infectious Fever with a Tincture of Bat's Wings?" John slipped into his mad scientist's persona. "Not rot of ages with a side of pen-nu-monia?"

"Neither of those," Cynthia beamed. "Just a plain, ordinary, grumbling appendix. That's all." They smiled at one another. "I'm fine. Completely fine. Really."

"I'll bet there's a confused Scouser out there searchin' for toffees and cigs who'd beg to differ, y'know."

"Poor George." Cyn sniffed again. "I think I terrified him. He didn't expect me to erupt into waterworks, and truthfully, neither did I."

"He grew up in Speke. He'll manage."

"It's just that….well, I thought you'd…I thought we'd…be alone, y'know. I mean I assumed…"

"I've been alone and plenty of it," John smiled suggestively. "It's *you* I'm after thisavvy, luv."

The first kiss was gentle and protective. But John soon forgot that Cynthia had been an invalid for days as she wrapped her arms around his neck. A quarter hour dissolved, and neither of them thought once of George, the hospital staff, the crushed flowers in between them, or the anxiety of illnesses past.

"I missed you incredibly," Cyn whispered, touching John's lower lip with her forefinger. "I thought you'd never get here."

"Sorry I couldn't come before." John took a deep breath, inhaling her scent. "Al insisted on makin' a demo to take to Hamburg, and we had to complete it before his departure, y'know."

"A recording?" she stiffened.

"Yeah, a promotional tape – somethin' to showcase Al's bands to the various club owners, as it were."

Cynthia felt worse just thinking about it. "So...Al's found some interested German businessmen, then?"

"A couple."

"I told you he'd bring the mountain to Mohammed."

John smiled and tucked her hair behind her ears. "You're a fuggin' fortune teller, aren't you, Powell? From now on, we'll call you Nostra Dame, us."

"Well," she forced a smile, "tell me about it. What was it like – the tape? What'd you sing? And who were the other groups?" She crossed her fingers that they were better than The Beatles.

John rubbed his hand across the coverlet as he talked. "The usual lot," he said. "Gerry Marsden 'n his group. The Cassanovas...'n some folk group who call themselves The Spinners...as well as this trad jazz bunch. It was a motley crew."

"And?"

"And Al set up this 7 ½ i.p. recorder – downstairs in the Jac...this mad machine with two track reels – all the latest in technology, y'know."

"Is it safe to come back in now?" A voice sounded from the hall.

"Come in!" Cynthia called. "George!" She smiled warmly this time.

"Y'must've gone to bleedin' America for a bleedin' pack o' Camels!" John teased. "You've been gone the last half decade, haven't you?"

"But I thought you wanted me to..."

"Come on in, George. Ignore him. Have a seat." Cynthia waved John off. "We were just talking about the recording session at The Jacaranda."

George took a few tentative steps forward and handed Cynthia a small box of wrapped candy. "This was with *my* money, Cyn – not John's. I mean, I had it for you...even before I went out."

"Thank you," she blushed. "I'm awfully sorry I..."

"It's all water under the bridge, isn't it?" George grinned and sat on the chair where Lillian Powell had been sleeping each night. He tossed John the commissioned cigarettes along with several matchboxes and two Cadbury's Flakes. "So John's been fillin' your head with our great and glorious future, eh?"

"The toppermost of the poppermost," Cynthia winked.

"Did he tell you how much trouble we had figurin' out Al's recordin' machine...how it was all a big jumble – that session?"

"I was just up to that." John tucked the cigarettes in his shirt and ripped open one of the long, thin chocolate bars.

"You couldn't get it to work?" Cynthia's hopes rose in spite of her good intentions.

"None of us could," George said.

"Paul was pacin' about and havin' second and third thoughts about our musical selections, and Stu just kept on sayin', 'Let's have a bash at it,' as if he'd suddenly learned to play," John explained, "but no one could figure out how to get the fuggin' recorder to work...no matter what we tried."

"Al kept askin' *me* to operate the bleedin' machine," George leaned in, "just because I worked as an electricians' mate for a few days, y'know."

"But none of us," John said, "had ever seen anythin' like that fuggin' contraption, had we, George?"

Cynthia rubbed John's arm, "So what then?"

"Well, right in the middle of it all, Al was called away to one of his other clubs." John was now animated. "And he gave us this serious, rally-the-troops speech about how our future depended on gettin' that effin' machine to do its thing...how he'd rented it for one night and one night only, and how we'd better find a way to make it work, or all fuggin' deals were off!"

"And we just did," George shrugged.

"Mother of invention and all that." John sniffed. "We not only made the contraption work, we even recorded a song for you, Powell."

"For me?" Cynthia blushed. "What was it – an appendix to your play list?"

"Nice," John cut his eyes at her. "But strangely enough, the circumstances of the last few days really did fit. I've named it, 'I Call Your Name.'"

"If we weren't in hospital, you and George could sing it..." she almost expected him to do so. But the nurses would have none of it, she was certain.

"It'd lack a certain *je ne sais quoi*, as Mim always says," he gestured at the green concrete block walls.

"It'd lack musical accompaniment as well," George smiled. "All you'd hear is *him* singin'...a precursor to a relapse," he teased.

"John singing?" Cynthia squeezed his arm. "That's the first and best remedy."

"Let's just hope the Krauts think so." John was back to Hamburg.

"Right," Cynthia bit her lip and tried to be supportive, "let's hope."

"We *really* want to go to Hamburg, y'know," George's eyes sparkled.

"I know," Cynthia said. And she did.

But it didn't make her happy. Being away from John for weeks, maybe months, on end wasn't a bit appealing. For her, it only meant worry and loneliness and days with nothing to look forward to. Being without him in hospital for only two days had been bad enough. But weeks...

"Sounds like 'I Call Your Name' might become my song, not yours," she said softly.

"Nah," John cut an eye toward the door, on the lookout for nurses, "If I were allowed to sing you the song…"

"But you're not," Cynthia said quickly. The rules were hard and fast.

"But if I *were*, you'd see it's not about separation as much as it's about blame."

"You didn't cause this attack, John," Cynthia sighed. "You didn't make me sick."

"He couldn't sleep nights," George offered.

Cynthia smiled in spite of herself. "And how do *you* know?"

"Grouse," the boy returned, making a face and pointing at John behind his hand.

"Well, you'll have to get used to that, won't you? I mean, if you two plan to share a flat in Hamburg?"

"I hope he won't start callin' *my* name!" George grinned.

"Don't flatter yerself, Sonny Jim," John said.

"I'll have no part in this!" Cynthia threw up her hands.

And despite the lingering pain in her side, the uncomfortable surroundings, and the very real possibility of Hamburg on the horizon, she found herself once again completely happy. John always made her smile.

The facts concerning Allan's attempt to woo financial supporters are documented. But the Gambier conversation between John and Cynthia is, of course, imagined. Cynthia did experience a "grumbling appendix" while with John in Gambier. He did walk her to Lime Street Station and then visit her in the hospital on Sunday. The events with John, George, and Cynthia are recorded exactly as they occurred.

All facts about the recording that Allan prepared for his Hamburg trip are also authentic.

"I Call Your Name" was written during this time frame. Inspired by a grumbling appendix? Perhaps! Who knows?

6 August 1960
The Grapes Pub
Mathew Street
Liverpool

As a drummer, Norm Chapman was even more talented than Allan had imagined, and first day with The Beatles, he seemed to fit. A Scouser – full of dry wit and subtle expressions – he was well suited to the lads' antics. Norm's rapid-fire personality matched John's own.

But just as the five lads began to work together as a group, the government intervened and whisked Norman away "to do his duty to his country."

The military! John shuddered at the prospect. *Poor, fuggin' Norm.* He shook his head. *Here we are on the verge of gettin' a chance at fuggin' Hamburg, and where'll Norm be? Flirtin' with a gun. Travelin' in a tank. Norm woulda loved Hamburg, and Hamburg woulda loved him!*

As if Norm's loss had somehow been The Beatles' fault, Allan claimed no responsibility whatsoever for finding them a replacement. Furthermore, he made it clear that if The Beatles wanted a shot at Hamburg – or any venue beyond Merseyside – then they were going to have to get a drummer...and quickly.

John, scribbling on a thick, cardboard beer mat, mulled it all over.

Who in the fuggin'ell can we conjure up at this late date? Who'd drop everything – work, family, the whole bit – for a gig in a foreign city? Most everyone's entangled one way or another...a girl, a nine-to-five...

John could count on one hand the number of drummers he knew who had their own kits and were able to travel.

Tommy Moore was still Merseyside, but he was unquestionably out. And besides, Moore added nothing to the group's charisma or camaraderie.

Moore...a drag. John shook his head.

Pete Best had performed with them, now and again, at his mum's Casbah Club, and Pete owned his own drums as well, but was he spontaneous enough, madcap enough? John wasn't sure.

"Done here, then?" Pat, the barmaid at The Grapes, gave John a well-honed glare. John had been in the cozy Mathew Street pub for an hour, nursing one pint the entire time, and in Pat's estimation, the bench could well be filled with more profitable customers.

"I wudden mind another." He grinned at her, his slight overbite brushing his lower lip coyly, like a little boy.

"Did they institute table service when I wasn't lookin', then?" She grabbed his glass away. "If it's a drink y'er after, John Lennon, get up to the bar and pay like everyone else."

"C'mon." He dipped his forehead, the way he always did for Mimi. "Givvus a Black and Tan, luv. Can't y'tell when a man's wrestlin' with prolific profundities, as it were?"

"I can tell when a man's fuggin' freeloadin'!" She tossed her honey-brown hair.

"So that's what it's come to?" John lost his smile and his charm. "Workin' for the rentfeller, eh?"

"That's right. What of it?"

"I pay me effin' dues here at The Grapes, night in and night out, as it were...."

"Yeah, right!" she scoffed.

"...so if you're bootin' me," he went on, "just because I'm light this once, I might be well-inclined to direct all future business over The White Star's way."

"Buggeroff, Lennon!" She wiped the table with a large, wet terry towel. "You don't frighten me."

John, striding to the bar, pulled some assorted coins from his pocket and shook them in his hand. "Another lager, barmaid." He slammed the money on the counter and glared at Pat. "I'll play your lousy game."

"Money talks." She walked over and filled his glass. Flashing a sardonic smile, she slid the pint across the slick hardwood surface. "Cheers, luv," she hissed.

"What's up, John?"

"'Ullo dur!"

It was Paul and George. Like everyone else at dusk, they migrated to the busy pub just off St. John – popping in for a quick Guinness, Bass, or Black and Tan, and a "birrov" lively conversation. The Grapes was the watering hole for secretarial pools, trendy movers and shakers, and staunch, dyed-in-the-wool Scousers.

"Pint wudja, Pat? How're ya, luv?" Paul clicked his cheek and winked, quickly sliding his money over to the girl.

"For me as well," George grinned and paid up. He offered John a cigarette from a brand new pack, and John's eyebrows lifted appreciatively. Paul checked his reflection in the large mirror behind the bar and unruffled his hair from the Mersey's havoc. Even though it was only August, fall was already in the air. The nip had come early this year, intimating a cruel winter.

"Sláinte!" He touched John's glass in an Irish toast.

"Cheers," John lifted his in return.

"To a new drummer!" George clacked glasses and broached the subject on all their minds as they returned to John's table and straddled the low, cushioned stools.

"I would've paid had y'come in earlier." John took the bench seat against the wall and stretched his legs out. "You shoulda been here when I was carryin'."

"And when was that?" Paul knew the truth.

"1957, I believe," George teased.

"Yeah, he was loaded back then," Paul nodded with a serious face.

"I heard he had a five nicker once, all in one day."

"But he spent it all on a six-string, mail order guitar," Paul winked.

"Fuggin' hilarious," John drank deeply. "Go on. Amuse me, jokers. I'm up to here with problem solvin'."

"Any leads, then?" Paul knew exactly what John was talking about.

"Pete Best…he's the only answer we've got."

"He's got a good, steady beat – Pete." George looked on the bright side. "Ken Brown's always goin' on about him these days. Says Pete's a phenomenon with the female fans, a real attraction 'n all that."

"We're runnin' a band, George, norra bordello." John put the Scouse on.

"Yeah, but Ken says…"

"As if there's tremendous weight in the words of Ken Brown," John snapped. He'd never forgiven Ken for ducking out on a gig he'd promised to play with The Quarry Men at The Casbah about a year ago, a gig Ken had missed on the excuse of a "sore throat." The Quarry Men had played the gig anyway, but afterwards they'd adamantly refused to pay Brown his share for the night. Only the iron hand of Mona Best had wrangled Brown's three pounds from the Liverpool boys, and John would never forget the incident, no matter what. John was an expert in long-term grudges.

"Well, I did hear Pete play only recently," George abandoned the Ken Brown endorsement, "and he's not bad, really."

"Sure, he's all right – Pete," Paul chimed in.

"But that's just the point, isn't it!" John paused to wave to Eddie Porter, the amiable waiter from the Odd Spot Club where Twitchy worked now and again. Everyone knew everyone at The Grapes. There was always an unofficial reunion going on. "'All right' isn't enough, y'know…that is, if our gettin' beyond Liverpool and beyond Hamburg's the actual plan. I mean, *anyone'll* do in the short term…but it's the long run that's ultimately crucial, isn't it?"

"'Ullo, lads. Cheers." Eddie took a table close to theirs. He unzipped his lightweight windbreaker and made himself at home.

"Eddie," Paul toasted. "How's tricks?"

"I mean, we coulda kept Moore if it's just a drummer we're after," John interrupted, all business. "I coulda convinced him to 'take us back,' as it were." George and Paul exchanged skeptical glances. "And Chapman was great 'n all that," John went on, "but things bein' as they are, Chapman's out, and I'm looking for somethin' different this time…a real chemistry of sorts…."

"Look John," Paul leaned on his elbow, "it's not a ring-and-rice-forever kind of decision, is it?"

"But it fuggin' *should be*, shouldn't it?" John argued. "I mean, as it is, we're shufflin' members in and out every few weeks, helter-skelter. It's ludicrous. We have to have some fuggin' stability, as it were! It'd take me a full half hour to recount everyone we've seen come and go – Bill, Rod, Eric, Len, Nigel, Colin, Ivy, Pete, Tommy, Norm! We've got to get a core group, don't we? A group that's more than 'all right'…a group that has fuggin' charisma!"

"As far as charisma goes," George edged in, "I think you'd be happy with Pete. I mean, he's got this real James Dean draw…this aloof, untouchable appeal that makes the girls cry."

"Oh, fantastic." It was Paul's turn to throw his eyes to the ceiling. "Another Stu. Just what we need."

"As a matter of fact," George said quickly before John could react, "Pete's group, The Blackjacks, are on at The Casbah tonight – and what's more, it might be their last performance for some time, actually."

"What are you – their fuggin' manager?" John was having none of it.

George grinned and shook his head. "It's just that Ken Brown said…that is…I heard a rumour that Ken's takin' a job in London, and Chas Newby's got one lined up somewhere in Essex as well – Harlow, I think it is. Anyrate, they're on the verge of breakin' up, as it were. At least that's the scuttlebutt I heard."

"Well," Paul toasted John with the old Liverpool adage, "if you're not rich, you're lucky, mate. You might get yerself a drummer after all."

"And," John drained the last of his lager and wiped his mouth with the back of his hand, "since Grosvenor backed out on our gig tonight, it appears we're free…it also appears we have all our equipment at the ready, lads. So, what say we do Mo Best a favour and pop 'round The Casbah – just fer old times' sake?"

"Just like any other Saturday night," Paul agreed.

"Just a friendly visit to ole West Derby," George smiled.

John grabbed his wet beer mat and hopped up on his stool, balancing as he pressed the cardboard mat firmly against the stucco ceiling. It hung there like a medallion, affixed firmly, or at least until the liquid dried later on. By then, The Beatles would be miles away in suburban West Derby, scrutinizing the work of Randolph Peter Best and eyeing his expensive drum set. By the time the precarious mat lost its suction and fell on unsuspecting Grapes' patron, John's decision would have been made. But right now, everything hung in the balance.

****

The Casbah Club
8 Hayman's Green
West Derby

John chewed gum and nodded thoughtfully. He stared at Pete's sparkling new Blue Pearl Premiere drum kit. It was outstanding.

"Well, as you said, no surprises." Paul shrugged, "I mean, we've heard Pete play a hundred times before, right?"

John didn't answer. He swigged the Coca-Cola that Mona Best had given him in return for "a short set" that Paul, George, and he had played when The Blackjacks were on break, and he studied Pete with judicious eyes.

Upturned collar, Elvis coif, cool pout…Pete had the look, all right. But John wanted to see him "sell it." Right now, Pete was drumming and minding his own business, oblivious to the crowd around him. As far as Pete was concerned, the audience might not have even been there.

John watched without comment.

"Mo says Pete's not goin' back to school after all, John." George gave the update. "She says he's set on makin' a career as a professional drummer. She says he doesn't see the sense in goin' on with school when drummin's all he really loves 'n that."

"Right." John continued to observe.

As each song ended, The Casbah crowd shouted encouragements, friendly insults, and requests at The Blackjacks.

"They seem to think he's 'best,'" George nodded towards a large group of girls who screamed at Pete and waved from the sidelines.

"A pretty face," Paul winked. "Failsafe."

"So, what do y'think, lads?" Mona joined them – her long, dark hair swept up attractively for the evening. "Our Pete's fantastic, isn't he?"

"Just what John here was sayin'," Paul nodded. "His very words."

"Well, he's right then, isn't he?" Mona beamed at John and gave his shoulder a quick squeeze. "He can't paint worth a mite – your John – but he's got an excellent ear for music, as it were." She still saw glossy spots on the matte walls around The Casbah where John had "assisted" with the refurbishing last summer.

The music began again, and for the moment, conversation was useless. George nudged John and mouthed something about "steady beat." Paul tapped his toe and folded his arms across his chest.

But their reactions were moot anyway. In reality, they had no other option. Pete was the right man in the right place at the right time. He was able and available. He owned his own drum kit, and he'd played with them before. If the Beatles were going to go to Hamburg at all – and they were determined to – they would have to take Pete with them.

At the next interval, John broached the subject. "Listen, Mo," he cleared his throat, "We've got this chance to play in West Germany...Hamburg, in fact. Al's workin' out the all details even as we speak."

"Al? Allan Williams? Bah!" Mona brushed them off. "He's all talk and no do – that one. Don't count on it, John. He'll lead you 'round the rosy, will Al."

Paul leaned in closer, his eyes earnest. "But if it *did* materialize, Mo, if it actually did come about..."

"We'd be needin' a good drummer, as it were." John jumped in and made the official offer. "Someone who'd be free to go along for several months, without any other entanglements, as it were."

Mona put her hands on her hips and smiled at the three boys who called themselves The Beatles. It was her dream come true, the break that Pete had been waiting for. Hamburg was the golden egg, the chance of a lifetime for her son. *And though he's too damn good for the likes of these raspy Beatles, at least it's an opportunity,* she thought.

"Well...that'd be up to our Peter," was all she said. The expert promoter took control. "He's on his own these days, lads. I can't even begin to imagine what he'd tell you. I mean, he's very much in demand, y'know."

"Isthasso?" George innocently began. "But Ken Browne said that..."

John, knowing the ritual dance, cut in quickly. "Right, Mo. Well, we'll just have to ask Pete then, won't we? Perhaps at the end of this set – that is, if he's got the time."

"You could do." Mona shrugged.

"And of course, if he's interested 'n all," Paul spelled it out, "we'd need him to come 'round for an audition within the week."

"For Al's benefit," John was quick to add. "Because like it or not, he's our manager, y'know."

Mona's retort about Allan Williams was swallowed up in the first chords of the next song. But without even hearing it, John knew exactly how she felt. There was no love lost between the two powerful promoters. But John also knew that any animosity between them would be readily shelved to serve their own ends. Allan and Mo were smart and savvy.

As the next song ended, Mona shouted to John above the applause,

"*Your aunt's* actually letting you go off to Hamburg, John Lennon? The notorious city of sin and vice?"

"Well, she doesn't have much choice, does she?" John leaned back casually against a support column, "Just like Pete, y'know, I'm on me own these days – makin' me own decisions, as it were."

"And *you're* going as well?" She turned to the rosy-cheeked George Harrison.

He shrugged and offered a hint of a grin. "If everyone else goes, I go. We're The Beatles, y'know."

"Are you even old enough?" Mona tried to remember the boy's age.

"Al's workin' on that as well," John answered for his friend. "He's makin' arrangements for work visas or student visas…or somethin' along those lines…"

Mona folded her arms and nodded, her eyes full of suspicion. Allan Williams was a known wheeler-dealer, an entrepreneur not unlike herself. They both pushed for what they wanted, and at times, let the chips fall where they may.

So despite what she'd told John about Pete's autonomy, if Pete agreed to audition with The Beatles, Mona would be there. She'd be there controlling any agreements and ascertaining the benefits, pitfalls, and grey areas in between. Mo would always be in the shadows. She would always a part of the drummer who smiled at her from his rostrum.

****

The Blue Angel
Liverpool 8

The following Friday, 12 August, Pete performed his ritual "trial run" with John, Paul, George, and Stu at The Blue Angel. Allan took notes, nodded, and rubbed his dark beard. Mona sat beside him, judiciously squinting her eyes and making notes of her own. It was all to the letter.

At the end of the day, John and Pete shared an off-handed comment or two and a few laughs before John promised to ring him up "within the twenty-four." Pete hung around to chat a while with Stu, whom he'd seen less than the other three, and Paul and George seemed genuinely pleased with the audition as a whole.

But it was laughable, really – a show, a pretense. Bruno Koschmider, the owner of Hamburg's Indra Club and Kaiserkeller Club had already signed The Beatles for a two-month run, just as he'd signed Derry and the

Seniors before them. A drummer wasn't a luxury for The Beatles; it was a contractual necessity, plain and simple.

Whether Mona knew it or not, whether Pete knew it or not, the deal was done. Pete Best, the newest of The Beatles, was already on his way to Hamburg.

I spoke with Pete Best by phone from the Grange Hotel in Aigburth in March of 1989 and tried to arrange an interview. Pete's fee for a one hour interview was cost-prohibitive for me at that time (though not unfair), but I have since read both of his books and heard him speak at The Fest for BeatleFans, 3 April 2004, where I took extensive notes during his question and answer sessions.

All events are factual and documented. All conversations are conjecture.

16 August 1960
The Harwich Ferry
Newhaven, England

"D'ya think the Germans will take to The Beatles, there Al?" John's eyes hinted mischief. "We've no saber scars, y'know."

"You'll wanna forget about the war, John." Al's voice reflected the anxiety he felt about this venture. The Beatles were, at best, an "on-again-off-again" group with as many dismal failures as triumphs. They were hardly seasoned musicians, whether their egos would allow them to acknowledge it or not, and Hamburg was out of their league. "Tell 'im to take a bit of the acid out, McCartney, or *his* ass is out, as it were," Allan warned.

"Take a bit o'the acid out, Johnny." Paul mimicked Allan's voice.

"Or *your* ass is out!" George finished it off. The boys snickered, enjoying themselves.

For them, it was a red-letter day. As far as they knew, they were the chosen ones; they were "the band of bands" selected for a venue in a foreign, metropolitan city. They were the ones handpicked for the honour, the very cats about to divvy up a fat, prized canary. And they were acting just as contrary and conceited.

Only Allan knew it was a gift – a chance The Beatles didn't deserve. Only Allan knew the boys had won the trip by default. Rory Storm and the Hurricanes had committed for the entire summer at Butlins Resort in North Wales; Cass and the Cassanovas were still off completing their Duffy Power tour, and Gerry Marsden had turned Allan down flat when Hamburg had been mentioned. So The Beatles had been chosen, but they were Allan's very last choice.

But the kicker is, they aren't one bit appreciative! Allan silently fumed. *Not a snippet of appreciation among 'em, even after I took their fuggin' tape to Hamburg, met with Koschmider, and persuaded him to take them on – in spite of the fact that the fuggin' tape wouldn't play a note! I sold these scruffs, bag and baggage, to one of the most prominent club owners in Germany despite reels of garbled noise – more 'n likely muddled by the unprofessional tapin' techniques of that sod, John Lennon. And look at him now, so smug and full of himself! Look at 'em all!*

Al shook his head. He lit up an Embassy and strolled down the pier, leaving The Beatles to their own too clever devices. *What the hell,* he thought, flicking ashes onto the Newhaven dock. *Why should I lose sleep over what John Lennon says about the Krauts? So what if Lennon insults 'em a time or two? They pummel 'im good, just fer old times' sake, and that'll teach him respect. Besides,* Al tossed the hardly smoked cigarette into the water, *I can't be babysittin' this lot forever. I've more important fish to fry.*

Watching the dilapidated green and cream road van slowly hoisted by large carriage straps onto the Harwich ferry, Al sucked his breath in and held it. Atop the tiny minibus, all of their luggage and equipment waggled to and fro, threatening to plunge at any minute into the murky English Channel below. Al only hoped that Lennon had loaded the gear better than he'd masterminded the failed Hamburg demo tape. *Another fiasco,* he thought, *The Beatles don't need.*

John had actually donned his glasses and stepped forward, calling out encouragement to the dockworkers. "C'mon mate! Yeah, that's it. Great, great! Good on yer." John's body English guided the minibus up and over, on to the ferryboat with great care.

When a rough plop announced the minibus safely aboard, John removed his specs and tried to look casual. He flashed Al a toothy grin but kept one eye on the dockworkers unfastening the vehicle hoist.

"All right, Manager," John said, "It's off to the Hook of Holland then, isn't it?"

"Right," Allan nodded, "off to the bright lights of The Reeperbahn. And if The Caribbean Steel Band and Derry and the Seniors aren't inflatin' the truth, it's off to riotous livin', fame, and fortune for you lot…none of which you deserve."

"Ah, the legendary Valhalla!" John recalled the Nirvana of German folklore that his Uncle George had told him about so often.

"Yeah, yeah. Whatever you say," Allan shrugged. Half the time, he had no idea what John was "on about." He checked his watch and excused himself to see how much longer the loading process would take.

"I can't believe Williams bleedin' expects us to travel all the way to Hamburg in that peeled-paint rubble of a half-baked minibus!" The West Derby sound of Pete Best's voice came from behind John's back. John turned to find the drummer shaking his head. "I mean, first it's Al's relatives hornin' in on the trip, right? And then some London interpreter's comin' along as well. And that West Indian…"

"Lord Woodbine to you," John interjected. "Woody to us."

"Whatever," Pete shrugged. "All I know is…we'll be Branston Pickle before we're there. We won't be able to turn around and breathe, will we?"

"Y'shoulda been there on the nine-day tour of Scotland," John stretched and yawned. "It was this and more – day in and day out. We rode in the minibus; we changed in the minibus. We slept in the minibus. We did every fuggin' thing but shit in the minibus."

"Yeah?" Pete's voice took on an edge. "Well, I wasn't invited on the tour of Scotland, was I? So I wouldn't know."

"That's right," Paul joined them. "Good ole Tommy Moore was along that trip. Now *that* was a drummer."

"Actually," John deadpanned, "it couldn't be further from the tooth." He and Paul smiled at each other knowingly.

Pete ignored their secret, inside joke. "Well, all I can say is, we'll never bleedin' make it in a rattletrap like that."

"If you don't make it," Paul's eyes twinkled, "can I have yer space, then?"

"I think he's beginnin' to look a bit peaked already." John walked around Pete, examining him intently.

"A bit green around the gills, I'd say," Paul agreed.

"Ah, he's done for." Stu overheard and joined in the initiation rite.

"I just hope it's not contagious – that." George winked and grinned.

Pete muttered something none of them could hear, then ambled away to the far end of the pier to look out over the grey, choppy channel. He squatted down, picked at a splintered spot on the weathered dock, and stared. Though he wouldn't admit it, he was already a little homesick. Only George was younger than he on this venture, and George had the advantage of history with this group. George was part of the band – part of The Beatles' inside jokes, tag phrases, and group references. George belonged.

Pete turned and looked at them all. John and Stu were standing together, their heads leaning in as they talked quietly and shared a common cig. George was laughing with Allan over the punch line of some unheard joke, and Paul was chatting comfortably with Beryl Williams, her brother Barry, and their newly acquired German interpreter, George Steiner. Even the unusual Lord Woodbine, who sat alone, meditating over an unhurried smoke of some sort, looked at ease in his self-imposed isolation. They all seemed to fit.

"All in!" a voice called from the ferry. "Hoooooook o' Holland!"

"That's you bunch!" Allan waved them all aboard.

John and Stu began singing "Bye, Bye Blackbird" and Paul joined in, belting the lyrics out, pub-style. Al added his high, Welsh tenor to the mix as George directed the combo with an invisible conductor's wand and Woody laughed loudly and deliciously. Beryl and Barry applauded when John did a quick soft-shoe. Then Paul whistled the bridge, and they all joined in the song again, just as if the performance had been planned and rehearsed.

Pete hurled the wood chip he'd freed into the water, watching it plop and float away from the dock. He wondered if he'd made the right decision after all. He wouldn't be home until at least October, possibly later. And August had just begun.

"C'mon, Best! We haven't all day, lad!" Allan hailed him from the gantry.

"Yeah, c'mon drummer!"

"Right. Pick up the beat, son!"

"Let's go!"

"Move it, Sonny Jim."

Pete stood up slowly and made his way back, dreading the rough channel crossing ahead and the inevitable moment when all ten travelers would have to squeeze into the unbearably tiny minibus for almost a two-day ride.

****

On the Road to Hamburg Germany

When Allan led them in the Welsh national anthem, they tried their hand at harmony, and when Paul followed with Bill Haley's "Rock Around the Clock," they all found something to pound on. They whistled, stomped, and sang at the top of their lungs. Every inch of the minibus reverberated.

They were tourists, traveling the road to Hamburg, speeding along in a dilapidated, dented minibus filled with cameras, a tin of Louise Harrison's scones, suitcases, guitars, amplifiers, an art case, and one shiny set of blue, mother-of-pearl drums.

Without warning, John burst into the bawdy Liverpool folk tune,

Ole Maggie May,
They have taken her away
And she'll never walk down Lime Street anymore,
Oh, the judge – he guilty found her...

Beryl, Barry, and the entire company – excluding George Steiner who didn't know the words – joined in the raucous lyrics about the notorious Merseyside "prossy." They took turns improvising and changing the lyrics to fit the moment, and as they sang, John produced his mouth organ, while Pete tapped out a backbeat on the seat cover and the ceiling. They sang until they had nothing left to sing, until the songs slipped into conversation and catnaps.

Al discreetly pulled a folded letter from his pocket and looked it over again, guarding it against his chest. It was a note, and a nasty one at that, written by Derry and The Seniors – with the notable exception of Howie Casey, their lead singer – protesting The Beatles' assignment to Hamburg. It was a hate letter, pure and simple, and Allan would have to decide how to deal with it once the lads were settled in.

The Beatles, the letter insisted, were "a bunch of five-chord merchants" who would be best "panderin' their wares" in "two-bit shops" like Grosvenor Ballroom, Neston Institute, or The Casbah. Merseyside groups, The Seniors had asserted, were making a reputable name for themselves in Germany these days, and they didn't want standards lowered by the likes of Lennon, McCartney, Harrison, and Sutcliffe. The "band without a drummer" was not welcome in Hamburg, it seemed…and that was that, in no uncertain terms.

Allan folded the paper and tucked it back safely into his pocket. *How quickly they forget!* he thought, recalling that only two weeks ago Derry and the Seniors had been the ones "cold shouldered" by Larry Parnes, the very ones who'd been forced to drive to London seeking employment from a friend of Allan's – a friend who owned the "Two I's Coffee Bar."

In fact, if my mate, Tommy Littlewood, hadn't been decent enough to let the fuggin' Seniors take the stage at the Two I's Bar in London that evenin' without prior contracts or agreements, they'd be nowhere! The fact that Bruno Koschmider – the very club owner from Hamburg that I'd already contacted – was actually sittin' in the fuggin' audience that night was one in a million! It wasn't talent or skill or premeditated preparation on The Seniors' part that led them to Germany. It was luck, pure and simple…luck and my unparalleled salesmanship, naturally! Al patted himself on the back. *It was my tellin' Bruno that Liverpool bands were better 'n fuggin' Elvis that cinched the deal! It was my persuasive genius that paved the way for The Seniors to go to Germany – no argument, no doubt about it!*

Allan was fascinated by kismet in the grand scheme of things. He often mulled over the balance of coincidence and fate, and he wondered how much luck or predestination had led them all to this very moment.

To meet up with Koschmider that night and then to accidentally find a German waiter, George Steiner, workin' in the bar right next door to the Two I's was all part of the grand coincidence, I suppose. Steiner was fuggin' invaluable translatin' for me that evenin'! And he will be on this trip as well.

Allan stared out the window of the tiny mini-bus and watched the lush Dutch countryside fly by. He caught his reflection in the side-view mirror and smiled. He grinned to think how things had all fallen into place, one by one.

Had Allan not flown to Hamburg with The Beatles' tapes in June, had the tapes not flubbed, had Allan not had to embellish the talents of his group in the absence of concrete evidence, had Koschmider not fallen for Allan's tales of greatness, had Allan not forgotten to tell Koschmider what city he was from, had Koschmider not flown to London instead of Liverpool to find Allan, had Larry Parnes not rejected Derry and the Seniors at The Blue Angel audition, had Allan not driven The Seniors to London to try their luck at the "Two I's," had Koschmider not walked into the exact coffee bar that Allan walked into that very night, had Koschmider not recognized Allan and come over to his table, and had the translator, Steiner, not worked next door, none of this would have transpired! A thousand golden wires pulled on the puppets and made them dance. Was it chance or was it direction? Allan wondered.

Whatever the impetus, the deal that Derry and the Seniors signed with Koschmider was primarily fortuitous. Any airs that they now had about their superiority to "the likes of the Beatles" would have to be dealt with once they all reconnoitered. Allan was used to the egos of musicians. He'd find a way to smooth it all over.

"How much longer, then?" George Harrison called up to Woody, who was taking his turn at the wheel.

"At least ten centimeters longer'n yours, boy!" Woody laughed uproariously. He intentionally swerved the wheel and sent them all crashing into one another. Then he burst into indecent laughter all over again.

"Me blood's congealed in the extremities," George complained again, massaging his calves and trying to readjust so that he was marginally comfortable.

"Right. It's bleedin' miserable in here, Al," Stu joined in. "How's about a cuppa, eh?"

"All right, all right!" Allan waved them off and leaned over to Woody. "If I'm not mistaken, there's a war memorial just ahead. I saw a postin' for it a coupla minutes back. Let's give the lads a rest when we get there."

Woody smiled widely. "Suits me fine. Then *you* can take the wheel for a spell. How's that?"

"Pffft! Like I haven't done *more* 'n my fuggin' share! I've been drivin' the whole fuggin' trip!"

"This trip or an imaginary one?" Woody laughed again.

"Look Woodbine…"

"Belt up, both ya," John barked without even opening his eyes, his head wedged against the window. "It's like sleepin' in a field o' fuggin' magpies around here."

"Caw! Caw!" Paul called.

George chirped up with various fowl-like whistles as Stu flapped his wings.

"It's madness – this," Pete said softly.

"That's right," John opened his eyes and sat up. "It's madness!

Madness! We're all prone to madness!" He laughed a hyena's laugh.

"If I don't get out of here soon…" Pete began.

"Stop the bus and let him out!" John yelled.

"Set him free!" Paul began pounding his feet. As John broke into a chorus of "Let My People Go," Woody followed the signs for the Arnhem War Memorial, slowed the minibus, and gratefully pulled to a halt.

Paul hit the pavement first, turning his wide collar up against the unexpected chill of the late German summer. George followed, shivering and buttoning his street coat over the trendy shirt his mother had bought him for the trip. Pete stretched, reaching into his jacket for the last of his cigs. Beryl, Barry, and Woody unloaded the hamper of cheese and bread from the rear of the van. Only Stu, John, and Allan remained behind.

"C'mon Lennon – y'er holdin' up the fuggin' show!" Allan stomped his feet in the cold and waited to lock the door. "Get off the fuggin' bus!"

"I'm goin' down with the ship," was the only reply.

"All right, Lennon. That's it. Get out!"

"In a minute, Al…" Stu began, but Allan had had all he could stand.

"Not in a minute!" Allan exploded. *"Now!"*

"Look, if he'd rather not…" Stu tried again.

"Bloody fuggin'ell!" Allan spit. "Why the fuggin'ell not? I thought you wanted out the van! Well, here we are…so get out!"

"It's the memorial…" Stu raised an eyebrow meaningfully, but Al was past subtle hints or sympathy.

"I know where we are, Sutcliffe!" Al raged back. "All the more reason we should all stop and pay our respects and all that. It's Arnhem, y'know – the war…brave British boys dyin' here for the likes o' you layabouts! Get off the fuggin' bus, John!"

John opened his eyes for a moment and glanced up the hill at the endless rows of crosses blanketing the green lawn like tiny, hand-stitched squares on Mimi's quilts. He stared for a minute and then closed his eyes again, tucked his arms under his armpits, and let his head fall back against the window.

"I'm not interested in that sort of thing," he offered, hoping the explanation would be enough.

"Look, for the last time," Allan fumed, "get…out. Get out 'n act human for a change. Have some bread 'n cheese and a cuppa tea and at least pretend to…"

"Here!?" John's eyes flew open again, his face flushed, *"Here!* Surrounded by *them?"* He scooted to the edge of the seat. "You're actually gonna stand around with yer casual jam butties and yer cups of tea and yer restin'-up-for-the-journey conversations when *they're* out there?" John motioned towards the graves. "You're gonna stand around and have a fuggin' chat while they're six feet under with no fuggin' hope of reprieve? Is that it?" he yelled.

Allan and Stu stared without a word.

"Go on, then." John glared with real invective. "Go on and mingle in yer managerial, sleeveless sweater vest. Go have yer little tea in the graveyard, as it were. Just leave me out of it! I'm stayin' on the bus."

"Right. All right, John." Stu swallowed hard. "Yeah. Great. C'mon Al."

"Pfft!" Allan muttered. "*Great? How is that great?* How is anything he does great?"

But Stu didn't answer, John didn't open his eyes, and Allan gave up talking to either of them. He slammed the minibus door and left John behind.

"He's not gettin' out, is he?" Paul ambled up, his hands pulled up inside his sleeves.

"Not in this lifetime." Allan raked his hand through his hair.

"Didn't think he would." Paul's eyes met Stu's. "Not here."

"He knows death a bit more intimately than most of us," Stu said quietly.

Paul kicked at a crushed paper cup someone had tossed on the sidewalk before his eyes met Stu's. "More than most," Paul nodded, "but not all, y'know."

"Beryl says she wants a photograph, Al," George joined them. He handed cups of tea to Allan, Paul, and Stu.

"Ta," Paul blew on his.

"Cheers!" Stu lifted his cup, but Allan only scowled.

"Hey Al," George repeated, "Barry's brought his camera, and Beryl wants him to snap us at the monument – y'know…as a memento 'n all that…that is, if the rest of you would oblige us with a bit of the hurry up, as it were."

"Yeah, right. No rest for the weary, is there?" Allan took a long slurp of tea. He wished for a good, stiff shot of "Irish" to spike it…anything that might help take the edge off of dealing with John Lennon. But he hadn't dared cross international borders with libations in tow. Whiskey would have to wait until they reached Hamburg.

"Where's John?" George's eyes wandered back to the minibus.

"Gaurdin' the gear, mate," Paul winked.

"It's not his scene." Stu gave the straight answer.

"But…if he doesn't get out, he won't be in the photograph," George began to protest before Al's glare stopped him, mid-sentence. John's absence had obviously been a point of contention. George's arms flopped to his sides, and the words trailed off.

The group walked towards the monument in silence and took their places for Beryl's picture. Barry Chang toyed with the light meter as the group stood solemnly, Only George and Pete chatted quietly.

Paul sat alone "centre stage" on the concrete steps, his teacup still in his hand while George and Pete found a roost a couple of steps up and to the right. Allan, Beryl, and Stu, all in sweaters and white shirts, stood clustered around Woody, who lounged on the far left, his elbows resting on his knees. And behind them all, the monument wall rose up to Beryl's shoulder height, filling the photograph and entirely blocking all but a few of Arnhem's headstones from the picture.

It was an imposing memorial, a thick, white marble backdrop against which their dark, Liverpudlian attire stood out vividly. Barry's black and white film would do justice to the setting. In fact, it was perfect.

Engraved in the wall behind them was a quote that began at Stu's left hand, a quote that saluted the soldiers who had sacrificed their lives in the battle. Stu noticed the inscription first, and he read the words aloud. "Hey, look at this," he read, "'Their names liveth forevermore.' If John were here, he'd swear it was some kind of foreshadowin' or omen – that."

"He'd say it was fate," Paul nodded.

"A harbinger, a portent of things to come," Woody grinned.

"The toppermost of the poppermost," George repeated, giving the wall a quick glance over his shoulder.

"Bigger'n Elvis – the fabulous Beatles!" Pete snickered and shook his head.

But George didn't find it humourous. He believed in John's vision, and he repeated the quote again. "'Their names liveth forevermore,'" he said, almost to himself.

"It's uncanny – that," Stu agreed.

"Hold still, please," Barry instructed. "One, two, three!"

George's and Pete's smiles lingered for Barry's camera while the rest looked serious, rather grim, as if the group photo had come at an inopportune time or an extremely maudlin moment. They stared into the lens with haunting expressions, and Stu never even removed his sunglasses.

"Kind of eerie that we'd stop and have our photo made here, considerin' the 'liveth forevermore' 'n all that?" George followed Stu and the others back to the van.

"Not really." Stu stretched one last time at the bus doors. "I mean, nothing's really coincidence, is it?"

"Y'can save the ethereal crap." Allan wedged behind the steering wheel. "It's hard enough to navigate the wrong fuggin' side of the highway without the Dalai Lama and company holdin' forth in the back seat, as it were."

But George ignored him. "Hey, you shoulda been there, John!" He wedged into the tiny space allotted to him. "You shoulda read the words on that monument back there. It was all about us..." he began.

Allan revved the engine and glared in the rear view mirror. "If Lennon had wanted to see the fuggin' monument, Harrison, he had two able legs, didn't he?"

"Yeah, but it said…" George began.

"Give it a rest, George." John never opened his eyes. "As far as I'm concerned, the less I know about that monument, the better."

And as Allan popped into gear and careened back out onto the road with the mad carelessness that had cost him his license, the group hung on. They all fell into white-knuckled silence.

All facts are documented in The Man Who Gave the Beatles Away, *including the singing of "Bye, Bye, Blackbird," and "Maggie Mae." Only the conversation is conjecture.*

The photograph described can be found in several sources. The best rendering of it is in The Anthology, *p. 66.*

17 August 1960
Hamburg
Germany

"Where're all the bombed-out ruins, anyway?"
"Yeah, where's the rubble, Al?"
"I thought Germany *lost* the fuggin' war!"
"It's bleedin' *cosmopolitan* – this!"
"Too fuggin' good for the fuggin' Krauts!"

Hamburg, West Germany was no war-seared Liverpool. It was alive – a morass of elevated railways, billboards, flashing advertisements, and crowded streets. While the port on the Mersey lay gashed and wounded from Hitler's assaults, Hamburg glittered its reflection into a ship-stoked bay, beckoning sailors with freshly painted bordellos and ladies dappled to match. It was as vibrant as Liverpool had once been – before the lacerating blitzkrieg nights.

As last light faded from the sky, a neon borealis flared before them. Nightspots, strip clubs, restaurants, and theater houses dazzled competitively. The whole town flashed and writhed in coloured lights as the tiny, paint-chipped Austin minibus cautiously crept by, its passengers gawking at the oddities filling Hamburg 4. Without an ounce of shame, the town displayed its seamy wares with aplomb, and the Liverpool boys took it all in – amazed.

"Prossies, transvestites, and now Scouser musicians!" Allan chuckled. His eyes gleamed at the parade of deviant humanity. "The rag-tag and bobtail of human existence, lads! You can buy anything or anybody in Hamburg 4. All you have to do is imagine it!"

"Well, how's about imaginin' an 'A to Zed' for starters, then?" John was tired of their aimless wandering. Even though Allan had been to Hamburg before, he'd lost his way in the intricate web of streets. He needed a road map before lost became hopeless.

"Look, Lennon, I'm doin' the fuggin' best I can!"

Wham! Their necks lurched with the sudden jolt.

"Fuggin'ell! Not *this* again!"

"How do you say *déjà vu* in German?" Paul asked.

"It's Scotland revisited," George monotoned.

"You've wrecked the van there, Manager." John put the boot in. "The first thing *you'll* see in Hamburg's the inside of the lock-up, as it were. It's the end of the line for you, Sonny Jim."

"Shirrup, Lennon!" Allan barked, fishing for his passport. "Bloody hell, what a fuggin' miserable trip! Thirty-six hours and now this!"

The driver of the injured vehicle in front of them advanced towards the minibus, waiting impatiently for Allan to alight and explain himself. Her crossed arms and sour expression didn't bode well. Allan donned his most diplomatic smile as he frantically sifted through the debris in the cluttered glove compartment. The woman refused to smile in return.

"She seems like a nice German lady."* Even George was enjoying Al's dilemma.

"*Ja, ja, jawohl!*" From the back seat, John winked at the woman. Paul and Stu waved at her as if she were some long lost cousin.

Al ignored them, retrieving the documents he needed, scrambling to get everything in order. But one inadvertent glance in the rearview mirror revealed George and John with their faces plastered against the windows. They were busy pulling expressions at a crowd that had started to gather.

"You'd joke on the bloody rim of hell,* wouldn't you?" Allan sputtered. "Especially if it were *me* ferryin' 'cross the River Styx. What do you care, right? Just sic Cerberus on Al and larf it up."

But Al's rumblings were unfounded. The German motorist was reasonable and in fact, stoic. She spoke a bit of English and got down to business, inspecting her bumper and gathering information from Allan. Neither car had suffered noticeable damage, and with a smattering of German here and there, the drivers reached detente without having to call in reinforcements.

All smiles and good humour, Al returned to the minibus. The Beatles and their entourage cheered loudly as he opened the door.

"She'll make no trouble," Allan assured his wife. Beryl patted his arm and smiled as he settled back behind the wheel. "What's more, she even supplied us with directions, as it were. I asked after The Kaiserkeller, and believe it or not – I was only slightly off course. The Grosse Freiheit's just a couple of blocks up and to the left."

"Last leg o' the trip," George applauded. "We've finally made it!"

"I was beginning to like it in here, all sandwiched in," Paul smiled.

"Cozy, isn't it?" Stu nodded.

"Drive on." John pointed a finger forward.

"To the Grosse Freiheit!" George smiled.

A quick jaunt, turn, and zigzag, and the long-awaited haven of nightlife sprawled before them. The Grosse Freiheit Strasse – the Street of Great Freedom – was aptly named. It was an illuminated midway of depravity, a collection of weapons' shops, adult cinemas, and whorehouses. It was a promenade for transvestites, hired killers, traders in white slavery, and drug dealers. Here the unthinkable was reality, and the bizarre, commonplace. The Grosse Freiheit was the very heart of Hamburg 4 – but a dark heart beneath a sequined veil.

"There y'have it, lads!" Allan slowed the van and swept his hand panoramically. "The bleedin' 'big time,' as they say. Take it in, lads. The whole thing's yours, that is as long as you keep fuggin' Koschmider happy!"

"There's a guy wearin' ladies' gear over there,"* George announced with some concern.

"Right, get used to it." Allan hardly missed a beat, glancing at them in the rear view mirror as he lectured on. "Remember that Koschmider's booked you in his Indra club for two months flat, but my guess is he'll keep you…as long as you're worth his lousy one-fifty quid a week. 'Until boredom do you part,' if you catch my drift. It's up to you lot whether you stay here or not." He looked pointedly at John. "I fuggin' did my bit to get you here. But from here on out – make it or fuggin' break it, as they say – it's all up to you, y'know."

"There're more Maggie Maes here than one can shake a stick at." John ogled the sidewalks.

"Did you hear a word I just said, Lennon?"

"It's up to me," John paraphrased.

Allan sighed and scanned for The Kaiserkeller sign. "At any rate, until 16 October, this is hearth'n'home, lads. And it's a home like none you've ever known!"

"Like none other, indeed!" Woody chuckled deeply, his heavy Caribbean accent filling every word with mystery. "Handcuffs, whips, and feather dusters…there's nothing Hamburg hasn't got!"

"Just make sure it doesn't give *you* a thing or two you don't want!" Al grinned.

"There it is, Allan man, straight ahead. Right where we left it, eh?" Woody had spotted the huge, brightly blinking sign. It read:

Kaiserkeller
Derry and The Seniors von Liverpool

"Hasn't budged an inch, has it?" Allan smiled, manoeuvring the van over to the curb and slowing to a stop. A cluster of childish "prossies" waved and giggled as the rattletrap vehicle and its predominantly male cargo came to a halt. Allan chuckled, winked, and gave them "thumbs up." And when Beryl smacked him on the arm, the girls twittered and flounced around in their thigh-high skirts. "It does appear they've missed us, Woody…got the welcomin' committee out in the street, as it were."

Woody quickly wriggled into his jacket and popped a stick of gum in his mouth. "Stand back, lads! One minute longer, and I'd break a thousand hearts." He was the first on the street.

"I'll take the lads round to meet Koschmider," Allan called out after his friend.

"You do that," Woody yelled over his shoulder. "And later on, I'll take 'em round with me, and we'll make the *really important* introductions."

"Make mine Greta!" Paul shouted, eyeing a buxom blonde on Woodbine's left.

"'Ullo Heidi! How's your grandfather 'n them?" John said.

The girls, who spoke only limited English, covered their mouths and giggled. But when Woody displayed an impressive collection of ten pound notes, the females burst into enthusiastic German and led him quickly down the street. Lord Woodbine's contagious laughter covered The Beatles in smiles.

"Tch, tch, *mein Herr*!" John turned to Pete as the others chuckled and filed off the van. "Goosestep it up, son. Sieg one, heil two, sieg three, heil four. Get on with it, eh?"

"Bugger off," Pete snapped, his nerves frayed by the cramped, aromatic quarters, "I've had enough of your banal commentaries."

"Off the bus, both o'you!" Allan intervened. "Koschmider's not waitin' around while the two of you square up. E-fuggin'-nough!"

Pete disembarked, looking slowly this way and that over hunched-up shoulders. He wondered what Mo would have to say about the element in which he now moved – the crowd of degenerates hustling to unspeakable destinations illuminated by bright marquee lights. He moved cautiously, feeling out of place, jumping as Allan slammed the minibus doors.

John stretched on the sidewalk and grumbled about leaving the gear unattended on the van roof.

One of their amplifiers, the Vox, was "on loan" from Liverpool College of Art. The other, a brand new Alpico, had been recently purchased to highlight the sound of McCartney's new, if inexpensive, solid body guitar. Both amps were covered with a stained, thin tarpaulin and attached to the van with a rope, but that was far from adequate on the Grosse Freiheit. It was not the place to leave valuables unattended.

"Barry! Hey Barry!" Al hailed his brother-in-law, motioning him over. "Keep an eye on this stuff, eh? Harrison's got his mum's tin o'scones on board, y'know. We'd hate to lose *that*, right?"

"Yes, they're all I've had to eat all day." Barry rubbed his hollow belly and smiled. "I'll stay here and guard it with dear life."

Allan grinned and elbowed his brother-in-law good-naturedly.

"Who's laggin' behind now, manager?" John upbraided him from The Kaiserkeller entrance.

"Right, c'mon Al." Paul chipped in. "We're all dead creased, y'know."

"Let's get on with it," Stu sighed.

"I want to hear Derry in action." George thumbed towards the door.

"I thought you were worried about your miserable little amplifiers here," Allan fumed. "In y'er in such a fuggin' rush, I can disregard directions to Barry and let that Alpico of yours take a solo tour of the city, McCartney. I'm sure there's plenty around Hamburgy-berg who'd love to show it the sights, as it were."

"Yeah, yeah, yeah," John opened the door and waved Allan in ahead of them. "Great job. Good security. We bleedin' love you. Let's get on with it."

"Right. On with the show." George echoed.

Allan shook his head, but he followed the boys inside.

****

The Kaiserkeller
38 Grosse Freiheit
Hamburg

Bruno Koschmider was John's worst nightmare – a bull-necked, humourless cripple. He was a man without a smile or even a hint of one, a veteran of Hitler's Panzer Division, a tyrant who belted out orders with a hand-held truncheon to back them up. Rumour had it that Koschmider had once been a circus clown and a fire-eater, but there was no evidence of carnival frivolity now. The man before them was all business and authority, a far cry from the accommodating Allan Williams whose only iron clad rule was to have no rules and who feigned toughness while befriending his clients.

The interpreter traveling with The Beatles, George Steiner, made the formal introductions while Koschmider nodded, evaluating The Beatles as if purchasing a crew of able-bodied field hands. His eyes glistened, and he licked his lips. Nobody, except Allan, said much of anything. It was apparent that even though Allan chattered on pleasantly, Bruno Koschmider understood little and wanted to understand even less.

As John watched the short, square-bodied German size him up with his squint-eyed stare, John's flesh crawled. Vice and licentiousness were not foreign to those who knew Liverpool 8 well, but that didn't begin to describe the aura Koschmider emanated.

"Cor! Great place, eh?" George nudged him.

John looked around, trying to submerge his thoughts about the club owner and concentrate on the club itself. George was right. The Kaiserkeller was incredible. The room was twenty times the size of The Jacaranda, and it actually had a décor – a nautical theme. Draped netting – encasing sparkling blue and green glass floats – hung from the ceiling, and captain's wheels adorned the walls. Brass portholes gleamed. Customers laughed and talked and clustered around ample tables. And the bar, as large as The Jacaranda itself, was carved in the shape of a ship.

"Put yer eyes back in yer head, lads," Allan cautioned as they slowly turned and looked around them, "Y'er not playin' here, remember?"

"It's bleedin' fabulous – this!" Paul was radiant.

"You're *not playin'* here," Allan tried again.

"'Ullo, Al. 'Ullo, Beatles." It was Howie Casey, Derry and the Seniors' lead singer. He was taking a short break between sets. "Welcome to The Reeperbahn, lads, home of vice and vice versa!"

"Casey." John acknowledged him.

"It's fantastic – this!" George smiled at Howie and Koschmider in turn. Koschmider nodded at the obvious admiration the British boys had for his remarkable club.

"Yeah, it's great – The Kaiserkeller." Howie shook hands with Allan. "Al done all right by us...up to now."

"Up to now!" Allan sputtered. It was easy to push his buttons.

"This is goin' to be great – this place." Pete played air drums enthusiastically.

"But you realize you're not playin' here, right?" Howie raised an eyebrow at Allan.

"I've tried to tell them that," Al shrugged.

"You're on at The Indra," Howie emphasized. "On *down* the Grosse Freiheit, at the other end. This is number 38. You're at 58, mates."

"Yeah, what of it?" John chewed his gum nonchalantly.

"Didn't you tell 'em, Al?" Howie asked. Then he looked at John. "Didn't he tell you The Indra's a strip club...just like the New Cabaret Artistes, y'know?"

"Shite!"

"C'mon Al!"

"It's a fuggin' joke, right?"

"It's not a strip club," Allan raised his hands to fend them off. "It's a..."

"Bugger of a place – the Indra." Howie rubbed the back of his neck where the guitar strap had been rubbing for several hours. "Ugly, quiet, off the beaten path. No one much goes down there. No one normal, anyrate."

"No one goes to Indra," Koschmider understood that much and repeated it loudly. "But," he pointed at The Beatles, "*you* will make it Kaiserkeller."

"Hell of a long way to come for somethin' like that, isn't it?" Howie shook his head.

"Hell of a long way," Stu repeated.

"We go now." Koschmider pointed to the door.

"Do somethin', Al! We aren't up for that sort of gig!" Paul stepped up.

"Yeah, Al," George looked worried. "Straighten it out."

"It's not all that bad," Allan began, nervously. "I mean, it's a venue, isn't it – a foreign venue just like you asked for?"

Koschmider slapped his thigh with a meaty hand. "We go now."

"Better do as he says," Allan urged them forward. "Let's just go check it out, right? Have an open mind, yeah? Look at it as a challenge. A provin' ground, of sorts."

"This way, Peedles." Koschmider limped awkwardly towards the door.

"*Jawohl*," John muttered under his breath, but when Bruno turned on him, John threw the club owner a large Cheshire grin.

"It appears we're off." Paul fell in line.

"Right. It appears," Pete sighed heavily.

Howie Casey watched The Beatles slouch away. Even though he had refused to be a part of the letter that The Seniors had written to Allan about the band, Howie nevertheless expected the worst. The Beatles weren't equal to the challenges and rigours that Hamburg demanded. In fact, they'd *never* been "up to par" with the other Liverpool groups. The Beatles, he was certain, would make a miserable showing in Hamburg. They didn't have the repertoire, the stamina, the talent, or the charisma to make it in a town like this.

****

The Indra Club
58 Grosse Freiheit
Hamburg

The minibus puttered out of the neon into a hushed, streetlamp section of the Grosse Freiheit Strasse. The crowd was thinner here, tougher. At one corner two Aussie sailors were "puttin' the boot in" on some brute who looked like he probably deserved anything he was getting. Still, none of them could watch it. Stuart turned away.

"And for the last fuggin' time, regardless of what Casey has to say," Allan went on, "it's *not* a fffuggin' strip club! I mean…it was once, all right? But that's all water under the bridge, as they say."

"No worry, Peedles." Bruno had joined them in the van, sitting in

Woody's accustomed place, "Indra has not strippers there. Be sure."

"Well, we won't back them, y'know," Paul told his new employer, smiling as much as his tone would allow.

"We've had enough of that, ta very much," John spat out bluntly, although he smiled and batted his eyelashes.

Bruno gave directions in German, and Steiner passed them along to Al. "He says to slow down. Over there. Yes, to the right. Edge up a bit. Park there."

Koschmider nodded towards a dark, apparently deserted building – a structure of little note except for its neon Indian elephant, hanging over the street and emitting a weak, pea-green light.

"Indra Club!" Koschmider announced, waving his hand demonstratively.

"That's no club." Pete's face was solemn.

"Where's the marquee and our names all illuminated, then?" George leaned forward and squinted as if his eyes were playing tricks on him.

"Names…in…lights," Paul spoke slowly to Koschmider as if he were talking to a child. "Mar - quee? Beatles von Liverpool, y'know?"

George Steiner rattled off some phrases in German, and Koschmider nodded. He motioned them all to follow him inside.

"No one'll even bleedin' know we're here,"* Pete muttered.

"Yeah, well, they found The Casbah all the way out in West fuggin' Derby, didn't they?" John shot back.

Allan raised an eyebrow at the unexpected optimism. Allan would've never expected the boy to be so tolerant. Lennon was obviously playing the hand out, down to the very last card.

Once inside the lobby, Koschmider grinned a wide jack-o-lantern grin and pointed to a small poster affixed to the Indra's interior wall. "There! Names!" he said.

"Ah! 'The Famous Beatles from Liverpool, England!'" John read in his best thespian's voice.

"Great! Great. Now that's all right, isn't it, wacks?" Allan tried to sound cheery.

"But it's *inside* – this advertisement!" Paul thwacked it with the back of his hand. "Shouldn't it be on the exterior of the building, y'know? *Outside?*"

"And it's microscopic as well," Pete complained.

"Let me grab me specs!" John teased, leaning forward and straining to see, "Oh, there it is! Remarkable advert, Herr Koschmider."

"Don't get eggy, John," Allan warned.

"I don't like this place much,"* George sniffed.

"What's to like?" Paul echoed.

Bruno pushed the interior door open and nodded. "Come in, Peedles! Come in. You will see!"

"I think we're obliged to trail after him," Stu looked back at the others.

"Into the bowels of the place, as it were," John said.

Paul took a deep breath and held his nose as if going for a dive. "Here goes, then."

And one by one – silent, disgusted, deeply disappointed – they filed in. John's jaw clenched in a vice-grip as he scanned the place for any shred of possibility. His eyes moved rapidly, trying to find a saving grace.

"The Kaiserkeller it isn't," Stu was stunned.

"Dead awful," George whispered.

"Right," was all Paul could manage to say.

A low, raised landing that John supposed was a stage of some sort made an ungainly lump in the worn carpet. John stepped up on it and raised an imaginary flag. "I hereby claim this land for Mother England! Long may we rave!"

"Look," George flicked one of the tattered, red-shaded table lamps on and off with feigned wonder. "Here's a nice, little lamp. And all electric, y'know!"

"Electric, is it?" Paul joined him. "Let's have a look at that."

"And curtains as well," George moved around the empty room like a detective. "Premium stuff. All brand new...once...ages ago."

"Ah, tatty velvet. Excellent!" Paul trailed along behind him.

"Thick enough to totally muffle any hint of sound." Pete shook his head in frustration. "Could they possibly be any thicker – these drapes?"

"Bruno," Allan saw his opportunity to get in a bit of confidential business. "You did manage to get the work permits, right?"

"Per-mits?" Bruno threw a confused look in Steiner's direction. Steiner conveyed the word in German.

"Ah, yes, permits." Koschmider turned back to Allan. "Not needed. Everything okay."

"Not needed?" Allan's face went a deep red, "*Not needed?*" His eyes flicked rapidly from George Steiner to Koschmider and back again, "Listen, Koschmider, George Harrison's underage, as I've told you repeatedly before. He's only uh – seventeen, y'know. We'll all be hauled off in a fuggin' battle-taxi, if the German police get wind of this. We can't just shrug it off and be done with it! We've got to have legal papers, as it were!"

Steiner translated to the club owner.

"Listen," Allan went on as soon as the translation had ended, "I had one fffffffuggin' helluva time just crossin' the effin' borders with the lads in tow. It took genuine, Welsh finaglin' to convince the local powers-that-be that the lads were just students on holiday. With all those amps and guitars strapped to the fuggin' roof and the nine of us loaded to the gills inside, they were hard fuggin' pressed to believe a thing I had to say. But I pulled it off – relyin' on the fact that it would be the *only* time I'd skirt the law, as it were. I trusted we'd have the legal paperwork as soon as we got here!"

Steiner translated again, and Koschmider responded rapidly in German.

"Trouble here?" John's voice cut through the various languages. He had radar for disaster where his band was concerned.

Allan and Bruno stared at one another for a moment. Neither of them wanted to divulge their secrets. The contract had been signed, and the primary parties were satisfied. The Beatles had been transported to Hamburg, and the authorities had discreetly looked the other way, even on the flimsiest of excuses. Why stir up discontent this late in the game? Why involve John?

"No trouble." Allan forced his face to relax. "And I don't remember invitin' you into this conversation, Lennon."

"What's up?" Paul was at John's elbow.

"There's some sort of trouble here…" John began.

"Everything o-kay," Bruno insisted, slapping his palm emphatically with the back of his other hand. "We go now."

"Where now?" John was sure they weren't being told everything. "What's up, Al?"

"We *go!*" Koschmider repeated, pointing to the door. "Bambi Filmkunsttheater! Now!"

"What's that, and why're we goin' there?" John refused to budge.

"Whatever it is, I'm all for it." Pete followed Koschmider. "Any place is better 'n this, right? I mean, there's no way it could get worse."

But it did. The Indra was a hundred times better than Number 33 Paul-Roosen Strasse, the Bambi Kino Filmkunsttheater. It was a dive. Crumbling and disgusting, littered with debris and graffiti, the old cinema building shamefully squatted in its own deterioration.

"The Bambi!" Bruno pronounced before launching into a soliloquy in German. George Steiner listened and translated.

"He says," Steiner told the group, "he owns this building. He uses it as a cinema for American westerns. He says westerns are very popular these days."

"Well, *I* wouldn't go in there…even if Gene Autry himself were live and in person, y'know." Paul said it for them all.

"Filthy, isn't it?" John leaned down and gave the building the once over through the mini-van glass.

"Worse than the last place," George sighed. "And I didn't think *that* was humanly possible."

"Why are we here?" Stu looked pointedly at Steiner.

It was John who had the answer. "Don't you know, son?" He gestured his thumb towards the building, "It's hell, y'know. We've all died, and this is our just desert. We should've eaten our peas and learned our catechisms when we had the fuggin' chance. Now we're in for it, as it were!"

"Shirrup, John!" Allan smiled at Koschmider, hoping the man's

English was as rudimentary as he pretended. This deal had been too difficult to negotiate to see it go sour this late in the game.

But whether Bruno understood The Beatles' comments or not, he was unfazed. He merely opened the minibus door and lumbered towards the building, never glancing behind him. "Inside Peedles! Bring things. Come."

They had no alternative.

Gunfire and the sound of horses' hooves filled the paltry, ill-furnished cinema lobby. The Bambi smelled more of urine than popcorn, and there were no uniformed ushers with torches waiting to show customers to their seats. In several places, the faded maroon carpet was completely worn through to concrete beneath, and the portion that was still intact was heavily stained. Cigarette butts were crushed everywhere. A large, dark bug of some variety crawled nonchalantly up the wall.

Koschmider nodded for them to follow him down a cramped hallway off the lobby, and John stayed on his heels, imitating Koschmider's limp when the German's back was turned.

Near the end of the narrow, concrete hallway, Koschmider and the line of Liverpudlians came to an abrupt halt. Here the sounds of the American movie were even louder.

John turned and informed the group, "The Diddyman's daft, y'see. He thinks we want to be in films."

"I've always had a certain amount of yee-ha and giddyup," George smiled. The others laughed lightly.

But all humour vanished as Koschmider shoved a door open and pulled at a suspended light bulb hanging from the ceiling, illuminating a six-by-eight foot storage cell directly behind the movie screen. The windowless, concrete cubicle housed two camp beds and a dilapidated, ripped, and faded sofa – nothing more.

"You sleep here," Koschmider told them.

"But there's gunplay in here," Paul hoped it was all some sort of joke. The noise from the movie screen was assaulting.

"We're not janitorial, y'understand," George teased.

But Koschmider didn't hint a smile. He stared at them with cold eyes.

"Hear, hear, there's only two cots in here, Herr." John tossed his bag on one and nodded for Stu to take the other. George rapidly claimed the sofa.

"So what're *we* supposed to do, then?" Paul was wide-eyed, incredulous.

"Come." Bruno moved on.

Two smaller, darker, dirtier closets opened at the very end of the hall. Although no door hung on the empty hinges and no cots were visible, the five-by-six cells appeared to be their final destination. Paul fumbled inside one doorframe, searching for a light switch, but all he retrieved was a handful of grit. He reached up for a pull string, but brought down only a sizeable cobweb.

"Koschmider says you'll be *sleeping* here," Steiner translated to Paul and Pete, "so there'll be no need for lights, per se. By the time you get back here each evening, he says you'll be more than ready to fall asleep."

The tension in the tiny hall was incredible. The boys stared at Allan and then at Koschmider with defiance that had been simmering since their first glimpse of the mini-van days ago. With gunfire and Indian war-whoops blaring in their ears, confrontation sizzled all around them.

"Absolutely ludicrous!" Pete was the first to explode. "You're expectin' *us* to live in total, bleedin' darkness like bleedin' bats in a bleedin' cave? Is that it?"

"I wouldn't do that fer a big clock!" George's old Scouse adage had never been more appropriate. "It's sordid – this place."

"The Black Hole of Calcutta," Pete went on.

"You're out of yer fuggin' mind if you think…" Stu began.

"Look lads," Allan stepped up, his eyes pleading, "You're right, you're absolutely right. I don't blame you a bit for bein' put off, as it were. I mean, this isn't exactly what I anticipated when the contract stated 'adequate lodging.' But for right now," Allan employed every ounce of managerial finesse, "why not give it a whirl, eh? I mean, you've come this far'n all. And it's not like you lot haven't bunked on the tables at the New Cabaret Artistes, with only Woody's rancid tablecloths pulled up around yer shoulders, right. Remember that?"

He had their attention.

"And in that minibus 'cross Scotland, you slept God knows where and God knows how. Truth told, Stu's flat isn't *that* much cleaner than it is right here, is it?"

They chuckled a little.

"Cummoffit!" Stu pretended to be insulted. "Just because they call the place 'The Beatnik Horror…'"

Allan smiled at them. They were softening. There was a little hope.

"Look lads," he said. "I'll admit it's no fffffuggin' Adelphi Hotel – but what the hell, right? It's a venue. All the way, yeah?"

As Allan conferred with his group, Koschmider turned and roughly elbowed down the tiny hall. He didn't care what "The Peedles" thought about the premises, and he didn't wait for the consensus of the band. As far as he was concerned, The Bambi was home for the five straggly, British boys.

They could like it or not. This was all he had to offer and all he would offer. Williams had signed the contract, and the deal was final.

"One more thing," George Steiner stepped forward. "As we entered the lobby, there was another hallway, off to the right. If you take that hallway, Koschmider says, you'll find the cinema toilet. Since the cinema will be closed by the time you return each evening, Herr Koschmider has explained you may consider it yours…to wash up."

"A…public loo?" Stu almost stammered.

"And what if we want to wash up, say mid-afternoon?" George asked.

"Then you'll have to learn to share," Steiner shrugged.

Without waiting to hear more, John was off down the hall, across the lobby, and over to the other side of the theatre. He wrestled with the sticky loo door, finally kicking it open. The tiny, box of a room reeked of urine and had only one milky, broken mirror.

"There's only a fuggin' urinal here!" John's veneer of optimism was wearing thin. He turned to the others who'd followed him.

"But plenty of cold water," Steiner stated. "And Koschmider said each of you will be given a towel."

"I'll spit in his eye and blind him!" John lapsed into Scouse.

"Right. We'll put 'im in a sling – Koschmider," Paul agreed.

"We'll put a fluke's gob on 'im!" George joined the word-assault.

"Yeah…marmalise the fuggin' bastard!"

Then suddenly, without explanation, the luckless Beatles began to laugh. They laughed hysterically, punching each other playfully and shoving Allan about in the miserable, squalid hallway. Stu leapt onto John's back and made a mad charge for Paul. Paul ducked out of the way and spun around, brandishing an invisible matador's cape. George applauded and cheered them on as Pete jabbed at the bull with an invisible sword.

There was no use explaining the antics of The Beatles to the befuddled Germans. There was no use trying to make sense of them to an outsider. Allan backed up and let the boys work it out for themselves.

"Home, sweet fuggin' home!" Stu yelled at the top of his lungs.

"Break the news to muvver…"* George began.

"…tell'er that I luvver, tell'er that I'll never more roam!"* John shouted back.

"Hang me hat, Maggie, and bring me a pipe!" Paul sing-songed, making up a tune. "Fetch me the slippers. I'm home for the night!"

Koschmider hobbled up rapidly, "shushing" their shouts and laughter, speaking quickly in German, and signaling them to be quiet. But Al intervened.

"Listen, Bruno," he put a hand on Koschmider's shoulder, "Let 'em be, all right? I mean, there's a few things lackin' here, as I see it. Hot water, blankets, showers, lights, towels…"

Steiner followed them and began to translate. But the negotiations were cut short by John's voice behind them.

"It's all right, Al." John's almond eyes were at peace. "What's done's done, isn't it? Never mind the details. We'll just play our music and see how it goes.* That's what we came here for, right?"

"But…"

"We'll take it as it is." John held both hands up. "What the fuggin'ell, right? As you said before, we'll give it a try."

"Who knows?" Paul looked at the others for confirmation. "We might be able to rent somethin' better after a bit...when things are lookin' up, y'know."

"You will get towels, blankets...and three more cots," Steiner translated Bruno's latest offer. "And...you're free to use The Indra facilities as well. There's hot water over there."

The boys nodded.

"Yeah, all right," John said.

"Well, if all's settled here, then," Steiner stepped forward, clapping his hands together, "Herr Koschmider says we're a bit behind schedule. We'll need to leave as soon as possible."

"Leave?" It was Allan's turn to be taken by surprise.

"For The Indra." Steiner hated to say it. He was sure they'd kill the messenger this time.

"Show!" Koschmider barked. "Show tonight! Beatles von Liverpool!"

"Now look here," Allan's cheeks flushed all over again, "that's fuggin' lunacy, Koschmider! It's been thirty-six hours since any of us've slept! Our wheels got stuck in a tram track, and we were almost knocked down en masse! We tangled with a woman whose boot we bumped, and we've ridden in a fuggin' pencil box for days! The *last* thing the lads are prepared to do is put on a show at this point in time!"

Koschmider look at Steiner, and Steiner looked back. No one had to translate Allan's anger. It was hard to miss.

Pulling a long, folded document from his coat pocket, Koschmider licked his thumb as he flipped through the pages. Then he pointed rapidly to one section and held it over for Steiner to read. The interpreter's lips moved as he scanned the paragraph at the bottom of the page. His face blanched.

"It's your contract, Allan." Steiner took the document in his own hands and held it out. "Look. Look at this section."

And there it was, in black and white. The Beatles were to perform every night, Monday through and including Sunday, four and a half hours every weeknight, six hours on Saturday and Sunday nights, beginning 17 August and ending 16 October 1960. There was no getting around it. Today was 17 August on anyone's calendar.

Allan read it several times, running his hand through his curls.

"Yeah, all right...I *see* it," Allan admitted, "but surely you..."

"Let's get on with it then." John's voice sounded behind Allan's shoulder. "If we came here to play rock'n'roll, then what the hell're we doin' in the fuggin' loo of some rancid theatre?"

Allan turned and looked at the boys, reading their tired, gaunt faces. He hesitated – afraid to take Lennon's word as gospel. So often, John pushed them beyond their endurance. Al waited for confirmation.

"John's right," Paul nodded. "We've come all this way to work, and if that's what we're here to do, let's do it, then."

"We've a show to put on, y'know," George grinned quickly.

"At the soon to be 'famous' Indra," Stu smiled.

"And the longer we're here," John pushed past Allan, "the longer it'll be 'til we're back again. Y'er holdin' up the wheels o'progress, Manager."

"Off we go!" George tagged along after John.

"You're actually quite decisive these days, aren't you?" Paul was on George's heels.

"Thasso?" George smiled.

"It's his way." John pushed out the front door of The Bambi Kino and headed for the van. "C'mon, Koschmider!" he called back over his shoulder. "We've an empty house waitin' on us, son. We've a fuggin' show to do for no one!"

And laughing because of and in spite of their fatigue, The Beatles settled into the minibus one more time and began to discuss the first song on their play list.

Lewisohn and Miles have the Kaiserkeller at 36 Grosse Freiheit and the Indra at 58. Harry and Giuliano have the Kaiserkeller at 38 Grosse Freiheit and the Indra at 34. Allan Williams gives no address. I have used Lewisohn's and Miles' addresses because Williams emphasizes that the Indra was in a completely different part of the Grosse Freiheit, not just a few doors away.

Williams says The Beatles had three rooms at the Bambi Kino. (Clayson, who relies upon Stu's sister as a primary source, agrees.) Lewisohn and Salewicz mention only one room and Goldman says they had "a couple of unlit cubicles." Miles says they had "two rooms."

Bill Harry gives great details about three rooms, and his account matches Pete Best's perfectly. I have used details from Best and Harry in this chapter.

*I have tried, when possible, to use the actual language of The Beatles in this chapter. When I have quoted from Williams' excellent account, The Man Who Gave the Beatles Away, *I have used the asterisk to indicate that.*

I have also employed Pete Best's fascinating Beatle! *as a primary source. Both Best's and Williams' books go into much greater detail than I have and should be read in their entirety.*

Some of the conversation in this chapter is, of course, imagined. All events are documented.

Recommended viewing for those interested in this chapter of Beatles' history: "Backbeat"

18 August 1960
The Bambi Filmkunsttheater
("The Bambi Kino")
Hamburg
3:00 am

John lay perfectly still on the rickety camp bed and stared into the darkness. With the slow motion of extreme fatigue, he raised his right arm, took a drag on the last of his Woodbines, and too tired to exhale, let the hot air smoulder in his chest.

It was a strip club after all, he thought, finally exhaling in a tight line. *Or at least it was 'til tonight.*

Only yesterday, on the fantastic hopes that "The Fabulous Beatles" would transform The Indra – just as Derry and The Seniors had transformed The Kaiserkeller – Koschmider had fired his entourage of strippers. But he'd never informed his patrons about the new directives or the changes they entailed. And tonight, when the peep-show aficionados shuffled in to see "their girls" in action, there had been no girls to see.

It was a disaster all 'round, John rolled on to his side, unable to sleep, though he was exhausted beyond all imagination. *A crap place and a crap audience...eight or nine randy, old men who trudged down to the dark end of The Reeperbahn in search of mounds of fatty flesh. And all they found was five men performin' rock'n'roll in a language they couldn't even understand! Agggh.*

He rolled over on his side and tucked his arm under his head in lieu of a pillow.

No wonder The Seniors were so fuggin' smug! They've got the Kaiserkeller...and what d'we have? Eight, furious ol' bastards who hate us even more than we hate them! I mean, even at The Casbah, in someone's basement with no liquor license at all, we had hundreds and hundreds in a night. But here we are – in the fuggin' middle o'The Reeperbahn with tipplers en masse – and what've we got? Eight lousy patrons!

"Asleep yet?" Stu knew he wasn't.

"Yeah, fuggin' snorin'." John rolled onto his back again.

"It was just the first night, y'know."

"First night in hell's no different from the last, Stu."

"And no worse, either."

"How's that help?" John took another drag on his cig. "You're sayin' I'll get used to it, then?"

"No." Stu leaned on his elbow and looked at the direction of John's voice in the darkness, "I'm sayin' you'll *change* it."

"Change hell?"

"You'll find a way."

"Right." John quoted *Paradise Lost.* "'Better to reign in hell than serve in heaven.' Is that it?"

"Somethin' like that." Stu flopped back down on the mouldy tarp. "Blasphemous, but determined."

For a moment, there was quiet.

"I thought I'd wring Bruno's neck if he yelled 'Mak show!' at us one more time," George piped up from the couch.

John sat up and tossed his cigarette onto the floor. It was too dark to see where it had landed or crush it out.

"As if something magical would happen if only we played harder and harder," Stu agreed.

"At least Rumplestilskin had straw to transform into gold." John scratched his shoulder where the torn, wool blanket irritated his skin. "A fuggin' alchemist, I'm not."

"Isthasso?" Stu rolled towards the wall, overtired but determined to find sleep somehow. "Well, we'll see about that."

Someone down the hall coughed in the silence. And there was more scratching as the course blankets did their worst.

"We'll have to put a few new songs together, y'know." John collapsed back onto the flimsy cot. "I mean, I know we played on no sleep at all tonight – but face it, we were shite. And we were flat outta songs by the last set."

No one answered. Someone was breathing heavily.

"Toward the end, I woulda resorted to "Happy fuggin' Birthday" if there'd been anyone in the club celebratin'! When we dredged up "Cumberland Gap" from the tombs of skiffle, I knew we were done for. We'd played everything we knew – twice."

Soft, muffled snoring.

"Stu!"

John got no response.

"Sutcliffe!"

"Give it up, John," George's drowsy voice answered from across the room. "We'll deal with it all tomorrow, y'know."

"Yeah," John stared wide-eyed at the ceiling. "First thing

tomorrow…first thing, we're goin' over to The Kaiserkeller…as soon as we're up."

"Yerrokay. Right."

"And we're askin' questions of The Seniors, and we're stealin' every fuggin' song and chord progression they know."

"Yeah. Right."

"And then we're comin' back here and…"

"Can't we just *do* it, John, and not talk about it, then?"

Silence. George took the opportunity to roll towards the wall.

"We've only got one day," John muttered, "one day before we have to play a six-hour set, and we could barely make it through a coupla hours tonight, as it were!"

"Y'er sayin' everythin' but your prayers in there, John!" Paul yelled from down the hallway. "Give it a rest, right?"

"Shirrup, y'cack-handed son of an Irishman!" John yelled back.

But John stopped the chatter and began strategizing instead – devising ways to change their act. When he fell asleep, he was listing out all of the songs he'd like The Beatles to learn to play. He could think of at least a dozen, right off the bat.

****

The Indra
58 Grosse Freiheit Strasse
Hamburg

They gave "Hound Dog" the standard treatment, and Bruno wasn't impressed. He marched around the club scowling, his demeanour reminiscent of his Panzer days, and his large, wooden truncheon repeatedly slapping his palm.

"*Mach shau! Mach shau!*" he screamed when the sound died away. And the sparse audience muttered and mumbled in agreement.

"Too Much Monkey Business" and "Long Tall Sally" were mediocre. Bruno goaded the band to press harder, to give more. He shouted and waved the bludgeon wildly.

"What's he want now?" George looked at John with confused eyes. Their act had always been good enough for the Liverpool crowds. The audiences in Scotland had seemed pleased with them. What had changed here in Germany, just a few hundred miles away across the tiny channel?

"I'll tell you what he fuggin' wants." John talked with a cigarette in his teeth. "He wants the five of us here to turn this filthy, God-forsaken place into another bleedin' Kaiserkeller – that's what he wants! He told Pete so just the other day."

"But," George objected, "The Kaiserkeller's got decorations, paper napkins, a real marquee, and a great location! It's got atmosphere, hasn't it?"

"Well son," John waved his hand at the hideous room around them, "at The Indra, that's us. *We're* the atmosphere. We're the attraction, as it were."

"And how're we supposed to do that on four hours of sleep and two pounds fifty per day?" Paul was just as discouraged.

John drained the last half of his lager in one long gulp, leaving only a splash that he poured into his hair. Then he turned back to the microphone and screamed at the top of his lungs, laughing hysterically when the dozen or so patrons in the bar startled, wide-eyed.

"Let's...*mach....shau!*" John yelled, imitating Bruno's voice. And with another crazed scream, he launched into a raucous cover of "Money."

The audience hardly moved, convinced that the boys on the stage were having a breakdown right in front of them. Tired and disgusted and full of angry adrenalin, John began running and sliding across the low platform as he sang. Paul turned up the Alpico, full throttle, and joined John as they danced and rammed each other, head on. Pete drummed with an intensity that threatened to damage the skins. Even George and Stu laughed together at the nonsense.

For the next three hours, The Beatles ripped through their play list, screaming at the audience, laughing with each other, and hurling themselves into chaotic music. They heard the word "lunatics" bandied about. They writhed and jumped all over the stage and gave Bruno more than he'd ever demanded.

That night, there was talk on the street of a drummer with baby-blue tortoise shell drums whose eyes could "read your soul." There was gossip about a pool-eyed, left-handed guitarist who was as beautiful as he was talented, and about a strange, wispy lad in dark glasses whose surrealism excited the imagination. There was talk of a band from England, and someone said they were down at The Indra.

"The Indra? Nein, that's a strip club, is it not?" the puzzled would reply.

But many claimed The Indra had changed. The following evening, the crowd at The Indra swelled to twenty-two. Thirty-five patrons found the club the evening after that. And on the following night, every single one of the tables at the remote club was taken.

The word on the street was that the metamorphosis was something to see.

****

"Be Bop A Lula" went down with contorted, Gene Vincent gyrations. John could make himself into the Igor of rock'n'roll with very little effort. In fact, he scared some clients.

Then he shape-shifted into another persona – the confident rocker who screamed out "Hippy, Hippy Shake" in a way that seemed immoral, even on The Reeperbahn. With ruthlessness in his voice, he tore through "Slippin' and A-Slidin'"" as his eyes raked over each female in the crowd. Giving the lyrics a suggestiveness no one could miss, John made the performance an invitation. It was perfect for Hamburg. John was in his element.

By the time Allan, Beryl, Barry, and Woody prepared to depart at week's end, The Indra had an audience, and Bruno was ecstatic. People were filtering down to the building with the dull neon elephant sign to see "The Fabulous Peedles," to evaluate the band for themselves.

Curiosity had pulled them in, but once there, they stayed. Stu said it was the alchemy he had predicted John would perform. John and Paul chalked it up to hard work.

"All right, then," Allan got the five boys together to issue his final edict, "You've gotten what you fuggin' asked for, right? You've made it to Hamburg, as it were. Now y'er on yer own…and we'll see what you can do before October rolls around."

"I'd say we've done quite well already, haven't we?" Paul's eyes swept the room, brimming with people – all new customers, all *their* customers.

"Pffft! Y'er the new kids on the block, McCartney, that's all!" Allan waved them off, "You're still baskin' in the charm of novelty. Nothin' to write home about…yet."

"Tell that to John!" Paul slapped his friend's arm. "He's been writin' home, *volumes*, every day…and not to Auntie Mimi, if you get me drift."

John shoved him and mumbled something Allan didn't catch.

"Yeah? Isthasso?" Allan turned on John, "Look Lennon, just keep yer randy little mind on the business here at hand, son. My advice to you is – do yer job and let the home fires stoke themselves, as it were."

"Sod off." John was already famous in his own mind. "I don't take instruction from you."

"Well, you'll take this!" Allan's face burned a bright red. "If yer concentration's not on what y'er doin', and if once I'm gone you revert back to standin' on that stage like one o'Lewises, that'll be the fuggin' end of the fuggin' Beatles, as far as I'm concerned. If you blow it here – after all I've done – then that's *it* for me, then. You're finished, as it were."

"And I thought Polonius was dead." John threw his eyes to the ceiling.

"Furthermore," Allan raged on, "don't think I won't know what's what over here! I've asked George Steiner *and* Bruno to send me updates and to keep me informed."

"German spies," George mumbled. "I shoulda known."

"And what's more," Allan wagged a finger at them, "don't think I won't be back...when you least expect it..."

"For a surprise inspection of the troops," Stu grumbled.

"It's very popular in these postwar days," Paul joined in.

"*Jawohl!*" John saluted.

"Pfffft!" Allan threw up both hands, exasperated. "Laugh it up, lads. But you'll be cryin' in your cups if you carry on in a casual manner over here. Any two-bit band with a buzz-on can grab a mike and sing rock'n'roll as well as you do! And that's the god's truth. So if you're really out to reach the 'toppermost of the poppermost' like you're always on about, you're gonna have to *mach shau,* as Bruno says. You're gonna have to rattle the fuggin' cage, lads! Be different! Stand out somehow."

"That's why we have Stu, isn't it?" Paul grinned.

"Ta very much," Stu flushed.

"All right, all right..." Allan began again.

"Goodbye, Al." Paul nodded towards the exit. "So long. Lovely visit, wasn't it?"

"There's the door, manager." John popped his chewing gum and looked bored.

George laughed softly and clapped Allan on the shoulder. "Glad you got to see us, Al!" he teased. "Come back anytime."

"Ungrateful bunch o'swine!" Allan muttered, but a smile played on his lips.

On the sidewalk, Beryl hugged them all. She reminded them to stop in at The Seaman's Mission for a breakfast of cornflakes and a cup of tea, and she mandated that they wash up at The Kaiserkeller at least once a week. Barry and George Steiner shook their hands and wished them luck. Woody gave them, once again, the name of his favourite physician.

When the goodbyes began to grow maudlin, John grabbed Allan by the arm and dragged him towards the minibus.

"Flee, Allan, flee!" he yelled madly. "Save yer family and yerself! Don't think of us! We'll stay here and wait for the reinforcements!"

And as the minibus pulled away from the curb to the sound of John singing "Oh Britannia" at the top of his lungs, Allan watched Paul and George saluting on the sidewalk and Pete chatting comfortably with Stu.

As he adjusted his rearview mirrors and crawled out into the heavy traffic, Allan wished he had the luxury of remaining in Hamburg for at least one more week...just to see what would happen at The Indra. If he knew The Beatles as well as he thought he did, Bruno was in for a long line of misery. And the German audiences were in for the show of their lives.

All events are documented; the conversation is conjecture.

3 October 1960
The Indra Club
Hamburg, Germany

"So that's it then." John feigned depression. "First they tell us to bring down the fuggin' house…"

"Like honest, good little lads," Paul injected.

"…then they give us *das boot* for makin' too fuggin' much noise and creatin' too fuggin' much furour, *mein Führer*!"

"Yeah," George rolled the amplifier cord carefully, looping it methodically over his elbow and shoulder, "we only did what we were told, and now we're bein' packed off…to The Kaiserkeller."

"Right." Pete threw his eyes to the ceiling and tried not to smile. "Imagine that!"

"It's all too easy – The Kaiserkeller," John mocked.

"At least here at The Indra," Paul carried the Art College's purloined Vox amplifier towards the door, "we had a bit of a challenge, y'know."

"Yeah. The Kaiserkeller's all too fuggin' easy…regular stage, huge crowds, and a marquee people can actually see…" John smiled.

"Yeah, who needs it?" George joined in.

"Well, rambullon, all o'ya," Pete laid a stained tarp across his calfskin drumhead, "but I'll be glad to give it a shot, if y'don't mind."

"Not you!" John gasped. "You wouldn't, would you? Not the rugged Pete Best?"

"I would, and I am," Pete returned, point-blank. "I'm up to here with dungeons and dirt! I'm tired of comin' to work in a rat hole half the size of me mum's basement, and makin' Koschmider wealthy when he's barely givin' us enough space, water, or bleedin' sunlight to keep us alive."

"So young to fade away," Paul sniffed.

John wiped an imaginary tear from his cheek.

"Hey, when's Rory 'n his group comin' to town, then?" Stu was as thrilled as the rest of them that The Hurricanes were headed to Hamburg to share the bill at The Kaiserkeller with them.

"Read for yerself, son." John dug in his pocket and handed his friend the latest Williams' post. Stu tried on his best Allan accent.

> *Dear Lads,*
> *Congrats! I'm happy to learn that your time in Hamburg is turning out as beneficial to you as well as Mr. Koschmider.*
> *However, I must say I warned you lot that you were playing entirely too loudly for The Indra Club. The ramifications of which have come back to haunt you. But truthfully, the blame is not all on your shoulders, as one cannot imagine a rock and roll band performing, as one would do in a morgue.*

They chuckled and shook their heads.

> *But a word to the wise: for the sake of your contract, I remind you to heed to all Koschmider tells you. He wrote to me asking if you lot would like your contract over there extended somewhat.*

"No," John sarcastically jammed his tongue behind his lower lip, "We'd all like to go home straight 'way and twiddle our thumbs for a fuggin' while, if ya don't mind. Ta."

"Always a popular pastime, that," Paul nodded.

"Shirrup, both ya," Stu began again.

> *I hear from Herr Koschmider that you boys only gyrate about the stage when unobserved, no one is in the audience...this is stupid and a suicidal attitude for any band to adopt*.*
> *I'm sure I've always preached to you that the public demand performers who can give them a show as well as play good music.*

"He's always pointin' that out, isn't he?" Paul looked at John. John patted his head and rubbed his belly in reply.

> *And trust me lads, I am repeating this once again because...*

"Because you're redundant and dead borin', as it were," John cut in.

> *...because Rory Storm and the Hurricanes are on their way to Hamburg and they have no inhibitions at all, period. Therefore, it would hurt me deeply, personally,* if I happened to discover that you lads were becoming second*

> *fiddle to The Hurricanes. And I'm one hundred per cent certain that this will be the case if you continue to stand about like one o'Lewises.*

"D'ya hear that Georgie?" John wagged a finger.
"If you stand about like one o'Lewises," Paul narrowed one eye, "you'll be hurtin' Allan deeply…"
"And personally as well." John straightened George's shoulders and lifted his chin.
Stu chuckled and went on with the missive.

> *I sincerely hope that you Beatles heed these words of advice as I take management of all my groups very seriously and such unimaginative behaviour could quickly cancel your future plans in Hamburg, lads… and unfortunately, with me as well.*

"We closed down an entire club because of outrageous performances!" Stu shook his head and handed the letter back to John. "We played our guts out in this rotten, god-forsaken hole. And here, Al's still about warnin' us that we'd better give it all we've got!"
"I'm thinkin' of firin' Pete here out of a cannon the next time Al's around," John looked serious.
"That's a stupid and suicidal attitude for any person to adopt, y'know," Paul mimicked Al.
George snickered and then hurried to kick the Indra's warped front door open as Paul and John dragged equipment out onto the sidewalk. Pete walked in and out as well, carrying his drum kit and placing it right where he wanted it. Stu walked the perimeter, doing one last check around the club – making sure they'd left nothing behind.
In record time, they'd emptied The Indra of everything Beatle. And they left it just as they'd found it – dirty, ragtag, and dark. None of them lingered to say goodbye. Not one of them stood looking back with nostalgic eyes at the nightspot that had been their home for the past six weeks.
Laughing, talking, and spilling nonsense, they gathered on the sidewalk in a tight circle. They smoked, stamped off the cold, and waited impatiently for Bruno's man to arrive with their transportation.
"So," Stu carefully eyed the shops and apartment windows all around them, "which one o'these buggers complained about the noise to the police, d'ya think?"
"They're all under suspicion until further notice," John stage-whispered.
"And we thank you, one and all!" George yelled as loudly as he could. "We're off to The Kaiserkeller, y'know! That's what your calls and letters

to the authorities have done for us, then! John, Paul, Stu, Pete, and me greatly appreciate the unsolicited endorsements! Good on yer...whoever you are!"

"I think it was that little old lady – right up there." Paul pointed to a lace-curtained window.

"Nah," Pete shook his head, "she's completely deaf – that one. Can't hear a bleedin' thing – that lady."

"But it makes for a great legend, doesn't it, son?" John grinned. "'We've heard 'twas the old lady above The Indra who had'em tossed out!' That's what they'll all say when we're rich and famous and livin' in the lap o'luxury."

"But it *wasn't* her, was it?" Pete gestured to the hundreds of other apartments topping the Grosse Freiheit shops. "It was almost certainly someone else altogether...or lots of someone elses, what have you."

"But that's the story we're goin' with." John shivered as the wind kicked up a bit. "History's half myth, y'know: King Arthur's sword, George Washington's cherry tree, Fin McCool's magical powers. It's the legend that lasts, son."

"Hey there, Grandma!" George yelled up from the street. "When we're famous, we're takin' you with us, Nin!"

"You'll be in all the books!" Paul shouted.

"Half as famous as the famous-famous us!" John yelled.

Pete tossed his cigarette down and shook his head at their insanity.

"So there y'have it, Randolph Peter." John bumped him gently, "Majority wins again. The old lady's in, as it were. It's a good story. It plays to a crowd."

"Speakin' of playin' to a crowd," Paul zipped up his jacket and folded his arms, "is Al comin' over when Rory arrives?"

John motioned the transport van to the curb, "As far as I know, the Williams watch-word hasn't been given."

Bruno's driver double-parked, and then edged between cars, moving with what speed his huge frame could muster.

"*Sieg heil*!" John raised a hand. "How's tricks in the baths these days, mate? We heard it's all a gas, as it were."

The driver scowled and gestured for them to load their gear. He wasted none of the few English words he knew on this bunch of ragged teenagers.

"'ullo there!" Paul nodded and grinned. "Lovely day, isn't it?"

"In the bus, Peedles." The man glared at them with condescension. "Hurry. Quickly. You are due."

"Y'know...you're like a muther to us all." John batted his eyelashes and grinned madly.

"Second only to Bruno, of course," George nodded.

"No conversation! Load gear!" the driver barked as he tapped his watch. "Tonight you play Kaiserkeller! Tonight on time!"

"Y'know, believe it or not, we've done this all before, Sonny Jim," George hissed. "It's only routine – this. We know gear-loadin' like back of our hands."

"But we wouldn't dream of bein' late." Paul winked and clicked his cheek.

"Not for a fuggin' date with fuggin' Bruno!" John shoved the last piece of equipment in and slammed the van door.

"Get in!" The driver ignored their barbs. "We must go now. Tonight you play The Kaiserkeller."

"Really?" George raised an eyebrow. "We'd no idea!"

"But it couldn't have come at a better time." John tapped the man's watch.

"Or to a better group," Paul nodded.

"Drive on, driver," John jumped in the van. "We've places to go."

"And hopefully," Paul held his hands up in prayer, "people to see."

The letter from Allan Williams is paraphrased. The actual letter may be seen in The Man Who Gave The Beatles Away, p. 160-161.

*Two phrases in this letter are actual and are quoted from Allan Williams. They are "this is a stupid and suicidal attitude for any band to adopt" and "it would hurt me deeply and personally."

All events are documented, except one:

Many sources supports the statement that an elderly lady living above The Indra complained about the noise that The Beatles made, and had them evicted from The Indra.

However, Pete Best and Bill Harry vehemently deny that the "the old woman upstairs story" is true. Because Pete is the singular primary source for this chapter, I have taken his word but have written one possible explanation for the Beatle myth.

The conversation is conjecture.

9 October 1960
The Kaiserkeller
Hamburg, Germany

For weeks The Beatles had talked about little else, fantasizing about standing on "the real stage" where Howie Casey, Derry Wilkie, Lu Walters, Frank Wibberly, and Brian Griffiths – Derry and the Seniors – had been allowed to perform.

"Y'know, if we were at The Kaiserkeller..." most of their complaints had begun. But now that The Kaiserkeller was at last theirs, it was destroying The Beatles.

Their first week had passed disastrously, and Bruno was at his wits' end. He'd even contacted Allan Williams and insisted that Allan return to Hamburg immediately and light a fire under the boys. After all, Bruno had George Steiner say, Williams was the one responsible for "the do-nothings."

But even Allan, with Rory Storm and the Hurricanes in tow, had no ready answers. Instead he sat in "The 'Keller" and knocked back drink after drink, squinting his eyes, staring at the stage, and studying The Beatles with increasing ire.

As he listened to them dole out songs without an ounce of exuberance, his red-veined cheeks shone, and he had to pace to keep his temper at bay. He slapped his sides and sighed repeatedly, heavily.

What the fuggin'ell are they up to? he fumed. *I've seen more life in the corrugated John Wayne in The Odeon Cinema lobby!*

"What the fuggin'ell's the matter?" he screamed over the music, waving his hands at the band. Then he flopped back on his bar stool again, shook his head, and muttered to himself, *They're miserable tonight – worse than miserable! In fact, they're almost as bad as in the early days of The Jac.*

As the song ended and obligatory applause sputtered up here and there, Allan looked around the room at empty tables surrounded by empty chairs, at bored patrons fidgeting, at the lifeless band shuffling their feet. He rubbed his hand over his eyes, trying to make some sense of that which made no sense, trying to explain the Beatles' loss of enthusiasm and *joie de vivre*.

In The Jac, the lads had been hungry and determined. And over in The Indra, the Beatles had been electric. Now they hardly emitted a spark.

On stage, John walked over to Paul – turning his back on the audience for a private conference of some kind – and Paul nodded, turning away as well. A murmur rose from the sparse and disgruntled crowd.

George listlessly tuned his guitar and said something indistinguishable to Pete. Pete tossed him a cig in reply and then lit one of his own, while Stu stared down at the floor.

Two couples got up to leave.

"Shite!" Allan couldn't stand it a minute longer. Several heads turned in his direction. He stood up and yelled towards the stage, "E-bloody-nough! Sing! Move! Do somethin', y' lousy bunch o'scruffs! What's the fuggin' problem here? *Mak show*, lads! Do what you came here to do! *Mak fuggin' show*!"

The audience picked up Allan's Scouse-German and ran with it. It came first from one corner of the room where an enamored fan from The Indra repeated the request like a plea: "Peedles! Peedles von Liverpool! *Mach shau! Mach shau!*"

Then a large, tattooed man with two heavily perfumed dates shouted it as a demand, "*Mach shau*, Peedles!"

One inspired patron waddled towards the stage, his fingers crooked around five sloshing beer steins. He grinned and plunked them right at John's feet. "This," he grinned a toothless grin, "for 'Hound Dog.' You *mach shau*, right? Drink…*mach shau*, Peedles!"

The applause this time was genuine. Everyone left in the club whistled and cheered the man's gesture. Even The Beatles smiled, grabbing the steins and toasting one another, downing the warm, bitter brew in greedy gulps. The crowd laughed and yelled again as John waved a hand towards their benefactor and the bulky, toothless German took a bow.

"Go on!" Allan shook his head. "Efuggin'nough already! Just play the bleedin' music! *Mak show*!"

"*Mach shau! Mach shau! Mach shau! Mach shau!*" The crowd began to chant. Another patron brought a second round of ales to the stage while "Hound Dog" made the room ring. And after Paul's screaming rendition of "Long Tall Sally," The Beatles downed yet another round.

After his third pint, John began to run and slide on his knees across the stage. He came within inches of flying off the edge and landing in an exotic looking fraulein's lap, but she only squealed and urged him on.

By the fourth round, The Beatles forgot how large The Kaiserkeller had seemed, how intimidating the upscale décor and immense, polished bar had appeared, and how nervous they'd all been. They forgot how small they'd felt in the midst of it all and began to concentrate instead on the ringing applause in their ears and the blur of the moving crowd below.

John offered up "Mr. Moonlight" until his vocal chords trickled blood. Then he diluted the pain with something liquid proffered from a British sailor's glass. And something else ordered by an aging prossie in a worn bustier.

As midnight approached and Beatle music diffused onto the sidewalk outside, the crowd began to grow. New customers sent up drinks as they saw others doing, and The Beatles quaffed down everything put in front of them.

"Roll Over Beethoven" had never been so unruly. George winked, grinned, and did a "retreat back three steps, stomp forward three" sort of dance. John and Paul began to challenge each other to "feats of valour" – leaping off the stage, jumping into splits, flailing like madmen, and shouting epithets at the audience. They acted as if they'd been born in The Kaiserkeller, as if they'd been doing this all their lives.

Nodding his head and smiling, Bruno joined Allan at the bar. "Much better Beatles!" He slapped Allan on the back.

"Yeah, right. Pissed to the gills Beatles, all of 'em." Allan shook his head. "Lennon's as lushed as the landlord's cat on Sunday, and Louise Harrison would murder me in me sleep if she saw Georgie this way."

"Beer," Bruno nodded, making a quaffing gesture.

"Yeah, I understand. Beer, indeed." Allan lifted his own glass. "That's the fuggin' crux of the matter, isn't it, Koschmider?"

Bruno wrinkled his brow.

"I mean," Allan leaned towards him, shouting over the music, "what'll y'do with them tomorrow night when they're all hung over…and the night after that and the night after the night after that, as it were? You saw how they were a while ago. They were as frightened as day-old chicks! I think they're fuggin' terrified at the sheer size and magnitude of this place! So how'll you continue to ward off stage fright without turnin 'em all into to sots, tell me that?!"

"Pfffffft!" Bruno shrugged. "Fright? No problem here. We have ways."

"*Ways?*" Allan swung completely around in his chair. "This isn't World War II, Koschmider! What d'ya mean, 'we have *ways*'? This isn't about torture and intimidation, is it? Because if that's what y'er on about, I'll have them all back in Liverpool before the cock crows three – contract or no fuggin' contract! Understand?"

Bruno fished in his pocket and produced a handful of assorted pills, pills of all colours, shapes, and sizes – one tumbling over the next in abundance.

"Preludin," Bruno explained. "No headaches. Much energy."

Allan eyed the owner of The Kaiserkeller warily. "We don't hold with those as a general rule – pills. They're not addictin' or fuggin' black market, are they? I want no run-in with the authorities, y'know…a blemish on my record I can well do without."

"Preludin! *Mach shau!*" It was the only explanation Bruno was willing to give, but he brandished the pills so blatantly that Allan assumed they weren't illegal.

Paul and George were doing a polka of some sort, stomping on the hollow Kaiserkeller stage and making the room clatter. Pete kept beat enthusiastically and Stu let out the western "Yippee!" he'd overheard in the interminable movies that interrupted his sleep. Then goaded by shouts and whistles, the band of unleashed maniacs charged into the next number.

Paul's "A Taste of Honey" was more than a little slurred, but the crowd loved it. George's "da-doo-m-dooes" were not quite on time, but they were accompanied by a full smile instead of the boy's traditional shy grin. Stu clunked his boot heel and laughed while Pete employed a heavy backbeat.

But John was a different story. Al squinted his eyes and watched the boy carefully.

John stood alone, his hair dripping wet and his eyes, a dazed animal's. Although John maintained his wide, confident stance, he was visibly wobbling. Al could see that the alcohol was beginning to do its worst.

"Boys need Preludin? No worries." The pretty dark-eyed, blonde barmaid delivering Allan's drink patted his hand and winked. "They are slimming capsules. More energy. Very good. Only, they make great thirst. And then," she beamed, "more lager!"

Allan snorted. "Pfffft! Pills, lager, and rock'n'roll! Sounds like a fuggin' dangerous combination to me, girl!"

"No, no problems. Green bombers…or red or black. All legal. All very safe."

"Yeah?" Allan glanced towards the stage, "Safe if you've the personality for it…safe if you're not highly fuggin' volatile to begin with, right?"

The waitress had no idea what the ruddy Englishman was talking about, but she nodded and smiled pleasantly anyway. And Al gave up trying to explain that the new German "slimming pills" might ruin a musician altogether. He'd seen far too many entertainers destroyed by drugs. And calling them slimming pills, bombers, or Prellys didn't make them any less lethal. For certain people, they were poison.

Al cut his eyes to the boy at the far right of the stage and observed John carefully.

John had moved far beyond glee, far beyond enthusiasm. While the rest of The Beatles rioted and guffawed, John stood motionless in a dark realm, full of warning.

Lennon's always reacted more adversely to alcohol than the others, Allan thought. *And tonight's no exception. John's demons're legion…always itchin' for any port of entry. I mean, just look at him now, with only lager to mar his somewhat merry veneer! He's so lushed, he's probably even forgotten it's his fuggin' twentieth birthday! Bevvied beyond all belief, is Lennon. Nallered.*

Allan puffed his cheeks and sighed again and worried.

Who knows what Bruno's "magic pills" might unleash in Lennon on an unsuspectin' world? Who knows what might happen once he goes down that fuggin' road? Will he be able to handle it or will he come back to Liverpool, changed for the worse?

Wild applause jarred Al and John from their respective reveries and for a second, their eyes met across the room. John raised an eyebrow to his manager, and Allan smiled back slightly, raising his glass. "Better!" Allan mouthed. And John smirked, looking around the room victoriously before faded back into the fuzzy world of inebriation.

In both Beatle! *and* Drummed Out, The Pete Best Story, *Pete makes it quite clear that he did **not** participate in the use of Preludin or Benzedrine. This claim is backed by Allan Williams in his primary source book,* The Man Who Gave the Beatles Away. *Any references to the use of drugs in this and future chapters do not include Pete Best.*

This event actually occurred on October 10, 1960. I took "author's license" to move it to the 9th so that it would fall on John's birthday. On 9 October, The Beatles were playing The Kaiserkeller just as they are in this chapter. Allan, however, was there on the 10th.

All events on the 10th happen as stated here. All conversation is conjecture.

11 October 1960
Hamburg

"S-s-s-say, J-John Lennon!" A voice hailed him from the sidewalk.

John spun around, in no mood to socialize. Bruno's new pep pills had his head still buzzing, mid-afternoon.

"Rory!" John immediately recognized the lanky, blond, lead singer for The Hurricanes. Storm was a celebrity in Liverpool circles. His good looks were outdone only by his affability. No one could be rude to Rory Storm. Rory was one of those people who always made you smile.

"S-say John, did A-Al put you in the fuggin' dungeons, like he-he did us? It's, it's, it's unbearable, that's what it is!"

"Unbearable, is it?" John grinned. "Could be y'er used to Butlins Resort – with all those plushy summer camp amenities, as it were!"

They walked side-by-side, John taking two strides for Rory's one. "N-n-not us," Rory elbowed John good-naturedly. "We've uh-uh-seen it all, y'know. But this is b-bleedin' awful! We-we're s-sleepin' on chairs pulled together, an-and Ringo's threatenin' to go home...straight away."

"He's soft, isn't he – Ringo." John directed Rory down an alley shortcut to The Kaiserkeller. "Tell 'im for me we've got vermin at our place pre-datin' his very existence...and fat German ladies, with braided armpit hair, elbowin' us out of the fuggin' loo! At least you're stayin' at The Kaiserkeller. We're livin' in the back o'some piss-n-stench cinema, holed up in a filthy utility closet!"

"Geez!" Rory's face was genuinely sympathetic. "I-uh-uh-I didn't r-realize! B-bad luck, right?"

"Or," John grumbled, "bad management – you tell me."

John nodded to the right, and the two threaded their way through The Reeperbahn as if they'd grown up there. John had spent the last six weeks learning the quickest routes to The Seaman's Mission, The Kaiserkeller, and The Bambi Kino.

"Y-you really know yer uh-uh-way around, don't you?" Rory followed, looking for street signs and landmarks, trying to memorize the route.

"Well, it'll come to you as well. There's not much else to do here…except practise, perform, and ogle the bairds on the Herbertstrasse."

"Yeah," Rory chuckled. "They-they're somethin', aren't they? G-g-girls with whips and chairs, as-as it were…"

John narrowed his eyes. "And girls with man-eatin' plants, and girls who never were girls in this fuggin' lifetime! I've seen enough of it to put me off sex forever! It's getttin' old, y'know."

They rounded the last turn and discovered The Kaiserkeller just off to their left. John led the way, holding the door open for the experienced performer.

"'ullo, Lennon!" It was Ringo Starr, The Hurricane's sophisticated, renowned drummer. His pencil-thin mustache, beard, shiny stage slacks, and starched, French-cuffed dress shirt proved him every bit the professional. He leaned suavely against the foyer wall and smoked.

"'ullo, Ringo," John returned the greeting. "What'd they do – give ole Horst Fascher the boot, as it were, and sign you on as the effin' bouncer, then?"

Ringo smiled broadly, flashing his nugget-adorned hands. "I could bounce all right! I'd whack 'em with me rings and have done with 'em. It's not likely the scruff of Hamyburg'd last more than a round with these fisticuffs!"

"H-hey, Ring," Rory began, "J-J-John's group's installed in a-a pit, as-as it were…s-s-sleepin' in a uh-uh-movie house c-closet."

"And that's supposed to cheer me how?" Ringo tapped his cig into a glass ashtray. "They're 'at one' with pigsties – The Beatles. But we're above all that, y'know."

John affected his best Scouse accent, "Yeah, right! Comin' from the land 'whur they play tick wid'atchets,' Hamburg's all muther's milk to you, isn't it, Ringo?"

Ringo chuckled his deep, throaty chuckle and blew a line of smoke in John's direction. He liked Lennon's quick retorts and smart remarks. He liked the impudence of the wack, even if John was from poshy Woolton. John Lennon was always razor sharp and ready to bandy words. Ringo liked that.

"S-so h-how's it's goin' with the uh-uh-stage, then?" Rory nodded towards The Kaiserkeller's expansive front room.

"We've just about destroyed it," John reached over and filched a single cigarette, a "loosie," from Ringo's shirt pocket. Ringo swiped at his hand but missed intentionally.

"That'll be the night of the day that never was!" Ringo chortled. "You Beatles're no match for a stage like that."

"*W-we'll* be the ones to smash it up!" Rory smiled. "G-Good money's o-on *us* to be the group to finally uh-bring down that ramshackle str-structure."

"It's a wager you're sure to lose, Stormy." John lit his filched cig and took a long draw. "We'll have that victor's crate of German champagne."

Ringo snorted. "Y'er wastin' your time, aren't you, Lennon? We all know Rory's far more athletic than you lot and," he flexed his bicep inside the expensive stage shirt, "much more muscular, as well."

"That all depends," John looked down his nose, "on which muscle you're referrin' to, Starkey. *The Beatles'* references come from the local tarts, as it were."

Ringo chuckled. "With that mug? You've a face like a dollop o'mortal sins, Lennon! The only tart you've had's apple."

"Balls to you, drummer. I'm fireproof!"

"B-but no-no matter," Rory got back to the wager at hand, "no-no matter who smashes up the stage, we-we all win…as long as the bleedin' thing gets uh-uh-uh destroyed."

"Right." John leaned out the front door and tossed the last nub of his cigarette into the street. "We're doin' all of us – includin' Bruno – a favour by crashin' it."

"I-it's dead rotten – that stage," Rory agreed

"Hazardous to me health," Ringo said.

"I-I was poundin' it so-so hard last night," Rory walked towards the feeble platform, "tha-that the piano was t-teeterin' way over…like this."

"Paul and I were doin' flamenco dances," John wouldn't be outdone, "and stompin' so hard we were virtually drownin' Pete out in the process."

"You wouldn't dare drown *me* out," Ringo smirked.

"We would if we could…but we can't," John returned.

"Yeah, that's right, *that's* the ticket!" Ringo puffed up playfully. "Powerhouse drummin' – that's what I'm known for! Takes a man, not a shirt button, for that sort o'sound, y'know!"

John put on his announcer's voice. "Ladies and Gents, now appearin' in live and in person…Ringo Starr and his Manly Drums!"

Ringo smiled and gave the "air drums" an exaggerated roll.

But John only sniffed. "Wasn't a bit masculine – that roll. In fact, I've an idea if I blew me nose, you'd fall over."

"Co-come on, b-both of you," Rory grinned. "Let's walk out and…uh-uh…grab a bite to eat, yeah?"

"On our budgets? There's only Willy's Café." John pointed the way. "Follow me…for the specialty of the house…"

"Which is?" Rory asked.

"Cornflakes." Ringo threw his eyes to the ceiling.

"Co-cornflakes it is, then!" Rory laughed. "I-I-I think even *I* could afford that! A bowl for-for uh-uh each o'you!"

Ringo cut his eyes at The Beatle. "I believe it's John's turn to buy a round, as it were."

"Don't get eggy, Ringo," John returned. "I haven't seen you puttin' the mitts in yer moneybags, as it were!"

"Well, rumour has it," the drummer shot back, "you've had your pockets combination locked!"

And the three musicians, shouldering together, ambled out onto the Grosse Freiheit Strasse. They plotted against Bruno's dilapidated, orange-crate of a stage, railed against Allan's management, complained about their accommodations and unbearable work conditions, and one-upped each other at every turn – three Liverpudlians trying to best one another in the age-old Scouser game of banter.

Rory and his band, including Ringo, did share the Kaiserkeller stage with The Beatles during this time. Living accommodations were exactly as reported. Willy's Café and its famous cornflakes were there. The plot to destroy The Kaiserkeller stage is well documented.

Only the conversations are imagined.

11 October 1960
Evening
The Kaiserkeller
Hamburg, Germany

The Hurricanes and Beatles played alternating ninety-minute sets – competing, comparing notes, and spelling each other in symbiosis. And because an hour and a half wasn't really long enough to go anywhere or do anything, the British boys spent the evening draped about the 'Keller's front row tables – watching each other perform. In only a matter of days, the two Liverpool bands became a tight, cohesive group.

Before performances, Ringo and Pete sat at a table of German girls, laughing and ordering up drinks. Pete, whose German was fairly competent, gave "Ring" the verbal specifics when body language didn't quite do. And Ringo exuded all the charm the two drummers needed, and then some.

John, George, and Paul huddled with Johnny Guitar, guffawing and disparaging the clientele around them. And Rory often chatted with Stu as they packed things away at closing time.

"The Beatles ha-have taken it u-up a notch, y'know." Rory was frank. "I mean, n-not that you were bad or-or anything. It's just that the group is uh-uh-much better than before."

"Can we take that as a compliment, then?" Stu raised an eyebrow.

"Y-you know what I mean." Rory slapped him on the back. "Th-they all go b-bleedin' crazy when you Beatles do "What I'd Say" or "L-L-Long Tall Sally."

"And how about 'Love Me Tender'?" Stu smiled wryly. It was his vocal solo.

"El-Elvis sleeps at night," Rory teased.

The admiration between the two groups was mutual. John was impressed with The Hurricanes' repertoire and lost no time "cadging" their arrangements, tempos, riffs, and lyrics. When George pointed out that John was "borrowin' rather heavily" from The Hurricane's style, John just grinned, "I only steal from the best. It's to be expected in situations like this, y'know."

Ty Brian was, now and again, teaching Paul the new German hit,

"Wooden Heart," and Ringo and John continually sparred with one another – jabbing and cuffing in Scouse verbiage. Though Lu Walters had offered to work with Stu on his bass riffs, Stu had been working instead on a sketch of Rory. And Paul shared cigs and stories with Johnny Guitar, whom he'd known since the days when Guitar had been simply Johnny Byrne. Miles from home, the ten Scousers grew less homesick when they "knocked about" together. They worked, ate, composed, practised, and got into trouble as a group.

Of the ten, it was John who had first noticed the tentative German lad in The Kaiserkeller shadows. He had pointed him out to Rory who had, in turn, alerted Paul to the "w-wide-eyed, ra-rather nervous lookin' wack in the uh-uh-leathers."

The boy's clothes – eloquently cut and trendy – marked him as a stranger to the Reeperbahn. He was clearly out of his element in the rough-and-tumble.

"He's over there again – starin' again," John leaned over to George between songs. "What about that, eh?"

"I dunno," George smiled and nodded at the stranger. "He seems harmless enough, doesn't he?"

"Probably after our Prellys, if you ask me…shite…*now* you've done it, George! He's fuggin' comin' over!"

"'Ullo," George nodded in the stranger's direction.

"Don't encourage him!" John hissed.

"Shirrup, John," Stu intervened. "That's Klaus – Klaus Voormann. I met him the other night. He's all right." Stu walked to the edge of the stage. "'Ullo, Klaus. Welcome! Glad y'er back."

"Hello," Klaus shook Stu's hand. "I have brought friends tonight."

"Oh yeah? Well, great. Ta." Stu waved to a lovely blonde girl and a few assorted others, all decked in black and sitting at a rounder.

"Yeah, ta." George nodded as well and waved. "We need all the fans we can get."

"Slummin' again, eh?" John turned around and faced Klaus. "Back to rub elbows with the Teds, eh? Well, you'll have to rent yerself a fuggin' bomber jacket if this keeps up, won't you, son?"

"Lay off, John." Stu hated to see anyone ridiculed.

"Yes, a jacket," Klaus smiled shyly. "I have wanted to tell you…I have designed a record jacket. I thought you might like to know…"

"Oh really? Thasso?" George looked at him with new eyes.

"He has, y'know." Paul walked over, smiled at Klaus, shook hands, and nodded.

"Go on!" John removed his guitar and placed it in the stand. It was The Hurricane's time to take the stage.

"No really. He has." Paul nodded. "It was a jacket for John Barry Seven…for 'Walk, Don't Run' – the German version."

"Is that right?" John mangled his chewing gum. He studied Klaus with genuine interest this time. "Thasso, Klaus?"

"Yes," Klaus beamed. "I have designed it."

"Well...I'm impressed, son," John said, nodding briefly.

"And y'should be." Removing his guitar strap, Paul shrugged his shoulders several times and rolled his neck side to side.

"Klaus is an artist..." Stu flicked his amplifier off, "...one who's had commercial success. Imagine that, John! An artist who makes money!"

"Yeah?" John was still skeptical, "Well...what's he doin' here? With a reputation like that and those upper class kecks he's got on...what's he doin' in the fuggin' Kaiserkeller instead of hangin' about in some uptown coffeehouse, as it were?"

"He likes us," Stu grinned.

"Right," Paul agreed. "He likes our sound, y'know. He thinks *we're* commercially successful as well."

"The toppermost of the poppermost, remember?" George teased.

John cut his eyes at the German. "Well then, Klaus, since you've done so well, then – how's about a round or two for us all, son? We're spittin' feathers up here, aren't we?" Both bands had been jumping riotously on the stage all night in hopes of finally breaking through the splintered boards. But so far the platform held its own.

Paul spoke into John's shoulder, "This time you've picked the right nudge. He's the son of a physician – Klaus. He can well afford a lager...or two or three."

John leapt from the stage and slapped an arm around Klaus as if he'd known him for years, and Paul was right behind them, pushing through the crowd to Klaus's table.

"So, what's the prediction, John?" Paul nodded towards the stage. "Is it givin' way at all? Have the crates got enough fight left in 'em for another night of Scouse torture?"

"Nah, it's nearly collapsed." John patted his pockets for a cig. "But from here on out, we'll have to use discretion. I watched Bruno, and he's catchin' on. The last thing we need is for the fuggin' repairs to come out of our fuggin' paychecks!"

"Are y'sure he's on to us?" Paul handed John the last of his Embassies.

"He gave me the evil eye...and earlier tonight, he told me, 'Not so much *mach shau*, Peedle.' He told Lu and Rory as well. 'Warned them' might be the better phrase."

Paul pulled out a chair and sat down. "Yeah? Well, if you take a looksee, you'll find Johnny Guitar's not exactly influenced by that directive!"

Up on the stage, The Hurricane's lead guitarist was pounding his left foot solidly into the wooden planks as he sang, slamming his boot heel over and over again on the platform's weakest spot. Up on his rostrum, Ringo watched The Beatles and smiled – the Cheshire cat grinning broadly from the Wonderland tree.

"Yeah, well they can pound all they want," John assured Paul as he flipped Ringo the backhanded V, "but they'll never break through this set. My bet's on the stomp o'midnight…and that's us!"

But Paul had lost interest in the contest. He was taken instead with the exotic, elfin blonde seated directly across from him.

"'Ullo, luv," he smiled at her. "I'm Paul. And this reprobate here's John."

"This," Klaus leaned in and yelled over the music, "is my fiancé, Astrid Kirchherr. She, too, is a student of art."

"Hello." Astrid offered her hand to each of them. "I like your music very much." She smiled from deep within dark lashes.

"Ta," John hardly acknowledged her, his attention on The Hurricane's antics. "Y'bunch of fuggin' vandals!" John yelled over his shoulder at the stage as Rory leapt into the air and crashed to his knees with all his might.

"Allow me to introduce myself." A latecomer smiled at the girl. "I'm Stu. Stuart Sutcliffe. Also an artist. Also of The Beatles."

"Hello." Astrid extended her hand. "Your band is very good. I think you have very much talent."

"It isn't really my band." Stuart squeezed a chair in next to hers. "I'm just along for the ride, y'know. I mean, I'm truly only an artist actually…on holiday from Liverpool College of Art…"

"Klaus has told me." Astrid played with the wispy strands of hair fringing the nape of her neck.

Stu leaned closer to her and shouted above the music, "I've been interested in talkin' to someone about artistic avenues here in Hamburg…about ways into the art scene. Klaus tells me you're the one to ask, as it were."

"Perhaps." She smiled and dipped her head. Her blonde hair was cropped close, and it made her look every bit the sprite.

"Great then." Stu finally let go of her hand. "Perhaps we could talk someday soon."

"Perhaps…we shall see." Astrid leaned back in her chair. "But for now, we listen to the rock'n'roll. Right?"

"Right," Stu smiled and held her gaze.

John, catching the scene, folded his arms and chewed his gum ferociously. Another side interest Stuart didn't need, and this blonde looked every bit like a first class distraction. As Stu gave the girl a lingering look, John nudged him and redirected his attention to The Hurricanes on stage.

"Pay attention, son," John barked. "There's serious business at hand, right?"

"Yeah, serious," was all Stu said.

****

Willy's Café
12 October 1960
1:15 a.m.

"Next set we really hafta put the boot in!" George was resolute. "You *do realize* that If The Hurricanes collapse that stage before us, the five of us'll have to come up with the funds for all that champagne!"

"A clear financial disaster, if ever there was one," Paul nodded. He tipped his bowl of cornflakes and milk so that he could scrape out the dregs. Willy's was the only place the bands could escape for a quick "nosh-up" between sets. It had become The Hurricanes' and The Beatles' primary home away from home.

"Look, I'm savin' up for that fuggin' Rickenbacker," John protested.

"You're in with the rest of us, John." Paul was adamant. "In fact, this whole thing might've been your idea, if memory serves."

"Look McCartney, you can drown yerself in that fuggin' bowl of surreal as far as I'm concerned, but I'm not about to spoon out ready cash when I'm this close to purchasin' that Ric, as it were!" John picked up his bowl and noisily slurped the last of its contents.

"Then we'll just have to make sure *we're* the ones who crash through." George leaned forward, always the peacemaker. "We can do it! We've all but done it thus far, haven't we? John said it would go 'round midnight. Well, it's past that now, and we've got the last set, haven't we?"

John nodded, digging into the pocket of his tight jeans and pulling out a few random coins. He tossed them onto the table and wiped his mouth with a wad of the thin, paper napkins from the metal dispenser. "That's right," he said, nodding towards the clock. " We're up in less than a quarter of an hour."

"But unhappily," Paul looked out the window towards The Kaiserkeller, "my money's on Rory. I've been expectin' shouts of victory for a while now."

"Don't be a fuggin' traitor." John pushed his coins and the bill towards George. "Just because Storm's six-fuggin'-foot-two doesn't mean he's…"

But the sound of unadulterated celebration not so far away ended all debate. The three Beatles threw their eyes to the ceiling and shook their heads as the volley of cheers, laughter, and triumphant "whoops" grew closer and closer. George put his head down on the table and groaned. The door swung open.

"It's done!"

"We've done it! We've beaten fuggin' Koschmider!"

"It's smashed ter bits – that stage!"

"We've done it at last!"

"There'll be no more rock'n'roll tonight!"

The Hurricanes tumbled into the café with all the force of their stage name. "I just about killed meself!" Ringo was still picking splinters out of his stage jacket. "Drums collapsin' and Lu here fallin' on top of me – addin' insult to injury."

"W-w-we've done it, lads!" Rory yelled, waving his arms in the air.

"You shoulda been there, John!" Stu emerged from the back of the group. "They all vanished in a crash – instruments 'n all! Bruno was effin' speechless when it went!"

"T-t-took her down durin' 'Blue Suede Shoes!'" Rory beamed, his face still red from exertion. "I-it's the *shoes* that turned the tide!"

"You're a marred bunch o'rotten rockers." John tried to sound angry. "Breakin' and destructin' property! Smashin' up material goods!"

"Right back at ya, John!" Lu Walters yelled, and the group cheered. "We were all in this together, weren't we? Hurricanes and gale force destruction! Beatles and a plague on the land! Never was so much done by so few, eh? It'll be a long time before Bruno fuggin' Koschmider forgets us, right?"

"N-n-now B-Bruno's got to build a re-real stage in that place," Rory smiled, pulling up a chair. "Somethin' uh-uh-worthy of Mersey music, right?"

"A real stage!" they chorused.

"Up the 'Pool!" someone shouted.

"Scousers all!"

"S-s-smashin' victory!"

"Take that, Bruno! We won the bleedin' war!" John yelled.

Absorbed in heroics, smoke, and camaraderie, none of them saw George Steiner slip in and out of the café, and not one of them suspected that there might be recriminations.

****

The Kaiserkeller
1:40 a.m.

The most dangerous characters on the entire Reeperbahn were the nightclub waiters and bouncers employed to keep the peace. Vicious, thick-necked, bulldog men, they ached for opportunities to inflict pain under the guise of justice. They waited for moments when their coshes, billy clubs, and brass knuckles would enhance the sheer momentum of their fists. Hired for their "act now, ask later" responses, Hamburg's bouncers waited hungrily for any provocation that might invoke a boot to the skull or a nightstick to the ribs.

These capable mercenaries served Bruno Koschmider in several capacities. Some, in stiffly starched aprons, waited tables; others mixed and poured drinks. Still others, like Horst Fascher, stood and perused the nightclub crowd, his hawkish eyes scanning for any hint of irregularity.

Now, armed with an assortment of weapons – legal and illegal – Koschmider's battalion of henchmen gathered at The Kaiserkeller door, ready to exact blood payment from the two Liverpool bands who'd purposely demolished their employer's stage. The Hurricanes and The Beatles had willingly conspired to destroy Koschmider's property. In fact, the boys had been overheard celebrating their triumph openly. Now Horst Fascher gathered his accomplished pugilists, his comrades from the Hamburg Boxing Academy, and readied them to square the insult.

Fascher had every provocation to act and act swiftly, but as he rounded up his men for the mêlée to come, Horst, for the first time in years, felt the slightest twinge of guilt. He tried to steel himself, recalling George Steiner's account of The Beatles and The Hurricanes cheering and congratulating each other at Willy's Café. But unfortunately, over the past few weeks, the British boys had "rubbed off" on Horst. It was difficult not to like them.

Paul, the clown, the *lustig*, always greeted Horst with a smile and an anecdote. George, the *schuchtern*, the baby of the group, was eager and optimistic, amenable to just about anything. And Rory, the tall, strong lad with the big, broad smile, never had a mean word for anyone. They weren't bad – these boys. They were just mischievous.

All the waiters had taken to Richie, as they called him – the one the English boys referred to as Ringo. Richie was "of the earth," Horst always said. He was solid, natural, and always ready with a handshake or a proffered cigarette. In fact, out of all the British rockers, it was Richie who knew the names of every employee at The Kaiserkeller. The lad fit in any group.

The Liverpool boys laughed constantly, amusing each other and Horst as well, taking the dinginess off things in the Reeperbahn. And once – when Horst had taken the five Beatles home to meet his mother, brothers, and sisters – the lads had won his family over with their antics and laughter.

Now Horst paced back and forth, clenching and unclenching his fists, just as he used to do in the old days, before his title bouts. His jaw flexed and his breathing accelerated slightly, but tonight his spine didn't tingle with the old anticipation. He didn't have "the edge" as he contemplated what was to come.

In fact, he dreaded the encounter. He dreaded facing John Lennon. In John, he'd found a bit of himself, a kindred spirit, a friend. Horst had dubbed John the *zyniker*, the fighter, and it was the highest compliment. The nickname denoted tenacity, determination, courage. If John had grown up in Hamburg, Horst had once told him, he would've invited John to join his elite group of *zynikers* known as "Hoddel's Gang." But now Horst was directing members of that very group against Lennon and his friends. It felt wrong.

Horst paced and watched Bruno nervously for the sign. He squinted his eyes and put on his game face.

Not so many years ago, Horst had fought his way to the featherweight championship of West Germany, eliminating opponent after opponent with skilled ease. But in all of those title bouts, he'd never faced a friend. This was a first. The fight tonight would be different.

Inwardly, Horst hoped the *zyniker* in Lennon would be equal to his own. He hoped John's abrasiveness ran as deeply as it appeared to run. But Horst was a trained boxer and more importantly, a realistic man – a fighter who had once accidentally killed an opponent. It was a credential that Bruno valued and Horst secretly despised.

And it was the fact that worried him most when Bruno shouted, "*Schnell gehen!* Go!"

****

Willy's Café
2:28 a.m.

They were "well into their cups" when the word came that Bruno's armed henchmen were headed for Willy's. Champagne bottles dotted the tables – most of them empty. The Hurricanes and The Beatles were "nallered." Pissed, excited, ready for action – they jumped to their feet and began talking, all at the same time.

"U-u-use the chairs, lads!" Rory directed, pointing this way and that.

"Skwur up! Get fuggin' ready!" Johnny Guitar yelled.

"Push the tables up in front!" Ringo took action. "Make a holdin' line!"

"Make 'em come to us!" John barked. "No one breaks out alone!"

"Get 'em lads!" Paul encouraged.

"Hey, watch the fat one with the lame eye, right?" Lu warned. "He's tricky, that one."

"Eck! Eck! Here they come!"

"Fuggin'ell!!!"

"Up the 'Pool!"

Willy watched as chairs, tables, his old coat rack, champagne bottles, and storage crates became lethal weapons. The Liverpudlians fought with battering rams of furniture. They defended themselves with shattered bottles, with forks and knives. The boys hurled anything they could lift and throw. Bruno's waiters were initially amazed.

George Harrison's pointed winklepicker boots delivered sharp blows to shins, groins, and chins. And Johnny Guitar fought beside him, laughing and screaming as if it were all some sort of lark.

Paul and Pete rammed the bouncers with the coat rack while Ringo plunged into the fracas, his days in the Dingle not forgotten. And Ty Brian used a table as a shield, fending off the relentless whacks of the waiters' coshes as he pushed and shoved towards the open door.

The sheer size of Rory Storm was overwhelming, but his physical prowess was something no one had anticipated. The waiter who had been designated to face Rory was falling back. Rory had been trained and trained well on the streets of Liverpool 8.

"Fuggin' bastards!" John screamed. "You and all yer effin' relations!" He lunged and kicked and flailed without any rational fear of the consequences.

"John!" Stu watched his friend lose control. "Keep yer head about ya! Watch out!" He knew John's anger could trip him up.

John shoved, spit, bit, punched, and screamed – risked too much and reserved too little. He fought without plan or strategy.

When Horst felt that a lesson had been learned and that the boys had had enough "to remember them by," he whistled for his group to retreat before any serious damage could be done. Shouting threats and promises of what would happen "next time," Bruno's henchmen fell back, breathing heavily.

"That'll teach you to mess with us in our kip!" Paul yelled after them, his shirt torn in several places, his shoulder aching.

"Right!" George seconded it. "You couldn't knock the skin off a rice puddin'!" But the boy's voice quivered, and he staggered to the curb to collapse.

Ringo sat down beside him, draping an arm over the kid's shoulder, offering George a cig and a light. "Well now, that was a proper doodle, wasn't it?" Ringo smiled. "But we fetched 'em home, didn't we, son?"

George grinned and nodded, but his nose was bleeding, and he was still breathing heavily. He wanted to say something clever, but he was shaking too hard to speak.

"Shite!" John tripped out onto the sidewalk, a bloody hand to his lip.

"Where'd they mizzle off to just when we'd hit our fuggin' stride?"

"Ah, you'd had enough." Ringo eyed him from the curb. "You're bleedin' from stem to stern, Lennon."

"Isthasso?" John shot back. "Well, you're fuggin' ugly, Ringo. What's your remedy for that, drummer?"

In spite of their wounds and exhaustion, the group laughed. They collapsed together on the street, taking in deep gulps of October air and leaning on one another, pretending they were champions.

"W-w-well, a-at least we'll get a s-stage out of it all," Rory grinned, sweat dripping from his chin.

"Yeah, right. I'd say we earned it," Stu panted from the doorway, his clothes in complete disarray. "In fact, I'm sure I'm half dead over here."

"They weren't so bad, those bouncers," Paul chuckled.

"Yeah," George echoed, "they weren't so awful bad."

"We gave as good as we got, right?" Pete shoved Paul playfully.

"I-I was es-especially outstandin'," Rory laughed.

"And so," John employed his announcer's voice, "another evenin' in Hamburg comes to a close as our heroes – the lads from Liddypool – mauled but happy, bloody but unbowed, stand together against the forces of German domination – each Scouser mangled but triumphant and each eagerly anticipatin' a new stage in their lives."

"That's bleedin' awful, John," Ty groaned.

"Bring back the bouncers and spare us the Lennonisms!" Ringo yelled.

"We've had enough for one night, John." Paul shook his head.

"R-r-right. I-I'm dead creased," Rory agreed.

John wore a serious face. "That's what you say. But I've heard, it's only a stage y'er goin' through…"

The group turned on John, and within minutes, the tussle was on again. But this time, it was all in fun.

This incident is well documented in Williams' brilliant book, The Man Who Gave the Beatles Away. *(No one tells a story like Allan does.) But obviously I have had to improvise on the conversation. Otherwise, the events are as they were.*

[As a side note, in the summer of 2004, my husband and I were two of a small group of VIP viewers on the front row of Ringo's "Good Morning America Summer Concert" in Bryant Park, New York City. I had made a poster to catch Ringo's eye; I wanted it to be something that would show him I knew more about him than the fact that he sang, "Boys." So I wrote on the poster, "Richie, congrats on crashin' The 'Keller stage before the Beatles!" During his practise performance that morning, Ringo was performing "With A Little Help From My Friends" when he happened to see the poster. He read it and chuckled. It was a great moment!]

12 October 1960
Willey's Café
Hamburg, Germany
Noon

Allan had summoned Rory and John to Willey's for a lecture on the evils of destroying one's employer's property. But now Al was sorry he'd invited Lennon over at all. John was on the rampage – another one – already pressing for the "next big thing" he wanted Al to do. John was launching an all-out campaign to convince Allan to locate and book a recording studio for them. The time had come, he insisted, for cutting their first record.

As Allan attempted to reprimand the two boys about the busted stage and the expenses involved in repairing the café, John merely waited for Allan to take a breath. And when the waitress brought Al's "ham sarnie" and milk, John stole the moment to harangue.

"Having a gig's all well and good," he was in Allan's face, "but makin' a record…well, that's the stuff Elvis is made of, isn't it? I mean, recordin'…*that's* the way a band moves from bein' merely entertainment to…"

"Look, Lennon," Allan pointed a finger at him, "don't start with me. I haven't any fuggin' connections in the record industry over here! You'll just have to wait 'til we're all back Merseyside…that is, *if* I can afford deals like that after all the destruction you lot caused here last night!"

Allan tried to take a bite of his sandwich, but John pushed the plate aside and leaned in. "We *can't* wait 'til we're back Merseyside, Al!" He moved Allan's mug of milk away as well. "Everythin's about timin', y'know, and Rory here says we have to strike while the fuggin' iron is hot!"

"Rory?" Allan shot him a look as he pulled the plate back again. "Pfffft! I suppose *he's* your manager now."

"I-I only said that J-John should…" Rory began, blushing.

"Enough!" Allan waved them off. "You'll both have to *wait* until after the holidays when we're all back in Liverpool, got it? Then I can ask Bob Wooler, Ray McFall, and all the powers that be."

"They don't have studios." John didn't like the idea.

"And who do *you* know over here that has one?" Allan talked with his mouth full. "Back home Merseyside, Wooler knows everyone who's everyone, and we owe each other tits for tat, as it were. As does McFall. I've already got a foot in the door with them, and we can make it happen over there. But here...I've no fuggin' idea where to find a recordin' studio!"

"Look, we've already promised to record with Wally and Ringo, and they're not goin' home when we're goin' home, now are they?" John badgered.

"Ringo, is it?" Allan cut his eyes at Rory. "Why Ringo? You've got yer *own* drummer, haven't you? I already filled that bill for ya, didn't I?"

"No – Paul 'n George 'n me found Pete...and don't get sidetracked." John said, "And don't look at Rory, either. It isn't about whose drummer's whose! We're all in this together – The Hurricanes and us."

"Is that right?" Allan eyed the boys suspiciously. "I thought the whole idea of a recordin' was to promote *a band*...that bein', in your case, Lennon, the fuggin' Beatles."

"Yeah well," John fumbled for logic, "Ringo wants to play for us, and Wally's in as well...because it was his idea. He has a coupla numbers he wants to do...and we've all agreed to back him up, as it were."

Allan took another bite of his sandwich and said nothing, imagining the colourful things Mona Best would have to say about a vinyl from Hamburg featuring all The Beatles, except Pete. It spelled trouble, a record like that, and trouble from Mona Best, Allan didn't need.

"No record," he said succinctly.

"C'mon, Al," Rory flashed a winning smile. "Mull it over, eh?"

"Look Al," John pressed on, "who knows when we'll all be in the 'Pool again, right? With The Hurricanes tourin' in one direction and us performin' in another, who knows when we'll all get the chance to do this thing, as it were?"

"But why do you need to record with Ringo and..."

"*All* we're asking you to do is find us an effin' studio! That's *it*, right? We're not askin' you to go out and get us a fuggin' recordin' contract, are we?"

"All we're asking you to do, all we're askin' you to do..." Allan mimicked John's voice. "God Almighty demands less of me than you, John Lennon! You're downright pushy, more often 'n not!"

"And *that's* how it's done." John leaned back in his chair.

"If you'd really like to know how *it's* done," Allan exhaled audibly, "it's done like this. I'm the manager. You're the client. I get the gigs. You say 'ta very much' and perform admirably. I decide when you're fuggin' ready to record a vinyl, and you keep workin' 'til I fuggin' do! I make the connections, and in due time, you reap the just rewards."

"Thasso?" John refused to take "no" for an answer. "Well, realize this then. We're fuggin' ready! We've got a song all prepared 'n Ringo's been practisin' it with us. Wally's worked out the details, and all we really need at this point's a bleedin' studio…if that's not too much to ask, that is."

"I'll say when you're ready to record." Allan hissed. It was a face-off.

"Say it, then."

"I'll say it when I'm ready."

"It's your *job* to be ready."

"It's not your job to tell me *my fuggin' job*, Lennon!"

"Then do your job, and I'll lay off."

"Pfffft! That's a bald faced lie!" Allan swallowed the last of his milk and wiped his mouth. "You'll *never* lay off! You'll *never* be fuggin' satisfied with fuggin' anything! With yer last dyin' breath, John Lennon, you'll have some project y'er pushin', promotin', and fightin' for…every inch of the way!"

"So…" John allowed a hint of a smile, "you'll locate us a studio, then?"

Allan had had enough. He knew he'd have to face Mona Best down on this one, but Mona was there and John was here, and Al was tired of sparring with the relentless kid. Shaking his head, he pushed away from the table.

"I'll find you a studio," he spat out, "and all for a buck'n a dime, I suppose…but anythin' for a little peace and quiet in this corner of the world!"

"Great," John grinned. "Ta very much. And of course – we'll all perform admirably…as instructed."

"And you…you're all right with this, Rory?" Allan scrutinized the boy.

"A-all right?" Rory opened his hands magnanimously, "I-I'm so all-all right with it, that I'll, uh-uh, come along for the bleedin' ride!"

"If y'can't beat 'em, join 'em!" John smiled at Al and Rory.

"Speakin' of beatin' things up, Lennon…" And without giving the boy a chance to interrupt, Allan launched into another sermon on the cost of stages and cafés.

One can only imagine what Allan had to say to Rory and John when The Kaiserkeller closed for repairs. The conversation above is conjecture, but John's desire to record with Ringo and Lu Walters is confirmed by several sources. John, Paul, George, Ringo, and Lu were all pushing Allan to find them a studio in Hamburg. Stu did not participate.

Saturday, 15 October 1960
The Kaiserkeller
Hamburg, Germany

"You're serious, then? The back of a railway station?" Paul's eyebrows lifted.

"That's where all the good studios are these days." Ringo's gemstones glittered over the stub of his cigarette.

"Sounds like a drag." George was easily elated and easily crushed, swayed by the moods of John and Paul. "What sort of studio would situate next to all that rail-rumblin', I'd like to know? It's bound to be less than ideal."

John ducked in from the hallway and summoned them, his brand new Rickenbacker in his hand. "I've got the directions...and the name of the man we're supposed to contact. Let's get down there before the fly-by-night studio ups and flies by night."

"Slow down, son." Ringo showed John his bare wrist. "It's barely afternoon by my watch."

"Fuggin' hilarious, Ringo," John growled, but a hint of a smile played at his lips.

The group continued to smoke and lounge about.

"C'mon, c'mon then!" John banged his hand against the doorjamb. "Get on with it! Chop, chop! Car's waitin', y'know."

Lu Walters, "Wally," stood and limped gingerly towards the door. "Listen John, I don't care what you say...I'm takin' it slowly and carefully. I don't know about the rest o' you, but I'm still achin' from Bruno's ghastly goons."

"Yeah, Rory's gorra a shiner as big as me fist!" Johnny Guitar, who'd decided to come along for the ride, followed them out.

"Stu's a bit worse for wear as well." Paul grabbed his amp en route.

"Now who'd want to smash up Stu?" Wally shook his head.

"Ah, they're all sadists, that bunch." Guitar spelled it out.

"I'm 'saddest'..." Ringo punned, "saddest that we didn't do more damage when we had the fuggin' opportunity!"

"Yeah, we could have finished 'em off...if they hadn't run," John fantasized.

"Rule Britannia!" Paul gave him thumbs up.

George rubbed his neck. "Speak for yourselves. I was afraid of fear itself, and I don't mind admittin' it to FDR or anyone else who'd care to listen. In fact, I was thrilled when they retreated. It was gruesome – that fight." George had his guitar and Paul's in hand, and he looked around to make sure they hadn't forgotten anything. "Hey!" he yelled towards the retreating group. "Someone's left a cord in here, y'know."

"It's all right," John yelled from the door. "Paul's got an A minor we can cadge when and *if* we ever get there. C'mon!"

"It's like talkin' to Morecambe and Wise," George muttered, throwing his eyes to the ceiling and adding the forgotten coil to his arm. "Someday we'll hafta have a real roadie. Someone as famous as me can't be doin' this sort of thing. I've bigger responsibilities, y'know."

****

The Akustik Recording Studio
57 Kirchenallee
Hamburg, Germany

The Akustik Recording Studio, once they'd found it, was hardly more than a sound booth, hardly more than one of those "serve-yourself" photo closets John frequented to send snapshots home to Cynthia. Quietly sequestered at 57 Kirchenallee, behind the railway station, The Akustik was seriously ramshackle.

Paul poked around the meagre establishment, pulling at the thick, musty curtains that were supposed to dampen the sounds from the terminal. The fabric reeked of mould and threatened to disintegrate in his hand. He doubted that the draperies enhanced the sound quality one iota, and on the down side, they made him cough.

"It's lousy – this place," he said.

"Some recordin' studio you've got here, John!" Ringo poked at the stained, broken acoustic wall panels.

"I've been in larger jowlers, haven't I?" Wally stretched out his arms in the close confines, just to see if he could.

"You *have* larger jowlers," Ringo punned, pinching Wally's cheeks to George's amusement.

"Get off, Ringo!" Wally shoved him away with a grin.

"He'd love to son." John was busy arranging the amps. "But it's all too cramped in here for that, isn't it?"

"It's not bad…in a way." George mirrored John's enthusiasm. "Sort of like singin' in the shower – lots of reverb, y'know."

"You heard the man," John nodded. "There's reverb in here. It's fuggin' ideal – this studio."

"Oh yeah, right," Ringo snorted, pretending to look the place over as if he were deciding to purchase it. "I'm comin' here for all me recordin' needs from now on. No EMI or RCA for me, as it were. From now on, it's The Akustik or nothin' at all."

"Yeah, we're done with those large studios, aren't we?" Johnny Guitar's eyes twinkled.

"Yeah," Lu agreed.

"Love it here," Paul smiled.

"You are ready?" The German attendant knew very little English, but he knew that he had a schedule to keep.

"Yerrokay…in two." Ringo made some final adjustments.

"Y'see, Mr. Recorder Man," John flashed an imbecile's grin in the attendant's direction, "it's taken a while in here, as it were. It's just that we're not used to all this elbow room, y'know."

"Five minutes," the bewildered man said. "We record then." And without waiting for assent, he disappeared.

Wally stepped up to the microphone and adjusted the height. "'Summertime' – test one two, one, two, two, two…"

John tested his own mike. "The Beatles do Gershwin!" he said.

"*I'm* no Beatle, Lennon," Ringo yelled from the side cubicle where his drums had been placed.

"All right. The Beatles *and* Ringo do Gershwin," John corrected loudly.

"I'm not a…" Wally began, but John was ready this time.

"Comin' to you live from the fabulous Akustik in fabulous Hamburgyberg," John cut him off, "Lu Walters sings 'Summertime.' Instrumentals and vocal accompaniment provided by that ever-popular, fab quartet, John, Paul, George, and Ringo. How's that?"

"Might do," Ringo shouted.

"Sounds good…" Paul agreed. "It's got potential."

"I think y'er all daft, that's what I think." Johnny Guitar squeezed into a rusted, metal folding chair. He settled in.

Lu glanced at his watch and then cleared his throat a few times before launching into the first song.

They recorded "Summer Song" with only a few hitches, and "Fever" didn't go badly, but "Summertime" was another story. Generally one of Lu Walter's favourites and a showcase for his vocal range, the song was today his undoing. The harder he tried to remember the words, the more they eluded him. They recorded the number five, six, seven times.

Ringo, sequestered in his separate cubicle, was having trouble hearing the rhythm and getting into the phrasing without being a physical part of the group. His drumming thudded unimaginatively from the disconnected space.

He wrinkled his nose at the playback. "*That* wasn't me, was it?"

"Yeah, that's you," George grinned. "It was him, wasn't it, John?"

"Giddyup, Black Bess, only a few more miles, I guess!" John teased, drumming out horse hooves with his fingers on the wall.

Paul stomped his feet while John whinnied, "Sounds a bit like Custer's last stand, Ringo!"

"Ah, bollocks, all o'ya!" Ringo waved them off. "What do you bunch know?"

"So how's it goin' lads?" Allan strode in, ready for the short trip back to The Kaiserkeller.

John grabbed Wally's arm and looked at his watch. "We haven't even recorded the first one yet! You're back too soon, that's how it's goin'."

"Haven't recorded the first one yet!" Allan exploded. "It's fuggin' four o'clock! You're all due at The 'Keller in less than an hour...or have you forgotten there's a real world outside, and you've got a job to go to, as it were. Get on with it! *Shite!*" He shook his head in annoyance.

"It's my fault, Al," Wally shrugged sheepishly. "I'm just bleedin' nervous in front of this inhuman machine! Give me an audience, and I'm totally in control. But this thingy, here… I dunno. It comes on – I turn off."

Allan had his soft side. He was an easy mark for anyone with a genuine hard luck story. His anger immediately abated.

"C'mon, Wally!" He led the kid over to the microphone. "Just concentrate and relax. You know the song. You've got it down pat." He adjusted the mike a little and gave Wally a slap on the back. "I'll be the audience, right? Just look over at me and sing the fuggin' song the way y'always do. C'mon. Off you go!"

And with Allan in the studio, watching him perform, Wally delivered "Summertime" as if he were working The Kaiserkeller on a Saturday night. The recording was almost perfect.

"You are happy this time?" The German technician searched each face.

"Yeah right, thrilled." Allan spoke for them. "Let's just get on with it. We'll take nine copies. You can do that, right?"

"Yes." The man nodded and made notes on a clipboard. "Nine. I can do this."

"And now Ringo and I'd like to record a couple of other numbers as well," Wally piped up, encouraged by his success.

"Half four, Wally, half four!" Allan slapped his watch. "The Kaiserkeller, remember? Koschmider and his band of merry men?"

"Bastards all!" Wally's lips tightened.

"Round two with that lot we can't afford." George rubbed his right bicep.

"We could always use that warm-up recordin' of 'Fever' for side B, couldn't we?" Paul asked.

"Or that next to last take of 'September Song,'" George suggested.

"I suppose we'll have to settle for one o'those," Ringo shrugged. "Regardless of what I said earlier, I'm not really up for another round with Koschmider's Panzers."

"Yeah," John lit a cigarette, "there's shag-all hope of us survivin' another bout with *that* group. Especially if Rory's not in the mix."

Allan pushed for a timely departure. "You still have to load the gear and transport it all back, y'know."

"All right," Wally conceded. "'Fever' it is."

But the end result was not what they'd anticipated, and the five of them grumbled all the way back to the club. Wally and Ringo were perturbed that the pressing had been done on a 78-rpm commercial recording rather than on the traditional 45-rpm vocal disc. John was highly insulted that the B-side was not "Fever" at all, but a sales promotional for leather handbags and shoes. And The Beatles – who'd wanted to record a number of their own backed by Ringo – were frustrated that they'd lost the opportunity. They were already badgering Allan for a repeat performance.

"Not listenin', *not* fuggin' listenin'! You had yer chance!" Allan began to sing the Welsh national anthem to himself. He drove like a madman, weaving in and out of traffic and checking his watch every few minutes.

"But we worked out a coupla songs with Ring, and we'd really like to…" Paul began.

"Not hearin' you, McCartney!" Allan sang even louder.

"And Ringo wants to record with *us* as well," George yelled over the song, tapping Allan on the shoulder as he talked.

"Wales! Wales! Fav'rite land of Wales!" Allan's lovely tenor filled the bus.

"We want Ring! We want Ring!" John, Paul, and George chanted to the beat.

"All here…and all *out!*" Allan announced, slowing the vehicle to a stop in front of The Kaiserkeller. "Out, all o'ya!"

John refused to budge as the others scrambled. "Listen Al, we…"

"Shirrup, Lennon!" Allan banged on the roof. "*Get us to Hamburg, Al! We want to play The Kaiserkeller, Al! We need to cut a record, Al! We want Ringo, Al!* Try bein' satisfied for once! Try givin' it a fuggin' rest!"

John brushed by, carrying his Ric and the Art College's amplifier. But Allan knew the boy would have the last word.

"You're only postponin' the inevitable, aren't you?" John snipped from the sidewalk.

"Consider it postponed."

"But we…"

"…will talk about Ringo once you've done what you came to do."

"I'll remember that," John wagged a finger.

And Allan knew he would.

All events in this chapter happened exactly as they are portrayed with the exception of these points:

Barry Miles mentions that Stu was present during the recording, but Allan does not mention Stu attending at all. Furthermore, Clayson and Sutcliffe do not mention Stu's presence at The Akustik in Backbeat.

Bill Harry says that Johnny Guitar and Ty Brian were there as well and sang on "Summertime." Barry Miles only mentions Johnny Guitar attending. For certain, we know that the six young men included in this chapter were definitely present.

The conversations are conjecture.

17 October 1960
The Seaman's Mission
Hamburg, Germany

Saying little, staring out the window, they lingered over tankards of milk. George yawned. Paul rubbed his eyes with his palms and lit a cig.

John leaned forward, chin in hand. Barely blinking, he stared at the stormy horizon. When motivated he listlessly picked at the faded, yellow paint chipping from the windowsill. But mainly he watched the lightning intersect the bay as a colourful fraternity of harboured boats rolled and clacked each other in a rising wind.

Sailors with thick, upturned collars scampered here and there, battening down hatches, checking tie lines, and preparing for the rain that was sure to come. They were as varied as their winter uniforms but they all reminded John of the man who'd more or less vanished at sea all those years ago. Vagabonds just outside his window – sailors who had sons back home somewhere, sailors with sons they'd little time for…

Alfred, Fred, Freddie, Pater, Daddy…where the hell've you been all these years?

"More milk?" Frau Prill, in her wilted pink Seaman's Mission uniform, hovered over them.

"I'll have an Oxo cube in mine, ta," George said charmingly.

Paul simply nodded and offered a smile.

John waved a hand over his glass. "I'm all cow-juiced out," he said, tersely. He continued to stare at the harbour, hardly glancing at the others.

"He's gorra cob on," George stage-whispered to the concerned woman whose brow furrowed in motherly concern.

"Too much of a good thing, y'know." Paul's eyebrows moved up and down quickly, painting a picture of excess.

"Oh!" Her face settled into disapproval. She clucked, shook her head, and walked away. Paul and George shared a chuckle.

But John had no energy to defend himself. And he couldn't have cared less. He was totally exhausted, fagged out.

Frau Prill can think what she wants, John looked away. *But it's no hangover, and it's no mood. I'm just tired. Tired of everything.*

The Beatles had just renewed their contract at The Kaiserkeller until 31 December. But the extension didn't cheer him the way he'd imagined it would. Another two months with Koschmider. Another two months in the Bambi Kino. Another two months without Cyn. Success wasn't all it had once seemed.

John was – they all were – drained from the sheer intensity of the last sixty days. Stamina was almost beyond them. Practising, performing, *mach shau*-ing…they endured a murky purgatory.

"Here!" Frau Prill returned with a steaming platter. "Eat! Eat now!" She had a plate piled high with eggs, steak, toast, and real British chips. It was a far cry from the accustomed bowl of cereal that The Beatles could afford, and on a normal day, John would've been elated. But today it had no aroma or appeal. John stared at the eggs, and they stared back at him with grotesque, bulging eyes.

"Eat," Frau Prill repeated. "Eat now."

She'd seen it before – the languor. She'd seen it on sailors just in from tankers – the big boats that remained at sea for a very long time. She had seen more than her share of men who'd lost their zest for living, who plodded down to The Seaman's Mission and stared out at the sea with eyes as empty as this boy's. She put her large, wrinkled hand on John's shoulder and pushed him closer to the table.

"Looks fantastic – that!" George gave her a smile.

"Almost as good as the chippy in the Penny Lane roundabout." Paul paid her the ultimate compliment. "Worth every pound – a meal like that!"

Frau Prill snickered. *Worth every pound!* The nominal two-marks-eighty that she charged her patrons barely covered the cost of milk. The meal was actually her form of charity. *But no matter!* she smiled to herself, keeping the secret. Generosity was what the Seaman's Mission was all about.

"It is for *John*," was all she said before turning to the table behind them.

George reached for a slice of toast as Paul offered the daily challenge. "A game of arrers, then Mr. Harrison?"

George grinned, "Why not? If we keep at it, you just might edge me out and win one – one of these days. You never can tell."

"Isthasso?" Paul got up from his chair, "Well, if you're of *that* mind, how's about a game of table tennis, then?"

George followed his friend out the room. "If you insist…but I was tryin' to leave y'with a bit of pride, y'know…"

John stared down at the food before him. He poked at the fried egg with his fork tine until the liquid oozed and ran like one of Stu's oil creations. Taking a deep breath, he steadied his stomach as the bright yellow eked under the steak, filling the entire plate with the gaudy colour.

Automatically, he began to eat. The chips were all right. Not too hot, not too crisp. They reminded him of Mim's.

Mim...ole bag o' bones! he smiled a little. *I wonder what she's up to this mornin'...it's half ten there. I wonder what Cyn's doin'...*

He'd gotten Cynthia's latest string of photos from the Woolworth's booth, and he pulled it from his pocket. Pouty, provocative, very Brigitte Bardot-like...

It'd be a hell of a lot easier stayin' here another forty days and nights if I could just forget about Powell!

But the visions of Cynthia weren't erased easily. They flashed through his mind like the worn black and white movie cells on The Bambi Kino screen.

Hoylaker! he grumbled, polishing off the last of his eggs. *What's she doin' here in Hamburg, anyway? What's a girl like that doin' in a place like this?*

John finished his toast and got up in search of the twangy, upright piano in the next room. The Seaman's Pub would be deserted at this time of day, and he'd have it all to himself.

Maybe working on a song would help him shake this colourless funk. He scuffed his heels and walked with his head down.

Right...no one in the room. Fantastic.

John screeched the piano stool across the wooden floor and lifted the Wurlitzer lid carefully.

The pub was musty-cold. October was as raw in Hamburg as it was in Liverpool, and they didn't light the bar heaters until two in the afternoon. The sour ether of day-old cigarettes permeated the room, and John breathed deeply, taking in the poison. Exhaling, he barely whispered the words to a song he'd written four days ago.

They'd sounded stronger when he was drunk. Sung in daylight, in solitude, the poetry was immature and wobbly. But John repeated it quietly, hardly putting voice into his whisper.

Then he waited. He drummed his fingers on the piano.

He played the first few lines over and over, finding a haunting, minor sound for the confessional...a sound that said how little time there was...for rest, for happiness, for...

And the words just started falling into place. They wrote themselves. They conjured up a sanctuary, a refuge. They led to a place where he was safe. They took him deep inside himself, where inevitably and always, they led to her.

John kept humming the tune while he walked to the bar to grab a handful of napkins. He found a pen on the heavy, brass cash register, and before he'd even made it back to the piano, he was writing the lyrics down, reworking the rough spots – finding a way to make the rhythm work.

He could hear Paul and George laughing and trading insults down the hall. The sound of a table tennis ball ricocheted back and forth; it was his only backbeat, his only percussion.

Memory directed the lyrics now. They cried out for her, as his songs always did – imagining something hopeful, imagining some impossible reunion.

They sang of a tomorrow where sorrow had no power, where loneliness and sadness didn't exist.

It was the same old futile fantasy. But John let the lyrics wander where they would. Hoping. Hoping that perhaps this time the ending…

John stopped and laid his head on the piano. And for a couple of minutes, he sat – resting a hand on the keyboard. Then he wrote, "I love only you."

And he sat in the darkness – remembering, biting on a fingernail.

Mimi used to say to him, "Wherever you go, John, there *you* are."

And she was right.

No matter how he tried to escape, no matter far he traveled, she would always be there.

Julia was always with him.

The Beatles did frequent The Seaman's Mission (or Seaman's Society in some sources) for breakfast. There really was a Frau Prill, table tennis, and a Seaman's Pub (with a piano) where the fire wasn't lit until 2 p.m. John's homesickness is documented in his letters home to Cynthia and in the sources listed in the footnotes.

Tim Riley's book, Tell Me Why, *places John's composition of "There's A Place" in this time frame. This chapter suggests one way that it might have been composed Play the song, listen, and imagine.*

20 October 1960
The Bambi Kino
Hamburg, Germany

"Who's up for a round of brag?" John challenged, shuffling and invert-shuffling the cards in the semi-darkness of The Bambi Kino closet that Pete and Paul called home. They'd found a crate in the alleyway to use as a table, and John began to deal out the cards on the wobbly wooden surface.

"I'd rather not, if you don't mind." Paul shook his head. But he pulled up one corner of Pete's army cot anyway. "Y'know, it's suspected you're cheatin' somewhat, here and there."

George wedged in beside Paul. "It's more than suspected," he agreed, picking one of the hands up and studying his cards casually. "It's widely rumoured."

"Borderin' on fact." Paul picked up a hand as well.

John flashed a buck-toothed grin before discarding two cards and picking up two new ones. "Covetous little bastards, aren't you?" He used his old man's voice.

"You're a bad influence, y'know." Paul discarded. "Me dad said so from day one."

"Bad influence on the purse strings, that is." George took his turn.

John laid down his hand in quick triumph. "Ta-da!"

"Suckered again!" Paul looked at George.

"I think there's more here than meets the eye!" George shook his head in disgust.

"Pay up, both o'ya." John held a hand out.

The losers tossed in their coins, and Paul reached for the deck, determined to deal the next hand himself. But the outcome was always the same. When Pete returned, an hour later, John's stack of coins was impressive.

"The two of you'll never turn around and learn, will ya?" Pete slid up another rickety crate to use as a stool. "It's a fool's game – playin' against John."

"So...out rubbin' noses with the natives again, eh Peter?" John dealt Pete in.

"You three ought to try it sometime, y'know. It's a helluva lot better'n spendin' day in and day out in muckin' about like three bats in a bleedin' cave, as it were."

"*You* speak the lingo." George discarded. "We don't."

"Well, you could always learn." Pete waved his hand to pass. "It's not that far off English, y'know. You'd recognize half the words if you gave it a go."

"You know a few words, don't you, John?" Paul smiled, taking his turn.

John clicked his heels and picked one card from the deck. "Zee oven is hot now."

"Look," Pete tossed down a worthless hand, "what's the use of insultin' the very people who're employin' us – the ones we're supposed to be entertainin', as it were? The war's over and done with, John! What d'you have against the German people, anyway?"

"Disrespect, disenchantment, and disfuggin'ease!" John hissed

"What about Astrid and Klaus?" Stu's voice came from the doorway.

John slammed down another winning hand. "He's got both legs in one knicker, has Klaus."

"C'mon! You haven't given him much of a chance..."

"And I won't." John dangled a wrist while the others laughed.

"You're wrong, you know!" Stu walked to a cot and sat down. "Klaus has a great mind. And he's tremendously creative as well. You'd like him, John! He's unique...a thinker...a leader in the new angst movement that's sweepin' Germany these days."

"Sounds complicated – all that." Paul got up to stretch his legs.

"Sounds like shite to me." John stood as well.

"Well, it isn't shite." Stu's face flushed. "It's serious. The Exis are champions of individual freedom in the meaninglessness of the universe, as it were. They believe in what we believe...in canvases and poetry and *guitars* speakin' out louder than words – in art providin' the only sense in a world that's lost touch with true worth and value."

"Good on yer, lad!" John patted Stu on the head. "There's a Nobel Prize for you in all that fraternization, y'know. Hands across the water and all that crap."

"If you'd only talk to Klaus...or Astrid..." Stu began. But John, dressed in only his white, drop-panel long underwear, grabbed the newspaper and strode out the exit door into the street. The others roared at the latest in a long string of Lennon absurdities.

But Stu, who read John's message quite clearly, didn't find it a bit amusing. Instead Stu blushed for the German people who were being so clearly reviled. He blushed for Klaus, for Astrid, and for The Exis...and inexplicably, he found himself taking it as a personal insult.

****

The Kaiserkeller

"Hey! Yew!" John's slurred speech did little to attract the Kaiserkeller waiter. The booze and Prellys swirled everything into a Van Gogh. People moved at half speed, oblivious to his needs. "Hey, yew!" he yelled again.

"Ah, he won't crack on." Ringo, heading for the stage, brushed past John. "He knows you're dead skint, Lennon, and they've only ears for payin' customers 'round here. You grammar school lads shoulda figured that one out by now."

"But me credit's first rate!" John shouted as Ringo hopped up on Bruno's new wooden platform. "In fact, I'm widely known as a credit to Mother England, as it were!"

Ringo knelt down to tighten a screw on his drum kit and chuckled when John resumed his vocal demands for tableside service.

"John." Stu's voice interrupted the shouts.

"Yeah?"

"Astrid wants to have a word with you, all right? I-in private, as it were."

"Astrid!" John spun in his chair, a sardonic sneer poised for action, but the look vanished when he saw the girl.

Tiny, pale, very feminine, mysterious – the German existentialist was wrapped in a long, black leather coat, black stockings, and worn, black ballet slippers. Her pixie eyes, too, were heavily charcoaled, and they hinted magic.

"Hullo John." She smiled briefly and brushed her wispy, blonde hair self-consciously off her forehead. Cropped hair, elfin hair...it suited her personality. It suited the round eyes that sparkled with a secret she never told. It suited the tiny, tipped nose. It suited a girl with a name like Astrid.

John stared.

Stu dropped her hand and looked at her questioningly. She nodded and motioned for him to leave. Without waiting to be invited, Astrid took a seat, cupped her chin in her hands, and looked at John full on, demanding his attention. He begrudgingly obliged.

"You are aware that I have photographed Stuart, are you not?" she began.

"Is that what they're callin' it these days...photographin'?"

"And," she moved on, unfazed by John's innuendo and unwilling to banter with him, "I would like to photograph your group as well."

"It's not my effin' group," he answered back, still trying to catch the waiter's eye. Astrid raised one finger, and the waiter nodded.

"Oh, but it is," she insisted, never backing down. "I have seen you perform. I have watched you on and off stage, here in the club. It is your group. It is *your* band. And I would like your permission to shoot photographs. Will you accept?"

"What sort of photographs are we talkin' about?" John watched as the waiter delivered a pint to Astrid. With two slender fingers, she pushed the glass in John's direction and paid for the drink from a tiny, leather pouch that hung from her shoulder by an elegantly braided string.

"Cheers, luv," he toasted her.

"I wish to do stills..." Astrid explained, returning the pouch to her side, "life studies – juxtapositions in black and white."

"None of that Exis crap, right?" John's animosity was thinly veiled. Astrid was monopolizing Stu's time, and John recognized her for what she was – the competition, the enemy.

"Just photographs, John," Astrid smiled sadly. "There is no reason to be so afraid."

"I haven't been afraid since yer fuggin' bombs stopped crumblin' me neighbourhood at night, luv."

"They weren't my bombs, John."

"Oh, but they were." He satirized her words. "I've seen you perform. I watched you here in the club, and you are German."

"Your hostility makes me sad." Astrid never lost his gaze. "It makes Stuart sad as well."

"Right. Well, of course, you'd know all about Stu, wouldn't you, Miss Kirchherr?"

"I know enough to know he is worried about you. We are *both* worried about your constant anger, John." She paused with tremendous control and then asked the question again. "Will you come and bring your band to pose for me tomorrow? I need to know if you will accept."

"Right." John gulped down the dark German beer, slamming the pint on the table. "Why not? I accept. How's that for your freedom of the individual in a meaningless world, as it were?"

But instead of answering, Astrid only nodded, rose, and walked away. She dissolved from John's line of vision as silently as she had appeared.

"T'rah John!" Stu's voice called from the shadows at the back of the room. "See y'tomorrow...for the photographs, eh?"

But John pretended not to hear. Without looking up, he returned to his lager and his swirling, Van Gogh world. "Play us a number, Ringo!" he shouted.

And Ringo, who was just settling in to the rostrum, shook his head and laughed softly.

All events in the chapter are accurate including the game of brag, Astrid's clothing, and Pete's ability to speak German. The conversation is conjecture.

There is a photograph taken in Hamburg of John in his underwear, reading the newspaper on the street, in Williams' The Man Who Gave the Beatles Away.

21 October 1960
Der Dom Park
Hamburg, Germany

John didn't know what he'd expected from the photo session, but it wasn't this. There was no studio, no pull-down backdrops, no lights, no props or paraphernalia, no inducements to make them smile. Smiles, in fact, were never mentioned. The Beatles huddled together beneath the overcast skies cupping Der Dom Park in the hushed anticipation of a storm, and they talked quietly to one another, their hands in their pockets. Astrid rarely spoke to them as she studied the boys through her Rollercord's eye.

The icy Westerweg crosswinds buffeted the small leather-clad group. John squinted and hunched his shoulders. George stomped his feet. Astrid drew deeply on a short brown Stuyvesant cigarette for warmth.

"Drag on yer fag, luv?" John walked over and reached out in anticipation.

"Here." Astrid dug into her coat pocket and handed him one of his own. "But quickly, please. We have much to do."

"Look!" Stu spread his arms and turned full circle for John's perusal. "The jacket's great, isn't it?"

John lit his cigarette and nodded at the coat Stu had purchased from him. "It's more you than it ever was me. I was never really right for suede, y'know."

Astrid ignored the chatter, surveying the bleak, early winter backdrop for possibilities. Der Dom Park was liberally doused in shades of grey that created a haunting stillness. It was eerie, dramatic.

"Shall we begin at the carousel?" Astrid directed the question to them all.

"Actually," Paul leaned in as if divulging a confidence, "John'd be more at home in front of the freak show…given the choice, y'know."

"Y'er a regular George Formby, aren't you, McCartney?" John flicked ashes at him.

"I've been known to raise a chuckle or two, in my day."

"Hardee har har," George smiled.

"See?" Paul shrugged. "I'm always appreciated by the common man."

"I resemble that remark!" George pretended to bristle.

"This way, please." Astrid secured her beret and motioned for the boys to follow her. Pete hoisted his snare drum, and the others, carrying guitars, tagged along behind, pausing only when Astrid paused, waiting as she looked through her viewfinder and consulted her hand-held light meter.

At the base of a deserted, gigantic Ferris wheel, she finally announced, "We will begin here. It will be good, this shot."

"Right, then. How's this?" John assumed a Napoleonic pose.

Astrid smiled slightly, put a hand to her temple, and shook her head. "I will arrange the pose," she decided.

Within minutes, she'd aligned them all, shoulders cocked at odd angles, eyes stern, chins lifted. They were all James Dean. They were all Elvis. The bantering Liverpool lads were serious and silent – aloof and dangerous and full of rock'n'roll.

"No...look away, please," Astrid would direct them when they tried to pose for the lens. "Forget the camera. Stand as you are."

They stood about in their dark plimsoles and black bomber jackets, looking tough and out of place in the childlike, carnival atmosphere of Der Dom Park's semi-annual funfest. In a terrain of Ferris wheels and calliopes, The Beatles were the only serious elements on the sawdust midway. It was a clever juxtaposition, a paradox of moods.

"I feel a ruddy fool," Pete stood off to one side, posed with the others on a fairground wagon, his snare drum at his side and his drumsticks in one hand.

"And you look it as well." John was no help.

"Thasso?" Pete was tired of the constant "mickey talk." "Well, you're no Savoir Faire either, Lennon..."

"No talking." Astrid admonished. "Stand still."

The wind swirled around them. Stu shivered. George's teeth chattered audibly. "Are we there, yet?" he complained.

"Lift your guitar higher," was Astrid's only response. "John, look to the right...as if you've seen someone you know. Good. Very good. Hold, please."

The camera clicked.

She posed John and George on the back of a festival lorry. Stu, in dark sunglasses and a lost, pensive look, took the foreground. Black and white musicians against a pale grey sky, they formed a tight triangle that intimated the strength of their music. They were rock'n'roll personified.

As the shadows lengthened, Astrid loaded them in her tiny car and drove them to the marshaling yards that the RAF had targeted all through the war. In front of barracks, on the bonnets of heavy troop trucks, and in between huge tanks, she posed the British boys and their gear.

"How come Sutcliffe's out in front again?" Not even Astrid escaped the Lennon tongue. "I thought it was *my* fuggin' band! You've forgotten that, haven't you, photographer?"

Astrid smiled coyly. "He is out front because he is the most beautiful," she stated, never blushing nor hesitating in her honest appraisal. "He is there because he has the most magnetism."

John looked at George, and they broke into adolescent laughter. "He's gorra face like a ruptured custard!" George pronounced.

"As pallid as Spencer's ghost – is Stu," Paul said.

"More mirage than man, truth be told." John also put the boot in.

But Astrid never laughed, and she hardly took her eyes off Stu. She posed him in the background of almost every picture. She posed him nose to nose with John on the new stage of The Kaiserkeller. She posed him in doorways, in her mother's attic, and in the dim light of the fading afternoon sun. And last, almost as a *piece de resistance*, Astrid posed Stu where he most belonged.

It was a cunning portrait of John, a silhouette that captured his denied innocence and cynicism, the study of a man with hard eyes that screamed resentment and whispered sorrow. John sat alone, glancing offhandedly at the camera with a mouth that had forgotten how to smile, with the first furrow of a determination line between his thick, unruly brows. His looked as if he dared the world to confront him, as if he dared Astrid to take the photograph.

But without hesitation, the camera clicked, and Astrid stepped forward, clicking the Rollercord again and again and again.

Posed in the distance, blurred, with his guitar bowed, stood Stu, ever relinquishing centre stage to his friend, following in John's footsteps. Stu stood in the foggy edge of the Rollercord's vision, always there, always just within reach, but removed – a figure in the shadows, looking on.

It was Stu's most perfect portrait. And whether he would admit it or not, it was also John's.

All facts are well documented including the date, place, make of camera, locations, weather, clothing, and so forth. Every shot described is an actual shot from the portfolio, "Die Beatles in Hamburg," by Astrid Kirchherr.

The only point of conjecture is the conversation.

The photo on the cover of this book is one of the shots taken by Astrid Kirchherr on 21 October 1960. I have used the photo with permission of Ms. Kirchherr through her agency, Retna, Ltd. in New York City. My sincere appreciation to John Rauch at Rockstore, Sarah Field at Retna, to K&K Center of Beat in Hamburg, and to Astrid Kirchherr for making it possible for me to share the hauntingly beautiful work with you.

23 October 1960

Dear Cyn,

I love, love, love and miss you like mad. How long's it been? Three decades now? My imagination's runnin' amuck inventin' all the things we'll do (ahem!) when (and **not** if) I get home. (I miss you.)

As it happens, Al's signed us on for an extension (sorry, luv) 'til 31 December. I know that's shite with Christmas and all...but just think of the fame and fortune waitin' for you down the road as a famous rocker's luv, luv. It'll all be Wool-worth it some day. In any event, Bruno's got me through the holidays, so be a good girl and hold the holiday pudding 'til I get home. We'll poke about for plums then.

Good news! I love you.

On a lighter note (C major), we've been having some conversations with this other club owner, Peter Eckhorn, about the possibility of us playin' at his new venue, The Top Ten Club. It's massively huge...in this great building called The Hippodrome... and rumour has it, it's destined to be the hottest place (besides one I can think of) in existence...a venue that could rescue us from the shite Koschmider's been shovelin' out. Tony Sheridan of the famous Tony Sheridan has agreed to headline there...and we get on well. Even ole Horst (our loyal bouncer) Fascher has defected to the Eckhorn (enemy) camp. So all things considered - as well you know I have - we're thinkin' of makin' the move ourselves.

Besides, Al and Koschmider have been knockin' about the idea of us playin' in Berlin after the New Year, and **who the fuggin'ell wants Berlin?** (I want you.) It's Hamburg that's the "with it" rock'n'roll scene these days, and it's The Top Ten that'll soon bee attractin' all the bzzzzzness around here. So that's where we bee-long, as it were.

In fact, we dropped 'round The Top Ten lassnight after our set at The 'Keller and had a go with Sheridan...an ~~Arry Freeman,~~ "with nothin' exchangin' hands...but great fun and a great sound, nevertheless. (I'd forgotten what it's like to play where there are actual acoustics, y'know. That's an extra Bruno'd never spring for.) In fact, Stu said (and I quote) that we sounded as good as Sheridan's "Jets" – his London backin' group. (Although you can't go by his opinion these days. All he's hearin', seein', and contemplatin's the lovely German Astrid.)

I'm contemplatin' the lovely Hoylake you.

Cyn, you'd hardly recognize Stu really. He's all done up in this "Exis" garb Astrid promotes...collarless jackets, tied-up shirts, velvet gear...dressed up like some medieval gadfly with that pale skin of his even paler under the lovesick pallour of unrequited lust. (I wish he'd just shag her and have done with it!)

And Astrid's obviously mad for him as well. I mean, she's decent to all of us...havin' us round for eggs 'n' chips or beans 'n' toast at teatime. But Stu's been asked to move lock, stock, and barrel (aye, there's the rub!) into the Kirchherr home...leavin' behind us squalid types who knew him 'before he was.' (If only we'd secured his autograph, photograph, phonograph, or graph paper when we had the chance. It's all too graphic to dwell on now.)

I wudden mind his goin' off under ordinary circumstances, but he's losin' concentration on the band, y'know. And what's more, he's back to paintin' again...usin' Astrid's loft as a studio of sorts...which is all well and good, except that we're here on business, and Stu's not all that focused on the band...much less when there's art and Astrid on the brain.

As I wrote yesterday, we did that recordin' with Wally and Ringo at the

Akustik. Well, Al had nine pressin's made up, and he dropped them 'round for us before headin' back to the 'Pool, so you'll be receivin' an exclusive, recorded concert on Boxing Day or thereabouts. (How's about comin' up to hear me pressings, luv? They're sure to impress, me impression of a rocker, and even if not, there's more pressin' matters I can press on you, as it were.)

I can't think what else to write right now, so I'll close and post this posthaste. Hello to Phyl and that lot. My best to the odd sods and bods at the art college. Tell Ballard we're makin' "millyns" and that Stu's well taken care of, or will be any day now. (Lucky bastard...I miss you.)

All my love forever and ever...and ever and ever... and ever...and ever... and (quoth the Raven) ever more.

I love you!!!!!!!!!!!!!!
—John

This letter is completely fictional, but Coleman tells us that John wrote Cynthia every day. To create such a letter, I studied John's letters printed in Coleman's book as well as a letter written by John to his sister, Julia Baird, which was shown to me by Allan Williams in March 1993. These letters, coupled with a study of John's writing style in his three books, In His Own Write, A Spaniard in the Works, *and* Skywriting by Word of Mouth, *have enabled me to construct this letter.*

All of the events mentioned are factual.

31 October 1960
The Kaiserkeller
Hamburg, Germany

Koschmider sat with George Steiner, their heads together over pilsners of warm Bitburger. Over the past few months, Steiner had remained in Hamburg as a liaison between Koschmider and the British groups, and he had become a trusted ally in the Koschmider dynasty. Moreover, he'd become Bruno's friend.

It was mid-afternoon, and The Kaiserkeller was quiet. Only Rosa doddled along, her antiseptic spray pungent and her vacuum cleaner the perfect white noise for the conversation the two men were having. Steiner punctuated his recommendations with quick, jerky gestures, and Koschmider nodded, listening and lodging a thumbnail between his front teeth.

"Ungrateful boys!" Steiner's German was accented with disdain. "Self-serving opportunists, eh!"

"And to think," Koschmider narrowed his eyes, "that I gave them a chance! Brought them here when *no one else* on The Reeperbahn would have had them!"

"Gave them the opportunity to prove themselves," Steiner motioned towards the stage.

"And now," Bruno slammed a meaty fist into the pocked pub table, "they thank me with this! Blatant deception!"

"Deception!"

"Desertion and lies!"

The night before, Steiner had seen the evidence himself. Young entrepreneur, Peter Eckhorn, had invited The Beatles down to his lavish, new Top Ten Club at 136 Reeperbahn where the lads had willingly taken the stage and performed with Eckhorn's star – British singing sensation, Tony Sheridan.

"So you're telling me," Koschmider reviewed the facts again, poking the table top as he spoke, "that they openly and willingly broke contract…that they sang on stage for Eckhorn and performed for crowds who could have been *here* instead of there?"

"For over an hour – for seventy minutes!" Steiner nodded. "They 'jammed,' as they say, with this Sheridan and another man called Ian Hines, also a Brit."

"For pay?" Koschmider's eyes were darting back and forth excitedly.

"I saw no money exchange hands," Steiner shrugged. "But I did hear them talk contracts, and Eckhorn seemed to be suggesting they...jump ship."

"Unforgivable!" Koschmider grabbed his glass and headed for the bar. "They've all been well-informed they're not permitted to work anywhere within a twenty-five mile radius of The Kaiserkeller...nor can they work anywhere on The Reeperbahn for thirty weeks after they leave here! I put it all in writing. I went over it very carefully with Williams."

"But," Steiner shrugged, "Allan Williams is away, and these boys are hungry for riches and fame."

"They'll *think* hungry..." Bruno threatened. He reached for the tap and overfilled his glass. Then he slammed the handle back into place and swore loudly.

Bruno's strategy for dominance of The Reeperbahn had already been severely impeded by the opening of Eckhorn's new Top Ten in the former sex-circus, the Hippodrome building. Compared to the expansive, glamourous Hippodrome, The Kaiserkeller now looked shoddy, second-rate – outdated.

When young Eckhorn had wooed Bruno's experienced bouncer, Horst Fascher, away to the glitzy, new nightspot, he'd wounded Bruno severely. Then Fascher's minions had also defected to the new location. Rumour had it that even Rosa was soon to follow.

Bruno's only real remaining defence against Eckhorn's appeal was the retinue of popular Liverpool performers who graced The Kaiserkeller stage. With The Hurricanes and The Beatles in his employ, Bruno was still assured of crowds and a steady income – no matter how The Top Ten dazzled, no matter how Eckhorn packaged his entertainment.

"A club is, after all, only trappings and backdrop," he'd told Steiner earlier in the week. "The draw that keeps The Kaiserkeller in the black is Rory Storm's group and The Beatles. Everything else is show. We have the essentials, the *hauptbestandteil*."

But now, Koschmider was losing his biggest draw.

Just days ago, The Hurricanes had politely refused to sign an extension contract with Koschmider and had packed up for home. The long hours, poor living conditions, and low pay that they'd endured since October had taken a toll. Although Bruno had scurried to offer better wages and more suitable lodging, nothing had persuaded Rory, Johnny, Ty, Wally, Lu, and Ringo to re-up.

Bruno knew that if the popular "Peedles" relocated to The Top Ten, it would ruin him financially. At two pounds fifty per day, the Liverpool boys exacted almost nothing in wages, and their upkeep at The Bambi Kino was negligible. But the crowds that they had pulled into The Kaiserkeller night after night kept the cash registers ringing non-stop. Never had Bruno seen such a steady influx of customers from all walks of life. Sailors, tourists, college students, and locals all packed The 'Keller to watch the antics of the flippant ruffians from Northern England. The loss of the charismatic Beatles would be the final blow

"Hmphffing" into his glass, banging against anything in his way as he bulldozed back to the table, Bruno clenched and unclenched his jaw.

"Eckhorn was quite taken with The Beatles," Steiner continued his story. "They began singing 'What I'd Say,' and everyone in The Top Ten joined in…the whole crowd. Those who weren't up and dancing were clapping their hands and moving at tables. And McCartney zeroed in on this group of girls who…"

The sound of Bruno's chuckling stopped George Steiner in mid-sentence. He snapped his head towards his business associate, who was now laughing loudly. Bruno had dissolved into a gale of hysterics.

"What did I say?" the confused Steiner began. "Everything I've told you was just as I've said…"

"Yes, yes you've told me exactly what they did. But now, I tell you…The Beatles von Liverpool will soon be singing a different tune altogether." Bruno grinned and wagged his finger back and forth in front of his face. "Understand this, my friend. No one survives the Reeperbahn without protection. No one is safe – even from his own shadow – in this corner of the world without a guardian, a covering, a bodyguard!"

Steiner nodded. "So I've heard," he said.

"Thus far and up to this moment," Bruno's eyes twinkled, "The Beatles were under my invaluable shelter. But now…let us see how they can fend for themselves, these young – these very young – British boys, now that the hedge around them is about to be lifted."

All events are factual. But once again it's a battle of details. Allan Williams says that The Beatles weren't allowed to play anywhere in a 25-mile radius of the Kaiserkeller, and Norman, Pawlowski, and Lewisohn agree. Bill Harry says the distance was 45 miles. In any event, The Beatles broke their contract, and retribution was sure to follow.

The conversation is conjecture.

November 1960
The Bambi Kino
Hamburg, Germany

"John," Stu reached for Astrid's hand, and she took his, "we're engaged! Y'know, spoken for…on the road to wedded bliss 'n all that."

Astrid smiled and dipped her head.

John looked at them without expression. He'd known for weeks that Stu and Astrid were "involved," but he was still blindsided by the rush of it all. He stared at their interlocked hands – the two modest gold bands they wore. He sized up the giddiness in Stu's eyes. This was no joke.

"See?" Astrid extended her hand for John. "We have exchanged rings. It is the German way. It is the one tradition I keep without challenge."

"Yeah," Stu's eyes held Astrid's for a moment before turning back with a grin, "*you'll* go back to the 'Pool with German boots and a Rickenbacker as a souvenir. I'll have…" he grinned and gestured towards Astrid, "somethin' a bit more wonderful, as it were."

John blinked and looked away.

"Well?" Stu sat down on the dirty camp bed next to John. A long, sliver of diluted light filtered into the storeroom from the hallway and fell just shy of John's face. "What d'ya have to say, then? What d'ya think?"

"Congratulations." John stood up. He leaned on the cracked concrete wall beside the bed. "I'm sure you'll be shag-all happy, the both o'you."

"Stuart still loves you, John." Astrid's voice sliced through the morass of things unsaid. "Nothing takes that away. Something has been added, but nothing has changed."

"Nothin's changed?!" John turned and glared at her, anger gripping his throat. "Tell that to Klaus!"

"Klaus knows," Astrid said quietly and evenly.

"He wants her…and me as well…to be happy, John," Stu muttered.

"Well, that's fuggin' generous of him, isn't it?" John hissed. "Plays well with others – Klaus. Very well adapted – Klaus."

"You must not insult him, even with sarcasm, "Astrid said.

"Why the fuggin'ell not?" John yelled. "You sure as hell have! You've tossed him a fuggin' grenade, sister! And look…y'er wearin' the pin ring, aren't you!"

"Nothing has changed, John," the girl said again.

"It's *all* fuggin' changed!" John raged. "You're wearin' rings! You're fuggin' committed! Stuart here's about to become a married man with fuggin' responsibilities and parameters and expectations! Don't tell *me* nothing's fuggin' changed!"

"I'm not leavin' the band, John, if that's what y'er on about." Stu stood up.

"Pffft! You will."

"Will not!"

"Y'er only fuggin' foolin' yourself, Sutcliffe!" John's voice was cold. "At least have the fuggin' gall to admit what it is you're about to do!"

"We want a long engagement, John," Astrid spoke up. "Stu wants to finish his art studies before we marry, to try for an apprenticeship, to learn all there is to learn…"

"Fanfuggin'tastic!" John kicked at Stu's former bunk, booting it over onto its side. "Astrid *and* art, eh Stu? Is that where we are these days? And here I thought you'd come to Hamburg to play in the fuggin' band!"

"I play in the band!" Stu's volume went up as well. "I play hour after hour and day after day! I rehearse and perform and do whatever it is you fuggin' tell me to do! What else do you want? What more do you want me to give?"

"He wants it all." Astrid grabbed Stu's hand. "He wants your attention, your presence, your commitment…"

"It's not like that…" Stu began.

"You're callin' me a fag?!" John moved towards the German girl with his face contorted and wild. Stuart stepped between them, but Astrid continued, unabashed.

"I am saying," her voice was strong and even, "that you love Stuart. I am saying that you are jealous of me. I am saying that you are afraid of losing him."

Stu put a hand on John's chest, but John shoved it off.

"And what I am saying," Astrid stepped out from behind her fiancé, "is true. Admit it, John. You know it. You love Stu. That is the reason you are so angry."

"If you were a man, I'd smash yer fuggin' face and walk away exonerated!"

"You love him." Astrid hardly blinked. "That is why you are enraged by me. But sexual preference is something entirely different. It is often outside the realm of love. Sex, in itself, is not love any more than any other bodily function is love. I am not saying you desire Stuart sexually." She blinked as John stepped forward, invading her space. "And I am not saying you are anything other than his friend. But I am saying that you love him. And you are jealous needlessly. Nothing will be different, John. Nothing will change."

"Change is all there is, Astrid Kirchherr." John's nostrils flared. "You never put yer foot in the same effin' stream twice, right? Isn't that how the adage goes?"

"You think I am your enemy John." Astrid's eyes confirmed the sincerity of her words, "But you are wrong. I am your friend."

"I don't *have* any fuggin' friends!" John shot an angry glare at Stu. "It's all rubbish – friends. It's all shite!"

John turned to walk away.

"John," Stu pleaded, "we came here to tell you first…before anyone, y'know. Before we even rang up me mum or sisters. Before Astrid's family even…"

"How about Klaus?" John said. "You destroyed him, didn't you…before you came for me?"

John slammed out through the metal fire escape into the street, angry percussion echoing behind him in the tiny hall, punctuating the silence and then falling away into emptiness.

"He will be back." Astrid stroked Stu's arm. "He will come to accept it in time."

"Nah, you don't understand. John thinks…he thinks everyone deserts him eventually." Stu put his arm around her shoulders and pulled her close. "I mean, all his life, Astrid, everyfuggin'one who shoulda been there, wasn't."

"But you are not going anywhere, Stuart. He will see that."

"Yeah…right."

"You can say no more," she went on, "and words are not proof of anything anyway. Time will prove your heart."

"Yeah," Stu leaned his head against Astrid's, drawing strength from her calm assurance. "Yeah, y'er right. John'll have to find that out for himself…"

"You will always be there for him."

"I hope so," Stu whispered. "Dear God, I hope so."

****

George and Paul were hysterical. In fact, George was laughing so hard that the hand he held to the ceiling shook, the candle wax splattered, and the final "e" smeared so violently that it looked more like an "i" than an "e," really.

"The *Beatlis*?" John leaned against the doorway, supervising their craftsmanship.

"This'll be worth millyuns to Bruno, one of these days!" George predicted. "He'll be down here givin' tours and chargin' for a glimpse of the wax autograph on the walls where The Beatles once stayed."

"He'll be proclaimin' how he knew us 'way back when,'" Paul gave George a hand as he jumped down from the stack of fruit crates they'd piled up to reach the ceiling.

"But *that's* not us," John flopped onto his camp bed and folded his hands under his head. "It says 'Beatlis,' not 'Beatles.'"

"Have some imagination," Paul prodded. "We *were* actually beat-less once. You remember it, don't you, George?'

"It's an eventuality I'm prepared to remember," George teased, using his favourite bit of Scouse gobbledygook.

"Oh yeah," John rolled over on his side, "that was back when we had less of Moore and fell short of Best."

"Yeah, those were the days!" Paul threw his eyes to the ceiling.

George stood back and surveyed the signature they'd scrawled on the ceiling in wax and smut. Then he grinned, wiped his hands on the seat of his wrinkled, black jeans, and began sliding the crates out into the hallway, hiding the instruments of their vandalism.

"That won't save you, son." John never opened his eyes as he pronounced judgement. "You've gone and vandalized property, haven't you?"

"And the wrath of Bruno will be upon you!" Paul made himself comfortable on George's sofa bed.

"Hey, it was *both* our decisions to write our names up there!" George protested.

"Just look up, Havva," John teased, using George's nickname. "The evidence speaks for itself, son. Plain as the nose on Ringo's face…there it is…yer very own handwritin'…for all the world to espy."

"And when Bruno espies it," Paul wagged a finger, "sad to say, you're off to the scuffer, lad."

"Down to the cop shop," John echoed.

"It's uniforms for you!" Paul leaned back and grinned.

"Ah, but they've a lovely stripe, haven't they, Macca?" John opened one eye.

George's smile had faded. "But it was really Paul's idea!" he insisted.

"Bruno'll have his revenge on you, Georgie Harrison," John warned.

A voice came from the doorway. "He already has."

They turned to find Pete holding a legal-sized document, a paper that looked official. Pete's face was colourless; his eyes were full of fire.

"Bruno's threatened to can us," he stated flatly.

"Y'er jokin'…"

"Fuggin'ell!"

"What's this?"

John jumped up and grabbed the paper from Pete's hand. He reached under his pillow and grabbed his glasses.

"What's it say?" Paul was at his shoulder.

"Read it aloud." George scanned the document, too.

"For 'jeopardizin' their employment'...'for failure to adhere to the non-fraternization clause,'" John ran his finger down the page and scanned rapidly.

"What's that mean?" George looked from one to the other.

"It's fuggin' revenge, that's what!" John's spat it out.

"It's ridiculous," Paul shrugged. "When did we fraternize and with whom?"

"When we turned around and jammed at the Top Ten with Tony Sheridan, that's when and whom." Pete spelled it out for them. "Read on down...that part about the twenty-five mile radius of The Kaiserkeller."

"He'd punish us for *that*? For one jam session on our own time and for no pay whatsoever?" George couldn't believe his ears.

"Wait 'til Al hears this!" Paul was indignant.

"It was only the once!" George whined.

"Yeah, well the once," John flapped the paper angrily, "or a fuggin' thousand times, it's all the same to Koschmider."

"He'll never can us!" George looked around the room for confirmation. "We're his meal ticket, aren't we?"

"Don't bet on it, Sonny Jim," John warned. "He'd as soon see us in hell..."

"Or in Liverpool," Paul interjected.

"...as see us over at The Top Ten," John finished.

"Well, happy holidays to us, eh?" Paul's dejection was their common denominator.

"If we go home, at least Father Christmas'll know where to find us, right?" George tried to smile.

"Back Merseyside," Pete lit and cigarette and stomped out the match with his new cowboy boot. "Back to square one."

"Hey, wait 'til Stu hears!" Paul looked over at John. "It'll break him to bits, the thought of leavin' Astrid behind, as it were."

John turned towards the wall, sick of everything. "Yeah, well that's highly unlikely," he answered over his shoulder. "In fact, as things stand now, whether we go or whether we stay, it won't affect Stu at all."

"How's that?' Paul glanced at the others. They only shrugged.

"Stu's fuggin' engaged. He's given Astrid a ring. They're as good as married, and he's already plannin' to go back to his art studies and 'learn from the masters' – all that crap."

"So y'er sayin'..." Paul was almost afraid to ask, "he'll remain in Hamburg, then?"

"I'm sayin'," John hissed, "that Stu'll be wavin' us a fond farewell from the railway platform, as it were. No matter what he tells you right now, Stu's out of the fuggin' group!"

No one knew quite what to say. George folded his arms and sighed. Pete shook his head and wondered if they should confront Bruno face to face.

"Look," John said into the wall, "if we're accused of playin' The Top Ten...we might as well, right?"

"Yeah," George's eyes brightened. "If we talk go and to Eckhorn and tell him what's happened, he might just take us on straight away."

"But then...Stu...he'd remain in the group then, wouldn't he?" Paul couldn't resist asking.

"Forget Stu!" John barked. "No matter what transpires in the next few days, Stu's out. We're down to four now, and that's the way it is."

In The Anthology, *Paul states, "Round about this time, Stu and I got a little fraught, too. I claim that I was making sure that we were musically very good...People would now call that the perfectionist in me. I see it as trying to get it right, but not obsessively so. That did create a couple of rifts on stage, and I could have been more sensitive about it. But who is sensitive at that age?" (p. 53)*

In Backbeat, Clayson and Sutcliffe say that with his engagement, however, Stu had reached a stage where he no longer cared: "He no longer bothered to strain his ears to catch Paul and George's murmured backstage intrigues. They could get John to sack him now for all he cared." (p. 113) With his engagement to Astrid, Stu continued to play with the group, but less frequently and with even less conviction.

All facts about Bruno Koschmider and the contract are accurate. Only the conversation is conjecture.

Monday, 21 November 1960
The Bambi Kino
Hamburg, Germany

Roughly shaken from a deep, mid-morning sleep by intolerant *Polizei*, George Harrison was required to produce his work visa and documentation proving that he was of legal employment age. Visibly terrified, the seventeen-year-old tumbled out of bed onto the icy, concrete floor and dressed with shaking hands. He was jostled this way and that and ordered to accompany two very no-nonsense officers to headquarters for further interrogation.

Without even brushing his teeth or grabbing an overcoat, George staggered to a waiting car where stone-faced officers – their glares and growls permitting no discussion whatsoever, not from the accused, not from the other boys around him – began berating the boy for attempting to work illegally in a foreign country. The *Polizei* shouted and turned deaf ears to the young Beatle's stammered explanations and entreaties. And within a matter of hours, he was found guilty.

The rosy-cheeked lad from Speke – George Harrison – was on his way back to Liverpool.

Astrid and Stu alone were permitted to accompany the youth to the train station, but even then, a stern, uniformed officer looked on with arms folded as the British boy accepted a farewell basket of apples and biscuits from his confused friends.

Back at The Bambi Kino, the remaining Beatles huddled together on George's vacated sofa and tried to make some sense of the last few hours. Paul suggested that they phone Allan as soon as possible. But John was past discussion.

"What's the fuggin' use?" He threw his sparse belongings into the worn, green duffel bag that was beginning to grow mould in the dank, windowless room. "This is more'n likely the first in a series of arrests, y'realize. Bruno doesn't have it out for George exclusively. We're all movin' targets here!"

None of them had any delusions about the source of the *Polizei's* information regarding George. The Germans had had months to investigate the legality of The Beatles' work visas, yet they'd chosen to look the other way. Now suddenly – after a heated argument during which Koschmider threatened to have The Beatles assassinated if they dared perform at The Top Ten Club again – information about the band's work visas had mysteriously "come to light." For months George had performed without the slightest hint of censure. Now in one fell swoop, he was gone, and the Beatles had lost their crucial lead guitarist and their friend.

"So what're you sayin'?" Paul shook his head as John dredged up a dirty shirt from the space between his cot and the wall. "You're just givin' up? You're leavin' then?" John continued to pack. "And where'll you go exactly? The Seaman's Mission? Astrid's? We can't exactly afford a hotel room, John."

"I'm movin' to The Top Ten."

"Isstharrafact?" Paul raised an eyebrow.

"C'mon, John," Pete held up his hands, "if y'just walk out, what'll we say to Al?"

John grabbed a pile of dirty socks and jammed them into the top of his bag. He reached for his cap, pulling it down low, obscuring his face. "Tell him the jig's up. Tell him we've no lead guitarist. Tell him we're bein' hunted by a man who has paid assassins at his fuggin' beck and call…and who's threatened to have us terminated, *literally*! Tell him it's well past contracts and agreements now…it's all a case of survival, as it were."

"Oh, splendid lecture, Professor Messer!" Paul was frustrated.

"Y'er really goin'?" Pete looked surprised. He watched John tug at a rusted zipper. "And what are we supposed to do here while y'er over at Eckhorn's…livin' the good life, as it were?"

"Why would you be here?" John's snapped. "Read the writin' on the wall, son. The Boogey Man *is real,* and he's out there, and his name is Koschmider. If I were you, I'd get the hell out."

Pete and Paul threw their eyes to the ceiling and tried to snicker as John grabbed up his coat, but their levity was forced, and it faded too abruptly into awkward silence.

Paul forced a yawn. He settled into George's sofa and crossed his arms.

Pete sprawled on John's bed, testing it for improvements over his own, and watched John exit in silence. But as soon as the door banged shut, he turned to Paul. "Well, *I'm* not turnin' around and goin' anywhere, that's for sure. I'm dead creased, aren't you?"

"Right," Paul hardly moved. "I was almost asleep when the scuffers broke in to pay George their courtesy call."

"Yeah, I'd just about dropped off meself…"

For a while, the only sound in the room was the movie on the other side of the wall. Talking, gunfire, more talking, more gunfire.

"John's crackers, right?" Pete asked.

"Yeah," Paul didn't sound convincing. "Yeah, sure. You know John."
More talking.
More gunfire.
Horses' hooves.
Gunfire.
Quiet.
"Shite!" Pete spat out angrily. "John's bleedin' right, isn't he?"
"Ummmm," Paul muttered.
"He's *dead* right, and we both know he's right." Pete confirmed his own suspicions. "I mean, we're finished here, aren't we? End of story! Done! Bruno'll find a way to incriminate us in somethin' somehow. And who knows? Perhaps it'll be even worse than George's…"

"Or perhaps not." Paul was exhausted. He only wanted a few minutes' rest. "Look Pete, half the time, John's convinced the world's out to get him. I've known him a bit longer'n you – and he's fantastically paranoid – John."

"But come to think of it, doesn't he have a reason to be?" Pete sat up. "I mean, most people *will* stab you in the back, given half the opportunity, won't they? And Bruno…well, he might not wait for a well-presented back to come along!"

Paul's feet thudded to the floor in exasperation. "All right then. Come on. Collect yer things!"

Pete began to feel his way towards the door in the darkness.

Bruno hadn't replaced their single light bulb for weeks, and the umber of early winter made the room barely navigable.

"I think it's the only thing to do," Pete began, tripping over a boot someone had kicked off. He lost his balance and banged his shoulder into the wall. "Cor!" He hopped on one foot. "It's the bottom of an effin' well in here!"

"Exactly why we have these, right?" Paul said.

Pete heard rustlings and movement, the sound of paper being torn, and the scritch of a match against the concrete wall. He knew precisely what Paul was doing. It had been their only dependable light source for the last month or so.

They'd discovered that a well-inflated, inexpensive "French letter" burned just long enough to wedge one's boots off and find a cot. A couple of the prophylactics ignited in the corners of the room provided enough light to manoeuver successfully for several minutes. The condoms weren't as long lasting or as practical as traditional candles, but on The Reeperbahn, they were always available, and they served the purpose.

"There!" Paul rubbed his hands together. "That should do. But let's get goin', eh? These won't last tremendously long, y'know."

"Ugh! That smell!" Pete shook his head. "Burnin' rubber – rancid!"

"Yeah, but around here, who'd notice?" Paul lit another condom and fixed it to the wall of their room. In the dim light it gave, he found his duffle bag, kicked it a couple of times to scatter the mice and water bugs, and then hoisted it onto his bunk.

"Yeah," Pete located his bag as well and began packing as quickly as he could. "It's been hell – this place."

"A sojourn into the bowels of depravity."

One of the condoms sizzled and sent stray sparks up into the ragged material that covered the theater walls – material that had been ratty even when it was new. Now the fabric hung in shreds – kindling. The flame traveled instantaneously up the wall, igniting a small fire.

"Shite!" Paul grabbed his bomber jacket and began to beat the flames. "Take that! And that! And that! Ow!"

Pete shoved the last of their belongings into the hallway and then hurried to gather up some of George's things.

"Anythin' we do to this dungeon," Pete yelled, "would only be improvement, y'know!" He grabbed one of George's shirts from on the sofa and a pair of socks from a flap in the torn fabric. "C'mon McCartney. Save yourself, right? Let's get out of here."

Paul was right behind him. "I wudden mind if I do."

"We're out, then!"

And within a matter of seconds, they were gone. Only a few of George's things remained behind. Had it not been for their smudgy, wax signature on the ceiling and the small fire still burning in the back room, one could hardly tell that "The Beatlis von Liverpool" had ever been in The Bambi Kino at all.

All incidents are documented, but…

Allan Williams says that it was Paul and George who were deported for setting fire to the Bambi Kino. Every other source, including Pete Best and The Anthology *say that it was Paul and Pete.*

Lewisohn indicates that Paul and Pete let the fire burn intentionally using terms like "fiendishly decided to ignite" and "deliberately ignored" the flames. He also says that the boys lit the tapestry directly. And Peter Brown tends to agree with that assessment. He writes: "The drapes began to smoulder. Paul and Pete hightailed it out of the theater without bothering to mention it might burn down. The fire was discovered and put out before much damage was done."

Allan Williams says that the lads merely lit a French letter and "the walls were so dusty that there was a woosh and a flare-up." And Phillip Norman also takes that same view: "Paul struck a match in order to see." He even quotes Pete Best as saying that some filthy drapes on the walls ignited but "smouldered only a bit."

Official Beatle biographer, Hunter Davies, sees the whole incident as quite harmless. He quotes Pete Best as saying, "Paul and I were just clearing out of the Bambi…we were getting a light to see what we were doing, and we must have started a fire. It wasn't much." And Barry Miles agrees: *"Paul and Pete accidentally set their rooms on fire."*

On p. 55 of The Anthology, *there is a copy of a letter that Paul wrote to the Polizei in 1961 (in an effort to return to Germany) explaining this whole incident. He maintains that the fire was set just as I have explained it in this chapter, but he says that he and Pete put the fire out completely, and then went to sleep in the Bambi Kino.*

Was it an accident or arson? We'll never know. The facts are that some part of the Bambi Kino storage room burned…and retribution was soon to follow.

The conversations are conjecture.

1 December 1960
8 Hayman's Green
West Derby

Pete Best and Neil Aspinall had been form-mates at the Liverpool Institute and friends for years. But the two were nothing alike. Neil was an accounting student, meticulous and detailed. Pete was more compulsive – intuitive and spontaneous. Neil spent his nights completing correspondence courses for an accounting degree. Pete spent his nights in one cellar or another, pounding drums.

In August, when Pete left for Hamburg and adventure, Neil stayed behind in rural West Derby. He moved into the spare bedroom Pete had vacated at 8 Hayman's Green and went to work for Mo – taking tickets, filling Coca-Cola cups, running errands, making change, assisting The Casbah bands in their set-ups and knockdowns, and lining up entertainment for the month to come. With Pete away, Neil found himself slipping gradually into his friend's world, enveloped in skiffle and rock'n'roll.

Pete wrote very little from Hamburg to Neil or to anyone, but Paul McCartney was always dashing off quick posts that kept Mona and Neil abreast of the Beatles' accomplishments and "feats of valour." It sounded like quite the life – Hamburg – but Neil secretly wondered if things were really as fantastic as Paul painted them.

Then in November, when Derry and the Seniors returned Merseyside, the colourful McCartney tales became black and white truths. The Beatles were, in fact, "rockin' the German nights away down at The 'Keller." They *were* the biggest act in town, just as Paul had intimated! According to The Seniors, The Beatles were literally smothered by adoring fans.

"They're *big*, Mo, unbelievably big!" Neil threw his hands up. "And this from the Seniors...whom you'll remember resented the boys at first, right?"

"Jealousy," Mo nodded.

"Well," Neil continued with hardly a pause, "now Derry's singin' out of *their* book, as it were. He's goin' around tellin' everyone, 'Just wait 'til The Beatles come back!' I mean, he as much as admitted to me that The Beatles are better'n The Seniors these days!"

Mo tapped the last of her coins into the paper-tight roll required for business deposits and marked the total in her "Casbah Accounts Receivable" book. She closed the ledger with a thud and slid it onto the allotted shelf.

"And you expected less?" she smiled, removing the reading glasses she only used for bookwork. "With Pete havin' his dad's charisma and my unrivaled brand of determination, I'd be surprised only if he *weren't* destined for the top!"

"Right." Neil didn't offer logic for a mother's pride, but he wondered if Mona realized how many skiffle and rock'n'roll bands swarmed the available Northland venues these days. Scores and scores of would-be musicians were drumming and strumming in the hopes of being discovered someday. They all dreamed of playing The Kaiserkellers and The Jacarandas of big cities.

Yet somehow, against the odds, The Beatles had done just that. They were, amazingly enough, becoming a local legend. They were inching their way to the top, one gig at a time, just as John Lennon had always predicted they would.

That evening, Neil shoved his accounting aside, spread out the materials he'd purchased in a West Derby art shop, and began a project that really excited him. At Mo's suggestion, he began a "public relations programme" designed to welcome Pete back in high style. Neil began hand-lettering posters to be distributed throughout Merseyside in the months to come, posters that would broadcast the return of his friend's newly famous band.

"The Return of the Fabulous Beatles!" Neil meticulously printed.

"The Return of the Fabulous Beatles!" he scrawled all night long. The words imprinted themselves on his brain as he worked.

"The Return of the Fabulous Beatles!" he wrote over and over again. And the more he wrote it, the more he believed it.

With an enthusiasm that Neil had never felt for accounting, with a racing thrill he'd never experienced before, Neil threw himself into rock'n'roll publicity. He made each poster slightly different and used vibrant, contrasting colours especially selected to catch the eye. He worked with the precision of one to whom details matter.

The next morning when Mona brought in his usual breakfast, Neil was still working. He was exhausted, but not a bit sleepy. He was alert – far too excited for bacon butties or Irish Breakfast tea.

"Just another hour or so, Mo," he waved her off, continuing to work with paint all over his arms and shirtsleeves. "It's…impossible to stop right now."

"But the lads won't be comin' home for months!" Mo clucked. "Paul only just wrote about them renewin' their contract, right? And once Koschmider releases them, they have that winter-spring engagement at The

Top Ten. You've got all the time in the world, luv."

Neil kept right on lettering. "Well...as you say, there's no harm in bein' prepared, is there?"

"Prepared, yes," Mona chuckled, pleased that he'd been listening to her advice, "but you've got the turn signal for Upper Parly on in Aigburth, luv!"

"So, I'm little early," Neil smiled back. "That's all right, isn't it? The early bird always gets *somethin'*, as I recall."

"A worm." Mona affectionately laid a hand on his shoulder. "It's only a worm, y'realize."

"Right. A worm," Neil grinned. "All right. Not bad."

"Well, if you should decide on breakfast over the worm, it's right here on the table. Don't let it grow cold."

"Ta, Mo." He bent his head over another poster and began penciling in the letters. "I'll have it...in a while."

But it was almost noon before the posters were finished, and it was mid-afternoon before Neil realized he'd eaten nothing since teatime the day before. As he munched mindlessly on the cold stack of toast, Neil stretched and thought about the publicity sweep he'd engineer for The Beatles. By the time they returned from Germany, he'd have it all planned. He'd have every last detail worked out.

Bill Harry is one of my sources for this chapter. He says, "Mona Best asked Neil to make some posters announcing, 'The Return of the Beatles.'" Similarly, Mark Lewisohn, in his The Complete Beatles' Chronicle *states, "[At] The Beatles first engagement following their return from Hamburg...Neil Aspinall, Pete's trainee-accountant friend, covered the club with hand-drawn 'Return of the Fabulous Beatles!' posters..."*

Interestingly, there is no mention of Neil Aspinall's work on behalf of The Beatles in Pete Best's book, Beatle! *Instead, Pete's first mention of a poster bearing the words, "The Fabulous Beatles" gives the credit to Sam Leach (p.89). Sam Leach, in his book,* The Birth of The Beatles, *calls Neil "the Beatles first and most loyal roadie" but he mentions nothing about Neil making the posters that were so prominently displayed all over Liverpool on the boys' return.*

When I interviewed Bob Wooler in 1994, he claimed to have originated the catch phrase, "The Fab Beatles" or "The Fab Four," and Bob Wooler was known for alliterative and catchy language. However, he said nothing about making posters or distributing them.

All conversations are conjecture.

Friday, 2 December 1960
Liverpool 3

It was an unorthodox place for a nightclub, a place that only Allan Williams could have selected.

Soho Street – a brief U-shaped loop off Islington, just blocks from Liverpool's City Centre district – was miles from the established nightlife in Liverpool 8. It was several miles northeast of the art college crowd that congregated on Hope, Rice, and Canning; north of the bustling Lime Street shopping district; and southwest of the residential suburbs. Soho was, in fact, north or south of anywhere that mattered. A part of Liverpool 3, it was more or less a border district – a tough, urban cluster of unattractive row houses, indistinguishable businesses, and dilapidated storage centers.

It wasn't as glamourous or trendy as Seel or Slater Streets where Allan's other coffee houses thrived, and it was certainly not as safe. But Soho reminded Williams of the "colourfully seamy side of Hamburg," and he envisioned a re-creation of the Reeperbahn right under the noses of the staunch, British City Fathers.

As Allan carefully picked his way through the neighbouring streets, sidestepping cut-jaw toughs who leaned against the walls and watched his every move, he could imagine the sort of money these latter-day Teds had to spend. He could imagine the abundance of ill-gotten loot that the gangs around Soho, Langsdale, and Rork Streets could put their hands on at any given moment. Armed to the teeth and menacing, these teens were hungry for a place to meet and carouse. And their pockets were never empty.

With this in mind, Allan had purchased a long, rambling warehouse – formerly a bottle-washing shop – at 100 Soho Street, and he'd christened the new venture, "The Top Ten Club." Like Hamburg entrepreneur, Peter Eckhorn, before him, Allan believed that the name would serve as a good omen, but he'd ensured the club's success by booking only the most clamoured-for Northern talents: Davy Jones, Terry Dene, Garry Mills, and Michael Cox.

Allan had even hired respected compère, Bob Wooler. Bob's lilting voice, clever alliteration, and quick puns made him one of the most sought-after disc jockeys in Merseyside entertainment, and Allan had offered a tidy sum to bring Wooler in on the project.

"Not much in the way of looks, is it?" Paul McCartney sat waiting for Allan on the wobbly, wooden steps leading to the bleak Top Ten building.

"Pfffft! It's as good as most on The Reeperbahn!" Al was defensive. "The Indra, for example – how was that?" He tugged at his leather gloves and retrieved a single key from the inner pocket of his coat.

"I was only…" Paul began.

"Yeah, right. You Beatles are all worldly wise these days, aren't you? It's all champagne and starters for you, isn't it?" Allan nodded for Paul to follow, and using caution, they navigated the tottery stairs. In one spot, there was no board at all, and they had to take two at a time.

Paul gripped the handrail tightly. Paint flakes chipped off under his hand and floated to the sidewalk below. Someone had scribbled fresh graffiti on the landing just above them, and a couple of empty Scotch bottles rolled in the pushing wind.

"Great ambience." Paul raised an eyebrow.

"Yeah, rugged appeal – all too natural charm."

Paul put his face against a window and peered inside. "Oh, it's every bit of that – rugged."

Allan wrangled with the lock and then booted the door open. "There y'have it, McCartney. The next home of The Beatles!" he said. He held his hand out. "Go on. Have a look-see."

They moved tentatively into the immense, featureless room – a wide expanse of paint-splattered planking. A wharf rat bolted across the floor. Boards creaked. Spider webs jiggled – the only lovely feature in the whole room.

"Could do with decorator, couldn't it?" Paul nosed around.

"Pfffft!" Allan pushed back his long, wool coat and hitched his pants up authoritatively. "It'd only be lost on the sort we'll have here! The gangs of Soho'd never appreciate embellishments. It'd be pearls before swine"

"So," Paul winked with a quick nod of the head, "it's the barren motif then." He sniffed. "Right, well…you've achieved it then, haven't you?"

"Not bad, eh?" Allan chuckled.

Paul walked over to the new platform stage that Allan had had constructed and kicked it as if testing the tires on a used car. "Rory-proof," he smiled.

"Vandal-proof," Allan corrected, including The Beatles in that category. "Vandal proof, ready, and waitin' to be the next St. Pauli – The Reeperbahn of Liverpool, as it were!"

"Oh, right. I can see that." Paul threw his eyes to the ceiling.

"Al, y'do realize it's hell's kitchen – this place? I mean, I know I told you we'd play here now and again, but…" Paul squinched his face.

"Don't be such a finnyaddy, McCartney!"

"It's not that. It's just…look, only you and John could love a place like this."

"And speakin' of the ffffuggin' devil himself, where is Lennon anyway?" Al checked his watch and then motioned Paul back towards the door. He'd promised to meet Bob Wooler at The Grapes in Mathew Street at half-six. They had only a quarter hour to get there. "When's he comin' back? And how about Stu…I suppose he's with John as well?"

Paul shrugged. "I dunno. I haven't heard from either one of 'em, really."

"Well, what the ffffuggin'ell are they still doin' in Hamburg?" Allan fumed. They exited, and Allan bolted the entrance door behind them, zippering the key into his coat pocket and double-checking the lock. This was not a neighbourhood for carelessness. "Lennon's got no fffuggin' band or gigs over there, and if I know him right, he has absolutely no fuggin' money to his name about now either. He swears he's madly in love with Lady Muck of Muck Hall, the long-suffering Cynthia Powell…."

"That's the griff." Paul followed Al down the stairs.

"…and yet he's still in Hamburg, isn't he!"

Paul zipped his bomber jacket and turned up the collar. It was brutally December in Liverpool. "That's about the size of it," he shrugged. "I've heard zilch."

"Well, I think it's all strange!" Allan spat. He'd wanted The Beatles to be his headliners at The Top Ten over the Christmas holidays. Prominent acts such as Don Fox and Danny Rivers would fill the bill until then, but no one except The Beatles would agree to work during Christmas week. He'd counted on John's hunger for fame to take care of that gap in his entertainment calendar. "And I imagine Mimi Smith thinks it's strange as well…wonderin' why the rest of you little lambs 're all back home while her lone black sheep's still wanderin' about aimlessly."

"She *doesn't* wonder, as far as I know. She doesn't know we're back." Paul followed Al as they edged through the crowds in London Road and moved into Lime Street. He tucked his face in his jacket, trying to escape the blowing cold. "I mean, I've no reason to ring her up, and I'm sure George hasn't. She's never fancied George for some reason. She literally despises him."

They passed a frozen Salvation Army band honking out an F-sharp rendition of "O, Come All Ye Faithful." Allan dropped a handful of coins into the bright, red pot and gave the bonneted bandleader a respectful nod.

Paul smiled as well. "I haven't really had time to be ringin' people up, y'know. I mean, I've taken that driver's mate job on the lorry, and I'm dead creased by five o'clock. It's all I can do to get home and serve tea for me 'n Michael 'n Dad. It took all I had to drag meself here thisavvy."

"You *are* still a young man, aren't you?" Allan admonished. "C'mon, McCartney! Pick it up, lad." But no matter what he said, Al couldn't see any perceptible change in the boy's pace.

At St. George's Hall, they cut across Lime Street and angled in the direction of Victoria. The five-story Washington Hotel with its hundreds of tall, brick chimneys cast deep, cold shadows over them. Night was falling fast on Liverpool.

As if on cue from some backstage manager, a wisp of snow began to fall – a gauzy, windswept dusting. All around them, Scousers tucked their heads and quickened their paces, eager to reach destinations before the real storm began. But Paul, enjoying it all too much to hurry, dug his hands deeper into his pockets and began to hum. He hummed "The First Nowell," an old Welsh tune Allan knew well. By the time the pair reached the black-lacquered door of The Grapes, they were singing the last verse.

Paul stomped and shook the snow out of his hair. Allan brushed it off his shoulders. Through the large, multi-paned window, they could see Bob Wooler already ensconced at a table next to the fireplace. Allan waved, and Bob gave a tiny, pert salute.

"C'mon then, Al, you'll be late," Paul teased, hurrying inside.

"Pfffft!" It was the traditional Allan answer.

Old and unimaginatively decorated, The Grapes in Mathew was still the best place to stop for a chat and a pint. It was the only place to discuss business, and everyone knew it. Cordial, warm, crowded – full of oak and noise – The Grapes was just loud enough to be completely private. Serious conversations passed almost unheard in the babble. Solicitors, business managers, entertainers, promoters, entrepreneurs…everyone flocked there.

"What'll y'have, McCartney?" Allan headed towards the bar.

"Pint of Carling. Ta." Paul sat down by Wooler and shook hands with him.

"And I'll have a pint of anything lubri-cacious!" Bob shouted in Allan's direction.

"Motor oil, then!" Allan yelled back.

"In that case," Bob cupped a hand around his mouth, "Splurge! Make it a full quart, if y'don't mind!" The round-faced disc jockey with the precise bowl haircut turned and slapped Paul soundly on the back. "Good to see yer, lad! Glad y'er back! How was horridly hedonistic Hamburg? As lusciously and lewdly lascivious as ever, I take it?"

"All that and more," Paul winked.

"I heard that yer mate, John Lennon's, still over there, then." Bob knew everything about everyone Merseyside. "What's he doin' – applyin' for bleedin' citizenship?"

"Nah, they wouldn't have him. We Liverpool Irish aren't exactly in favour over there, are we?"

"And especially not John fuggin' Lennon!" Allan returned, three glasses in hand. "He's *sieg-heiled* once too often for his own good, has John."

"Well, I don't mind sayin', he's throwin' a real spanner in the works."

Bob slurped the heavy foam off the rim and then whacked his glass on the table several times to froth it up again. "I've got plenty of jobs for you lads...but we obviously need the whole group, right? I've already told Allan that Litherland Town Hall was all wide-eyed and agog when I told them all about 'The Fabulous Beatles von Hamburg!'"

"Von Hamburg?" Paul raised an eyebrow.

"Ah, a little mystery and panache never hurt anyone." Bob winked, his cheeks flushed with excitement.

"*I'll* provide the fuggin' panache when there's fuggin' panache to be provided!" Allan sputtered, his face getting red again. "I'm their fuggin' manager, Wooler!"

Bob's elfin eyes twinkled with amusement. "Of course, you are, Al. We all know that. The manager of the The Jacaranda, The Angel, The Beatles, and now...Liverpool's own Top Ten!"

"Dead straight." Allan was appeased.

"Well then," Bob smiled, "To the success of Top Ten, then!"

"Right. All success!" Paul nodded.

"Cheers, lads! Ta." Allan beamed. They drank.

"Enjoy what you do," Bob quoted, "then you'll never go to work."

"Good one!" Paul nodded. "I'll drink to that!"

And for the next few hours, drink they did.

****

Hamburg, Germany

"What I'd give for Mimi's eggs 'n mushrooms with a side of cooked Irish potatoes!" John leaned the ladder-back chair and closed his eyes.

Stu smiled. "Astrid'll feed you...or her mother will."

"Nah. I'm tired of handouts." But John rubbed two fingers together anyway, asking for a cig. "I'm tired of it all, really...tired of worryin' about Bruno...tired of bein' fuggin' famished, day 'n all night."

Stu paused. "Y'er goin' home, aren't you?" He knew the answer before John said it.

"Look Stu," John began, "it's different for you, y'know." He leaned over and took the loosie Stu handed him. "You've got a life here. You've got Astrid."

"Eckhorn said he'd give you work..."

"I've got to get back to the band." John lit the cig and took a slow drag.

Stu went to the smudged window overlooking The Reeperbahn and stared into the darkness. The lights of The Top Ten below flashed on and off, on and off, on and off, colouring the wet street with dazzle. They reflected on Stu's face and gave him a ghastly tinge.

"Well...you'll call me Mum, then?"

"Nah," John said, "you'll always be Stu to me."

Stu turned and cut his eyes at his friend. They smiled. They tried to laugh.

"Tell her I'll be comin' home soon – straight away, spring at the very latest. Tell her about Astrid...about Klaus and Jurgen and The Exis...about all the fans, the *intellectual* fans we've drummed up...all the great friends we've made. And tell her I'll..."

"Yeah," John interrupted, "I'll be the fuggin' town crier, Sutcliffe."

They were silent.

"I wish you didn't have to go," Stu spoke.

"I wish you didn't have to stay." John was uncharacteristically candid.

Then silence prevailed. Stu watched a string of Christmas lights dance over the street as a cold front raced in from the harbour.

"We'll hafta have a new bass player, y'realize." John took a drag on his cig.

"Yeah, I know," was all the artist said.

"I could ring up ole Ken Browne," John teased.

"Or," Stu almost whispered, "you could let Paul have the job. He never wanted me..."

"That's not true."

"It's true. You know it's true."

"He just didn't like it because you were always shite."

"Right," Stu chuckled. "There's that."

More silence.

"Looks like it's snowin' out there." Stu cupped his hands against the window and made a tunnel for clearer viewing. He watched the frosted flakes fall in geometric swirls against the streetlights; he blurred his vision slightly and made them into white scarves tossed by the unpredictable drafts. "Come look, John. It's nice, this...the snow, the lights, the night, the breeze..."

"I'm short on money." John cut him off. "I don't even have enough for an effin' ticket home."

"I'll ask Astrid." Stu continued to watch the dance of the snow-scarves.

"Just ask her for enough for the train ticket." John became matter-of-fact. "And tell her I'll pay her back. I'm good for it."

"It doesn't matter, John. She won't see it as a loan. We'd give you anything we've got. You know that."

"Right." John rubbed a finger across his eyebrow. "Well in that case, tell her I could use a bit of fuggin' luck then. I'm fresh out these days."

"You've got luck...all sorts of it," Stu said. "You've a band that's exceeded all expectations. And friends, real friends…George 'n Astrid 'n Paul 'n Pete Shotton 'n Bill Harry… and me." He turned to face John. "And then of course, there's Al." They both smiled. "But most of all, in case you haven't thought of it lately, you've Cyn."

"Ah, the lovely Miss Powell," John said.

"So you'll get no sympathy from me, John. I don't feel sorry for you. I never have."

"Then don't." John hunched his shoulders. "I never asked you to. I never asked for anythin' but train fare."

Stu turned towards the snow again as the wind rattled the panes. And as always, he let John have the last word.

****

251 Menlove Avenue
Mendips
Woolton

Mimi paid the cabbie. In her nightdress and cap, she fumbled down the driveway and paid the exorbitant fee the man was demanding for a fare from Lime Street Station.

"Look luv, I ain't squabblin' wit ya!" The dour-faced East Indian showed her his watch. "It's half-two, luv! No cut rates this time o'day! Not in this friggin' weather, luv!"

"Indeed." She counted out the money and scrimped on the bonus. She handed the man his due and slammed the passenger door with aggravated fervour.

"Don't get eggy, sista!" he yelled from the driver's side and flashed his lights brazenly a time or two.

Mimi turned her back on him and marched towards the house.

"Happy Christmas to ya, then!" The cabbie screeched out of the driveway and blasted his horn several times before disappearing into the Woolton night. And just as Mimi had feared, a light came on in the house adjoining her own. She hurried inside.

So…home at last! She shivered and bolted the door behind her.

"John's home, Tim," she told the stretching cat. "No more law and order around here. Home only minutes, and already it's roolya-boolya as usual. Horns honking, cabbies shouting, neighbours awakened from sleep! It's a fine madness he carries with him – your John."

A clonk sounded in the room upstairs, then a drag and another clonk.

Mimi frowned, worried about the boarders.

She pulled the belt on her housecoat tighter and sloughed to the kitchen. Tim followed in search of an early morning treat, but he knew Mim. He didn't hang his hopes on it.

Mimi chewed her bottom lip over the embrace she hadn't received, over the brusque "pay the man outside" that had supplanted even the briefest "hello." She frowned over the expensive cowboy boots she'd seen John wearing coupled with his lack of funds for common transportation. Pouting, she poured herself a tiny glass of milk and tried not to cry over the immediate seclusion of the boy she hadn't seen in months. Silence hovered all around her now.

Tim left the kitchen in search of the boy he loved, and Mimi knew he'd climb the stairs and meow outside John's room until John opened the door. Tim wasn't embarrassed to ask for attention. He only wanted John to let him in.

Nearly three a.m.! Mimi finished her milk and then washed the old juice glass and set it upside down in the drying rack. Switching off the kitchen light behind her, she tried to resist temptation. But it had her. She had to try.

"John!" She rapped on the door lightly. No reply came from inside.

"John!" she tried again, her voice a pointed whisper. But there was no response.

"John!" Exclusion got the better of her. "Where's that famous hundred pounds a week, John? No cab fare, eh? And you…with all that ready money!"

"Just like you, isn't it?" came the voice from behind the door, "Just like you to go on about cab fare when it's obvious I'm completely exhausted!"

"Have it your way, then." She spoke to the keyhole. "But this discussion is tabled, not ended. First thing tomorrow morning we're sorting out the details in this quizzical situation."

"Yeah? Well, we'll see about that," was John's terse reply.

"Yes, we will," Mimi hissed. Then she flounced down the hall and snapped off the landing light.

The information about The Top Ten Club is authentic. But the scene between John and Stu is imagined, and the conversation is conjecture.

The scene between John and Mimi is well documented…including the cab fare, the time John arrived, the boots, etc. Only their conversation is conjecture.

Tuesday, 13 December 1960
Mendips
Woolton

The telephone rang once, twice, three times.

John swore.

He didn't want to talk to anyone. He didn't want to explain why he hadn't come home rich and famous or why Stu was still in Hamburg or why anything. He just wanted to be invisible for a while.

He knew Cyn still expected him to return around Boxing Day, and he had no inclination to tell her otherwise. He wasn't sure why.

Cyn. At times he thought of nothing but her. Yet he wondered if he loved Cyn the way he was supposed to. He wondered if he even knew what "that way" was.

What's her draw, after all this time? he asked himself. *And why don't I want to ring her up? Why'm I even thinkin' of her right now?*

John wished he understood what loving Cyn or loving anyone really meant. Oh, he'd had enough Sunday school lessons to know the lingo: "Love your neighbour as yourself." *But loving yourself's always the bottom line, isn't it? The part that makes it tricky.*

John tried to remember if he'd *ever* loved himself. He'd spent the better part of the last twenty years blaming himself...for Julia's relinquishing him, for his dad's disappearance, for Mimi's arm's length brand of guardianship – even for Uncle Ge'rge being taken away so suddenly. He had a reservoir of guilt.

But I've no overflow of love to hand out randomly, he thought. *And I've had no practice lovin' others, really. It's* not *lovin' I'm the expert in."*

John sat up on the side of the bed, his bare feet cold on the oval, braided rug and his naked shoulders goose bumped with chill. He squinted and scanned for his glasses. He scuffed his hand through his hair and slowly edged his feet across the floor.

It was noon, and John knew exactly what Mimi was thinking: "High time John was up and about – up and looking for gainful employment!"

"John!" The expected voice on the other side of the door still startled him.

"Yeah?" He found the glasses, neatly folded and placed, as if in a carrying case, inside his left slipper. "What is it?" He cleared his throat.

"Cynthia Powell rang. And strangely enough…she sounded rather surprised to find you home. She said she'll speak with you when you've a moment. You *have* been corresponding with her, haven't you?"

John ignored the question. "What'd you tell her? Did you say I was here, Mim?"

"Yes, of course. I told the truth."

"Which was?"

"That you'd been here for days. That you were upstairs sleeping your life away – sleeping, eating, and doing virtually nothing else."

"Great. I'm sure it was the Christian thing to do."

"Watch yourself, John."

"No," John jerked the door open, "Watch *yerself*, Mimi!"

He pushed past her and charged down the stairs in a panic. His ragged bathrobe hung open, and the frayed belt followed behind him like a whippet, close on his heels.

"The boarders, John," his aunt cautioned. "Remember the boarders."

"There are no borders with you!" he yelled back. John sat down beside the parlour phone and picked up the receiver.

The house was silent now. No one moved. John could hear the parlour clock ticking as his tabby, Tim, sauntered soundlessly into the room and stretched in front of the fire. John took the receiver in his hand and tried to think of something to say.

What do I tell her? What do I say? How do I fuggin' explain why I haven't rung her up?

Upstairs, a floorboard creaked. The toilet flushed in the loo. Beside him the fire hissed and crackled, and when a log rolled off the stack and split in two, it sent orange cinders flying.

Pinching the bridge of his nose, John whispered a few rehearsed words. Then with a deep breath, he dialed the number and waited.

"Hullo?" It was Cynthia's breathy whisper.

"Cyn?"

"John! John, I'm so glad you're home! I've missed you so much! I can't begin to tell you how much. It's just fantastic to hear your voice, to know you're here, back home, only miles away…right here, breathing the same air I'm breathing."

John let his head fall back against Mimi's hand-crocheted doily, closed his eyes, and drank in the sound of her voice – the sound of unconditional love, complete acceptance. Then the words came. He began piecing together the story of his last days in Hamburg – George's deportation, Paul's and Pete's arrest, Bruno's thugs, the *Polizei*, the attic of The Top Ten, and Stu's decision to remain behind with Astrid.

The words that had seemed so impossible stepped over one another as they tumbled out. And Cynthia listened.

As John talked, Tim relaxed, too. He lowered his lids and finally let his shoulders slump. He gave way to a deep rhythmic purr. Eventually the old cat's ears quit moving, and he fell asleep listening to John unravel.

The Top Ten Club
Liverpool 3

"So *this* is the famous Top Ten." John kicked through the charred rubble, the collapsed boards that had recently been a building.

"Yeah, rough luck, isn't it?" Paul brushed the snow off the singed remains of a guitar neck. "Al was quite on about the whole thing, actually. He really believed in this place."

John's toe found what was left of a drum kit. He flipped it over in the ash-washed snow.

"Yeah," George knelt, picking up bits of debris. "It was goin' to be our new Hamburg – this place – the new home of The Beatles."

"But it's all in ruins now." Allan's unexpected voice lifted their heads.

"Hullo, Al."

"Sorry. Tough break, Al."

"We woulda come sooner, if we'd known…"

"Thanks, boys, but what d'ya do, y'know? What's done's done. That's the way it goes, isn't it? Y'win some, and I lose all the rest."

"We'll stick by you, Al," George volunteered, his boyish smile sincere.

"Open a new place, and we'll be there," Paul pledged.

"Yeah," John stood up and walked towards the club owner. "One for all, and all for Al. That's what I always say, right?"

"About time you got home Lennon," Allan smirked. "I thought you'd applied for fuggin' citizenship over there."

"How's Bob takin' all this?" Paul changed the subject, offering Al a Woodbine.

"Unemployed and nervous," Allan shook his head. "But other than that… all right. I mean, he's a survivor – Wooler. We both are. Fuggin' unbreakable."

No one knew quite what else to say, but Allan kept the conversation rolling.

"Actually, Bob's already been 'round to The Cavern in hopes of pickin' up some compère work in Mathew Street." He bent over and fished something shiny from the debris. He examined it for a moment and then quickly put it into his pocket. "The owner, Ray McFall, and Bob go a ways back, y'know…"

"Yeah," Paul agreed, "Bob knows practically everyone Merseyside,"

"He'll have no difficulty securin' a venue," George nodded.

Allan sighed and ran his fingers through his thick, curly locks.

"But what about us?" John still had a band to consider. "Where do *we* go now that our new club's all ash?"

"Bollocks to you, Lennon!" Allan's cheeks immediately flushed. "I lose my fuggin' dream, and you want to know…"

"Look, whatever's happened," John refused to be chided, "you're still our manager. Regardless of circumstances and things as they are…" he motioned to the rubble, "that hasn't changed."

Allan exploded. "Five lousy days ago, my dream club was burned – obliterated – after being open for only five days!" He picked up the charred marquee and tossed it at John's feet. "Now it's a loss all 'round – with nothin' left to rebuild, as it were – and *you* want me to…"

"You'll spring back," George encouraged.

"That's right," John never relented, " and you'll spring back because you've still got us."

"Pffffft! The Beatles!" Allan ranted. "The what-becomes-of-us-we-could care-less-about-you-Beatles! The…"

"Right…what *is* to become of us?" A slight smile played at John's lips. He nudged the irate manager with his shoulder. "I mean, now that you've burned down our new home, as it were…where do we go from here?"

"*I* burned down?" Allan's eyes grew instantaneously wide. "What d'ya mean *I* burned down?"

"Yeah, Al, you old arsonist!" George winked at John. "Buy us a drink at Ma's…or we'll spread it 'round town that it was *you* who ignited The Top Ten."

"For the insurance money, Sonny Jim!" John used his pensioner's voice and rubbed his hands together greedily.

"We're well acquainted with the details of arson, y'know." Paul clapped a hand on Allan's shoulder. "Just ask Bruno. He thinks we're quite accomplished in that arena."

"Pfft!" Allan tried not to smile, but he shook his head and crooked a corner of his mouth anyway. "All right. Let's go," he tried to sound begrudging. "But one drink only. That's it!"

Tripping each other and hurling insults, the four manoeuvred the tiny street that led to the rear of the majestic Empire Theatre. John pitched a snowball at Allan and hit him squarely between the shoulders. Allan bellowed before slinging one back.

"Look, it's Allan Williams, isn't it?" A man in a double-breasted, wool overcoat pointed in their direction.

Al cut his eyes at the pair. "What's left of him, wack! Only what's left!" he said, brushing the snow off his coat.

"Heard about your club, Williams. Rotten luck, that!" one of them offered.

"Yeah…well ta anyway." Allan kept on walking.

"Better luck in the new year, mate!"

"Right…better luck!" The man's companion added as well.

"C'mon lads." Allan pulled open the heavy, wooden door of the Skelhorne Street bar. "That's the thought we'll cling to, eh? Better luck in 1961, right? Let's drink to that."

All events are documented. But here again, "the facts" are fuzzy. Salewicz says that Allan's Top Ten was uninsured. Bill Harry states that "Williams claimed there was an electrical fault in the wiring, [but] rumours around the scene in Liverpool at the time suggest it was arson." He goes on to say, "Williams didn't have it fully insured and only received 1.086 pounds in compensation."

In The Man Who Gave The Beatles Away, Williams clearly states that the fire was accidental (due to the aforementioned electrical fault). He mentions nothing about insurance money.

Even the tiniest details of this incident differ from biographer to biographer. Williams says the club was open for 8 days. Phillip Norman says it was open for 6 days. Bill Harry says that the club opened on Thursday, 1 December and burned at 11:30 p.m. on Tuesday, 6 December…five days.

Whatever the length of the club's existence, we know that The Top Ten was plagued by threats from local toughs who wanted "protection money" from Williams to keep the place "running smoothly." And we also know that Allan Williams was never one to submit to threats of any kind.

This incident between John and Cynthia is imagined. The incident between The Beatles and Allan, however, is well-documented in his book, The Man Who Gave The Beatles Away. *Conversation is conjecture.*

17 December 1960
The Grapes
Mathew Street
Liverpool

"Picture perfect! Good job, Neil!" Bob Wooler held the posters at arm's length, examining them as one would an artist's original. "We'll use them, of course. 'Return of the Fabulous Beatles!' I like that!"

"Yeah, well," Neil smiled quietly, "I wanted 'em to come home with a splash."

But the boys had returned without fanfare.

Disjointed, disillusioned, and dejected, the Beatles had wandered back to Liverpool, embarrassed. In fact, they felt like failures.

Here they were again, back Merseyside, working for beans in Pete's basement as if Hamburg had never even happened. It was a let down, a demotion.

"We'll use these adverts at Litherland on Boxing Day. They'll be perfect for givin' the lads a boost of morale 'n all."

"Good but...they weren't designed to flatter, y'know," Neil shrugged. "I meant every word of it. The Beatles're damned good, aren't they?"

"Absolutely," Bob winked, but not patronizingly. Bob never patronized anyone. "Hamburg's rearranged them all...even the unswerving John Lennon."

"Yeah, they've all improved." Neil turned his wooden stool towards the fire crackling in The Grapes' Delft fireplace. He leaned in and warmed his hands, rubbing them together vigorously.

"Too good for The Casbah – all apologies to Mo Best," Bob nodded. "Even too good for The Jacaranda these days."

The front door swung open and a red-cheeked Joe Flannery hurried in, followed by a blast of frigid air. Bob waved at the tall, broad-shouldered Aigburth promoter, and Joe smiled back. It was almost five o'clock. All the regulars would be making their way to The Grapes within the half hour.

"Yeah," Neil fished in his pockets for change. He was ready for another pint. "But I guess, all in all, things could be worse, right?"

"Yeah, the lads coulda spent the remainder of the winter shut up tight as a clamshell in a German prison, couldn't they? They coulda vanished – and we'd've never really known what happened to 'em!" Bob got up and stretched. "It's lucky their friend, Astrid, had all the right connections."

"So…" Neil headed towards the bar, "Litherland Hall at seven pounds ten is the best offer on the table, then? The only venue so far?"

"Unless Williams can work wonders we've only wished for," Bob ordered a pint as well. Then he began to roll and band Neil's posters for storage.

"Wait!" he stopped, his hand tracing the "Fabulous Beatles" lettering. "That's *it,* Neil! That's it exactly!"

"What's it?" Neil set two pints down on the tiny, ringed table.

"Here! You'll need yer artwork back, lad," Bob's eyes were shining, "You'll need to do a bit o' touch-up, as it were."

"How's that?"

"Right here," Bob pointed. "Right here where you wrote 'The Fabulous Beatles.'"

"Yeah?"

"Well…underneath, go back and paint in, 'Direct from Hamburg.' Paint it on every one. Make it as large as you can."

"'Direct from Hamburg'?" Neil smiled slowly. "Oh. Right. Yeah, I see what you're after."

"E by gum!" Bob's smile was warmer than the fire. "'Direct from Hamburg!' That's the phrase we need! Tack that on, and then we'll see how it goes, won't we? We'll just see what the locals down at Litherland have to say about a bunch of German toughs all decked out in leathers and greased-back coifs. *That's* the group we'll be sellin'!"

"The Fabulous Beatles von Hamburg, right?" Neil raised a toast.

"Right." Bob winked again. "The very ones."

****

25 December 1960
Liverpool

Litherland Town Hall was just a town hall. It was a long, two-story building, a double-chimneyed brick edifice, highlighted by a steady row of upper floor Paladians and a lower floor of boxy windows without shutters or decoration. A single flagpole adorned the front entrance, and small, unimaginative, anemic evergreens lined the walk. Quite unspectacular in every aspect, the building seemed hardly the place for a rock'n'roll band to perform. It looked like the last place that teenagers would want to frequent. But frequent it they did.

Twice a week, scores of young people filled the hall to dance to the sounds of The Deltones, The Searchers, or The Del Renas. Promoter Brian Kelly – who also supplied the bands for Lathom Hall in Seaforth and Alexandria Hall in Crosby – booked groups well in advance for these sell-out shows, and he maintained rigorous standards to which his performers had to adhere. He wasn't overly amiable, even with the groups he liked.

And Brian Kelly didn't like The Beatles.

Over a year ago, in order to accept the tour with Johnny Gentle, The Beatles had cancelled a Kelly booking without adequate notification, and Kelly had never forgotten the insult. He didn't care about Williams' excuses of "a rare opportunity" or "a once in a lifetime chance." And he wasn't ready to forgive or forget the irresponsible boys and move on.

But Bob Wooler – whom Kelly genuinely liked and respected – had assured him that The Beatles had changed. Bob gave his personal word that the lads would arrive on 27 December – on time, in tune, and with enthusiasm. The band, Wooler claimed, had just returned from Germany where they'd wowed audiences up and down the famed Hamburg Reeperbahn, and the teens of Litherland were in for quite a performance.

On that endorsement, Kelly had conceded. But he was still wary. He didn't trust Allan Williams, and he didn't trust The Beatles. They'd always seemed arrogant, in his book, as if they were the greatest rock'n'roll band ever to hit the music scene. He couldn't imagine where they'd adopted that notion. He'd never seen any evidence of it.

****

27 December 1960
Litherland Town Hall

It had become second nature to them now, the gyrations, the antics, the connection with the audience that left them panting and breathless. The show itself had become their music.

As the Litherland curtain slid anonymously aside, Paul dominated the stage. He was already perspiring, his Elvis pompadour dripping at the sideburns. His eyes were round and wide. Breathing deeply, gathering reckless velocity, he hurled his words at the audience. It was a rocker's cry. It was the dark passion of Hamburg coming home to the port of Liverpool.

John hurled himself down on one knee, the half-split challenging the seams of his pants. Swathed in black leather, wrapped in sensuality, he moved without decency, without caring. He moved, reeling the audience in, enchanting them as the viper does his prey.

George had to smile at the spectacle. It was great to be together like this again! It was great to have an audience once more! Watching John and Paul clown and work the crowd, George laughed out loud. It felt like home – this. It felt right.

Pete winked now and again, tossing a nod here and there, dipping his head, and glancing about with cool reserve. And Pete's mate, Chas Newby, sitting in on bass guitar, did a little dance step he'd devised for the occasion...a quick one-two, with a stomp and a slide.

"Human dynamos!" Bob whispered to Kelly, both of them mesmerized by the scene.

"Just look at 'em!" Kelly agreed. The Beatles leapt and pounded all over the stage. They utilized every square inch of board space.

And then it happened. Without warning. Without explanation.

The crowd, totaling over 1,500 teens, surged towards the stage, their dance partners abandoned, their plans for mixing and mingling forgotten. Several girls started to scream as the song ripped to its close. More screams rose as John tore into the next number.

Bodies pressed forward heedlessly – shoving, elbowing, pushing without regard – plowing to edge closer, jostling for position.

The crowd was drawn to the power that emanated from the stage. They were pulled to the dais, to the boys, to the energy.

For the next half hour, sound piled upon sound. Screams vied with drums for domination. Guitars were diminished by wails. The crowd unraveled, lost control.

Neil Aspinall moved closer towards the back door, pulling Rory, Pete's younger brother, with him. Mo would have his head on a royal platter if anything happened to Rory. And tonight the place was chaos. Bedlam!

"What the fuggin'ell?!" Kelly mouthed to Wooler and the Beatles' driver, Frank Garner, as if they had answers, as if they knew. But no answer could be heard above the shouts of a thousand voices. Nothing.

It was all and everything – the screams. It was all and everything – the high-pitched wails and stomps and shouts. It was all and everything – the press of hundreds and hundreds of bodies. It was reckless, amazing.

"We've a situation here," Kelly muttered to himself, looking anxiously towards the exits.

Fuggin' dangerous is what this is, Garner thought.

But although Bob put his hands over his ears to muffle the sound, he found it hard not to smile. This was thrilling! This was phenomenal! This was the stuff fame was made of!

I believe we just might have the beginnin' of a real mania here, he thought. *A mania born at Litherland of all places! Litherland Town Hall!*

Who would've believed it?

All events are documented. Only the conversations are imagined.

1961 !!! Some thyme in January

STU!!!!!!!!!!!!

When r u ending the great Beatle Schism and coming back, son?

We've been gettin' some gigs. And Chas Newby is playing guitar in your abscess. You know the score, musician. You're being irreplaced.

Come home.

We've played The Casbah and Litherland as well. You shoulda been there. They screamed.... **fuggin' screamed** as if possessed! (Back fiends! I've got hot-crossed garlic, and I'm not afraid to use it.)

Al's doing his best (quoth Al) to get us readmitted to Hamburg come spring (or as soon as the embers cool). And Eckhorn's tryin' to make it all a reality as well. So tell Astrid we'll be back before the Exis rotate on their Axis, as it were.

How is she? Tell her I asked. I know she thinks I don't like her or something equally adenoid. As far as I'm concerned, she's all the **rage**.

You remember Ray McFall and The Cavern Club in Mathew? Welllll...Baa-Bob Wooler and Mo have booked us there for cash performances. Money up front and all that! The powers that be in The Cavern think we're bleedin' German, Stu! "Direct from Hamburg!" our posters say. They even told George he speaks good English! (I think he fuggin' murders it...he's gonna mouth like a parish oven...and all that Scouser lingo... I don know a blind werd e says.)

Look Stu...

We've lined up The Casbah-umbug.
We're on at Litherland.
We've got Wallasey comin' up...
And Lathom and Blair Hall...
Where the fuggin'ell are you?????????????
Quite this shite and get back to makin' music, son.
So that's it, thin. You've been summoned.
Yer muther misses you. We all do. Even Mim. Even the one with (and without) the glasses. You remember him?
Come home NOW. Command performance. R.S.V.P. (a.s.a.p.) (S.O.S.) (abcdefghijklmnopqrstuvwxyz....now I know me ABsee's. Tell me what you think of me.) (Or do I want to know?)

From,

John

Letter style is mimicked from a letter to Stuart found in Davies' book (108-109), from other Lennon letters found in Ray Coleman's Lennon *and from a letter from John in Allan Williams' possession shown to me during an interview in 1993.*

Tuesday, 21 February 1961
The Cavern Club
Mathew Street
Liverpool

The crowd murmured and fidgeted. They were ready for the lunchtime show.

John took a bite of his jam butty, and offered it to an unfamiliar, almost-too-young girl in the front row. "Sunblest Bread, luv...naturally wholesome, thirty-two ways," he batted his lashes. "Ask yer sister, she's had plenty," he said, suggestively. "Haven't ya, Maggie?"

The Fazaerkley pair giggled, wrinkling their noses and shrugging their shoulders coquettishly.

On the other side of the boards, Paul gnawed on a cheese roll and tapped the microphone twice. "One, two," he said. "Two, two, two."

George swung his amplifier cord around behind him and practiced moving without tangling his feet in it. Pete bit his bottom lip and waited.

"Anyone seen The Swingin' Blue Genes lately?" John shouted. He talked as he chewed. The audience laughed, responding to the boy's show of confidence.

The Beatles, not The Swinging Blue Genes, were The Cavern's house band these days. Thanks to Mona Best's phone calls and letters and Bob Wooler's endorsements on their behalf, The Beatles were now playing The Cavern once, if not twice, daily – almost every day. It had been that way since the end of December.

Watching from the sidelines, Bob Wooler smiled. The Cavern crowds loved Lennon. They loved all The Beatles. It made Bob's job of compèring relatively easy; there were no silent moments to fill with patter, no awkward situations to gloss over. Once The Beatles were on stage, all was well.

A guitar chord blared, full volume.

"Good afternoon, ladies and gents!" Paul pointed and winked at the secretaries in the front row.

"How's every little thing thisavvy?" John's nasal voice intoned.

"We'd like to welcome you all to The Cavern Club..." Paul began diplomatically.

"Ah, purra zipper on it," John interrupted, holding his guitar high against his chest, "and just play the fuggin' song, son!"

The audience roared with delight.

"But we haven't as yet heard the theme music, have we?" Paul smiled at Bob who'd suggested that the group acquire an introductory song, a calling card of sorts.

And right on cue, Wooler turned the volume up, letting the William Tell Overture fill the packed, smoky room. The lunch set sprang to their feet and cheered, and The Beatles bowed, waved, and accepted kudos from the crowd.

Then their cowboy-booted feet sprang into action with John and Paul dually vamping on rhythm guitars, meeting at mid-stage and slamming into one another as they played. Screams filled the narrow tunnels of The Cavern. Screams snaked up the stone-lined stairs and filtered into the all-too-bright daylight of Mathew Street above. Screams bounced off the wet walls of the tiny cubicle below.

Saturated to the skin, John grabbed the microphone at the end of the first song and yelled, "Don't give us the clap. Send money!" George pitched a half sandwich at him.

"For the next number…we'd like to do…" Paul began. Scattered screams. He wiped his forehead with the palm of his hand and carefully avoided his Elvis locks. "Back at you, luv!" he winked. More squeals. "The next number we'd like to do is one that was very popular back in Hamburg…"

"Right," John grinned maniacally, his tongue jammed down into his lower lip. "It's called 'SS Men are Breakin' Up That Old Gang of Mien Herr.'"

"It's called 'Hully Gully,'" Paul ignored him. "And if you know the words…"

"…then shut the hell up!" John finished with a cackle.

The room exploded in laughter and cheers. And the music began.

Leslie Condor sat back and absorbed the insanity around him. It was a welcome change of pace – this window of nonsense and music in his otherwise structured day. He sipped his Coca-Cola and watched a perspiring blonde receptionist unfasten the two top buttons of her blouse. *It's bleedin' swelterin' in here,* Leslie thought, *and the temperature's unbearable as well.*

"Gissalite, luv?" A pretty Irish brunette with heavy eyeliner leaned over to him. She held out her cigarette, and Leslie lit it for her, in hopes of a bit more interaction. But the sound of John's voice pulled the girl away.

"Pipe down, plebeians!" John fought with squealing feedback.

"Y'er upsettin' the apple carts topside, y'know," Paul confided. Mathew Street was no longer a sleepy little alleyway for fruit markets, vegetable stands, and produce warehouses.

"Bad fans, bad!" George wagged a finger. And when the heavy backbeat of Pete's drums interrupted him, the shy lead guitarist danced a bit and began to drone out "Roll Over Beethoven."

Neil Aspinall leaned against the arched stone column closest to the stage. He crossed his legs at the ankles and smoked casually, as if the room around him were hushed and sedate. Over the past four weeks, he'd grown accustomed to the frantic behaviour of Beatles' fans. He'd learned to expect shrieks. He'd learned to anticipate bawdy requests yelled from the audience. He'd learned to expect the customary rush on the stage. As he'd gradually fallen into the role of roadie – following Pete from venue to venue – Neil had learned to deal with almost anything from the growing cult of Beatle enthusiasts.

At Aintree Institute more than a dozen girls had lipsticked Neil's touring van, leaving phone numbers and graphic messages in greasy red. A week or so ago in Mathew, the crowds had passed a toilet paper roll along the queue, each fan writing her own message, phone number, and address on a tiny square. And every afternoon, while Neil unloaded his mates' equipment, eager girls quizzed him – flirted with him for a chance to meet "the lads." They promised him virtually anything just for the opportunity to chat up one of The Beatles von Hamburg.

"And for our last number…" Paul began. A chorus of "boo's" and hisses filled the room. "So sorry," Paul smiled and shook his head. "I wudden mind stayin' round for a while, but it's me mate here." He motioned towards John. "He's got a live one waitin' up at Edge Hill…that's what we've all heard."

"And she's got up-de-entery eyes, eh!" A lanky stock clerk from Speke yelled from the back of the room.

John held his cigarette between his teeth and flipped the backwards V. Several girls screamed, and John screamed back. He picked up his Coke bottle and toasted them, letting his cigarette fall to the stage as he swigged the warm liquid down in one gulp.

Then finding his place at the microphone, he belched, tapped the mike, and pronounced flatly, "This is the last song we're doin' thisavvy. If you haven't had enough, come 'round to The Cassanova this evenin' or out to Litherland later on, if you're still on yer feet. We're the fuggin' band that never sleeps! Just a bunch of coffeehouse layabouts…with *three* fuggin' gigs a day!"

"We'll be there, Johnny!" some girl yelled.

"Y'can count on us, luv!" another pledged.

"Well then…this one's for you then." John began to stamp his feet. "Maybe you've heard of it. It's a little number called 'Twist and Shout' and it goes like this…"

In March of 1993, I was interviewing June Furlong at The Pump House Pub in Liverpool. A gentleman sitting at a nearby table called me over and told me that he had been to countless Cavern Club sessions and would give me details about what he had seen there. He did so. His name was Leslie Condor, and it was through his vivid eyewitness account that I was able to write this chapter. "Ta" to Leslie for permission to use his name and information. Best wishes.

Some of the incidental information included in this chapter – The Sunblest bread and the cheese roll, for example – can be found in The Anthology.

One note of trivia…the group that John mentions, The Swinging Blue Genes, changed their name to the Swinging Blue Jeans in March of 1961 when they gave up skiffle and began to play rock'n'roll. However, the "Cavern Diary" (found in Thompson's excellent book on The Cavern Club) continues to list the group under its skiffle name. The Swinging Blue Genes continued to play The Cavern, though not as often as The Beatles. In 1963, they had a huge hit: "Hippy, Hippy, Shake."

22 February 1961
The Grapes Pub
Liverpool

It was hard to complain. They were playing somewhere every day – often twice a day, and sometimes three…Hambledon Hall, The Grosvenor Ballroom, The Casbah. There were lunchtimes at The Cavern Club and evenings at Aintree Institute, Alexandria Hall, and The Jacaranda now and again. On one occasion, they played for a whopping audience of six at The Palais Ballroom in Aldershot.

The Beatles went everywhere and anywhere, determined to play for anyone.

But Merseyside wasn't Hamburg. And even the steamy Cavern cellar wasn't The Top Ten Club. More and more every day, John missed Hamburg. He missed the excitement and freedom it provided, the intense edge-of-reality existence of The Reeperbahn.

But most of all, he missed Stu.

They sent letters back and forth, and Stu had plenty of time to write. He was in hiding now. Bruno's henchmen had been instructed to "find the last Beatle" and "act accordingly," but Astrid kept her fiancé carefully sequestered. She feared for his safety – even urged him to return to Liverpool for a while.

"You've got to set things right with the Germans, Al!" John exhaled smoke as he talked. The Beatles were between shows, stretching their legs a bit at The Grapes. "Stu's still over there, y'know," John insisted. "And it's not safe. Y'can't just leave him to the wolves, can you?"

Allan rubbed his finger around the edge of his pint. He raised his eyes to meet John's. "And as I see it, *y'er* the ones responsible for Stu and anythin' that happens to him, as it were. Y'er the ones who broke yer fuggin' contract and ran off, willy-nilly, to Eckhorn and The Top Ten without my by your leave. Y'er the ones who ignited Bruno's property and left it to sizzle – who crashed his boards for a fuggin' case of cheap champagne!"

"Yeah, yeah, we've heard it all before." John brushed him off.

"John's right, y'know." Paul scooched his chair up, wedging into the tiny table. "You've got to step in, Al. You've got to write to the authorities. We want to go back over there, y'know! We've got great opportunities in Hamburg."

"It's a town we love – Hamburg," George chimed in.

"It's where we belong," John agreed.

"You Beatles have absolutely no idea when you're well off, do ya?" Allan got up to get another drink. "You're playin' literally here, there, and fuggin' everywhere! You've got more gigs than any other band around – more of a fan base, more publicity…"

"Yeah, we're tired of municipal halls and churches," George complained.

"We're tired of bein' tired," John said. "We want to go back to bein' wiped out, fagged out, dead creased, exhausted, and mutilated from an overdose of rock'n'roll. We want to get back to Hamburgy-berg."

Allan was sick of their whining and nagging. "I'm workin' on it," he said, curtly. "I'm doin' the very best I can."

"Which leads us to the crucial question," John smiled innocently. "Is yer best good enough, manager?"

"Meaning what, Lennon?" Allan narrowed his eyes.

"I dunno. You tell me."

But everyone at the table understood exactly what John meant. Unspoken as it was, the threat couldn't have been clearer. It was time to make some important decisions about the future of the group.

Should Stu be in this chapter? Pete Best says Stu returned to Liverpool in mid-January, and this is confirmed by Pauline Sutcliffe and Alan Clayson's book, Backbeat. *Lewisohn says it was late February. Davies says Stu returned in early 1961, but gives no dates. Because of the number of letters exchanged between John and Stu, I tend to agree with the February date, but no one can be completely sure.*

As an aside, please note that The Beatles were playing only lunchtimes at The Cavern at this point. Their first evening appearance was March 21, 1961 when they performed with The Swinging Blue Jeans.

All conversation is conjecture.

Saturday, 25 February, 1961
Aintree Institute
Aintree

"I haven't the least idea what I'm doin' back here." Stu held his Hofner President bass as if it were an alien thing.

"Savin' yer bleedin' neck, that's what!" John kicked at the tangled web of electrical cords at his feet. "Stayin' one step ahead of Bruno – that's what."

"Runnin' away's more like it." Stu hung his head. "Leavin' Astrid to deal with who knows what."

"Koschmider's no threat to her." John looked at Stu straight on. "Her father's a fuggin' physician, Sutcliffe! The Kirchherrs are all too visible for anythin' to happen to them, aren't they?"

Stu hoisted himself onto an amp and sat there, hangdog.

"Truth told," John pulled a rickety three-legged stool over and balanced one foot on it so that he could tune his Ric, "she's safer without you, son. By leavin' the country, you've disassociated her from the evils of the errant Beatles *von* Liverpool, as it were."

"Yeah, I realize that, John," Stu grumbled, "but I still miss her."

John spat on the scuffed ballroom floor. "That again? Same tale, eh?"

"Nice," Stu scowled. He knew exactly how John meant it. But he bit his tongue to keep the peace.

"All right, then." John strummed a few bars, tentatively. "Let's try 'I'm Gonna Sit Right Down and Cry Over You.' After all, it appears to be yer fuggin' theme song, doesn't it, artist?"

"Sure, if you say so." Stu shrugged. "Whatever. Let's do it."

But John knew it wasn't cooperation Stu was offering. It was resistance…passive aggression.

Stu was miserable. He found it unbearable being back Merseyside, being back in the band again. He didn't enjoy the set ups or the breakdowns. He didn't enjoy the audiences or the gigs. It had been bad enough in the days prior to Hamburg when he'd been asked to sacrifice his weekends for the band, but now The Beatles were performing almost all the time.

As a result, Stu hadn't painted a single stroke in a week. And now it looked as if he wouldn't have an opportunity to slip away today either. As soon as they were finished here at Aintree, they'd have to head directly over to Lathom Hall.

This's our so-called "free time," as it were, Stu groused silently. *But here we are – goin' over the same ole songs again, hammerin' away as if one more practise could actually make a difference in the way we perform.*

But John believed it could. He was serious. And he was intense, throwing himself into rehearsal – belting out lyrics and badgering tunes from his "wooden box 'n strings" with a gusto generally relegated to live performances. John always performed.

And his Ric obediently filled the room with reverberation, while Stu's Hofner twanged a beat behind – reluctant, tone shy, and devoid of any emotion, except melancholy.

****

Lathom Hall

In the last few weeks, The Beatles had become somewhat of a local phenomenon. In fact, they'd taken to using bodyguards of sorts to screen the swarm of promoters and dance hall managers who surrounded them before and after every gig.

Even Brian Kelly, who'd looked down his nose at the group ten months prior, was now quietly delighted to book The Beatles at Litherland, Lathom, Aintree, or any of his venues. In fact, he felt "damned lucky" to get the popular Liverpool band to perform in his dance halls.

Well over an hour before performances now – far more punctually than ever – the five black-jeaned and leathered Beatles and Neil Aspinall arrived to unload their marred, scuffed amps and hideous guitar cases. They'd learned to work quickly and efficiently. They had, somewhere along the line, become entertainers.

Tonight, Bob Wooler moved among them like a coach, making suggestions, joking with the lads, going over their game plan. And "Nell," as they often called Aspinall, had them chuckling over a caravan of fans who'd doggedly followed them from the Aintree Institute gig that afternoon. The brash Scousers loved it – they reveled in their newfound popularity. They bragged and strutted and let it go to their heads. But never once did they let the dialogue slow them down. The Beatles set up the stage in just under half an hour.

Since Valentine's night, Wooler had suggested that the group reposition Pete closer to the front of the stage, setting his drum kit on equal footing with the guitars and giving the fans a better view of the sultry drummer. And tonight, a new niche was being cut for a fifth member of the group – Stu.

Kelly carefully studied this new lad, this Sutcliffe – a thin, puzzling kid lingering in the wings. Withdrawn, quiet – anything but a rebel rocker – the boy seemed out of place in the pre-show mêlée gyrating all around him.

"Yer amp's loose again, John." George kicked a dangling electrical cord with his boot.

"Yeah, well so's yer muther." John pulled a face.

"That's seemingly rude and ineffectual," George sniffed. "Especially on me birthday."

"*Ineffectual*, eh?" John slipped into his old man's voice. "You've been readin' books again, haven't you, Sonny Jim?"

Stu chuckled at the nonsense and shook his head.

"Laugh on, Mr. Bass Player Man," John turned on him. "But a *serious* question remains...have you learned to play *anythin'* all the way through, yet, son? Did you practise, all those months in Hamy-berg?"

"He knows 'My Bonnie,'" George grinned.

"Nah," John corrected, "he thinks he *is* 'My Bonnie'...it's that part about 'lyin' over the ocean' that has him mesmerized, as it were."

"Geroff, John!" Stu smiled a little less.

"Everyone's sayin' that these days," George pointed out.

"But as far as I can tell," John strummed his guitar once for effect, "no one's doin' a fuggin' thing about it!"

Outside the curtain, the William Tell Overture began. The Lathom Hall crowd began to rumble – spurts of anticipation erupted here and there. A shout. Chants. Stomps and whistles.

John stuck one hand through a small rip in the curtain and waved, and the room resounded in a chorus of squeals. Then he put his boot through the hole instead, just to hear the crazed reaction.

"Ah-one, two, ah-one, two, three, four!" Paul gave the standard count, and right on cue, the curtain began to move. John hopped on one foot, attempting to extract his cowboy boot from the hole in the fabric. The others, less occupied, gave their full attention to the song.

Despite Kelly's new security, girls ran to the edge of the stage. They swooned at Pete's every move. They screamed "Georgie!" and winked at him. They cried and shoved and elbowed each other to get to the band.

When Paul sang a ballad, he could hardly be heard over the screams. And John's edgy "Twist and Shout" had them digging fingernails into their faces, their cheeks red with delighted agony.

But tonight, it was Stu who excited their imaginations. The new bass player in the dark squared-off glasses intrigued them. They learned his name quickly and used it. They jumped up and down and waved to him.

They threw things in his direction and tried to get a reaction. And the more Stuart withdrew, the more he attracted ardor. The girls were as fascinated with Stu as he was put off by them.

"What's he got that we haven't got?" John nudged Paul as the curtain closed on the performance.

"Magnetism?" George suggested.

"Sunglasses," Paul shrugged.

Stu laughed softly, placing his guitar carefully in its case.

"Stealin' the show, are ya, Sutcliffe?" John gave him a nudge.

Stu shoved back. "I didn't do anythin' at all!"

"Yeah, that's what they all say – the guilty ones!" John walked around, heckling him.

Stu needed an ally. "Me and George were just mindin' our own business, weren't we, George?"

"Well…I was," George grinned.

"Show stealer!" Paul wagged a finger at Stu.

"Hidin' behind dark glasses and an all too innocent smile!" John teased.

But before Stu could respond, Neil came slamming in from the alley, rubbing his hands together, and blowing into his palms. "It's colder 'n a witch's tit out there! And I've heard we're in for snow – maybe ice – within the hour as well." He looked worried. It was a long drive back to the Liverpool suburbs – more to West Derby.

"I'm ready." Stu hoisted his amp on his back and headed for the door.

"You would be!" John yelled after him, "First to the van, first with the bairds, first in the hearts of yer countrymen!"

"Cannon balls to you, John!" Stu yelled back over his shoulder. "How's that for a revolutionary concept, eh?" And, pun delivered, he slammed the heavy metal stage door solidly behind him.

"Y'know, y'should lay off Stu once in a while, John." Pete moved his drum kit closer to the exit. "He's not that happy here, y'know, and he's got a bit on his mind these days…"

"Isthasso?" John's nostrils flared. "And I suppose no one knows him 'best' than you, right drummer?

Pete threw John a look. "Yeah, you *know* him, all right, but you…"

"John was just teasin', that's all." George leapt to John's defense. "Stu knows that. He reads John like a book, as it were."

"Yeah? Well, they'll both lived happily never after then." Pete insisted.

"The end." John glared at the drummer and kicked the exit door open with his boot.

Almost at once, he heard it. He heard it above the whine of the wind through the alleyway. He heard it above the engine purr. He heard it with sickening clarity. Someone was being pummeled.

Thuds and grunts. Growled, angry threats punctuating long, low moans of pain. John's mind raced, trying to make sense of it all. His eyes worked to adjust to the sudden darkness. Suddenly, his amp and guitar case crashed to the concrete, and instinct took control. He ran towards the sound, ran towards what he knew it had to be.

Stu!

Just past the rumbling van and its white exhaust screen, John saw them.

Five, maybe six men – each bigger than Stu – loomed over the body on the ground. They huddled over the whimpering man and took turns smashing his skull, football-style, with heavy brogans. They spat on him, taunted him, delivered one brutal kick after another, laughing and egging one another on.

"Get yer hair cut, lass!"

"Yeah, lay fuggin' off our bairds!"

"Go back to fuggin' Germany, y'fuggin' Kraut!"

"Yeah, y'lousy, fuggin' sod!"

John hit them without warning. Shoving, kicking, swearing, he plowed in, screaming hideously, letting years of latent hatred blossom fully.

Within seconds Pete had joined in, full on, and the gang began to run...never looking back, scrambling into the darkness, taking cover since the odds had evened out a bit. Pete turned and screamed for help. He banged on the stage door and shouted for someone, anyone, to call for an ambulance. John fell to his knees.

Stu lay lifeless, bleeding heavily on John's dark jeans.

"Sutcliffe!" John shouted. "Sutcliffe, answer me! Answer me, Stu! Wake up! Open yer fuggin' eyes!"

Blood poured from Stu's mouth and trickled from his ears. For a minute, John didn't think he was breathing. There was only the wind and the fast clack of approaching footsteps.

"How is he?" Paul knelt beside them. George stood off to one side, his face a white orb of fear.

"How d'ya think?" John barked. "He's fuggin' dying – that's how he is! He's fuggin' dying, that's what!"

"I'm not," Stu managed coherence. His blood-smeared lips parted with great difficulty. Already both eyes were swollen shut. His face was twice its normal size. Even in the darkness, John could see disfigurement warping his friend's features. Stu's face was pulp.

"You look bloody awful, don't you?" Paul offered, trying to smile.

"Yeah, grotty." George knelt down, too. He reached out and gently touched Stu's leg.

"Get off him! Get back! Ring the fuggin' medics!" John was shaking. He cradled Stu against his chest. The blood saturated John's shirt.

"No." Stuart struggled to sit up, his breath coming in cough-gasps that only produced more blood. "No physic, John. I mean it. Me mum...we can't afford the..." He sank back down. "It isn't...as bad as it looks. Really."

"That's crap!" John shouted at the injured man. "Look at you! Y'er bleedin' from the ears, the mouth...it's not just cuts and bruises, Stu!"

"Ta for the good news." Stu pushed himself up again and tried to labour to his feet. Paul and George grabbed his arms and helped him steady. He wobbled, but once upright, he held his ground.

"How is he?" Pete returned with Neil in tow. "Ambulance is on the way, John."

"It won't be long, Stu," Neil reached out to touch his arm. "Hang in there, lad."

"I'm fine," Stu muttered. "And...call them off...please. I-I don't...I don't want a fuggin' medic."

"He isn't fine!" John was still kneeling in blood. "He's in shreds. He doesn't even know what he's sayin'! He's out of his fuggin' mind!"

"It's all right, John." Stu was still standing, though weaving more now. His speech was slurred, and he held a hand over his eyes as if it were bright daylight. "Look, I've got one eye in a whelk, and...a rack of rattled bones...whatever..." He tried to take a step and stumbled. Pete caught him before he fell. "But I'm all right," Stu insisted. "No doctor...no 'ozzy. Promise John....promise that."

"Listen Stu, I..."

"*Promise!*" he yelled with the last reserve of strength. Then Stu collapsed into the tiny rivulet of water that ran through the service alley. He folded in half and sank to the concrete without another word.

"He's out." Neil checked Stu's eyelids and pulse. "Alive...but just barely..."

"They did a number on him." Pete helped lift Stu's limp body into the van.

"As if Stu ever did anythin' to deserve somethin' like this." George gave him a hand.

John still knelt on the concrete, his hands and clothes turning dark brown. He rubbed his forehead, smearing blood across his face. "Someone ring the effin' ambulance," he sighed, "and tell 'em to forget it. Tell 'em..."

"But you can't..." Pete started.

"I promised!" John hissed. "Do it!"

Ordinarily on their return trips, The Beatles smoked, played Radio Luxembourg, rehashed the evening's encounters, or stopped off for a nightcap or two. But tonight they hardly made a sound. Paul tried to hum quietly for a while. George attempted small talk a couple of times. But mostly, they were silent. They stared out the van windows and avoided each other's eyes. They coughed now and then and tried to ignore Stu's moans. They concentrated on the road and bit their lips in the darkness.

John raged against the irony of it all. Astrid had sent Stu away to

Liverpool to hide from the dangers of Hamburg, to escape being brutalized by Bruno's gang. But here at home, surrounded by friends, Stu had met with exactly the same fate. *Worse, probably,* John thought.

He turned and adjusted the coat that Paul had tucked around Stu's neck. He looked for any signs of improvement. John wanted to believe that Stu was asleep, that he'd given into exhaustion in the silence of the ride. But deep inside, an old voice whispered about loss of blood, the ramifications of shock, and the danger of trauma to the head. John sat back, closed his eyes, and tried to press the fear down deeper where he couldn't hear it. He folded his arms across his chest and tried to breathe.

His arms. John wasn't sure when he'd begun to notice, but by the time he was really aware of it, the pain was enormous, throbbing with every heartbeat, moving up to the elbow. His knuckles stung, raw. His swollen fist refused to clinch or un-clinch, and clearly the little finger on John's right hand was broken.

How they'd play Litherland in two days, John had no idea. Neither he nor Pete nor Stu would be able to move. John shifted his weight and tried to close his eyes. He leaned his aching head against the window and tried to rest.

Without warning, the van hit black ice and spiraled into the curb, jarring them, slamming them into one another without warning. John sucked his breath in sharply, swearing and turning quickly towards Stu, reaching out to secure him. But there was no cry of pain from the limp body next to him. Stuart was unconscious.

"Watch the fuggin' road, Aspinall!" John spat out. "Yer only fuggin' job is to drive the fuggin' van, right?"

"Yeah, yeah. Right, all right. But it's wicked out here, y'know. It's snowin' on top of ice, and *ice* I can't even see. It's…" Neil gave up trying to explain and slowed the pace even more. He squinted through the darkness and squeezed the wheel tighter. His shoulders ached; his neck ached. Neil wiped the windshield with the back of his hand and leaned in, nose almost to the glass.

It seemed to take hours to manoeuver the narrow streets, back home, southward. They crawled along…navigating slowly, inching back to the security of familiar surroundings.

When the snow began to fly faster over Liverpool and the van finally whooshed to a sliding stop in Sefton Park – in front of the old, Victorian Sutcliffe family home – only George and Paul had enough energy left to carry Stu inside. Pete was cut and badly bruised. Neil was limp from the harrowing drive. And John, holding his gouged arm and broken finger to his chest, was fighting a racing heartbeat that skipped and pounded and left him fighting for air as he watched his best friend being carried away. He watched until the porch light finally came on and Stu was taken inside. Then he closed his eyes and let the fuzzy darkness pull him under.

There seems to be a great deal of disagreement about this particular episode. Bill Harry denies that it ever happened, calling it an "apocryphal Beatles story." He states that Stu was never kicked in the head, and that his later headaches were the result of a fall in Hamburg. He quotes Neil Aspinall as saying there was indeed a fight at Lathom Hall in Seaforth, but that it was "a mere skirmish in May of 1960 in which John broke a little finger."

Alan Clayson and Pauline Sutcliffe (Stu's sister) recount the event as it has been told above, but they place the event at Lathom Hall. They quote Mike Evans as saying, "It was one of the few times when the aggressive Lennon became really violent as opposed to 'violent in his manner.' It was on this occasion that he, if you like, rescued Stuart from this attack – but by this time Sutcliffe had been kicked about the head and was bleeding."

Allan Williams tells the exact event recounted in this chapter, but he places the event at Litherland Town Hall. Phillip Norman also agrees that it took place at Litherland, and Norman adds that John had a sprained wrist after the incident.

Here are the facts:

1. Neil Aspinall did not join the group until Dec. 27, 1960, so if he observed the incident (as Bill Harry indicates) it had to have occurred after that date.

2. According to Lewisohn, Stuart did not return to Liverpool until late February 1961. If this is correct, the incident could not have occurred at any of The Beatle's December or January appearances at Litherland – 27 Dec. 1960 or 5 Jan. 1961 or 26 Jan. 1961.

3. All accounts by any source report that there was a group of jealous thugs who accosted Stuart. (Clayson says that they were additionally riled by Stuart's reply of "good evening" to their "Ulllo.")

4. All accounts of a fight report that John furiously defended his friend. And all accounts say that in this process, John broke a little finger (which was later indeed crooked) or sprained a wrist, or both.

5. Pete Best tells of such an attack at Lathom Hall in which Stuart was accosted and John's finger was broken.

6. All accounts – including Bill Harry's documentation of a fall in Hamburg – mention that Stu suffered a blow or several blows to the head.

In light of these facts, I chose the Lathom Hall venue in late February 1961 as the setting for this chapter. Telling this story does not preclude Stu's fall in Hamburg as an additional and actual piece in the puzzle leading to Stu's brain trauma. The essence of the story remains. Somehow Stuart Sutcliffe suffered severe head trauma. After that date, Stu began to suffer from horrid headaches, blurred vision, and mood swings.

Friday, 3 March 1961
Liverpool College of Art Canteen
Liverpool

When Stu had come home to Liverpool in February, Cynthia had hoped he would reconnect with the Art College and find a reason to stay. She had hoped he'd settle in and convince Astrid to come to Liverpool instead of vice versa.

But Stu had only remained Merseyside a scant two and a half weeks. Then he'd returned to Germany. And John had already begun talking about Hamburg again.

Since the end of December, Chas Newby had been filling in for Stu on bass – and making a success of it. A friend of Pete's and a former member of The Blackjacks, Newby possessed more skill than Stu. But even wearing a borrowed leather jacket with an upturned collar, he lacked the air of mystery that Stu had always emanated. Chas lacked the charisma of shy hesitancy Stu seemed to have invented.

On top of that, Chas had informed John that he was going back to college to finish his chemistry degree. Truth told, he'd only stepped in on bass as a favor to Pete. If The Beatles wanted a permanent bass player, they would have to trek to Hamburg and get Stu back again.

Hamburg! Cynthia sighed slowly, resting her head in her hands and gazing around the canteen at the other students on break. Discussing exams, projects, classes, and professors, they were busy with university lives. None of them were worried about bass players or German groupies or rock'n'roll contracts or work permits. None of them lost sleep over exotic foreign women who took marvelous photographs and led existentialist geniuses. Cynthia felt very alone.

Once upon a time – quite some time ago it now seemed – Cynthia had dreamed of becoming an art teacher in a large, cosmopolitan classroom. She had wanted to work in Birmingham or perhaps London, sketching in her spare time and exhibiting works in a few well-respected galleries here and there.

But three months ago, John had come home from Germany debating the reality of human existence, sniffing a Vick's inhaler that kept him agitated for hours, and raving about the delights of something called *The Kama Sutra*. He'd come home with enthusiasm for things that a girl from the Wirral had never entertained privately, much less discussed openly. And now he constantly badgered Cynthia to open her mind, enlarge her world, think bigger!

She had tried. She had tried not to say how dismayed she was about John's new philosophies and continental attitude, Instead, she had let her bangs grow down into her eyes, lined them her with kohl and applied extra mascara. She had worked to achieve an Exis "look" without adopting Exis ways.

But somehow, even that had backfired. The Beatles were playing St. John's Hall in Bootle this evening, and although Cyn looked fantastic – no, because Cyn looked fantastic – John had forbidden her to accompany him. A gorgeous, unescorted blonde in Bootle was only asking for trouble, and John couldn't watch Cynthia and do his job at the same time.

It was logical, but Cynthia resented being separated from him. She knew their nights and days together were numbered.

Inadvertently, through Pete, Cynthia had discovered that the boys were gathering tomorrow afternoon at The Jac for a heart-to-heart with Allan, for a serious discussion over their suspension from Germany. They were going to pressure Al into doing something about the situation – to get them back into the clubs on The Reeperbahn sooner rather than later.

But John hadn't said a word about these plans.

Oh, he'd started practising some of the songs that were popular in their Kaiserkeller shows, spending hours writing to Stu each day, and working up new numbers that the Bootle and Litherland crowds didn't really relish. Cynthia had even heard Paul humming "Wooden Heart" a few days ago. But no one had out and out told her that Hamburg was so imminent. Cynthia just knew it.

John was getting ready to leave again. His thoughts were far away. Half the time, he was already there.

And so was Cynthia.

She'd decided that if John found a way to go back to Germany, she would go with him. Of course, she couldn't abandon the term entirely, but she'd go at Easter break and find a way to make it a bit of an extended stay.

If John were determined to go, she would let him. But she wouldn't pine away back home, hoping for the best, and she wouldn't surrender either. John had worked hard to make his dreams come true. And Cynthia was just as resolute.

She didn't care that John hadn't invited her, that they weren't engaged, that her mother wouldn't like it, that Mimi – if she found out – wouldn't approve. She didn't care that a trip like that would interrupt her preparations for final exams and cost her an arm and a leg. Cynthia only cared about being with John. That was all that mattered. John was all that mattered.

While in Liverpool, Stu had, in fact, attempted to return to his studies at Liverpool College Art, but that the school refused him admittance. (They accused him of having stolen the college's amplifier.) With no possibility of pursuing art in Liverpool, Stu was, therefore, free to return to Astrid and to Hamburg.

All information in this chapter is documented. Only Cynthia's private thoughts are conjecture.

Saturday, 4 March 1961
The Jacaranda
Liverpool

"All right, all right – this is *it*, y'understand!" Allan brandished the letter in their faces. "No more badgerin'. No more, 'Al, do this' and 'Al, do that!' No more fuggin' pressurin' me about Hamburg!"

"Let's hear it, Al." George never agreed to anything without reading the fine print.

"Yeah, read us what you've got, and then we'll let you know." Paul took a drag on the cig in his left hand.

Allan cleared his throat and prepared to read aloud the letter he'd written. His eyes swept the expanse of the empty, Saturday afternoon Jacaranda, as if there were a crowd assembled, as if a roomful of invisible listeners were perched, waiting to hear his discourse.

"Just read the fuggin' thing!" John barked, folding his arms. Cynthia had been inexplicably moody for the last two days, and it had him in a snit as well.

"Yeah, get on with it," Pete seconded.

"It's addressed to, and I quote, 'The German Consul, German Consulate, Church Street, Liverpool,'"* Allan began, importantly.

"How's *that* get us back to Hamburg?" John exploded. "How's writin' to someone here, Merseyside, have any affect on *anyone* over there?"

In disgust, Pete tossed his cigarette butt onto the scuffed, wooden floor. "You need to turn around and write to the authorities in Hamburg, Al – just as Mo's done! Just as I've done! I've said it all before! I've told you exactly who to contact…"

"Is that right?" Allan puffed up with instant anger.

"Look…why don't we give Al a chance, eh?" Paul intervened. "We haven't even heard what he's written yet, have we?"

"*If* it's all right with you," Al huffed.

"Go on, Al," Paul encouraged.

"What he said." John motioned for Al to continue.

Allan began again. "To The German Consul, German Consulate, Church Street, Liverpool. Dear Sir, On behalf of a group of musicians…"*

"That's us," George grinned.

"Not so fast. Let's hear your scales." Paul wagged a finger at him.

"On behalf of a group of musicians," Al repeated, "I would like to apply for permission for them to obtain work as professional musicians in Hamburg…"*

"Professional, is it?" George breathed on his fingernails and polished them on his shirt.

"Now we're gettin' somewhere." John propped his booted feet up on the captain's chair in front of him.

"May I *read* the fuggin' letter?" Allan was close to the boiling point.

John rolled his hand like royalty.

"Pfffft!" Allan sputtered. "Where was I?"

"The Jacaranda," George mumbled.

Al cut his eyes at the boy and read a little louder. "They have recently worked for a Mr. Koschmider…"*

"Not him again," John interrupted.

"I thought he was a bad dream." George reached for a cig.

"*This* is the bad dream!" Allan exploded. "Listen, all of ya…fuggin' *shut the fuggin'ell up* 'til I'm done! Not another fuggin' word!"

"Yeah, Harrison, y'er bein' rude and disruptive, aren't you?" John looked down his nose at the boy.

"Me?" George mouthed, silently, pointing to himself.

"They have recently," Allan repeated, "worked in this capacity as musicians in Hamburg for a Mr. Koschmider. This engagement with Mr. Koschmider was unfortunately disastrous as Mr. Koschmider broke the playing times; he did not give them decent accommodations…"*

"An outright lie!" John jumped up. "Some found it the ideal habitat! As I recall, all manner of vermin loved it there!"

"And," Allan ignored him and read on, "he was responsible for obtaining work permits…but this he had not done."*

"Yer tenses are jumbled, Manager," John fell back into his chair. "And grammatical errors? Legion!"

Allan ignored him. "I think I have made it clear that Mr. Koschmider did not abide by the contract, he deliberately tried to stop the musicians from working at another club, but was not able to completely stop…"*

"There – split infinitive." John flashed a quick grin.

"… but was not able to completely stop the musicians from doing so."* Al turned his back to John entirely, reading to the others as if John had ceased to exist. "'He reported them to the police for a minor mishap the musicians committed…"*

"Right. It was only arson, y'know," the nasal voice from behind Al chorused.

"…and as a result of this, two of the musicians were requested to leave the country."*

"Three! *Three!* What about *me*? I was deported as well, remember?" George piped up. "Why's everyone always leave me out of everythin'?"

"I've noticed that," John egged him on. "Have you noticed that, Paul?"

"Noticed what? Who? Where?" Paul searched under the tables and chairs.

"I can assure you," Allan read on, "'all the musicians have very good characters…'"*

"Make mine Badger and Mole, the White Rabbit, and the Walrus, if y'don't mind," John smirked.

"'…and come from first class families…'"* Al was undeterred.

"Here! Here!" Paul put his hand over his heart.

"…and they have never been in any trouble with the police in this country."*

"We've always outrun them…or outwitted them, one." John cupped a hand to his mouth in a stage aside.

"You've been very much on the sly, haven't you?" Paul dragged a chair over next to John and pretended to take notes.

"I'm well recognized for my incognito." John pulled his leather cap down lower, just over his eyes.

"That's it I'm done!" Allan sputtered. He threw the letter down on the oak pub table and glared at them all. "If you lot know so fuggin' much, then…let's hear *your* plan of action, then!"

"Well," Pete shrugged, "what Mo and me've *been* doin' is talkin' directly to Eckhorn, right. Convincin' *him* to persuade the authorities that he's got to honour the contract he signed last November – which clearly states we're playin' The Top Ten come April."

"Eckhorn! Pfft!" Al threw his eyes to the ceiling. "Great influence he has not!"

"But furthermore," Pete continued, "I've been writin' directly to the West German Immigration Office and requestin' a one-year suspension of the deportation ban against us. I've also been petitionin' for special concessions and…"

"Yeah well, that's one avenue," Allan was defensive. "There're others."

"Pete's right, though, y'know," Paul sighed. "It's four March already, Al. We haven't got that long to work it out if we want to make it back by our contract date, do we?"

"Don't overwhelm me with yer fuggin' appreciation, McCartney!" Allan hissed. "I really can't take all this praise and adulation from the four of ya all at once! It's fuggin' overwhelmin' – this!"

"Just post the letter, Al," John directed sternly. "And then try what Pete says and ring up Eckhorn as well…as a secondary, back-up measure."

"Since when do I take orders from you, Lennon?" Al barked.

"Since we became 'the *fabulous* Beatles,'" John pointed his cig at Al.

"So you've let that shite go to yer heads, have you?" Al fumed. "Well, believe me, y'er no more fabulous than y'ever were! It's all hype and poster board – that."

"Look Al," John's nostrils flared, "y'can give rant 'n rave'n give fuggin' orders 'til y'er blue in the face, for all I care. I don't give a fuggin'ell *who* does what around here…or how it's done or why! As along as all roads lead to Hamburg…that's all that fuggin' counts."

Allan hated to agree with anything John said. But he had to admit: any road leading The Beatles back to Germany and out of his hair sounded wonderful – too good to be true.

No wonder Bruno had 'em fuggin' deported! If only I could think of a reason to have 'em shipped out; I'd be down at the cop shop now filin' charges and signin' on the dotted line! A ban on The Beatles! How fanfuggintastic would that be?

* *The excerpts from the letter written by Allan Williams were taken from* The Man Who Gave the Beatles Away *(p. 204). I highly recommend reading the entire document. In fact, Williams book, as I have said before, is a "must read" for Beatles fans!*

The Top Ten contract was negotiated directly between The Beatles and Peter Eckhorn while the group was in Hamburg in November of 1960. The Beatles later insisted that this engagement was not one that Al had negotiated for them, and thus, they denied him the standard ten per cent manager's fee. Pete and Mo Best's work to secure the gig formed the basis of the opinion that Allan was not an integral part of their Top Ten booking.

In Williams' book, The Man Who Gave the Beatles Away, *Williams does not mention that Pete was involved in management, and Allan asserts that he was still managing the group completely.*

In Best's book, Beatle! The Pete Best Story, *Pete says, "I had become more or less acting manager of the Beatles, lumbering myself with all the paper work and attention to details. The rest of the group just let me get on with it, and Allan Williams gradually faded from our scene."*

6 March 1961
The Cavern Club
Mathew Street
Liverpool

John studied the timetable in his hand, scanning Pete's characteristically rapid scrawl. The list covered two pages, front and back, and it reeked of routine, repetition, and sameness.

Club	Date	Set	Promoter
Cavern Club	6 March	Lunch	McFall
Liv. Jazz Soc.	Same	Eve	Leach
Cavern Club	8 March	Lunch	McFall
Aintree Institute	8 March	Early Eve	B. Kelley
Hambleton Hall	8 March	Late Eve	Hill/Anton

Hamburg had been one thing, with Prellys in abundance and the adrenalin of the crowds to inspire them. But back Merseyside, the gigs felt increasingly like work. John ran his finger down the page until he found the weekend schedule, and he made a mental note of the details for Cyn.

Club	Date	Set	Promoter
Cavern	10 March	Lunch	McFall
Grosvenor	10 March	Early Eve	A. Williams
St. John's	10 March	Late Eve	Forshaw
Aintree	11 March	Early Eve	B. Kelly
Liv. Jazz Soc.	11 March	Late Eve	Leach
Casbah	12 March	Early	Mona Best
Cassanova	12 March	After	Leach

Then he joined Paul on the cramped Cavern boards. "You've read this, have you?"

Paul gave it a scant glance. "Yeah, right. Pete read it out earlier, before you arrived."

"Yeah, well look – there's Leach, Kelly, McFall, Forshaw, and A. Williams here, but he writes out *Mona Best*, in all her entirety. She's the only one with a Christian name in the whole list, as it were."

Paul and George smiled as they worked on the new arrangement for "A Taste Of Honey." They were adding the tune to their late show this evening.

"Ah, but Mo *deserves* full billin', doesn't she?" George said, good-naturedly. "I mean, she's the one doin' most of the work these days, isn't she? Mo and Bob Wooler."

"Yeah," Paul shrugged. "It does seem Al's cut us a bit adrift."

"Well, as we can see from this manifest," John hit the gig list with the back of his hand, "the ship sails on…with or without him."

"D'ya think we can we do it, John – all these engagements?" George peered over John's shoulder. "I mean, The Cavern every lunchtime – 13, 14, *and* 15 March – and a gig or two every night as well? I mean, it's wearin' on Nell – this nonstop routine."

"Too fuggin' bad," John rummaged through the pile of guitar cases, tarps, and gig bags, searching for his microphone stand. "He's a roadie. It's his job to be worn."

"*Volunteer* roadie!" George reminded him. "He's uniquely free of charge is Neil."

"And y'think *we're* fuggin' paid?" John huffed. "At ten pounds, eight?!"

"I made more workin' on the lorry," Paul nodded.

"I made more trimmin' Mim's hedge…on a bad day."

"Yeah," George pulled a tarp off the floor and uncovered the lost stand. "I suppose there's no revenue for anyone in all this, is there?"

"But," John forced himself to say it, "where are we goin'…I mean, ultimately, in the grand scheme of things?"

"Nowhere fast, it seems."

"Where are we goin', son?" John repeated, a little bolder.

"Oh, not that again," George threw his eyes to the ceiling. "I'm too tired to…"

"Just say it and get it over with," Paul advised. "You're only makin' it hard on yerself, y'know."

"Where *are* we goin', lads?" John yelled to the room at large.

"To the toppermost…or so we've heard." George shook his head, smiling a little in spite of himself.

"And where's *that*?" John barked louder, cupping his hands around his mouth.

"To the toppermost!" George shouted back. "To toppermost of the poppermost!"

"Wrong." John held one finger high above his head. "We're goin' to *Hamburg*, son."

"Right," Paul nodded, as if he'd known the correct answer all along. "Everyone knows that. I knew that. You knew it, didn't you, John?"

"Ah, bushwa!" George waved them off. "You're daft, both ya."

"So it's been said," John nodded. He butted George playfully with his shoulder. "And so it shall be. Work without end. Amen."

But John wished he had some certainty about returning to Hamburg.

Every other day, pages and pages of scribbled handwriting arrived from Stu - news of some angle Peter Eckhorn was taking with the various German government officials. Every day Pete kept them apprised of Mona's efforts on their behalf. And every evening at The Cavern, Bob Wooler brought them up to date on his latest phone calls and contacts. But so far, The Beatles were getting the royal run-around, and the long, dull list of Merseyside venues continued to grow – binding them to Northern England with gigs in nondescript dance halls, gigs that made every night seem just like the night before.

The gig at Grosvenor Ballroom on 10 March proved to be the last gig booked by Allan Williams for The Beatles. They were, at this point, transitioning into other realms of management.

The gig list in this chapter was compiled from information provided in Lewisohn's The Complete Beatles Chronicle. *Only the conversation is conjecture.*

21 March 1961
The Best Home
8 Hayman's Green
West Derby

Pete put the receiver back into its cradle with a triumphant flip of the wrist. "It's a go!" he beamed. 'Signed and sealed,' as they say! Done!"

"We're goin' back!" Paul whooped and gave him double thumbs up.

"Three cheers for Eckhorn!" John could hardly believe it.

"*And* for Stu'n' Astrid," Pete added. "They're sendin' us cash for five railway tickets straight away. No ramshackle minibus for us this time! No knees tucked under the chin, as it were."

"And just when I'd grown accustomed to it all!" George, sitting on floor, drew himself up into a ball. The others laughed.

"Right. Well…when do we go, then?" John asked.

"One April." Pete explained. "For four weeks…more if we're successful. Less if not."

"And the arrangements?"

"We'll all be upstairs at The Top Ten."

"Where all good beetles belong," Paul teased.

"How much're we gettin'?" George rubbed two fingers together. "And how…"

"And who else'll be playin' The Top Ten?" Paul pulled up a chair.

"And how much are *they* gettin'," George asked, "compared to us?"

Pete took a long drag on his Embassy and slowly exhaled a trail of smoke. "All right. It's like this. We're playin' with Tony Sheridan, naturally, right? And lucky to back him, as I see it. I mean, face it, he's the headliner, right? We're only, y'know…" He took another drag.

John flipped his chair around, straddling it. "What else?" he asked.

"No days off," Pete spelled it out. "And no holidays, right? On stage every night, 7 to 2, Mondays through Fridays and 7 to 3, weekends. We've fifteen minutes off each hour…not twenty…not even sixteen. And other'n that, it's the usual, right? Free lager, free lodgin'.."

"Free fräuleins," Paul clicked his cheek.

"And a few free for alls, as well." John couldn't resist.

"And the money?" George pressed on.

"Not bad," Pete shrugged. "Three pounds per man per day, right? No paid expenses. Nothin' unusual…just base and standard fare. Just what The Pacemakers got when they were over."

"And the Hunchback of Notre Lame?" John pulled a face, his best Koschmider imitation. "What's to keep his fuggin' claws off us – once we're back within his sadistic, little reach?"

"Eckhorn says Bruno's dropped all charges," Pete said. "No one knows why. And no one cares, right? I guess we're old news to Bruno now. He's well past us."

"Nah, it's just he knows he's wrong!" Paul was still infuriated by the whole episode. "I mean, we couldn't have burned that place down with a gallon of petrol, could we? It was all concrete – The Bambi Kino."

"Arsonist," John sneered at him.

"And after all we did for Koschmider!" Paul fumed. "The crowds at The Kaiserkeller! The money we made him! And what'd we end up with? The serious end of a battle-taxi!"

"Torcher," John said a little louder. Then he turned on George. "And you…larkin' about and pretendin' to be of legal age, as it were. It was deceit and treachery all 'round, wasn't it? Lads with lies and men with matches."

"Yeah, well I'm old enough to work legally now!" George let John get at him once again.

"And how do we know that?" John feigned concern. "C'mon. Let's have a look at yer lifeline, sonny."

"Geroff!" George batted him away as John grabbed his hand and tried to examine his palm.

"Speakin' of legal," Paul turned to Pete. "Al *is* gettin' us work permits, right?"

"He says he's put in the paperwork and rung up all the right government agencies," Pete shrugged.

"But we don't have the permits in hand, now do we?" Paul was skeptical. This was too much like last time.

"Nah, not yet," Pete frowned, scratching his neck nervously.

"Al's been a bit tied up, as it were," John was uncharacteristically tolerant, "what with the authorities fuggin' breathin' down his neck about that blaze at The Top Ten."

"Says he," Paul protested. "But, if you'll notice, he had plenty of time to arrange Gerry Marsden and the lads' trek back to Hamburg…and to get gigs for everyone else we know."

"Yeah, Paul's right," Pete argued. "Al's been lukewarm to us for months. I mean, *I'm* the one who's rung the German authorities. And I'm the one who turned 'round and had the bleedin' drum kit located and salvaged before Koschmider sold it out from under us."

"Good on yer. It does belong to you." John threw laurels at no one.

"The point is," Pete ignored John's sarcasm, "Al's had very little to do with our gettin' back into Germany, y'know."

"Yeah, right," John nodded.

"And in light of that," Pete got to the point, "I can't logically see our cuttin' Al in for the full ten per cent of take, as it were. Not when we'll only be makin' fifteen lousy pounds per day, right?"

"Right." Paul agreed. "I mean, Ray McFall at The Cavern's booked us more often than Al the past few months."

"Even Sam Leach's done more for us than Al lately," George added.

"And Bob as well...there's always Bob," Paul said.

John gnawed on a fingernail, "But...Al did write that letter to the German consulate. None of us can deny that, right?"

"I wrote letters," Pete argued.

"And *I* wrote a bit of a missive to Eckhorn meself," Paul said. "I even rang him up once, if you recall."

"But you rang him from The Jacaranda, didn't you, son?" John reminded him. "And you charged the call to Al, as it were."

"As I see it, we had that phone call comin' to us, John!" Paul said. "Al owed us at *that* at the very least...in light of The Bambi Kino, the *Polizei*, and all the sordid rest."

"Admit it, John," Pete pointed a cigarette at him.

"Yeah, he owed it to us – did Al," George echoed.

The germ of an idea had begun to form. None of them wanted to say it outright, but all of them were thinking the same thing. Whether he knew it or not, Allan was on tenterhooks. The only real consideration was how to release him with the least amount of aggravation.

There is much debate about who was right and who was wrong in the way Allan Williams was treated when The Beatles returned to Hamburg in April, 1961. Williams in The Man Who Gave the Beatles Away says, "If it had not been for my Trojan work with the German authorities in Liverpool, they never would have been allowed back in Germany. And who was it scurried round getting the signatures of the next of kin to legalise the whole affair?"

Similarly, Cynthia Lennon, in her 2005 book, John, says, "Allan Williams came to their rescue. He wrote to the German consulate, praising the boy's musical ability and characters, and explained they'd been exploited on their previous visit. This time, he said, they were going to work for an honourable businessman, Peter Eckhorn, owner of The Top Ten club."

In his book, Beatle! (pp. 88-89) Pete writes, "Paul and I decided to try and do something about having the slate wiped clean [in Hamburg]. We wrote to the immigration authorities and called on the German Consul in Liverpool, pouring out our tale of woe...By this time, I had more or less become acting manager of The Beatles, lumbering myself with all the paper work and attention to details. The rest of *the group just let me get on with it and Allan Williams gradually faded from our scene."*

All conversation, however, is conjecture.

10 April 1961

Dear Allan,

    In light of the fact that our recent engagement with Peter Eckhorn was negotiated solely by us during our stint at The Kaiserkeller last fall and confirmed by calls from us this past Spring, we can see no legitimate reason to follow your directive to deposit ten per cent of our salaries into your Hamburg account. We cannot justify this financial loss since you neither transported us here nor paid for our tickets nor had any part in arranging our lodging or establishing our job requirements. We cannot justify compensating you as Manager for the group when in actuality we served as managers for ourselves in this venture.
    All of us appreciate what you have done for us in the past but at present we not longer feel a need for your services.
    We are enjoying our booking at The Top Ten Club and hope that if you are in Hamburg you'll drop in on us.

                Most Sincerely,

                Stuart Sutcliffe

*I was unable to find a copy of the actual letter written to Allan in any sources. This letter is compiled from information provided by Allan, Bill Harry (*The Ultimate Beatles Encyclopedia*) and Clayson and Sutcliffe's* Backbeat.

11 April 1961
The Top Ten Club
Hamburg, Germany

Everything in Hamburg had changed, and nothing had changed. It was almost as if they picked up on chords still reverberating from last December.

Same songs, same antics, same bottles of dark, bitter, gratuitous lager. Same covers of Carl Perkins, Chuck Berry, and now and again, Ray Charles. Same cowboy boots. Same Beatles. Same John, Paul, George, Pete, and Stu. They clashed and twanged again, vending the raw sound that had made them a Reeperbahn legend.

But this time, it was The Top Ten Club, not The Kaiserkeller. It was Peter Eckhorn, not Bruno Koschmider. They were second fiddle to Tony Sheridan now, not headliners. Even as immensely popular as The Beatles had become on the Herbertstrasse, here at the prestigious Top Ten, they weren't quite "top bill" material.

But being subordinate had its benefits. They were less cautious about being always on their game.

"Look, it's ole Horst Fascher!" John shouted as the former Kaiserkeller bouncer strolled into the Top Ten. "Giddyup, Horst!"

"Greetings von Liverpool, Horst!" Paul winked.

"Shut up, you lousy Beatles. You are no better than last year." Fascher suppressed a smirk. "Rude boys. All that noise! Bah! You give me headache!"

"Ah, you love us!" John crowed. "Rumour is, you were effin' miserable while we were away."

"You stink, Beatle!" Fascher bandied. "Same as always. Stink very bad."

John lifted his nose, sniffing the air like a bloodhound. "Nah. It's not me, it's him." He pointed to Paul.

"I showered, y'know." Paul brushed some imaginary dandruff from his shoulder. "We have those this time around – showers."

"Yeah. Just when we'd grown used to the mod cons of cinema toilets and cold, filthy cinema sinks," John sneered.

Horst brushed past them, shaking his head and chuckling gruffly.

"What's up with him?" George ambled back from a break, sipping a bottled Coca-Cola through a straw.

John jumped, startled at the lead guitarist's sudden appearance.

"Sorry." George bit his bottom lip to keep from laughing. "Didn't mean to disarrange you, John."

"Don't be a lurker, son," John warned. "Men've been knifed on the Herbertstrasse for less than that."

"I wasn't lurkin'…I only just went for a Coca-Cola," George shrugged. He yawned and looked around the room. "Where's Stu? Hasn't he arrived, then?"

"Stu?" Paul looked around as if he hadn't noticed. "Hmmm, must be at Astrid's for a change."

John's lips were tight.

"But he's performin' with us tonight, right?" George glanced at his watch.

"I am." This time they all jumped. Head down, guitar in hand, shoulders slumped like a condemned man, Stu plodded towards the platform. He stepped up on the stage, knelt down, and unsnapped his guitar case – lifting the heavy Hofner out by its neck.

"Welcome to The Top Ten," John gestured towards the huge room. "Perhaps you've heard of us. We're The Beatles."

"Piss off, John." Stu wrinkled his brow. "Don't act like I'm not part of the group. I've been here every fuggin' night for the last ten days!"

"And absent every fuggin' day for the last ten days." John spelled it out.

"I told you where I'd be today. I told you I was workin' on gettin' an apprenticeship. I told you this was my one and only opportunity to connect with someone important…"

"I thought *we* were important," Paul mumbled.

"How'd it go, Stu?" George tuned as he talked.

"I've finally gotten an interview with Paolozzi…tomorrow mornin'," Stu tried to restrain the smile he felt, "thanks to Astrid and her family's connections, as it were."

"Edouardo Paolozzi, eh?" John sniffed. "Cultural elitist!"

"Cut it out, John." Stu's smile vanished. "I'm not bein' pretentious, and you know it. You're as familiar with Paolozzi as I am."

John shouldered his guitar. "The only Paolozzi I've heard of's a fuggin' sculptor."

"That's right," Stu nodded. "That's the one."

"Yeah?" John chewed gum and adjusted his guitar strap at the base of his neck, "Well, what's a sculptor like him got to do with a painter like you?"

"Same thing that a crooner like Sheridan has to do with a rocker like you. It's all art, John…whatever medium."

"Right." John turned away. "All right then – let's run that intro to 'Kansas City' a coupla times."

"That's the congratulations I get?" Stu's hands fell to his side.

"No," John fired back, "that's the *slack* you get. That's the unusual amount of consideration you get! That's the support you get from all of us here – allowin' you to be completely excused while we're stuck here day in and day out, workin' on bein' a band instead of workin' on somethin' else entirely!"

"Not that you'd be shown any partiality, mind you, Stu," Paul spat out.

"But…but it's *my career* I'm workin' on!" Stu started.

"Now there's a new one!" John cut him off. "We've never heard that one before. Tell us all about it, Mr. Sutcliffe."

"Ah-one-two, ah, one, two, three, four!" Paul truncated the argument with the countdown into "Kansas City," and the music began. Stern-faced, Stu reluctantly shouldered his Hofner and joined in.

A few bars into the number, Paul walked over and tapped his foot pedagogically, indicating the beat he wanted Stu to play. John took up rhythm alone while Stu followed Paul's direction and tried to match the pace.

Only Astrid, standing in the shadows at the back of the room, could see how impossible it all was, how awkward and hopeless the situation had become. Stu hadn't a bit of interest in the band. He was tired, and his drawn face showed ennui.

John, in contrast, was performing – even in the middle of the afternoon, even with no one in the club. Legs wide apart, shoulders squared, and knees slightly bent, he tossed his head defiantly while supplying close harmony to Paul's melody line. He flashed a Cheshire grin and bounced a bit in his stance.

As soon as Paul resumed his place, Stu took a couple of steps towards the back of the stage and let his head fall lower over his instrument. He nodded at Pete, and in doing so, faltered for a second in the bass line. His face flushed; he scrambled to catch up.

"How are they?" Klaus arrived, touching Astrid's arm above the elbow.

"Hello, Klaus." She smiled and reached over to squeeze her former fiancé's hand. In spite of everything, they were still best friends.

"They sound good today, yes?" He returned her gaze fondly. Anyone could see he still loved her. And in loving Astrid, he loved those she loved.

"Yes," she removed her hand, "they sound good…but truth, Klaus…it is only veneer."

"Veneer?" He lifted an eyebrow.

"You have heard the saying, 'Believe half of what you hear'? There," Astrid motioned towards the stage, "that is the perfect example."

Klaus shrugged. "I hear nothing different." He listened for a minute and then shrugged again.

"Then," Astrid said, "they have succeeded, and you are duped." She smiled sadly. "Nothing on that stage is as it appears, Klaus. Not one of them is what he seems to be. You know them well…but they have fooled even you. They have persuaded you with play-acting and charmed you with their music. Look at their faces, Klaus. Look in their eyes and tell me what you see."

For the next few minutes, Klaus studied the band as a cat traces the wriggling of a sparrow in tall grass. John whooped, did a dance step, and lunged into a vaudeville bow. Pete tossed his drumsticks in the air and caught them. Paul waved to an imaginary crowd while George applauded for him. He cheered and clapped enthusiastically.

"Do you see it?" Astrid whispered. But before Klaus could answer, she explained. "Stu is not happy in that group. And Paul clearly wants him to go. But John will not let him go, although John is miserable, too. Stu is not right for the band, and John knows it. But John will not turn him loose. He will not release Stu to lead a life of his own."

Klaus looked at her and listened.

"And with Pete, there is some tension as well," Astrid continued. "Some sort of struggle for identity or influence. Even with George – who wants to get along with everyone – there is a sense of being unappreciated by the rest. Nothing is good about the way things are right now." Astrid pronounced. "Nothing is right."

"But…what will happen, then?" Klaus frowned. "What can make it the way it was at The Kaiserkeller – the way it used to be?"

"It was never 'the way it used to be,'" Astrid shook her head. "Since the very first, it has always been like this. George has always felt left out. Pete has always been outside looking in. Paul has always wanted Stu to go. John has always wanted Stu to stay. And Stu…"

Klaus brushed a bit of his bowl haircut behind his ears. "Why *does* he stay?" he asked.

"Because he loves John." Astrid shrugged in resignation. "Part of his heart belongs to me, but part of Stuart's heart will always belong to John Lennon."

"And so…he will remain in the group?"

"No," Astrid shook her head. "Stu has already decided that he must tell John he is leaving the band. He is only waiting for the right time. And sadly for them both, that time is coming very soon."

This is not an actual event but a "representative" moment in the days just after The Beatles returned to Germany. Stu did secure an interview with Paolozzi, and was planning his exit from the band. The Beatles did reconnect with many of their former friends, including Horst Fascher. The incidents in this chapter did occur, but perhaps not all on the same day. The conversation is conjecture.

A. R. Williams
jacaranda enterprises
21 Slater Street Liverpool 1/Royal 6544

20ᵗʰ April, 1961

Dear Lads,

    I am extremely put out to hear you are considering not paying my ten per cent commission for your engagement at the Top Ten Club.
    May I remind you, in light of the fact that you are all letting your own publicity go to your heads, that the clubs of Hamburg, Germany, would never have been open to you and yours if I had not flown to Germany with the demo tapes, talked you up to Koschmider, and negotiated the contacts on your behalf last year. Might I also remind you that it is against the law for you to negotiate a new contract through an initial contract.
    We all know that, with things as they were with Bruno and the Polizei, the only way you got back to Hamburg – period – was through my hard work and intervention on your behalf.
    So you can understand how peeved I am that you should turn out so unappreciative and should take your debt to me so lightly.
    If you decide not to compensate me for the work I have performed on your behalf, I must warn you that I will move heaven and earth to have you removed bodily from Germany within two weeks. And this is no idle threat, lads.
    Furthermore, I plan to document your behaviour to the Agency Members Association here in England, which protects Agents and Managers from those who do exactly the kind of thing you are trying to pull off here.

So if you want to ever perform Merseyside again, you'd better rethink your position. I have a great deal more power than you imagine I might have, and I won't hesitate to use it. Period.

Finally, and you'd better listen to this, I have an associate who is sponsoring a Ray Charles tour throughout England very soon...perhaps in September. I had planned to recommend The Beatles as a touring band for Mr. Charles, but if you cannot keep your contracts as promised, you will be only a vague memory to me. I will make sure that Rory and the Hurricanes fill the slot you would have taken. It will be a pleasure to do so.

I believe that in your newfound "fabulous" state, you've forgotten that I can make or break you Mersyside. I am the one who can get you where you want to go. All the other promoters locally are merely mimicking my lead. You may be besieged right now with promoters who have turned your heads, but when push comes to shove, who will be there for you?

I have always had a fondness for you lot and helped you because I thought you were honest lads.

We have had a good relationship in the past, and I don't want bad blood between us after all this time, but I have no use for those who violate contracts and fail to keep their promises. I hope you will reconsider your rash actions.

Yours sincerely,

A. R. Williams

"That's blackmail, y'know." George let the letter fall onto the waxy, checkered tablecloth beneath his elbows. He nervously brushed back a tousle of hair that had fallen over one eye. "He can't do that, can he – all those evil things?"

"He can do." John slurped up a lukewarm bowl of The Seaman's Mission's "soup of the day." He turned his overlarge spoon sideways and shoveled the liquid in, reaching for a handful of crackers and crumbling them into his bowl. "He's got the clout *and* the fuggin' connections. But will he take the trouble – Al? Will he put himself out just to save a bit of fuggin' pride and compensate for a few pounds, as it were?"

"Right," Paul nodded, blowing steam off his bowl. "If he did turn us in to the authorities, he'd have to admit he got royally skunked...shanghaied by the 'lousy, layabout Beatles.'"

"He'd get the worst of it by the time the story circulated Merseyside," John said.

George listened and nibbled on a cracker. Prellys had left him queasy, not famished, as John always seemed to be. The smells from Frau Prill's kitchen nauseated him this morning.

"Yeah, I suppose y'er right." George took a deep, cleansing breath. "But *we* don't come off all that lovely in the episode either, now do we?" He nudged Al's letter over to John.

"Ah, that's just classic Allan." John pushed it back. "And *he* woulda done exactly the same thing, given half the chance. If he'd been in our shoes, he woulda chucked himself as manager ages ago."

George was hardly convinced, but he didn't press the issue. He turned and stared out the window at the slate blue and green-grey dinghies bobbing recklessly at the pier. Their lullaby motion only exacerbated his discomfort, and he put his head down on the table, resting his forehead on his arms. "Ugh," he moaned. "I really hate losin' that Ray Charles tour, as it were," his muffled voice complained.

John sputtered. He covered his mouth with his hand and tried not to spew liquid across the table. When he could finally swallow, he choked out a guffaw.

"What's so terribly funny?" George sat up and blushed. Paul was smiling, too. "You think there never was any Ray Charles tour. Right?"

"I think it's all high expectations and low realizations," John wiped his mouth with a napkin. "Al's pie in the sky. He's 'once upon a time' and 'somewhere over the fuggin' rainbow.'"

"He's a *promoter*," Paul reminded George.

"Oh," George swallowed a tad of a cracker. "Well...it sounded good on paper, didn't it?"

George picked Al's letter up and read it one more time, mulling over each paragraph. Then he folded it and slipped it into his pocket as a memento, a reminder of things as they were in the real world.

"Anyroad," he chewed his bottom lip nervously, "I hope it's all unfounded – those threats. I mean, it sounds ugly and dangerous, what he said."

"It's only rhetoric." Paul yawned and looked out over the dark Hamburg bay that was growing grimmer by the minute.

"The roaring of the injured," John assured him.

"Who says he's out to ruin us," George whined. "Who says he's out to get us blackballed Merseyside."

"But behind the dark and tasseled drapery," John shoved his empty bowl aside, "is a real man playin' the part of the great and terrible Oz. And no matter how many lights he flashes or how many promises he makes, he hasn't the enchanted, red shoes you need, Havva – and he can't drop a fuggin' house on your family, either."

"He's not half as evil as he seems," Paul smiled. "It's all smoke 'n' mirrors."

"If you say so," George mumbled.

"Knowin' Al," John leaned back and belched, "he's already brushed himself off and moved on. We're the least of his concerns."

"Yeah," George admitted, "that's right. Al's no vengeful Koschmider, is he? He's not that way, right?" He looked at the others.

"Just keep tellin' yerself that, son," John said, "but have a furtive glance over yer shoulder now and then, anyway." And he chuckled as George blanched and started worrying all over again.

This is a paraphrase of a letter that Allan sent to The Beatles in April of 1961. To read the actual letter, look in Williams' book, The Man Who Gave the Beatles Away, *p. 206-207. All conversation is conjecture.*

21 April, 1961

To Mim It May Concern:

Dear Madam, greetings from Hamburgy-berg! We're all safe and sound of mind. Paul sends warm regards. George says you'd be happier if he didn't. So he doesn't. Stu sends his Best...but we needed him here to drum, so you'll have to manage on yer own, madam. I send a request for clean socks (fur-gyle, isn't it?) and an advert from the news about The Beatles at The Top Ten. Save it always.

Just a missile to say that Cyn's comin' over at the Easter break...didn't want you to hear it from Paul's dear ole dad at the Penny Lane Woolies.

I'll have her a respectable place to stay, and it's all kosher, although we were Anglican, last time I checked. You don't have to go ter bits over it.

She's comin' over by rail with Paul's girl, Dot Rhone, or so the rumour goes. And, yeah, Mrs. Powell knows all about it – so no need to ring her up and spread the good news to a waitin' world.

We're on our own now, The Beatles, these days... Allan Williams isn't managin' us anymore. And that's all right because we saved his ten per cent, didn't we? Less for him, more for the Queen! (God save!) And even without him, we're gettin' on famously here. There's even talk of recordin' somethin' with Tony Sheridan (the star whose sheridan the stage with us) before we head back Mersey-Side B.

Hope y'er well.

How does yer garden grow? Or have you heard that one before? Give me love to the cats, and say hello to Shennon if you happen to see him. Until we meat and potatoes again.

Best wishes, cheers, and fondly all love,

John

This is not an actual letter written by John but one compiled from studying his writing style in Sky Writing By Word of Mouth, *his letters in Coleman's book, and letters shown to me by Allan Williams during various interviews in 1993 and 1994.*

Easter, 1961
Top Ten Club
Hamburg, Germany

John flipped the perfumed letter onto Paul's bunk. "Appears it's all arranged and done, McArtrey...they're both comin' over."

"That *was* the plan when we left, wasn't it?" Paul nodded.

"Yeah, well Dot and Cyn've even rooked your dad into drivin'em to the fuggin' station...and Cyn's mum's goin' along...for the final words of admonition, as it were."

"Good man, our Jim," Paul clicked his cheek. "Always the fatherly, 'put-it-there' sort, isn't he?"

"For girls like Cyn and Dot, he's all about chivalry – your dad."

Paul smiled, glancing around their ten-by-ten room above the noisy Top Ten. It was little more than a monastic cell: a primitive dresser, a three-legged chair, two bunk beds, and a stack of suitcases. There was just barely enough room in the attic for George, Pete, John, and him to manoeuver after work. There wasn't an inch of extra space for two girlfriends complete with rollers, makeup, and God knows what else. He was a little worried about it all.

"So...what'll you be doin' with Cyn, once she arrives, then?" Paul asked.

"You figure it out."

"I mean," Paul threw his eyes to the ceiling, "where'll you be *puttin' her up*, as it were? She'n Dot can't stay here. We've nothin' in the way of privacy...not even a divider to change behind, as it were."

"All too unrefined for the likes of Hoylake, eh?" John bristled.

"I wasn't sayin' that." Paul flopped down on George's bunk. "For Cyn *and* Dot...I mean...we have to have some place more appropriate."

"I've already asked Astrid if Cyn could stay with her in Butler Strasse...I thought the two of 'em might hit it off, as it were...y'know, two artists and all that."

Paul tugged at his boots and plunked them, one by one, onto the concrete floor. "But they're very different – Cyn and Astrid – aren't they?" He raised his eyebrows. "I mean, art school aside, what do they really have in common?"

"Well, it's not a fuggin' engagement, McCartney! It's only holiday break."

"Right, all right." Paul slipped off his socks and wiggled his toes. "But there's still the matter of Dot, y'know. I don't suppose Astrid would…"

"There's no room in the inn, son."

"Your generosity's overwhelmin', John."

"As are yer feet. Put yer effin' shoes back on!" John pulled a pillow over his face.

"Right. Well…I guess I'll just go ask Rosa then. She's mentioned a houseboat of some sort, hasn't she?"

"Don't count on it, son." John peeked out from under his pillow. "Rosa'll have nothin' to do with your little schemes. Y'won't budge the anchor of her respectability…you and your trysts and yer filthy, British ways."

"What filthy ways are these?" George trudged through the door, his eyes bleary from lack of sleep.

"McArtrey's," John said.

"What's he up to now?" George played along.

"He's plannin' to sequester the lovely and Liverpudlian Dot Rhone – the famous chemist's assistant – away on Rosa's houseboat."

"She's really comin' over, then?" George took Paul's bunk since Paul had his.

"Yeah…she 'n Cyn both. John just got the telegram." Paul yawned and talked at the same time.

"That's fantastic! They'll absolutely love it here! The Top Ten 'n the Exis 'n Astrid 'n Klaus 'n Tony Sheridan 'n all!" George imagined the sightseeing walks they might all go on together.

"Yeah, before we left home, Dot was always on about Hamburg and the things she wanted to do over here. I think she wanted *me* to come over just so she could tag along!" Paul sniffed, pulling himself up from the bunk and beginning to tug on the dark, rumpled jeans that had become The Beatles' staple uniform. He kicked a pile of mildewed clothes, looking for a passably clean shirt. "It appears we'll have to do a bit of laundry before the girls arrive, y'know."

"You do it. I'm too nallered to care." John rolled towards the wall.

But a week later, John was far from apathetic. In fact, he was the first one across the long, wooden platform when the wheels screeched to a slow, whooshing halt. Wearing a rare Lennon smile, he grabbed Cynthia, suitcases and all, and held her in a clutch that left no room for modesty, burying his face in her hair. He refused to let her go.

Behind them, Dot's giggles and whispers mingled with Paul's words. The sound of a train gaining momentum throbbed dully. People hugged each other and laughed. Families reunited and conversed. A conductor issued a boarding call over the wail of a frustrated baby.

John savoured the moment. He breathed deeply, surrendering to the spicy scent Cyn always wore. He wrapped his arms around her tighter, pulling her even closer against him. Even when she pretended to fuss, he held on.

"John! You're all beery. Let go!" Cynthia playfully tusseled.

He picked her up and swung her around. She laughed and blushed.

"John!" Her eyes danced under the long, blonde bangs. "Can you believe I'm actually *here*? Can you believe I've made it to Hamburg after all this time?"

"Can you believe our parents actually *let us* is more to the point!" Dot's cute, pixie face beamed. She draped an arm around Cynthia and one around Paul, making the couples into a foursome. "I thought mine would *never*!"

"It *is* rather incredible…when you think about it," Paul agreed.

"It's fanfuggin'tastic, that's what it is!" John pulled Cyn away to himself.

"I can't wait to see Hamburg!" Dot nuzzled in under Paul's arm.

"I can't wait to get to Astrid's," Cyn flirted, ducking her head meaningfully.

"No sooner said than done." John pointed the way to the exit.

"Fourteen days…and it's only just begun," Paul did a smooth waltz step.

"Fourteen days," Dot exclaimed, "and fourteen thousand things to do!"

"Fourteen days," Cyn pouted sexily, "and it won't be nearly long enough." And although John was too macho to admit it, he had to agree.

****

Eims Butteler Strasse
Hamburg, Germany

"You look lovely." Astrid stood behind Cynthia as they stared into Astrid's full-length, ebony, oval mirror. She rested her hand on Cynthia's shoulder and smiled with quiet satisfaction at the metamorphosis she'd performed.

Draped in a floor-length vest of black velvet, a loosely knit, crocheted blouse with tightly fitted sleeves, and a pair of Astrid's body-clinging black jeans, the girl from Hoylake now looked every bit "the Exis." Posh conservatism had been replaced by artistic trendiness. No hint of the Wirral remained.

"*Trés chic!*" Astrid stroked Cynthia's long, blonde hair admiringly. "Black suits you well."

Cynthia bit her bottom lip. "But...what'll John think, I wonder?" Cynthia's hand traced the pattern of cording that swirled across the breast of the intricately patterned vest.

"He will think you are beautiful...even more beautiful than before," Astrid whispered.

"It's just...it's not *me*, you know – all this." Cynthia's eyes scanned the foil-lined walls of Astrid's third-floor studio apartment and then returned appraisingly to her own reflection in the mirror. She sighed and let her shoulders slump. "I mean, you're extremely kind to lend me these things, Astrid, but..."

"You are an *artist*, are you not?"

"So they say," Cynthia shrugged. "It's what I'm trained to do."

Astrid went to the black-draped credenza and lit a tiny, purple votive candle. She blew the match out slowly, elegantly, and watched the curls of smoke rise into the glare of the overhead spots. "And John knows this?" She faced Cynthia again.

"I suppose so," Cynthia curled an errant string from her sleeve around her finger and pulled on the garment with a quick tug. "I mean, he knows who I *was* when he met me, and he knows how I've tried to change for him, in dozens of ways."

"But what you have altered has not changed you?" Astrid frowned.

"It's hard to say," Cynthia sat on the edge of the bed and sighed. "Since I met John, I've been in a virtual *downpour* of creativity...music, art, poetry, drama, rock'n'roll...I've literally been drenched in it – drenched!"

"And?" Astrid took a seat beside her, rubbing her hand slowly over the black velvet bedspread.

"And somehow it's never managed to find a fissure in my brightly shellacked surface." She laughed softly at the image. "No matter how thunderous the shower or how prolific the rainfall... in all this time, I've never quite managed...to get wet."

"You see," Astrid smiled, "*that* was art."

Cynthia nodded. "I do have my moments."

The girls smiled at each other for a second. Then Astrid reached out a hand to her new friend.

"You know," Astrid lowered her voice, "it will not be enough to pretend for John. It will not be enough to masquerade...'to act like' an artist."

Cynthia lowered her heard. "You're saying I'll lose him eventually, then?"

"I am saying..." Astrid took a deep breath, "that I have never known anyone like John Lennon, ever. Not Paul. Not George. Not Jürgen. Not Klaus. Not even Stuart. And that is saying a great deal."

"Because he's a genius?"

"Because he is frustrated, angry, determined, irreverent, tragic, beautiful, passionate, rebellious, brilliant…but most of all, painfully honest. John only respects those who are what they are. And if you are one thing outside and another thing inside, you will lose him. You will lose it all." She paused. "But I do not need to tell you this. You know it as well as I do."

Cynthia stood and walked to the tall, single window three stories above the street and paused as swaths of bright fuchsia and indigo tinged the sky. Night was falling. The ancient, iron streetlamps along the elegant Eims Butteler Strasse glowed, flickering orange, and beyond them, the gaudy neons of Hamburg's Reeperbahn began their evening debaucheries. It was almost time for the girls to leave for The Top Ten.

"Stuart wrote to me," Cynthia began, hesitantly, "and urged me to come to Hamburg straight away."

"Yes, he likes you very much," Astrid nodded. "And Stuart knows how much you love John as well."

"But more than that," Cynthia went on, "Stu wanted me here for another reason." She paused, but Astrid motioned her to go on. "He wanted me to remind John of what he'd left behind in dear, old Liddypool. To put it bluntly – Stu wanted me here to belay a change he sensed in your threesome – to stop a twist of events that he worried just might transpire…if things went on as they were."

Astrid stared at a tiny, white moth that had suddenly appeared and now flitted too close to the purple sandalwood and myrrh votive on her desk.

"John's letters," Cynthia spoke slowly now, "are full of you, Astrid."

The moth darted about just above the tiny flame.

"He writes about your photographic experiments, your strange literature, your music, your clothing, your *avant garde* circle of friends, your wonderfully unpredictable behaviour, your *Kama Sutra*…even your haircut…and your eyes."

Astrid met Cynthia's gaze.

Cynthia returned to the bed and sat down. "Astrid, I've been jealous of you beyond all belief. The way John writes, I was beginning to believe the sun shone from your backside!"* The girls smiled at one another. "I was beginning to believe that…well, I thought that by coming here and…intervening of sorts…I thought I might be able to head off any infatuation that had inadvertently reared its ugly head."

"And now?" Astrid barely whispered.

"And now, I'm convinced that John was, and is, absolutely right. You're remarkable."

Astrid stood and walked to the closet. She reached for the scuffed, black ballet slippers that were her trademark. She bent over and slipped them easily onto her feet.

"But John does not love me." Astrid stood and ruffled her hair. "He is only intrigued. He is *that*." She motioned toward the moth, "John is a curious creature drawn to a bright flame."

"But…he might eventually come to love you, right?" Cynthia asked.

"If you let him," Astrid agreed.

"Astrid, it's no secret how I feel…I want to marry John. I want to have a life with him. *I* want to be the one he's infatuated with."

"Then," Astrid ran her fingers through her short, pixie cut, "you must decide who you really are, and it is *that* life you must live."

"Even if it's not avant garde? Even if I'm not an artist, after all?"

"What I have seen of John tells me this." Astrid pulled on her soft, black beret. "He has no use for shams. He has no dealings with those who are false. He is drawn to Stu because Stu is real. He is drawn to me because I am who I am. He is drawn to those who do not care what others think. John is drawn to self-confidence…to those who know where they are going."

"But I've always tried to be what *he* wants," Cynthia said.

"Try being what *you* want." Astrid opened the door and flipped off the ceiling light. "Try being who you are. Try being Cynthia Powell for a change. You are lovely, Cynthia. When you are honest, John will find that intriguing."

Dot Rhone, according to Paul's brother, Michael, (in Thank You Very Much*), was Paul's "first real sweetheart."*

Again, there is some debate about when this trip occurred. Barry Miles in The Beatles' Diary, Volume 1, *places it between June 1-30. But Bill Harry and Philip Norman both say that the trip took place over the Easter break since Cynthia was still enrolled at Liverpool College of Art. In Cynthia's book, A Twist of Lennon, she says that the trip was a two-week stay (p. 58) and that "Dot and I had gone on our trip to Hamburg during the Easter holidays," (p. 64). In her 2005 book, John, Cynthia states, "It was the Easter holidays, and I had two weeks off from college," (p. 61).*

* "I thought the sun shone from your backside" is an actual quote from Cynthia, found on page 53 of A Twist of Lennon.

The story line in this chapter is also told in the wonderful film, Backbeat, *based on the book by Pauline Sutcliffe and Alan Clayson. I cannot recommend the book enough. And the film is excellent as well.*

The facts in the scene between John, Paul, and George in the attic of the Top Ten are authentic (Rosa's houseboat, the letter from Cyn, Paul's father driving them to the station and Mrs. Powell going along). But the conversation is imagined, as the scene at the train station is imagined.

May 1961
The Top Ten Club
Hamburg, Germany

"How now, Sir Real?" John nudged Stu, who slumped, his head in his hands, over one of the Top Ten's wooden tables.

"Yeah," came the muffled voice behind the fingers. "What's up?"

"What *off's* more like it...and she is...back to the arms of 'er dear, ole mudder."

"Cyn? She's gone, then?"

"On the one after 909." John gave a nod to the song he'd co-authored with Paul.

"Did you tell 'er...did she understand why I couldn't come 'round to see her off?"

"She knew yer head was the size o' Lewises, as it were." John sat down beside his friend. "She knew you'd had a few too many and a few too many after that."

"I'm *not* hung over, John!" Stu tried to focus, but his eyes wouldn't cooperate. "I told you before... I'm sick."

"Sick, is it? Well, we're all sick these days."

"It's not the Prellys! It's not the lager! It's not even the interminable workload..."

"It was *your* choice to take those classes with fuggin' Paolozzi on top of the gig..." John had inherited a penchant for lecturing. "*You're* the one who chose to..."

"There was no choosing about it...I couldn't afford *not to*, John. I couldn't just walk away from a grant doled out by the Hamburg fuggin' City Council, could I?"

"No, you'd rather welsh on the band."

"I haven't *welshed* on the band! I've been there every time you've taken the stage, haven't I?"

"But you're backin' out on the Bert Kaempfert recordin' session, aren't you, son?" John let the bomb fall.

"How'd you know?" Stu lifted his head with agonizing determination. He'd wanted to tell John himself. He'd wanted to explain that he just couldn't cancel day classes with Paolozzi, regardless of Kaempfert's impressive offer to let The Beatles record with Tony Sheridan. "Who told you?"

"I dunno."

"It's all too obvious, isn't it?"

"Right. Well, he'll be forced to play the effin' bass in your stead if you walk out on us at this stage o'the proceedin's."

"Forced, is it?" Stu let his head fall again. "That's rich."

"He'll do what he has to do."

"He'll dance on me grave, and enjoy it."

"Look, Stu…" John began again, "you can't be everywhere and do everythin', can you? Have done with this Paolozzi shite!"

"Thank you, Auntie Mimi," Stu shot back.

"It's not the same thing! It doesn't begin to be the same thing! I'm not sayin' you're without talent, or I don't believe in your ability to be great. What I'm sayin' is, you've signed on for too *much* in too fuggin' little time! You look like hell…and y'smell even worse! You're a shell of what you once were. You're no fuggin' good to anyone, not even Astrid it seems."

"What d'you mean by that?" Stu raised himself up on one elbow and forced himself to focus.

"She says you bleedin' smacked 'er, son!"

"I…I-I was sick." Stu teared up rapidly. "I was fuggin' sick! Shite!"

"Yeah? Well, she says y'er always sick…y'er always in a rage…more'n half the time these days. She says y'er throwin' tantrums 'n' screamin' 'n'…"

"She's right." Stu slumped back to the tabletop. He grabbed his head with both his hands and rocked inconsolably. "But I don't know what's wrong. I *honestly* don't know what's wrong, John! I'm out of control, that's what. I'm racked!"

"The beans, then?" John had seen Stu popping more than his share of Prellys in the last few weeks.

"Nah, it's more'n that." Stu thought for a minute, choosing his words carefully. "It's somethin' else…."

"Battle fatigue." John crossed his arms. "A case o' the fuggin' nerves."

"If only I thought it was exhaustion, I'd grab on to that hope and hold on for dear life."

"Then what? You're bound to know."

"I *don't* know! It's just these…headaches – these blindin', gut-punchin', savage bitches! These white-hot, steel bands grippin' me tighter and tighter around the brain! I've daggers borin' eight-inch holes into me skull, John!"

"You should see a surgeon."

"Don't you think I already have?" Stu collapsed back into his chair, his voice weaker than before, perspiration beading on his forehead. "Don't you think that might've possibly occurred to me – even to someone as muzzied as I am?"

"And…what's the bottom line?" John's face had gone white.

"Oh, an incredible cure. Really. Stu took a quivering breath. He told me to fuggin' *rest*! He told me to try relaxin'…to try 'n quit pressin' so hard. He told me to take a picnic in the country – to smell the fuggin' roses and pluck the fuggin' daisies, as it were! *That* was his remedy for the hell that is my life!"

"It's all that art." John stood and began to pace, his boots making hollow sounds in the cavernous pub.

"No…it's the *lack of!*" Stu was perspiring heavily. His shirt was splotched with dark, wet patches. His skin was mottled. "It's tryin' to fit the art in at odd hours and catch-as-catch can moments. It's sandwichin' all *I* want to do in between the demands of all *you* want me to do."

"You're breakin' me heart."

"It's Mum tellin' me to come back to Liverpool and Astrid tellin' me to get on with the important work I'm destined to do and Paul mumblin' jabs… when you're not…and *you* tuggin' on me to get here and be there and dance when you pull my fuggin' strings! It's Paolozzi tellin' me to concentrate, and the lot o' you tellin' me how to run my life and live out the myriad fantasies you've all so conveniently preconceived on my fuggin' behalf!"

"You had an agreement with the band."

"No, *you* had an agreement!" Stu slammed his fist into the table, spinning it sideways and onto to floor. "I was never asked!"

"You agreed to…"

"I was bleedin' dragged along! It was *you* who decided I'd play bass…it was you who decided I'd give up art to chase down some dream I *never even had*! It was you who said I'd be in the band, John…you who said I'd leave school and come here and sacrifice every fuggin' thing for the sake of rock'n'roll! I *never* agreed to it! Not once!"

John stopped dead still and looked at Stu as if seeing him for the first time. He stared for several seconds, taking in the sweat, the shaking hands, the pallour.

"You're out, then." John pronounced quietly. "Paul'll play bass from now on. And come 23 June, we'll do the Kaempfert session without you."

"Right," Stu exhaled relief. "I'd appreciate that."

John stood up tall. "Yeah? Well, how about when our record comes out and your name's not on it? How'll you feel then?"

Stu had no answer, and John had nothing else to say. After several minutes, John sat down again.

"Cyn wanted to say goodbye, y'know. She was hopin' you'd show up, right down to the last minute."

"I wanted to…I really tried, John…I….ugh, these headaches! God help me!" Stu gagged violently – dry heaves. Sweat ran down his sideburns, and his shoulders trembled. John had seen him collapse in a seizure once before, and now adrenaline pumped furiously as he watched, anticipating another episode.

"C'mon, Stuart. Breathe," he offered. He didn't know what else to say.

"Tell Cyn…" Stu almost whispered. "Tell her 'sorry.' Wouldn't want her browned off at me. She's a good friend."

"She's a fuggin' distraction…" John tried levity. "All assets and titillation, as it were."

Stu looked at John with eyes that water-coloured everything. He pushed an anemic laugh past his lips. "Is that how it is, then? A distraction, eh?"

"Yeah. With her gone and you replaced, I'll be back on track again, won't I? Focused!"

"Rock'n'roll as usual, right?"

"Yeah."

"And you're really doin' a record with the famous Bert Kaempfert, then?"

"Yeah, Sheridan's arrangin' the whole thing. All that's left's the fine print." John got up and clattered towards the stage, eager to begin his first set in two weeks without Cynthia's watchful eye. But once he'd shouldered his guitar, he turned back to Stu and whistled between his teeth. "Hey, son! Wake up! Pull yourself together and get out o' here. You're only draggin' me down, y'know."

"Sendin' me packin'…just like y'did the lovely Miss Powell?"

"Yeah, I'm chuckin' the both ya." John jammed his tongue down behind his bottom lip in his famous grin.

"Right." Stu struggled to chuckle, wobbling as he stood. "And y'would! Except for the fact that you fuggin' love us."

"I'll get over you." John strummed his distinctive open chord.

Stu stumbled a few steps towards the door.

"And now ladies and gentlemen," John yelled to an invisible crowd, "as the famed Mr. Stuart Sutcliffe takes his leave of us, we end Act One and pause here for a short intermission and an elaborate change of scenery."

"House lights up!" Stu yelled, and he staggered towards the door in semi-darkness, his limited vision browned into a softly rolling fog.

In Backbeat, *Alan Clayson, and Pauline Sutcliffe write, "Stuart had been feeling off colour for some time. Those closest to him had noticed with more than a little concern his frequently ghastly pallor and a habit of closing his eyes as if in pain…he would insist that nothing was the matter, though nausea, dizzy spells, insomnia, increasing pains in his head, chronic indigestion, and bouts of depression were plaguing him persistently," (p. 145). Stu was very ill.*

This was not the last time that Stu played with The Beatles, even though Paul immediately assumed the role of bass player, borrowing Stu's Hofner President bass until he could get one of his own. Stu played one or two more times with the group, but only out of friendship. He was never again considered a regular member of the band, although he did continue to write missives to Allan on behalf of the group when they had something to communicate that they didn't want to tell Al.

While all events are documented, conversation is conjecture.

Friday, 23 June 1961
Friedrich Ebvert Halle
Hamburg, Germany

Point of truth: John never expected anyone to be anything other than self-serving.

That's why Bert Kaempfert worried him. The man didn't need The Beatles or even Tony Sheridan. He was already a millionaire.

Kaempfert's "Wonderland By Night" had just recently made it to Number One on the American music charts. Mimi's boarders had it endlessly on the record player. It was all over the airwaves these days – the handsome German composer-orchestra leader was legitimately famous in his own right.

So what's he want with us, then? John watched the rain-washed streets flying by outside the taxi window. *What's he want with a bunch of Liverpool scruffs…or even a somewhat well known rock'n'roller like Sheridan? What've we got to offer that he couldn't get on his own – just by writin' another movie theme or composin' another soulful love ballad, what have you?*

John rubbed a finger across one bushy eyebrow and shook his head, trying to keep his eyes open.

It was 8 a.m., and he was nallered. They all were. For the last eighty-eight days in Hamburg, The Beatles had performed without a single day off, without a single full night's sleep. John had done the calculations. By the time that The Beatles planned to depart Germany on 2 July, they would've played over 503 hours on The Top Ten Stage, not counting practise sessions. It was crushing.

Paul, seated next to him, had nodded off, and George, by the window, was fidgeting – fighting sleep. Pete and Tony were in the second taxi just behind them, but John was sure that for them the scenario was the same. None of them had had more than two hours' rest the previous evening.

Why would Kaempfert want to record Sheridan? John sat up again, shaking his head and clearing his throat. *And why would Sheridan ask us in as his back-up band, as it were? Have we become as good as all that, and I haven't noticed?*

It was all...unexpected. Kaempfert had even alluded to the possibility of signing them to a one-year recording contract if things went well today. John shook his head again. *Too fuggin' good to be true.*

The tick of the blinker and the crunch of taxi wheels plowing through gravel roused Paul. He stretched and leaned forward as the vehicle rolled up the circular driveway of an unimaginative, red-orange brick building with concrete keystones over the windows.

"*This* isn't a recordin' studio." John rolled the window down and took a second look.

"It's...a school, isn't it?" Paul yawned.

"A school," John sneered.

"I thought we'd done with all that – schools," George droned.

The taxi paused, and Tony jogged up from the rear with Pete close on his heels. Studying a small, torn slip of paper, he rapped on their window. "Perhaps there's some error," he mumbled, glancing in confusion at the building. "But...no...no, the address is correct, all right. Friedrich Ebvert Halle. This is it."

"It's an infant's school, Sheridan." John chewed gum obnoxiously and stared at Tony.

"It's a school, y'know," Paul echoed.

The taxi driver turned to eye them impatiently. His fare had ended, and he was eager to move on. He held out his hand indicatively and nodded towards the door.

"C'mon," Pete waved John out. "We might as well go in and have a look-see, right?" He scratched his neck. "I mean, if the famous Bert Kaempfert said to meet him here, then like as not, we can take him at his word, right?"

"And what word's that, son?" John edged out of the vehicle.

"School," Paul teased. "It must be 'school.'" He brushed himself off as if he'd been traveling in an open buggy over dusty roads.

"Right," George nodded, tumbling out as well. "That *would* be most the appropriate adjective, I believe."

"Noun," John corrected, looking down his nose. "Person, place, or thingy, son – noun. Where were you the day they gave out grammar?"

"Maybe I was with your girlfriend," George teased.

John flipped him a backhanded V.

"Ee-nough! C'mon," Tony impatiently motioned them towards the entrance. Beatle banter at any o'clock was always exclusive and hence eventually irritating, but this early in the morning, the Liverpudlian wordplay was flat annoying.

"We'd just like to know somethin' once and for all, Sheridan," John said as Pete removed his gear from the rear taxi and slammed the boot shut. "Why is it that a man like Bert Kaempfert's after recordin' us, anyway? Tell us that, if y'don't mind."

"I know that!" George grinned. "It's because we're the fabulous Beatles, that's why,"

"*Beat Brothers*! Beat Brothers!" Tony corrected. It was the name Kaempfert had suggested they use when functioning as Sheridan's back-up group.

"I'll do what I want with me brothers – ta just the same," John muttered, picking up his guitar case and amp.

"Beat Brothers – it sounds rather nasty, doesn't it?" George grimaced, collecting his gear as well.

"Yeah?" Tony fired back, "Well, if y'ask me, it's a helluva lot better than bein' called The Peedles all over bloody Germany!" The phonetics of the word 'Beatles' had never worked well in translation. The connotations were awful, and German fans had enjoyed many a joke at the band's expense.

"I dunno," Paul grinned, moving towards the door, "Peedles isn't all that bad. I've heard John called worse on a good day...by his dear ole Auntie Mim."

"Good morning! Good morning, everyone!" Thirty-seven year old Bert Kaempfert strolled out to greet them. Tall and broad-shouldered, with a high, wide brow, a thick shock of light hair, and a crinkle-eyed smile, he offered Tony a handshake and nodded warmly to the rest. In a cream silk shirt, striped tie, and elegant pleated-front trousers, he smiled and looked them each in the eye, as if he were genuinely thrilled to see them.

The "Beat Brothers" shuffled around, muttering small talk – trying to make polite conversation with their cords, amps, and guitars still in hand. Tony delivered the "thank yous" for the group and politely inquired after Alfred Schacht, a mutual acquaintance of his and Kaempfert's at Aberbach Music Publishing. John, who always listened intently when successful people talked, immediately made the connection between Kaempfert and the director at Sheridan's publishing organization.

So, that's it, he finally understood. *It's this Schacht who's inadvertently gotten us the gig. He must've recommended Sheridan, and Sheridan must've recommended us. Right place, right time. All kismet. Or guidance. Who knows?*

The others – their equipment growing heavier and heavier – were quickly losing interest in the conversation. Pete finally rested his drum kit gently in the gravel, and Paul set down his Alpico.

"Oh – so sorry..." Kaempfert noticed. "Where are my manners? Please...please come inside." He gestured towards the door. "Shouldn't be wasting minutes, anyway...I know you're all slated to return home by the end of next week...far too little leeway for correcting or reworking anything we do today..."

It was the cue they'd been waiting for. John followed Kaempfert and Sheridan into what appeared to be an auditorium, and the others quickly stacked up behind him, eager to set eyes on the studio hidden behind the walls of this grammar school façade.

But what they found inside was an ordinary school assembly hall, a regulation room with rows of folding wooden seats featuring faded and stained green cushions. An elevated stage, beggaring any exact description, sat empty between two thick panels of heavy maroon drapes. Nowhere was there a sign of a recording studio. It was just a school auditorium, plain and simple.

"Gentlemen," Kaempfert smiled, undismayed, "follow me, please."

He led them up and across the stage and into the wings where a board of red lights blinked at regular intervals and archaic machines hummed monotonously.

"Must be some relic from the British army occupation," John whispered in Tony's ear.

"Shhh!" the singer cautioned.

"A radio bunker of some sort," John tried again.

"Shhh!" Tony warned. He elbowed John in the ribs.

"Is this it, then?" George asked, dumbfounded. None of them could believe the primitive conditions.

"Yes," Kaempfert smiled at the boy. "This is where we'll make the record that will change the world!"

They all chuckled – The Beatles, half-heartedly.

The sure-to-be-fantastic Kaempfert studio they'd all fantasized about huddled before them – a mess of wires and antiquated equipment shoved into the wings of the old school stage. It twinkled and buzzed and appeared to be alive, but the contraption was far from state-of-the-art.

"I think the train station had it all over this," John mumbled to Paul.

"At least it's quiet this time," George whispered.

"I told you we were destined for the stage," Paul said out of the side of his mouth.

"We'll begin in twenty minutes," Kaempfert announced, "…as soon as the technicians arrive and settle in."

Tony nodded, with a tenuous, quivering smile plastered across his face – a smile that tried to hide the disappointment and skepticism they were all feeling.

They'd all been so thrilled on the way over, so sure that the recording Kaempfert planned to make of "My Bonnie Lies Over the Ocean" would propel them to fame. Tony especially had counted on the session to be the hallmark event that secured his future. Now, standing in the wings and watching The Beat Brothers take the stage, he wasn't so sure. It was hard to believe that anything worthwhile would ever emerge from this makeshift collection of lights and dials. Things weren't going according to plan.

"Great studio, Sheridan." John caught Tony's eye as Kaempfert exited. "It's an infant's school, y'know."

"Yeah, so you've said," Tony hissed, "and your support's been duly noted."

"Right," Paul winked. "We're known for our dual notes, aren't we, lads?" Paul hit a high note and George supplied low harmony.

And the banter went on. The Beat Brothers chattered their way through the entire set-up. They laughed at the limited technology, and they upbraided Tony – trying to rattle his cage.

Ah, never mind them, the experienced performer tried to tell himself. *It's not that bad here, really. And no matter where it's made, this record'll top the charts.*

Yeah, that's right...top the charts! The Beatles can laugh all they want, but in truth... the only questionable part of this whole production's them, as I see it.

But okay then. Once Kaempfert puts their vocals in the background and their names in fine print, no one'll ever think of them again, will they? I'll score a hit with this, and then it's on to greater horizons. And the lads from Liverpool? They'll be back in Scouseland...back to the semi-obscurity from whence they came!

Tony Sheridan and The Beat Brothers cut the record in only three takes. In fact, the recording went so well that Kaempfert graciously allowed The Beatles to cut several songs of their own. They chose "Cry for a Shadow" (the Lennon-Harrison instrumental) and "Ain't She Sweet" (John's lead vocal). However, the all-Beatles record was not destined to matter half as much as "My Bonnie Lies Over the Ocean" in which the only distinguishable Beatles' voice is Paul's...offering up a "whoop" in the background.

All information in this chapter is documented. Only the conversations are conjecture.

Friday, 14 July 1961
The Cavern Club
Mathew Street
Liverpool

If the temperature had fallen in the July night outside The Cavern Club tunnel, none of the patrons inside could vouch for it. Waiting impatiently for The Beatles to begin, the restless mob fought for air – air that was thick and muggy and ripe with funk. But the odours and heat were hardly a deterrent for the effervescent Bob Wooler. He moved quickly and well. He smiled and waved to those he knew. He spun up the crowd for the show.

"Welcome to The Cavern Club, the best of cellars!" Wooler articulated into the tinny microphone. His voice, however, was anything but tinny. It was melodious. It rung with exhilarated self-assurance.

"Ah, welcome yerself!" someone yelled back.

Bob flashed his boyish grin at the heckler. "So, you've come to ballyhoo the bountifully beautiful Beatles, eh?"

A few feminine shrieks shot up.

"We've come fer a bit o' fookin' music, norra lot o' lip!" an impatient male voice returned.

"Cut to the fuggin' chase!" came another.

"But first," Bob ignored them, "here's a new one from that fabled, fantastic favourite son, Cliff Richard. Ladies and gentlemen, let us venture into The Shadows."

But the platter that spun into sound was not Cliff Richard and the Shadows at all. In fact, it wasn't even rock'n'roll. It was military music – a recording of parade drills. Loud, abrasive, and clearly out of place, the record was obviously the handiwork of John Lennon. *Damn him!*

Bob quickly removed the selection from the turntable and tossed it aside. He shook his head and repressed a smile. *Ah, the prank of the day,* he thought. *Only to be expected! Now* all *the platters'll have to be examined, one by one, and I'll have to re-sort the entire stack! If I didn't like that lousy layabout so much, I might plan to seek retribution on him one of these times.*

But no matter! Bob never lost his composure in front of an audience.

He simply chuckled with the crowd and shuffled efficiently through the bundle of 45's, splaying them in search of the Richard disc. "Ah, variety, variety, a never-ending musical variety!" he stalled for time. "Come to The Cavern to see it all, *hear* it all! See, hear! See, hear!* It's The Cavern Club for *all* your musical selections! Our platters are replete with a ready range of repasts!"

And in less than a minute's time, the sound of The Shadows began to fill the sweat and cleanser-soaked room. Three girls in the front row of wooden chairs shared a compact and put final touches on their make-up. An acne-faced clerk hopelessly attempted to chat up a coworker whose steno pen was stuck decoratively in her hair. A delivery boy from Toxteth – his hair greased back loosely, one lock falling free – brusquely jostled his way into the ninth row. Sitting shoulder to shoulder while "Cavern dandruff" filtered down from the ceiling, hordes of damp, uncomfortable young men and women squirmed and talked and waited for the show to begin. It was just about time.

"It's another houseful out there." George had cracked the band room door as he munched on one of his mum's bacon butties. Until recently, he would've been out mingling with their female fans, "The Beatlettes," as John now called them. But since The Beatles' return from Hamburg eleven days ago, Bob had put an end to such fraternization. The Cavern compère had insisted that the lads remain sequestered backstage prior to performances, creating a tension between the band and the audience, making the fans wait until the lads were formally introduced.

"Isthasso?" Paul raised an eyebrow. "Let's have a look-see, Havva." He headed towards the door.

"We're not supposed to, y'know," George closed it and stepped away.

"You're both damagin' the magical mystique created by our mystical invisibility." John over-articulated as he sketched yet another hideous scene – a congregation of deformed, drooling fans transfixed by the antics of a grossly misshapen band of rockers. "You'll all but ruin the suspense, won't ya?"

Paul peeked anyway. "I only want to see if Pete's kit's blindin' the punters, y'know." A recent coat of bright orange paint had made the drums somewhat a focal point on the tiny, barely elevated boards. Pete smirked.

"Bob's up to the introduction part now." George looked over Paul's shoulder. He could hear the William Tell Overture, their calling card, begin. John and Pete stood and tugged at their clothes. John ground his cig out on the rough concrete floor and grabbed the other half of George's bacon butty, wolfing it down in a bite. Pete glanced at his James Dean coif in a bit of broken mirror.

"And now," Bob's voice lured them towards the tiny entranceway, "it's time for everybody's favourite rock and dole act...." There were screams and cheers and a few vulgar retorts, all in good fun. "The one, the only...the *fabulous* Beatles!"

"That's us!" Paul crowed.

John kicked the door open, and Paul followed, his new Rossetti bass polished to a high gleam. "Gang way, mates!" He shoved John aside.

"Bonsai!" John hooted, running for the stage.

Whistling at the cheering crowd, waving and winking, John and Paul plunged towards the boards, with George – raising a hand now and then and grinning from ear to ear – right behind them.

Pete sauntered out casually and took his place, adjusting his drumheads with cool reserve – never completely acknowledging the girls who reached out for his attention. Even the desperate, whining pleas of "Pete! Pete! We *looove* you, Pete!" did little to engage him. He scratched the back of his neck every minute or so and offered a quick nod in the crowd's direction.

John knelt on one knee, crouching close to his amplifier, attempting a final tune-up. Leather-clad, sideburns already wet from the heat, he was every inch the *mach shau* rocker that Allan Williams had once insisted he be. Expressionless and haughty, John was intent. He was insular, connected only to his guitar. He took his time, making the world wait for him, and though the crowd shouted and clapped and urged him on, he refused to rush.

Pete lit a cigarette and let it dangle from his mouth. Paul gave a wave to a group from Allerton who considered him their own.

Finally, John pushed himself up into his wide-legged commander's stance, glanced at George and Paul, and blurted out, "We'll be doin' this first one, for Bob Wooler, here, whom I've only recently discovered is me long-lost dad."

A murmur spread through the crowd, and Bob played along, smiling, waving, and nodding convincingly at John's nonsense.

"It's a tune by that bandy legged Liverpudlian, Charles McBerry." John had his mouth close to the mike. "Maybe you've heard it. It goes sumthin' like this..."

"Oh Maybelline!" Paul began. And another Cavern show erupted into action.

John's journalist-friend Bill Harry sat in the third row and watched the crowd rock with hysteria. He and his girl, Virginia – a pert, Hayley Mills sort – never missed a night at The Cavern. But tonight, especially, they were there. They had come to celebrate the launch of "Mersey Beat," to toast the first issue of the magazine they hoped would become a "must-read" for fans of Mersey music. They had come to celebrate the beginning of their dream.

Virginia laughed her double-dimpled laugh. She flirted with Bill and watched as John made faces, George made music, and Paul did Berry better than Berry himself. She giggled and laid her head on Bill's shoulder when George and John square-danced and yelled jokes to one another over the rock'n'roll.

And when John screamed out "Shakin' All Over," as if it were the last tune he'd ever sing, when he threw back his head and let the song tear through him with raw, sexual intensity, Virginia's deep green eyes watched as the girls around her flew into hysteria or melted quietly. It was something a woman would notice.

"Tightened the act quite a bit, haven't they?" Bill had to yell to be heard.

Virginia nodded, gripping his arm affectionately, letting her soft, auburn flip fall onto his shoulder.

"Much, *much* better since Hamburg," he observed again. "Improved!"

Virginia nodded.

"I mean even without Stu they've still got this certain charisma, this..."

"Hey!" John stopped playing and yelled from the stage. "What d'ya think this is, Harry...the fuggin' social hour at yer fuggin' local?"

Paul and George snickered, and Bill held up both hands sheepishly as if to proclaim his regret. The rest of the audience strained to see the man who'd interrupted their concert. Some began to catcall and hiss.

Bill stood up, grinned, and took a sweeping bow, waving off his nay sayers before turning to John with a hands clasped in pardon. "All apologies, Mr. Lennon, sir...but if you'll resume, I'm quite done now, sir. You can carry on, as it were, sir."

"Right." John smacked gum and looked down his nose. "Will fuggin' do."

"Hello thur, Virginia!" Paul winked, always the ambassador of good will. Virginia rippled her fingers in reply.

"Let's have another go at it!" George suggested, kicking his feet out in a quickly stomped dance step.

"Right," Paul nodded. "I'm in."

John let a chord rip, and all was forgiven and forgotten. The music absolved and covered them completely.

It was Pete's turn to solo, and he'd chosen Carl Perkins's "Matchbox". He called it "the ideal drummer's tune" since it opened with the line, "I'm just sittin' here watchin', matchbox hole in my clothes." As the music began, he offered a shy smile. Girls shrieked as if in pain. A couple tried to rush the stage, but The Cavern bouncers would have none of it.

"Up next..." Paul took the mike at the end of Pete's song.

Screams.

"Up next," he tried again, "one of me favourite ballads, y'know." He winked and smiled charmingly. "Ideal for those...in a romantic sort of mood." Squeals again. He pointed in that direction, though he couldn't see them for the lights. "This one's for you...and it goes like this..."

"Play 'Searchin,' Paul!" A unison of female voices, his Allerton contingent, called from the back of the room.

"How's that, luvs?" Paul put a hand to his ear.

"Play 'Searchin,' Paul!" The demand came again.

And without further ado, Paul abandoned the wistful acoustic ballad he'd chosen, reconnected his amp, and plunged into the requested tune. George and John quickly readjusted, joining him after a bar or two. And Pete found them easily, in almost no time at all.

By the time Paul had finished "Searchin'" and then pulled the audience into the Ray Charles hit, "What I'd Say," John was in rare form. He crouched for cover when George hurled a stale butty at him and cackled outrageously anytime any one of them hit a "joke chord." When the audience screamed, John screamed back. He tapped his foot and bounced as he sang. He yelled epithets at the fans.

And when Paul took a breath, John "chanka-chanked," uninvited, into "Soldier of Love," one of their biggest Hamburg hits.

Bill Harry watched The Beatles closely, trying to remember every detail of the performance for his review in the next Mersey Beat. Honestly convinced that he was observing a phenomenon that would someday put Liverpool on the map, Bill *worked* to remember it all clearly, to capture every nuance, every word and gyration. He had already decided that his next cover story would be The Beatles' recent recording session with Bert Kaempfert, but he realized that this was the mere "tip of the iceberg." The Beatles, he believed, were on the verge of something huge.

Bill had seen their list of engagements for the next three months: The Cavern, Aintree Institute, Litherland Town Hall, Blair Hall in Walton, St. John's Hall in Tuebrook, Hambleton Hall, The Casbah, and on and on. Incredible lines queued in Mathew Street for hours prior to Beatle performances, and Bill doubted if even members of the royal family would attract such a gathering on a Liverpool workday. The Beatles were rapidly developing into what some called "a cult following." They were booked, day and night, for weeks ahead.

Giving a soft-shoe step, a lunge, and a snort, John concluded the opening set and exited the stage, the others following suit. Bill applauded with the rest, watching his friends retreat before turning to Virginia with a curious writer's eye. "D'ya think he's happy – John?"

She tucked a long strand of auburn hair behind her ear and dipped her head, hiding her eyes behind a shock of blunted bangs. "As happy as John Lennon *can* be…especially with Stu over there and John over here."

"Yeah, right. They're almost brothers – those two."

"And I think," Virginia's upturned nose met his levelly, " I think your John looks exhausted. I mean, they've never a day off, do they, Bill?"

"Yeah, but…I mean, that's what he's always wanted, isn't it?"

"Right." Virginia bit her bottom lip. "But we all want things, don't we, luv? I mean, I once thought I wanted a pet monkey – way back when."

"*You*?" Bill smiled his crushingly charming smile and raised a thick, dark eyebrow.

"Right, me," she said. "But it wouldn't have been practical, would it?"

"Ah," he nodded, understanding. "The old 'be careful what you wish for,' eh?"

"Yeah, you just might get it…and then some."

"Are we still talkin' about John here?" he frowned. Mersey Beat had been their dream for months, almost years. *Was she worried that it would somehow go awry?*

"I'm talkin'," she squeezed his arm again, "about all of us…about John 'n how The Beatles'll most definitely change him…about you 'n me and how Mersey Beat'll lead us away from Liverpool someday and take us to a life we've never imagined."

"Good or bad?" His handsome visage clouded.

"With you, always good. Always good." And kissing him perfunctorily on the cheek, Virginia clipped away to the less than lovely Cavern loo, clicking her prissy, tiny heels on the concrete floor.

With the first set of the evening still fresh in his memory, Bill pulled a small notepad out of his pocket and began jotting a few notes. He scribbled more than half a page. Then, as an afterthought he added a few "to do's" for the week to come.

1. Call Allan Williams. Find out what he's up to these days.

2. Mention Pete's second solo, "Pinwheel Twist"…extremely well received tonight. {Don't forget to write a birthday cheer for Rory's drummer, Ringo.}

3. Quote Bob Wooler as saying, "The Beatles are the biggest thing to have hit the Liverpool rock'n'roll set-up in years." Note that he compared Pete Best to "a sort of teenage Jeff Chandler" and called the group as "the hottest property any Rock promoter is likely to encounter."

4. Get quotes from fans…follow up on lead that an Official Beatles' Fan Club is being formed…ring Bernard Boyd straightaway.

5. Arrange a meeting with John. Brian Kelly's comment that "The Beatles have lost their luster without Stu" seems unfounded; except for J.W.L. Must encourage John to write something for next "Mersey Beat" issue. A follow-on to his history of the group…

You can still read the original copy of "Mersey Beat" and all the issues that followed in Bill Harry's Mersey Beat: The Beginnings of the Beatles. *In August of 2007, just as this book was going to the publisher, Colin Fallows at John Moores University in Liverpool (formerly Liverpool College of Art) was kind enough to give me Bill Harry's e-mail address. (As always, thank you, Colin.) Within hours, Bill graciously responded to my inquiries about Liverpool College of Art, and he also gave me information to complete this chapter and the October 1958 chapter as well. He spent a great deal of time giving me photos of his lovely wife, Virginia, and himself, and supplying the details that helped make this story realistic and alive. Having written many, many books about The Beatles, Bill Harry was quite generous to share his time and expertise with me. I owe him a great debt of appreciation. In a world where most people are out for "number one," Bill was inordinately kind and generous with a writer he'd never even met. Remarkable.*

*Similarly, in March of 1994, I had the great privilege of interviewing the late Bob Wooler in Lark Lane, Liverpool. Having been the compère at The Cavern Club during the Beatle years, Bob was the authority on the events that transpired there, and he is the one who gave me the information for my chapters on The Cavern Club. Bob was also gracious enough to share with me several songs he'd written about Liverpool (one includes the line "See, hear!" that I used in this chapter) and an original D.J.'s request card from The Cavern days. His memory was flawless; his wit, fantastic. We talked "Beatles" for about four hours and then adjourned to Keith's Wine Bar where he, Allan Williams, my husband, and I shared enough wine to make me glad I'd brought a tape recorder and didn't have to rely upon memory.

The Beatles did play The Cavern Club on this evening. And Brian Kelley's comment, the Wooler quote, the "Pinwheel Twist," and the play list is all documented.

The conversation is conjecture.

30 July 1961
Mendips
Liverpool

...I remember a time when everyone
I loved hated me
Because I hated them so what
So fucking what.
I remember a time when belly
buttons were knee high
when only shitting was dirty
and everything else was clean and
beautiful.
I can't remember anything
without a sadness
so deep that it hardly
becomes known to me,
so deep that its tears
leave me a spectator
of my own STUPIDITY
& so I go on rambling
on with a hey nonny
nonny nonny no.*
love,
John

Along the edge of the last two lines, John scribbled eighth notes with all-seeing eyeballs, and he scrawled the page number in the upper left hand corner. "Page 10," he wrote. Then scratched it off. "Page 11," he corrected. It was one of his shorter letters to Stu.

Then John remembered one more thing, and he hastily began to sketch a caricature of himself at the bottom of the page. Warted, claw-fingered, leather-booted, and posed in a grotesque marionette squat, the misshapen John Lennon spewed mucous from his mouth and nose. He smiled hideously as hair fell into his eyes and mouth, and he wore the national issue glasses John never let anyone see.

"Done," he said, but John scribbled one last quick note in his erratic scrawl. *There y'have it, Sutcliffe – John Lennon, Mersey Beat author, a.k.a. 'Beatcomber' himself. Y'may've known him as the mad Cavern rocker or the former Liverpool college of artist or the randy Hamburg heartthrob, as it were. But here he is, revealed for your eyes only, son. John the misanthrope, John the miscreant, John the mistake-I-was-ever-born-John. I am not what I appear to be. See above.*

He folded the stack of lined sheets and sealed the letter up with a smack of his hand. It had been an hour and a half – maybe a little more – and Mimi would soon be up the stairs, raging about "the utter loss of time sequestered away, doing absolutely nothing worthwhile." It was her ritual homily, surpassed only by her longstanding favourite – the "dripping down the drain, falling to ruin, and amounting to nothing in life" sermonette.

John had them both memorized.

At times, when especially peeved, Mimi alluded to heredity and John's genetic connection to "that shiftless Fred Lennon." On other occasions, she merely skirted the issue, pointing out that she'd heard Peter Shotton had left the police force and had "taken gainful employment" at The Old Dutch Café on Smithdown Road. In either event, she was short on subtlety.

John tossed the letter on his bedside table and picked up his old, acoustic guitar. He strummed it, tuning the strings and glancing at the clock, wondering what to do.

Sundays were hauntingly quiet Merseyside, in contrast to the never-ending rush of Hamburg life. On Sundays, Liverpool cocooned. The pubs locked up tight. Most restaurants – except the Adelphi's elegant dining room – were closed for the day. Entertainment of any sort was at a premium. The streets were literally empty.

The Beatles had, in fact, one of the few bookings in the area that day. They were to appear at Blair Hall in Walton for the last of three Sunday evening performances for Peak Productions. But that was hours away.

"John..." the anticipated voice sounded behind his bedroom door. "You realize you'll have to take tea soon if you intend to make work on time."

"It's not work!" John snapped, though lately it had been.

"Exactly," Mimi agreed, "but it's a commitment nevertheless, and you wouldn't want to be late."

John opened the door and leaned against the doorjamb. "You can suck the life out of practically anythin', can't you, Mim?"

She stared back at him with no-nonsense eyes. "I have no idea what you could possibly mean."

"C'mon. A clever girl like you?" He folded his arms. "Don't play the fool, Mary Elizabeth."

"Soup's on," was her only answer, and she flounced into retreat.

"And mandarin duck's off!" he called after her.

But instead of following the smell of an early supper down the stairs, John returned to his room and picked up the notepad he'd been using.

Dear Stu, the new letter began, *There is no oppression like the oppression of Mary Elizabeth Smith. She would be well equipped to run a small country. Is there one immediately available anywhere?*

The opening segment of this chapter in John's handwriting is part of an actual letter written to Stu. And the sketch discussed is in fact on that page. You can view it in Hunter Davies's official Beatle biography entitled, The Beatles, *page 108. The final lines of this chapter in John's handwriting are imagined, as is the small segment that begins, "There you have it, Sutcliffe…"*

John was living back at Mendips in the summer of 1961. The Beatles were playing Blair Hall on that Sunday evening. Pete had taken a job at the Old Dutch. Liverpool on Sunday is exactly as I have described it, believe me! But the conversation between John and Mimi is conjecture.

Thursday, 21 September 1961
Litherland Town Hall
Litherland

"And how is Ringo thisavvy?" John pulled a chair up beside The Hurricane's scrappy, bearded drummer.

"All right," Ringo picked at the unwrapped fish and chips tenuously balanced on his lap, "despite the fact me mitts 'r achin' from overuse…one too many gigs after one too many others."

"Beatin' the skins again, eh?" John used his old man's voice. "Y'know you'll go blind like that, Sonny Jim."

"I've heard that one before, if you don't mind, Lennon."

"Well, I do mind," John sniffed

"And I," Ringo chuckled as he ate, "couldn't give a lousy, red meg!"

John smirked and pulled out a cig as Ringo gorged on the greasy, pre-show meal. Neither felt the need to talk. They were comfortable just sitting together and staring into space.

Here at Litherland, there were few amusements for a visiting band. A town hall converted into a weekend dance venue, the place was stiff and unyielding. From the rectangular bed of boxwoods and staid perennials at the front doorway to the white, wrought iron railing that trimmed the place, Litherland was as far from the The Cavern as rock'n'roll was from "yer granny's woolsey knickers." There wasn't even a place to have a pint before the show – nowhere to congregate. The musicians perched like birds on any bit of equipment, waiting miserably for show time.

"Who's up first tonight, then?" John broke the quiet.

"I dunno. The infamous Brian Kelly doesn't take me into his confidence as a general rule." Ringo motioned towards the promoter who was busy giving last minute directions to one lackey or another.

"Ah, Brian Kelly, the great stone face of the live jive hives," John quoted Bob Wooler as Kelly concluded some consultation with Rory Storm. "He's had it out for us ever since we jilted him over a year ago for that Johnny Gentle tour, y'know. You'd think he'd give it a rest. That was the fuggin' Dark Ages, wasn't it?"

"Well, don't think y'row that boat alone," Ringo said, mouth half full.

"Kelly doesn't like anyone I know of. And trusts even less."

"Yeah, well it appears he's settin' you up as the *openin'* act over there, Ring...meanin' we're headlinin' tonight, son! You Hurricanes must be even lower on his totem pole than even we are!"

"Hey!" Ringo yelled to Kelly's hired help who were jostling his drums across the stage. "Don't go shovin' me gear about like that! Just wait one, 'n I'll handle it meself."

"I wouldn't call it *gear*, actually." George joined them, settling onto a backstage crate that had been pushed up against the wall. He smiled at Ringo. "I wouldn't even call those drums average, y'know. 'Bunged up' might be the phrase I'd choose, if I had to choose a phrase."

"Is that right?" Ringo raised one eyebrow. "And what would *you* know about gear, our kid?"

"Hey Johnny," George appealed for back-up, "he's gettin' nasty – that drummer."

John grinned, flicked his cig away, and popped a stick of clove gum into his mouth.

Ringo continued to eat.

"Hey drummer!" George heckled a little louder. "Me lips are movin'. I'm talkin' to you, as it were!"

"Get on wit' ya!" Ringo fought back a smile. "I'll burst ya."

George made a bicep. "You never!" he grinned. Then he turned to John. "Have you made the decision yet, John? Are we incorporatin' 'Hey Good-Lookin' into the play list tonight?"

John nodded. "Yeah. We'll give it a go. It's good enough for Litherland and Brian Kelly, as it were."

George's eyes lit up. "I've been rehearsin' the Perkins sound on it all afternoon, 'n I was thinkin' it'd come off more naturally if we just slow the whole thing down somewhat 'n ease up on the tempo, what have you. Y'know...blues it up a bit."

Ringo interrupted, speaking to an imaginary audience around them. "D'ya hear that folks? A new song from the legendary Beatles von Hamburg and a new arrangement from their fab lead guitarist, a lad only nineteen months old."

John picked up the ball and ran with it. "That's right, jadies and lents," he grinned at Ringo, "y'er all guinea pigs, y'lovely audience, you!"

"I'd advise y'to run!" Ringo took the give and go. "Run while you still can! Get out! Get away with yer miserable, little lives!"

"That's dead rude," George sulked.

"Are they at you again, Georgie?" Paul ambled up, looking wilted. They'd played The Cavern the previous evening, and all of them were growing dark circles under their eyes.

"How's it goin', McWack?" Ringo crumpled his waxy wrappers and pitched them, reaching for a cigarette.

"Not bad, Ring," Paul smiled weakly. "'ullo, John."

"You look fuggin' miserable, son." John bypassed tact. "The wreck of the fuggin' Hesperus, as it were!"

Paul straightened and tried a grin. "Oh lovely. Ta."

"Yeah," George teased. "We hardly knew ya – Johnny and me."

Paul lifted an eyebrow and sniffed. "Well, if I'm so bleedin' unrecognizable, then how's it Ringo here knew me straight off, eh?"

"I only knew it had to be you or Pete," the drummer smiled, "and Pete's always in top form, no matter what."

"Isthasso?" Paul looked around. "Well, where is he, then? And where's Neil – and the van and the gear?"

"Late," George whined. "Van trouble."

"*Déjà vu* all over again, isn't it?" Paul threw his eyes to the ceiling.

"It's only a fifteen pound van, y'know." John grabbed Ringo's Embassy for a long drag.

"Yeah, well lately it hasn't been worth even *that*." Paul shook his head. "I'd sooner rely on our old Raleigh two-wheelers. At least they always got us where we wanted to go."

"That was yours." John got up, returned the cig, and tugged at his jeans. "Mine stopped at every fuggin' palm shop along the route and veered into every alleyway. It was truant and habitually tardy – that bike. I could never manage to conform it to any sort of punctuality…and neither could good Queen Mim."

At the sound of an engine sputtering, George jumped up and headed for the stage door. "They're here! And look, it's only half six!"

"Now maybe you lot'll get to grace the stage," Ringo yelled after them, "as soon as *I'm* done with it! Yeah, it's not all that bad, is it – comin' in second place?"

"Balls to that!" John yelled back. "You're openin' for *us*, Starkey! Face the music, son!"

Ringo cupped his hand around his mouth and had the final word. "Y'know, if I'd known you was comin', Lennon, I'd've brought along me autograph booke!"

John flipped him the backhanded V and a snarl, and Ringo laughed loudly, taking a last, delicious drag on the cigarette in his jeweled hand. Then he stood and sauntered towards his drum kit to finish the job Kelly's men had clumsily started.

"H-how goes it with the-the prima donnas?" Rory gestured towards the door. "A-at each other uh-again? Familiarity breedin' contempt, and-and all that?"

Ringo glanced over his shoulder and broke into a grin. "Ah, they're all shit-hot, accordin' to them. If they weren't so fuggin' likeable, I'd have nothin' to do with 'em at all."

"R-r-right!" Rory laughed. "But who could hate The-The Beatles, eh?

E-e-everyone loves 'em. *I* think they're uh f-f-ffuggin' great!"

"Oh yeah?" Ringo gave his drums a final shove and took a seat beside his friend. "Well, we think *you're* fuggin' great, Stormy – Johnny Guitar and Ty and me…in fact, we *know* y'er fuggin' great! The great-*est*!"

Rory slumped back in his chair and let his eyes glaze over in thought. He watched The Beatles unloading as Kelly marched back and forth with a clipboard in his hand. He looked at them as if they were actors in a drama for which he had the only ticket.

Lately Rory had felt himself slipping further and further into a distant place, removed from those around him. It had been lonely there at first, but recently Rory had begun to like the isolation, to yearn for escape to the haven where his thoughts took him.

"I mean it, Rory," Ringo nudged him. "No one around Merseyside's got your moxy or charisma, mate. You're heads and tails above the likes of those swaggerin' Beatles, y'know."

"L-listen, Ringo," Rory smiled slowly, patting his friend's back. "Yer tongue's s-s-silver, and yer heart's fuggin' gold, b-but it's dead obvious…yer-yer singin' in the rain there. I-I'm all right Merseyside…but that's wh-where it ends, y'know. The Beatles are out t-t-to be uh big – bigger 'n I'll ever be."

"So they say." Ringo tried to laugh it off.

"So they are," Rory smiled.

"Ah, you're only buyin' into their hype!" Ringo encouraged. "That 'toppermost of the poppermost' shite! They've done a number on you, lad!"

"S-s-six months ago," Rory explained, "B-Brian Kelly over there said he'd ne-never have 'the fuggin' Beatles' on his stage again. An-And now tonight, th-they're not only here, th-they're closin' the set! They're the headliners, Ring!" Rory sighed. "*We-we* used to be the ones, y'know. We used to be the ones who-who could a-a-afford to d-drag in late and uh scramble to set up." He paused for effect. "I-It's The Beatles' day now, Ring."

"So?" Ringo shrugged. "Tomorrow's another one. It comes, and it goes. We'll close the show next time, Stormy."

"N-n-not the next," Rory smiled a bit. "And not the one a-after that either. I-it's The Beatles. I know the truth. But you? You've got what it uh takes. You could uh-uh-uh, be one of 'em."

****

Fifteen p…a lousy three shillings…less than you'd pay for a pound of butter, less than you'd pay for a haircut in Penny Lane. Three insignificant shillings for three full hours of entertainment. That was all Brian Kelly charged for admission.

But tonight, he could have easily charged double. For handsome, blonde, lanky Rory Storm and his Hurricanes alone, Kelly could've asked the published fee. For Liverpool's tremendously popular Gerry and the Pacemakers, three shillings would have been a bargain. But to top the show off with The Cavern Club's Beatles, the price of admittance was ridiculously low.

"It's a capacity crowd!" Kelly beamed at The Beatles' unofficial road manager, Neil Aspinall. "We could've done at least *two* shows tonight. Three! Done it without so much as a blink of the eye."

"*You* might could," Neil surveyed the horde of teenage bodies jammed into the room, "but The Beatles couldn't, I'll tell y'that. They played The Cavern until close last night, and they were right back up on the boards, lunchtime today."

"And you can tell it as well." Kelly checked his watch. "They look battle worn – the four of 'em. I told Bill Harry…and I still mean it…I think they're losin' their fuggin' lustre with that Sutcliffe gone. Sometimes I think they're only goin' through the motions."

"If you're talkin' about John…" Neil began.

"John Lennon *especially!*" Brian slapped his palm with his hand.

"Right…but Stu's bein' gone hasn't changed Paul or Pete drastically, has it?"

"Well…not that much," Kelly admitted.

"And George," Neil pressed on, "he's still as adept and talented as ever, right?"

"Right, but…"

"So it's really only John y'er talkin' about, then. Just John."

"Right," Kelly admitted, "but Lennon's the…"

"He's fagged out, Brian," Neil defended him. "He's knackered. They're all knackered…workin' nonstop with no end in sight."

"Right, well…that's not my problem, y'know. And if that's how it is, then someone ought to speak to their manager about reinin''em in a bit, as it were. If it's still Allan Williams or Mona Best or whoever – Bob Wooler, perhaps, I dunno – you need to let 'em know the lads are on a collision course with breakdown."

"They haven't a manager right now." Neil folded his arms.

Kelly raised an eyebrow. "But I thought I'd overheard Sam Leach was makin' an overture of management of sorts."

Neil shook his head. "Nah, he's tryin' to buy a record company – somethin' of that nature. *That*'s his big interest these days."

Kelly gave a nod to Ron Appleby, his compère, and Appleby turned and walked towards the stage. "Leach *is* looking into Troubadour Records," Kelly admitted, "but he has been for years. It's old news in the music world – that purchase."

"Well, who knows?" Neil shrugged and leaned against the wall as Appleby stepped up to the microphone, centre stage. "Maybe The Beatles'll be his first recordin' group, as it were. Time'll tell."

"Whomever..." Brian insisted. "They'll have to have *someone* soon." But as the house lights went down and Appleby's announcements began, Kelly turned away, focusing on the performance at hand.

With a heavy-handed drum roll, Rory Storm and The Hurricanes charged into action astride the backbeat of charismatic Ringo Starr. Rory sang flawlessly, without a single stutter, almost swallowing the microphone as he tossed his head back and set a song free. Johnny Guitar leaned into the sea of fans – almost falling off the stage – and a pony-tailed blonde screamed his name when he winked at her.

In the mêlée, Neil tried to edge along the wall, tried to squeeze backstage to have a few words with the headliner band. He wanted to tell Pete about his conversation with Kelly – to urge Pete to speak earnestly with John.

Now more than ever, Neil was convinced that The Beatles would have to find a full-time manager – someone to promote them properly, to coordinate their efforts, to know when to say "yes" and when to say "no." None of them, his old grey and maroon clunker of a van included, could continue with things as they were. It was all just too much.

Note: Hunter Davies says that Neil Aspinall's van was an eighty-pound purchase. Pete Best, who further describes it as a maroon and grey battered model, places it at fifteen pounds. Since Neil was Pete's closest friend, and Neil lived in his home, I am using the facts supplied by Pete.

Sam Leach, mentioned in this chapter, doesn't get enough credit in the Beatles' saga. He was one of the most important and colourful promoters Merseyside. For more of his story, read his book, The Birth of The Beatles.

The description of Litherland comes from several visits I made to the facility in the 1990's. I was informed that the building had changed very little since the Beatles were there. See photo in appendix.

Rory Storm's group, The Hurricanes, continued to "decrease as the Beatles increased" to paraphrase the Gospel writer, Matthew. After losing his drummer, Ringo, to the Beatles, and after losing his father that same year, Rory and his mother were both found dead in their home. Rory's tragic story is told beautifully by Allan Williams on pages 226-229 of The Man Who Gave the Beatles Away. *All conversations are conjecture.*

October 1961
Mendips
Woolton

It was a chance to see Stu again, maybe the only one he'd get for ages, and John wasn't about to pass it up. Rehearsals, gigs, and aspirations could be hanged. For once, the band came second.

Generously endowed by "Mater" – his Auntie Elizabeth in Sutherland, Scotland – with forty pounds for his twenty-first birthday, John had just enough money for the channel crossing and two weeks on the Continent. He'd just enough money to make turning twenty-one into an occasion.

And he had funds enough to take someone with him. But it wouldn't be Cynthia.

Over the summer, when Cyn's Mum had moved to Canada to live with relatives, Cyn had become a boarder at Mendips. She'd found a job at the local Woolworth's in Smithdown Road, near the Penny Lane roundabout, and she'd walked there each morning and returned each afternoon. Trying desperately to please Mimi and to fit in, Cynthia had helped with the household chores. She'd worked the garden and folded the clothes. And in the evenings, she'd eagerly offered to cook and clear the diner table. She had worked tirelessly to fit in, to win Mimi's good graces. But by the time Cyn finally vacated Mendips for her Aunty Tess's home, she had become disturbingly domestic, more domestic than John was ready to enjoy.

Besides, Cynthia was now back full swing in her last semester of art college and couldn't afford a mini-break. It was simply easier, John convinced himself, to ask Paul to go on holiday instead.

He'd warned Paul not to tell Cynthia a thing about the trek. And he'd also cautioned him about breathing a word of the escapade to George, Pete, Bob, or Neil. John figured they'd find out soon enough when two of the four Beatles didn't show for the dozen of scheduled gigs over the next fortnight. He saw no use in arguing about things beforehand.

Stu had mentioned Paris as a rendezvous point. Their mutual friend, photographer Jürgen Vollmer, had already made plans to be there on assignment in late September-early October, so Stu hoped he might be able to slip away and join them for a few days. He needed a rest from the cyclone's eye of studies, work, and painting, and Paris seemed as good a place as any to forget.

Stu's recent letters had been infused with fatigue. He'd confessed he'd lost weight, had no appetite whatsoever, and blacked out frequently. The headaches he'd developed in May grilled on, and rarely was there a day without fantastic pain. But his failing body couldn't stifle his creativity. Stu painted as if he had a deadline.

Recently he'd become more inventive and amenable to new ideas. He'd begun to experiment with films, "moving pictures" as he called them – art in motion rather than art in stasis. Stu had borrowed a camera from Astrid's cousin, Theo, and had begun to work in black and white celluloid, dramatically expanding the technology of his canvas, stepping into the realm of three-dimensional art. Working in pain, Stu craved beauty.

John had to admit he was jealous of Stu's impulsive world. His own life in Liverpool plodded along unceremoniously from Mendips to The Casbah to The Cavern and back. Always a dance hall, sometimes an institute, frequently a town hall or a club on the edge of town...almost always a van, sometimes a bus, rarely a car. To John, the days were redundant.

But Stu never did the same thing twice. He rarely worked on two successive projects in the same medium.

Lately, in fact, he'd been writing a novel about John and himself entitled *Spotlight on Johnny*, and he'd used John's letters to capture John's restlessness, depression, and anger. He'd sent the first draft over to John for his approval and now two days before his trip to Paris, John stood at the upstairs bedroom window and read the scrawled manuscript.

> with john it was different. he was unlucky. given the breaks other people have, he would have been all right. as it was, he brooded, trying to find the right answer. he was born old. he dried up before his time. he wilted because he knew that someday he would wilt anyway.

"Fuggin'ell!" John hurled the manuscript onto his bedspread and looked at himself in the silver-streaked antique mirror above his bureau. "I *haven't* wilted away, and I won't, either! I'll make Stu take that out – first thing, first day in Paris!"

"Keep it down, John," Mimi enunciated from the corridor. "You'll wake the boarders. *They* have jobs, you know."

John exhaled heavily and flopped down on his bed. He couldn't wait to get to away and cut loose. He couldn't wait to wave his arms and scream at unsuspecting tourists, laugh with Stu, and be free of the watchful eye of women. He couldn't wait to revel. He couldn't wait to prove to Jürgen, Paul, and Stu that he wasn't drying up or wilting away. He couldn't wait…

****

9 October 1961
Paris, France

But Stu didn't come to Paris. And John began to drink.

Traipsing through the jumbled maze of the Montmartre flea markets in search of sleeveless sweaters and corduroy jackets similar to Jürgen's, John and Paul wore the inebriated smiles of young men away from home and country. They staggered into reckless nightspots; they drank gallons of cheap, dark wine that had never seen a storage cask.

Jürgen, his *pilzen kopf* haircut framing his face like an overturned bowl, laughed constantly at the two Brits. Their spontaneous cavourting, their naïve sense of adventure, their Epicurean curiosity amused him, and he watched them as one does a couple of toddlers out on wobbly legs.

John seemed happy. "Well," John finally broached the topic over a swill of Prellys, Port, and lemons, "So how *is* our friend, Sir Stuart of Sutcliffe, then?"

Jürgen averted his eyes, searching for the right words. "He is…" he took a slow sip of his sweet Riesling, "…not well, John."

"How's that?" Paul twisted a cellophane cigarette wrapper around his finger. "He seemed well enough when he was Merseyside with Astrid in the spring."

"Yes," Jürgen nodded, "but that was then." He shifted his eyes. "This is now."

John felt his gut tighten, and he picked at the fabric of his new, green corduroy coat. "Same old migraines, eh?"

"He is a skeleton, John." Jürgen pinched his own wrist

demonstratively. "He is...thin. Pale – dark under the eyes. Astrid would tell you he has become an *invalide*." He used the French pronunciation. "Stuart is a sick man."

"But he writes about his special projects...his art..." John leaned forward.

"All true," Jurgen nodded. "He is working better than you have ever seen him do. In fact, quite fantastic. But it is draining the lifeblood from him."

"Sounds like The Cavern, doesn't it?" Paul tried to lighten the mood.

John and Jürgen glanced at him without a word. The three of them sat in awkward silence.

After a moment, Jürgen held his empty glass up for the waitress to see. Then he turned to John with a sympathetic smile. "But Stuart asked after you, John. He wants me to 'get all the news and details.' He wants to know all about The Beatles and Cynthia, and someone called Mimi..."

"Yeah, well he fuggin' knows it all already," John snapped.

"Tell him we've got a fan club these days," Paul tried again. "Tell him John's evolved into a famous writer as well. I mean, he's got his own column in Bill Harry's 'Mersey Beat' publication under the pseudonym..."

"Cut the fuggin' shite!" John rasped, too loudly for a restaurant. "Tell 'im to fuggin' eat! Tell 'im to fuggin' sleep! Tell 'im *that* why don't you...and tell 'im all this crap is makin' *me* fuggin' sick!"

"You tell him, John." Jürgen met him straight on. "*You* try to reason with him. I have tried. All of his friends have tried. We have even heard that Paolozzi has tried. Stuart will listen to no one. He works and works and grows steadily worse. But...if *you* try to speak with him, perhaps he will listen to you. You are his brother...more than that."

"And Lady Astrid – how does she fuggin' react to all this?" John desperately needed someone to blame.

Jürgen swilled the last sip of wine in the bottom of his glass and then swallowed it. "She is...helpless...as frantic as you are...angry at everything and everyone."

"I'm sorry, mates, but I'm dead creased." Paul rubbed his hand over his eyes and yawned, even though he tried to suppress it. "It's half-three, y'know. Half-three. Look!" He held up his watch.

Three a.m. in Paris was different from three a.m. in Liverpool. At three a.m. Merseyside, the clubs would be just turning out the last customers – hordes of them – onto the streets. The bouncers and waiters would be washing down floors and walls with garden hoses and joking with each other. And bands like The Beatles, packing away their equipment, would be discussing where to adjourn for a nudger and chips.

But here, sitting at a table on the street, talking quietly, sipping wine, three a.m. felt heavy-lidded and cold. It felt long past midnight.

But John pressed on. "Listen, Jürgen, Stu's got to chuck it in – this art!

He's got to get to a medic and look after himself...to consult a specialist, a practitioner, what have you..."

"The Kirchherrs," Jürgen tried to remain patient with John, "have seen to all that, you must realize. In fact, Stuart has been examined by the Director of Medicine at one of our finest hospitals in Hamburg, one of the very best."

"Right!" John was angry now. "Straight from Dachau."

"Peter Hommelhoff," Jürgen sat up very straight in his chair, "is a brilliant man and physician...the most excellent doctor the Kirchherrs could find...very astute."

"And with his astute on the line, what'd he come up with, then?"

"Unfortunately," Jürgen's voice softened, "a great deal." He looked at John with pity. "A shadow on the lungs. Gastritis...a chronic infection of the stomach lining brought on by excessive use of alcohol. Various nervous disorders from the overuse of Preludin...imminent collapse, general ill health. Dr. Hommelhoff says that in his entire career as a physician, he has never seen anyone – young or old – as destroyed as Stuart Sutcliffe. He has never seen anyone as tainted by tobacco, drugs, alcohol, and complete exhaustion. He has never seen a human body so abused."

"Christ." John whispered. It was more of a prayer than a curse.

"But," Jürgen offered almost apologetically, "he has stopped drinking. I will give you that much. And he has given up the Prellys as well. He has even relinquished smoking in hopes that the dark shadow on his lung will retreat."

"Yeah, well fuggin' felicitations, Stu!" John yelled. "Now you can waste away by degrees rather than goin' all at once, son!"

"C'mon John," Paul tried to spin it up, "I think it's good Stu's done all that. I mean, he's makin' the effort, isn't he? Cleanin' up the act, as it were."

"Yeah, balls to that!" John lashed back. "*Anyone* can give up cigs and shots, but when it gets right down to it, it's the fuggin' *art* that's smashin' him up, isn't it! And he won't give it up, will he? Even though *it's* what's fuggin' killin' him!"

"Sounds familiar," Paul mumbled.

John ignored him as he turned to Jürgen. "So what's he sleepin' these days...two, three hours at the utmost?"

"A few hours each night, perhaps," Jürgen nodded.

"And does he ever eat?"

"On most days," Jürgen almost whispered, "his digestion is too destroyed to have a meal."

"But canvases..." John's eyes narrowed, "how many of *those* has he digested in the last month?"

The waitress, keeping her distance from John, gingerly placed a full glass of wine in front of Jürgen. The photographer dug into his pockets for the last of his coins. It would have to be the end of the evening when this was gone.

"Canvases?" he came back to the conversation. "In truth, I have not counted – I am not sure Stuart has either."

"Hazard a fuggin' guess!" John barked.

"How many songs have you played in the last month?" Jürgen looked in John's eyes. "How many have you sung? How many times have you performed or practised or played a tune in the time you have off?" John didn't respond. " So…you see how it is, then." Jürgen took a sip from his glass, "It is impossible to know…even more impossible to control. The physicians, John, have recommended a great many treatments to Stuart: hydrotherapy, massage, rest, change of scenery. They have recommended surgery to remove his appendix at once. They have suggested many avenues to make things better. But Stuart is too busy tossing coal dust and crumbled cakes of sand on top of wet paint. He is too obsessed with oils splashed in violent, triangular reds. He is deep in a baptism of art, while the doctors and Astrid stand on dry land, wringing their hands."

"Well then," John leaned so close that his stale wine-and-cigarette-smoke breath assaulted Jürgen's nostrils, "you can tell the artist fuggin' *this* then…whatever his 'grand obsession' is, whatever it is he's up to…tell him he's *not about* to leave me here and piss off somewhere else! *I won't stand for it this time!* I won't have it again! Tell him that for me, would ya – word for word."

And without paying his part of the tab, John stormed away, shoving chairs and tables in his path…swearing and unsettling the sleepy, late-night clientele on his way out.

All information, including the items that Paul and John purchased, the drink they were consuming, Jürgen's haircut, and Stu's diagnosis is factual. Only the conversation is imagined.

Friday, 13 October 1961
The Casbah
West Derby

"Look now," Bob Wooler tried to reason with George, "I realize what they did was errant, but what's done's done, right? It won't do any good to go on shunning them, y'know. You'll only hurt yourselves in the process – you 'n Pete – because relish it or not, you need the conglomerate *four* of you to 'band it all together,' as it were."

George continued to push tiny water droplets off his Coke bottle. "They left us in the lurch without a word. They left us with the graft while they trekked off on holiday."

"Maybe *all* of us would've liked to've run off 'n rested up a bit," Pete grumbled, "but we weren't given the opportunity, now were we? So George and me, we turned around and thought that perhaps we weren't considered 'good enough' to be privy to their special, private plans."

"Right. I understand." Bob held a stepstool securely in place as Pete changed light bulbs in the ceiling sockets for his mum. The Casbah needed constant attention. It didn't have the staff that more commercial ventures like The Blue Angel, The Iron Door, or The Cavern Club had, but it needed the same care and repair. Pete and his brother, Rory, were the legmen, and there were always plenty of tasks to be completed.

"Well, if y'understand, then, here's another fact for you," George added, "I haven't an overlarge sack of money lyin' about the last time I checked...and it cost me quite a lot of what I *might've had* – all those cancelled gigs over the last fourteen days."

"Not to mention," Pete jumped down from the stool with a defunct bulb in his hand, "the damage to our professional reputations, y'know."

"Yeah, right. Now *there's* somethin' that was fuggin' unblemished!" It was John. He stood leaning against the doorway. His arms were crossed – his face, half hidden in backlight.

"Oooze he?" George looked at Pete with a blank expression.

"Good question – that." Pete turned his back on John and continued to work.

"Ah, it's the Parisian playboy home with trinkets and travelogues!"

Bob walked over and pulled John in. "The wandering minstrel back with song and ceremony!"

"Bravo," George clapped cynically, just once.

Pete glanced at John and then gawked in disbelief. "What the hell d'ya call *that* coverin' yer head?"

"Look, Peter!" George snickered at the wispy locks of ungreased hair falling across John's forehead in a sort of bowl cut. "It's ole Klaus Voormann come for a visit…or Jürgen or one of the other Exi, as it were."

John pulled out a wooden chair and sat down, crossing his legs at the ankles, brandishing a new pair of boots, front and centre. "If I'm not dead wrong," he said, "and it's unlikely that I am, *you* had Astrid arrangin' *your* hair just like this in Hamburg, Harrison."

George, still angry, folded his arms across his chest. "Right. But as I remember it, mine looked a whole lot better 'n yours, y'know. It's all in the eyebrows, John. Mine are sculpted. Yours are…how shall I say it…densely bushy."

"Y'look effin' ridiculous," Pete spat out. "Johnny Lennon, little Prince Albert."

"Y'know, I was only borderline about keepin' the look up to now." John narrowed his eyes.

"Cor!" George jumped up and came closer to examine John's feet. "Now *they're* fantastic!" Souvenirs from a quick stopover in London, John's polished, black Flamenco boots looked custom made.

"Staccato heels, eh?" Bob walked over. "Cubans! Rat-a-tat-tat! They conjured up a considerable cost, didn't they, lad?"

"But worth it." John arched a knowing eyebrow, turning his feet a bit so they could see the detail work, right down to the leather back tags. "They called to me from a place on Charin' Cross Road, 'n I fuggin' fell in love with 'em."

"Well, I hope you'll be very happy together," Pete smirked.

"It's a shoe in." John cut his eyes at George, trying to make him smile.

"Take 'em off and hand 'em over," George demanded.

"Buggeroff. Get yer own, son!" John stretched his legs out in front of him and grinned. "These two're spoken for."

"I might *could*," George said, "if only I had the tidy sum I missed out on durin' these past two weeks when we've had *no effin work*, as it were."

"Look…" John felt little remorse, "we're playin' Albany Cinema come Saturday and then straight off to Hambleton Hall with no break. Then back to The Cavern on Monday and The Cavern on Wednesday, Friday, Saturday, Tuesday, Wednesday, Thursday, and quoth The Cavern, evermore."

"Yeah…there's that," George acquiesced.

"And we're booked through the entire month of November – every single day – except Tuesday the second, Monday the twentieth, and

Saturday the twenty-fifth. *Every fuggin' day* without a fuggin' break, Havva! Isn't that enough for ya, then?"

"I dunno," George relented, smiling his crooked smile. "Depends on how much those boots're gonna set me back."

"Well," John swiped at him playfully, "boots or no...you'd *still* be on the outer fringe of fashion unless you're sportin' bell-bottomed kecks! They're all the rage in Hamburg, y'know. Jürgen was paradin' a pair around Paris, as if he'd stepped off a fuggin' American sailin' ship!"

"Paris, eh? Bell bottoms, eh?" George was wide-eyed. "You and Paul and Jürgen in Paris with bell-bottoms! I'm almost glad I missed it."

Pete's voice came from behind Mona's old box fan where he was hunched over, replacing a frayed cord. "And how about Stu, then? Was he along as well? How's he these days?"

"You tell me." John's good humour dissolved.

"What d'ya mean?" George wrinkled his brow. "We naturally guessed you'd gone off to meet him."

"Wasn't he on holiday with the 'in crowd,' then?" Pete asked.

"We'd heard rumours that..." Bob began.

"Oh, he was there all right," John hissed. "Only invisible...an apparition, hoverin' above our heads and insinuatin' himself into every fuggin' conversation."

George looked at John with eyes dawning forgiveness.

"Ah, that's a loss," Bob shook his head.

"His loss." John rubbed his jaw nonchalantly. "I mean, the three of us...me 'n Paul 'n Jürgen...we had an unbelievable time. We..."

"Oh, sorry, John." George swallowed hard.

"Save it!" John snapped. "It was great. It was fanfuggin'tastic! Stu missed out, that's all. He shoulda been there when we sat just three rows back for Johnny Hallyday at the Olympia or when we climbed the effin' Eiffel tower or when we posed for snapshots with three buxom bairds that made Astrid look fuggin' anemic! He shoulda been there...he shoulda been there for me twenty-first!"

"So then," Bob changed the subject as quickly as he could, "where do we get them then – these fantastic Flamenco boots?"

"Anello and Davide." John remembered a name for once. "Some address in Charin' Cross with 9's. You'll have to ask Paul later on. He's got the details, as usual, committed to McMemory."

"*He's* got boots as well?" George was clearly envious.

"Not just the boots," John pointed to his hair. "This, too, son."

"Yeah, well that's it then!" George beamed. "We're *all* goin' Exi, aren't we?"

"*You* might do," Pete scowled, "but y'can leave me out of it."

"C'mon Pete," George wheedled, "it'll be mad – this look."

"Mad's the perfect word. You're only embarrassin' yourselves, and you'll find out exactly what I mean when the crowd at Knotty Ash gives ya the boot...don't mind the pun."

"Still one for rugged individualism, eh different drummer?" John stood up and pulled his pants legs down over his boot tops. "Well, don't come mewlin' to us when we're all the rage...and you're all the aged."

"When we've got all the bairds..." George began.

"Yeah, pffft!" Pete snorted. "That'll be the day!"

"Just remember where that kind of philosophy got good ole Buddy Holly, son." John broke into his pensioner's voice. "Better see the error of your ways and venture out, Sonny Jim, or you'll find the show passin' you by."

"I'm not too worried, as it were." Pete scratched his neck.

John mimicked Pete's motions, just to be aggravating. "Well, y'might want to *get worried* then, because *we're* all gettin' on board. You heard Georgie here. It's our new look – these boots and this hair. And if I were you, I'd make it a fuggin' point to stay up."

"Rambullon, Lennon," Pete said, bending down to check the wiring on a floor plug.

"I don't mind if I do," John retorted, and motioning to George, they went upstairs together for a bit of fresh air.

In her 2006 book, John, *Cynthia Lennon says that John and Paul ran into Jürgen Vollmer "by accident" in Paris, but in his 1985 book,* Beatle! *Pete Best states, "One of the attractions of Paris was that an old Exi friend from Hamburg named Jürgen Vollmer was there at the same time, a fact that John Lennon gleaned from the regular and lengthy correspondence he kept up with Stu." Similarly, Lewisohn states, "In a letter from Hamburg, Stuart had mentioned to John that Jürgen Vollmer would be in Paris...John and Paul were eager to meet him again and wasted little time in getting there." Finally, Bill Harry writes, "Stuart Sutcliffe had informed John by post that Jürgen Vollmer, their friend from Hamburg, had moved to Paris, and he provided them with his address."*

The concert that John, Paul, and Jürgen attended is spelled Johnny "Halliday" by Harry (quoting a letter from John) and Johnny "Hallyday" by Lewisohn. Bill Harry (p. 511, The Ultimate Beatles Encyclopedia*) provides an excellent excerpt from a letter from John while he was in Paris covering this topic.*

There is some controversy about whether John and Paul actually missed any gigs during their holiday in Paris. In his book, Beatle! *Pete writes, "John, feeling flush with some money sent by an aunt in Scotland, suddenly took off to Paris with Paul...leaving George and I to fend off broken bookings." But Bill Harry in* The Ultimate Beatles' Encyclopedia *writes, "Some reports have suggested that the two of them left without informing George and Pete...This isn't actually so, John and Paul had planned the trip, and no bookings were made for the period while they were away." All accounts of the return of John and Paul from Paris depict Pete and George as being angry with them. But George and Pete might have been resentful simply because they were left out of the trip. There is no conclusive information proving whether actual gigs were missed during this time frame.*

There are myriad theories about why Pete was eventually released from the Beatles. Entire books have been written about just that one topic. One of the most interesting is Drummed Out! The Sacking of Pete Best *by Spencer Leigh. Was Pete penalized for refusing to wear the* pilzen kopf *hairstyle? Were the others jealous of him because he was the most popular with the female fans? Was his drumming considered less than first-rate? Was Ringo more compatible? No one knows. And maybe, it was no one thing, but a combination of many factors.*

Sincere thanks to Carol Ghesquire who, after reading the first edition of this book, found a rare copy of a Johnny Hallyday record and mailed it to me. This 45 rpm clearly showed that the correct spelling of the singer's name is indeed Hallyday.

Monday, 16 October 1961
North End Music Stores
Whitechapel Road
Liverpool

It was the only economical way to learn lyrics. None of them had ready cash for record purchases, so spending an afternoon at the glass-fronted North End Music Store in Whitechapel – located at the heart of Liverpool's shopping district – was the only way to enhance their play list. Listening to a record over and over, John could learn the chords, George, the lead riffs, Pete, the backbeat, and Paul, the lyrics. They'd developed a technique.

The NEMS shop owner – crisp, immaculate, twenty-seven year old Brian Epstein – seemed less than thrilled about Liverpool's rock'n'roll bands "lolling about" his place of business. He called them "trespassers with no earnest intent to buy." But since the boys violated no rules by asking his female clerks to spin records, and since they behaved themselves – at least when he was around – the soft-spoken, manicured Mr. Epstein could do nothing to bar the freeloaders from the premises.

But truthfully, although he would never openly admit it, Epstein considered the Scousers' presence somewhat of a compliment. He prided himself on stocking absolutely every record in the top forty of The Hit Parade. He reveled in the knowledge that his inventory was unrivaled in northern England and – he hoped beyond all hope – in the whole of England itself. The fact that rock'n'roll bands from miles around swarmed *his* tiny downtown Liverpool shop only endorsed his managerial acumen, an endorsement he dearly needed.

Brian Epstein had not come upon success by serendipity. He'd no knack for his family's furniture business. He hadn't been successful in the army, either. And although he'd wanted to desperately to shine, Brian had not succeeded at the Royal Academy of Dramatic Arts in London. In fact, he hadn't blossomed anywhere, until now. But home in Liverpool, here in Whitechapel, running the NEMS music store seemed to come naturally to him. He loved organizing, cataloguing, and ordering stock. Brian loved music and critiquing new records for the local newspapers. In fact, he enjoyed everything about running the North End Music store...even, secretly, the presence of edgy rock'n'rollers.

And they were there quite frequently.

Since Whitechapel Road intersected Mathew Street just a few paces outside the NEMS front door, The Cavern bands wandered to NEMS before their lunchtime gigs or on off days. The Beatles made NEMS their home away from home. They spent some time there almost every day, enjoying the remarkable inventory of platters and adeptly avoiding interaction with the owner who, though only six years John's elder, seemed decades older in his expensive suit and polished, black wingtips.

When Mr. Brian was on the floor, The Beatles were in and out in a hurry. But they'd discovered that after their lunchtime gigs, later in the afternoons, Epstein was usually absent. Just before teatime, several days a week, the quartet stopped by the shop to learn a song or two and to chat up the lovely assortment of NEMS clerks.

"'Ullo, there." A leather-jacketed John Lennon with a bit of a five o'clock shadow thrust a disc at a young, Irish shopgirl in the pale green sweater set. "Let's have this one, if you don't mind."

"Right," she beamed. "Y'mean you'd like me to play it…or is it one you're considerin' *purchasin'*, as it were?"

"It's one," he smirked, smacking his gum. "And I *am* considerin' things… even as we speak." The girl blushed and sauntered towards the "listening room," letting her hips swing seductively inside her modest tweed skirt.

"Wait one…" It was Paul, his new *pilzen kopf* haircut in disarray from the bold, October winds. "We'll have this one as well, please." He held out a second disc.

"And this one, if y'don't mind." Pete proffered a third.

"Right," she lowered her lashes at the boys and smiled. "Y'know, you'll be hearin' nothin' at all if Mr. Epstein gets wind of yer game, lads. He's practically on to ya already. He asked me only yesterday what you lot were doin' in here so frequently, as it were."

"Tell'im I've a mad crush on him, dearie." John fell into his old man's façade. He flashed his Cheshire grin and batted his eyelashes rapidly.

"Tell 'im we're undercover taxmen." George leaned on his elbow and stared into her eyes. "Tell 'im that he's recently fallen under certain observation."

"You!" The girl giggled and waved them off. "You won't do, you lot!"

"That's where you're wrong, luv," John deadpanned. "We will do, and we have done. You've only to say the word."

Smothering another round of giggles, the clerk grabbed all three selections and turned towards the gramophone. *This bunch,* she thought, *is as oblivious to rules as Mr. Brian is to frivolity.* She only hoped that she could keep the two factions from colliding in the tight confines of the Whitechapel store.

Mr. Brian's office was on the second floor, and he habitually chose late afternoons as quiet time for "necessary paperwork." So right now the lads were in the clear. But Epstein seemed to have an extraordinary business sense that always kept him on his toes. She kept one eye on the door as she worked.

Just as the New Orleans-style hit, "Ya Ya" began to play, Beryl Adams, Mr. Epstein's assistant, whisked past the booth towards the front counter.

"Eck! Eck!" the fair-skinned Irish girl whispered to the boys. "Miss Adams! Look like y'er interested in purchasin' for a change! Rattle some coins or somethin' of that nature."

Petite Beryl Adams glanced surreptitiously in their direction as she perused the record racks. Double-checking Mr. Epstein's detailed system of strings and cardboard tabs, and carefully placing orders for selections that were not fully stocked, Beryl kept the shop current. It was a job Mr. Epstein entrusted to no one else and a practise that had earned NEMS its reputation. Mr. Brian knew that the pretty and efficient blonde took her job very seriously; even though she was only twenty-six years old, she was as efficient as she was attractive. Beryl saw everything that happened in the shop but only interfered when it mattered, and The Beatles were one of the "things" that Beryl chose to overlook. She barely gave them a second glance.

"Not speakin' to us, is she?" Pete observed.

"I think she's mute," Paul suggested.

"She thinks yer mut-ant." John never missed an opportunity.

"It's a mute point, regardless," Paul returned, sniffing.

"I dunno. I think she's speakin' volumes," John observed.

"She doesn't cotton to the likes of us," George pouted. "We're not her variety."

"Go on, then." John instructed the clerk. He had already forgotten Beryl Adams. "Play the next selection," he said.

Tonight The Beatles had a rare evening off without a gig, and John had promised Cyn a movie at the Abbey Cinema. He was on a tight time schedule. But he wanted to learn the rest of "Only the Lonely" before they played the David Lewis Club in City Centre the following evening.

"It's that one there," George showed the girl. "You know, the big one by Roy Orbison. We love Roy. We think he's got a sound – Orbison."

The clerk obliged their request, but at regular intervals, she glanced nervously over her shoulder, keeping an eye out for Mr. Brian.

While the record played, Paul jotted down the lyrics and Pete drummed with his fingers on the countertop. John listened for a minute and then exited the booth, walking to the front counter and immediately returning with the latest copy of Bill Harry's "Mersey Beat."

"Here." He unfolded the publication and shoved it at the girl for inspection. "If y'er so fuggin' worried about us bein' around, show this to yer famous suit – yer famous Mr. Epstein. Show him this, and tell him this is me!" He pointed to his "Around and About" column, penned under the pseudonym, Beatcomber. "Tell him that 'the lurker and vagrant' he's groused about so much shares a page in print with him, as it were."

And sure enough, right next to John's column was Brian Epstein's own musical critique entitled, "Stop the World – And Listen."

"Oh!" the girl breathed a bit easier. "I've read yer column, luv! But I must admit, it's over me head. For example, whatja mean by 'Froliche Fussboden Her Vollmer'? What's *that* about, eh?"

"It's code," John touched his nose with one finger.

"He's on Her Majesty's Secret Service – John," Paul winked.

"Yeah, right," the spirited clerk threw her eyes to the ceiling. "More like Her Majesty's public jester, if I'm not wrong."

George tapped the girl on the shoulder and smiled. "We're all done here. Ta very much."

"Yeah," Paul clicked his cheek as he rolled his lyrics sheet up and tucked it inside his leather coat. "Lovely time. Wonderful to see yer. Ta."

Pete offered his jealously given, disarming smile. "Tarrah, then," he said. "It's been what it's been."

And John backhanded the copy of "Mersey Beat," pointing once more to his name. "Beatcomber," he repeated. "Remember the name, sista. See ya in the funny papers!"

And as if on cue, the four boys piled out of the booth and out of the store almost as quickly as they'd arrived. The tiny entrance and exit bell jangled as they closed the door behind them, and George waved through the glass.

Shaking her head, the clerk waved and smiled. She made a mental note to get back to the lunchtime show at The Cavern as soon as she could.

It was extremely difficult, almost impossible, to slip off for a solid hour in the middle of the day, but Mathew Street *was* only a couple hundred yards away, and The Beatles were hilarious. She loved their music, but she loved their antics even more. Perhaps if she managed to convince Mr. Brian that she simply *had* to keep a medic's appointment, she might be able to finagle it. If she told him that…

"Sandra Joy," Beryl Adam's lovely Scouse accent dispelled all daydreams, "if y'wouldn't mind refilin' the records that those lads were considerin' *purchasin'*…" She raised a meaningful eyebrow.

"Oh, right. Not at all," Joy smiled shyly.

"But wait one," Beryl took the top disc, turned it, and examined both sides. "Roy Orbison, is it? *Roy Orbison?*"

"Yeah," Joy nodded. "They love him. They said he has a sound."

"Isthasso?" Beryl jotted a note on her clipboard. "Mr. Brian'll be very interested in that, I'm sure."

"Does *he* like Roy Orbison, then?" Joy's eyes widened.

"Well…he's interested," Beryl smiled, "if Orbison sells."

"Well, in that case," Joy grinned, "how about The Beatles, then? They're all the rage Merseyside! Would he be interested in The Beatles as well?"

"The Beatles?" Beryl looked out the window towards Mathew Street. "I seriously doubt Mr. Brian knows who they are, really – and it might be best, y'know, if we keep it that way. If y'want your friends to keep comin' 'round for free samples, as it were, you'd best keep them on the 'q.t.' as long as possible."

"Oooh, but Miss Adams, they're really…"

"Sandra Joy," Beryl smiled wisely, "your ways are not Mr. Brian's. In fact, if I recall correctly, *you* even have a birrova a crush on that bearded, ringed drummer in the Rory Storm band, haven't you?"

"Ringo," Joy blushed heavily.

"Yeah, Ringo," Beryl sighed and shook her head.

"So, y'er sayin' that's a bad thing?" Joy was a little hurt.

"No, no, no," Beryl placed a gentle hand on her employee's shoulder, "but it's not…classical music…and that's Mr. Brian's genre. Sibelius…that's where his heart lies."

Joy took the three platters and began to file them away. "Well, there's no accountin' for taste, now is there, Miss Adams?"

"No," Beryl smiled, "none at all." And she hurried off to begin the intricate process of mini-inventory as the NEMS wall clock ticked towards five.

Brian's column was originally published under the name "Stop the World – And Listen to Everything in It." Later, it was called "Record Releases." Fans who can still procure a copy of Bill Harry's Mersey Beat: The Beginnings of the Beatles *will actually get to read the ads, articles, and columns written by John, Brian, Paul, and many others. It's a fascinating bit of history! You can also visit Mr. Harry's website. See foreward for address.*

The Beatles were regular customers at NEMS at exactly the time of day and in exactly the same manner as recorded here. Beryl Adams is real and is just as described. She is a dear friend and supplied many of the details for this chapter during interviews at The Grange in Aigburth in 1993 and The Buttons in Liverpool, March 1994. The conversation is hypothetical.

Tuesday, 17 October 1961
Mendips
Woolton

The gibberish was baffling, even to John. Stu's letters were becoming less and less coherent – squiggled lines of bizarre free-association, blurred bits of jumbled thoughts. Stu now addressed John as "John the Baptist" and signed his letters "Jesus." It was all very strange.

> dear john the baptist,
> you must forgive me for not writing very good letters…it's very difficult now because i'm never alone for long enough

John hardly knew what to make of it. He only knew Stu was not himself.

> i have been liberally endowed with the sutcliffe or cronin temper, and at times have allowed it too free a hand consequently, people suffer and often they are shocked.

John wondered – worried – if Astrid had become one of "the suffering."

When John received word that Stu had written to Allan Williams, asking Allan to arrange a one-man show for him at The Jacaranda, John's worst fears were confirmed.

How could Stu have asked *anything* of Al if he could recall writing to Al on The Beatles' behalf – firing Al as their manager? Had Stu blocked that out, along with Allan's ensuing bitterness and anger? Or had Stu completely forgotten the last few months? Entirely?

John chewed his thumbnail and glanced at Mimi's mantle clock. He still had a half hour before he needed to shower for his City Centre gig. And from the sound of running water in the pipes, one of the boarders was occupying the loo anyway.

He pulled his bare feet up into Mimi's parlour chair and sat cross-legged, folding himself into the cushions. Snuggling against the warmth of the tiny fire, he read Stu's letter one more time, searching through the morass of disjointed thoughts for some hint of the friend he'd known.

> i am prescribed a regimen of sedatives, bland food, and naps after lunch sometimes i lie down fully clothed it doesn't matter i don't sleep
>
> my impression of john moores is that of crap i don't know whats happening to painting here in germany its all the same they paint good but unoriginal
>
> there is nothing intellectually stimulating here at the moment. i feel in a torpor, well and truly drunk.

John lifted his eyes from the page and watched the fire play. He stared and wondered what, if anything, he could do. It was obvious: Stu was floundering. He was calling out for help, but John couldn't think of *any way* to help from this distance.

Sure, he could encourage Stu to come home, but how would that change things?

In Liverpool, Stu would be in competition with the talented Liverpool school of artists and writers who were progressive, forward thinking, and extremely talented. Greats such as Roger McGough, Adrian Henri, Alun Owen, George Jardine, and Arthur Ballard were gathering international notice and acclaim. If Stu chose to return home and join their clique, he would have to reestablish his ties, make them forget that he'd been accused of stealing the Liverpool College of Art amplifiers and burning art school furniture for heat in Percy Street and Gambier Terrace.

After walking away and leaving Liverpool flat for studies in Germany, Stu would have to work diligently, fiercely, to regain respect. He'd have to work even harder than he was doing overseas to break back into the local ranks.

More importantly, John wondered if the physicians Merseyside would be as good as the fabled German Director of Medicine, Hommelhopf. If the Kirchherrs were indeed providing the very best medical care that money could buy, how would Stu be able to afford something comparable back home, on his own paltry – almost nonexistent – income?

And most crucial of all to Stu's well-being...Astrid. John worried that Astrid might not be willing to leave her work, friends, and family to move to northern England at a moment's notice. The Exis were a tight fraternity. John doubted Astrid would agree to leave Germany for good and forever.

John had no answers. The only thing he was sure about was that there was nothing in Liverpool for Stu.

John unfolded himself from the tapestried chair and grabbed a notepad and pencil from the library table. He raked his hands through his new *pilzen kopf* and frowned, trying to think of an appropriate reply to Stu's letter. He tried to think of something wise without sounding wizened. He tried to think of something Stu might actually listen to.

Dear Stu, he began...

STUpendous achievement! We've been chosen "Number One" Merseyside out of all the bands that be. Announced in "Mersey Beat" just this savvy. And what will that get me? A free round or two at The Grapes. Yeah, right.

We all put stock in bullshit, y'know. We kill ourselves to achieve things that don't fuggin' matter.

We've been booked as part of "Operation Big Beat" at the New Brighton Tower Ballroom. And...yeah, we have a fan club. Does any of that count?

Think.

Life's no different here, y'know. It's all the same as yours. It's all a shitty deal. You and me...we can fuggin' destroy ourselves chasin' after fame 'n acclaim, or we can pace ourselves and go for the long run, son.

Which will it be?

Unfortunately, I think I know.

Here's one for you: "The reasonable man adapts himself to the world. The unreasonable man persists in trying to adapt the world to himself. Therefore, all progress depends on the unreasonable man." That's ole George Bernard Shaw, as it were. Brilliant, eh?

We can be "the unreasonable man," you and I. We can sacrifice ourselves on the altar of success. But will it be worth the price we'll pay? And if we die tryin', who'll fuggin' remember us?

If you give up Paris to paint...if I sacrifice happiness to write or to sing in a cavernous club, what'll we have to paint and sing about eventually?

If all we do is work, are we missing the point(alism)?

Is it worth it... bein' the unreasonable man?

I dunno. I've lost the ability to reason.

                        Love,

                        John

These short snippets of letters written by Stu are found in their entirety in Clayson and Sutcliffe's monumental and scholarly work on Stu called Backbeat. *One quote is actually from a letter to Pauline, and the other was written to Stu's mother.*

John's letter is purely fictional. The only real quote from John is. "It's all a shitty deal." However, I have studied John's letters to many other people (both published and unpublished) in addition to his prose in Skywriting by Word of Mouth. *This letter was created with those in mind.*

Thursday, 19 October 1961
Liverpool

It was all so "settled."

Cynthia had nested in the tiny apartment that she shared with Paul's girlfriend, Dot Rhone. Cleaning, arranging, and adding pink light bulbs "for a rosy effect," Cyn had cleverly turned the tiny, archaic bed-sit with a one-ring cooker into a cozy little home. She'd scrounged to purchase a somewhat threadbare, once-velvet chair and a musty, beige sofa, and she'd found quilts and coverlets that disguised them rather nicely. With a "sprig of this and a throw of that," Cyn's overgrown closet of a flat took on a rather homey appeal.

And, much to John's chagrin, she'd transformed herself as well. The leather mini-skirted blonde had lately donned sensible shoes and trim, plaid wool skirts for her practise-teaching at a Garston secondary school. Hitching three different busses to work each morning and three home again each afternoon, Cynthia dutifully arrived each day with the punctuality of seasoned instructor. Her lessons prepared and papers graded, "Miss Powell" had blossomed into a force to be reckoned with.

It made John uneasy.

Now when he stared at Cyn, she seemed less intriguing – more domestic and "housewifey." *She was a teacher, of all things!* And when she offered him cups of tea, removed his plate, and dialed in his favourite radio programmes, it didn't feel soothing – it felt wrong. Less and less the leathered, blonde temptress he'd lusted after, Cynthia was becoming a sweet helpmate. But it was help John wasn't ready to receive.

Without realizing it, John began distancing himself from her.

He continued to schedule gigs twice a day and to practise in between. The Beatles now played The Cavern on Mondays, Wednesdays, and Fridays from 12 noon until 5 p.m. and then performed there at least two evenings each week. On Tuesdays and Thursdays, when The Beatles were free, John began spending time with the new Beatles Fan Club, and when the opportunity presented itself, he ventured into photography, using some of the more eager members as models.

Persuading the inexperienced girls to pose, to unbutton a button or two, or to discard a blouse altogether, John discovered "a bit of a rush" in semi-nude shots of his infatuated Cavern groupies. He felt the exhilarated thrill of doing something dangerous and prohibited…just the way he used to feel with Cyn in Stu's flat.

John was trying almost anything to drown out the ancient voice that had lately returned, the voice that whispered that perhaps rock'n'roll was not what he wanted after all – that the band was not going to make him as happy as he'd dreamed. John was trying anything to hush the familiar, terrifying chant that predicted he would *never* be happy…not ever. He was feverishly searching for ways to be ignited.

****

Litherland Town Hall
Litherland

"So this is the plan, then," John was overly animated, moving back and forth at Litherland like a man possessed. "Pete, you'n Freddy'll split the drummin'. And Paul, you'll have rhythm, right? George, you'll have lead. And Gerry, you'll handle the vocals on most numbers…unless it's one y'er not well versed in. Les, you'll take on bass while Maguire comes in on saxophone."

"And what'll you be doin', Lennon?" Gerry Marsden folded his arms, chuckling at the prospect of combining their two bands for one evening. "Conductin' with a big, black sorcerer's wand, as it were?"

"Piano, son." John wiggled his fingers. "Ticklin' the fuggin' ivories!"

"Zarrafact?" Gerry raised a bushy eyebrow. "Well, that's news to us Pacemakers. We didn't know y'could! Maguire's the keyboard man 'round these parts."

"John's absolutely *keen* on keyboard!" George vouched for him. "He practically invented that song, 'Chopsticks,' y'know."

"Ah, great." Gerry rubbed his forehead. "It's Lenn-erachi, is it? If only we had a candelabra and a birrova velvet cloak for 'im."

John booted an amplifier into position at the front of the stage. "Yeah, well who effin' cares what we do anyway, right?" he shrugged. "It's only 'Slitherland' and we've only played here a million and a half times, so it seems."

"Yeah, it's not The Albert Hall, y'know." George backed him up.

"Just another drab dance hall in another drab town, dutifully drab and dull," John scowled.

"Just waitin' for us," Paul place one hand over his heart and sighed, "to rush in and drown out the droneness."

"I think y'er all daft – you Beatles!" Gerry smiled, shaking his head. "But," he held his hands up in surrender, "I can't fight all o' you, even if you *have* gone stark, ravin' mad! We'll have it your way and make it one band tonight, one mee-raculous group…The Beatmakers! But if it all goes to hell in a hand basket…y'can be sure I'm blamin' it all on Johnny B. Lennon here!"

"I'll take it," John said. "These days, anythin' for a birrova laugh. *Anythin'* but more slog."

****

An hour before concert time, John had also recruited Karl Terry to abandon his Cruisers and join The Beatmakers' ranks as a second vocalist. The montage group was becoming formidable, and John predicted it was going to be a performance that unsuspecting ticket holders would never quite forget.

"And here's another twist!" John was on a roll. "We'll have costumes as well!"

"Bollocks to that!" Pete was conferring with Freddy Marsden, and both drummers grew stone-faced at the prospect.

"As if those indecent, German leathers of yours aren't costume enough!" Gerry eyed George's leather pants. "Can'ya imagine me in kecks like that, eh? I'd actually die of sheer suffocation – if the public ridicule didn't ruin me first!"

"Then I suppose you'd be more or less averse to wearin' a thing like *this*?" Paul held up a moth-eaten, faded blue nightie that Freddy employed as drum padding.

"Ugh. I wouldn't wear that for a big clock!" George shook his head in disgust.

"I dunno." Paul shrugged, "It's got a certain crowd appeal – this nightie."

"It goes with yer eyes," John deadpanned.

And at half-seven, when the Litherland curtain parted on the unsuspecting crowd, The Beatmakers appeared in full regalia. Gerry Marsden had donned George Harrison's black, fitted leathers and Cuban boots while George had purloined a brown, woolen, hooded monk's robe from the backstage wardrobe bin. Paul was draped in the sad and faded nightie, while John played the opening number on a scrap of newspaper and an old pocket comb. The audience gawked, stunned.

By the time that Gerry and John plunged into harmony on "Whole Lotta Shakin' Goin' On," the audience "winked back." Laughing, clapping, and hooting as John squatted and tried to play guitar while crawling underneath the piano, the Litherland crowd began to respond in kind. They became as mad as the boys on stage.

Cheering louder and louder as first Pete would drum for a bit and then Freddy Marsden would pick up the backbeat from his own rostrum, the crowd whipped into a frenzy. When the two drummed simultaneously, the room shuddered.

John was a hyena. He cackled, howled, and ran his elbow up and down the keyboard à la Jerry Lee Lewis. On "What I'd Say," he hoisted one booted leg up on the piano top and hopped about on the other. In true Hamburg fashion, the rockers gave all to *mach shau*. Only George performed in his accustomed role and place, but mysteriously hooded, he looked as berserk as anyone else.

For the moment, John was happy. He forgot that he was due at The Cavern Club the next morning for the usual set-up. He forgot that he was playing The Casbah yet again, day after next. He forgot that by performing he was earning a suitable living, a living that his aunt was pleased with and that his steady girl – a demure Garston schoolteacher – was duly proud of.

All events are documented...right down to the costumes and instrument assignments. Only the conversation between Gerry and the Pacemakers and The Beatles is conjecture.

Saturday Morning, 4 November 1961
Mendips
Woolton

The 2-16 November issue of Bill Harry's "Mersey Beat" featured a column by Cavern Compère, Bob Wooler, entitled "The Roving I," reviewing the recent and rather extraordinary performance of The Beatmakers at Litherland Town Hall. It read:

It had to happen sometime. It was just a question of the right time and the right place...and the sharing of a carefree mutual mood of cooperativeness. Well, it happened at Litherland Town Hall during the Thursday night jive session on 19 October. The curtains opened, and the Beatmakers exploded on an astonished crowd with a sound that was bigger than the guns of Navarone. You've never heard of the Beatmakers? Well, it may never happen again that the Beatles and the Pacemakers (the Beatmakers) are feeling in a sufficiently crazy mood to go on stage together in one terrific jam session. Gerry wore George's black leather outfit and capered about in a hilarious Faron-cum-Rory-cum-Karl Terry type of act using the hand mike; Paul wore a castoff nightie that Freddie acquired from his mother to pack his drums with; John did a Marx Brothers style piano act; Freddie, in a railwayman's rig-out was on one drum kit. Pete was on the other George wore a hood and played lead guitar, Les was on rhythm. The other Les was blowing wild on his sax. The whole thing was a gas, a riot! The octet zipped through four romping numbers "Whole Lotta Shakin'," "What I'd Say," "Red Sails," and "Hit the Road, Jack." The crowd stopped jiving and went wild. Like I said it may never happen again. It was one of those things that now and then swings.

John, in the leisure of a Saturday off without a lunchtime gig, slurped up Kellogg's Corn Flakes and read Wooler's words again.

The article had been on the newsstands since Thursday, but this was

John's first chance to see it. All Thursday had been spent in rehearsals, revamping the play list and adding a few new numbers. And on Friday, of course, they'd had the usual afternoon stint at The Cavern. But today was his.

He shuffled to the counter, and poured himself a beaker of Earl Grey from the pot Mim had steeped. He let the steam warm his face – inhaling deeply. And closing his eyes, he thought about what he'd do for the next few hours.

His old "blood brother," Pete Shotton, had rung him up twice this week, suggesting that John drop 'round his Old Dutch Café in Smithdown Road for "a chat" with "two fantastically interestin' working' girls" whom Pete had met. John had to admit, the prospect was enticing. The girls, it seemed, were strippers in Liverpool 8, and as such, they piqued his interest. Rebels, free spirits – the pair were just the sort of diversion John needed right now. Unfortunately, Paul had other plans for the afternoon.

Paul had suggested that he and John pick up Dot and Cyn for "a stroll through NEMS" in search of lyrics to Phil Upchurch's new song, "You Can't Sit Down," and "a coupla at The Grapes" when the pubs opened, late afternoon. But John was sick of doing the same ole thing. Pete's idea sounded better.

John returned to the breakfast table and propped his heels on the chair rung. He adjusted his glasses a little lower on his nose, and slowly began flipping through the pages of "Mersey Beat," slowly scanning each ad and article.

On page eight, the usual ad for "The Colony Club" made John smile. "80 Berkley Street...featuring Lord Woodbine," it read.

A con man with a velvet cloak of come-ons, John thought, shaking his head. *But Lord Woodbine? That'll be the fuggin' day!*

On page 6, Brian Epstein's NEMS advertisement vied for attention with Hessey's Music Store, and on page 4, the traditional "Cavern Club Kalendar, Evening Sessions" occupied a large block on the page. John flipped to the next section quickly. He didn't want to be reminded of work today.

When the telephone sounded, he tried to ignore it.

"John –you know it's for you!" Mimi called from the other side of the swinging door.

Reluctantly, John scuffed to it.

"Yeah, hello?" he barked.

"Old Dutch Café, Woolton. Shotton here!" Pete's familiar voice always made John smile.

"Young Scouser, Mendips. O'Lennan this end," John returned.

"Hey!" Pete lowered his voice a notch and cut straight to the details. "Pat'n Jean'll be here at half-two, and *you'd* better be here as well, son. I said it was all arranged. I said one of the famous Beatles'd show up."

"So," John cupped his hand around the phone and tried to talk so that Mimi couldn't hear, "they're up for a few mortal sins, are they?"

"Cor, you've forgotten more than I realized!" Pete lamented, "It's you who's supposed to be *up*, wack!"

"At the very thought of it," John grinned.

"Right." Pete said, "Now that's the Johnny they'll know and love."

"Biblically, as it were."

"Yeah, right." Pete lowered his voice again as the entrance bell to the Old Dutch rang in the background. "Be forewarned about these bairds, son. Hoylake virgins, they ain't..."

For a moment, there was silence. Pete had said the one thing that reminded John how really wrong this all was: *Hoylake*.

"Y'still there, Winnie?" Pete felt the tension on the other end of the line.

"Yeah." John glanced at Mimi's wall clock. He had to make a decision soon. If he were not going to meet Cynthia after all, he'd have to concoct a plausible alibi.

"C'mon, John...y'deserve a birrov fun," Pete began. But there was no answer. Pete waited for what seemed like ages. He could even hear John breathing.

"All right then," Pete sighed. "Give me love to Cyn. Wish'er all the best and all that..."

"Y'er a filthy, black-hearted bastard with filthy ways, aren't you, son?" John smiled sadly.

"Most of which I hope to use thisavvy," Pete agreed.

"If only y'were lucky like me," John told him, "you'd be headed for a leisurely walk around NEMS in Whitechapel."

"Ah, but I couldn't take that much excitement in one afternoon, could I?" Pete threw his eyes to the ceiling.

"Me neither," John complained. "But as usual, I will."

All information is documented with the exception of whether John made that liaison or not. (See Pete Shotton's book, John Lennon: In My Life, *p. 69 for the real ending to this story).*

At a Lark Lane interview with Bob Wooler in March of 1994, Bob gave me information about his "Mersey Beat" article above. As per Bob, the article is accurate.

All conversation is conjecture.

Saturday Afternoon, 4 November 1961
NEMS, Whitechapel
Liverpool

Brian Epstein stood with his hands clasped behind his back and stared at the poster tacked just inside his shop. The swarm of weekend customers filled the rows between the counters. Shop clerks bustled back and forth with requested selections, and cash registers chinged. But Brian stood transfixed, examining Sam Leach's cardboard advertisement for a colossal "rock and roll" undertaking – a musical super show scheduled for 10 November. According to the poster, it was to be known as "Operation Big Beat."

The upcoming programme was billed as a monumental event. Featuring two licensed bars, a full buffet, and "late transport to Liverpool, the Wirral, and Cheshire," the fantastic concert of concerts was labeled "a showcase for Merseyside's top five groups: The Remo Four, Kingsize Taylor and the Dominoes, Rory Storm and the Hurricanes, Gerry and the Pacemakers, and The Beatles.'"

The Beatles. Brian almost smiled at the double entendre that he assumed the name implied. *The Beatles.* Ah, but they'd been a thorn in his flesh for the last seven days.

One week past – on 28 October – Brian had been quizzed about the enigmatic Beatles by no less than three customers, and to his great mortification, Brian had had no knowledge at all of the musicians or of their music. His unquestioned authority had been questioned.

The scrupulous Brian Epstein had been embarrassed.

****

Saturday, 28 October 1961
NEMS, Whitechapel
Liverpool

"Have ya the new disc by The Beatles, then?" Raymond Jones, a frequent customer and printer's apprentice, asked.

"Beetles?" Brian blinked three times. He knew that Jones generally asked after country and western artists, specifically Carl Perkins. *Beetles, Beetles*…he couldn't recall a single country group by that name. "I'm sorry. I'm afraid I'm not familiar with that particular ensemble. Might you be able to give me…"

"They're no ensemble," the eighteen-year-old explained with a slight throw of the eyes. "They're a group, a rock'n'roll group…from right here…right Merseyside, y'know."

"Indeed?" Brian pulled out an index of British recording artists and quickly flipped through to the "B" section.

"Yeah…indeed." Jones smirked at Epstein's formality. *He's a ruffler, a real and truly 'oly Joe,* Ray thought to himself. *But of all places to buy records in the whole of th' Northland, this 'un's the best. No question about it.*

"Beetles, Beetles, let me see…" Brian ran his finger along the column of printed names. "Beetles? No…no group by that name listed in the directory, I'm afraid."

"B-e-**a**…" Raymond suggested.

"Oh, B-e-a-" Brian repeated, scanning again. "No, nothing under B-e-a as well. No listing at all, and this is quite current."

"Yeah well, if y'don't mind me sayin', that proves nothin'…because they've got a disc, as it were. I've heard it."

"Heard it?" Brian's pride was wounded. "Heard it where?" *Who in the Northland has a better selection of records, I'd like to know?* he fumed.

"Hambleton Hall. Heard it there Friday last. And at The Cavern, as well. Bob Wooler's spinnin' it daily down there."

"Wooler?" Brian felt his throat tighten. His solid ground was growing shakier by the minute.

The boy nodded. "Yeah, Wooler. Bob Wooler. The Cavern Club compère? Y'must know Bob…"

"And this Cavern…" Brian lifted a hand to halt the lad's diatribe. "You're referring, I presume, to the jazz venue? Ray McFall's nightspot?"

"It's not a jazz club anymore." Jones shook his head. "It's a 'jive hive,' Mr. Epstein, a rock'n'roll club. And a good one, too. Cor, it's right over there!" The boy pointed out the front window. "Just there...in Mathew Street. Straight ahead o'yer face, y'know."

"And these Beatles are performing *in* The Cavern Club, you say?" Brian stared at the youth, as if to wring the truth from him with an intense look.

"Yeah, three times a week of a lunchtime. Two or three times a week of an evenin'."

"So it's B-e-a..." Brian spelled the name again as he wrote it down.

"Yeah, right...just like that there." Jones pointed to a large, cardboard poster lying face up on the counter top. It was an advertisement that promoter Sam Leach had dropped off earlier in the day. He'd come in with a stack of tickets to be sold to something called "Operation Big Beat," and Brian had agreed to offer the tickets to his clientele and to post the flamboyant poster in his shop as well. And there it was – The Beatles – right in front of him...right on the poster.

"Yes, I see," Brian's cheeks burned with humiliation as he kept on writing. "And the name of the illusive disc, then, Mr. Jones?" He looked up.

"'My Bonnie,'" Raymond enunciated clearly. "Y'know, 'My bonnie lies over the ocean,' 'n all that. You know the one...you've heard it." And he hummed a few bars just in case Epstein was as unclear about folk songs as he was about Liverpool's biggest rock'n'roll band.

The Beatles – My Bonnie, Brian scribbled, and he underlined the note while the boy continued his rendition of the song.

"Yes, yes, I believe I have it now." Brian nodded curtly. "Thank you very much."

"Great, wonderful." Raymond smiled. "So...I'll be back when it's in, then?"

"Try midweek," Brian suggested.

"Right. Midweek. Ta!"

But it wasn't midweek before The Beatles emerged again. In fact, they resurfaced that very afternoon.

"Mr. Brian," the flushed clerk rapped twice at the entrance to his office. "I've two customers on the floor who're inquirin' about a disc I've never even heard of..."

"A disc of which we have no recording, Diana," Brian corrected, looking up from his paperwork.

"Yeah, that." The fair complected girl with the light sprinkling of cinnamon freckles blushed deeply.

"And it is?"

"The title's 'My Bonnie,' and these gerls out here claim..."

"These young ladies…"

"These young ladies out here claim it's by The Beatles, but they're…"

Brian's expression changed, and he stood up abruptly. "If you wouldn't mind," he stepped out from behind his desk, "I'd like to handle this situation myself, Diana. Just a matter of sheer curiosity, you understand…and not because I think for one minute you're incapable of placing the order appropriately."

"Yeah, awwright. Uh, I mean…yessir, Mr. Brian." The oval-faced girl brushed back a wisp of prematurely soft grey hair that had fallen out of her French twist, "They're over there. This way."

But Brian could have guessed who had made the inquiry, even with no direction. Two cosmetic school types nudged each other and giggled as he approached. They smiled widely in anticipation.

"Good afternoon," Brian tightened the Windsor knot in his navy blue silk tie. "I understand you're seeking a new recording by a group called 'The Beatles.'" He got the spelling right in his head this time.

"Yeah, right." The shorter girl answered, smacking gum. She smiled coyly at the "deep-pocketed," smartly dressed storeowner with the Kirk Douglas cleft in his chin.

"It's 'My Bonnie,' chooks," the other girl, a blonde in a black, wool A-line dress and black thick-heeled work shoes, answered. "Mr. Bob Wooler said to ask for it in person, y'know."

"It's all the rage, ducks!" the first girl – a shrillish redhead – winked at Brian. "You've 'eard of it, avenue?"

"Indeed I have," Brian cleared his throat, "*and* of the immense popularity of the local artists who produced it."

The two girls exchanged amused glances.

"Oh, yeah?" The short redhead stared at him with laughing eyes.

"In fact," Brian straightened his already erect posture, "you are the second and third customers today inquiring about the aforementioned recording."

"Isstharafact, luv?"

"But unfortunately," Brian used his hands awkwardly in apology, "I haven't that particular disc in stock at the moment."

"Oh nice." The taller one – an ash blonde with piercing blue eyes – let out a sigh that lifted her bangs. "Birrova letdown, isn't it, luv?" She fingered absently through the pile of Operation Big Beat tickets on the glass countertop.

Fighting the urge to grab the tickets and stack them back into a neat, straight pile, Brian glanced away and repeated the commitment he'd made to Raymond Jones earlier. "Yes, indeed, and I do apologize. But…if you'll return midweek, I feel certain I can have the recording for you then."

"But we've come 'round from Upper Parly, y'realize!" the no-excuses blonde protested, as if the length of her walk would change matters somehow.

"I-I do understand." Brian took all complaints seriously. NEMS was his very last chance in the family business as far as his father was concerned. There was no margin for error. None. And although his voice was reassuring and in control, Brian's porcelain skin blotched with hives. "Please permit me to custom order your request and have it shipped rush-delivery…no extra charge."

"Yeah, awright chooks." She dug into her coin purse and plunked several fat coins onto the counter, one by one. "We'll just have tickets to Operation Big Beat, then. I'm thinkin' that'll have to do for now."

"Certainly." Brian proffered his hand for the stack of tickets. "And how many will you be needing?"

The girls glanced at each other and giggled. "Two, luv! Unless, of course, *you'd* like to…"

"Yes, yes, two. Here we are." Brian crimsoned. He took the stack and removed two tickets, busying himself with the money, keeping his eyes lowered. The girls giggled again.

"Yer otter come 'round to The Cavern and hear The Beatles yerself, y'know." The blonde batted her eyes at Brian and leaned over provocatively, her ample breasts almost grazing the countertop. "I mean, since they're as close as they are 'n all…"

Brian registered the sale in his ticket ledger.

"Yeah," the cagey redhead chimed in. "Myras well come 'round fer a looksee and a lissen, y'know."

"And then you could hear the record as well," the blonde winked. "Though no record could ever replace the sight of our lads in all their lovely live-ness, as it were – in those tight leathers they've been sportin'…and those Cuban heels!"

"The boys in all their sweat-drenched glory!" her friend sighed.

"Yes, quite." Brian cleared his throat. "Well, I uh appreciate the invitation, and naturally, your business with NEMS…and uh, your patience."

"Don mention it!" The redhead primped her hair. "It was *our* pleasure, wasn't it Lis-er Lou?"

"Yeah, our pleasure, luv."

But as the girls began to muster yet another chorus of giggles, Brian glanced purposefully at his watch, then nodded, retreating briskly to his small upstairs office.

There, he unfolded an ironed, Irish linen handkerchief from his pocket and dabbed his forehead three, no, four times. And closing his eyes, he drew a long, shaky breath, holding it as long as he could, slowing his heart rate down with practised concentration. When Brian finally exhaled – almost a full minute later – he moderated the deliberate release.

Then picking up the tele to ring London, Brian sat primly in his swivel oak chair and tried not to slump or inordinately wrinkle his trousers. He had an evening engagement that would not permit an unkempt appearance. That sort of thing would never do.

****

That had been eight days ago. And still Brian had failed to locate the disc.

None of his sources had discovered any information about a record entitled, "My Bonnie" by The Beatles. Brian had failed to unearth a single copy of the sought-after platter. His telephone calls to agents, North and South, had been useless. His scans of catalogues had turned up nothing. Now, more than a week since Raymond Jones and the chatty Scousers had first requested the mystery disc, Brian stood staring at the "Operation Big Beat" poster and struggling with mounting frustration.

"Still lookin' for 'My Bonnie,' then, Mr. Brian?" His "weekends only" clerk, Ruth – an attractive green-eyed recruit from the art college – followed Brian's gaze to the advertisement near the window. When he didn't answer, the coed folded her arms and simply waited. In the last few months, she'd learned to read her employer's volatile moods. Used to working with artists, she'd learned when to speak and when to retreat strategically. It was a balancing act, to be sure. Mr. Epstein blew hot and cold.

"Yes," he pursed his lips, "but with precious little success, I'm afraid." He turned away from the poster. "And that hardly reflects Favourably on NEMS, does it? It doesn't validate our claim of having *all* the latest recordings by *all* the latest groups...or our promise of twenty-four hour access to the same."

"Well," the soft-spoken blonde hesitated, "there must be a way...I mean, it's an actual disc. I've even heard it myself."

"You?" He gave her the same look Peter Pan gave Wendy Darling when Pan discovered that she could reattach severed shadows.

"Y-yes sir." Like her employer, she blushed easily. "I hate to admit it, but...all right...I'm a bit of Beatles fan myself, actually."

"Really?"

She had his full attention now. *An intellectual fan! A fan from the art college! Now* this *is interesting!*

"I am," she smiled, "primarily because of their patronage here in the shop."

"*Here?* In Whitechapel?" Brian blinked. "You're saying The Beatles have been *here*?"

"Oh sure, quite often. You know them, Mr. Brian...those four rogues who're always loiterin' and listenin' to songs...the ones who stay and play and stay and play, but never purchase. Why, two of them were in this very afternoon – with their girlfriends."

"But...I'm sure those lads are German." Brian was confused. "They're a popular combo from...from Hamburg, I believe."

"Oh that!" The girl's emerald eyes glistened. "That's legend." She tossed her pageboy as she talked. "Actually, they're all from Merseyside – Allerton, Woolton, Speke, and West Derby. They've only been to Hamburg now and again. Entertainin' in the clubs, as it were."

"Hamburg?" The solution to Brian's problem suddenly surfaced. "*Living* in Hamburg?"

"That's right," Ruth shrugged.

"And during their time in Hamburg," Brian had turned investigator, "might they have recorded a disc, do you know?"

"I uh...I have no idea."

"Miss Anderson," he took a few steps towards her and lowered his voice, "have you ever been to The Cavern Club?"

"The Cavern Club?" Ruth tried to decide how best to answer the question. Was it something of which Mr. Brian would disapprove? She swallowed and stalled for time.

"Yes, The Cavern Club," he repeated. "The one in Mathew. Ray McFall's..."

"Oh, that Cavern!" she smiled feebly. "The one in Mathew, then."

"Yes, *there*! I've just said that! Have you been there or not?"

"Well...perhaps once." She didn't lie well. "Once or twice... if memory serves."

"And could you..." Brian lowered his voice even more. "Could you speak to someone who would promise me admittance there this Thursday, the ninth...for the lunchtime session – no questions asked, no red tape, no inquiries or nonsense at the door?"

"Well," she met his gaze, "I could try. I could speak to Mr. Paddy Delaney..."

"Who is?"

"Who is the doorman...the bouncer, so to speak."

"*Absolutely not!*" Brian vetoed the idea without a blink. "In fact, that's just the sort of person I'm striving to avoid! You'll have to do better than that. I need you to go straight to Cavern management with this request."

"Cavern *management*? You want *me* to speak to Cavern management?" The twenty-one year old blanched. "I...Sir...Mr. Bob Wooler couldn't pick me out of a crowd of three or four! And Ray

McFall...well...I'm not exactly a regular at the club, you understand...and I'm by no means a celebrity, by any stretch of the imagination!"

Brian fought back a smile and looked away. He relaxed a little at the girl's ingenuous admission. "Yes, of course." He found his composure. "And I won't rely solely upon your petition to Mr. Wooler. But any 'preparation' that your speaking to him might afford would be most appreciated, Ruth. You see, I've never been able to tolerate making a scene, and although I'd like to attend a lunchtime performance, I *couldn't* do so if it would generate a public stir of any magnitude."

"Well...all right then," the girl nodded. "I'll see what I can do – though I can't imagine anyone objecting to a businessman of your caliber..."

"Thank you, but..." he interrupted her. Praise always made him antsy. "We can discuss this later...after you've talked to the powers that be at The Cavern. But right now, there's a more important matter at hand."

"Yes sir?"

"I'd like you to check each and every import catalogue available...every source we have for records published in foreign countries during the past twelve months. Please give special attention to discs imported to the U.K. from Germany, and see if you can locate 'My Bonnie' in that arena."

Ruth made notes on the pad Brian had used earlier. "Still determined to track it down, then?"

"I am," he nodded. "There *has* to be a way to find this illusive disc."

"Well, if it's out there, you'll locate it, won't you?"

"Miss Anderson, since acquiring management of NEMS, I've never been thwarted in the delivery of a customer's request. And I certainly don't intend to start now. I can't have a local band like The Beatles marring a unsullied reputation."

"To keep your record, you must find theirs," Ruth smiled.

"Exactly," Brian said. And he offered his reticent but lovely smile in return.

In the years since Raymond Jones wandered into NEMS, Whitechapel, rumours have emerged alleging that Jones never existed.

In their book, The Walrus Was Ringo, *Alan Clayson and Spencer Leigh assert that Raymond Jones was and is real. He was originally, they say, from Huyton and worked his way up from printer's apprentice to owner of his own printing shop in Burscough. He is now retired and lives in Spain. And according to them, he did request "My Bonnie" from Brian personally on October 28, 1961.*

It's interesting to note, according to Mark Lewisohn's The Beatles Chronicles *(p.34), that on 28 October, when Raymond Jones and the two girls described above (the names I have used are fictitious) petitioned Brian Epstein for copies of "My Bonnie," The Beatles themselves were busy preparing for an evening gig at Aintree*

Institute...completely oblivious to the enormous impact that such inquiries would have upon their lives.

All facts, including the description of the poster are accurate. However, the clerks were not named Diana and Ruth. And all conversation is conjecture.

If you're interested in what happened at Operation Big Beat, by the way, read pp. 122-125 in Sam Leach's colourful book, The Birth of the Beatles.

Thursday, 9 November 1961
The Cavern Club
Mathew Street
Liverpool

"All right, he's out there!" Bob Wooler poked his head inside the door of the tiny band room behind The Cavern stage. "Look lively, lads. Give it yer all!"

"Yeah, right." John continued to tune his guitar, an art he still found elusive, even after all these years. He missed Eric Griffiths or Rod Davis taking care of it for him.

"I mean it, Lennon!" Bob knew that tone of voice. "He bleedin' owns a record store, y'know! His father owns two 'n three! He's got influence, money…and clout to boot. Brian Epstein could put you lot on the Merseyside map, if he had half a reason to!"

"We know all that information," George droned, unmoved. "We've been to his store, y'know. We've heard his many records."

"We've seen his black valise as well…and the shiny patent shoes." Paul moved his eyebrows up and down.

"And we're not impressed," John added. "He's no Bert Kaempfert. He's no Peter Eckhorn either, is he?"

"Yeah? Well, y'er no Lonnie Donegan yerself, are ya?" Bob snapped.

"Ta." John smirked, unfazed. "Because ole Lonnie's passé, as it were. He's all washed up and gone these days."

"Showtime!" Pete wedged in the doorway behind Bob.

"Right. Make it count!" Bob waggled a finger and then disappeared to the compère's booth.

"Hey Pete, Mr. Epstein's in the audience, y'know!" Paul told him.

"Who?"

"Epstein…'Mr. Brian'…Epstein of NEMS, the record man…Whitechapel." Paul spoke a little louder as the William Tell Overture began to blare. The boys gathered their things and began threading their way to the boards.

"*That* one, eh?" Pete glanced around for a familiar face. "What's he turned 'round and come here for – a man like that?"

"It appears he's come to see us." George smiled at three fans who called his name. He waved and wrapped an arm around his waist, as if to take a bow.

"He's come to free the slaves, son." John clasped his wrists together in imaginary manacles. "He's come to save us from the bowels of this darkly, cavernous hell of cacophonous pandemonium, he has!"

"All that, eh?" Pete shrugged. "Good then. Right. We could use some savin' about now."

"But George here…is he old enough for that sort of activity, we ask." Paul nudged him playfully.

"Only just." John grinned and fluttered his eyelashes in George's direction. "He's still in the full blush of youth – our kid."

"Get off." George smiled in spite of himself. "I'm years older than you'll ever be."

"Clever lad." Paul applauded.

They jumped up on stage and rippled fingers at The Beatlettes.

Pete sat and adjusted his cymbals. He ran a few practice rolls between the snare and the tom-tom. Paul lit an Embassy and offered a drag to a girl in the front row who wanted to touch anything Paul touched. With a wink at a girl with an American snapshot camera, George hoisted himself atop Paul's squatty amplifier, scooched into place, and centered his guitar perfectly. The Beatles were constantly in motion.

John stepped to the edge of the platform and squinted into the audience. "Did y'come here for the show, then?" he bellowed to no one in particular.

"Yeah!"

"That's right, mate."

"Get on with it!"

It was the usual Liverpool patter.

"Right then." John stopped suddenly and stared at a group of immaculately attired office workers who were laughing and chatting together under the first archway. "Hey! you…yeah, that's right…you in the bleedin' tweeds. Shut the fook up before I come down there and, as they say in dear, ole Bootle, 'purra lip on ya.'"

The crowd roared with derisive laughter as the cluster of accountants was squelched. John continued to glare at them while George ran a lick on his Gretsch.

Paul tapped sharply on the microphone, three times, then cleared his throat, and pronounced the customary, "One, two….two, two, two."

Someone applauded and shouted, "Next selection, if ya don't mind!" The Beatles smiled.

"Good afternoon then," Paul chuckled, winking, tossing his head. "Welcome to The Cavern Club. Glad y'er with us for a birrova lunch, as it were. My name's Paul…" he waited for the whistles and whoops to subside, "and that over there's John… and George…and back here, Pete. We're The Beatles!"

Mad applause. A few screams peppered the room.

John retired to his place and swung his Rickenbacker into position, untwisting the strap and shrugging his shoulders repeatedly to adjust the angle of the instrument. He took one moment to scan the crowd for the NEMS owner, but the lights prohibited him from seeing all but the first few rows, and no one unusual was there. It was all the standard fare – a delicious assortment of sweater sets and hosiery. If Epstein lurked in the audience, John couldn't find him.

"We've this little number we'd like to do," Paul began.

"*He'd* like to do," John corrected, throwing his eyes up sardonically. A cluster of girls giggled.

"All right then," Paul lowered his guitar from the ready. "What've *you* got planned, as it were? We're all ears, Mr. Lennon. Go on."

The "Paul faction" in the room bounced in their seats and chalked one up for their jaunty hero. John merely turned his back and began to fiddle with his guitar.

"As I was *about to say*, then…" Paul leaned into the microphone. But the sentence never ended. It was cut short by the raspy sound of John Lennon's voice.

> *Sweet Sixteen Lisa!*
> *Hearts lay in the sun,*
> *Her sister said she was sixteen…*
> *But the men said…..Twenty-one!*

The audience supplied percussion with their hands and feet, and Pete had no choice but to join in. George was next on board, his amused grin only half hidden in the concentration he always gave to his work. And at last, the irked emcee himself joined in the fracas, slapping out a bottom bass to complete Lennon's selection.

The song was an immediate success. The crowd leapt to its feet. Someone hoisted a flimsy, wooden Cavern chair in the air and shook it. One boy, jammed against the first slimy stone arch, whistled through his teeth while a shop girl with wet hair slipped a folded note up on the stage and shoved it in Paul's direction. Even John's rebuked accountants nodded and clapped to the beat. And camouflaged in the far corner, sitting with Alistair Taylor – his personal assistant – Brian Epstein of NEMS sucked his breath in sharply and stared at the hullabaloo in horrified, fascinated amazement.

****

The rest of the set was the same. The Beatles, in black polo shirts, black leather jackets and pants, and two-inch Cuban heeled boots, "mucked about" and did exactly as they pleased. They requested jam butties and ate them on stage. They smoked and drowned their cigs in half-bottles of Coca-Cola. They shouted, sweated, argued, swilled chaos with rock'n'roll, and waged verbal battles with one another. As Paul jiggled the mike back into its stand after Ray Charles's hit, "What I'd Say," Bob Wooler stepped up onto the tiny, cramped podium and interrupted the programme.

"Ladies and gentlemen…" Wooler cleared his throat and waited for the noise to subside. "Ladies and gentlemen, I'd like to introduce a very special visitor we have with us this afternoon…somewhere out there in the vast sea of faces." He put one hand over his eyebrows. "I was informed earlier by Mr. Bill Harry of 'Mersey Beat'…" Cheers went up. Everyone loved Bill Harry. "I was informed that Mr. Brian Epstein of the North End Music Store in Whitechapel is actually in the audience this afternoon. Mr. Epstein, if you would please stand and be acknowledged…"

For a moment nothing happened. But when Wooler started to make the announcement again, Brian reluctantly slid his chair back and stood for a second only.

"Mr. Epstein, please accept a round of applause, if you will," Bob went on. "Ladies and gentlemen, a considerable Cavern welcome for Mr. Brian Epstein of NEMS!"

The crowd responded politely but with a murmur of curiosity. Several girls turned to stare at his sleek attire. Others merely nudged their friends and giggled.

John watched the blurred figure rise and stand and take his seat again. Epstein was out of visual range, beyond John's field of focus. And John found the man's motivation for attending the performance equally difficult to perceive.

What's Epstein here of a lunchtime for, especially in the middle of a workday, in the middle of a work week? He's never given us the fuggin' time of day. In fact, he's made it perfectly clear he doesn't want us lurkin' about in his place, as it were. Well, that door swings both ways, doesn't it? Yet here he is…in our shop…uninvited.

And without waiting a second longer for Wooler to expound on Brian's local fame and prestige, John began the count-in to the next song.

"Ah one, two, ah one, two, three, four…" The music began again, pulling the audience back to the stage.

Under the watchful eye of their prestigious visitor, Paul went full tilt with his *mach shau*. He leaned into the crowd and hung out over the edge of the stage as he'd often seen Rory and Johnny Guitar do. He winked and nodded and smiled coyly while Pete hammed it up on "Pinwheel Twist," and George waggled his guitar a bit to enhance his three-count stomp-step-hustle. But John did what he always did...stopped songs in midstream, changed the play list at will, and took off on musical tangents without warning.

Alistair Taylor – a bit bored by it all – leaned over and tried to make conversation with his employer. But he was waved off. Brian stared at the stage and hardly blinked. He sat motionless, strangely agitated, his eyes following John, finding it hard to focus on anything else but the disaffected, arrogant boy.

When Alistair followed Brian's line of vision to the conceited, rhythm guitarist, John was shouting at a fan, the veins in his neck bulging as he yelled. Sweat rolled down John's sideburns and soaked his collar. His leather pants clung to his legs.

Yeah, the lad's got charisma all right, Alistair thought. *They all do. But stars? I mean, they're basically a bunch o' five chord merchants."*

"And now," Paul McCartney announced from the stage, "we'd like to do a little number we wrote – a tune from John'n me called 'Hello Little Girl.' So, hang on, then....here it is, and here we go..."

Brian turned and looked at Alistair for the first time since the set had begun. They simultaneously raised their eyebrows and nodded. A group that writes their own songs! This was starting to get interesting.

The Beatles had just upped the ante.

****

George watched his diffident approach. The man was head-to-toe elegant, but thoroughly embarrassed.

"'Ullo there." George shook Brian's hand. "What brings Mr. Epstein here?"*

Brian smiled a quiet smile, one to match George's own.

"Actually," the businessman self-consciously adjusted his tie, "I'm here on a bit of research, as it were."

"Research, is it?"

Brian was sure George's expression was one of ridicule. He blushed deeply.

"Yes, yes..." Brian faltered. "You see...I'm – uh – interested...or one of my *customers* is interested...in a disc you're rumoured to have released – a cover-cut, a rendition of the popular folk song, 'My Bonnie.'"

"Yeah, that's right. We cut that."

"Excellent." Brian waited for more information, but George offered none. They stared at each other uncomfortably. "Well, then," Brian voiced the obvious, "where might I possibly secure a copy of the record?"

"Paul's got one," George teased. "You might try askin' him."

"Paul?"

"Yeah, that one." George pointed to his comrade. "The good-lookin' one, the one over there chattin' up the bairds."

Brian stared. The one named Paul was indeed enmeshed in an all-out flirtation with three bold, young women. He was quite involved, and Brian couldn't dream of interrupting.

"He's got it back in the band room – that record." George spoke over Brian's thoughts. "He keeps it handy for the compère 'n all….y'know, if Mr. Wooler needs to fill a musical lull, what have you."

Brian focused on George again. "Yes, of course – quite shrewd." Brian meant it. *Just what I'd do if I'd intentions of having a chart topping record someday,* he thought.

George nodded.

The conversation bottomed out again. George stared at the man's expensive tie, and Brian brushed the back of his hand across his face nervously.

"I uh…I would love to hear the record, actually." *This is grueling,* Brian thought. But he refused to give up. "In fact, it would help me a great deal if I could possibly have a glance at the disc…that is, when the moment's convenient."

George could just imagine what John would say if he left the stage now to go into the band room on a "hunt-search" for Paul's record. John had little patience with "suits," NEMS or no NEMS. So George, reining in his overanxious vanity, shrugged nonchalantly. He pretended not to care that someone, ostensibly an important someone, was actually asking after their record.

One glance at Epstein's wrist told George all he needed to know. Their break was almost over, and the second set was about to begin. John would be back any moment now, and he wasn't in a great mood this afternoon. The curious, Liverpool businessman would just have to wait.

"The record? Sure, right." George's right cheek twitched out a smile. "I'll dig it out for you. Right after the next set."

"The…next set?" Brian was taken aback. He was rarely put on the back burner by anyone.

"The next part of the show." George wasn't sure the shop owner understood rock'n'roll lingo.

But in truth, Brian understood only too well, and he was dumbfounded. He wanted to give the impertinent lad the tongue-lashing he deserved and spin on his heels in a wounded huff. He wanted to say, "Thank you very much, but never mind then," and storm off in a rage of indignation, but Brian was too intrigued.

John strode onto the stage and picked up his guitar. He balanced his cig on an amplifier and tossed his sweat-tangled hair back with a quick thrust of his hand. For a moment, his almond eyes met Brian's, and he sized up the shop owner without expression.

Brian stopped breathing and stared back.

One of the club cleaners, a matronly sort who'd taken John under her wing, stepped up to the stage and swatted John's leathered legs. He turned and knelt down to talk with her.

"What's shakin' there, Aggie?" He employed one of his Goon voices. "A good bit more 'n the leaves on the trees – isn't that right, gerl?"

She giggled at his flirtatious nonsense and swatted him again.

"So wot wujja like then, luv?" John could be very Scouse when the occasion called for it.

"Somethin' by that ole Gene Vincent!" Aggie spit as she talked. Her salt and pepper head bobbed with enthusiasm. "Somethin' just fer me, somethin' for the one what gets you butties now and again."

"Can do," John bartered, "fer a plate of chips, luv."

"Fer a plate of chips and a smuggled half-pint as well, I suppose?" Her eyes twinkled.

"Find a pint 'n y'er on, Ag!"

"Ah yew!" she laughed. "You'll get the Cavern lunch and a Coke! That's what you'll get, Jack Lennon."

"The Cavern lunch!" Paul hopped up on the stage and joined in the banter. "Ah, John, y'er a lucky, lucky man! My dream's out, Aggie."

"The Cavern lunch!" George grinned. "I've always wanted one of those."

Feigning frustration, Aggie shook her head and waddled away as John stood up and stamped his boots in a quick Spanish dance. George laughed and did the same, and Pete took his seat at the rostrum while Paul polished off one last swig of his lukewarm Coca-Cola.

Brian saw no purpose in standing there, ignored. So he walked briskly back to his table, trying to decide if he should stay a minute longer.

"Here's one," John blurted out suddenly without preface or further introduction to the second part of the show, "Here's one for our Aggie! Aggie, Aggie, dear ole Aggie, she's the girl wit' her foot in a baggie."

The crowd chuckled, cheered, and whistled. And from the far tunnel, Aggie curtseyed.

"Be Bop A Lu La!" John screamed, and the song was instantly everywhere. John pushed it into the room with a force that put Brian firmly in his seat. The entire audience moved to the blues-rock melody. In the cruel, suffocating Cavern heat, in waves of smoke and rancid perfume, in the tangle of perspiring bodies, in the humid darkness, John swayed with a guttural sound that was completely primitive.

Among the fumes of cleanser and urine, he sang a song for Aggie. He sang as if there were no one else but Aggie in the world. And he sang in a way no one else would've bothered to sing.

Brian forgot to stalk off indignantly, to be inconvenienced or even provoked. And when next he glanced at his watch, it was ten past two. The afternoon was well over, and in The Cavern Club, the second set of the day was just coming to an end.

****

NEMS
Whitechapel Road
Liverpool

"Wait, wait...here it is...I've got it!" Alistair Taylor pointed with an index finger to one of the listings in NEMS' large Continental Catalog. "Look, Brian: 'Tony Sheridan and the Beat Brothers, My Bonnie.'"

Brian peered over Alistair's shoulder and read aloud, "Polydor Records, Germany, Number 24-673." He nodded. "That's it, that's the one! That's exactly the one the Harrison boy showed me...precisely the name on the label."

"But Polydor..." Alistair shrank from questioning one of Brian's decisions. "You know how their stipulation, Brian...they'll require us to order an entire sealed box. Twenty-five records, after all!"

"Place the order, Alistair."

Alistair hesitated, then said it. "It could mean a great whackin' loss. We could feasibly end up with twenty-three discs gatherin' the dust of ages in the back room, y'know."

"That's always a possibility," Brian stiffened. He hated to be challenged by anyone. "Even with an Elvis Presley release...there's always a calculated risk."

"But The Beatles...or should I say The Beat Brothers," Alistair protested. "Aren't they a bit different from Mr. Presley?"

"Completely different." Brian's voice changed. "*Completely* different." He walked to his second-floor window and stared out at Whitechapel below. "Eccentric, captivating, magnetic, exciting..."

"So...you're still intent on offerin' them management of some sort, then?"

Brian had divulged his plans over lunch at Peacock's the previous day. Alistair wasn't sure then that the magic would last the night, but apparently it had.

"I'm still intent on *meeting* them and speaking with them further," Brian corrected.

"Meanin' what?"

"I'm not sure yet." Brian bit his bottom lip. His fingers played with the edge of the Venetian blinds. "I mean...managing The Beatles would require a great deal of work...I'd...I'd have to set up a separate company, a management company per se. And naturally, I couldn't ask my family to be involved in such a risk – I couldn't do it under the auspices of NEMS. I'd have to ask Rex Makin to help me create a separate business entity..."

"Right," Alistair nodded. "And even with your solicitor's help, runnin' a record shop while managin' a new company *and* a rock'n'roll group at the same time would be absolutely overwhelmin', Brian."

"Yes," Brian nodded solemnly, "which is exactly why I'd like you to join me, Alistair. No, no, let me finish. I've given it some thought, and I'd like to offer you two and a half per cent of The Beatles' contract...that is, if it all works as I hope, and *if* a contract indeed emerges, as I anticipate it might."

"But...I've no money to put into a scheme like that." Alistair shook his head. "And no matter how you approach it, Brian, it's gonna cost a bleedin' fortune to bring this all to fruition, as it were."

"I don't want your money, Alistair – just your loyalty." Brian turned to face him. "I need someone I can depend on – someone I can trust one hundred per cent."

"But you've already got that, haven't you? Just pay me a decent wage, and I'll be happy. I work for *you*, Brian – not NEMS. Whatever you do, I'm along for the ride."

Brian turned back to the window and looked out towards The Cavern Club. "There's an uncanny link, you know," he almost whispered, "between NEMS here in Whitechapel, Bill Harry's 'Mersey Beat' right over there in Renshaw, The Cavern Club straight ahead in Mathew, and The Beatles. We're all *right here*, Alistair, in a tight triangle...all within a few blocks of each other...all interrelated, interconnected like cogs and gears. It's all right *here* waiting to come together somehow. All I have to do is discover how to set the machine in motion."

"Well...while you're at it," Alistair suggested, hoping it wasn't too soon to commence being the person Brian could trust one hundred per cent, "y'might want to discover how to put a birrov polish and *je ne sais quoi* on those lads of yours, as it were. I mean, don't get me wrong here – they've a certain amount of raw appeal 'n all that. But even as energetic as they are, they're a ruined bunch o'schoolboys, Brian – crackin' one-liners and wearin' those sinister black leathers from head to toe. You've got to admit it, really...The Beatles wouldn't go down well at the Royal Variety Performance Show, would they?"

"No," Brain turned and smiled slightly, "I can't imagine that they would." He nervously rubbed the back of his hand lightly across his forehead. "No, not even on the best of nights. The Beatles wouldn't do well at all at The Royal Variety."

During a 1995 interview with Bob Wooler, he pointed out to me that Pete did not sing "Peppermint Twist." According to Bob, Pete, in fact, sang "Pinwheel Twist." Who knows?

Bob also talked about John's reticence towards Brian Epstein. John was sincerely interested in and impressed by successful people (Michael Issacson, June Furlong, Rory Storm). But, like Julia before him, John was also wary of authority figures. And he was always very concerned about maintaining control of his group.

Another conflict of facts arises: In his book, Yesterday, My Life with the Beatles, Alistair Taylor says that the Beatles' set at The Cavern lasted only "twenty....mind-churning minutes" and "it was over." He doesn't mention staying for a second set. Of course, that does not mean that he and Brian left the Cavern at this point.

But Philip Norman states that Brian "stayed at the Cavern through the Beatles' second session, until 2:10 P.M." and Pawlowski states, "[Brian] forced himself to remain for the second show and found himself liking them more and more."

In The Anthology, none of The Beatles specify how long Brian remained at the lunchtime show, though George does state that Brian "afterwards came 'round to the band room." In Beatle! Pete Best states, that "at the end of a set" Brian "braved his way forward...and managed to have a word with George Harrison," but Pete doesn't indicate whether Brian remained for another set or not. Lewisohn, Coleman, Goldman, Brown, Geller, and others give no time frame for Brian's visit to the Cavern.

I elected to go with Norman and Pawlowski in this chapter. But what the truth is, we may never really know.

All events are documented except the song sung by John. That was not original. The song he actually sang was "Sweet Little Sixteen" by Chuck Berry. The song in this chapter is "Sweet Sixteen Lisa" by Rande Kessler.

*Most of the conversation is conjecture, although this one sentence is authentic. (Epstein, Cellarful of Noise, p. 47)

Wednesday, 15 November 1961
The Cavern Club,
Mathew Street
Liverpool

The Beatlettes were always there, part of the aura of the place – as much a part of The Cavern as The Beatles themselves. The girls seemed to live on Mathew Street, to belong to the tangled warehouses and narrow alleyways whose smoky brick walls were lined with weathered, wooden vegetable crates and pungent produce. Between sets, the girls nosed about the entrance of their underground haven and clustered in cliques. They lingered on long after the lunchtime show, gossiping, waiting, counting the minutes until the evening performance began.

Two, sometimes three hours before The Cavern opened for the night, they queued in Mathew, pressing chest to back as they nudged closer to the door, vying for position – competing to get choice seats in front of the tiny stage. Carrying small train cases crammed with make-up, hairspray, and brushes, the Beatlettes waited in hair rollers and amused one another, reliving lunchtime escapades and fantasizing about a night alone – even an hour alone – with their favourite Beatle.

Most of them were hungry. Admission to two sessions required all the money they had. Most couldn't afford the "nudger and loop de loop" that comprised the Cavern lunch. Their flat, young bellies were empty.

"Eh!" They spied local promoter Sam Leach, with a half-eaten Eccles cake in his hand, on his way to The Grapes. "Eh yew! Give us a bice!"

"See 'im! He's loaded!"

"Yeah, c'mon! Y'orta! Give it up, luv!"

"We're all dead skint here!"

Leach quickened his pace and looked in another direction. He had no fondness for Bob Wooler's "punters," male or female. Wooler was his primary competition Merseyside, and these girls were feeding the fire of The Cavern's popularity. Leach's Brighton Tower Ballroom needed The Beatles as much as The Cavern did, and Sam had tried every tactic in the book to sign the lads at his own facility. He'd no sympathy for the Mathew Street "bairds." These hangers-on were Wooler's patrons.

"Scrooge, yew!" a girl with pink sponge curlers tied up in a flimsy green scarf shouted after him.

Sam drew his teatime sweet closer and dared not take a bite of it.

"Where's yer 'urry, mate?" Another tried a softer approach. "Come back, eh? We're all friends here, right?"

"Ah, eez got moths in his wallet, Jeri!" A shivering girl with a ponytail shook her head.

"He wooden givyerra spot iffnee 'ad pimples," said another.

"Yer," came Jeri's high-pitched complaint, "His pockets are all sewn up – that one!"

"Ee won't crack on! Ee's all Mutt and Jeff."

"Eh, mister!" came a last desperate cry. "Givvus sum, right?"

But Sam had reached the black lacquered door to The Grapes and disappeared inside without a glance in their direction. The girls booed, hissed, and cursed his very existence and then continued to complain, trying to distract themselves from the cold and the aching in their bellies.

"I'm gazumped, how about yew?"

"Yeah, I'd love to visit the back o'me eyelids fer a few."

"Me head's gorra train runnin' through it. Anyone have an asperro to loan?"

"Sorry, luv. I'd gladly give it if I was carryin'."

The late November afternoon passed slowly for the line that snaked its way down the broken, uneven street. Shadows converged from the towering buildings on either side of Mathew, and breath became frosty at sunset. But in this narrow valley between high, brick walls, the biting Mersey winds were mitigated. In a still cold, the girls huddled and blew on their hands.

Tony Jackson, the handsome bass guitarist for The Searchers emerged from The Grapes brandishing a sheet of lyrics he'd scribbled out for Paul McCartney – "Some Other Guy." He cocked his head with a grin and waved to the crowd. Some of them squealed at The Searcher's thick, dark hair and polished good looks. Others only yelled out inquiries about The Beatles.

"Hey Tony, where's Paul thisavvy?"

"Have y'seen John 'round yet, Tony? He should be here by now, y'know."

"Where's Pete, Searcher?"

"More important," Tony shouted back, "where're yer coifs, luvs? Curlers? For the likes of Tony Jackson? Y'er drippy, all of ya!"

They giggled at his insults. They posed and pretended to primp their rolled up locks.

"Y'er a perve, Tony Jackson!" one yelled.

"Geroff, Searcher!" bantered another.

In the friendly squabble, few of them saw John Lennon approaching from St. John Street, a cigarette hanging from his bottom lip, his squinted gaze conjuring up James Dean. John walked quickly – his hands deep inside his pockets and his thoughts several hundred miles away, in Hamburg.

He'd had a letter from Stu this afternoon, and he carried it in his pocket right now. As close as John could gauge, it weighed well over a thousand pounds.

Long before he could see them, John could hear the girls laughing – their pitches shrill, their inexpensive perfumes part of the winter air. He looked at the blur that was the queue, growing clearer as he grew closer. Shapes became outlines; outlines, bodies; bodies, familiar friends. He knew most of them by sight and many of them by name, and ordinarily, he would've stopped and come to Tony's aid. But today he hoped to slip past them all unnoticed.

"Hey, it's Johnny!" One of them spotted him.

"John!"

"'Ullo, John Lennon!"

"And does yer muther know y'er out, Paige Lynette?" Despite his mood, John tried to be pleasant, playing on the words from an old British pub song.

"Yeah," she quipped back. "She's queued up as well…way back there!"

The others laughed.

He stopped and gave the lanky blonde a slow once-over. "And here I thought she'd gone off to the Mounties."

The crowd giggled at the obvious sexual innuendo.

"Ah, that's where y'er wrong, luv." The Bardot-like girl moved closer and touched the front of John's jacket. "That was *me*, y'heard about. Me mum's gorra face like an ole man's knee!"

John smiled feebly, then cupped the girl's hands in his calloused, nicotine-stained palms and moved her gently away. He stepped towards The Cavern door.

"Wait John!" an unfamiliar voice called out. "I - I bought yer record in NEMS. D'ya mind signin' it for me, then?"

A shy wisp of a girl who looked far too young to be eighteen stepped forward, held out a disc, and offered a pen. Her hands trembled. John walked over and took the record and pen from her.

"D'ya have a name then, luv?" His dismal face softened.

"Margaret. Margaret Dorothy," she stammered. She looked at him from under a fringe of heavy, blunted bangs.

"Ah, Maggie May," he smiled sadly at her. "'ullo Maggie. Pleased to meet ya, luv." The bawdy sailor's song hardly fit the girl, but she smiled back, complimented to be compared with the sexy lady of Lime Street.

To Maggie, Luv Ever, John, he signed the record. Then he held it for a moment, staring at her pale cheeks and disoriented eyes. It was almost more than he could stand today, especially in light of Stu's news.

"And what've y'had to eat thisavvy, Margaret Dorothy?" he asked.

"Um," she glanced at the others, "not much really. None of us have, y'know." She indicated the first six girls in the front of the line. "We've been *here* all afternoon, from lunchtime on. We were afraid of losin' our place in th'queue, as it were."

"We knew that if we went off," Paige explained, "there'd be plenty others in front of us when we came back."

"Takin' our place – bargin' ahead as they will do," said another.

Paige told the truth. "We can't afford two Cavern sessions *and* a cob o'chuck as well."

"No…we'd rather see *you*," Margaret admitted.

"We'd rather starve to death…"

"That's so much shite!" John exploded, his already dark mood taking a nasty turn. "That's crap, all of it! I'm not fuggin' worth it! None of us are! We're just a band…not some kind of gods here…we're a rock'n'roll group, that's all! *Miss* a show now and then! Get out o'the fuggin' cold, as it were! Quit makin' it more'n it really is! Quit puttin' me up here," he lifted his hand, "when I'm only just here – just like you, just like everyfuggin'one else!"

"Wha…" Margaret was stunned.

"We won't leave!" The sixth Beatlette in line, a heavy-set, olive-skinned girl with dark brown eyes, shouted.

"We *won't* do!" came another. "You can't make us, John Lennon!"

"We won't go off somewhere 'n shove down lukewarm Scouse and sordid beets when y'er up on stage singin' 'Soldier o Love'!"

"I can't *believe* you'd ask us to go away!" Paige started to cry.

John didn't know how to respond to any of it. He didn't like tears, and he didn't know how to deal with them. The only women he'd ever known – the Stanley women – were strong, iron-willed, stoic, and firmly in control. But these glazed-eyed girls were surrendering their dignity and health in an uneven trade for blind obsession. Just like Stu.

Just like Stu…

"Fuggin'ell!" John spat out. Then he lunged towards the red, metal door of The Cavern without another word. He barged past doorman Paddy Delaney without the usual "hello" or chat and quickly skirted down the concrete stairs.

"Hard knock, yew!" one girl called out as the door clanged behind John.

"Stadium lad!" screamed another.

They berated him loudly as he took the narrow steps to The Cavern below. They hurled taunts that he tried not to hear. They yelled from the top of the stairwell – their insults just as dangerous as the full-blown infatuation they'd lavished on him only minutes ago. Both extremes had the potential to make him *feel* again, and today John wanted only to be numb.

Skidding a bit as the street-grit on his boots met the concrete Cavern floor, John stopped and let his eyes adjust to the underground room. He dug into his snug pants pockets and scrounged for loose change. But a small handful of coins was all he could manage.

"Seven bacon butties, Clifton, if y'don't mind." He slammed the money on the water-ringed snack bar. "And seven cups o' tea – sugar only…"

"For?" Cliff raised one eyebrow.

"It all goes up to the street. First seven girls in line, right?"

"Sure, right. Will do."

"And Cliff," John lowered his voice, "whatever you do…keep me fuggin' out of it, son."

The coins that John had coughed up were clearly ten bob short, but the experienced waiter began to fill the order anyway, wondering how The Beatles' enigmatic rhythm guitarist would manage the wee-hours bus fare all the way home to rural Woolton with pockets empty.

Lennon'd better hope Aspinall shows up with that tricky road van, as it were, Cliff mused as he worked. *It's a long fuggin' walk from here to Menlove Avenue and a right cold night to walk it in!*

****

"How goes it?" Paul's question was really an observation. It was an acknowledgement of the mood written on John's face.

"How d'ya think?" John smacked his gum and looked away.

Paul stood silently, lighting a cig and waiting for an answer. John would get around to it eventually.

"Stu's not comin' back Christmas." There. It was out. But sayin' it only made it worse.

Paul shifted his weight, took a drag, and listened. He clenched and unclenched his right hand in his coat pocket trying to exercise it back to warmth. The Cavern was still afternoon-cold. It was a full hour before the first punters would be admitted. Everything was empty and damp.

"Yeah?" he raised an eyebrow. "Not comin', is he? Not even for a few?"

"He can't fuggin' travel." John never made eye contact. "He's too ill for the ferry, even if that were a financial option."

"Said Astrid?" Paul pulled up a chair.

"Said Stu." John drew a sheet of paper from his jacket pocket and shook it. "Here. Have a look. And happy fuggin' chrimble to me!"

Paul crossed a boot over a knee and drew on his cig while he took the letter. He scanned it slowly, not really reading…stalling for time, searching for something positive to say. "Well…all right, then…in the spring, right? There's always that, y'know."

"There *isn't* that!" John snapped, his eyes now locked on Paul's. "Stu'll be pushin' up a gravestone by then! It'll be a word here and a word there and bless him thrice with handful of gravel on a coffin lid, as it were."

"He was well enough to write this, wasn't he?" Paul flipped the letter in his hand. "So it can't be all that bad…"

John almost whispered. "He doesn't know breakfast from Thursday. It's all a jumble of rave – that."

And Paul could see it was true. Stu's jagged, uneven lines of cursive trailed off into blurs and blobs. The irregularity of the letters, the points and valleys that filled the page geometrically hardly resembled handwriting at all.

> dear john
> very sad i cant write now….s precisely. i feel so sick and stupid and i…dfa astrid will have to pay thous…n doctors bills they say i must once back home when strong enough and examine mentally, i mean but….to, im not abler to come home for christams please exaplin to pauline, joyce, and all im not made as i keep saying…how many illness are caused thourgh physchological!
>
> im always sick
> i dont care if they put me in an insane asylum or…or a coupel of months im

always sick and then pain for a moment retreats but comes back with increased vigour

my illness is almost all psychological your understand mental i'm not mad or anything just not well adjusted
cant paint. cant walk very well without falling over the only thing is these headaches...
meanwhile, i go mad

you have a sadness that goes too deep for tears so deep it hardly becomes known to you think of me at christmas...we will be sad together

    Paul chewed his bottom lip and thought. Almost always, he managed to gloss over life's rough spots somehow. But what consolation could he offer for this?

    "Right." Paul finally raised his eyes from the page and handed it back to John. "All right. Seems rough…worse than it was a while back…worse than Jürgen made it seem in Paris…"

    "Worse? It's fuggin' *tragic*!" John cut him off. "And to think… 'I knew him, Horatio…a man of infinite jest.'"

    Paul pinched the bridge of his nose. "Yeah…Stu…a great artist, Stu. Great."

    "Is that all he is these days?" John snorted, looking away.

    Paul waited, knowing any answer would be the wrong one.

    "Stuart Sutcliffe, great artist," John sneered. "Stuart Sutcliffe – dearly beloved – painter, writer, cremator of furniture, one-time rock'n'roller…a man who thumbed his nose at the rest of the effin' world, who dressed as he pleased and lived as he liked. An artist who made his own fuggin' rules his own fuggin' way and fell in love with a pixie girl who transfixed him and stole him from the magical Beatles – and from his very best friend."

Paul took the last drag on his cig and tossed it down. "Yeah? Well, if he's all that, John…then you're bound to believe he'll…go on…to whatever's out there for someone as great as him."

"Huzzah." John's nostrils flared. "They'll likely make him Saint Stu and do a post mortem, a one-man show down at The Walker. They'll canonize his fuggin' birthplace and set laurels all around – leavin' only *me*, of course, to comfort Astrid 'n shut out a thousand things I wish I'd never think of again. To act unaffected and get on with me life…business as fuggin' usual! And never again to…" John's voice cracked. He waited a moment. "They'll act duly sad and say gratuitous things about him. But no one'll really give an excrement, of course…except that unlucky git, John Lennon, who'll be more of a corpse than Stu'll ever be."

John crumpled the letter and hurled it as far as he could.

If John had had any money at all, he would've hurried to The Grapes and knocked back as many Black and Tans as he could afford, blunting the pain with alcohol just as Stu, miles away, dulled his torture with liberal morphine. But up in Mathew Street, seven laughing girls were finishing the supper that John's money had supplied, and none of them would ever know the tremendous price their benefactor had actually paid.

This incident is modeled after a story related by Hillary Williams in Coleman's Lennon *(p.132).*

Stu's letter is a compilation of several letters written home to Liverpool in the winter of 1961. These can be found in Clayson and Sutcliffe's thorough, accurate, and excellent book, Backbeat.

The conversations are conjecture.

Tuesday, 21 November 1961
The Cavern Club
Mathew Street

He didn't know why he'd come here again. Really, there was no explanation. He didn't enjoy crowds or confusion or teenagers, and he loathed the claustrophobic heat. He gagged on the turgid smells that the "Cavern dwellers" called "pong." Nor had he come for the music. He didn't like rock'n'roll. Its immature rhythms and melodies fringed with simplistic rhyme were, in Brian's estimation, time-wasters.

But most of all, Brian hated the way The Cavern made him feel. He hated being different – being whispered about, pointed to. He resented being made to feel old at twenty-seven – being regarded as stuffy and strange.

Brian Epstein despised everything about The Cavern. Everything except The Beatles.

Sunday last, Brian had confided to his family that he envisioned some sort of business connection between the NEMS Top Twenty Chart and the Cavern Club groups. He'd explained to them that beat groups were springing up like wild mushrooms in the dank Liverpool clubs – beat groups with fans, beat groups with purchasing power in their clientele. Brian had explained all of this confidently to his father, Harry, his mother, Queenie, and his younger brother, Clive. But now – alone in a Cavern corner – Brian knew that was not the real explanation for his interest in the band.

His motivations were many and complicated – a candy jar jumble of desires.

Never successful at anything his parents had ever expected him to do and never happy with their choices, Brian had reached twenty-seven without fulfilling any expectations, even his own. He'd been expelled from school, hastily discharged from the army, dismissed from the Royal Academy of Dramatic Arts, and even relieved of his duty as furniture store manager for the Epstein conglomerate. Nothing he'd ever done had won his father's approval or equaled his brother's natural competence; nothing had merited the maternal love his mother never rescinded.

In all aspects of life, Brian considered himself a failure.

Oh, he dressed smartly enough – was the epitome of polish, the dictionary definition of "gentleman." He moved in all the right circles and in all the right ways. And he adeptly managed the Whitechapel music store.

But he knew and they knew that Brian ran NEMS only because no other outlet could be found for him. He had been relegated to Whitechapel only because he'd failed every other endeavor.

Being Jewish in a highly Roman Catholic and somewhat Anglican town was off-putting enough. Being wealthy in a town of working class families was yet another degree of separation. But being homosexual was the final curtain that draped Brian away from the world and left him desperate to prove his self-worth.

"Sorry, I'm tardy, Brian…orders…pressed me later than expected…and well, you know how it is. But here *you* are as usual – bang on time." Alistair Taylor fumbled with the wooden chair, negotiating the tiny corner space against the wall.

Brian sputtered from his reverie. He glanced at his watch. "You're fine," he said softly. "They're just about to begin, anyway. No apologies."

"It's a real pea souper out there, isn't it?" Alistair settled in. "Very January for a November. I can't say I remember when I…"

"They're starting." Brian held up his hand to silence conversation, but the club noise swelled to a roar. As the tiny door to the right rear of the platform stage opened and The Beatles emerged, cheers, applause, whistles, squeals, and screams arose. Paul waved. George gave a coy smile and eagerly hopped up on the stage. Pete nodded in his jacket of "cool." But John skulked to the boards without a glance at his constituents.

Brian's forehead wrinkled. He watched Lennon move towards his guitar, shoulder it, and then stand blankly, without enthusiasm, at the microphone. He didn't goad the audience or shout back at them. He wasn't even chewing gum. The boy's eyes were fish-dead. Something was wrong.

George's skillful lead sounded, giving the screams a melody, and the crowd noise diminished. Paul and Pete synchronized the bass and backbeat. And then John began to sing. He sang without caring, and he played a listless rhythm. Tonight nothing that was John was in the song.

But a girl near Brian and Alistair didn't notice, didn't care. She threw back her head and sang out loud, "That's what I wa-a-a-ant, yeah, and that's what I want!"

"Got'em goin', hasn't he?" Alistair cupped his hands and shouted over the furor. Brian nodded mechanically. But still, he watched John.

Paul was up next with a song Brian actually knew, "Till There Was You," the ballad from "The Music Man." It was a tune Brian generally enjoyed, and Paul's arrangement was quite nice, but it was impossible to concentrate on the offering. Brian watched John's eyes – dark and empty.

Now, George Harrison – the lad with whom Brian had spoken on his first visit – stood before the centre microphone and introduced the third selection. His back-in-the-throat, Scouse accent was so thick that the words congealed, but Brian deciphered "Hamburg" and "icy sea" and saw John's face twitch as the words were spoken.

"So then," George finished up, "this one's fer Stu 'n Astrid, then...'n all our mates over there, y'know. We're thinkin' of them thisavvy, from here to there and there to here – we wish 'em well. So here it is then...a song for Stu and all of you and for us as well...'A Taste of Honey.'"

Paul sang with clear, crystal control, negotiating the ballad into a Beatles' swing-rock rhythm that made it unique. But try as he might to like the innovation, Brian found it distasteful. He shook his head and scribbled on a napkin to Alistair: "I can't say that I admire this enormously."

Alistair smiled but shrugged noncommittally, trying to agree with his employer without criticizing the heroes of the moment.

And so the session went – almost identical to the last. The play list and arrangements were, by and large, completely predictable. The antics were the same. Virtually everything was as it had been on the ninth. Only John Lennon was different. Aloof, quiet, and removed, he was not the caged animal Brian had eyed a week ago. The boy was torpid, lethargic.

Until this very moment, Brian had decided to risk everything – to propose management of the musical group. But now he questioned the wisdom of it all. Was he making the right decision? Was the rhythm guitarist a risk he could afford? Would he be able to control the taciturn singer? Would he know how to deal with John's complexities?

Brian took a deep breath and straightened in his chair, weighing his liabilities, trying to decide what to do. The crowd around him laughed and clapped and swayed to the music without reservation, and none of them seemed to notice John's metamorphosis. They seemed as entranced as ever. Brian began to wonder if he were imagining it all, if he were – as his mother always insisted – merely stirring up a tempest in teapot.

When the last chord of the set sounded, and Alistair said, "Ready then?" Brian stood slowly. And as they began to thread their way back to the band room, he walked slower and slower. Brian would make the offer, just as he had planned, but without joy, full of misgivings – petrified he was making the greatest mistake of his life.

****

John's shirt was soaked to the skin, and it clung to him, cold and uncomfortable. With pinched fingers, he extracted it from his body, but immediately it sucked back in again – limpid, wet, and slimy. John shivered and rummaged through the band room debris for even the stub of a cig.

He hated being cold. His bent was toward warm and comfortable: scruffy slippers, worn tweed jackets, tattered robes two years past their prime, blankets that smelled of pets and winter fires, Ovaltine in thick white beakers with fat handles, and high-backed pub benches that hoarded heat. He liked tub baths, cafés with fireplaces, sweaters with turtleneck collars, and socks against an icy floor.

What he didn't like, Liverpool served up generously. Both Liverpool and Hamburg delivered bone marrow cold. *Hamburg.* He closed his eyes and took a deep breath. *Hamburg.*

"What now?" he barked at the knock on the band room door.

"Come in," Paul shouted almost simultaneously.

It was two men in suits and ties. John hardly looked at either of them. He lit a short, discarded fag, and sat down to wipe off his fret board.

"Hello," one of them offered.

"It's you again, eh?" George's voice had a smile in it. John glanced up briefly.

The one John now recognized as Brian Epstein from NEMS cleared his throat and fumbled over a few words. "Yes…I-I wanted to say to you all…that is, I wanted to formally introduce myself. I'm Brian Epstein, and this is my personal assistant, Alistair Taylor."

"Hello," Pete nodded cordially.

"Hello there," Paul walked over and shook hands with both of them.

John lifted his head again. He gave them a slow, once-over that sprouted splotches above Brian's collar.

"I want you to know that I've heard you sing several times," Brian avoided John's eyes, "and quite honestly, I think you're great."

The boys looked at each other. Screams they were used to. Applause they knew how to accept. But this one-on-one with a businessman was a little awkward.

"Right. Thanks very much," Paul nodded.

Brian cleared his throat and tried again. "I'd like to meet with all of you in the near future at my offices in Whitechapel…for a chat…to discuss the possibility of…of a mutually beneficial association with your group."

No one said a word.

"I think I might be able to be of some assistance to you – to promote you, as it were, in a positive way, to offer some rather valuable advice and direction."

They looked at one another.

"And when would this meeting be, then?" Pete stepped forward.

"Well," Brian took a breath, glancing briefly at Alistair, "how about 3 December, then…a Sunday afternoon?"

"Sorry." Pete shook his head. He knew their schedule for the next three weeks by heart. "We've a gig at The Casbah that night."

"We'd have to be done in time to set up, y'see," Paul explained.

"It takes time – settin' up," George offered.

"Yes, well...our business would be concluded long before your evening programme would begin," Brian assured them. "And it needn't be a long, protracted meeting, you understand, just a casual chat – a chance to organize our ideas."

"Three December?" Pete shifted questioning eyes to John. "Yeah, all right, we'll be there."

"Whitechapel NEMS," Brian stated redundantly, fiddling with his tie.

"I think we can find that well enough," George grinned.

"Sure, why not?" Paul gave a warm smile and a toss of the head. "Three December it is."

"Yeah...we'll come and see *you* next time," George teased with a straight face.

"Yes, yes of course. Great then." Brian edged his way out of the room. "Three December, in the afternoon."

"Nice meeting you all." Alistair threw in. "Tarrah then."

"Yeah, t'rah," one of them responded.

It wasn't until the door closed that Brian really began to breathe again. John Lennon's glare had almost unnerved him entirely. He'd almost lost the resolve to suggest a meeting after all. He'd almost forgotten everything he'd planned to say.

But at last the fantasy that had been swirling around in his head for eleven days had begun to take shape. He had delivered his proposal and made the first move towards reality.

Of course, my next conversation must be with Rex Makin, Brian noted. The long-time family solicitor would be essential to his business plan.

But beyond the obvious legal assistance, Brian realized that he also needed to chat with all of the Liverpool promoters who'd had any dealings with The Beatles in the last few years. Bob Wooler, Charlie McBain, Sam Leach, Brian Kelly, Joe Flannery – he'd made a list of names that had been linked with The Beatles on his colourful NEMS posters. He'd invited Bill Harry over for a sherry as well; no one knew the ins and outs of Merseyside as well as Bill.

But most of all, Brian wanted to have a long, serious talk with The Beatles' former manager, Allan Williams. Before plunging headlong into an investment that could cost him his last pound and his last vestige of family pride, Brian wanted to know the truth about the boys Williams had sent off to Scotland and Hamburg, Germany. He wanted to hear all the facts from the man who knew The Beatles better than anyone else.

Brian was not too proud to admit that he needed Williams' help...especially with the mercurial John Lennon. With John in the mix, Brian was vulnerable – dangerously so.

I have tried to stay faithful to Brian's version of this story. However, the conversation is imagined. I refer you Epstein's book A Cellarful of Noise *(p.41-48) for any details I might have missed.*

Friday, 1 December 1961
The Adelphi Hotel
City Center
Liverpool

Tastefully draped in seasonal evergreens and fat butter cream lights, the Adelphi's Grand Dining Room was elegantly lovely. Sheltered beneath wedding cake layers of white dental moulding, the voices of Liverpool's elite were hushed; the clink of Waterford crystal, muted. Even the exquisite candled chandeliers, two stories above, were polite – casting a kind glow on the mature diners.

In shaded nooks of the immense room, tuxedoed waiters stood obsequiously, seeing nothing but noticing everything, serving anonymously, personifying trite expectations of service right down to the linen hand towels draped dramatically across their forearms. Dining at The Adelphi was an affair.

But for the Epsteins, it was simply a family tradition, something to be expected rather than celebrated, something to be enjoyed. It was merely another Friday evening together – an occasion almost taken for granted.

"Yes, it *was* helpful." Brian leaned towards his brother, two years his junior, "albeit lengthy and tiring. I mean, any trek into London has its downside, doesn't it? But it gave me the opportunity to speak directly with the manager of His Master's Voice in Oxford Street about The Beatles and…"

"Ugh!" Harry had already heard enough to convince him that his son's latest obsession with rock'n'roll was just another of Brian's many "flings." Drama school, classes in fashion design, art studies – the boy's fits of passion wearied him.

Brian flushed. He sat back in his chair and daubed the corners of his mouth with a thick, linen napkin.

"And…" Clive ignored his father's skepticism, "what advice did he give you?"

"Yes, dear, what did the man in London say?" Queenie Epstein turned her full attention to her eldest son.

"A great deal, actually," Brian began, his left eye tick betraying him.

"Both he and the manager of Keith Prowse's music shop were extremely helpful…very practical in spelling out the various duties and responsibilities of a manager."

"*I* could've told you the duties of a manager!" Harry Epstein growled. He sliced his minted leg of lamb with aggravated fervour.

"Yes, and most of what they said," Brian continued, "*was* redundant. Old news. I already knew most of it from watching you…and from talking with Rex Makin."

"Rex!" his father exploded. "You've gone so far as to insinuate *our family solicitor* into this nonsense? This fly-by-night…"

"Harry," Queenie said quietly. She placed her soft, jeweled hand firmly on her husband's arm.

"Well…of course, I-I had to…" Brian began to stammer, but Clive cut him off.

"Right, of course! And I'm sure Mr. Makin agreed that you ought to give it a whirl…thought the venture feasible." Clive hoped his assumption was correct. Brian needed some validation – quickly.

"Actually," Brian cut his eyes at his father, "he did not."

No one said a word. A mustached waiter refilled the tall, perspiring water goblets and then disappeared into the shadows once again. One goblet wobbled tenuously, threatening to spill, but with a single motion, Queenie stilled it.

"Rex called The Beatles' project, if I remember correctly," Brian drew himself upright in his chair, "'just another Epstein idea.'"

Harry groaned and began to massage between his eyebrows. Queenie nudged her plate of cinnamon-spiced roast beef and braised asparagus away with one finger and stared at her son.

"And *is it*, Brian?" she asked. "*Is* this new infatuation a…a fleeting interest?"

"Something," Harry echoed, "you'll lose interest in once the real work begins…once you're out there pounding the streets for recording studios or wading knee-deep in paperwork and sorting through the red tape of contract negotiations?"

Brian was accustomed to his father's disapproval, but his mother's doubts jabbed deeply. She was the one person he'd never disillusioned, no matter what. She was the only one who still believed he could do anything he imagined.

Brian folded his napkin and placed it on the table. He gathered his thoughts.

"The way I see it," he cleared his throat, "against all odds that I should ever be impressed by a collection of rock'n'roll musicians, four untrained local lads managed to spin up such a whirlwind of publicity around themselves that I – an established entrepreneur – took notice and gave them an audition, of sorts."

Queenie nodded. Harry "hmmpfed."

"Knowing a great deal about music in general," Brian looked at Clive who was nodding in agreement, "although admittedly very little about rock'n'roll in particular, I was, nevertheless, impressed with the group's live performance. I found them...energetic and compelling – even stunning in their own way. Full of excitement. Unique."

"'Special,' I believe you said," Clive offered.

Harry sighed and leaned on the tapestried arm of his chair. He looked at his two sons with fatigue.

Brian went on. "Once inside The Cavern Club – The Beatles' primary venue in Mathew Street – I watched as two hundred teenagers reacted vehemently to the group, as they became enamoured not only with the music these four young men played but with the very *personalities* of the musicians-slash-actors."

"Actors?" Queenie asked.

"That's right," Clive jumped in. "Brian says they cavourt all over the stage...telling jokes and shouting at the audience...interacting with the patrons, the groundlings, as it were...just as in Shakespeare's day."

"The very least of their charm, however," Brian frowned. It wasn't a detail he would've chosen to share with his parents.

"And the very thing a good manager should discourage!" Harry hissed.

"Quite." Brian nodded. "One of the things I intend to change."

"But managing a musical group..." Harry gave the idea credibility by even considering it. "It's a job, Brian...a *job*, not a pastime! It's a serious commitment to four other people who would be entrusting their careers into your hands, into your *inexperienced* hands, if you will."

"I realize that, Father." Brian knew he had an audience now. "But it's also a once-in-a-lifetime shot at something beyond Whitechapel, beyond Liverpool – perhaps beyond England."

"A Scouse rock'n'roll band *beyond England*?" Harry closed one eye sardonically. "A bit overblown, isn't it?"

"Let me ask you this." Queenie raised a hand demonstratively and then placed it on Brian's arm. "Has this group of young musicians ever had or wanted to have a manager heretofore? Would *you* be the first manager they've worked for? Do they see value in having someone direct their career paths? Do they *want* that kind of interference?" She took a short breath. "What do The Beatles think about having a manager?"

Brian withdrew an engraved, sterling cigarette case from his inside coat pocket and opened it, offering his mother the first selection. She declined, but Clive and Harry joined him as the waiter emerged from invisibility – lighter in hand.

The pause gave Brian a minute to consider his mother's questions.

"All right," he began, taking a slow drag and then releasing it over his left shoulder, "Yes, no, and I'm not sure, three times – in that order." Brain smiled a little, for the first time all night. Then he took another drag on the cigarette. His hand trembled perceptibly.

"Bore me with the details, son," Queenie commanded.

Brian stalled. It was hard to know where to begin.

"All right," he smiled at her. "No, The Beatles have no manager at present, although I'm told several local promoters are crouched, waiting in the wings. I've heard rumours that Sam Leach, who directs extravagant rock and roll shows at Brighton Tower Ballroom, has designs on the group. And several others are interested as well. But for the time being, they've all adopted a 'wait and see' attitude."

"Because?" Harry rolled his hand.

"Because, for one thing, they're intimidated by the powerful presence of one of the lads' mothers...a lady named Mona Best, the former wife of boxing promoter, Johnny Best. She owns The Casbah Club in West Derby and is, by all reports, a clever, undaunted businesswoman who stands guard over her son, Pete, and over the rest of the boys...in a maternal sort of way."

"So *she's* serving as their manager at present?" Harry leaned in.

"No, she hasn't officially assumed the role," Brian explained, "but she has secured several bookings for them in the last year. And I know that raises the obvious question: since Mrs. Best is in the perfect, key position to become The Beatles' manager, why hasn't she done so?"

"Spot on." Harry shifted his weight in the armchair.

"*My* questions first, Harry." Queenie insisted.

"All right, all right." Brian's animation increased. "You asked me if The Beatles have ever had another manager, and the answer is yes, they have. About a year ago, The Beatles were sent on a tour of Scotland and then on to Hamburg, Germany, by a rather flamboyant, Liverpool-born Welsh entrepreneur. Actually, you both may know him or know of him...Allan Williams?"

"The Jacaranda owner," Clive added.

"And the owner of The Blue Angel in Seel Street," Brian said.

"Williams." Harry crushed out his cigarette in the flat, silver ashtray bearing the Adelphi coat of arms. "I've heard of him. Who hasn't? Lots of rumours surrounding the burning of his club in City Center some months ago, you know."

Brian nodded and took a sip of water. "Williams is shrewd. From what I can tell, he's a survivor in the business world."

Queenie leaned back from the table as the waiter cleared the plates and brushed crumbs into a silent butler. "Well if he's so shrewd, Brian, then why did he relinquish your beat group? If they're all you say they are, and if *he's* so savvy...then why did he let them go?"

"I don't know the answer to that question, Mother," Brian admitted. "But I intend to find out. As a matter of fact, I've an appointment with Mr.

Williams tomorrow evening at The Blue Angel, right after I close shop."

"Good," Queenie smiled. "Get the answers."

"All right, back to Mrs. Best," Harry redirected.

"Mrs. Best." Brain sighed, trying to give an honest answer. "I think Mona Best has her hands full. I mean, she's single-handedly running a teen club – a very successful teen club – right in her own home." He paused momentarily as the waiter delivered his pot of tea. "Night after night, so they tell me, teens pour into the Best's Casbah out in West Derby, and Mrs. Best is responsible for supplying refreshments, providing a safe, clean atmosphere, booking a host of energetic bands to entertain the crowds, and so forth. Quite simply, I think she's over-extended at the moment."

"Brian, Brian, Brian." His father shook his head. "There are so many holes in that story, it could function as a fishing net." The table fell silent. Brian knew his father wasn't wrong. "Is it possible, son," Harry's voice softened, "that you would listen to me, just once?"

Brian's face was impassive. His eyes met his father's, but they revealed nothing.

Taking the silence as consent, Harry leaned into the family circle with voice lowered. "If I were you," he said, "I would approach this venture as if it were the *last thing* in this world I actually wanted to do. I would let myself be swayed into managing The Beatles only if the merits far outweighed the risks."

"Um-hm," Brian nodded.

"And if things don't progress as you imagine they will," Queenie reminded him, "you know you can always run the record store, dear. Whitechapel NEMS belongs to you."

"Yes," his voice was small. "NEMS."

"I realize that seems unglamorous, Brian," Harry signed the check the waiter brought him, "but trust me, son…you can always sleep easy at night when you run a reliable business."

"Your father knows." Queenie smiled at her husband. "We both do. There's something to be said for security, you know – for respect in the community, for the comfort of solid reputation."

Brian nodded and took a sip of his tea. Clive gave him a nudge of courage under the table.

But before the nudge could spawn a rebuttal, Harry stood and helped his wife from her chair. He offered her his arm and began the slow, traditional Friday evening exit from the dining room. Saying goodnight to friends and associates, nodding at those less familiar, and being careful to ignore no one, Harry and Queenie Epstein moved through the room with dignity.

Behind them, the two Epstein boys walked together, talking quietly and nodding politely to those bound for performances at the Empire or Philharmonic.

"Never mind that I hadn't finished my Darjeeling," Brian whispered to his brother.

"Ah, you'll have to move quicker next time, won't you?" Clive grinned.

"Story of my life so far," Brian shook his head. "Harry…always at the helm."

"Only *so far*?" Clive smirked handsomely.

"Yes," Brian nodded, "because it's all about to change, Clive. This time *I'm* going to be in control. I've thought it through carefully and outlined a plan, and in the next ten days, everything will fall in line. Mother and Father may be skeptical – you all may be – but I promise you, this liaison with The Beatles is going to be a real turning point for me. It's going to be a whole new future for us all."

"So?" Clive patted his wallet and smiled. "Should *I* invest in the project, then?"

"Yes," Brian said with certainty, "without a doubt. Trust me, Clive. You'd be well advised to do that."

Although the primary source for information about Brian Epstein is his autobiography, A Cellarful of Noise, *I also recommend reading Debbie Geller's definitive work,* In My Life: The Brian Epstein Story. *Her interviews with family members, close friends, and business associates reveal many aspects of this talented, complicated man.*

The Epsteins did, in fact, have a tradition of dining at The Adelphi on a Friday night. And Harry's reticence is also authentic. Brian had traveled to London to visit Keith Prowse's shop and the manager of His Master's Voice in Oxford Street prior to this dinner. And he had actually talked with Rex Makin and scheduled the appointment with Allan Williams as well. The holiday decorations are authentic, described from my trip to Liverpool in late November 1999. Only the family's conversation and menu selections are conjecture.

Saturday, 2 December 1961
20 Forthlin Road
Allerton

Jim McCartney wasn't sure why he objected, really. "It's just…I can't understand why an established entrepreneur like Brian Epstein of *the Liverpool Epsteins* would be interested in your kind of music at all!" He paced and debated with his son.

"Well, he does own a record store, y'know." Paul was annoyed. He'd never anticipated reservations on his father's part.

"And I play jazz! But that doesn't make me an aficionado of rock'n'roll, now does it? And it certainly hasn't inspired me to become the manager of a rock'n'roll band!"

Paul folded his arms. "But then you aren't Brian Epstein, are you? I mean, he makes his livin' sellin' rock'n'roll records, doesn't he? He writes a regular article for Bill Harry's 'Mersey Beat.' And his store's situated only steps from The Cavern…right in the middle of it all!"

"And for years I've worked in the vicinity of a chimney sweep's, son, but you don't see me wearin' a top hat and flyin' down flues." Jim plopped into his favourite, overstuffed chair and picked up the daily *Echo*. Flicking it open, he disappeared behind the football scores. Paul waited his father out.

"What's the man proposing exactly?" came the tired voice from behind the newspaper.

"Nothing yet," Paul sat down and brought his socked feet up onto the sofa while his father wasn't watching. "We're to meet him, all of us, tomorrow in Whitechapel. We're to think about mutual interests…ways in which we could all be beneficial to one another."

"To what end?"

"I dunno…he only said he wants us to meet with us."

"A meeting with no agenda?"

"I suppose he wants to offer us management, as it were."

Jim moved the paper to aside. "He suggested that?"

"In a way."

"In what way, Paul?"

"Well…he mentioned a 'liaison' as he called it… an agreement between us and him that could have a mutual advantage for all concerned."

"Good God! It sounds as if he's trying to sell you life insurance!"

"Right! Yeah. I'll bet that's it." Paul pinched his nose a couple of times quickly. It always tickled madly when he was aggravated.

Jim closed the paper and folded it in half. Then he leaned towards his son, his arms resting on his knees. "Remove your feet from your mother's sofa, and I'll tell you what we'll do." He had softened his tone. "You'll go to that meeting tomorrow, and you'll listen very carefully, won't you? Then, if you're truly interested in what he proposes, we'll have your Mr. Epstein in. And…we'll have Olive 'round as well."

Jim stood and clasped his hands behind his back. He began to pace slowly as a plan unfolded. Olive Johnson was the neighbourhood social sanctioner. She was Forthlin Road's "Ambassador to the World." Having done more and experienced more than her provincial Allerton friends, she was the first and last word in respectability. Olive Johnson knew an imposter when she met one – or so she said, and so everyone in Forthlin Road believed.

"Oh, right, Olive!" Paul threw his eyes to the ceiling. "Now there's a *real* authority in the realm of contractual agreements."

"You *do* want my permission, young sir?" Jim stopped and raised an eyebrow.

"Yerrokay. Right." Paul sighed and let his head fall back into the soft cushions.

"Olive'll be just the one to sort this all out…" Jim mused.

"Great. Good. Invite 'er over then!" Paul threw up his hands. "By all means, invite the world over, if that's what it takes."

"The world wouldn't be interested, son," Jim said, dryly.

"Oh, I think they might," Paul said. And he wasn't kidding. He was pretty sure this was a "Colonel Tom Parker" kind of decision. Both he and John were convinced that this was a decision that the world would have a real, vested interest in.

****

25 Upton Green
Speke

"He's *rich*, y'know!" George sat with his mum at the worn, green Formica table. His eyes danced as they always did when he was talking about the band.

"Right, but is he decent – that one?" his mother asked. She unfolded trading stamps, dampened them with a sponge, and plastered them into the yellowed redemption book. "I mean…is he the sort man who…"

"He drives a Ford Zodiac, Epstein does," George emphasized.

"And *that* makes him a good man?" Louise paused, lowering her chin questioningly.

"Well, if not good," George grinned, "then at least not daft!"

"You need a *good manager*, Georgie." Louise had thought so for some time now. She wasn't always happy with the decisions that Mona Best made for her son's band. But Mona was a woman not to be wrangled with. Louise always gave Mona Best and Mimi Smith wide berths.

"We need a manager, *period*," George agreed. "We can't keep sortin' it all out for ourselves, can we? We're all hit and miss these days."

"Right, right. A manager's the only way to get to London," Louise nodded.

"Well, actually," George got up and gave his mother a quick hug, "there are the rails, y'know."

"Oh the rails," she smiled a sweet Scouser's smile. "Of course the rails! I'd almost forgotten all about them."

****

The Kardomah Café
City Center, Liverpool

John almost fell into the shabby Glastonbury chair. Tossing his packages on the floor and kicking his feet out dramatically, he exhaled audibly, puffing both cheeks.

He'd been out for almost three hours Christmas shopping for Cyn, and it had been punishing. The stores in City Centre were burgeoning this close to the holidays, and John had quickly exhausted his tiny reserve of patience with the questioning, clutching, shoving Yuletide hunters and gatherers. He was tired of hearing, "Happy Christmas, luv!" and "Cheers to you and yours, wack!" John needed a shot of caffeine, quickly.

"Hey gerl!" he barked at the Kardomah waitress. He was in no mood to be polite.

"Yeah, yeah." Toweling off a table and daubing her face with her shirtsleeve, the wiry Scouse girl balanced a stack of teacups and saucers in one hand. "What'll y'have?" she asked perfunctorily, but when she turned to look at the boy beside her, a smile threatened her dour lips. John's thick, purple mohair sweater was the strangest thing she'd seen all day.

"Givvus a java," John spat. "And while y'er at it…a packetacigs as well." He needed nicotine, too.

The waitress bit her lip and tried not to laugh at the wack's odd garb. "Fags're over there," she offered wryly, nodding to a cigarette dispenser in the corner.

"Yeah right," John grumbled, too tired to clue into to the girl's innuendo. He struggled out of his chair like an injured man. "Yer service is amazin'ly above and beyond, isn't it?"

"*Least* I can do," the girl returned.

"The very," John hissed. Then he dragged himself across the room to the vending machine, regretting every antic he'd performed at The Casbah the night before. His calves and hamstrings ached. His lower back was stiff and unforgiving. Even the tips of his calloused fingers stung as he unraveled the slick plastic wrapper.

"Well, well, yes – John Lennon, yes! You've aged a bit, now haven't you…now that you've left the sunny world of art for the seamy side of life?" It was June Furlong, John's friend from his art school days. He hadn't seen the lithe model in months, not since The Cavern had become his only palette. But the months had only been kind to the willowy thirty-one-year old. Even bundled in her layered December garb, she was a "dazzler."

John hunched his back and hobbled towards her dramatically, using an invisible cane as he went. "But even at half the man I once was…" he cackled, "I'm moreova a man than you'll ever get from anyone else, Junie June."

"Oh right, right…is thasso?" June unwrapped her silk scarf and smiled at his fun and nonsense. It was good to see John as cocky and confident as ever. June had always found the boy roguish. She liked Lennon both in spite of and because of his arrogance.

"Order up!" The waitress set a lone cup and spoon in the middle of John's table.

"Yeah, well we'll have another…and a plate of biscuits as well for the famous model here." John pointed to June. "You *will* join me in a cuppa, won't you, Miss Famous Furlong?"

"I dunno! I dunno! With you all decked out in that lady's sweater, as it were?" June raised an eyebrow and clucked. "No, no, no…I think I'd better disassociate myself from that unusual get-up, as it were!"

"It's a *man's* sweater!" John's nostrils flared. "And an expensive one, at that!"

June could see she'd hit a nerve. John loved to tease everyone else, but he always had a tear of a time on the receiving end. June had frequently seen the boy jump to his own defense, even when no defense was called for. John Lennon always "had his back up," and today was no exception.

"Pfffffff!" June brushed him off. "It's very much a lady's sweater, isn't it? I know a lady's sweater when I see one. But quite nice – that – lovely."

"It's straight out of a *men's* store in St. John Street!"

"Borrowed it from Cynthia, did you, then?" June goaded him.

"Look!" John began to peel off the plush, purple mohair, right in the middle of the café. "Read the fuggin' label, Furlong! What's it say? Right there. Read *that*!"

"Yes, yes, all right. Austin Reed Haberdashery. Nice, quite nice."

"Austin Reed…that's a *men's* store, isn't it?" he insisted.

"Yes, all right, yes. Very masculine, Austin Reed. Great store, Austin Reed. Great." June removed her plum coloured coat and took a seat at his table. There was a time to rattle John's cage and a time to retreat. The boy was irascible. You could only push him so far. Like every great artist with whom June had worked, Lennon had to be managed.

"Hey yew! Keep yer clothes on inside The Kardomah!" the waitress yipped as she delivered June's coffee.

John pulled the sweater back over this head. "Only if you'll givvus a kiss, luv!" He batted his eyelashes rapidly and pursed his lips, but the harried girl ignored him.

"Oh yes, John Lennon, yes! As incorrigible as ever, aren't you?" June stirred a teaspoon of sugar into her cup. "Always up to no good!

"Incorrigible!" John sat down beside her, smiling at his uncle's pet word. "How'd ya know that's me effin trademark?"

"Takes one to know one," June smiled. "Cheers, luv." Their ceramic beakers clinked.

John took a large gulp of the burnt black liquid, reached in his pocket and donned his glasses, and looked with June over Whitechapel for moment. Shoppers, businessmen, children just off school, delivery boys on rusted bicycles – all Merseyside spun before them like a board of game whirling tops, colourful and pivoting madly into one another. John and June took it in – relieved to be still for a while.

"So," he cut his eyes at his friend, "how's the world of ole Van Gogh these days, life model?"

June leaned back in her chair. "Great, great, lovely as usual…but we ask ourselves from time to time what's become of you, y'know!"

"It's more believable you ask what's become of Stu." John cupped both hands around his beaker. "He's the one the art world always kowtowed to – George Jardine, Arthur Ballard, Teddy Griffiths…"

"Oh yes, yes, and you're the misbegotten, mistreated pariah," June smiled. "Persecution stalking you at every turn. It's rough – that. Rough."

John slurped his coffee. "I never was a favourite son at Liverpool College of Art."

"And you were never nose-to-the-grindstone either, were you now?"

"Why work myself into an early grave," John's voice razored, "the way Stu has?"

"So it's true?" June was instantly serious. "He's not well – Stu?"

"Y'wouldn't even recognize him."

"But…at first…we'd heard great things! Great, great, amazing things. We'd heard Eduardo Paolozzi had taken him on as an apprentice and…."

"Right." John's removed his glasses. His eyes narrowed. "The only problem is…death's graciously agreed to take him on as well."

There was nothing either of them could say to mitigate the tragedy at the table. They nursed their coffees and avoided each other's eyes.

When the bells on The Kardomah door clanked as someone exited into the cold, June jumped. And John, reawakened to the moment, assumed his best Rob Wilton voice and plastered on a comedian's smile.

"The day the war broke out," he mimicked the famous comic, "me missus says to me, she says, 'Now what are *you* going to do about it?'"

Then just as quickly, the hollow smile vanished.

June took a deep breath. "You can't do anything about Stuart, John. No, no, no – it's all out of your hands. Out of your hands completely." She searched for the right words to say, but everything seemed insufficient. "It's all…fate, what happens to us. All…"

"Yeah," John's voice was bitter, "and so was the war, Junie June. But that's the punch line of the fuggin' joke, isn't it?"

For a few minutes, they said nothing. They listened to the couple next to them reviewing their shopping list and checking off presents purchased. Licorice Allsorts for Nigel, a gauzy scarf with raised, velvet flowers for Auntie Beryl, and naturally, a Liverpool football club scarf for Oscar's Uncle Ned. The husband repeatedly said, "Check!" after each name discussed.

"So…how's John Lennon, then?" June asked. She rarely ever called him John; it was always "JohnLennon" as if his name were all one word. "How's the band?"

"We played the Merseyside Civil Service club last month," he said, throwing his eyes to the ceiling.

"Oh, fantastic! Right! The coveted Merseyside Civil Service Club! The pathway to fame and fortune – that!" she laughed the laugh of one who is grateful for humour.

"Actually," John slid his cup to one side and leaned across the table, "there *is* a bit of news, as it were."

"Right? Yeah? Good. Go on." Anything to distract him from Stu.

"We've been offered a manager."

"Offered a manager?" It was a weird way to phrase it. June couldn't tell if John was pleased, annoyed, or amused.

"Yeah, someone wants to manage us, y'know…manage the group."

"Great! Great! Wonderful!"

"Except it's Brian Epstein," John divulged, "the record man. North End Music Stores, y'know. That one." John assumed his radio announcer's persona. "North End Music Stores! The finest record selections in the North, NEMS now open Thursdays 'til 6 P.M. and Saturdays, 6:30 P.M."

"Very good, that." June relaxed. She leaned back in her chair and ran her fingers through her hair. "So…what about this Brian Epstein, then? Shop owner, record man. Epstein of the furniture Epsteins. Rather odd match-up, wouldn't you say?"

John looked around and lowered his voice. "I'm afraid that's the operative word."

June frowned.

"Word has it," he glanced at the couple beside them and then leaned in closer, "…rumour has it Epstein's a bit…light on his feet, if y'know what I mean."

"Oh?" June's eyes widened. Homosexuality was a topic rarely discussed in mixed company, in any company.

"Airy-fairy, as they say," John continued.

"And?" June waited for John's appraisal of the situation.

"And so…we're in limbo, as it were." He leaned back in his chair, confession over. "None of us can decide what to do."

They sipped their coffees.

"Can he manage a rock'n'roll group – this Epstein?" June was ever practical. She'd been responsible for her family fortune since her early twenties and had realized, early on, that prejudice had no place in business decisions whatsoever.

"Well, he runs the music store, doesn't he?" John shrugged. "And he's made a lot of money, I'm told. I mean, the man wears expensive suits and drives his own car, what have you."

"And his employees?" June interrogated. "How do *they* react to him? More to the point, how do they act when he's not around?"

"I dunno," John gave it some thought. "They seem to like him in a strange sort of way. They seem to think ole Cap'n Blye runs a tight ship…but they appear to respect that. I mean, they call him Mr. Brian, not Mr. Epstein. And they all do what he says…in their own creative ways, y'know."

"And is that the sort of leadership you could live with, John Lennon?" the model raised an eyebrow. "Could *you* get along with a Cap'n Blye?"

"I don't know, now do I?" John said honestly. "And I wouldn't know until I'm well into it, would I? Until well after I'd signed on the dotted line, as it were."

They were quiet again.

"Have you ever had a hit record, John Lennon?" June's high cheekbones lifted as she smiled.

"Not yet," John shot back.

"Ever made it to the hit parade? Ever been on a radio programme, on television – on the BBC, as it were?"

John knew exactly where the experienced model was taking this. "You know I fuggin' haven't," he nodded, "and what's more, you know I'd fuggin' love to!"

"Well, then," June paused. "What have *you* got to lose?"

John cut his eyes at her and began to smile.

"Right," he said quietly. "What have *I* got to lose? What the fuggin'ell has any of us got to lose at this stage of the proceedin's?"

"Those who have much are often afraid to risk," June elaborated.

"Ah, the Haves of the world," John said hoarsely.

"Right, right, yes…the Haves, the Haves! The ones who won't risk their medium sacks of gold on even an amazing, incredible toss of the die!"

"Afraid to gamble it away."

"Reticent, close to the vest…" June waved a hand. "But *you, you…*"

John finished the sentence for her, "Have no sack…and wild aspirations!"

"And gambling," June made her point, "is the only way…"

"To the toppermost of the fuggin' poppermost!" John shared his watchword with her.

Considered in that light, it all seemed so simple. John was a little irritated he hadn't seen it for himself.

George had given up his electrician's apprenticeship. Paul had walked away from a promising career as a teacher. Pete lived only to drum. And The Beatles were all John had.

"And if it all bottoms out, eventually?" June suggested.

"Then all right, then," John said. "Because I'll already, in some sense, have had it all, won't I?"

"Exactly," June said. "Exactly what I think. Exactly what I've always thought."

And the two old friends smiled at one another.

This story was lovingly shared with me by June Furlong, and June has read this chapter and made corrections so that it is completely accurate. All details, including John's purple mohair sweater from Austin Reed's, are true. Only the conversation is imagined. The quote, "What have you got to lose?" is authentic.

Saturday Evening, 2 December 1961
The Blue Angel
Seel Street
Liverpool

The Blue Angel's piano bar was comfortably intimate. Washed in pale turquoise light, Allan's pianist, Duggie, offered up a blend of old favourites, hit parade songs, and jazz tunes – and the clientele sang along, when they knew the words, when they felt like it.

Brian didn't feel like singing, but he hummed a bit. He relaxed in his chair and nursed the "rocks Bacardi" Allan had sent over, compliments of the house.

Everything at The Angel was relaxed and cushy. Thick, turquoise curtains accented with concealed lights broke the monotony of the textured, stucco walls. Ultra modern, cone-shaped beams threw blue shadows up and down – pouring colour onto the floor and splashing it onto the ceiling at random. Recessed eyespots shown dramatically on clean-line sofas while thin-legged, contemporary chairs stared at each other across low and highly polished conversation tables. And against the wall, a curved, futuristic bar gleamed ebony.

The Angel was Liverpool's answer to New York's poshest nightspots, and even the great Judy Garland had found Williams' Seel Street club "charming, definitely charming."

At The Angel, everyone was anonymous. A twenty-seven year old in an expensive suit fit in. Young executives were the norm, not the exception. No one pointed or introduced or watched or fawned. In fact, until Allan took a seat beside him, Brian was lost in a world of his own.

"So…The Beatles, eh?" Allan's eyes twinkled mischievously. He pointed to a quiet table away from the music, and the two men relocated. Allan raised a finger, his bartender nodded, and two drinks were delivered, only moments after the businessmen had settled in.

"Yes, The Beatles," Brian nodded, offering Allan a cigarette from his monogrammed case. "The Beatles it is. Or 'The Beatles von Hamburg,' as I've recently heard them referred to."

"Von Hamburg, my ass!" Allan ruffled. "Pffft! Von Scousers is more like it – layabouts, one and all."

"Yes, well…" Brian jangled his Bacardi, the ice cubes glittering in the blue lights.

"Layabouts to a man…" Allan repeated.

"Don't you think…" Brian began, "don't you find…they have magnetic personalities?"

The Welshman's eyes darted here and there as if he had too much to say and no way to verbalize it.

"Pfffffffft to that!" Allan finally sputtered. "*Magnetic*? The Beatles? Yeah, right! Fuggin' Will Rogers – every one of 'em!"

Brian blushed. The colourful Liverpool vernacular made him squirm. It had never been allowed in Queen's Drive.

"But their wit," Brian tried to explain. "I mean…they're completely…effervescent, aren't they? I mean, they've got this certain…"

"Oh, they've got somethin' all right!" Allan spotted several clients who'd just tumbled in off the blustery street. "Hey, you!" he yelled to the newcomers. "Shake the snow off *outside*, all of ya! We're not walkin' in yer lousy piddle all night, y'know! What kind of establishment d'ya think this is!"

The group yelled back good-naturedly and opened the front door to shake out their coats and scarves. Brian waited. Through the doorway he watched fat, white flakes falling on Seel Street and cars skidding about, their tire tracks crisscrossing the road like hearty flocked holiday garlands. It was strangely magical this time of year. Even though he didn't celebrate Christmas, Brian loved the flash and crinkle of it all.

"Sorry." Allan was attentive once again. "You were effervescin'."

"Yes. Well, uh…as I'm sure you've surmised," Brian cut to the chase, "I've come to ask for your advice."

"And advice doesn't come cheap, does it?" Allan smiled and toasted. "Cheers, mate."

Brian returned the toast half-heartedly, not certain if Allan were teasing or not. He blushed at the mention of money, but pressed on.

"Of course, you were the very first person to know…and to manage The Beatles." In his mind, Brian could hear his mother's admonition, "Pursue it, son. Get the answers." He could hear his father's warning, "Be careful, Brian. Approach this venture as if it were the very last thing you wanted to do."

"That's right." Allan took a long gulp of his Black Velvet and exhaled loudly. "And I've heard all about your checkin' the lads out….goin' the rounds down at The Cavern Club, as it were. I've heard you've even asked to meet Sam Leach at The Kardomah next week."

"That's true. I have," Brian nodded, letting the rum warm his throat. "But *you* were the first to discover them, Mr. Williams."

"Allan."

"Allan...you must know them extremely well. Better than Sam Leach. Better than anyone else."

Allan downed the rest of his Black Velvet, and wiped his mouth with the back of his hand. "Right." His eyes narrowed. "You might say that. Or at least I thought I did, once upon a time."

"Go on – please." Brian held his breath.

"Look Epstein, I don't know what you've heard about them or what you think you know about The *Fabulous* Beatles, but they're not all they're cracked up to be, the lovely lads...although it's not for me to go 'round tellin' tales,* y'know."

For days Allan had been nursing a cold, and this afternoon it had started to develop into something worse. His throat stung as the alcohol fanned out. He covered his mouth and coughed.

Brian waited. Then he leaned forward and forced himself to say it. "Is it true...is it true they cancelled your management agreement overnight – with no discernable reason, Allan?"

"Oh, the reason's discernable all right." Allan's voice went up a notch. "The reason's a breeze, wack! Money, that's why! Greed and money...the fuggin' root of all fuggin' evil, as it were!" His face had lost its natural mirth. "They wouldn't pay my commission...wouldn't pay me a lousy fifteen quid a week! *Me!* After all I'd done for 'em! They wouldn't've been *anywhere* without me!* There's no mystery to that, is there?"

"Perhaps," Brian stammered, "perhaps it was more complicated than that. Perhaps it was a...a general misunderstanding of sorts."

"And me auntie's the Queen of bleedin' Sheba, Epstein! They're all completely ruthless* – The Beatles – each and every one of 'em! Every one of 'em except poor ole Stu, and *he's* the one they got to do their dirty work for 'em!"

"Stu?" Brian was confused. His hands closed tighter around his highball, and he felt a tiny bead of perspiration trickle down the center of his chest. "Look...look Allan," he confided. "I-I've decided I want to take them over, to manage them, to push them as far as I can. I believe in them, you see. I..."

"Look what they did to me, Epstein! You'd have to watch'em every minute of the fuggin' day! You'd have to make absofuggin'lutely sure that what you were signin' with them was completely watertight, as it were."

"But they seem so..."

"But they seem so nice," Allan mocked, "Great lads! Cheers! Lovely lads! Salt of the fuggin' earth!" Allan snorted bitterly. "Just remember...when it comes to contracts with the lovely lads, you'll want to watch yer back, all right?"

"Yes, well...what I mean is...I suppose what I'm really asking is this. Should I take them over or not? Should I offer them management? Should I get involved? Your honest opinion."

"*My* honest opinion?" Allan chuckled. "*My* honest opinion? Don't touch'em with a fuggin' bargepole, Epstein!"*

"But they need someone…they need a manager desperately, you know," Brian whimpered. It was almost a plea.

There was a light smattering of applause as Duggie ended his set with the last vibrating notes of "Destiny." It was one of Allan's favourite tunes, a haunting melody that fit the moment.

"What The Fabulous Beatles need's a swift kick in the rear," Allan turned back to Brian. "I've no fuggin' sympathy where the lousy, Beatles are concerned."

Brian's blush spread to his neck.

"One last question, then…if you don't mind." Brian interlaced his fingers, as if in prayer. "And please, be totally honest with me."

"Right. Go on." Allan was becoming annoyed by it all.

"Do you still want to be associated with them? Do you still, in spite of everything, eventually want them back?"

Allan shoved his empty glass aside and leaned across the table, looking straight into Brian's eyes. He leaned so close that he could smell Brian's talc and see the pores in his clean-shaven cheek. Allan stared at the NEMS proprietor with such intensity that Brian glanced away nervously and then glanced back again.

"Listen, Brian," Allan laid it on the line, "*anyone* can fuggin' have them as far as I'm concerned. I want absolutely nothin' to do with any one of them! Is that clear?"

"Then…I think I'll take them on." Brian whispered. "I feel a great affinity for them…almost as if it's meant to be. I believe in who they are, in what they do, and in what they can do. As for the rest… well… I'm sure it'll all work itself out."

"Yeah, you keep thinkin' that." Allan gave him a wink. And without a word of goodbye, The Beatles' former manager got up from the table and walked away.

In March of 1993, I was privileged to interview Allan Williams on two separate occasions, and in March of 1994, we continued the interview in the presence of Beryl Adams. Allan told me in great detail about the meeting with Brian Epstein. I recorded the interview, and my husband took detailed notes.

The dialogue that I have used in this chapter comes directly from those three interviews. And it was comforting for me as a researcher to find the dialogue Allan used almost word for word in his book, The Man Who Gave the Beatles Away.

* These sentences mark the places where my research and Allan Williams work coincide. In the interview, he gave me some quotes that are not in his book. And some of the phrases that he gave me have been placed in different order in the book, but what you have just read is essentially the conversation that took place

between Brian and Allan.

Brian says in A Cellarful of Noise *that this conversation took place at The Jacaranda. Allan told me that it occurred at The Blue Angel.*

10 December 1961
Mathew Street
Liverpool

John sat on the broken brick street outside The Grapes and smoked. He took slow, deliberate drags on his cig and tried to calm his nerves. When he released the warm, silver smoke, his eyes narrowed, followed the trail into invisibility.

Anything to take his mind off the business at hand.

From somewhere down the street came the sound of a record playing. It was Bruce Channel's latest hit, one of John's favourites, "Hey, Baby" – a song built on a wailing harmonica base. John listened intently, even though he'd heard the tune hundreds of times. He listened for the sake of the harmonica, for the sound that was so familiar and comforting.

"Home at last, John!" A soft, worn, brown tweed. The Echo *pages turning. The crackle of the radio just before "The Goon Show." Saturdays at the picturedrome. A biscuit beneath the pillow. The minty aroma of aftershave. A bluesy harmonica whining behind a dairyman's cupped hands.*

"So, we're off to see the wizard, the wonderful wizard of NEMS!" Bob Wooler interrupted the reverie. Eyes shining and cheeks flushed, Bob held out a hand and helped John up. He reached over and brushed the ashes off of John's jacket, slapping the boy on the arm, grinning. "Ready, are ya?"

"Yeah, let's go." John struggled to readjust the ride of his jeans. "Let's follow the Mathew brick road...'n all that!"

"Except in this scenario," Bob winked, "none of you wants to click yer heels and be whisked away to Kansas, right? I mean, this is what you've waited for."

"Right. So lead the way." John assumed his announcer's voice. "To NEM-land! Second to the right and straight on 'til mornin'!"

"Now you've switched stories, midstream," Bob corrected. "That's 'Peter Pan.'"

John grinned mischievously. "The one about the boy who played with fairies? Perfect, as it were, for an occasion such as this!"

"John!" The compère wagged a finger reprovingly. "None of that today, y'hear! Brian Epstein's a refined and sensitive man, y'know."

"So I've heard." John made a lewd gesture. "So we've all heard!"

"Mind yer manners!" Bob barked.

"I don't mind them, and they don't mind me."

Bob had to chuckle. He knew the boy was on pins and needles. This appointment with Epstein was bigger than life for the aspiring lad. John was all nerves.

"No time like the present, eh?" Bob motioned John ahead.

"And no present like time," John returned.

They began to walk towards Whitechapel, clicking their boot heels on the cold sidewalk, hugging themselves against the wind. The day was bone-bitter. John tucked his hands under his armpits, but the gusts in Stanley Street buffeted him at the intersection. Bob tried clasping his gloves tightly behind his back and walking like a barrister, but nothing really helped. There was no way to keep warm.

The Beatles were to be in NEMS at 4:30 promptly. At the preliminary meeting the previous Sunday afternoon, Brian had remonstrated on adherence to schedule and avoidance of tardiness of any kind. In fact, he'd emphasized it so vehemently that he'd made it "an issue." Now, the closer they got to NEMS, the slower John walked.

"C'mon, Lennon!" Bob tugged at his sleeve. "You'll only irritate the Nemporer...and then you'll have to hear that spiel on punctuality all over again."

"He'll get over it." John took a last drag on his Embassy, tossing it to the ground and walking on it. He pulled his leather jacket tighter, tugging the zipper all the way up. It didn't help much. This was the coldest December John could ever recall, cold and wet. Thinking back, he didn't know when he'd seen the sun...days, weeks maybe. Fog and rain and flurries – Liverpool was smeared in Impressionist greys.

"Don't get eggy, John," Bob gave him the eye. "And don't get off on the wrong foot with Epstein, right?"

"Ah, more words of wisdom from me dear, old Dad."

"Not *that* again!" Bob groaned. "Y'er givin' me a complex, y'know! Do I really look as old as that sounds?"

"Older," John deadpanned. "If I hadn't set the record straight 'n told Epstein you were me dad, he might've taken you fer me granddad, Pop."

"Pfffff! Get off."

About a hundred yards from NEMS, Pete and George stamped impatiently, their hands in their pockets and their noses bright red. Pete pointed to his wristwatch, and George offered a half-wave.

"Y'er almost late!" Pete called out.

"It's almost half-four, Johnny!" George echoed, his body English urging them on.

"Listen to that!" John shoved at Bob playfully, "Our Georgie here's up to time-tellin'! Why, I remember when he was only a..."

"C'mon, let's go! Get a move on!" Paul appeared out of nowhere. His nose was running in the frigid air, and he sniffed every few seconds. "C'mon...we're past due, aren't we?" He directed the troupe down the last, quick block to Whitechapel. At the back of the line, John mimicked the parade following Paul, and catching his reflection in the NEMS window, Bob grinned.

They could all see Brian waiting for them, just inside the store. He was perfectly still, his arms by his side, his face pleasant but unreadable. It could have been a cardboard cutout of Brian – a life-size representation of the shop owner – but it was Brian himself, and when they began pressing their faces against the front glass, he quickly stepped forward to let them in.

Bob Wooler rested a hand on John's shoulder. "All right, then...son. You're on yer own now, as it were."

"Not comin' in?" George was wide-eyed with panic.

"Nah, you're all right," Bob said quietly. "My bein' with you last Sunday served its purpose. It told Epstein you've people watchin' out for you...people who expect him to be on the up and up. And he sees me here right now. So he knows. You don't need me muckin' about in your affairs."

The boys looked uneasy.

"And besides," Bob smiled, "I've got The Cavern to open, don't I? You lot *do* want to work tonight, right?"

"So here's where I leave home, eh Dad?" John wiped an imaginary tear from his eye.

"Go for it, lad. Get yerself a manager," Bob chuckled. "All the best...to all of ya!"

"Y'er a rill owld bastard, y'rill owld bastard," John teased under his breath.

"Right, see y'tonight, Sonny Jim!" Bob gave him a shove. Then he turned and hurried away.

"Right on time!" Brian waved them in, beaming with genuine pleasure. "Come in. Come in! I'm...extremely glad you could make it."

"Why not?"

"Yeah, right."

"Mr. Epstein."

"'Ullo dur."

The Beatles filed into the store. Paul offered a nod and a smile. Someone in the group coughed. John gave the entrepreneur a snappy, farcical salute, and Brian blushed under his gaze. It was all very unnatural.

"Well..." Brian cleared his throat, "all right, then." He rubbed his hands together nervously, "This way, please. We'll go right on up. Follow me."

Brian clipped to a small flight of stairs, and John watched the group traipse behind without speaking. Then he joined them, taking the stairs in two's, hurtling himself headlong the way he always did in Mendips.

The modest office above hadn't changed an inkling since last Sunday afternoon. Crisp, neat, and precise as before, it was a desk and a black leather ledger book, a marble-based fountain pen, and a calendar. It was a man in a starched, white shirt, tightly knotted silk tie, dark, expensive suit, and well-polished wingtips. It was a tiny room into which too many people were crammed – a tiny room too full to hold them all. John lingered at the door and worked for a deep breath.

The tiniest of rooms. Music echoing off the shower stall. Tiles volleying harmony. A vivid, yellow daffodil, hand-painted on the wall. A chorus of girls giggling over tinny banjo chords. The smell of spiced perfume. Rock'n'roll...and the moment she caught his eye and smiled...

"Well," Brian stood behind his desk. "Quite simply, you need a manager. Would you like me to do it?"

George looked at John. Pete turned to Paul. Paul and John exchanged glances and waited. Then someone spoke.

"Yeah." John's voice was husky. He heard it, but hardly recognized it as his own.

Brian turned his attention to the boy at the door. He wanted to hear it again, to make sure.

John met his gaze. "You're on," he felt himself say this time. "You're on. We're in business!"

"Yeah, right."

"Sure."

"That's right."

They all nodded, following suit.

"Right then, Brian," John decided to use the man's first name from the onset, to put himself immediately on equal footing. "Manage us now." A bit more control. "Where's the contract? I'll sign it." He walked assertively towards the desk.

Brian smiled shyly. "Well..." This was all coming out less smoothly than he'd planned. It was all moving too rapidly. He'd anticipated questions, reservations, explanations, and a good bit of discussion. He'd planned to talk more and to say it all better. But somehow in their presence the words jumbled and fell over themselves. "A contract? Yes, well that will take some time to draw up, won't it? In a few days, of course...due process. But... can I take it that I am now your manager? Is that correct?"

"Yeah."

"Yes, manage us, please."

"Yes!" John blared out, a bit impatiently. "That's right."

"Will it make much of a difference to us, actually?" Paul crossed one booted ankle over a knee. He looked at Brian with cautious eyes. "I mean, it won't make any difference...in the way we play, will it?"

"Of course not," Brian sat down and rolled his chair under the desk.

"I'm very pleased, anyway. You've real talent…ability. I only hope that you can take *my ability* on trust."

"Can you buy us into the charts, Brian?" John sneered the first of many sneers.

Brian went crimson. "No," he forced a smile, "but I do think I can do a lot for you." He leaned towards them, studying their faces. "You all know the score, of course. I've been quite honest, haven't I? I've never engaged in this sort of thing before. Never. But regardless…I promise you one hundred percent dedication. I promise you I will do everything in my power to…"

"You used to dread us comin' into this store, didn't you?" John interrupted, looking down his nose. His eyes searched Brian's, assessing the level of honesty there.

"Yes," Brian gazed back, "You were always…disruptive."

"Disruptive, is it?" John's mouth pulled to one side, but a smile slipped out anyway. "Well, that was just for starters, Manager. Wait 'til you really get to know us!"

Brian hesitated for a moment, then smiled back, releasing a slow breath, comfortable for the first time in almost a month. "I'm looking forward to it," he said levelly. And in all honesty, he was.

Probably one of the most highly documented chapters in this book, the events are factual. Only the conversations that take place prior to entering NEMS are conjecture.

But lest you think the facts are clear-cut in this chapter, let me add:

No one seems to know what really happened in December 1961, when the Beatles and Brian Epstein formed a loose managerial agreement of some sort. No one, including the people who were there, can tell the same story. Every single account is different, and the stories vary in large degrees.

All accounts agree that the meeting took place in early December, and they all suggest that one or more of the Beatles were late. Every account tells of two meetings prior to a contract signing, and all accounts begin in the Whitechapel NEMS store.

But from there, the stories take their own paths. Pete Best places them at The Grapes prior to the meeting with Brian, but Bob Wooler said that the pubs were closed from 3-5 P.M., so they couldn't have imbibed even if they'd wanted to. One account places Alistair Taylor at all three meetings, but most accounts place him only at the contract signing. Taylor sets the meetings in a stock room at NEMS. Best says they met upstairs in Brian's office. Brian says the first meeting began at NEMS but then continued at "a milk bar."

After the first meeting between The Beatles and Brian, Alistair Taylor says Brian (who was angry that Paul was late) "dismissed" The Beatles, and the lads left "crestfallen." But Pete Best, who mentions nothing about Paul being late, says The

Beatles were the ones who were unsure, who terminated the meeting to "think it over."

Brian's account has them parting as part of a mutual agreement, eagerly anticipating another meeting in three days. Yet Hunter Davies says that the four boys were only lukewarm to Brian's proposal.

No one tells the same story. Somewhere in the muddle, the truth is buried. But unable to discern that ONE truth, we end our story as we began it, surrounded by legend and mystery.

11 December 1961
The Grapes
Mathew Street
Liverpool

The customary late night popover at The Grapes was a celebration tonight. Word had it that The Beatles had acquired a new manager and that the manager was none other than the well-heeled Brian Epstein of NEMS.

The rumour had spread during The Cavern show like a Liverpool summer cold; by the second song, everyone had heard the news and embellished it a bit. The story had made its way up to street level by the end of the first set, and throughout the evening, it wound its way down Mathew and on toward Button, as far as The White Star.

By the time The Beatles swaggered into The Grapes, well after midnight, cheers met them head-on. Peers, fans, Bob Wooler, Neil Aspinall, promoter Joe Flannery – everyone in Mathew Street was in the mood for toasting. Lager, lime, and currant covered the floor and tables. John wore as much as he consumed, and by the time the fire burned low, he needed fresh air.

Outside, Mathew Street was deserted, except for a staggering shadow – a hobbled mendicant who reeked of an even stronger intoxicant than John did. For a moment, the beggar weaved and blundered in John's direction, looking for a handout. But as he approached and took a closer look at the leathered boy in the door light, the old grifter paused, then wandered away.

A rat leapt from a broken produce crate. It skittered across the alleyway, bound for dark corners, rustling among the heads of lettuce and bundles of chard. In its wake, a stack of leeks teetered, then scattered on the cobblestones. John paid little attention.

The air was breathable ice tonight. It hurt to draw it in, but John took a gulp anyway. He closed his eyes and shivered. He surrendered his shoulder blades to the frozen alley wall.

On down the block, the Irish pub overflowed with patrons, music, and nostalgia. John could hear them singing at the top of their lungs, slurring memories with the years to come, toasting trials past and better days ahead.

From another quarter, police sirens yelped, and the eerily deep, vibrating bass of a boat horn called long and slow, full of homesickness and regret.

Fifteen-two! Exotic New Zealand, lad! John could still hear it clearly, even after all this time. *Fabulous kangaroos and platypus ducks, Johnny boy! We'll hunt for shells on the shore, and I'll show you trees chock full of koalas. This time next year, we'll both be Down Under, you and me. But no matter where we are, we'll always love yer mother, won't we? And we'll think of her every time we sing, "When they begin the beguine..."*

"So, you're out *here*, then?"

John kept his eyes closed and said nothing.

"John?" Paul tried again.

"It was a fuggin' matchbox in there," John complained.

Paul leaned against the large, many paned window and studied his friend. "Is that what's wrong with ya?"

"You know what's wrong."

"Look, John...it's done, isn't it? I mean, we all agreed to it. We made the decision, right?"

"Yeah, right. Done."

"And we did all we could do. We checked Epstein out...we asked everyone we knew. We talked to everyone we possibly could, didn't we?"

No response.

"I mean, me dad even conferred with *Olive*, y'know." Paul tried to lighten the mood.

"Oh, Olive!" John opened his eyes and shook his head. "That's a relief."

They smiled a little.

"Cold as a witch's tit, isn't it?" Paul shivered.

"Yeah." John agreed for the sake of conversation. He'd hardly noticed.

Silence.

"So...what's Cyn think?" Paul tried again.

"Ecstatic is what she says."

"Says?"

"I don't believe her," John said. "She's...well...Cyn's the type who wudden say 'no' to a ring, isn't she?"

"What girl would, really?"

"The kind I need."

"The kind that Stu's got?"

"Somethin' like that," John said.

"Well...y'could always put out an advert, y'know: 'Independent and artistic girl wanted. Loves rock'n'roll and has a mind of her own. Apply in person. J.W. Lennon, Esquire.'"

John hardly smiled. "I think I'll just sit here, if it's all the same to you."

"Suit yourself," Paul shrugged. "Cig?"

"I'm the type who wudden say 'no.'" John took one.

Their cigarettes glowed orange and their breath billowed up before them, creating the illusion of warmth, but ice had completely frosted the windows of The Grapes. It was colder and later than it seemed.

From the docks, the boat horn called again, the triple blast of a ship leaving port. It called before leaving sailors behind. It called before pushing away into dark seas.

"He'll change us, y'know," John spoke up. "It's fuggin' inevitable. He'll change us, won't he?"

"Nah," Paul zipped his coat and pulled the sleeves down over his hands. "I asked him, didn't I? I asked him, and he said he wouldn't. He said he's 'pleased anyway.'"

"He'll change us. He'll have to."

"And why's that?" Paul twitched his nose twice to the left. It was a tell he always resorted to when he knew John was right. "I mean, what's wrong with us, I'd like to know?"

"Take a look!" John swept his hand from his wet, tangled hair down to the tight, revealing leathers that were their signature. "We're unholy! We're off the cuff. We *mach shau*. We rave. Epstein's...ethical. He's ironclad. He's RADA. The man choreographs!"

Paul dug a packet of cigs out of his pocket and lit it. He stared off into the night, not sure what to say.

"He'll change everything," John said again. "He'll have to, won't he?"

"Well, if you felt that way...then, why'd you say, 'Yes, manage us now!'...as if you'd heard it from on high, as it were?"

"Because of the group." John looked at Paul full on. "Because of the *group*, that's why." He struggled for words. "The four of us need Epstein...he has to be what he is in order to make us what we've always wanted to be. To get us where we've always wanted to go. To transform us into the topper..."

"Don't say it," Paul held up a hand.

"You know the rest."

Laughter chorused from inside The Grapes. Someone was singing a drunken cover of "Maggie Mae," and someone else attempted harmony – it was folk music, the music of Liverpool.

"Look, John, we've come a long way for this, haven't we?" Paul's large, dark eyes were serious. "The Levis Auditions, the Billy Fury thing through Scotland, all those cramped rehearsals in Julia's bathroom... some pretty fantastically terrible nights in the Garston Blood baths..."

John nodded.

"I mean, we've lived in rot and squalor in The New Cabaret Artistes *and* The Bambi Kino," Paul went on, "and we've played to almost every drummer there is! From Colin to Tommy Moore."

John groaned.

"And good ole Norm and Johnny Hutch. And once in a great while, the jeweled and jaunty Ringo."

"You forgot Peter Randolph Best," John threw in.

"I couldn't, could I?" Paul teased. "I mean, Mo'd never permit that sort of thing, would she?"

"You'd hang first."

"And I'd deserve it."

They smiled briefly in the darkness. They smoked and stared at their feet.

"A few years ago," John said quietly, "Mim gave me this handful of notes. It was back when I was livin' with Stu in Gambier – back when Rod and Stu and me were half starvin' to death, y'know…"

"Yeah, right. The good, ole days." Paul scratched a match across his boot sole and lit another cig.

"I'd gone home to Mendips for a couple – and when I got ready to come back, Mim pressed this crumple of bills into me hand, instructin' me to keep it all to m'self, as it were."

"Right. She would." Paul clicked his cheek. "Dear ole Auntie Mim!"

John reached over and took a drag on Paul's cigarette. He held it for a moment and then handed it back. "At any rate, I had this money on the tacit agreement I wouldn't use any of it – none of it y'understand – on anythin' remotely related to the band."

"So?" Paul looked at him.

"So this is the first time you've ever heard about it, isn't it? I used the fuggin' money! *I spent it all*! I never told anyone. Not Rod, not George, not you…not even Stu."

"And the moral of that tale, Mr. Aesop?"

"That I sold out…that I let someone in authority convince me to 'go along just once,' to do what Mim wanted. I let Rod starve. I let Stu starve! I let someone with money and power dictate what was right and what was wrong…what I should and shouldn't do."

"And…you think y'er doin' that all over again…with Brian?"

"Yeah," John almost whispered. "Only this time, I sold us *all* out – for fame, for power, for a handful of fuggin' money, as it were.

"It's not sellin' out to have a manager, John."

"It is if you give up who you are."

"All Epstein said is that he wants us to spruce up a bit…to end the fightin' on the stage and stop beratin' customers when they have requests. To quit eatin' and drinkin' while we're up there performin'…and other really trivial things like that."

"Go on," John insisted.

Paul flipped his hands up, as if he couldn't remember any more.

"Y'*know* the rest," John hissed. "He told us to quit swearin', to quit endin' songs halfway through, to quit actin' irresponsibly in front of the fuggin' fans – whatever that means – and…he wants us to quit wearin' 'those leathers.'"

"Yerrokay. There *is* that," Paul nodded. "But ultimately…I mean, he just wants us to be the best we can, John."

"He wants us to be different," John snapped. "He wants us to be somethin' other than The Beatles."

"Look John, everyone – even an individualist like Stu – has a Paolozzi to guide them, to shape them, y'know – to be a mentor."

"Paolozzi doesn't mandate what Stu wears or what he says or what he eats! Stu lives his life exactly as he fuggin' pleases!"

"That's not true and y'know it," Paul argued. "*No one* lives exactly as they please. Not even the Queen."

"Yeah?" John shot him a look. "Well, I knew someone who did."

"But," Paul waited a moment before he said it, "did this person do it at the sacrifice of everythin' else…of everyone else? I mean, how can you live exactly as you please and not shove someone else under a bus?"

John looked straight ahead and pretended not to hear.

"Look John," Paul folded his arms against the sting of a new wind. "You made the decision, right? We all did. And we did it –as you said – for the good of the group. If you didn't want to change, you'd be back in Woolton right now, back with Ivy 'n Len 'n Eric 'n Rod 'n Colin 'n Pete – still The Quarry Men, still playin' local gigs for local recognition, right? You'd still be droppin' round Woolies on a lunchtime, pinchin' pies at the roundabout, and livin' with Mim, right?"

"I'm not sayin' change is bad, and I'm not sayin' I'm afraid of change," John raised his voice, "but I want it to happen the right way, y'know. I don't want someone – Epstein – to rush in and obliterate everythin' I fuggin' recognize! I don't want him to annihilate us and make us over into somethin' we're not!"

"And what makes you think he will?"

"He's already started," John lamented.

"By slatin' a trip to London on our behalf… by goin' to Decca Records, as it were?" Paul raised one eyebrow to make a point the way his father did.

"I'll give him that."

"Then how? What's he done?"

"Nothing tangible – at least not yet."

"So as it stands," Paul went on, "you've nothin' actually to complain about, is that right?"

"Not yet." John looked away.

"And maybe not ever," Paul insisted.

"Come on, John," Paul wheedled, "don't you want to be…*can't* you be happy…ever? Even for a moment?"

But before the answer came, the door opened again. It was George. His head and shoulders popped out around the doorframe. "When y'comin' back in, Johnny?"

"Don't butt in with the men, George," Paul teased.

"C'mon!" George ignored the Scouse barb. "Ringo and Rory've challenged us to a soggy mat match, and they say y'er too afraid to come back and compete." It was the old trick of saturating cardboard beer mats and sticking them to the ceiling to see whose disc could cling the longest. John was a long-standing master at it.

"Pfft! There's no game in beatin' Rory, is there?" John pushed off the wall. "And Ringo? Bring 'im on, son! No one's half as *mat* as the fuggin' Beatles!"

"Hey Ringo!" George yelled back into the crowded pub, "John says no one's half as mat as The Beatles, like." A brief pause. "What's that? I dunno. I'll ask him."

George popped his head out again, all smiles. "Ringo wants to know what that means exactly – in simple, 'man-on-the-bus' terms?"

John headed for the door, clapping a hand on George's shoulder and giving him a gentle shove. "Tell 'im it's a joke, son…a larf, a snarf, a snide, a chide. Tell 'im that! And tell 'im that if he really wants to know, he shoulda been there."

"You shoulda been there, Ring!" George called to the corner table. "John says you shoulda been there!" Then he turned to Paul and John, brandishing his childlike, lopsided smile. "*I* was there, wasn't I?"

"George Harrison, isn't it?" Paul asked John.

"Right," John deadpanned. "I believe I recognize him,"

"I heard he was there from day one," Paul winked.

"In fact," John assumed his radio announcer's voice, "he'll be one of the ones to say how it was before it was and when it was and after it was. Amen."

"Yeah, I thought as much," George beamed. "I was pretty well convinced I was there. But it never hurts to make sure, y'know – just in case."

"We were all there!" Paul lifted an invisible toast.

"Legends in our own slime," John flashed a toothy grin.

"That's us!" George added. "Legends loomin' large!"

The boat horn sounded its final reprise from the Merseyside dock, but no one in Mathew heard it. The three friends had already disappeared into the noisy, overcrowded pub, yelling a mat challenge at Ringo and slamming the narrow door behind them. Mathew fell silent once again except for the muffled, animated voices of The Beatles and their fans. In the tiny, obscure alleyway, theirs were the only rhythms still heard in the late, northern, Liverpool night.

Footnotes

9 October 1940
Buskin, *John Lennon,*
His Life and Legend, 12.
Coleman, *Lennon,* 24.
Baird, *John Lennon, My Brother,* 10.
Goldman, *The Lives of John Lennon,* 29.
Norman, *Shout!,* 23-24.
Davies, *The Beatles,* 6-8.
Lennon, Pauline, *Daddy Come Home,* 35.
Whitworth, Rodney, *Merseyside at War,* 44.
Wootton, Richard, *John Lennon,* 7-8

November 1941
Coleman, 25-26.
Goldman, 40-41.
Norman, 27.

November 1943
Norman, 25, 27.
Lennon, Pauline, 38-39.
Coleman, 23, 25, 26.
Interview with Charles Lennon, The Grapes, Mathew Street, Liverpool, March 1995.

January 1944
Baird, Julia, 12-14, 175.
Norman, 27.
Goldman, 32-33.
Davies, *The Beatles,* 7-8.
Lennon, Pauline, 44-54.
Coleman, 19-20.

Spring 1944
Coleman, 26-27.
Baird, 13-14.
Goldman, 32-33.

June 1946
Davies, *The Beatles,* 8.
Lennon, Pauline, 66-75.
Baird, 14-15.
Coleman, Ray, 20-21.
Goldman, 34-35.
Harry, *The Ultimate Beatles Encyclopedia,* 382.
Harry, *The John Lennon Encyclopedia,* 480-481.

1947
Shotton, *John Lennon: In My Life,* 21-23.
Davies, *The Beatles,* 14.
Coleman, 26, 35.
Burrows, *John Lennon: A Story in Photographs,* 15.
Robertson, *Lennon,* 7.
Norman, Phillip, 20-29.
Davies, *The Quarrymen,* 5-7.

September 1948
Norman, 27.
Coleman, 26.

December 1948
Coleman, 33, 35, 39.
Lennon, Pauline, 85.
Norman, 21.
Goldman, 40.

Autumn 1949
Coleman, 56.
Shotton, 22.
Goldman, 40.
Tremlett, *The John Lennon Story,* 20.
Lennon, John, *Skywriting By Word of Mouth,* 96.

May 1950
Coleman, 29, 38, 41, 56.

Autumn 1952
Coleman, 32-33, 42.
Harry, *The Ultimate Beatles Encyclopedia,* 539.
Norman, 30-31.
Davies, *The Beatles,* 18-22.
Davies, *The Quarrymen,* 19, 32-33.
Shotton, 31-33.

Summer 1954
Davies, *The Quarrymen*, 20-21, 27.
Coleman, 27-28, 33.

6 June 1955
Harry, *The Ultimate Beatles Encyclopedia*, 610.
Coleman, 28, 30-31.
Norman, 23, 28.
Baird, 28-29.
Brown, *The Love You Make*, 19.
Goldman, 56.
Shotton, 23, 37.

Autumn 1955
Coleman, 32-33, 42.
Harry, *The Ultimate Beatles Encyclopedia*, 539.
Norman, 30-31.
Davies, *The Beatles*, 18-22.
Davies, *The Quarrymen*, 19, 32-33.
Shotton, 31-33.

August 1956
Coleman, 43-47.
Norman, 48-49.
Shotton, 33.
Harry, *The Ultimate Beatles Encyclopedia*, 528-529, 539.

September 1956
Shotton, 35-36.
Coleman, 43-44.

December 1956
Baird, 26-7, 47.
Shotton, 37-38.
Harry, *The Ultimate Beatles Encyclopedia*, 606.
Harry, *The John Lennon Encyclopedia*, 514.
Norman, 34.

February 1957
Shotton, 31-38.
Baird, 19-20, 26.
Norman, 32-33.
Coleman, 44.
Davies, *The Quarrymen*, 25.

Late February 1957
Norman, 71-73.
Pawlowski, *How They Became the Beatles*, 33.

Baird, 39-40, 48.
Shotton, 38.

Spring 1957
Coleman, 43, 54-55, 57-60, 82-83.
Pawlowski, 7-8.
Imagine video.
Shotton, 51-53.
Lewisohn, *The Complete Beatles Chronicles*, 14.
Harry, *The Ultimate Beatles Encyclopedia*, 187, 276, 539-540, 606-607, 688.
Davies, *The Quarrymen*, 10-11, 39.
Norman, 35-36.
Porter, Alan, *Before They Were the Beatles*, 22-23, 43.

May 1957
Interview with Dave Bennion, Calderstones School,
March 1993. Many of the quotes used in this chapter are taken, word for word, from this interview.
Description of building from tour of Calderstones and auditorium, March of 1993.
Salewicz, *McCartney*, 48-49.
Shotton, 53.
Coleman, 56.

Mid-May 1957
Coleman, 66.
Norman, 47-48, 55.
Harry, *The Ultimate Beatles Encyclopedia*, 402-403, 529.
Jones, *The Beatles Liverpool*, 23.
Shotton, 59.
Goldman, 71-72.

Late May 1957
Coleman, 43, 54-55, 57-60, 82-83.
Pawlowski, 7-8.
Imagine video.
Shotton, 51-53.
Lewisohn, 14.
Harry, *The Ultimate Beatles Encyclopedia*, 187, 276, 606-607, 688.
Davies, *The Quarrymen*, 10-11.
Porter, 22-23.

2 June 1957
Norman, 34-35.
Lewisohn, 12.
Coleman, 59.
Davies, *The Quarrymen*, 51-52, 256.
Porter, 47-48.
Buskin, Richard, *The Idiot's*

Guide to the Beatles, 89.

Sunday, 9 June 1957
Harry, *The Ultimate Beatles Encyclopedia*, 221, 276, 539.
Harry, *The John Lennon Encyclopedia,* 307.
Jones, 12-13, 15.
Coleman, 59.
Davies, *The Quarrymen*, 52.
Lewisohn, 14.
Norman, 42.
Telephone interview with Nicky Cuff, August 2005.

9 June 1957
Clayson and Leigh, *The Walrus was Ringo*, 19-21.
Description of Mendips from a letter written to me by the owners of the house in 1993. Letter in appendix.

22 June 1957
Norman, 38-39.
Davies, *The Quarrymen*, 52-53.
Lewisohn, 14.
Harry, *The Ultimate Beatles Encyclopedia*, 563.
Baird, 34-35.
Miles, *The Beatles Diary, Vol. 1*, 10.

6 July 1957
O'Donnell, *The Day John Met Paul*.
Baird, 36-7.
Salewicz, 43-44.
Buskin, *John Lennon: His Life and Legend*, 34.
Ruhlman, *John Lennon,* 17-19.
Lewisohn, 14-15.
Harry, *The Ultimate Beatles Encyclopedia*, 627-628.
Shotton, 55-56.
Norman, 55-57.
Coleman, 62-64.
Davies, *The Quarrymen*, 55-59.
Garry, *John, Paul, and Me: Before the Beatles,* 145-170.
Giuliano, *Two of Us*, 2.
Porter, 50-57.
Miles, *John Lennon: In His Own Words*, 18.

9 July 1957
O'Donnell, 141.
Norman, 44.
Giuliano, Geoffrey, *Two of Us*, 2-3.
Salewicz, 44-45.
Davies, *The Quarrymen*, 59.
Miles, *John Lennon: In His Own Words*, 18.

The Beatles, *The Anthology*, 20.

Late July 1957
Harry, *The Ultimate Beatles Ecyclopedia*, 139, 688.
Shotton, 55-56.
Thompson, *The Best of Cellars*, 9, 19, 21.
Lewisohn, 14-15.
Norman, 46.
Goldman, 68.
Coleman, 65.
Miles, *The Beatles:In their own Words*, 9.

7 August 1957
Coleman, 59-60.
Lewisohn, 15.
Salewicz, 45.
Shotton, 55-56.
Harry, *The Ultimate Beatles Encyclopedia*, 139, 539-40, 284, 187, 276, and 606-7.
Davies, *The Quarrymen*, 60, 68.
Miles, *The Beatles Diary, Vol I*, 11.
Thompson, 21.
Robertson, *Lennon*, 8.
Porter, 57-58.

September 1957
Descriptions of Liverpool from various trips to the city between 1993-2007.
Lewisohn, 15.
Shotton, 59.
Coleman, 66-67.
Stokes, Tucker, and Ward, *Rock of Ages*, 153.
Davies, *The Quarrymen*, 68.

19 October 1957
Lewisohn, 15.
Garry, 26-28.
Davies, *The Quarrymen*, 61-62.
Giuliano, *Two of Us*, 10.
Porter, 61-63.
Miles, *The Beatles Diary, Vol. I*, 12.

24 January 1958
Thompson, 124.
Lewisohn, 16.
Davies, *The Quarrymen*, 71-72.
Miles, *The Beatles Diary, Vol I,* 11, 13.
Porter, 69.

13 March 1958
Lewisohn, 16.
Giuliano, *Dark Horse: The Private Life of George Harrison*, 20.
Harry, *The Ultimate Beatles Encyclopedia*, 472.

Harry, *The John Lennon Encyclopedia*, 307.
Norman, 53-54.
Coleman, 77, 81.
Porter, 71-72.
Davies, *The Quarrymen*, 65.
Miles, *John Lennon: In His Own Words*, 25.
Miles, *The Beatles Diary, Vol. I*, 13.

April 1958
Baird, 46, 48-49.
Coleman, 57.
Pawlowski, 9.
Lewisohn, 16.
Davies, *The Quarrymen*, 70-71.
Miles, *The Beatles Diary, Vol. I*, 12.
Garry, 190.
Giuliano, *Two of Us*, 5.

15 July 1958
Norman, 71-72.
Baird, 44, 19-20, 50-60.
Brown, 29-30.
Coleman, 83-85.
Imagine video.
Shotton, 61.
Goldman, 77-78.
Harry, *The Ultimate Beatles Encyclopedia*, 383.
Harry, *The John Lennon Encyclopedia*, 126, 332.
Buskin, *The Complete Idiot's Guide to the Beatles*, 64.
Rose, "Long Gone John: Lennon and the Revelations," *The Lennon Companion*, 7.
Greenwald, *The Beatles Companion*, 14.
Robertson, 8.
Interview with Charles Lennon, The Grapes, Mathew Street, Liverpool, March 1995.

August 1958
The Beatles, *The Anthology*, 14-15.
Coleman, 77.
Goldman, 69-71.
Shotton, 61.
Norman, 54-55.
Harry, *The Ultimate Beatles Encyclopedia*, 250.
Riley, *Tell Me Why*, 300-301.

September 1958
Coleman, 87-92.
Davies, *The Beatles*, 49-50.
Goldman, 79-81.
Harry, *The Ultimate Beatles Encyclopedia*, 523.
Buskin, *John Lennon: His Life and Legend*, 43.

Miles, *John Lennon: In His Own Words*, 17.
Caserta, Tripod.com/beatlegirls/thelmapickles.

Mid-September 1958
Tour of the McCartney home in Forthlin Road, Allerton, 1999.
Salewicz, 47-48.
Coleman, 77-80.
Giuliano, *The Two of Us*, 6-7, 10-11.
Riley, 300.

October 1958
Coleman, 13-14, 70, 73, 99, 139-140.
Harry, 461, 476.
Clayson and Sutcliffe, *Backbeat: Stuart Sutcliffe: The Lost Beatle*, 48-52.
Goldman, 83-85.
Norman, 62-64.
The Beatles, *The Anthology*, 9, 11.
Information supplied by Bill Harry via e-mail and from Bill Harry's official website, http://www.mersey-beat.net.

Mid-October 1958
Coleman, 6-10.
Norman, 74.
Harry, *The Ultimate Beatles Encyclopedia*, 335, 375.
Lennon, Cynthia, *A Twist of Lennon*, 14-15.
Shotton, 61.
Davies, *The Beatles*, 51-52.

Late October 1958
Coleman, 5, 10-11, 68, 95.
Davies, *The Beatles*, 52.
Lennon, Cynthia, *A Twist of Lennon*, 14.
Harry, *The Ultimate Beatles Encyclopedia*, 375.
Norman, 57.

November 1958
Lennon, Cynthia, *A Twist of Lennon*, 15.
Lennon, Cynthia, *John*, 15, 16.
Coleman, 1-3, 7-8, 9-10, 14-15.
Goldman, 76, 82.
Interview with Helen Anderson in her home in Chester, March 1994.

Late November 1958
Coleman, 6-7, 16, 70-73, 100.
Norman, 74.
Buskin, *John Lennon: His Life and Legend*, 42.
Lennon, Cynthia, *A Twist of Lennon*, 16.
Lennon, Cynthia, *John*, 19.

Early January 1959
Coleman, 88-89, 91-92.
Goldman, 79-81.
Brown, 30.
Harry, *The Ultimate Beatles Encyclopedia*, 523.
Caserta, Jean, tripod.com/beatlegirls/thelmapickels This website has an excellent photo of Thelma and several interesting quotes from her.

Mid-January 1959
Harry, *The Ultimate Beatles Encyclopedia*, 259.
Clayson and Sutcliffe, 57.
Description of Mendips from a letter written by the owner, 1993. Letter in appendix.

April 1959
Coleman, 47-48, 70-72.
Goldman, 80-81.
Clayson and Sutcliffe, 49-52.
Interview with Helen Andersen in her home in Chester, March 1994.
Interview regarding Stuart Sutcliffe with Bryan Biggs of The Bluecoat School, Liverpool, 1993.

Early May 1959
Coleman, 4, 6-7, 73-74.
Buskin, *John Lennon: His Life and Legend*, 41.
Interview with June Furlong at The Pump House Pub, Liverpool, 28 March 1993.
Interview with Helen Anderson at her home in Chester, March 1994.
Details about Ye Cracke from many visits from March 1993 – present.

Late May 1959
Lennon, Cynthia, *John*, 20-23.
Lennon, Cynthia, *A Twist of Lennon*, 17-19.
Buskin, *John Lennon: His Life and Legend*, 45.
Norman, 57-58.
Coleman, 12-14, 94.
Goldman, 82-83.
Visits to Ye Cracke, 1994-2007.

Information about Gambier Terrace supplied via e-mail by Rod Murray, 2004.

June 1959
Williams, 14, 16-17.
Jones, 34.
Norman, 66-67.
Pawlowski, 5-6, 9-10.
Harry, *The Ultimate Beatles Encyclopedia*, 335-336.
Interview with Allan Williams and Beryl Adams at The Grange Hotel in Aigburth, March 1993.
Interview with Allan Williams at Buttons Restaurant, Liverpool, March 1994.
Interview with Woody, "Lord Woodbine," March 1994.

Late June 1959
Coleman, 93.
Pawlowski, 10.
Shotton, 57-62.
Lennon, Cynthia, *A Twist of Lennon*, 21, 25-26.
Williams, 24.
Davies, *The Quarrymen*, 66.
Lennon, Cynthia, *John*, 37.

20-27 August 1959
Coleman, 105.
Norman, 78-79.
Goldman, 98.
Lewisohn, 17.
Harry, *The Ultimate Beatles Encyclopedia*, 135-136.
Best and Doncaster, *Beatle! The Pete Best Story*, 16-20.
Best, Roag. *The Beatles: The True Beginnings*.
Leigh, *Drummed Out!*, 9.
Question and Answer Session with Pete Best at "The Fest for Beatlefans," 3 April 2004, The Meadowlands, New York. I was one of a large audience to whom Pete spoke.

29 August 1959
Coleman, 105.
Norman, 78-79.
Harry, *The Ultimate Beatles Encyclopedia*, 135.
Goldman, 98.
Lewisohn, 17.
Best and Doncaster, 16-26.
Best, Roag, 26, 31, 32. (You can see a picture of the Dansette record player on page 43.)

September 1959
Coleman, 13-14, 37, 77.
Baird, 7, 20, 23, 25, 26.
Lennon, Cynthia, *A Twist of Lennon*, 10, 20.
Interview with Helen Anderson at her home in Chester, March 1994.

November 1959
Coleman, 61, 102.
Furlong and Block, *June*, 115. Also, photographs of George Jardine from Ms. Furlong's autobiography.
Conversation with George Jardine, March 2000.
Interviews with June Furlong, March 1993-2005.
Sutcliffe and Clayson, 23-24, 33, 51.

14 November 1959
Compiled from interviews with June Furlong, Helen Andersen, Allan Williams, Charlies Lennon, and Eddie Porter.

15 November 1959
Coleman, 61, 102.
Furlong and Block, 115. Also photographs of George Jardine from Ms. Furlong's autobiography.
Conversation with George Jardine, March 2000.
Interviews with June Furlong, March 1993-2005.
Sutcliffe and Clayson, 23-24, 33, 51.

Christmas Eve 1959
Coleman, 250-251.
Letter from owner of Mendips, sent to me in 1993. Letter in appendix.

17 January 1960
Lewisohn, 18.
Brown, 32-33.
Coleman, 102-103.
Pawlowski, 5-6.
Shotton, 62.
Clayson and Sutcliffe, 65.
Harry, The *Ultimate Beatles Encyclopedia*, 635.
Harry, *The John Lennon Encyclopedia*, 875-876.
Davies, *The Beatles*, 59.
Norman, 64-65.
Jones, 34.
Information provided via e-mail by Rod Murray.

24 January 1960
Miles, *The Beatles Diary, Vol. I*, 19.
Salewicz, 85-86.
Giuliano, 13-14.
The Beatles, *The Anthology*, 41, 62.

Late January 1960
Harry, *The Ultimtae Beatles Encyclopedia*, 635.
Jones, 28.
Davies, *The Beatles*, 59-60.
Shotton, 62.
Pawlowski, 9.
Giuliano, 13-14.

3 February 1960
Lewisohn, 18.
Heatley, Michael, *The Immortal John Lennon*, 11.
Pawlowski, 33.
Coleman, 103
Harry, *The Ultimate Beatles Encyclopedia*, 65-66.
Norman, 74.
Beatles, *The Anthology*, 41.
Buskin, *The Complete Idiot's Guide to The Beatles*, 86-87.
Leach, *The Birth of the Beatles*, 35.
Interviews with Allan Williams in Liverpool, March 1993 and 1994.
Information supplied by Bill Harry via e-mail in August 2007.

16 April 1960
Lewisohn, 18.
Williams, 25-27.
Norman, 69-72.
Salewicz, 81-81.
Wootton, 23-24.
Tremlett, 28-29.

4 May 1960
Williams, 38.
Lewisohn, 18-19.
Norman, 72-73.
Harry, *TheUltimate Beatles Encyclopedia*, 471.
Coleman, 104-105.
Goldman, 94-95.
Interviews with Allan Williams, Liverpool, March 1993 and 1994.
Pawlowski, 12.

6 May 1960
Williams, 30.
Lewisohn, 19.
Norman, 74.
Coleman, 104.
Interview with Allan Williams, Liverpool, March 1993.
Beatles, *The Anthology*, 41.

10 May 1960
Ian Forsyth and Johnny Gentle, *Johnny Gentle and the Beatles First Ever Tour*, 28-31.
Williams, 38-47.
Pawlowski, 12-17.
Norman, 72-76.
Salewicz, 85.
Harry, *The John Lennon Encyclopedia*, 877-878.
Beatles, *The Anthology*, 41-44.
Davies, *The Beatles*, 65.
Brown, 37.
Coleman, 105.
Robertson, 9.
Goldman, 95
Wootton, 23-24.
Lewisohn, 19.
Interview with Allan Williams, Liverpool, March 1993.

19 May 1960
Williams, 49-53.
Goldman, 95-97.
Lewisohn, 19-20.
Pawlowski, 19.
Norman, 96-100.
Davies, *The Beatles*, 64-65.
Harry, *The Ultimate Beatles Encyclopedia*, 636.
The Beatles, *The Anthology*, 44.
Interviews with Allan Williams, March 1993 and 1994.

23 May 1960
Williams, 49-53.
Goldman, 95-97.
Lewisohn, 19-20.
Pawlowski, 19.
Norman, 96-100.
Davies, *The Beatles*, 64-65.
Harry, *The Ultimate Beatles Encyclopedia*, 263.
The Beatles, *The Anthology*, 44.
Interview with Allan Williams, March 1993.
The Beatles: The Long and Winding Road DVD, Part II: "One and One and One is Three"

29 May 1960
Williams, 49-53.
Goldman, 95-97.
Lewisohn, 19-20.
Pawlowski, 19.
Norman, 96-100.
Davies, *The Beatles*, 64-65.
Harry, *The Ultimte Beatles Encyclopedia*, 263.
The Beatles, *The Anthology*, 44.
Interview with Allan Williams, March 1993.
The Beatles: The Long and Winding Road DVD, Part II: "One and One and One is Three"

June 1960
Pawlowski, 17.
Coleman, 104-106.
Harry, *The Ultimate Beatles Encyclopedia*, 471, 475-476.
Norman, 78-79.

6 June 1960
Harry, *The Ultimate Beatles Encyclopedia*, 202.
Pawlowski, 19.
Norman, 78-79.
Williams, 54-57.

July 1960
Pawlowski, 19.
Williams, 74-107.
Lewisohn, 20-21.
Coleman, 109.
Brown, 39-41.
Interviews with Allan Williams, March 1993 and 1994.
Interview with "Lord Woodbine," March 1994.

Mid-July 1960
Pawlowski, 19.
Williams, 74-107.
Lewisohn, 20-21.
Coleman, 109.
Brown, 39-41.
Interview with Allan Williams, March 1993.
The Beatles: The Long and Winding Road DVD, Part II: "One and One and One is Three"

Late July 1960
Williams, 106-109.
Lewisohn, 21.
Lennon, Cynthia, *Twist of Lennon*, 27, 22-25, 33-35.
Scheff, *The Playboy Interviews*, 126-127, 144.

Brown, 39-41.
Interviews with Allan Williams, March 1993 and 1994.
Stevens, John. *The Songs of John Lennon*, 41.

6 August 1960
Best and Doncaster, 28-29.
Norman, 86.
Coleman, 109.
Lewisohn, 21-22.
Williams, 136-138.
Harry, *John Lennon Encyclopedia*, 113.
Harry, *The Ultimate Beatles* Encyclopedia, 90-91.
Pawlowski, 23.
The Beatles: The Long and Winding Road DVD, Part II: "One and One and One is Three"
"Best of the Beatles" video.
Information given in Pete Best's symposium and question and answer session at The Fest for BeatleFans,
The Meadowlands, New York, 3 April 2004.
Interviews with Allan Williams, March 1993 and 1994.
Interviews with Eddie Porter between 1993-1999.

16 August 1960
Beatles, *The Anthology*, 66.
Roberston, 9.
Williams, 148-150.
Best and Doncaster, 33.
Sutcliffe and Clayson, 85.
Norman, 88.
Pawlowski, 23.
Lewisohn, 22.
Interview with Lord Woodbine, Liverpool, March 1994.
Interview with Allan Williams, Liverpool, March 1994.

17 August 1960
The Beatles, *The Anthology*, 46.
Williams, 152-159.
Lewisohn, 22-23.
Coleman, 109-111.
Norman, 16, 112-113.
Best and Doncaster, 30-39.
Pawlowski, 24, 29.
Harry, *The Ultimate Beatles Encyclopedia*, 61, 365, 325-326.
Clayson, 86-87.
Norman, 76.
Giuliano, 13.
Robertson, 9.
Miles, *The Beatles Diary, Vol. I*, 24-25.
Interview with Allan Williams, March 1994.

18 August 1960
Buskin, *John Lennon: His Life and Legend*, 55.
Lewisohn, 23.
Williams, 158-160.
Best and Doncaster, 24, 37.
Davies, *The Beatles*, 76.
Interview with Allan Williams, March 1994.

3 October 1960
Williams, 159-161.
Norman, 93.
Best and Doncaster, 43-46.
Pawlowski, 25.
Davies, *The Beatles*, 77.
Lewisohn, 23.
Shotton, 65.
Coleman, 111.
The Beatles, *The Anthology*, 48.
Harry, *The Ultimate Beatles Encyclopedia*, 325-326.
Interview with Allan Williams, March 1994.

9 October 1960
Lewisohn, 23.
Williams, 159.
Shotton, 65.
Davies, *The Beatles*, 79.
Norman, 94.
Miles, *The Beatles Diary, Volume I*, 25.
Sutcliffe and Clayson, 103.
Best and Doncaster, 42-47.

11 October 1960
Lewisohn, 23.
Williams, 180-184.
Norman, 118-120.
Pawlowski, 24-25.
Coleman, 112-113, 123.
Goldman, 103-104.
Miles, *The Beatles Diary, Vol. I,* 26.
Harry, *The Ultimate Beatles Encyclopedia*, 359-360, 242, 559-561.
Sutcliffe and Clayson, 94.
Interview with Allan Williams, March 1994.

Morning, 11 October 1960
Lewisohn, 23.
Williams, 180-184.
Norman, 118-120.
Pawlowski, 24-25.
Miles, *The Beatles Diary*, 25-26.
The Beatles, *The Anthology*, 48-50.

12 October 1960
Norman, 95.
Lewisohn, 23.
Williams, 193-197.
Harry, *The Ultimate Beatles Encyclopedia*, 13-14.
Coleman, 254-255.
Miles, *The Beatles Diary, Vol. I*, 26.
Interview with Allan Williams, March 1994.

15 October 1960
Williams, 193-197.
Miles, *The Beatles Diary, Volume 1*, 26.
Harry, *The Ultimate Beatles Encyclopedia*, 13-14.
Coleman, 254-255.

17 October 1960
Norman, 117-118.
Scheff, 163.
Giuliano, 27.
Best and Doncaster, 56.
Davies, *The Beatles*, 78.
Lennon, Cynthia, *A Twist of Lennon*, 53-54.
Harry, *The John Lennon Encyclopedia*, 906.
Riley, 56-57.

20 October 1960
Coleman, 113-118.
Norman, 122-127.
Lennon, Cynthia, *A Twist of Lennon*, 52-53.
Brown, 45-46.
Sutcliffe and Clayson, 103.
Harry, *The Ultimate Beatles Encyclopedia*, 360.
Miles, *The Beatles Diary, Vol. I*, 27.

21 Ocotber 1960
Coleman, 113-118.
Norman, 122-127.
Lennon, Cynthia, *A Twist of Lennon*, 52-53.
Brown, 45-46.
Best and Doncaster, 66.
Harry, *The John Lennon Encyclopedia*, 452.
Harry, *The Ultimate Beatles Encyclopedia*, 360.
Clayson and Sutcliffe, 104-105.

23 October 1960
Lewisohn, p.23.
Williams, 197-198.
Brown, 46.
Harry, *The Ultimate Beatles Encyclopedia*, 213.
Norman, 122-124.

Coleman, 113, 115, 122.
Miles, *The Beatles Diary, Vol. I*, 26.

31 Ocotber 1960
Miles, *The Beatles Diary, Vol I*, 26.
Harry, *The Ultimate Beatles Encyclopedia*, 559, 653.
Williams, 198.
Norman, 100-101.
Pawlowski, 27.
Lewisohn, 23-24.
Interview with Allan Williams, March 1994.

November 1960
Norman, 127-128.
Lennon, Cynthia, *A Twist of Lennon*, 55.
Shotton, 66.
Pawlowski, 27.
Coleman, 123-124.
Interview with Allan Williams, March 1994.

21 November 1960
Miles, *The Beatles Diary, Vol. I*, 27.
Lewisohn, 24.
Norman, 101.
Williams, 198-199.
Best and Doncaster, 74.
Brown, 47.
Davies, *The Beatles*, 87.
The Beatles, *The Anthology*, 55.

30 November 1960
Lewisohn, 24.
Best and Doncaster, 72-75.
Pawlowski, 29.
Coleman, 124.
Lennon, Cynthia, *A Twist of Lennon*, 54.
Norman, 101-102.
Goldman, 107.
Interview with Allan Williams, March 1994.
Information also provided by Pete Best's speech and question/answer session at New York "Fest for Beatlefans," The Meadowlands, New York, 3 April 2004.

1 December 1960
Coleman, 195.
Miles, *The Beatles Diary, Vol. I*, 28-29.
Harry, *The Ultimate Beatles Encyclopedia*, 50-51.
Leach, 89.
Best and Doncaster, 122.
Interview with Bob Wooler, Lark Lane, Liverpool, March 1994.
Friede, Titone, and Weiner, *The Beatles, A to Z*, 11.
Lewisohn, 29.

2 December 1960
Brown, 48.
Lewisohn, 25.
Liverpool, A to Z Street Atlas
Best and Doncaster, 79.
Williams, 200-201.
Miles, *John Lennon In His Own Words*, 30.
Harry, *The Ultimate Beatles Encyclopedia*, 655.
Norman, 103.
Interview with Allan Williams, March 1993.

13 December 1960
Lewisohn, 25.
Williams, 200-201.
Brown, 48.
Pawlowski, 28.
Harry, *The Ultimate Beatles Encyclopedia*, 655.
Salewicz, 105.
Norman, 103-104.
Interview with Allan Williams, March 1994.

17 December 1960
Best and Doncaster, 80-84.
Williams, 202.
Davies, *The Beatles*, 90-94.
Greenwald, 37.
Lewisohn, 25.
Brown, 49.
Imagine, Part V, John Lennon talks about Litherland, explaining that the crowd assumed they were German.

January 1961
Norman, 136-138.
Davies, *The Beatles*, 94-99.
Brown, 49.
Lewisohn, 30.

21 February 1961
Pawlowski, 34-35.
Coleman, 132.
Greenwald, 93.
Williams, 203.
Davies, *The Beatles*, 98-101.
Brown, 49.
Best and Doncaster, 82-88, 90.
Lennon, Cynthia, *A Twist of Lennon*, 55.
Burrows, 25.
Harry, *The Ultimate Beatles Encyclopedia*, 639.
Miles, *The Beatles Diary, Vol. I*, 35.
Thompson, 126-129.
The Beatles, *The Anthology*, 57.
Weiner, *The Beatles: The Ultimate Recording Guide*, 10.

22 February 1961
Best and Doncaster, 85.
Harry, *The Ultimate Beatles Encyclopedia*, 369-370.
Norman, 102.
Williams, 76.
Coleman, 107.
Clayson and Sutcliffe, 121-122.
Jones, Ron, 56.

25 February 1961
Pawlowski, 34-35.
Greenwald, 93.
Williams, 203.
Davies, *The Beatles*, 98-101.
Brown, 49.
Best and Doncaster, 82-88, 90.
Lennon, Cynthia, *A Twist of Lennon*, 55.
Sutcliffe and Clayson, 119.
Harry, *The Ultimate Beatles Encyclopedia*, 637.

3 March 1961
Lennon, Cynthia, *A Twist of Lennon*, 58.
Lennon, Cynthia, *John*, 63-64.
Interview of Cynthia Lennon by Spencer Leigh, "Good Day Sunshine," Issue 75.
Norman, 113.

4 March 1961
Lewisohn, 30-31.
Norman, 112-113.
Best and Doncaster, 88-89.
Williams, 203-204.
Interview with Allan Williams, 1993.
Lecture and question and answer session with Pete Best at "The Fest for Beatlefans," 3 April 2004, The Meadowlands, New York.

6 March 1961
Lewisohn, 40-41.
Harry, *The Ultimate Beatles Encyclopedia*, 50-51, 374-375.
Coleman, 126-127.

21 March 1961
Harry, *The Ultimate Beatles Encyclopedia*, 371.
Williams, 205.

Pawlowski, 35.
Best and Doncaster, 88-89.
Lennon, Cynthia, *John*, 65-66.
Interview with Allan Williams, March 1994.
Lecture by Pete Best at "The Fest for Beatlefans," 3 April 2004, The Meadowlands, New York.

10 April 1961
Williams, 205-206.
Harry, *The Ultimate Beatles Encyclopedia*, 654.
Clayson and Sutcliffe, 127-128.
Salewicz, 107.

11 April 1961
Lewisohn, 42.
Best and Doncaster, 93-101.
Lennon, Cynthia, *A Twist of Lennon*, 63.
Norman, 144-146.
Davies, *The Beatles*, 102-103.
Miles, *The Beatles Diary, Vol. I*, 37.
Clayson and Sutcliffe, 108, 131-132.
Lennon, Cynthia, *John*, 71.

20 April 1961
Lewisohn, 32.
Williams, 206-208.
Pawlowski, 36.
Williams, 206-207.
Interview with Allan Williams, March 1994.

21 April 1961
Lennon, John. *Skywriting by Word of Mouth*.
Letter written by John Lennon shown to me by Allan Williams, March 1994.
John's letters in Coleman's *Lennon*.

Easter 1961
Lennon, Cynthia, *A Twist of Lennon*, 52, 56-57.
Norman, 144-145.
Shotton, 66.
Harry, *The Ultimate Beatles Encyclopedia*, 552.
Salewicz, 108.
Clayson and Sutcliffe, 133.
Lennon, Cynthia, *John*, 58, 67-71.

May 1961
Lennon, Cynthia, *A Twist of Lennon*, 23-24.
Miles, *The Beatles Diary, Vol I*, 38.
Clayson and Sutcliffe, 126, 130.
Norman, 115.

23 June 1961
The Beatles, *The Anthology*, 59.
Clayson and Sutcliffe, 96, 130-131, 139-141.
Best and Doncaster, 106-107.
Lewisohn, 42-43.
Wiener, *The Ultimate Recording Guide*, 10.
Norman, 146-147.
Davies, *The Beatles*, 104.
Salewicz, 109-110.

July 1961
Miles, *The Beatles Diary, Volume I*, 42-43.
Lewisohn, 43-45.
Coleman, 128, 139-142, 151.
Norman, 147-150.
Clayson and Sutcliffe, 149.
Best and Doncaster, 115-123.
Thompson, 49-52.
Pawlowski, 33.
Interview with Bob Wooler, March 1994, Lark Lane, Liverpool.
Information supplied by Bill Harry via e-mail.

30 July 1961
Davies, *The Beatles*, 107.
Clayson and Sutcliffe, 150-151.
Norman, 121.

21 September 1961
Lewisohn, 46.
Harry, *Mersey Beat: The Beginnings of The Beatles*, 8-9.
Best and Doncaster, 122.
Davies, *The Beatles*, 106-107.
Interviews with Allan Williams, March 1993 and 1994.
Interview with Bob Wooler, Lark Lane, Liverpool, March 1994.
Visit to Litherland Town Hall, March 1993.

October 1961
Clayson and Sutcliffe, 151-55, 165-66.
Davies, *The Beatles*, 107-110.
Lennon, Cynthia, *A Twist of Lennon*, 64-65.
Lennon, Cynthia, *John*, 74.
Best and Doncaster, 122-123.
Norman, 121.
Salewicz, 113.
Brown, 53.
Miles, *The Beatles Diary, Vol. I*, 44-45.
Harry, *The John Lennon Encyclopedia*, 949.
The Beatles, *The Anthology*, 64.
Harry, *The Ultimate Beatles Encyclopedia*, 511.

13 October 1961
Lewisohn, 34, 47-48.
Norman, 121.

Best and Doncaster, 122-123.
Lennon, Cynthia, *John*, 24.
Harry, *The Ultimate Beatles Encyclopedia*, 511.
Miles, *The Beatles Diary, Vol. I*, 44-45.

16 October 1961
Davies, *The Beatles*, 124.
McNally, David, 21.
Harry, *Mersey Beat: The Beginnings of the Beatles*, 22.
Harry, 11, 462.
Clayson and Sutcliffe, 154-160
Interview with Beryl Adams at The Grange in Aigburth, March 1993.

17 October 1961
Davies, *The Beatles*, 124.
McNally, David, 21.
Harry, 462.
Clayson and Sutcliffe, 154-160
Unpublished letter by John Lennon shown to me by Allan Williams, March 1993.
Letters by John in *SkyWriting By Word of Mouth*.
Letters by John in Ray Coleman's *Lennon*.

19 October 1961
Lewisohn, 47.
Harry, *The Ultimate Beatles Encyclopedia*, 265.
Miles, *The Beatles Diary, Vol I*, 45.
Norman, 120.
Best and Doncaster, 112-114.

4 November 1961
Best and Doncaster, 112-114.
Pawlowski, 43.
Harry, *Mersey Beat: The Beginnings of the Beatles*, 23-24.
Shotton, 69-70.
Lewisohn, 48.

Afternoon, 4 November 1941
Coleman, 39.
Epstein, *A Cellarful of Noise*, 43-46.
Best and Doncaster, 125.
Norman, 134-135.
Brown, 65.
Salewicz, 114.
Leach, 125.
Miles, *The Beatles Diary, Vol I*, 46.

9 November 1961
Taylor, Alistair, *Yesterday, My Life with the Beatles*, 10-13.
Best and Doncaster, 125-7.
Thompson, 55.

Epstein, 46-48.
Harry, *The Ultimate Beatles Encyclopedia*, 224-5, 642.
Norman, 170-172.
Pawlowski, 39-41.
Davies, *The Beatles*, 124-125.
Lewisohn, 48.
Coleman, 146-147.
Brown, 66.
Goldman, 111.
Miles, *The Beatles' Diary, Vol. I*, 46-47.
Geller, Debbie, *In My Life; The Brian Epstein Story*, 36-37.
Giuliano, *Dark Horse*, 38-39.
Interview with Bob Wooler, Lark Lane, Liverpool, March 1995.

15 November 1961
Lewisohn, 48.
Thompson, 49-52.
Clayson and Sutcliffe, 168-169.
Coleman, 132.
Interviews with Eddie Porter regarding The Beatlettes, March 1994-8.
Interview with Tony Jackson, at the Premiere Party for the movie, "Backbeat," Mathew Street, March 1994.

21 November 1961
Norman, 174.
Epstein, 41, 48.
Taylor, 14.
Pawlowski, 41.
Davies, *The Beatles*, 125.
Brown, 66-67.
The Beatles, *The Anthology*, 65.
Interview with Joe Flannery, March 1993.

1 December 1961
Norman, 175.
Davies, *The Beatles*, 125.
Jones, 16, 31.
Geller, 39, 44, 53.
Personal visits to The Adelphi Hotel between March of 1993-2007.

2 December 1961
Salewicz, 120.
Best and Doncaster, 127.
Norman, 176.
Coleman, 149.
Numerous interviews with June Furlong between March 1993 and 2005.

Evening, 2 December 1961
Norman, 175.

Davies, 125.
Jones, 16, 31.
Pawlowski, 37. (There is an excellent photo of The Blue Angel on this page for those interested.)
Epstein, 50-51.
Williams, 211-214.
Interview with Allan Williams in March of 1993 and 1994.

10 December 1961
Interview with Bob Wooler, March 1994, Lark Lane, Liverpool.
Epstein, 49-53.
Harry, *The John Lennon Encyclopedia*, 229.
Harry, *The Ultimate Beatles Encyclopedia*, 705.
Taylor, 14-17.
Best and Doncaster, 126.
Pawlowski, 41.
Norman, 185.
Davies, *The Beatles*, 126-127.
Coleman, 147-148.
Salewicz, 199-120.

11 December 1961
Epstein, 49-53.
Taylor, 14-17.
Best and Doncaster, 126.
Pawlowski, 41.
Norman, 185.
Davies, *The Beatles*, 126-127.
Coleman, 147-148.
Salewicz, 119-120.
Interview with Bob Wooler, March 1994, Lark Lane, Liverpool.

Historical Characters

Historical novels offer a blend of fictitious characters and characters who have actually lived (and in this case, are still living). Most of the characters in **Shoulda Been There** *are real people. Here, in alphabetical order, are all of the real people in the book. Note: These very brief biographies cover only the years of* Shoulda Been There *(1940-1961), with the exception of Paul McCartney, George Harrison, and Ringo Starr…and that other one…*

Adams, Beryl – Brian Epstein's secretary at the Whitechapel NEMS. Beryl was the only person that Brian trusted with his complex system of filing and ordering records. She was petite, blonde, smart, and extremely competent. Later, Beryl married Bob Wooler, the compère of The Cavern Club. (Picture of Beryl Adams, Allan Williams, and the author in the appendix.)

Aggie – Cleaner at The Cavern Club in 1961. Aggie was a great friend to all of The Beatles.

Anderson, Helen – (Known as "Heloon" to John) One of John's closest chums at Liverpool College of Art, Helen was a striking co-ed whose beauty and wit beguiled John and annoyed Cynthia Powell. Helen was part of John's close inner circle, including Geoff Mohammed and Tony Carricker.

Aspinall, Neil – Pete Best's best friend and an accounting student who assisted Mona Best with the running of The Casbah Club. In 1960 when Pete left for Hamburg, Neil Aspinall moved into the Best home at 8 Hayman's Green. In Pete's absence, Neil worked alongside Mona Best, Pete's mother, helping her run the busy teen club. In December of that year, upon learning how very popular The Beatles had become in Hamburg, Neil became interested in promoting and marketing the group. Before their return to Liverpool, he began making posters proclaiming them as "The

Fabulous Beatles." In 1961, Neil left accounting entirely to become a volunteer roadie for the group. Driving a 15-pound van, he transported The Beatles and their gear to all of their gigs. He became an integral part of the group and is often called The Fifth Beatle.

Ballard, Arthur – Liverpool-born, one-time middleweight boxer and influential art teacher at Liverpool College of Art. Known for his abstract landscapes, Ballard tutored Stu Sutcliffe in Gambier Terrace and was also a champion for John Lennon during college staff meetings. Ballard allowed John to attend his classes when no other professors would tolerate him.

Beat Brothers, The – Name used by The Beatles when functioning as a back-up band for Tony Sheridan at a June 1960 recording session. Under the direction of Bert Kaempfert, Sheridan and The Beat Brothers recorded "My Bonnie Lies Over the Ocean" at Frederic Ebvert Halle, an infant's school in Hamburg. Although The Beatles served only as a back-up band during the session, this record is the one that Raymond Jones requested from Brian Epstein on 28 November 1961 – the record that first alerted Epstein to the existence of The Beatles and led to his management of the group.

"Beatcomber" – Pseudonym used by John Lennon when writing articles for Bill Harry's "Mersey Beat." Under this name, John wrote an article for the first issue of the publication, the 6-20 July 1961 issue. It was entitled, "Being A Short Diversion on the Dubious Origins of Beatles," a farcical history of the group. Interestingly, Brian Epstein also had an article called "Stop the World (and listen to everything in it)" in that exact same issue.

The Beatmakers – One-night only group made up of The Beatles, Gerry and the Pacemakers, and Karl Terry of The Cruisers. They performed in outlandish costumes and playing instruments that they didn't ordinarily play. The Beatmakers were a group for one evening only: 19 October 1961 at Litherland Town Hall.

Bennion, Dave – "Head Boy" or Prefect at Quarry Bank School during the years when John was there. As liaison between the staff and student body, Dave was responsible for bringing John's myriad misbehaviours to the attention of the faculty. There was no love lost between John and Dave – who referred to John as "a salt" (in an open wound).

Berry, Chuck – (Mr. Berry is not in the book but is mentioned.) American pioneer of rock'n'roll, Berry had numerous hits including "Rock and Roll Music," "Johnny B. Goode," and "Sweet Little Sixteen" – all of which were covered by The Beatles in Hamburg and at The Cavern Club. They were all huge fans of Chuck Berry, and he was one of the greatest influences on the group.

Best, Johnny – (Mr. Best is not in the book but is mentioned several times.) Ex-husband of Mona Best, father of Pete and Rory Best. Johnny Best was a very successful and charismatic boxing promoter at The Liverpool Stadium.

Best, Mona – Wife of Johnny Best (later divorced), mother of Pete, Rory, and Roag Best. In August 1960, Mona opened The Casbah Club – a teen club – in her West Derby home. The Beatles performed for her on opening night. Through this association, they came to know her son, Pete, and eventually invited him to come with them to Hamburg, Germany for a gig at The Indra Club (and later, The Kaiserkeller). Mona was a savvy businesswoman and loosely served as The Beatles' manager for a time in the spring 1961, after ties with Allan Williams had been severed. (Picture of the Best home where The Casbah was located in appendix. Photo taken in 1992.)

Best, Peter – ("Pete") Oldest son of Mona Best and drummer for The Beatles in 1960-62. Pete lived with his mother and brother Rory (Roag was born later) at 8 Hayman's Green in West Derby, a suburb of Liverpool. After her separation from Johnny Best, Pete's mother converted the basement of her home into a teen nightspot called The Casbah. Pete, a drummer for The Blackjacks, entertained there frequently, as did The Beatles. In August 1960, Pete was invited by The Beatles to accompany them to Hamburg, Germany. During spring 1961, he returned with them to Hamburg to play The Top Ten Club. Best remained a member of The Beatles until August 1962.

Best, Rory – Younger brother of Pete Best, son of Mona and Johnny Best. Rory and Pete came up with the idea of a teen club in their basement. This eventually evolved into The Casbah Club. Rory and Pete both worked in the club with their mother.

Brown, Ken – Guitarist in The Les Stewart Quartet who met The Best family through George Harrison. Throughout summer 1959, Ken helped Mona Best and her sons convert the basement of their home into The Casbah Club. Because of his devotion to the project, he was booted from The Les Stewart quartet. Mona, therefore, asked The Beatles to let Ken play with them on The Casbah's opening night. John was reluctant to do so, but relented when he discovered that Ken owned his own amplifier.

Burnett, Phillip – English Master at Quarry Bank during the years when Pete and John were there. He was impressed with John's intelligence and aptitude. Burnett was a champion for John when most other professors considered him merely a delinquent.

Mr. Burroughs – John's and Pete's House Teacher (The Woolton House) at Quarry Bank.

Burton, Charles – Head of painting at Liverpool College of Art during the years when John and Stu were there. Born in South Wales and a talented artist in his own right, Charles Burton was never pleased with John as a student. He phoned Mimi Smith many times to report John's absences and failures and was influential in having John terminated from the college for non-attendance.

Caldwell, Alan – Leader of The Texans, a Liverpool skiffle group. The Texans performed on the same bill as The Quarry Men in March 1958 at The Morgue Skiffle Cellar. Caldwell owned the venue and arranged the programme.

Carricker, Tony – Student at Liverpool College of Art with John and Stu. Tony was part of the tight-knit group of friends who frequented Ye Cracke and carried out various pranks both at school and in the Hope Street/Rice Street area.

Cass and the Cassanovas – Popular Merseyside group led by Brian Casser (or Cassar according to some sources). The group was comprised of Brian Casser (vocals), Johnny Hutchison (drums), Johnny Gustafson (bass), Adrian Barber (guitar), and Casey Jones (rhythm guitar). They auditioned with The Silver Beatles for Larry Parnes at Allan Williams' Blue Angel in Seel Street, May of 1960. That day, Johnny Hutchison was "conscripted" by Allan Williams to drum for The Beatles whose temporary drummer, Tommy Moore, did not make it to the audition on time.

Casser, Brian (or Cassar, according to some sources) – Leader and vocalist for Cass and the Cassanovas, the successful Merseyside group who auditioned (as did The Beatles) for Larry Parnes in May 1960. Brian Casser was a favourite of Allan Williams and was influential in convincing Williams that the name The Quarry Men was out-of-date. Casser pointed out that all bands of the day listed the lead singer in the group name (Gerry and The Pacemakers, Buddy Holly and the Crickets, etc.). Brian Casser allowed his talented drummer, Johnny Hutchison, to play for The Beatles at the Larry Parnes audition (May 1960) when Tommy Moore – the drummer Allan Williams had secured for The Beatles – was late for the performance.

Chang, Barry – Brother of Beryl Chang and brother-in-law of Allan

Williams. Barry accompanied The Beatles, Lord Woodbine, Beryl, and Allan on the trip to Hamburg where The Beatles were booked at Bruno Koschmider's Indra Club. Along the way, Barry took the famous photograph of The Beatles at The Arnhem War Memorial. The group (minus John Lennon) are ironically posed in front of a wall that reads, "There names liveth forevermore."

Chapman, Norman – Amateur drummer who played with The Beatles for a short time in July of 1960. After losing Tommy Moore, the group was desperate for a drummer, and Williams heard about Chapman's ability; Williams thought he was a decorator. Chapman was, in fact, a frame maker. He was a witty Scouser and good drummer, and the boys hit it off well with him. He played with The Beatles several times at Grosvenor Ballroom. Unfortunately, soon after Chapman joined the group, he was conscripted into the army.

Charles, Ray – (Mr. Charles is not in the book, but is mentioned frequently.) American performer, pianist, and composer. Ray Charles had gigantic hits in the late 1950's and early 1960's including "What I'd Say," which was covered by The Beatles.

Chase, John – Student at Liverpool College of Art when John and Stu were there. Chase, a serious student and not one of John's cronies, was selected to star as "Prince Charming" in John Lennon's stage adaptation of "Cinderella" in 1959.

Cheniston, Roland – Regular customer at The Jacaranda, a friend of Allan Williams, and a photographer. In May 1960, Cheniston attended the Larry Parnes/Billy Fury audition at The Wyvern Social Club (soon to be The Blue Angel) at Allan's request. He took several photos of Billy Fury with Allan's Liverpool bands. One shows John Lennon asking Fury for an autograph.

Cochran, Eddie – American rock'n'roll pioneer who topped the charts with his hit, "Summertime Blues." On tour in England, Cochran and his best friend, Gene Vincent, were supposed to play a concert at The Liverpool Stadium (3 May 1960). Allan Williams was in charge of the venue and gave John, Paul, George, and Stu tickets to the event. However, on 17 April, Cochran and Vincent were involved in a car accident near Wiltshire, England, and Cochran was killed. Cochran's "Twenty Flight Rock" is the song that Paul McCartney played when he performed for John Lennon the very first time at St. Peter's Church Hall in Woolton and Cochran's "C'mon Everybody" is the first song Stu Sutcliffe ever learned to play on the bass guitar.

Condor, Leslie – Patron of The Cavern Club throughout the Beatle years. I met Mr. Condor at the Pump House Pub in Liverpool. He overheard me interviewing June Furlong and came over to introduce himself. He graciously gave me many details about The Beatles and their performances at The Cavern and is featured in a chapter about the club.

Connaughts, The – Band led by Nicky Cuff who auditioned for Carroll Levis at the Manchester Hippodrome in November 1959, competing with The Beatles. Group members included Gordon Conway, Martin King, Johnny State, Billy Jevons, Arthur Krowleson, and Nicky Cuff. The Connaughts garnered more applause than The Beatles, but the outcome of the competition will never be known. The Beatles had to leave Manchester before the final round of competition – in order to catch the last train home to Liverpool. They didn't have the funds to get a hotel room in Manchester.

Coward, Bill – Friend of Allan Williams and patron of The Jacaranda Coffee House in Slater Street, Liverpool. After reading the popular novel, *The Jacaranda Tree*, Mr. Coward recommended that Williams name his new coffeehouse in Slater Street "The Jacaranda." Allan did just that.

Cuff, Nicky – Diminutive (4'6") but hugely energetic lead singer for The Sunnyside Skiffle Group and later, The Connaughts. As leader of The Sunnyside Skiffle Group, Cuff competed against The Quarry Men at the 9 June 1957 Carroll Levis audition held in Liverpool's Empire Theater. John Lennon was so impressed with Nicky's antics on stage (including jumping up and balancing on his tea chest bass) that John directed The Quarry Men to "get a gimmick" and quit standing around "like one o'Lewises."

Davis, Rod – Quarry Bank acquaintance of John's who owned his own banjo and played quite well. Rod was invited to play with The Quarry Men because he owned an instrument and was talented. However, he and John squabbled over whether the group was going to play skiffle (Rod's choice) or rock'n'roll (John's). Rod was an excellent student in the A-stream at Quarry Bank; John resented this as well.

Derry and The Seniors – Very popular Merseyside band led by Derry Wilkie (lead vocalist). Members of the group included Howie Casey on sax, Lu Walters on bass, Frank Wibberly on drums, and Brian Griffiths on guitar. They were the first band to go to Hamburg from Liverpool and were not enthusiastic about The Beatles coming over to join them. They wrote to Allan Williams asking why "that bunch of five chord merchants" had to come over and ruin their reputation. Williams did not share this missive with The Beatles.

Donegan, Lonnie – Formerly the banjoist for The Chris Barber Jazz Band, Tony ("Lonnie") Donegan, formed his own band in 1956 and became a huge recording artist, instigating the skiffle craze. Known as "The King of Skiffle," Donegan had many hit songs, including "Rock Island Line" and "Cumberland Gap." The early Quarry Men emulated Lonnie Donegan and wanted to be as popular as he was.

Dykins, Jaqui – Daughter of Julia Stanley Lennon and John Dykins. Jacqui is John's half-sister, and spent many happy hours with him in her parents' home at 1 Blomfield Road, Allerton.

Dykins, John – ("Bobby" to Julia, "Twitchy" to John, also called "Jack") Father of Jacqui and Julia Dykins. While Fred Lennon was away from Liverpool for an extended amount of time, Julia Lennon fell in love with John Dykins, a handsome waiter at The Adelphi Hotel in Liverpool. When Fred refused to give Julia a divorce, Julia moved in with Dykins anyway. They had two children: Jacqui and Julia Dykins. For a short time, the couple lived with Pop Stanley at 9 Newcastle Road and then acquired their own home at 1 Blomfield Road in Allerton. John was with John Dykins and his sisters the night that Julia was killed. (House pictured in appendix)

Dykins, Julia – Daughter of Julia Stanley Lennon and John Dykins. Julia is John's half-sister and like Jacqui, shared many memories with her brother in Allerton. She later wrote a book about John: *John Lennon, My Brother*.

Eckhorn, Peter – German entrepreneur who, in late autumn 1961, opened a huge new nightclub in Hamburg's Reeperbahn area. It was called The Top Ten Club. Eckhorn not only began to take all of Bruno Koschmider's staff away from The Kaiserkeller – he also began to woo away Koschmider's entertainers. In December 1960, The Beatles played a free set for Eckhorn and infuriated Koschmider so much that Koschmider had George Harrison deported and Paul McCartney and Pete Best arrested for arson. The Beatles, nevertheless, signed a contract to play The Top Ten, April 1961. Tony Sheridan was Eckhorn's headliner at The Top Ten.

Brian Epstein – Son of Harry and Queenie Epstein of Queen's Drive Liverpool; brother of Clive Epstein. After trying many unsuccessful ventures (the army, the Royal Academy of Dramatic Arts, the family furniture business) Brian's father made the twenty-seven year old the manager of the Esptein's North End Music Store in Whitechapel Road. There Brian took great pride in stocking every record anyone could want. On 28 October 1961, a young man named Raymond Jones came into the store asking for a disc entitled "My Bonnie" by The Beatles. Brian had never heard of this record or of The Beatles – who were performing live at The Cavern Club only yards away from his NEMS store. On 9 November, Brian went to The Cavern to hear the lads perform, accompanied by his personal assistant, Alistair Taylor. In the days after this performance, Brian decided to offer management of the rock'n'roll band. His parents were convinced that the venture was another of his "flings" that would fail. The family solicitor, Rex Makin, was also reticent. His brother, Clive, however, believed in Brian's ability to make this a success. On 10 December, Brian offered to manage the group, and John Lennon (followed by all the others) accepted the offer.

Epstein, Clive – Younger brother of Brian Epstein. Clive was very supportive of his brother's decision to manage The Beatles. When Brian advised Clive to invest in The Beatles, he did so. Consequently, Clive became the highly successful Company Secretary of NEMS Enterprises and was known for his integrity and quiet, competent approach to business.

Epstein, Harry – Successful Liverpool businessman who inherited his father's furniture store, I. Epstein and Sons. Harry was an entrepreneur who he turned his father's single furniture store into a chain of furniture stores and then later opened the North End Music Stores in Liverpool. He married Malka (Queenie) Hyman, and they had two sons, Brian and Clive. The family lived at 197 Queen's Drive in Woolton. Harry was bitterly disappointed in Brian's many failures in the army, at the Royal Academy of Dramatic Arts, and the furniture store business. As a last ditch effort, he gave Brian the Whitechapel North End Music store to manage. There, Brian encountered The Beatles and decided to manage the local rock'n'roll band. Harry was extremely skeptical – was not in favour of Brian's taking on such a venture. (Photo of the Epstein family home in appendix)

Epstein, Queenie – Wife of Harry Epstein, mother of Brian and Clive. Born Malka Hyman, Queenie was the daughter of a successful businessman who ran the Sheffield Cabinet Company. Not surprisingly, she fell in love with Harry Epstein, another competent businessman. They settled in Liverpool and had two sons, Brian and Clive. When Brian announced his intention to manage a rock'n'roll group, The Beatles, Queenie was supportive but urged her son to speak with the group's former manager, Allan Williams, and to get all of the answers about the band.

Fascher, Horst – Bruno Koschmider's head bouncer at The Kaiserkeller Club in Hamburg, Germany. Horst led a very adept gang of fighters who kept peace in the club. They were former boxers known as "Hoddel's Gang." The gang took on Rory Storm and The Hurricanes and The Beatles after these two groups intentionally crashed through Bruno Koschmider's dilapidated wooden stage in The Kaiserkeller. Fascher, however, did not put his heart into the fight because he liked the boys. He invited The Beatles to his home on many occasions for dinner. In late 1960, he defected, with the rest of Koschmider's staff, to the new and glamourous Top Ten Club owned by Peter Eckhorn. He was delighted when The Beatles returned to Germany to perform there in the spring 1961.

Forrester, Mark – Assistant to Larry Parnes who contacted Allan Williams about selecting five of his best groups to audition for Parnes in May 1960. Parnes was looking for touring bands for his stars, Duffy Power, Johnny Gentle, and Liverpool-born recording star, Billy Fury. Forrester accompanied Parnes to Liverpool on 10 May 1960 for the audition at The Blue Angel in Seel Street and sat in on the audition process.

Furlong, June – Very successful Liverpool-born life model in London and on the Continent. At the height of her career, June returned to Liverpool to work at Liverpool College of Arts. She became a much-in-demand life model at Liverpool College of Art and was working on campus during the time that Stu Sutcliffe and John Lennon were there. John looked up to June as an example of a professional success and often sought her counsel. He once convinced her to contribute costumes for his stage rendition of "Cinderella." When trying to make up his mind about whether or not to sign with Brian Epstein in December 1961, John asked June's advice at The Kardomah Café. June's piercing question, "What have you got to lose?" convinced John to sign with Epstein. (1993 Photo of June with the author in appendix.)

Fury, Billy – One of Larry Parnes singing stars. Born in Liverpool as Ronald Wycherly, Fury had many hits, the most popular of which was "Halfway to Paradise." On 10 May 1960, he accompanied Mark Forrester and Larry Parnes to Liverpool for a talent audition of possible back-up bands. Cass and the Cassanovas were selected to back him while The Beatles were chosen to back Johnny Gentle. John Lennon was impressed with Fury – as he was with all successful people – and asked Fury for an autograph that day.

Garry, Len – One of the original Quarry Men, called in to play tea chest bass after Bill Smith had been dismissed. Len attended The Liverpool Institute, and on one occasion, when the school was on holiday, Len and Bill Turner were convinced by John to come to Quarry Bank with him, masquerading as new students. Len later wrote a book about his years with John and his Quarry Men days entitled, *John, Paul & Me: Before the Beatles.*

Gerry and The Pacemakers – Highly successful Liverpool group led by Gerry Marsden (lead vocalist). Members included Gerry's brother, Freddy Marsden (drums), Les Chadwick (guitar) and Les Maguire (piano). The Pacemakers auditioned with The Beatles in May of 1960 for Larry Parnes at Allan Williams' Blue Angel in Seel Street. Later, in 1961, they joined forces with the Beatles for one night at Litherland to form one band, a supergroup, "The Beatmakers." Gerry and the Pacemakers experienced great acclaim in the 1960's British invasion with hits such as "Don't Let the Sun Catch You Cryin'" and "Ferry 'Cross the Mersey." (Blue Angel pictured in appendix)

Gin, Auntie – Jim McCartney's sister, Paul's aunt. After the death of Paul's mother, Mary, Auntie Gin helped Jim with the care of his two sons, Paul and Michael.

Gretty, Jim – One of Hesssey's Music Store's most knowledgeable salesmen. He sold John Lennon (and his Aunt Mimi) his first store-bought guitar in the Whitechapel store in May of 1957. (Hessey's pictured in appendix)

Griffiths, Eric – One of the original members of The Quarry Men. Eric was one of the first boys invited to join The Quarry Men since he owned his own guitar. Later, Griffiths introduced Colin Hanton and Rod Davis into the group. Eric served as lead guitarist for The Quarry Men until Paul McCartney joined the band.

Griffiths, Teddy – Professor at Liverpool College of Art. Mr. Griffiths taught the Life Class in which June Furlong was the life model and John Lennon, a student. He was part of the panel of professors who decided to expel John from university for non-attendance.

Hague, Jonathan – Student at Liverpool College of Art with John and Stu. Hague shared a lettering class with John and Cynthia. He was also part of the Lennon-Mohammed crowd that frequented Ye Cracke.

Hall, Billy – Friend of Fred Lennon's during the time when Fred took young John to live in Blackpool. Billy and Fred devised a plan to move to New Zealand and sell ladies stockings. John was to go to New Zealand with Billy's parents and meet his father and Mr. Hall there. This plan was thwarted by Julia's arrival in Blackpool. John was taken back to Liverpool to live with Julia's sister, Mimi, and her husband, George.

Mr. and Mrs. Hall – Parents of Billy Hall who, in 1945, were supposed to take John to New Zealand to meet his father there.

Haigh, Jonathan – Student at Liverpool College of Art when John and Stu were there. Johnathan shared lettering class with John and Cynthia.

Hanton, Colin – First drummer of The Quarry Men, introduced to the band by Eric Griffiths. Through his friendship with Charles Roberts, Colin was able to secure The Quarry Men one of their first gigs – The Roseberry Street Festival on 22 June 1957.

Harrison, George – Lead guitarist for The Quarry Men and later The Beatles. A mate of Paul McCartney's at The Liverpool Institute, Paul admired Harrison's skill on guitar and invited George to attend the Quarry Men's performance at the Morgue Skiffle Cellar in March of 1958. Afterwards, he asked George (though three years younger than John) to audition for John. (Some sources list this event earlier in Feb. 1958.) George immediately became part of The Quarry Men and evolved into the talented lead guitarist and singer for The Beatles. George was always a close, personal friend of John's and Cynthia's and at Liverpool College of Art, he tagged along with them frequently. As part of The Beatles, George went on the Johnny Gentle Tour of Scotland and both trips to Hamburg. He emerged as a remarkable songwriter, gentle spirit, and shaping force in the group.

Harry, Bill – Handsome, Tony Curtis-like student at Liverpool College of Art when John and Stu were there. However, Bill Harry dreamed not of becoming a famous artist but of starting a news-magazine to cover the beat scene in Liverpool. He called it "Mersey Beat." The publication (first released July 6-20, 1961) was extremely popular, and John Lennon wrote many articles for it under the pseudonym, "Beatcomber." Bob Wooler also had a column entitled, "The Roving I," and Brian Esptein had one called, "Stop the World (and listen to everything in it)". Harry was a close friend of the Beatles and introduced John to his best mate, Stuart Sutcliffe. He was also present the day that Stu Sutcliffe suggested naming the group "The Beatles."

Harry, Virginia – Girlfriend (and later wife) of Bill Harry. Virginia worked arm in arm with Bill in developing and publishing the "Mersey Beat" news magazine in Liverpool, beginning 6 July 1961. She and Bill were intimate friends of The Beatles and attended virtually every Beatles performance at The Cavern Club.

Harvey, Lelia – Daughter of Harriet Stanley. Lelia was John's cousin and one of his close friends. She was with John on the day of his Uncle

George's funeral and tried to comfort him. She also returned from Edinburgh University to be there for John when Julia died.

Henri, Adrian – (Mr. Henri is not a character in the book, but is referred to several times.) Painter and a famous Liverpool beat poet of the 1960's. Adrian Henri loved Liverpool and helped foster the belief that it was a centre of culture, much like Concord, Massachusetts during the era of Hawthorne, Thoreau, Emerson, and Alcott. He was a friend of John's and Paul's and helped shape their belief that The Beatles were part of that movement of art, music, and poetry.

Holly, Buddy – (Buddy Holly is not a character in the book but is mentioned frequently.) American pioneer of rock'n'roll, Buddy Holly was the lead singer and composer for Buddy Holly and the Crickets. They had huge hits with "Maybe Baby," "Peggy Sue," "Cryin' in the Rain" and a song The Beatles covered, "Words of Love." One year after Buddy Holly died in an airplane crash, Stu Sutcliffe suggested that Johnny and the Moondogs (earlier The Quarry Men) change their name to The Beetles in homage to Buddy Holly and the Crickets. John Lennon liked the idea of spelling the group's name with an "a" (B-e-**a**-t-l-e-s) to employ the double entendre of beat and rhythm.

Horsefield, Nicholas – Art History professor at Liverpool College of Art when John and Stu were in attendance. Horsefield was one of a large group of professors who lobbied to have John removed from university for non-attendance.

Hutchison, Johnny – ("Hutch") One of the most talented drummers Merseyside, member of Cass and the Cassanovas. On 10 May 1960, Allan Williams requested that Hutch drum for The Beatles, whose temporary drummer had not shown up for the Larry Parnes audition. Hutch was reticent to do so (his group had already performed and it *was* a competition!), but he agreed, nevertheless, to help The Beatles for Allan Williams' sake. Halfway through the audition, the new drummer, Tommy Moore, arrived and stepped in.

Michael Issacson – Student with John at Dovedale Primary, Quarry Bank, and Liverpool College of Art. Issacson was an excellent scholar and a very confident young man. John once questioned him about what he had done to become so successful in his endeavors. John and Michael were not "friends" per se, but John admired Issacson's ability and determination. Michael was also a good friend to Cynthia Lennon.

Jackson, Tony – Very handsome lead singer and bass player for

Liverpool's The Searchers. Jackson wrote their hit song "Needles and Pins." Tony was a great friend of The Beatles and performed with them at venues all over Merseyside.

Jardine, George – Talented Liverpool artist who served as a professor at Liverpool College of Art during the time that Stu and John were there. Jardine was not a fan of John Lennon's and was one of a large group of professors who pushed for John's dismissal from the school for misbehaviour and non-attendance.

Johnny and The Moondogs – Name used by The Beatles for a short time in 1959. They were billed as Johnny and the Moondogs at the Carroll Levis competition in Manchester in November of 1959. John didn't like this name because he didn't think any one member of the group should be singled out. However, Allan Williams championed the name since Brian Casser of Cass and the Cassanovas had pointed out that most contemporary groups listed the leader's name before the band name (Derry and the Seniors, Cass and the Cassanovas, for example).

Johnson, Olive – Neighbour of Jim, Paul, and Mike McCartney's in Forthlin Road, Allerton, who was considered worldly-wise. When Brian Epstein offered to manage The Beatles in December 1961, Jim McCartney was very uneasy about the arrangement. He decided to invite Brian to the family home in Forthlin Road, Allerton, and to invite Olive in as well – to ascertain the genuineness of the entrepreneur. Paul was opposed to this idea, but his father was firm in the decision to do this.

Jones, Raymond – Lad who on 28 November, 1961 requested "My Bonnie" by The Beatles at NEMS in Whitechapel, Liverpool. The search for the disc that ensued alerted Brian Esptein to the presence of this popular local rock'n'roll group and prompted Brian to attend the 9 November 1961 lunchtime session at The Cavern Club. Jones was a printer's apprentice in Huyton who eventually owned his own printing shop in Burscough.

Kaempfert, Bert – Successful German composer/band leader. Kaempfert had a number one hit on the Continent and in America with his song, "Wonderland by Night." Through a mutual acquaintance, Albert Schacht, Kaempfert learned of the popularity of Tony Sheridan, and he visited The Top Ten Club in Hamburg to hear Sheridan perform. Kaempfert was impressed with Sheridan and offered to cut a record for the singer. Sheridan accepted and decided to use The Beatles (billed as "The Beat Brothers") as a back-up band. In June 1960, Kaempfert recorded Sheridan and The Beat Brothers singing "My Bonnie Lies Over the Ocean" at Frederic Albert Halle, an infant's school. This is the record that Raymond Jones requested at the Whitechapel NEMS (Liverpool) on 28 October 1960 – the disc that led to Brian Epstein's interest in The Beatles.

Kelly, Brian – Powerful Merseyside promoter of Lathom Hall, Litherland Town Hall, and Aintree Institute. In May 1960, Kelly booked the Beatles at Lathom Hall, but the lads reneged when they were offered the Johnny Gentle tour of Scotland. Kelly vowed never to allow the boys to perform in one of his venues again. But when the group became enormously popular, Kelly very reluctantly relented. It was at Lathom Hall that Stu was allegedly beaten after an early spring 1961 performance.

Kirchherr, Astrid – Fiancé of Klaus Voormann and a leader in the Exis movement in Hamburg during the early 1960's. Astrid Kirchherr was a beautiful and talented photographer who in 1960 photographed The Beatles at Der Dom Park in Hamburg. She was also influential in having them adopt an "out of the box," creative style of performing. Astrid cut Stu Sutcliffe's hair in an Exis *pilzen kopf* (bowl cut), and in October of 1961, John followed suit. This became the traditional "Beatle haircut." Stu and Astrid fell in love not long after they met, and they became engaged. When The Beatles returned to Liverpool in December 1960, Stu announced his decision to leave the band, and he remained behind with Astrid.

Koschmider, Bruno – German club owner of The Indra and The Kaiserkeller clubs. After The Jacaranda's Royal Caribbean Steel Band defected to Hamburg in the summer of 1960, Allan Williams traveled to Hamburg to convince club owner, Bruno Koschmider, to book several other of his Liverpool rock'n'roll groups. Unfortunately, Williams' reel-to-reel tape of the groups would not work. Williams was so convincing, however, that Koschmider had second thoughts about hiring the British bands, and he traveled to England to find Williams. Not knowing where Williams lived, Koschmider sought him in London on a whim. As fate would have it, Williams was in London that very evening, and the two men ran into each other in The Two I's Coffee Bar. Koschmider immediately booked Derry and The Seniors at his Kaiserkeller Club, and in August 1960, he also booked The Beatles at his Indra Club. The Beatles were so popular at The Indra that, in the autumn of 1960, they were moved to The Kaiserkeller to share the stage with another of Williams' groups, Rory Storm and The Hurricanes. Koschmider profited from the charismatic British groups, but watched each one of them defect (along with his staff of cleaners, waiters, and bouncers) when Peter Eckhorn opened the newer, larger, swankier Top Ten Club in December of 1960. When The Beatles broke their contract by performing at The Top Ten for an hour and a half on their night off from The Kaiserkeller, Koschmider had George deported for underage employment and accused Paul McCartney and Pete Best of setting fire to the Bambi Kino Theatre where he was housing them. He also obtained a work ban against The Beatles that made their return to Germany in the spring of 1961 extremely difficult.

Leach, Sam – Extremely successful promoter Merseyside, most often linked with The Iron Door Club (Liverpool Jazz Society). In the autumn 1961, Leach organized a gigantic rock'n'roll show entitled Operation Big Beat, featuring The Beatles. Brian Epstein was asked to put a poster advertising this event in his Whitechapel NEMS store, and this poster (along with requests for The Beatles' records) prompted Brian to go see the group for himself on 9 November. Leach, who had booked The Beatles on many occasions at The Cassanova Club, also toyed with the idea of managing The Beatles.

Lennon, Alfred – ("Fred" to Mimi, "Freddy" to Julia, written as "Freddie" by some biographers) Son of Jack Lennon, wife of Julia Lennon, father of John Lennon. Alfred was abandoned at an early age and reared in Liverpool's Bluecoat School for orphans. He fell in love with and married Julia Stanley of Liverpool in 1938. Their son, John, was born on 9 October 1940 while Fred was working aboard a World War II transport ship. During Fred's long absence from Liverpool, Julia became involved with another man, John Dykins, and asked Fred for a divorce. When Fred refused to grant her a divorce, she moved in with Dykins. John was sent to live with his Uncle George and Aunt Mimi in Woolton, a suburb of Liverpool. In 1945, Fred attempted to take his son to New Zealand to live with him. Julia found out about this plan and arrived on the scene before father and son could leave the country. She took John back to Liverpool to live with his aunt and uncle. Fred wrote to John many times throughout his childhood years, but John's Aunt Mimi thought it best not to upset the boy with these letters. Fred was a talented singer, entertaining the troops aboard World War II transport ships.

Lennon, John – Why are you looking for him in this list? See page 1.

Lennon, Julia Stanley – Daughter of George Ernest Stanley and Annie Sutherland Stanley, wife of Alfred Lennon, and mother of John Lennon. Julia was known to her sisters as "Judy." Although Julia ultimately relinquished her son, John, to her sister, Mimi, to rear in 1945, she had an overwhelming influence upon her son during his teen years. She played banjo and taught her son the instrument. She encouraged him to form a skiffle band. Julia taught John the value of creative thinking and of living life capriciously. Throughout his life, John worshipped his mother and wrote many of his best songs for her.

Levis, Carroll – "Mr. Star Maker" and host of the television programme, "Search" which highlighted undiscovered talent. On 9 June 1957, Levis hosted Liverpool auditions for his television programme at The Empire Theatre. One of the groups auditioning was The Quarry Men. They did not make the final round, but were bested by The Sunnyside Skiffle Group featuring the vivacious Nicky Cuff. This loss convinced John Lennon that his band needed to perform, not just play songs. In November 1959, Levis hosted another similar night at The Manchester Hippodrome, and The Beatles again performed. This time the group had to leave before the final round of competition because they had to catch the last transport home to Liverpool.

Makin, Rex – (Mr. Makin is not actually in the book although he is mentioned several times.) Prominent Liverpool solicitor with offices in Whitechapel. He was the family solicitor for the Epsteins. Consequently, Mr. Makin became the legal advisor for The Beatles. When Brian first consulted Mr. Makin about his decision to manage the rock'n'roll group, Mr. Makin flatly stated that he hoped this would not be "just another Epstein idea."

Marsden, Freddy – Brother of Gerry Marsden (both of Liverpool) and the drummer for Gerry and the Pacemakers. Freddy was one of the musicians who on the night of 19 October 1961 joined forces with The Beatles to form "The Beatmakers" at Litherland Town Hall. Freddy and Pete Best shared the drumming responsibilities that evening.

Marsden, Gerry – Leader (and lead singer) of Gerry and the Pacemakers, a popular Liverpool band. Marsden's group played with The Beatles on many occasions, including the 19 October 1961 Litherland Hall appearance in which the two bands combined to form "The Beatmakers."

Mr. Martin – John's art instructor at Quarry Bank. It was in Mr. Martin's class in the autumn 1955 that John passed Len Garry and Bill Turner (both from the Liverpool Institute) off as "new students" to Quarry Bank.

Mason, Ann – Coed who attended Liverpool College of Art with John. Ann was the girlfriend of John's close friend, Geoff Mohammed. As such, Ann was part of John's inner circle of friends.

May, David – Student at Liverpool College of Art who volunteered to teach Stu how to play bass. May tried to teach Sutcliffe the song, "C'mon Everybody" and in exchange, asked to measure Stu's Hofner bass so that he could construct one of his own.

McBain, Charlie – Promoter for The Clubmoor in Norris Green. The Quarry Men performed there in October of 1957 with a brand new band member, Paul McCartney. McBain tersely reviewed their performance that evening as "good and bad."

McCartney, James Paul – (also referred to under the stage name of "Paul Ramon" and nicknamed "Macca" by The Beatles) Incredibly talented guitarist and vocalist for The Quarry Men. A friend of Ivan Vaughn's at The Liverpool Institute, Paul McCartney could play guitar, tune guitar, and even write his own music. Vaughn wanted his friend, John Lennon, to meet this musician. So he invited McCartney to attend the Woolton Garden Fête in July 1957. Paul became a member of the Quarry Men about two weeks later. He later became The Beatles' bass player after Stu Sutcliffe left the group. Paul encouraged John to write his own songs, and the two collaborated on songs as well. Paul was a strong leader, and John was always worried that Paul would take control of his group. As part of The Beatles, Paul attended the Johnny Gentle Tour of Scotland, both Hamburg trips, and went with John on holiday to Paris in October 1961. Paul's strengths inspired John and always nudged him on to be more than he could have been alone. During The Fab Four years of The Beatles, Paul emerged as a prolific composer and performer, a strong leader of the group alongside John, and a charismatic star.

McCartney, Jim – Father of James Paul McCartney and Michael McCartney, husband of Mary McCartney. After his wife's tragic death to breast cancer in 1956 (at age 45), Jim McCartney raised his two young sons alone. He had played in a jazz band in his youth, the Jim McJazz Band (or Jim Mac's band in some sources), so he was enthusiastic over Paul's musical ventures. When Paul joined The Quarry Men, however, Jim was not thrilled about the influence of John Lennon on his son. Jim McCartney wanted both of his sons to do well in life and only allowed Paul to go on the two-week Johnny Gentle Tour of Scotland because Paul had told him that the Liverpool Institute was "on holiday" during that time. He was also reticent of the Hamburg trip and of Brian Epstein. He wouldn't allow Paul to sign a contract with Epstein until the man had visited their home and been approved by Forthlin Road's social arbiter, Olive Johnson.

McCartney, Michael – (Michael McCartney is not a character in the book, but he is mentioned.) Paul McCartney's younger brother who resided with him in Forthlin Road, Allerton. Michael was present during many Quarry Men rehearsals and knew all The Beatles well.

Mr. McDermot – Religious Instruction Master at Quarry Bank School for boys during the time when Pete and John were there.

McGough, Roger – (Mr. McGough is not a character in the book, but he is mentioned.) Liverpool-born poet. McGough was part of the burgeoning art scene in Liverpool during the late 1950's and early 1960's, when The Beatles were emerging. He co-wrote a book of Merseyside poetry with Henri and Patten, and he was a friend of John's and Paul's.

McKenzie, Phyllis – Co-ed who attended St. Peter's Church in Woolton with John and was at the Woolton Garden Fête where the Quarry Men performed in July 1957. Later, at Liverpool College of Art, Phyllis and Cynthia Lennon became best friends. Phyl encouraged Cynthia to follow John to Ye Cracke after their dance floor "tiff" at the End of the Term Bash in 1959. Only because of Phyllis's encouragement did Cynthia have the bravery to finally begin a relationship with John.

McKinnon, Duncan – (or Douglas McKenna in to some sources) Scottish representative for Larry Parnes on the Johnny Gentle Tour. At Dalrymple Hall in Fraserburgh, Scotland – 23 May 1960 – The Beatles were late arriving for McKinnon's venue. They had been involved in a car wreck on the A96. To make matters worse, their drummer had been hospitalized. McKinnon was furious and frantic, but John convinced McKinnon that even though Tommy Moore had lost his teeth, the drummer still wanted to play the gig. John urged McKinnon to go Moore released from the hospital. That is exactly what McKinnon did, and Moore had to play despite a swollen mouth and a great deal of pain.

Mohammed, Geoff – One of John's closest cronies at Liverpool College of Art. Geoff was a fixture at Ye Cracke, and he and John devised many pranks together. Geoff, of Indian descent, was extremely good-looking and very popular on campus. His steady girlfriend was Ann Mason. Though Geoff was as brilliant as he was handsome, he was ousted from the college for non-attendance, as was John.

Moore, Tommy – Merseyside drummer who worked at the Garston Bottle Works. Tommy agreed to drum for The Beatles at the Larry Parnes audition, 10 May 1960. However, he was detained in "collecting his drums" on the morning of the audition and arrived after The Beatles had already started performing – using Johnny Hutchison from Cass and the Cassanovas as a fill-in drummer. Tommy changed places with Hutch and finished the audition with them. When The Beatles were selected to tour with singing sensation, Johnny Gentle, Moore agreed to go along with them on the two-week tour of Scotland. During the tour, Moore lost all of his front teeth in a car accident. But John encouraged tour promoter Duncan McKinnon to have Tommy perform that evening, regardless of injuries. After the tour, Tommy swore never again to perform with The Beatles, especially John Lennon.

Moores, John – Extremely successful British merchant who began the Littlewoods Mail Order stores which evolved into the Littlewoods Empire. Each year in Liverpool, Moores hosted a prestigious art competition at the Walker Art Gallery. In late 1959 – early 1960, Stu Sutcliffe entered a painting in the competition entitled "Summer Painting." Not only did the painting win first place, but also Moores was so impressed with the work that he purchased it for himself at £65. John forced Stu to use this money to purchase a bass guitar and to join The Quarry Men – later, The Beatles.

Morecambe and Wise – (Morecambe and Wise are not actually in the book, but are mentioned) This popular British comedy duo was very popular during the 1950's and early 1960's. John admired their wit and often mimicked their humour.

Murray, Rod – Friend of John's and Stu's who attended Liverpool College of Art with them. The three art students shared a flat at No. 3 Gambier Terrace. Rod was considered as a possible bass player for The Quarry Men prior to Stu's getting the role. In fact, Rod had started building his own bass in anticipation of playing with the band. Rod and his girlfriend, Diz, were a part of John's group of close friends in Ye Cracke. (Gambier Terrace pictured in appendix)

Newby, Chas – Temporary bass player for The Beatles in spring 1961 when Stu Sutcliffe left Liverpool and returned to Hamburg. Chas, a friend of Pete Best's and a former member of The Blackjacks, was an excellent bassist, and he got on well with the lads. But Newby had no intention of joining the band. He was determined to finish his degree in chemistry. He could not be persuaded to go with The Beatles to Hamburg in April 1961 for their gig at Peter Eckhorn's Top Ten club.

Owen, Alan – (Mr. Owen is not in the book but is mentioned.) Liverpool playwright during the 1960's. Owen was an integral part of the group of artists, writers, and musicians who made up The Liverpool Scene. He was a close associate of Adrian Henri and Roger McGough. The Beatles admired Owen tremendously and later requested that he write the script for their first movie, "A Hard Day's Night."

Paolozzi, Eduardo – Scottish-born sculptor living in Hamburg when The Beatles were there in 1960. Paolozzi – who had achieved international success – agreed to take Stu Sutcliffe on as an apprentice and worked diligently to get Sutcliffe a grant from the Hamburg City Council. This was one of the factors that led to Stu's leaving The Beatles and remaining in Hamburg when John, Paul, George, and Pete returned to Liverpool in December 1960.

Pickles, Thelma – ("Thel" to John) Fellow art student at Liverpool College of Art when John was there. Thelma and John had much in common, including similar family situations. John respected Thelma's forthrightness and pluck. They dated during the fall and winter of 1958.

Pobjoy, William Ernest – ("Popeye" in The Daily Howl) Quarry Bank Headmaster who succeeded E. R. Taylor in 1956. Mr. Pobjoy had many encounters with John Lennon and Pete Shotton. He tried creative ways of dealing with the unruly twosome (instead of corporal punishment), including a period of suspension. He offered John's band, The Quarry Men, a chance to play at the 1957 Sixth Form Dance in an attempt to inspire the boy. Mr. Pobjoy was responsible for getting John into Liverpool College of Art. (Note: Some biographers list him as William Edward Pobjoy. Also of interest...Mr. Pobjoy was responsible for ending corporal punishment at Quarry Bank in 1961.)

Porter, Eddie – Waiter at The Odd Spot Club where John Dykins (Julia Lennon's second husband) worked. Eddie frequented The Grapes and knew The Beatles through Dykins. (Picture of Eddie Porter with Charlie Lennon – John's uncle – and the author in appendix.)

Powell, Cynthia – John's college sweetheart (and later, first wife). Born on the Wirral Peninsula in Hoylake, Cynthia Powell attended Liverpool College of Art. There the prim, sweater-set co-ed met rough and tumble John Lennon, and they fell in love. Cynthia and John dated from the end of the 1958 term until their marriage in 1962. Cynthia visited John in Hamburg during the Easter break, 1961. She was the inspiration for many of his songs and the father of his first son, Julian. Cynthia gave John the unconditional love that had been missing from his life. She "was there" when so many others "should have been."

Presley, Elvis – (Elvis Presley is not in the book, although he is mentioned frequently.) American pioneer in rock'n'roll who recorded initially for Sun Records. His vast number of hits in the 1950's (including "Heartbreak Hotel," "Blue Suede Shoes," and "Hound Dog," the latter of which The Quarry Men performed on their first gig at The Cavern Club in August 1957) impressed John Lennon. John admired Elvis more than any other recording artist and established Elvis as a benchmark of success. John constantly vowed that The Beatles would be "bigger 'n Elvis."

Pryce-Jones, The Reverend Maurice – Rector of St. Peter's church in Woolton. He organized the Woolton Garden Fête in July 1958, and at the suggestion of Bess Shotton, included her son's skiffle group, The Quarry Men, in the day's festivities. He asked them to be in the afternoon parade and to perform in the Scout field after the parade. That evening, they were also to play a few numbers at the church hall dance. (The Scout field, the church, and church hall are pictured in the appendix.)

Rhone, Dot – Paul McCartney's girlfriend in 1961. She traveled to Hamburg with Cynthia Powell over the 1961 Easter break and then later that year, rented a one-room flat with Cynthia in Liverpool

Roberts, Charles – Marjorie Robert's son and friend of Colin Hanton. Through Charles (and his friend, Colin Hanton) The Quarry Men were invited to play "a real gig" at the Roseberry Street Festival in June 1957. A group of "toughs," jealous over the popularity of the band, threatened to smash The Quarry Men up, and Charles (and his mother) helped the group exit the stage in safety.

Roberts, Marjorie – Chairperson for the Roseberry Street festivities in the Liverpool held on the occasion of the 750th anniversary of King John's giving the charter to the city. She was responsible for all entertainment for this "Founder's Day" type celebration (held 22 June 1957), and she chose a band known by her son, Charles. She chose The Quarry Men.

Rosa – Cleaner for Bruno Koschmider at The Kaiserkeller. Rosa had a crush on John Lennon, and he was always joking with her – dedicating songs to her. Rosa was kind enough to allow Dot Rhone, Paul McCartney's girlfriend, to live on her houseboat when Cynthia and Dot visited Hamburg in spring 1961. When Peter Eckhorn opened The Top Ten Club at the end of 1960, Rosa left Koschmider's Kaiserkeller to work at The Top Ten. She was thrilled when The Beatles returned to Germany in the spring of 1961 to perform there.

Royal Caribbean Steel Band, The – Group of West Indian musicians who performed at The Jacaranda Coffee Bar for Allan Williams. In summer 1960, Everett, Otto, Bones, and Slim – The Royal Caribbean Steel Band – deserted Williams' employ to defect to Hamburg, Germany where life on the Reeperbahn was more exciting. They sent Allan a letter urging him to come over and to bring more Liverpool groups to perform. This inspired Allan to travel to Hamburg and to promote his groups over there. It eventually led to The Beatles' gig at The Indra and The Kaiserkeller in

August 1960.

Sabine, Bruce – Graphics Arts Professor at Liverpool College of Art when John and Stu attended the school. Like almost all other professors with whom John was associated, Sabine believed that Lennon should be expelled from college for non-attendance.

Scott, Gerry – Driver/roadie for Johnny Gentle and The Beatles on the two-week tour of Scotland in June 1960. Gerry was not driving when the road van was wrecked on the A-96. He had taken a short break and Johnny Gentle was driving.

Shadows, The (more accurately, Cliff Richard and The Shadows) – One of the most popular bands of the late 1950's and 1960's in England. Bob Wooler at The Cavern played the Shadows' records constantly when The Beatles were performing there. Many of The Shadows most popular hits were instrumentals. John Lennon wanted his group to become as popular as The Shadows, and he and George Harrison co-wrote an instrumental wryly called, "Cry for a Shadow."

Sheridan, Tony – Very talented and popular British recording artist who was headlining at Peter Eckhorn's new Top Ten Club when The Beatles were in Hamburg, Germany in 1960 and 1961. Sheridan was offered a chance to record a platter with renowned composer, Bert Kaempfert, and he invited The Beatles to back him on the disc. He billed them as The Beat Brothers. The song that they recorded, "My Bonnie Lies Over the Ocean," was the record requested by Raymond Jones at the Whitechapel NEMS store, 28 October 1960. This request alerted Brian Epstein to the popularity of the Liverpool group and eventually led to Epstein's decision to manage them.

Shotton, Bess – Mother of Pete Shotton (John's best friend in school). Bess was a successful businesswoman, owning her own grocery store, wool shop, and finally, hair salon. She drove her own car as well. These were remarkable accomplishments for a female in the 1950's. The Shottons lived on Vale Avenue, very close to John's home in Menlove Avenue.

Shotton, Peter – ("Pete," later "Lotton") Neighbour of John Lennon's (residing on Vale Avenue) and acquaintance from St. Peter's church in Woolton. John and Pete became best friends throughout their school years and beyond. They were so inseparable that they were referred to as "Shennon and Lotton." Pete played washboard in The Quarry Men. After graduation from Quarry Bank, Pete became a Liverpool policeman and then the owner of The Old Dutch Café in Smithdown Road, Woolton. Pete and

John remained close friends throughout their adult years.

Shirley – ("Janice" in some sources) Stripper from Manchester who performed at Allan Williams' and Lord Woodbine's New Cabaret Artistes Club in Liverpool in July 1960. Her back-up band was The Beatles. Allan Williams, who hired her, calls her "Shirley" in his book, *The Man Who Gave The Beatles Away*, but in a letter to Bill Harry, Paul McCartney referred to her as Janice.

Smith, Bill – First tea-chest bass player for The Quarry Men. Because he was interested in football more than in the band, Bill was replaced by Len Garry and Ivy Vaughn.

Smith, George Toogood – Husband of Mimi Smith who served as a father figure during John's childhood. John lived with George and Mimi from 1945 on. George Smith ran the family dairy in Woolton. He played mouth organ, and taught John to play as well. "Uncle Ge'rge," as John called him, loved radio programmes and art, as did his nephew. He took John to the "picturedromes" against Mimi's wishes and hid biscuits for the child under the pillow at night. Tragically, George died in June of 1955, and John lost his best friend.

Smith, Mary Elizabeth Stanley – ("Mimi" to her sisters) Sister of Julia Lennon, wife of George Smith, and guardian of John Lennon. Mimi and her husband, George, took John to live with them (with permission from Julia) in their home, "Mendips," in 1945. When George died in June 1955, Mimi continued to parent John by herself. She was an avid reader and taught John to love books. She also instilled in him a strong sense of determination and organization. Although John ordered an inexpensive guitar from a catalogue, Mimi bought him his first real guitar at Hessey's in Liverpool. Mimi never approved of John's obsession with rock'n'roll as is often quoted as saying, "The guitar's all very well John, but you'll never make a living out of it." (Mendips pictured in appendix)

Stanley, Annie Jane – Mother of Mimi, Mater, Nanny, Harrie, and Julia Stanley, grandmother of John Lennon. Annie passed away in 1941, when John was only a year old. The loss of his wife left George Stanley devastated.

Stanley, Anne Georgina – ("Nanny" to her sisters) Third-born child of Annie and George Stanley and John's aunt. Nanny lived in Liverpool near Mimi and attended the Woolton Garden Fête with Mimi where they discovered John playing in a band – The Quarry Men – as part of the afternoon's entertainment.

Stanley, Elizabeth Jane – ("Mater" to her sisters) Second-born child of Annie and George Stanley and John's aunt. Mater lived in Scotland, and John was visiting her home when Uncle George passed away in the summer of 1955. Mater was also the one who gave John money for his twenty-first birthday that allowed him to make the trip to Paris with Paul McCartney and Jürgen Vollmer.

Stanley, George Ernest – ("Pop" Stanley to his family) Father of five girls: Mimi, Mater, Nanny, Harrie, and Julia and grandfather of John Lennon. John's first home at 9 Newcastle Road was with his grandparents. John also lived with his mother, John Dykins, and grandfather again for some months in 1944-45.

Stanley, Harriet – ("Harrie" to her sisters) Youngest child of Anne and George Stanley and John's aunt. Her daughter, Lelia, was John's close friend. Harrie lived not far from Mimi in Liverpool and visited John, Mimi, and George often in Mendips.

Starkey, Richie ("Richie" or Ringo Starr) Drummer for Rory Storm and the Hurricanes (and later, The Beatles). Born in 1940, and reared on Madryn Street in The Dingle area of Liverpool, Richie spent much of his childhood in hospitals and sanitariums. He suffered first from a ruptured appendix and later from chronic pleurisy. In hospital, he was introduced to the drums. By the time he was 17, he was playing drums for the Eddie Clayton Skiffle Group and in 1959, he joined the extremely popular band, Rory Storm and the Hurricanes. The Hurricanes were booked at Bruno Koschmider's Kaiserkeller Club in the autumn of 1960, and alternated sets with The Beatles on stage was another Liverpool group. Ringo became fast friends with The Beatles and even recorded a disc with them while in Hamburg at the Akustik Recording Studio. He joined The Beatles in 1962, replacing Pete Best as drummer. His witticisms and down-to-earth humour added as much to the group's appeal as did his excellent Northern style drumming.

Steiner, George – (or Sterner, according to some sources) German who worked next door to the Two I's Coffee Bar in London. On the night that Bruno Koschmider, owner of The Kaiserkeller in Hamburg, and Allan Williams, manager of many bands including The Beatles, accidentally ran in to each other at the Two I's, they needed an interpreter. Someone knew Steiner (who worked next door at the Heaven and Hell Coffee Bar) and suggested that he be invited over. Steiner, therefore, became the official interpreter for Williams and Koschmider and was invited to Hamburg when

The Beatles journeyed there in August 1960. He stayed behind to serve as Bruno's liaison with the British groups, including Derry and the Seniors, Rory Storm and the Hurricanes, and The Beatles. Steiner became Koschmider's trusted friend. It was Steiner who reported to Koschmider that The Beatles had played one gratuitous set at Peter Eckhorn's Top Ten Club in December of 1960.

Storm, Rory – Tall, blonde leader of Rory Storm and the Hurricanes. In autumn 1960, The Hurricanes were on the same bill as The Beatles at the Kaiserkeller in Hamburg. They became close friends. Both groups were managed, at that time, by Allan Williams. (Rory's drummer, incidentally, was Ringo Starr.) Rory was good-looking and very likeable. He struggled with a stutter when speaking, but never stuttered when he sang. His tragic death, by suicide, broke many hearts in Liverpool.

Sunnyside Skiffle Group, The – Nicky Cuff's original band (prior to The Connaughts). The Sunnyside Skiffle Group competed in the Carroll Levis "Discovery Night" at The Empire Theatre, Liverpool, June 1957 against The Quarry Men. At that time, the band included Nicky Cuff (band leader and tea chest bass player), Teddy Pickles (guitar), Brian Jones, and Norman Muten. The group's four-part harmony and wild stage antics "took the day" at the audition. John Lennon realized that his Quarry Men had to become as animated as Sunnyside Skiffle for all future performances.

Sutcliffe, Stuart – ("Stu" or "Stu de Stael," stage name) John Lennon's best friend at Liverpool College of Art. Stu Sutcliffe was an extremely talented artist who went on to study in Hamburg, Germany under Eduardo Paolozzi. In January 1960, he won the prestigious John Moores Art Competition at the Walker Gallery in Liverpool, and mogul John Moores even purchased his entry, "Summer Painting." John immediately forced Stu to spend that money on a bass guitar. Purchasing a Hofner President bass at Hessey's, Stu was enlisted into The Quarry Men, against his will. Later, Stu suggested the group change its name to The Beatles, in homage to Buddy Holly (and the Crickets). He went on the Johnny Gentle Tour of Scotland and then to Hamburg with The Beatles in 1960. There he fell in love with Astrid Kirchherr. When The Beatles returned to Liverpool at the end of 1960, Stu stayed in Germany with Astrid to study art under Eduardo Paolozzi. He suffered from extreme exhaustion and severe headaches, and his health began to fail rapidly from 1961 on. (Walker Gallery pictured in appendix)

Sytner, Alan – Manager of "The Cavern Club" from its inception in 1957 (as a jazz club). He booked The Beatles to play the club on 7 August 1957. Synter expected The Quarry Men to play skiffle, and when John Lennon launched into Elvis Presley's "Hound Dog," Sytner admonished them for playing rock'n'roll. Sytner sold The Cavern to Ray McFall in October 1959, just prior to The Beatles' heyday there. (Photo of The Cavern entrance, 1993, in appendix. Note: This is not the original Cavern Club, but the one presently on the premises.)

Sytner, Dr. Joe – Liverpool physician who played golf at the Lee Park Golf club where Nigel Whalley was the "apprentice golf professional." Whalley made it his business to befriend Dr. Sytner since Sytner's son, Alan, owned a jazz (and occasionally skiffle) venue in City Centre called "The Cavern Club." Through his association with Dr. Sytner, Nigel was able to secure The Quarry Men a gig at the Cavern in August 1957.

Swinging Blue Genes, The – ("The Swinging Bluegenes" in some sources) House band at The Cavern Club prior to 1961 when The Beatles evolved into the house band. The Swinging Blue Genes were tremendously popular in Liverpool and shared the stage at The Cavern with The Beatles many times. Later, their name changed to the Swinging Blue Jeans, and they had a number one hit with "Hippy Hippy Shake."

Taylor, Alistair – Brian Epstein's personal assistant at NEMS. On 9 November 1961, Taylor went with Brian to the lunchtime Cavern Club session to see The Beatles for the first time. Both men returned on 21 November for a second visit. Soon after that, Brian offered Taylor two and a half per cent of The Beatles as part of the contract negotiations. However, Alistair turned the offer down, pledging to work for Brian – no matter what the outcome.

Taylor, E. R. – Headmaster at Quarry Bank when John first arrived there. He frequently used corporal punishment to discipline John for misbehaviour and insubordination. Mr. Taylor left Quarry Bank at the end of the school year in 1955 and was succeeded by William Pobjoy. (Quarry Bank pictured in appendix)

Terry, Karl – One member of a popular Merseyside group called The Cruisers. On 19 October 1961, Karl was persuaded by John Lennon to join in on a bizarre conglomeration of musicians made up of The Beatles and members of Gerry and The Pacemakers. The combined band, known as The Beatmakers, performed one night only at Litherland Hall. They all wore outlandish costumes, and many of them played instruments they didn't ordinarily play.

Turner, Bill – Woolton neighbourhood friend of John's and Pete's who attended the Liverpool Institute. In the autumn 1955, John convinced Bill and Len Garry to spend a day at Quarry Bank as "new students" (on a day when Liverpool Institute was on holiday). The prank was discovered mid-afternoon, and all the boys were punished. Throughout their childhood years, when Bill failed to get John's jokes, John used to tell him, "You shoulda been there."

Vaughn, Ivan – ("Ivy") Friend of John's who occasionally played tea chest bass with The Quarry Men (shared job with Len Garry). Ivan attended Dovedale Primary with John and then went on to The Liverpool Institute with another young guitarist, Paul McCartney. He thought that Paul and John might like to meet each other, so he invited Paul to hear The Quarry Men perform at the Woolton Garden Fête in July 1957. After their performance, he introduced John and Paul to one another at the church hall across the street.

Vincent, Gene – American rock'n'roll pioneer greatly admired by all of The Beatles. The Quarry Men covered his hit tune, "Be Bop A LuLa", and Paul wrote down the lyrics of that song for John at their very first meeting in St. Peter's Church Hall, Woolton. Later, John, Paul, George, and Stu were given tickets by Allan Williams to see Vincent perform at The Liverpool Stadium on 3 May 1960. On 17 April, however, Vincent and his friend, Eddie Cochran, were involved in a serious car accident, and Cochran was killed. Vincent was heartbroken, but performed the concert nevertheless. John Lennon especially admired Vincent and emulated his style of delivering a song to the audience.

Vollmer, Jürgen – One of the Exis in Hamburg and a good friend of Astrid, Klaus, and The Beatles. Jürgen Vollmer was a distinguished photographer who was in Paris is October 1961. Stu and John – who had been given money for his twenty-first birthday – planned to meet at Vollmer's place in Paris, and John brought Paul along for the holiday. Stu was not able to make the trip due to poor health, but Jürgen, Paul, and John spent several days in touring the city. Jürgen was the first person to tell John how seriously ill Stu really was. Jürgen photographed The Beatles on many occasions. (One photograph of John Lennon standing in a Hamburg doorway was later to become the cover for John's "Rock and Roll" album.)

Voormann, Klaus ("Voorman" in some sources) Member of The Exis and the son of a Berlin physician. In autumn 1960, after having an argument with his girlfriend, Klaus Voormann visited The Kaiserkeller Club on Hamburg's Reeperbahn. There he saw The Hurricanes and The Beatles performing. He was so impressed with the Merseyside rock'n'roll that the next evening he brought many of his friends in The Exis movement and his girlfriend, Astrid, to the club. Klaus and Astrid became friends with both bands, and Astrid photographed The Beatles at Der Dom Park. Unfortunately for Klaus, Astrid fell in love with Stu Sutcliffe of The Beatles and the two became engaged in late November 1960.

Walters, Lu – (Wally) Bass player and vocalist for Derry and the Seniors. When The Seniors and The Beatles were both performing in Hamburg, Germany in 1960, Lu (called "Wally" by The Beatles) asked The Beatles to back him on a recording. They agreed and asked Allan Williams to secure a studio for them. Against much protest, Williams finally agreed to this venture. Lu, John, Paul, George, and Rory's Storm's drummer, Ringo Starr, recorded "Summertime" at the Akustik Recording Studio, 15 October 1960. Ten copies were made of the song. The B-side was an advertisement for shoes.

Webb, Janet –Student at Liverpool College of Art when John was there. Janet was a close friend of Cynthia Powell's and Phyllis McKenzie's.

Whalley, Nigel – Mutual friend of Pete's and John's, Nigel lived in Vale Avenue. Mimi approved of Nigel because his father was a policeman. After Dovedale, Nigel went on to The Bluecoat School, and he became the self-proclaimed manager of The Quarry Men. He got them their first real gig at The Cavern Club. Sadly, Nigel was a witness to Julia Lennon's tragic death outside of Mendips on 15 July 1958.

Wilkie, Derry – Leader of "Derry and the Seniors." Thanks to Allan Williams, Derry's group was one of the five groups auditioning alongside The Silver Beatals for Larry Parnes and Billy Fury at The Blue Angel on 10 May 1960. Members of The Seniors included Derry Wilkie (vocals), Howie Casey (sax), Lu Walters (bass), Frank Wibberly, (drums) and Brian Griffiths (guitar). The Seniors usually dressed in shiny jackets and black ties and wore patent leather shoes.

Williams, Allan – ("Al") Liverpool-born, Welsh entrepreneur who was very much involved in the beat scene during the late 1950's and early 1960's. Allan owned the successful Jacaranda Coffee Bar in Slater Street and allowed an ingénue group called The Quarry Men (later The Beatles) to play in his basement in exchange for the performance of odd jobs (including cleaning/painting the loo). Later he managed the group and gave them the opportunity to audition for Larry Parnes. This audition secured them a two-week tour of Scotland with recording artist, Johnny Gentle. A few months later, in August of 1960, Allan booked them at The Indra Club in Hamburg, Germany. After encouraging the lads to *"mach shau"* at The Indra – to perform instead of stand there lifelessly – Williams was able to secure them a booking at Bruno Koschmider's larger club, The Kaiserkeller. Williams was directly responsible for urging the lads to put everything into their performances. He also owned and managed The Blue Angel, an upscale nightclub in Seel Street, Liverpool, and The Top Ten, a Hamburg style nightspot in Soho Street (the rougher Liverpool 3 district). Absorbed with these pursuits, Allan lost interest in booking The Beatles in the spring of 1961, and they released him as their manager. Brian Epstein approached Allan in December of 1961 to ask Brian if he should manage the Beatles. Brian's advice was, "Don't touch them with a barge pole." (Picture of Allan Williams and the author in appendix.)

Williams, Beryl Chang – Allan Williams' wife. She always had a soft spot for The Beatles and fed them – free of charge and against Allan's wishes – at The Jacaranda Coffee Bar that she and Allan owned. She traveled with Allan and The Beatles to Hamburg in August of 1960.

Woodbine, Lord – (Woody) Native of Trinidad and business associate of Allan Williams. Lord Woodbine (or more affectionately, Woody) was not a Lord of any sort. He was an entrepreneur who encouraged Allan to open a strip club in Liverpool 8 entitled "The New Cabaret Artistes." The Beatles played back-up band there to Shirley (or Janice), the club's stripper. Woody also accompanied Allan on his trips to Hamburg, driving the van for The Beatles.

Wooler, Bob –Former railway clerk and friend/advisor to The Beatles. Bob Wooler was a man with the gift of gab. Known for his alliterative phrases and poetic puns, Wooler became a respected compère (or disc jockey) Merseyside. Allan Williams convinced Wooler to resign from his a railway job to compère fulltime at Williams' new Top Ten Club in Liverpool, December 1960. When the club burned down less than two weeks later, Wooler took at job as compère at The Cavern Club. He remained there for many years. Bob was a close friend of The Beatles and suggested that they get a signature song for entrances onto the stage ("The William Tell Overture"). He also suggested the lads remain in the band room prior to performances rather than mingling with the fans. He accompanied The Beatles to their first business meeting with Brian Epstein, and John Lennon often introduced Bob as his father.

Scouse Glossary

The first afternoon that I spent in Liverpool in 1993, I discovered that a road map was called an "A to Zed" and that literally everyone was referred to as "luv."

Liverpool's rich Scouse vernacular is a language all its own. During my ensuing seven trips to Liverpool, I studied and learned the lingo to avoid saying repeatedly, "What? Excuse me?"

If you want to learn more about Scouse and how to speak it properly, you may want to purchase the four books below. (And I might add, they are also great fun to read!)

Lern Yerself Scouse, Volume One. Frank Shaw with notes and translations by Fritz Spiegl and a pome by Stan Kelly. Scouse Press, Liverpool, 1965.

Lern Yerself Scouse, How to Talk Proper in Liverpool, Volume Two. Linacre Lane. Edited by Fritz Spiegl. Scouse Press, Liverpool, 1966.

Lern Yerself Scouse, Wersia Sensa Yuma? The Third Volume of the Scouse Press Thesaurus of Merseyside Words and Phrases. Brian Minard. Scouse Press, Liverpool, 1972.

Lern Yerself Scouse, The Language of Laura Norder, Volume Four of the Great Liverpool Tetralogy of Scouseology edited by Fritz Spiegl. Scouse Press, Liverpool, 1989.

The following are my own definitions – not as colourful as might be found in more exhaustive works – but utilitarian.

A to Zed – the street atlas or road map

Anyroad – anyhow

Battle taxi – police car

Bevvied up – intoxicated

Bird – (Also spelled "baird") girl

Black and Tan – a mixture of ale or lager and cider: This is a drink The Beatles enjoyed from time to time.

Black Velvet – a mixture of ale or lager and champagne: consumed by Allan Williams on occasion

Bonnet – the front of the car…the part of the road van that was crumpled in the Johnny Gentle tour road accident

Bonzer – excellent

Boot – the trunk of the car. When referring to "putting the boot in," however, it means to kick someone.

Browned off – angry

Bushwa! – bullshit!

Can do – can do it. The "it" is understood in Scouse lingo. Similarly, they say "I could do."

Carryin' - having ready cash as in, "Where was ya when I was carryin'?"

Cheeky – bold, impertinent

Chooks – a term of endearment for anyone of the opposite sex; also, "ducks" or "luv"

Cig – a cigarette, also "fag" or "ciggie"

Cor! – an expression of incredulity similar to the American "Wow!" or the British "Bloody Hell!"

Couldn't give a lousy, red Meg – couldn't care less

Crackin' the flags – extremely hot

Creased – tired; also "gazumped" and "knackered"

Cob o' Chuck – a piece of bread

Cuppa – a cup of coffee or tea

Coupla – several beers

Dead – very or extremely, as in "dead creased."

Dickie Liverpool – Lewis's Department Store in Liverpool's City Centre features a statue of a naked man above the store entrance. It symbolizes "Liverpool Resurgent," but its prominent physical attribute has been the brunt of many Scouse jokes. The nickname for the statue says it all.

Don't be at it! – Quit arguing! Quit complaining!

Dosser – sleeper

Dual carriageway – a boulevard

Eck! Eck! – an expression of warning similar to "Look out!"

Eggy – agitated

Fag – cigarette; also, "cig" or "ciggie"

Fagged out – tired; also "gazumped" and "knackered" or "creased"

Finnyaddy – a dandy, a fussy person; also "finnick"

Finnick – a fussy or picky person; also, "finnyaddy"

Flat – apartment

Gazumped – tired

Gettin' on me wick – irritating me

Give yer chin a rest! – Shut up!

Givvus a (whatever) – May I have a (whatever)? As in, "Givvus a light" for "May I borrow a match?" or "Would you please light my cigarette?"

Gnat's piss – Cheap, lousy beer or ale (usually used in the phrase "Y'er not werth a thimbleful of gnat's piss")

Gorra Cob On – in a bad mood

Graft – boring, humdrum routine…it's "the graft." George complains in the book that John went off to Paris leaving him with "the graft."

Griff – news or information

He won't crack on! – He's ignoring me!

(To) Have yer blinker for Upper Parly on in Aigburth – to do something long before it is necessary. (Upper Parliament Street is in downtown Liverpool. Aigburth is a suburb of Liverpool quite a few miles out of town.)

I wudden do that fer a big clock! – I refuse!

Judy – prostitute (This term is used with a small "j".) *In the book, John's mother, Julia, is called Judy by her father, mother, and sisters. In that case, it is merely a nickname for Julia and a term of affection.*

Jowlers – small alleyways (also, jowls or flabby cheeks)

Kecks – trousers

Kip – nap or sleep

Knackered – tired; also "fagged out" or "nallered" or "creased"

Loosie – a cigarette that isn't in a packet

Maggie May – famous Liverpool prostitute, the subject of several folk songs

Marmalise 'im – beat him up

Mickey talk – teasing someone, putting them on

(A) Mixer – troublemaker

Mod Cons – modern conveniences (used, for example, when referring to bathroom facilities)

Money for rope – getting nothing for your money or your efforts

Muck in, y'er at yer granny's – Eat up!

Nallered – tired (also, creased or knackered)

Not worth a light – useless

Nice! – an expression that means just the opposite

Nudger and chips – sandwich and French fries

'Oly Joe – (Holy Joe) a stodgy, formal person

One o' Lewises – a mannequin. Lewis's Department Store is one of Liverpool's prominent City Centre Stores.

Ozzy – hospital

Punters – the young patrons of nightclubs and dance halls

Purra lip on yer – hit you in the mouth

Rambullon – Keep talking, but I'm not listening.

Roolya Boolya – a riotous situation full of argument and discord

Ruffler – one who puts on airs

Sarny – sandwich

Shirrup! – Shut up!

Skint – without funds, broke (And "dead skint" is completely broke.)

Smash you up – beat you up

Sod that! – I'm not going to do it! (In New York this would translate, "Forget about it!")

Ta! – Thank you!

Takin' the Piss Out – teasing someone

Teds – (Also "Teddy Boys") In 1950's England, the Teddy Boys or Teds were "toughs" who sported tight, narrow ankled ("drainpipe") jeans and leather jackets. They had D.A. (duck's arse) coifs. The look that James Dean sported in "The Wild Ones" inspired their style. Teds were generally people to approach with caution. John Lennon and his group mimicked the look of the Teds, if not the ferocity.

The land whur they play wid'atchets – an affectionately degrading description of The Dingle, Toxteth, or Bootle, the "no go," tougher areas of Liverpool. Ringo was reared in The Dingle.

Thisavvy – this afternoon

T'rah! – Goodbye!

Twinnings – a brand of tea

Upper Parly – Upper Parliament Street

Wack – man

Well into their cups – inebriated

Wuden mind or **Wuden say no** – I accept or Sure, why not?

Yer – your

Y'er – you are

Yerrokay – (mildly) yeah, okay…or (more vehemently) for the thousandth time, I understand!

Appendix

The letter below was written to me on 20 March 1993 by the owner(s) of Mendips at that time (name withheld to protect privacy). I had written to them, asking to see John's home while I was in Liverpool. However, they gently refused me, explaining that it was private residence, a place only their friends visited. Heartbroken, I wrote back, pouring my heart out and explaining why seeing the inside of the house was so important. I was refused a second time. But...this letter was given to me as a substitute. It details everything about the house exactly as it was during John's childhood. And, as a consolation prize, the letter was even written on John's original stationery!

As you read the letter, you'll be able to see what Mimi could see from the kitchen window. You'll discover how many fireplaces there were, how the house was heated and so forth. The small bedroom to which they refer was John's bedroom. Note that it did NOT have a fireplace.

Today Mendips is open for tour (I will finally get to see it in November 2007) but for those of you who will never go to Liverpool, here is my gift to you, a copy of that intimate and lovely letter.

ORIGINAL   251 Mendips Avenue
Telephone   *Liverpool*
051-428-4302   L25 78A

20th March 1993

Dear Mrs. Kessler,

Most of the questions you ask in your letter will be answered when you take The Beatles Tour. As I told you – the interior section of the house at the front is virtually unchanged. The windows and porch are leaded lights – as is the one window at the side of the house. The woodwork inside the house as we remembered was white or magnolia.

The only thing in the kitchen was a sink unit – double drainer stainless steel sink with blue doors to cupboards, blue drawers. This was on the window side – which was a mirror image of the breakfast room window – extending the full length of the outside walls of the two rooms.

You will also see that there are four chimneys on the roof – telling you that there were four fireplaces one in each of the main rooms upstairs and downstairs which means, of course, chimney breaks, forming alcoves on each side.

There was also a chimney on the back for the breakfast room – that is no longer there. We had the fireplace and chimney break, etc. removed. The house was too cold for us as it was, depending entirely upon open fires for heating.

The previous owners (a man and his wife with two children under five – a boy and a girl) allowed the Gas Board to measure up for central heating before we moved in so we were able to have the system installed within a few weeks of moving.

The previous owners also had the garage built, thus altering the side garden to allow the drive to be extended for garage access. The only things we can remember being in view of the kitchen window were three white double lilac trees – two of which are no longer there; the third is just showing.

The small bedroom is now a lumber-room.

We are very private people, and I think you will have guessed by this lengthy letter that your wish to enter our home will not be granted.

It is not possible to recreate the house as it was in the 1950's – we did not see it until 1960 – did not know that John Lennon used to live here until after we had agreed to buy it – and must rush to admit, did not foresee the creation of "Beatle Tours."

None of our friends who visit have ever asked to see our entire home, just accept our hospitality and of course, use the facilities.

Please do not ask for any more information; writing is now so difficult for me – painful, and I am ashamed of the end result. Imagine the rooms as you look at the outside of the house. No one can contradict you. If you come inside you would see our home. You want to describe the home that Mr. and Mrs. Smith gave to John Lennon. We wish you every success with your book and enjoy your trip to Liverpool.

Photographs

Oxford Street Lying In Hospital,
Where John was born, 9 Oct 1940

Sam Flannery, Jude Kessler, Charlie Lennon, Eddie Porter – John's Uncle
Charlie offered to keep John while Fred was at sea.

Mendips, 251 Menlove Avenue – John came to live here with Mimi and Uncle Ge'rge

Quarry Bank School for Boys – John's "high school"

Prefect, "Head Boy." Dave Bennion from Quarry Bank and the author

The Head Master's office, Quarry Bank

Julia's house, 1 Blomfield Road

QuarryBank Auditorium, the scene of the Sixth Form Dance

In the background, Sefton General Hospital, where Julia Lennon died and where, years later, Julian Lennon was born

The Empire Theatre, where The Quarry Men auditioned for Carroll Levis

Liverpool College of Art

Paul McCartney's house in Forthlin Road, Allerton

George Harrison's house

Pete Best's home, 8 Hayman's Green, "The Casbah"

Allan Williams' "Blue Angel," Seel Street, Liverpool

Gambier Terrace, where John lived with Stu and Rod Murray near Liverpool College of Art

June Furlong, 1993, and the author

Litherland Town Hall

Ye Cracke, Rice Street, Liverpool

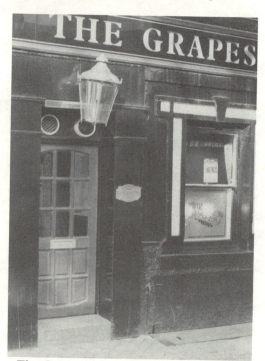
The Grapes, Mathew Street, Liverpool

Beryl Adams (Brian Epstein's assistant at NEMS and Bob Wooler's wife), Allan Williams, and the author

Pete Shotton's Old Dutch Café, Smithdown Road, Woolton

Ringo Starr's home, The Dingle, Liverpool

Strawberry Field...Forever.

Bibliography

Baird, Julia. **JOHN LENNON: MY BROTHER**. Jove, 1988. New York. ISBN 0-515-10250-4

Beatles. **THE ANTHOLOGY**. Apple Corps., 2000, Hong Kong. ISBN 0-8118-2684-8

Best, Pete and Doncaster, Patrick. **BEATLE! THE PETE BEST STORY**. Plexus, 1985. London. ISBN 0-85965-077-4

Best, Roag with Best, Pete and Best, Rory. **THE BEATLES: THE TRUE BEGINNINGS**. Thomas Dunne Books-St. Martin's, 2003. Italy. ISBN 0-312-31925-8

Buskin, Richard. **JOHN LENNON: HIS LIFE AND LEGEND**. Crescent, 1991. New York. ISBN 0-517-03590-1

Buskin, Richard. **THE COMPLETE IDIOT'S GUIDE TO THE BEATLES**. Alpha, 1998. New York. ISBN 0-2-862130-1

Brown, Peter and Gaines, Stephen. **THE LOVE YOU MAKE: AN INSIDER'S STORY OF THE BEATLES**. McGraw-Hill, 1983. ISBN 0-07-008159-X

Burrows, Terry. **JOHN LENNON: A STORY IN PHOTOGRAPHS**. Thunder Bay, 2000. San Diego. ISBN 1-57145-469-1

Caserta, Jean. **Tripod.com/beatlegirls/thelmapickles**.

Clayson, Allan and Leigh, Spencer. **THE WALRUS WAS RINGO**. Chrome Dreams, 2003. New Malden, Surrey. ISBN 1-84280-2056

Coleman, Ray. **LENNON**. McGraw-Hill, 1984. New York. ISBN 0-07-011788-8

Davies, Hunter. **THE BEATLES: THE AUTHORIZED BIOGRAPHY**. McGraw-Hill, 1968. New York. Library of Congress 68-9046

Davies, Hunter. **THE QUARRYMEN**. Omnibus, 2001. New York. ISBN 0-7119-8526-X

Epstein, Brian. **A CELLARFUL OF NOISE**. Pierian, 1984. Ann Arbor, Michigan. ISBN 0-87650-169-2

Furlong, June and Block, Jill. **JUNE: A LIFE STUDY**. APML, 2000. ISBN 0-9534461-1-5

Fulpen, H. V. **THE BEATLES: AN ILLUSTRATED DIARY**. Plexus, 1982. London. ISBN 0-85965-070-7

Garry, Len. **JOHN, PAUL, AND ME BEFORE THE BEATLES**. CG, 1997. London. ISBN 0-9695736-8-5

Geller, Debbie. **IN MY LIFE: THE BRIAN EPSTEIN STORY**. St. Martin's, 2000. New York. ISBN 0-312-26564-6

Gentle, Johnny and Forsyth, Ian. **JOHNNY GENTLE AND THE BEATLES FIRST EVER TOUR**. Merseyrock, 1998. Runcorn, Cheshire, England. ISBN 0-9532989-0-6

Goldman, Albert. **THE LIVES OF JOHN LENNON**. William Morrow and Company, 1988. New York. ISBN 0-688-04721-1

Giuliano, Geoffrey. **DARK HORSE: THE PRIVATE LIFE OF GEORGE HARRISON**. Plume, 1991. New York. ISBN 0-452-26700-5

Giuliano, Geoffrey. **TWO OF US: JOHN LENNON AND PAUL McCARTNEY, BEHIND THE MYTH**. Penguin, 1999. New York. ISBN 0-14-023460-8

Giuliano, Geoffery. **THE BEATLES: A CELEBRATION**. Wellfleet, 1986. Seacaucas, New Jersey. ISBN 1-55521-794-X

Greenwald, Ted. **THE BEATLES COMPANION**. Smithmark, 1992, New York. ISBN 0-8317-0717-8.

Harry, Bill. **MERSEY BEAT: THE BEGINNINGS OF THE BEATLES**. Omnibus, 1977. London. ISBN 0-86001-415-0

Harry, Bill. **THE JOHN LENNON ENCYCLOPEDIA**. Virgin, 2000. London. ISBN 0-7535-0404-9

Harry, Bill. **THE ULTIMATE BEATLES ENCYCLOPEDIA**. Hyperion, 1992. New York. ISBN 1-56282-814-2

Heatley, Michael. **THE IMMORTAL JOHN LENNON**. Longmeadow, 1992. Stamford, Connecticut. ISBN 0-681-41520-7

Jones, Ron. **THE BEATLES' LIVERPOOL**. Ron Jones, 1991. Moreton, Wirral, England. ISBN 0-9511703-1-7

Leach, Sam. **THE BIRTH OF THE BEATLES**. Pharoh, 1999. Gwynedd. ISBN 1-901442-30-6

Leigh, Spencer. **DRUMMED OUT! THE PETE BEST STORY**. Northdown, 1998. Borden, Hants. ISBN 1-900711-04-4

Lennon, Cynthia. **A TWIST OF LENNON**. Avon, 1978. New York. ISBN 0-380-45450-5

Lennon, Cynthia. **JOHN**. Crown, 2005. New York. ISBN 0-307-33855-X

Lennon, John. **IN HIS OWN WRITE & A SPANIARD IN THE WORKS**. Signet, 1964, 1965. New York. ISBN 0-451-16392-3

Lennon, John. **SKYWRITING BY WORD OF MOUTH**. Pan, 1986. London. ISBN 0-330-29719-8

Lennon, Pauline. **DADDY, COME HOME: THE TRUE STORY OF JOHN LENNON AND HIS FATHER**. Angus and Robertson, 1990. London. ISBN 0-207-16996-9

Lewisohn, Mark. **THE COMPLETE BEATLES CHRONICLE**. Harmony, 1992. New York. ISBN 0-517-58199-0

Miles, Barry. **JOHN LENNON: IN HIS OWN WORDS**. Quick Fox, 1981. New York. ISBN 0-8256-3953-0

Miles, Barry. **THE BEATLES DIARY, VOLUME 1**. Omnibus, 2001. New York. 0-7119-8308-9

Miles, Barry. **THE BEATLES: IN THEIR OWN WORDS**. Omnibus, 1978. New York. ISBN 0-8256-3925-5

Norman, Phillip. **SHOUT! : THE BEATLES IN THEIR GENERATION**. MJF, 1981. New York. ISBN 1-56731-087-7

O'Donnell, Jim. **THE DAY JOHN MET PAUL**. Penguin, 1996. New York. ISBN 0-14-025301-7

Pawlowski, Gareth L. **HOW THEY BECAME THE BEATLES**. E.P. Dutton, 1980. New York. ISBN 0-525-24823-4

Porter Alan J. **BEFORE THEY WERE THE BEATLES**. Xlibris, 2004. ISBN 1-4134-3056-2

Riley, Tim. **TELL ME WHY: THE BEATLES' ALBUMS, SONG BY SONG**. Vintage, 1989. New York. ISBN 0-679-72198-3

Roberston, John. **LENNON**. Omnibus, 1995. London. ISBN 0-7119-4981-6

Rose, Lloyd. "Long Gone John and the Revelations," **THE LENNON COMPANION**. Thomason, Elizabeth and Gutman, David, editors. Macmillan, 1987. London. ISBN 0-333-48255-7

Salewicz, Chris. **McCARTNEY**. St. Martin's, 1986. New York. ISBN 0-312-90451-7

Schafner, Nicholas. **THE BEATLES FOREVER**. MJF, 1978. New York. ISBN 1-56731-008-7

Shotton, Pete and Schaffner, Nicholas. **JOHN LENNON: IN MY LIFE**. Stein and Day, 1983. Briarcliff Manor, New York. ISBN 0-8128-6185-X

Solt, Andrew and Egan, Sam. **IMAGINE**. Warner Bros., 1988, New York. ISBN 0-02-63910-6

Stevens, John. **THE MUSIC OF JOHN LENNON**. Berklee Press, 2002. Boston. ISBN 0-634-01795

Sutcliffe, Pauline and Clayson, Alan. **BACKBEAT: STUART SUTCLIFFE: THE LOST BEATLE**. Pan, 1994. London. ISBN 0-330-33580-4

Thompson, Phil. **THE BEST OF CELLARS**. Bluecoat, 1994. Liverpool. ISBN 1-872568-16-5

Tremlett, George. **THE JOHN LENNON STORY**. Futura, 1976. London. ISBN 0-8600-7294-0

Whitworth, Rodney. **MERSEYSIDE AT WAR**. Scouse, 1988. Liverpool. 0-901367-30-3

Wiener, Allen J. **THE BEATLES: THE ULTIMATE RECORDING GUIDE**. Bob Adams, 1994, Holbrook, Massachusetts. ISBN 1-55850-414-1

Williams, Allan and Marshall, William. **THE MAN WHO GAVE THE BEATLES AWAY**. Coronet, 1975. Dunton Green, Seven Oaks, Kent, England. ISBN 0-340-21016-8

Willis-Pitts, P. **LIVERPOOL: THE FIFTH BEATLE**. AmOzEn, 2000. Littleton, Colourado. ISBN 0-9703118-0-X

Wootton, Richard. **JOHN LENNON: AN ILLUSTRATED BIOGRAPHY.** Hodder and Stoughton, 1984. London. ISBN 0-340-35875-0

Look for
Jude Southerland Kessler's next novel
In the John Lennon Trilogy

Shivering Inside

in bookstores
October 2010

If you are interested in learning more about self-publishing, layout and design, please write to:

Penin Inc Publishing, LLC
P.O. Box 9572
Dothan, Alabama 36304